WOLVES

WOLVES

D.J. MOLLES

BLACKSTONE

PUBLISHING

Copyright © 2016 by D. J. Molles
Published in 2016 by Blackstone Publishing
Book design by Andrew D. Klein

Printed in the United States of America
First printing: 2016
ISBN 978-1-5047-2591-0

1 3 5 7 9 10 8 6 4 2

CIP data for this book is available from the Library of Congress

Blackstone Publishing
31 Mistletoe Rd.
Ashland, OR 97520

www.BlackstonePublishing.com

For Laila

PART 1

THE WANDERERS

He stood at the northeastern corner of the field and looked out on his work, the labor he'd done under the sun. He felt satisfied. Fulfilled. Deeply content with all that he'd done, all that he'd accomplished. Stretching in front of him in a big, open expanse were his barley fields.

They were not his *barley fields, so to speak. They were the commune's. They were everybody's. But he'd been the one that staked it off. He broke the dirt. He dug the trenches. He broadcast the seed. He watched them grow every day with patience and excitement.*

Now, they were so close to harvest, the fields turned to a golden brown and the bearded heads of two-row were beginning to droop toward the earth.

"You did good," his wife said beside him, giving him a rub on the back.

He looked at her with a smile on his lips.

It had been a long time. A long time since they had been at peace.

His wife, Charity, on his left. His young daughter, Nadine, on his right.

His wife and daughter, both with the same wide, blue eyes, the same easy, broad smiles. They were both good people, better than he could ever be. Better than he deserved. He held on to them tightly.

The barley caught the glow of the setting sun behind it, and when he looked to his right and left, he could see how it struck their blonde hair, and he thought their hair was the same exact color as those fields, and it gave him a sense of great symmetry to his existence.

Hold on to this, *he told himself in that moment.* Always remember this.

And he did.

But memories fade.

CHAPTER 1

He is dying.

That much has become clear. Death sits in the aching tension in his muscles, how they refuse to propel him forward even one more step. He can feel it in the cramps in his stomach, and in the throbbing of his head.

It has been two days since he last tasted water.

Lost in this endless ocean of desert, and no matter his desperation, every horizon was only more desert. His desperation wasn't enough to get him to the other side. It had never been enough.

And so he falls, down to his knees, all the strength coming out of him, all of his miles given up, unable to put one foot in front of the other—that is what he has always told himself to do: *One foot in front of the other, Huxley. One foot in front of the other.*

He stares with hollow eyes at the sandy ground in front of him. Underneath that half inch of windblown dust, there is blacktop. Sometimes he could even see it, far ahead, little bits and pieces of it peeking out, only for the wind to cover it again in more sand. Constantly appearing and disappearing like a magician's trick.

His mouth is like paper. His lips cracked and peeling. His beard is long and unkempt. His dark hair is coated with desert dust, as it coats his entire body and all of his clothing, making him look like another piece of the landscape. He is tall, and skinny in the way that only a desert wanderer can be—every bit of fat stripped from him like all the soft things of the Old World, and the sun and wind have weathered him far beyond his forty years.

Maybe the next horizon …

Maybe there would be a town. Maybe there would be water.

Maybe there would be an end to these goddamned Wastelands.

But he will not know. He will not see the next horizon. He feels the certainty of his end like a buzzard's shadow cast over him.

I was weak, he thinks bitterly. *I was weak, and now I'm going to die.*

For nearly eighteen months he has tried, and he has tried, and he has tried. But he is not a match for these Wastelands. He has been blown back and forth in all directions, and time has slipped away faster than he could ever have imagined, and now the trail is cold, cold, cold, like a body long dead.

Eighteen months was too long to hold out hope.

And he feels like a fool for going on as long as he did.

Didn't he know that hope had died a long time ago?

He hears a voice calling out to him in the desert, but he knows it is not real. He doesn't want to look up to that shimmering eastern horizon. He doesn't want to look, because he knows who he will see, and he knows that she is not real.

She is gone forever.

He lays himself onto the ground, knowing this will be the place that he will die. He closes his eyes against the sun, tastes dust and heat, and tries to reach into his fading mind for the thing he promised himself that he would hold on to forever, the thing he would never forget.

Time and violence and misery have made it worn and faded.

The barley fields with the sun setting behind them. The glow of the barley, the glow of his wife's hair, his daughter's hair, all like smelted gold. The three of them standing there. Happy. Peaceful. *Hold on to this forever …*

His dying words are just a whisper: "I'm sorry … I'm so sorry …"

CHAPTER 2

Vaguely, the sensation of someone's hand, tilting his head up.

There is also the background ache of his body. The way it is nearly dead. The dryness on his tongue. The crust of the sand in his eyes, in his ears, in his beard. The warmth of the sun.

And also, the guilt of having given up. The recrimination of failing, breaking promises. *Weakness, you were weak, too weak to survive* ...

And something else he'd not felt before.

Something cold and hard. Like the diamond core that is left after a star burns itself out.

He thinks, *Why is someone touching me?*

Did I die?

Can you feel things after you die?

Water. Flooding his mouth.

It is a shock, almost electric.

He coughs and splutters at first, but on some instinctive level he knows he can't let that liquid escape his mouth. He opens his mouth for more, *more, please God, more!*

"Easy," a voice says.

A *real* voice.

Now Huxley opens his eyes.

Reality pries at his retinas. The day is still there, but it is fading, the light is dwindling in the sky, and shot through with oranges and reds. A face is hovering over him, indistinct. It is a man, and there is a canteen being set against his open mouth again and water is being poured in.

Huxley drinks, even as he feels terror.

People do not help each other in the Wastelands.

Weakly, Huxley pulls away, swallowing the water in his mouth. The man retracts the canteen and Huxley squints to try to get a better look at him. He can tell the man is very light-skinned, gone red from the desert sun. His hair is almost white.

"Why are you helping me?" Huxley croaks, his voice barely audible.

The pale man is watching him, but Huxley can't really see his eyes. The man's face is backlit by the orange-glowing sky. He tries to push the canteen to Huxley's mouth again, and Huxley wants it, he wants it badly, but he resists it for a second time because he doesn't trust this man, he doesn't know him …

There is the sound of a dry chuckle. "Drink the water, you jackass."

"Why are you helping me?" Huxley asks again, a bit louder.

"Because you'll die without me. Now drink the fucking water."

Huxley gives in. The pale man puts the canteen to his lips again, and this time Huxley leans into it, drinking as deeply as he can. Where did this water come from? Who is this man? And why is he helping a stranger on a desert road, where water and kindness are nowhere to be found?

Live or die, it doesn't seem to matter anymore.

The water is painful when it hits Huxley's stomach. He thinks that he's been poisoned, and unconsciousness creeps up on him again. It bats at the edges of his brain. One minute he is present, the next he is under.

He is being dragged. He feels his heels scraping across the road, then the soft sensation of sand. He can feel someone's hands hooked under his armpits. He tries to open his eyes, but he can't quite manage it. And Nadine's voice is calling out to him, as though through miles and miles of tunnel. Calling out to him as she always does in his nightmares, and in the half-light between sleep and awake.

No, she is gone. She has been gone for a long, long time.

He goes under again, this time to blessed blackness.

He stays there for a time. Swimming in nothingness. Floating in the dark.

At times, he comes up a bit from unconsciousness, and he can feel the hands on the back of his head, he can feel the water on his lips. More water than he can remember having in a very long time. And then he fades again.

The next time he opens his eyes, it is night. There is a tiny fire that warms his feet. He stares at it, blankly. Fire. Yes. It is fire. Why is this strange? His brain is scattered parts, trying to piece themselves back together. Things are not connecting just yet.

It's like he has truly died on the road and his brain broke apart and now it is reforming itself, gathering the pieces into a similar machine, but subtly different.

The fire. The fire. Did you make the fire?

I don't recall making the fire.

Where am I and how did I get here?

He can smell the night air around him. Crisp and cool, only very slightly tinged by the smell of the wood smoke. The front of his body is warm from facing the fire. His back is cold.

He shifts, plants his hands on the ground. He is sitting in sand.

When he moves, a shape stirs on the other side of the fire, causing Huxley to jolt, for fear to run through him like priming an engine. His hand goes to his belt, to the knife that he keeps tucked away there.

The shape rises up.

A man. A pale man. With white-blond hair.

Huxley stares at the man, his heart slamming his chest as his fingers lock onto the handle of his knife. He doesn't know this man. He is ready to gut him, except for the strange memory, the isolated image of this man hovering over him, pouring water into his mouth.

The man on the other side of the fire looks at Huxley's hand, gripping the knife. He holds up both hands to show he means no harm. In one hand, the canteen is held.

"Easy, brother," the man says.

Huxley forces himself to take long, deep breaths, trying to calm his heart. He needs a moment to piece things together. Something is telling him that he doesn't need to fight this man, but he is not putting everything together just yet, so he still keeps his hand on the blade.

"You," Huxley says, as concepts and images meld into actual memories. "You gave me water."

The man nods.

"Why?" Huxley says.

The man on the other side of the fire seems to realize that Huxley is not calm enough for him to approach with the canteen, so he just makes sure the cap is on tight and then tosses it over the fire. It lands in front of Huxley with a thud in the sand. Huxley can hear the water sloshing around inside. His mouth aches for it. He stares at it for a moment, but then he forces his eyes back up to the stranger.

The man has that type of coloring that borders on a complete lack of pigment. Even his eyes are pale. He has a certain ghostly aspect, but his skin is the thing that makes him real. It's suffered greatly in the sun and peels and looks painful. But despite all of that, there is something about his face that is ... friendly?

Perhaps that isn't the right word. More like ... familiar.

The stranger watches Huxley, as he is being watched, and then laughs, a short, sharp bark of laughter. He has big, white teeth. He seems like he smiles easily. He regards Huxley evenly, the smile lingering. "Look, brother. Maybe you're overthinking this a bit. You basically have two options. First, you can drink the water and live. Second, you can refuse the water, I take back my canteen, and you wander off into the night to die. It doesn't matter to me."

Huxley looks at the canteen, lying on the ground, just right there in front of him. "What's your name?" he asks, still looking at the canteen.

"You can call me Jay. You?"

Huxley loosens his grip on his knife. "You can call me Huxley."

That is not his real name, and it's also likely that Jay is not the stranger's real name. Everyone has their own reasons why they do this. For Huxley, his real name is something that doesn't belong to the Wastelands. It's something that lies behind him in the past. It was the name that his loved ones called him. It has become a sacred shrine.

"Well." The man called Jay lowers his hands. "Good to meet you, Huxley. What'll it be?"

Huxley's eyes jag up. "What do you mean?"

Jay gestures to the canteen. "You gonna drink? Or you gonna die?"

Huxley can still feel how his heart knocks—that heavy beating, like there isn't enough liquid in his blood for it to be pumped easily. He still feels light in the head, feathery in the chest. But he can feel the water the man has already given him—it is heavy in his stomach.

He clears his throat and reaches for the canteen. He takes it up out of the dirt, brushes it off, then uncaps it and takes a swig. There is maybe a quarter of the water left in it.

After another swallow or two, he caps it again and holds it up. "Thank you."

Jay walks around the small fire and takes the canteen, then retreats to his side of the fire, and sits in the dirt with a tired sigh. He stares into the flames.

Huxley licks what little moisture is left on his lips. He clears his throat and it doesn't feel like paper for the first time in two days. *It makes no sense, but it doesn't need to make sense. The man is right. I can take his water and live, or be stubborn and die.*

But what do I have left to live for anymore?

Huxley draws his legs up, props his elbows on them.

There is that feeling again. That feeling that his burnout has left him with a solid, dense core of something. Whatever it is, it is heavy. He can feel it like a weight on his chest. But there is also something comforting about it. A blanket can be heavy too, but it keeps you warm at night.

He looks around the little campsite. He can't really see much beyond the glow of the fire. There are a couple of rocks near them, and Huxley's back is against a small, withered tree. Other than that, it's just the fire, and the two men around it, like they are all that is left of the universe.

Jay breaks the silence. "Where are you headed, Huxley?"

Huxley considers the question for a moment before answering. "I don't know."

It is an honest answer. He has finally admitted that hope is dead, so there is no purpose for him now. No real reason to be going ... anywhere.

Jay prods the fire with a stick. "You don't know." He says the words slowly. Tasting them. "Seemed you were heading east."

"Yes." Huxley nods. "I was heading east."

Jay pulls the poker stick out of the fire. The tip of it glows red, then turns black and smokes. Jay watches it for a moment, then sets it down. He leans forward, clasping his hands together and looking at Huxley with those oddly pale, piercing eyes.

"I'm going to tell you something," Jay says, quietly. "You don't know me. I don't know you. But I'm going to say it anyway, because I think you need to hear it. Whatever has driven you this far, whatever you're hoping to find out east ... let it go. There's no hope out east. There's only blood and death. Trust me on this. Please, please trust me. If you cling to that hope, whatever it is … it'll drag you to your death." Jay leans back and grabs up his stick. Almost as an afterthought, he says, "Hope makes you weak. And the weak die."

Huxley stares into the fire, the words rolling over and over in his head.

Let go of the hope. It will lead him to his death. It will make him weak.

"What about you?" Huxley says. "Where are you going?"

"East." Jay smiles strangely at him. "But I have a purpose, Huxley. I have no hope. I don't know what's out there, but I know it's blood and death, and I don't expect anything else. In fact, that's exactly what I'm looking for."

Huxley shifts uncomfortably and doesn't respond. He is lost in thought and memories, filled with smoke and screams. They form a stage in his mind, occupied by three players.

One is his wife. One is his daughter.

The third is a shadow in the background.

A man. Huxley doesn't know the man. Can't picture him. All he knows is that the man has a scorpion tattoo on his neck. Huxley has pictured it many times, but even that is not firsthand knowledge. It was only words on dying breath. So in his thoughts, sometimes the scorpion tattoo looks one way, and sometimes another. Sometimes it is big and colorful, and sometimes it is small and black.

The man with the scorpion tattoo.

Huxley leans fully back into the tree. He feels sick to his stomach. The sensation of his body hovering around that moment between death and coming back to life. His whole body feels weak and shaky. He rests his hands on his knees so that Jay cannot see them trembling.

"Can I ask you something?" Huxley says, quietly.

Jay rubs his chin, then motions with his hand—an invitation for Huxley to speak.

"Have you ever encountered the slavers?" Huxley asks.

Jay is very still for a moment, his eyes locked on Huxley's. After a moment, the fingers of his right hand start to flick off of his thumb, a steady, purposeful movement. Like there is something on his fingers that he doesn't like the sensation of.

"Yeah." Jay's voice is flat. "I've encountered them."

Huxley puts a hand down into the sand and presses his fingers into it. Slavers. Ruthless men who come upon settlements and caravans, striking hard and fast. They kill the men, the infants, and the old. They take the children, and sometimes the women.

Huxley realizes he's gripping the sand. He lets it drain through his fingers. "Where do the slavers go?"

"East," Jay says. "They always go east."

"I know they go east," Huxley brushes the sand from his hand. "But where do they *go?*"

Jay seems to become cognizant of his flicking fingers, and he clasps one hand in the other, interlacing the fingers to still them. "You mean where do they take the slaves?"

"Yes."

Jay shakes his head. "I don't know. Somewhere east of us. Someplace that wants slaves."

Huxley's eyes glimmer with the flames. He is looking at the coals. The hottest part of the fire. The little bits and pieces that sit underneath everything and burn it up. They're so hot that nothing can even be near them without combusting.

Huxley's neck itches. That little concavity just to the right of his Adam's apple. Absently, he scratches it. "Then I'll keep going east," he says.

Neither man speaks for the rest of the evening.

Huxley tries to stay awake—he is not completely comfortable with Jay. But exhaustion takes a hold of him after a while and he sleeps. His dreams are of fire and ashes. He is running through burning fields. The ashes are thick. His feet sink into them. They clog his nose and his mouth. He can only keep slogging through those burning fields, unending, and listening as a voice screams for him. Things are crawling through the ashes, little lumps, like things moving under a blanket. They are tracking him, chasing him. He keeps trying to move, but he can't. They come out of the ashes. They are scorpions. Hundreds of them. They crawl over him and sting him.

Huxley wakes, gasping for breath, the feeling and the taste of the ashes still lingering in his mouth. A glance at the sky reveals a glimmer of dawn. Everything is that steady gray color that it achieves as it rises out of the blackness of night.

Beneath the sky is just another empty desert landscape.

It is cold this morning. It is late October, by his best reckoning. Here in the desert, the days are still hot, but the nights dip down into chill, and the mornings ache with it.

Huxley stands up.

Where do the slavers go?

The question burns in his head.

And the image. The picture of a man with a scorpion tattoo on his neck.

Those had been Charity's last words to him. Not "I love you," or some pleasant memory from their life together. Nothing good. Nothing beautiful. Nothing comforting. Instead, he had knelt at his wife's side, crying, weak and ineffective, and he'd cradled her head in his hands as the life flowed out of her.

"They took her," Charity had said, and the way her voice rasped and gurgled would never leave Huxley's mind. "A man ... a slaver ... he had a scorpion tattoo ..." Her words failed her, and her bloody fingers made a motion to her neck, and that was it.

She lived for another few minutes. Shaking. Making little noises of fear. Noises of agony.

And then ... gone.

The man with the scorpion tattoo.

Out east, there is only blood and death. Maybe Huxley wants that too.

He turns himself toward the dawn, and he almost takes a step. He thinks about leaving the stranger named Jay behind him and continuing on his own. To answer the question. To find out where the slavers go. By himself, and without the influence of a man whose pale eyes burn with something terrible.

But he stops himself. He turns and looks back.

The import of this decision glides by him, unnoticed as a black cloud at midnight.

Jay is awake, sitting up and regarding Huxley with curious eyes, barely visible in the weak morning light.

"You fixin' to leave?" Jay asks.

Huxley grinds his teeth together. It feels good to him. The grating. The pain in his jaw when he does it. It braces him. He doesn't respond to Jay's question directly. Instead, he turns back east. "It's dawn. And I'm heading east."

There is the sound of stirring behind him.

Boots stamping in the dust.

The sound of someone brushing dirt from themselves.

"Well," Jay says. "Let's go then."

CHAPTER 3

They are not the only ones on this road.

They take a break in the midmorning, and Jay takes a seat right there in the middle of the road, stretching his legs out in front of him. He has a certain lackadaisical manner to him. But it's a lie. His eyes are not lackadaisical. They are always searching. Always roaming around. It would seem that they are looking for danger, but sometimes Huxley thinks that they are looking for prey to devour.

Jay uncaps his canteen and swishes the contents around. He takes one mouthful. Holds up the canteen to Huxley, who is still standing in the road, cleaning dust and dirt out of his nose. Jay squints as he looks up at Huxley. "Probably another mouthful. You take it."

Huxley looks at it. Even just the few hours of walking have tired him. That is dehydration. It aches through him still. A belly full of water doesn't cure dehydration. It just gave him a little more time.

He takes the canteen, tips it back without hesitation.

Warm water fills his mouth.

Huxley holds it in his mouth, trying to allow it soak into his dry tongue before he swallows it. It tastes vaguely of the old plastic canteen. But it is not the worst water Huxley has ever had. Not by a long shot.

He looks to Jay, who is staring east, across that interminable expanse, probably wondering, much like Huxley, what lays on the other side. This great southwestern desert is a vast ocean that separates worlds. Those few people who have made it across come with different rumors every time. One would say there was a king. One would say there was a president. Another would say there was nothing but wooded badlands and barbarians seeking blood. No rumors seemed the same, and so, in Huxley's mind, what had happened to the rest of the country remained a mystery. Maybe the skyfire burned everything to the ground everywhere.

"You said last night that you had a purpose." Huxley leaves it open ended.

Jay sniffs, looks up at him. He holds Huxley's gaze for a time, then looks back east again. His hand begins to do the thing that it had done the night before—Huxley takes note of it again. The fingers flicking off his thumb.

"There's something on the other side of this desert, Huxley. And it's feeding on us. It's sucking us dry." *Flick, flick, flick.* "It doesn't think that we will come after it. But we will. *I* will. I can bite back."

Huxley stares at this stranger who has somehow turned into a companion. He can see the rage boiling behind Jay's eyes. This man is bitterness and hatred. He does a good job covering it up with a blanket of calm and a devil-may-care attitude. But it's there, and it only takes a little provocation to bring it out.

But his words stir Huxley. Stir that little coal-black center of him. The star that died and left a cold, carbon core. There is so little left to feel that even this phantom flame that flickers way down deep in him, even that feels heady.

What do I feel?

He has to ask himself the question. He has to search inside of himself for the emotion that he knows would make him human. He rifles through it like old junk in a basement—none of it works. The only working piece, he doesn't want. He keeps putting it off to the side.

Rage. He can feel that one clear as day.

Huxley has to force his teeth to stop grinding. "Let's keep going," he says. "The desert can't last forever. Maybe there will be an outpost. There has to be a town or a city eventually."

They keep walking.

Deep into the afternoon hours. Jay has a habit of humming tunelessly to himself. It is a quiet noise. Huxley should find it irksome, but the sound of another human on the road with him—one that doesn't seem to want to kill him—is pleasant.

Jay keeps looking around as is his habit, humming, and then falling silent for a while. Then he picks back up again. Maybe it is not so tuneless. There is a melody somewhere in there. Something old and familiar, but ancient and covered in the dust of memories. Some tune from the Old World. Something bluegrassy.

Jay hums. Then stops. He is looking behind them now. He squints into the west. Looks forward again. Then back behind them, scrutinizing. Finally: "Someone's coming."

Huxley stops and looks. "Where? What do you see?"

Jay shakes his head. "Not sure. More than one person though."

"Can you tell how many?"

"No. Several."

Huxley starts looking around. "We need to get off the road."

But there isn't anything to hide them. All around them it's just knee-high scrub brush, and an occasional tuft of dry grass. The rest is flat sand.

Huxley swears.

Jay is already moving to the shoulder of the road, hunching down. "Come on. Get low."

Huxley follows him. Moving low and quick, they put distance between themselves and the road. Then they start crawling on all fours, working their way through the low scrub. Distance is their friend now. They can't truly hide—if someone looks for them, they will be seen. But maybe they can go *unnoticed*.

They find a low point in the earth, a natural ditch carved by the rainy seasons and the scrub brush is an inch or two higher here, and thicker. It is situated about fifty yards off the road. They worm through the brush into the ditch and then squirm around to face the road again.

Huxley's belly is in the dirt. He can feel the sand, hot and gritty, working its way into his pants. He is breathing hard. The ground is hot, but he doesn't have enough moisture in him to sweat, so he just bakes, his pulse rising.

He peers through the scrub. The shapes on the road are taking form now, coming out of the mirage in the western distance, becoming solid beings. Like they are forming out of thin air. Jay was right. There are several of them.

Huxley does a quick count. "Ten," he whispers.

"Horseback," Jay says, matching Huxley's tone.

Huxley's heart speeds up again, feels his stomach turning. He can only think of one group that would go in number across the desert, and on horseback.

A rock is poking him in the side.

He refuses to move.

Five minutes pass by. Ten.

Now the men on horseback come close enough to see in detail. And the wagon that goes along with it. Huxley has seen these wagons before, these bastardized technicals that are pulled by teams of oxen, made from the chassis of old, defunct vehicles.

From both sides of the back corners rise tall poles, about ten feet high. Hanging from the poles is a jumble of shapes, tethered to the top. And Huxley knows what they are.

Jawbones. Taken from people.

"Slavers," he whispers, his voice barely more than a breath.

A sideways glance at his companion.

Jay is low to the ground, his chin almost touching the dirt. He stares through the scrub. His eyes are wide, but his eyebrows are cinched down. His whole body is tense and locked. But it looks less like fear and more like he might jump up and charge them.

"Jay," Huxley whispers. "Just let them pass."

Jay doesn't respond.

Another ten minutes go by, and now the wagon and the riders have drawn abreast of Huxley and Jay. The only thing that moves on Huxley is his breath, just barely stirring the dusty ground.

The rock jabs at him.

Don't move. Don't get noticed.

There is fear in him, still. But also anger. A burning thing. He finds himself thinking about the look on Jay's face, taking a sort of inspiration from it. But what could they do? There are nine riders, and a driver on the wagon, and every one of them will be armed. They will have rifles or scatterguns, and they will have revolvers.

Huxley has nothing but his knife.

And he suspects that Jay doesn't have anything.

They'd be gunned down before they could run ten feet.

No, Jay. There is a time for blood. And this isn't it.

One of the slavers on horseback is scanning around, and his eyes land on Huxley.

Huxley stops breathing.

Don't breathe.

Don't move.

If he could've stopped his heart from beating, he would have done that too, but it's only beating faster. He can feel his muscles trembling from being locked in this position for so long, the cords at the back of his neck aching and making his head shake.

The slaver will see him. He will see him moving, trembling in the shrubs like a scared desert hare and he will call out to his comrades and they will gun Huxley and Jay down without a second thought. Because they can, and for no better reason.

The slaver looks away. He's seen nothing.

Huxley feels weak with relief.

The wagon passes by. The driver is a woman, which is unusual. The slavers are a cruel lot. He wonders what this woman had done to earn their respect. What blood was on her hands? Whose wives did she murder? Whose children did she take? She is a tall thing, and Huxley thinks she could be beautiful in a cold sort of way. She has long, raven-black hair that she keeps in a braid that goes all the way down her back. A rifle lays in her lap, a bayonet on the end.

As the wagon passes, Huxley can see the cargo in its covered bed. There are two children there. A boy and a girl. They are dressed in rags and their faces are dark with soot and dirt. Where they've come from is a mystery. And where they're going is a mystery too. Two children seems a meager prize to Huxley. Perhaps the slavers ran out of supplies. Perhaps they felt they'd ventured too far into this ocean of sand. Perhaps they just planned to cut losses and pillage on their way back east. Who knew what their motivations were? Who knew what timelines and schedules they kept, what meetings they had to make to swap flesh and barter?

Huxley realizes his fingers are in the sand, delving into it, clenching it.

He imagines it is one of the slavers' throats. How he would like to get his hands on them.

But not now. Not yet.

The children stare out the back of the wagon. The landscape goes by underneath them, receding like a tide. Everything they ever knew is gone. Now they are in the desert. Now they are heading toward …

What?

Where do the slavers go?

"We could follow them," Jay whispers as the last rider in the group passes by.

Huxley shoots him a look. "What do you mean, 'follow them'?"

Jay turns his head, his eyes looking feverish and crazy for a second. "Follow them. See where they're going." He looks back after them, even as the image of the first horseman begins to shimmer in the heat coming off the road. "I bet they have water."

Huxley reaches up a shaky hand and rubs a bit of sand from his beard. "We can't just waltz in and take their water. There's only two of us. And we don't have guns. They have guns. They have *lots* of guns. They would murder us."

Jay makes a face. A sort of sneer that lasts for only a moment, as though he is just briefly disgusted by the situation. "Did you see the children?"

"Yeah. I saw them."

Jay shakes his head. "They're done."

"What do you mean?"

"The kids," Jay says. "They're done. They'll be dead or sold off in a month."

Huxley feels an old familiar pull in his soul. He wants to say something back, but he has trouble forming the words. After a moment he hitches himself onto his elbows. "Okay. We'll follow them—their tracks, anyway. See where they're going. But we're not going to sneak in and try to take their water. They'd kill us."

Jay rises from the dirt, slowly, and watches the slavers pass into the east. Because that is where the slavers go—they go east.

"Fine," Jay says. "But we'll need water eventually."

Huxley brushes dirt from his stomach, tries to shake it out of his pant legs. "We'll find water. We'll figure it out."

The slavers disappear into the horizon, leaving only their tracks to be followed. They are careless, these slavers. Because they have nothing to fear. Because they are the apex predator here. And the people of the Wastelands are the prey.

But Huxley is not prey. Maybe once he was. But in the time it takes for a man to lose everything he loves, he can grow claws and teeth.

I want what Jay wants. I want to make them bleed.

CHAPTER 4

It is close to sundown when they hear the gunfire.

Huxley and Jay stop in their tracks and stand stock-still in the roadway.

A breath. Another three beats of Huxley's heart. And then by some collective, silent decision, he and Jay both hunch down and move to the side of the roadway, off of the shoulder and into the old ditch that runs the side of the road.

Ahead of them, the sound of gunfire rolls, crackles, back and forth like an argument.

Maybe two miles away. Maybe even less.

A part of him wants to get up. Wants to run, but not away, like he would have before. He wants to run *toward* the sound of the guns.

From beside him, Jay squirms. "If I had a fucking gun, Hux ... If I had a fucking gun ..."

"I know," Huxley whispers.

Is it just his imagination, or are those screams?

His fingers go to his neck, scratching at that same spot. He doesn't register it until it starts to hurt. *Is there anything we can do? Anything at all besides lie in the fucking dirt?*

"We should get closer," he says, suddenly, coming up onto his hands and knees.

Jay looks at him. "What are we gonna do?"

He isn't asking because he's afraid. He's literally asking because he wants to know Huxley's plan. This is a man that doesn't care about the odds. His anger, his rage at the slavers is palpable in the air. He will do anything to make them bleed. Even if it's foolish.

Don't be foolish. Don't be rash.

Huxley gets up to one knee. Jay follows suit. Huxley points east. "We can creep up. While they're fighting. See what there is to see." He realizes he's breathless. He gulps air between sentences. The cool night air doesn't stop him from starting to sweat. He puts a hand to Jay's chest. "We're not gonna rush in, okay? We're not gonna do it, no matter what. Unless …"

"Unless there's an opportunity."

Huxley nods. "Unless there's a *real* good opportunity."

Jay has risen all the way to his feet. "Okay, brother. Let's go."

They move quickly, keeping low to the ground. It is tiring on their already taxed bodies, but fear and hatred keep them moving. They can be powerful fuels. They can stretch the body and mind. They can make a man go farther than he ever thought he could. They cannot sustain a body, but they can trick a body into thinking that it isn't dying of thirst, isn't starving.

They stop every hundred yards or so to look around, and listen. To triangulate on the sound of the gunfire. It is growing sparse now. But other things are growing louder, and now Huxley cannot blame it on his imagination. He cannot blame it on the wind. The sound of it is very clear.

Screaming.

There is a certain quality to it that Huxley has heard before and it strikes him down so hard, he actually halts and goes to a knee, feels like his chest is being compressed. It is not the screams of men. It is the screams of women and children. It is not mournful. It is electrically charged, and it makes his blood run cold and boil all at once. It is terror and anguish, with nothing left to hold it back.

"What are they doing?" he chokes.

"You know what they're doing," Jay hisses back.

Huxley knows. He knows very well what they are doing, because he's seen it before. Those screams are the sound of children watching their fathers' throats being cut, watching their mothers thrown to the ground and raped. It is the sound of men being as cruel as they can imagine how to be.

Huxley kneels in the dirt, shaking. *If I had a gun*, he keeps thinking.

But even if he had a gun, it would still be two on ten.

Ahead of them there is just the slightest berm in the dirt, and beyond that a dip in the land. Huxley knows that this slight valley is where the massacre is happening. It is less than half a mile from them, but he stays where he is.

Because there is nothing that he can do. Nothing but listen to the sounds and let them eat away at him.

He looks at dirt. Closes his eyes. *Be still*, he tells himself. *Be still and let it wash over you. You are a stone at the bottom of a river. You are hard rock. The water wears you down, but it only makes you smoother. And the smoother and harder you are, the less the flow can affect you.*

This is the only way to make it. This is the only way to *think clearly* in the midst of all of this. You have to harden yourself. You have to convince yourself that it won't affect you. It doesn't affect you. You are river rock.

After a time, the screams are not so horrible.

The gunfire tapers off. The screaming peters out. Now there are occasional shouts. The sound of laughter drifting over the desert wind. The sun dies in the west. In the east, a fire begins to glow.

"They're making camp," Jay says. He is sitting with his legs folded under him, picking at a piece of dry grass, his movements sharp and bitter.

"Maybe they're just burning things," Huxley says.

They stay put for another hour, and in that time all sound stops, and the glow of the fire wans. Huxley is thirsty, he remembers, because his tongue is stuck to the roof of his mouth. And he needs food. They cannot sit there forever. Even if it is dark. They are just sitting out in the open. And maybe …

"Maybe there's water," Huxley says quietly.

Jay makes an ugly noise.

Huxley labors to his feet. "I think they left. I don't think they're making camp there."

Jay flicks his fingertips. "Alright. Let's check it out."

They creep forward, quickly at first, but as they approach the top of the small rise that will provide them a view of the slight valley, they slow down and crawl on their bellies. At the top of the hill they look over at the dark land that spreads out in front of them. The only way they can tell anything is there in all the darkness is because there are two fires still burning, though the flames are low.

It is enough to just barely illuminate what is around. They cannot see details. But they can see the stillness. Whatever is around those two fires, it isn't alive. The slavers did not camp here tonight.

Huxley and Jay squirm their way over the top of the rise, so the blooming stars will not backlight their silhouettes and give them away, even though Huxley is almost certain that there is no one there. No one alive, anyway. He circles the camp a bit, heading north around it, and Jay follows. They keep their eyes on the fires, waiting to see any other shapes moving in the darkness, but again, there is nothing.

It is late into the night when Huxley and Jay actually step into the light of the dying fires.

It is a caravan of some sort. There are two rickety wagons made of wood and the bodies of old pickup trucks. It is these that are burning. The oxen that pulled these wagons are dead. Most likely gunned down in the fight as whoever was fighting used the poor dumb beasts as cover from bullets. They've been quartered, the meat taken sloppily, leaving giant pools of blood to be soaked up by the thirsty desert. They've taken only what they could eat before it spoiled, and the rest has gone to waste.

Huxley stands between the two burning wagons. The wood is still smoldering. The rubber tires are melted, smoking slag. It stinks of burning rubber and plastics, and it almost immediately makes Huxley nauseous. He moves out from between the cloying heat of the fires and into the blood bath.

There are six dead bodies. Five men, one old woman. They've been stripped nearly naked and piled off to the side, their bodies looted, their clothes and boots taken. They are stacked up like so many bags of trash, covered in each other's blood and shit. Two of the five men have had their jaws torn off—those are the ones that resisted.

Huxley stares. He covers his nose and mouth with his hands, the smell of his own musty, sweaty skin better than the smell of death and defecation. *You are a stone*, he tells himself. *A stone at the bottom of a river.*

What do you feel?

I feel nothing.

A sound of things falling over makes Huxley jerk and turn.

His hand goes to the knife at his belt.

Jay is behind him, at the back of one of the burning wagons. He has yanked a scorched but still-intact water skin from the back of the wagon and the charred wood had crumbled and caved in when he pulled the strap of the skin from where it was hooked on the wagon.

Jay staggers away from the cloud of sparks that rise up from the wagon.

He dances away from it and Huxley realizes that he must've singed himself to get the water skin. How the thing hadn't burned and burst is a mystery to Huxley, but the breath catches in his chest as he watches Jay pop the stopper out and upend the water skin into his mouth without hesitation or caution.

Huxley almost yells at him, but for some reason the funereal silence all around them makes him hold his tongue.

Jay takes two gulps and lowers the skin from his mouth. In the dim firelight, his lips glisten. His eyes look wild and unsettling. Like maybe it is not water that has found. But then he looks at the skin and nods once.

"Yeah," he says, huskily. "It's hot. But it's water."

He takes another gulp before handing the skin to Huxley.

Standing in other men's blood and the wreckage of their lives, the two men drink desperately. The water skin is a boon. It's big enough and full enough to keep them going for another day, maybe even two. When the madness for water begins to abate, they put the stopper back in and become more aware of what is around them.

"Do you think they left anything else?" Huxley asks, feeling like a carrion bird.

Jay nods to the oxen. "There's plenty of meat left on those things. And there's already a fire burning." He looks at Huxley and seems to sense the hesitation in him. The wrongness of it. He turns fully to Huxley and puts a hand on his shoulder. "Hey. Look at me."

Huxley tears his eyes away from the dead bodies. It is nothing he hasn't seen before. He looks at his strange companion. "What?"

Jay is very earnest. His eyes burn with a feverish intensity. "You wanna kill those motherfuckers?"

Huxley swallows. "Yes. I wanna make them bleed."

Jay gives him a little shove. "Then you gotta *live*, brother. These people are dead. I hate it. I hate that the slavers did this. But they can't use this shit anymore. And the only way they're ever going to get justice is if we live. And if that means eating their food and drinking their water, then fine. It's survival, brother. They died because they were weak. We are strong. We will live. And we'll make them bleed. For this and everything else."

Huxley grinds his teeth, but nods.

Jay points to the oxen. "See what you can get off those things. I'll see what else I can find."

Huxley sets to work on the ox nearest him. The slavers didn't bother to take the rib meat, which there is plenty of. Huxley pushes the huge gut bag out of the way with his foot and finds that there is even some loin left from the slavers' hasty hack job.

Huxley has an armful of bloody, dripping meat when he hears Jay utter a quick cry.

"Whoa! Hey!"

Huxley spins, bloody knife in his sticky hands, and he nearly drops the armload of meat in the dirt. Jay is at the pile of bodies and he looks like he's jumped back a bit. Now he's peering back at the bodies. From the pile, Huxley can hear a low mumble.

"Holy shit," Jay mutters. "Hux, this guy's still alive."

Huxley shoves the armload of meat onto the oxen's ribcage to keep it from getting dirt on it, and he runs to the pile of bodies. Jay is already there, pulling the top body out of place. Huxley can see a hand moving, just slightly in the tangle of limbs. The live one is two bodies down. As Huxley helps Jay pull the bodies away, he notices they are all dark-complected. He hadn't noticed it before.

Mexicans, most likely.

The man underneath the bodies is older, his face a craggy mess of wrinkles. He is covered in his own blood and the blood of his family and friends. He has been shot through the chest, twice. Somehow he clings to life.

Jay stares at the man, but speaks to Huxley. "He must've pretended to be dead."

Huxley cannot imagine. Lying under the people you loved. Waiting for the enemy to leave. He wants to weep for the man, but he can't summon up the intensity of feeling. Everything is numb. He still feels nothing.

The man's dry lips part, and he points with a shaking hand. East. Of course. "Los lobos," he mutters. "Ave María purísima. Los lobos."

Huxley shakes his head. "I don't understand. English?"

The other man blinks, fights pain for a second. His eyes go wide. "Agua," he says, spying the water skin slung over Jay's shoulder. "Agua, por favor."

Huxley understands that. "Water? You want water?" He reaches for the water skin.

Jay smacks his hand away. "What are you doing?"

Huxley looks at the other man. "He's asking for water."

Jay puts a protective hand on the skin. He speaks under his breath, as though the Mexican can understand them. "Huxley, this guy's dead."

"He looks pretty alive to me."

Jay bares his teeth with frustration. "I mean he's *going* to be dead. Giving him water would be a waste."

"It'd be mercy." Huxley reaches for the skin again.

Jay jerks it away. "Mercy would be putting him out of his misery, not giving him the stuff we need to survive. I'm fucking serious. I'm not giving him the water."

"Agua," the Mexican murmurs. "Por favor."

Huxley still holds his bloody knife in his hand.

Jay glances at it. "I'm not giving him the water. You gonna kill me over it?"

"I'm not gonna sit and listen to this guy moan for the next hour until he dies."

"Then kill him."

"I'm not gonna kill him."

"Then deal with it."

Huxley looks quickly between the dying man and Jay. His lips are tightened to a bloodless line. His jaw muscles bunching as he grinds his teeth away— that good, cleansing pain. This is Huxley's weakness: he is still trying to have pity. He is still trying to show mercy to people. But what place does that have in this world?

He hates the slavers for what they did. But that doesn't mean that this dying man is his friend. Huxley owes him nothing. And Jay is right. He will be dead soon enough. Giving him anything would simply be a waste of their resources.

Huxley takes a breath and looks at the old Mexican man. "I can't give you water. No agua. You are going to die anyway."

"Sí, agua," the old man says, pointing at the water skin.

For all Huxley knows, he is the original owner of the water skin.

But not anymore.

"No," Huxley says. "Not for you. You are going to die. You understand that, right? Comprende? You're going to die. But your water will help me live. And because I can live, I can find the people that did this to you." Huxley shakes his head. "I know you don't understand a word of that. Or maybe you do.

But that's the way it is." Huxley points the knife between him and Jay. "We're strong. We will survive."

The man falls silent, but breathes rapidly, shallowly.

Huxley turns his back on him.

Jay continues to pick through the wreckage looking for valuables left behind by the slavers. Huxley goes back to the ox carcass and the meat he had been able to harvest from it. He takes the meat, and he lays the pieces over a stick, and he holds the stick over the embers of one of the wagons and lets them cook. The meat chars and sizzles, fat dripping into the fire. Smoke lifts into the air.

What do I feel?

I feel ashamed. I feel ashamed that I am standing in the middle of all this death, and my mouth is watering for stolen meat, and I'm alive because of stolen water.

He should feel it stronger, he supposes, but it is a muted thing. A far-off cry.

The old dying man has been quiet since they walked away, but he begins to cry out, his voice dry and cracking. "Agua!" his voice hisses. "Amigos … amigos … por favor. Ten compasión. Agua! Agua!"

Huxley doesn't look. He keeps his eyes on the bubbling, crisping flesh.

The man's cries become faint, and then they are gone.

Huxley pulls the meat from over the coals. It smokes in the air. Huxley is starving. He cannot remember when he ate last, and whenever it was, it wasn't much. He's holding chunks of meat now, and nothing else matters.

He grabs a piece of the meat and starts shoving it in his mouth. It is burned on the outside, nearly raw on the inside. It doesn't matter. Blood and grease pour down his chin and into his beard. Jay appears at his side, drops a canvas satchel on the ground that clanks noisily, filled with pilfered items. Huxley gives him the other half of the meat. The two men squat down and tear at the chunks. If they'd been able to see themselves, they might've had pause. But their bodies need food. That is all they know.

They eat the meat. They drink more of the water. And it is only then when some of the madness of starvation has been put aside, that their eyes come up and see what is around them. Burning wreckage. Dead bodies. Blood everywhere. And out beyond the wreckage, shapes that scamper back and forth, eyes shining in the dark.

There are a lot of them.

Only when Huxley notices them do they begin to yip back and forth.

"Coyotes," Huxley says, reaching for his knife.

Jay shoves the rest of his meat in his mouth, his cheeks bulging. He chews manically, as though he would fight these beasts for it. When he has some room around the wad of food in his mouth, he stands up slowly and speaks. "They just want to eat. Just like we did. Let's just take what we have and go."

"Go out there?" Huxley isn't so sure, but he is standing with Jay.

Jay nods, carefully grabbing the satchel from the ground. "They won't fight us. Not with all this meat already dead. Why fight us when they can gorge themselves with no effort?"

Huxley pulls his knife from its sheath. "I'm not sure they think it through like that."

"Trust me," Jay says. "Let's just walk away."

Huxley doesn't know how much he trusts Jay, but he trusts him more than he did before, and he finds his feet following Jay's as they slowly move out of the center of the massacre. The coyotes yap and bark at them, but none come close. They stay at the edges of the firelight until Huxley and Jay have given it up, and then they slink in, growling. They test the ox by taking a bite of it and then dancing back. Then another, and another. And soon a dozen brown and tan shapes are moving through the camp, grabbing at the dead oxen, grabbing at the human remains.

By morning this whole scene will be a scattering of bloody bones and patches of skin and hair.

Huxley moves backward and sideways, but keeps his eyes on the coyotes until they are so far away that the coyotes are not even paying them any mind. They are barking at each other, but they don't fight for limbs. They are efficient. They don't waste time when they know there is enough for them all to feast. They have that cold sort of intelligence about them.

Huxley turns back into the night. Jay is a few paces ahead of him. He jogs to catch up and falls in step with the other man as they pick their way through the dark desert.

CHAPTER 5

That night, Huxley dreams of the barley fields again.

He is standing at the edge of them with his wife and daughter, as he always is in this memory. But this time his wife and daughter, they have no hair. It has been burned off of their scalps. Charity. Nadine. His beautiful girls. They look up at him. There is something off about their faces. Some little detail has been lost, like he cannot fully remember what they look like.

It terrifies him.

They look at him with their unfamiliar, undetailed faces, and their singed, bald heads.

They beg him for water, but he has none to give them.

"Water," a voice says, but it is neither of theirs.

This is a real voice, not a dream voice, and it pulls him through the membranes of reality and imagination ...

He blinks. He is looking at Jay.

Jay is standing over him. The sky is light with early morning. Jay looks angry.

"What?" Huxley says, heart thudding.

"I said, 'Where's the fucking water?'"

Huxley leans up into a sitting position, trying to shake off sleep and nightmares. Jay backs up a step, but he's still standing over Huxley.

"It's in the ... the ..." Huxley looks around for the water skin.

His eyes trace over Jay, and he realizes that the man is holding a knife.

Huxley reaches for his own, realizes the sheath is empty.

My knife. He's holding my knife.

His eyes go up to Jay's. "What the hell is this?" His voice is stone-cold.

Jay points at him with the knife. "Did you take the fucking water?"

"What do you mean?"

"I mean I went to bed with a half a skin of water and when I wake up it's gone. Did you drink it? Just be honest. Be honest, Huxley. Did you drink the water?"

Huxley lurches to his feet.

Jay backs up another step, still holding the knife.

"I didn't drink the water," Huxley grinds out. "Now you drop the knife or we're gonna have problems, Jay."

Jay is not going to drop the knife. He opens his arms wide. "Well then where's the fucking water? Where is it?"

Huxley wants to put his hands around the man's neck. "I've been asleep!" he snaps. "How the fuck should I know where the water is? You were the one that went to bed with it strapped to your body! I should be asking you the same question! Where's the water, Jay? Where the fuck is it?"

Jay shakes his head. "Don't try to spin this on me, Huxley."

Huxley looks to the ground. "Did you walk off to take a piss and leave it unguarded?" he demands. His eyes fall on a set of tracks that lead away from their little camp. He points to them. "You did, didn't you!"

Jay stares at the tracks.

"Jesus," Huxley kicks dirt. "You're about to gut me with my own knife and it's your own damn fault that the water got taken!"

Jay is looking at the tracks hard. He holds up a hand. "I didn't take a piss last night."

"What? You sleepwalk?"

"No," Jay is following the tracks with his eyes. "Those aren't my tracks."

Huxley goes quiet. He looks at the tracks.

They are steady tracks, carefully tread when they are close. But as they get farther away, they get sloppier. Just general impressions in the sandy dirt as the person that made them began to run. How long ago? How old were they?

The tracks lead up to a short pile of boulders, maybe fifty yards from them.

Huxley points. "There."

Jay nods.

In an instant, their argument is forgotten. They are both fixed on the boulders.

Jay very steadily hands the knife back to Huxley. Huxley takes it, holds it underhanded.

Huxley's voice is quiet. "You think they're still there?"

Jay shakes his head. "I don't know."

Huxley eyes the footprints in the sand again. It looks like only one set.

"Come on," Jay says, starting toward it.

The second he steps foot in that direction, a short, dark figure bursts out of concealment behind the rocks, sprinting away.

"Shit!" Huxley leaps forward.

"He's got our water!" Jay yells and hurtles himself toward the boulders.

Huxley's feet churn through the sand, but he gets his momentum up, and then he is flying across. This is the best-fed, most hydrated he's been in weeks. He feels suddenly unstoppable. And Jay may be a stouter man, but Huxley's strides are long, and they eat up distance.

He is passing Jay in a few seconds, and already gaining ground on the running figure ahead of them. Huxley can see it is a man, a dark-skinned man. The thief's clothes seem many sizes too large for his squat figure and they billow about him as he runs. He keeps looking back over his shoulder, and all that registers with Huxley is the way the man's eyes are so wide, so white, so terrified.

It makes Huxley run harder.

"I'm gonna fuck you up!" Huxley screams at the man.

The man looks back again. More ground lost. Every time he looks back, Huxley is closer, and the man knows it. His mouth is a wide O of fear. Huxley is closing in now, within yards. In another few seconds he will be able to reach out and grab the man. And he wants to catch him. He wants it so badly, he can feel the power of it, like a dog chasing a rabbit, he wants to get his hands on this motherfucker and rip the life out of him …

Suddenly the man stops and spins, holding up his hands. "No hay nada!" he screams, cringing away from Huxley. "Ten compasión!"

Huxley slams into the man as hard as he can. The two bodies go sprawling into the dirt, the thief toppling head over heels. Huxley slides on his belly, then rolls. He kicks sand and dust into the air as he struggles to his feet, still gripping his knife, ready to gut this thief.

The thief knows it. He jumps up from his hands and feet, trying to run again, but this time Jay tackles him, slinging him face-first into the ground.

The thief rolls, eyes squeezed shut, the skin scraped off his face, dirt and blood mixing. He holds his hands up as Jay staggers over, looking like he is about to stomp the thief's face into the dirt.

"Ten compasión!" he pleads again. "No hay nada!"

It registers through Huxley's rage.

"Wait!" Huxley reaches out and grabs Jay before he can plant his boot heel into the man's head.

"What?" Jay jerks away from Huxley. He wants blood. "He took our water!"

Huxley points the knife. "He's one of the Mexicans."

Jay opens his mouth to say something, then looks down at the man.

Huxley steps in, breathing hard. "You one of the Mexicans?"

The man looks up at Huxley. He has round, very dark features. A wispy moustache. There is something wrong with one eye. It's cloudy and the lid looks like it droops. He looks to be about thirty, if that. He is breathing hard, hands held up and shaking as he lies on his back.

"Sí, Mexico," he says.

"You speak English?" Huxley demands.

"Ah … a little bit." It sounds like *ah lihl bee.*

"The slavers," Huxley says, trying to speak clearly despite his chest still heaving. "Was it your group they hit? The slavers?" For some reason Huxley mimes the word "slavers" by making a gun from his fingers and pretending to fire it. "Was that your people? Your family?"

The man's face darkens. "Los lobos."

Jay spits into the dirt, dry and contemptuous. "This is bullshit. Where's our water?"

Huxley glances at his companion. The other man's pale, sunburned face is rocky and cruel. He doesn't care. He didn't care about the old man, and he certainly doesn't care about this one. He just wants the water. He wants to make sure that he and Huxley survive.

Can you argue with that?

Huxley addresses the lone surviving member of the caravan. "Where's our water?"

The man on the ground points to his voluminous coat. "Ayi. Lo siento. Por favor, no hay nada."

Jay kicks the man in the leg. "Speak English!"

"Sorry," the caravanner cringes back. "No hurt."

"You're *gonna* hurt," Jay says through clenched teeth.

Huxley bends over the man and pulls his coat open roughly. Inside, the water skin is hanging from the man's shoulder. Huxley rips it off of the man, feeling a little bit of his anger returning, though it's tempered now. How dare he take their water? But still … Huxley supposes it was *his* water first.

Huxley has to pull the caravanner's arm from the sleeve of his jacket to get the strap of the water skin off. When he pulls the water skin free, he hefts it, hears water sluicing around inside. It still has water in it, though less than Huxley remembers from the other night.

"Thirsty," the Mexican says.

Jay kicks him again. "No, you're not getting any more water." He fixes Huxley with his pale eyes. "Kill this wetback and let's get the hell out of here."

Huxley shakes his head. "It was technically his water."

"Technically?" Jay raises his eyebrows. "Fucking *technically?*"

Huxley glares at his companion. "Get a hold of yourself."

Jay becomes still. "I have complete control of myself, brother. Don't think that I don't. But when someone takes something from you, they need to die. That's the law of the Wastelands."

"Then he should've slit our throats last night."

Jay makes an angry noise in the back of his throat, but has no verbal response.

Huxley turns back to the caravanner. He doesn't want to kill the man anymore. But that doesn't mean Huxley has any kindness for him. He nudges the man with his boot. "Go. Get the fuck out of here."

The smaller man stands up, hesitantly at first, and then quickly. He stares.

Huxley and Jay both shoo him like a dog. "Go!" Huxley shouts at him. "Go on!"

The man runs. At first, it seems like he is trying to get away, but Huxley watches his pace slow, and then the man stops and turns and looks at them. Like he suddenly realized they let him live, which is probably far beyond what he would've gotten from anyone else in this world. And the Wastelands are a big, dangerous place for a lone man. Huxley knows this from experience.

"Fuck him," Jay says, and puts a hand on Huxley's shoulders, encouraging him to turn his back on the caravanner. "He's wasting our time now. Already wasted our water, now he's burning our daylight."

Huxley refocuses himself. *The slavers. That's what you're here for. To go east. To see where the slavers go. To find the woman with the black braid and make her pay for what she and her people did last night. And to find the man with the scorpion tattoo, and make him pay for what he did eighteen months ago.*

To find all of them, really. To make them all bleed.

Huxley and Jay walk back to their little campsite and grab the satchel of things Jay had pilfered from the Mexican caravan the night before. Then they turn themselves toward the road again. The tire tracks are still visible on the road. Wherever the slavers camped the night before, they continued on this morning, and it doesn't seem like they know they're being followed.

Good, Huxley thinks. *Let them get comfortable.*

The two men put themselves between the tire tracks again, and start walking.

Behind them, just a dark, ghostly smudge on the pale landscape, the caravanner follows.

CHAPTER 6

It is several hours later when Huxley realizes he can't see the tire tracks anymore. He stops where he is, in the middle of the road, and he looks all around. Here the landscape has actually begun to show some signs of improvement, rather than the bleak desert they came out of. Here there is actual soil, although it is a sandy loam. And there is more green growth.

Because there is less sand, the road is less swallowed by it. Here the road stretches and Huxley can actually see the concrete, a pale river of it, across the gradually rolling terrain, running east to west. And because there is no sand to cover the road, there are no tire tracks.

"Shit," Huxley says, staring down at his feet. "When the hell did that happen?"

Jay looks down, seems to realize it at the same moment. "Oh," he says.

Huxley looks east and can see no sign of the slavers or their wagon. Not even a rolling mirage of the ghastly thing and its poles topped with the jawbones of people that've fought back. Nothing. Like they never existed in the first place.

But they do exist. They're out there somewhere.

Where do the slavers go?

Huxley looks back west to see if maybe the trail is visible behind them. When he looks west he can see the shimmering figure of the Mexican caravanner, still following them. But no trail.

Huxley puts his hands on his hips, works some spit into his mouth. A strong wind out of the southeast has started to blow and it has been drying his mouth out, throwing dust into his eyes and chapping his lips.

Jay is looking at their follower too, shaking his head. "What are we gonna do with this guy?"

Huxley has no idea. "Why do you think he's following us?"

"Who knows?" Jay rolls his shoulders, stretches his back. "Probably just doesn't want to be alone out here."

"He is alone," Huxley says. "He's too far away for us to do anything if he was attacked."

"Well …" Jay looks east. "Chances are, we'd be attacked first. Maybe we're just convenient for him. Maybe we're clearing the way."

"Maybe." Huxley wipes grit from the corners of his eyes. "Maybe he's heading east."

"Clearly he's heading east."

"I mean for the same reasons as us."

Jay purses his lips, makes a thoughtful noise.

They wait in silence as the dark liquid figure of the caravanner continues to plod toward them, slowly but surely. He is still far away when he seems to realize that Huxley and Jay are standing there in the road. He stops and they can see his arms flopping about as though he is caught in some great indecision. Finally, rather than retreat or continue forward, he plops down in the middle of the road, in the bare sunshine, and crosses his legs underneath him, his wrists resting upon his thighs. Almost like he's meditating.

"Three is stronger than two," Huxley says.

"M-hm," Jay nods. "And harder to feed and find water for. Harder to hide."

Huxley cocks his head at his companion, squinting against the sun. "We're not hiding, Jay. We're not running. We're heading east. To find out where all those slavers are going and to make them bleed."

Jay flicks his fingernails. "Seemed like we were hiding last night."

"We were biding our time," Huxley corrects. "We were being smart. But imagine if we had more people, Jay? Even if we had five? Ten? We could've hit those slavers last night. Might even have hit them on the road when they first crossed our paths. We could've ambushed them, and they would never have massacred those caravanners."

"Three ain't ten."

"No, but it's a start."

Jay grumbles and looks at him. "I think you feel bad for him."

Huxley considers it. He looks into himself to see if Jay has spoken truth or not. *What do I feel?* But right now, the inside of him is as barren as the Wastelands themselves.

Finally, he shakes his head. "No. I don't feel anything for him. But I'd wager his feet are moving for the same reason as ours. He watched his whole family slaughtered. Probably watched sisters and daughters and sons, nephews, nieces ... rounded up and piled into the slavers' wagon with their family member's jaws rotting over their heads." Huxley tilts his head toward the distant figure. "He wants what we want."

"Well," Jay says. "If you're not gonna kill him, you might as well let him help. We'll see what his motivations are. But I'm keeping an eye on him."

Huxley watches the caravanner for another few seconds, then raises both arms up over his head and waves them twice. Far away, the other man perks up a bit. Huxley waves with one arm now, a beckoning gesture.

Cautiously at first, the man stands and begins to approach them again.

Jay gives it a minute or two. "We'll be waiting all day if he walks that slow."

Huxley waves again, more exasperated.

The man picks up the pace, but only slightly. Huxley can see him looking around. His pace slowing every so often as he tries to make sense of the situation. Why these two men are calling for him to get closer. Maybe they want to rid themselves of him. Maybe it's a trap.

That's the way you have to think in the Wastelands.

"Maybe that old man was his father," Jay says. "Grandfather. Uncle. Doesn't matter. Maybe he saw us let the old man die. Maybe he's just waiting to slit our throats tonight."

"He had that opportunity last night."

Almost begrudgingly, Jay says, "I'm still keeping an eye on him."

The caravanner stops about a hundred yards from them. The wind gusts again, flapping his over-large clothing around him. He stares at Huxley as he stands in the road. Huxley takes note of the man, the way his hands are empty and open and hanging at his side. He is not favoring anything, or holding anything. Huxley wonders if the man is even armed. He has a satchel on his back, it looks like, but that is about it.

"Oye," the caravanner calls out.

Huxley just stands there, watching.

The caravanner shifts his weight. "Amigos?"

Huxley doesn't respond, because they aren't *amigos*. They're just two people with shared interests. Maybe.

Huxley waves the man forward again. "Come on," he calls out, showing his hands. "We're not gonna hurt you. Come closer."

The caravanner waits, but Huxley doesn't give him anything else. Now they are both waiting each other out. But Huxley has the water. He has the friend. And the caravanner has nothing. Nothing but dead family behind him and empty, dangerous roads in front of him.

After about a minute of staring at each other in silence, the caravanner hitches up his loose pants and starts walking forward again, slowly. When he is close enough that they can speak without shouting, he stops again. His good eye is looking at Huxley, but Huxley is looking at the bad one. The clouded one. Maybe that is rude. He doesn't care.

"Amigos?" the man asks.

"The slavers," Huxley says, instead. "You know about them?"

The caravanner glances around, uncomfortable. His cloudy eye tracks with the same movements as his good eye, it just doesn't look like it works. "Los lobos," he says, darkly.

"Slavers."

"Yes. Slavers."

"Where do they go?"

The caravanner looks a little confused, but shrugs, and then points east.

"Yeah," Huxley says under his breath. "No shit." He holds up his hands again and crosses the distance between the two men until he is standing right in front of him. For some reason, he feels like he needs to speak quietly. He's not sure why. "Are you going east?"

"Sí." The man points east again. "I go."

"Are you going after them?"

"Qué?"

"The slavers," Huxley says with some irritation. "Are you going after them?"

The caravanner touches the corners of his moustache, deep in thought for a moment, his eyes—dark and light—looking away from Huxley. He is thinking something through. Sorting through his small repertoire of English words. When he finally speaks, he combines his words with exaggerated gestures.

"You call slavers," he says, carefully. "They take. Hermano. Hermana. They kill. I go. Take back." He makes a motion like he is gathering things close to his body. Then he forms a gun with his thumb and forefinger, fires it silently a few times. "Kill back."

Huxley searches the other man's eyes. He has a round face. Maybe even jolly once. But his drooping, cloudy eye lends him a harder aspect, and his good eye holds the same cavernousness in it that Huxley feels in his own gut. The same lack of feeling. There's nothing left in this man either. It's all been taken from him.

Huxley looks back over his shoulder at Jay. "Give him some water."

Jay, far from begrudging now, seems to be watching the other man with the same intensity as Huxley had. Seeing the same things. Recognizing the same emptiness. Huxley fully expects him to protest giving the man water, but instead Jay just takes the skin from his shoulder and holds it out.

The man hesitates, then takes it. He uncaps it hurriedly, like they might change their minds, and he drinks deeply.

Huxley watches the man's Adam's apple bob up and down as he drinks.

"Los lobos," Jay says, quietly. "You know what that means?"

The way he asks the question, Huxley can tell that Jay does.

Huxley shakes his head.

"It means 'the wolves.'" Jay crosses his arms over his chest. "That's what the slavers think they are. They think they're the top of the food chain. The most dangerous animal in the Wastelands. But they're wrong on that. Look at what they've done." He gestures to the caravanner, then to himself and to Huxley. "Look at what they've made." He laughs. "You take everything from a man and you leave him with nothing. Not even hope. And what does he have to live for?"

The caravanner leaves some water in the water skin, hands it back.

Jay takes it, caps it. Slings it over his shoulder. He looks between the newcomer and Huxley. "Desperate men. That's what they made us. And desperate men with nothing left to live for …" Jay pokes Huxley in the chest. "… *they're* the most dangerous animal alive."

Jay seems momentarily overcome by something. Some dark memory.

His fingers are flicking off his thumb, agitated.

He looks away from them.

Huxley stares at Jay's sunburned neck for a few seconds before turning back to the caravanner. "What's your name?" He pries at a little bit of Spanish in his memory. "Cómo se llama?"

"Soy Rigoberto."

Huxley sniffs. "How about just Rigo."

Rigo nods. "Is hokay."

"Okay."

Jay turns back to them. "His family was a trading caravan. He might know where to get guns."

Huxley raises his eyebrows to Rigo in question. "Guns? You know where we can get them?"

"Guns. Yes." Rigo points further on down the road.

East. Everything goes east.

"Borderline," Rigo says, overenunciating the word. "We go."

Huxley and Jay exchange a glance.

Rigo starts walking.

"Okay," Huxley says, falling in step. "Borderline we go."

CHAPTER 7

They happen across a sign that tells them they are leaving New Mexico and entering Texas. The sign is old and dilapidated, bent over on its rusted metal poles, the words scrubbed by years of wind and dust, and only just barely legible.

Huxley stops in front of the sign and looks at it.

"Texas," Jay says with a smile and a laugh. He has nothing else to add.

Huxley wonders if this is what Rigo had spoken of—the borderline between the two states. Perhaps this sign is a waypoint to a stash of buried weapons. But Rigo pays the sign no mind. He's traveled these roads before, it seems. He keeps walking.

Another hour or two passes. It is midafternoon. The sun is heating their backs. Huxley crests a rise and stops dead in his tracks.

"Holy shit," he says.

Ahead of them is a jumble of squat structures made from all manner of materials. Some of them are natural, and some of them are scrap. But if there is scrap, then there is civilization. And these little structures are surrounded by a wall.

"It's a settlement," Jay says, with some wonder in his voice.

"Does this mean we made it across the Wastelands?" Huxley asks.

Jay shakes his head. "Hell if I know."

Rigo realizes that the two of them are behind him, not moving. He stops and looks back at them, curiously. "Borderline," he calls back to them. "Is hokay. Vámonos."

The group of three stands in the center of the road and regards this small stand of civilization in the distance. Besides the occasional caravan, this is the first sign of other people that Huxley has seen in a very, very long time. He can't help but feel relieved by it. Huxley had run and hid from even the trading caravans, for fear that they were slavers in disguise. Jay was the first person he'd spoken to in over a month. Rigo the second.

Rigo continues on toward the settlement. There is this panicked moment in Huxley's mind when he doesn't want to get any closer. Other people mean danger, and he has spent so much time avoiding them. But then he remembers that he has nothing left to live for. He is not running anymore. He isn't hiding.

Just like Jay said. I'm the most dangerous animal alive.

As they approach the settlement, Huxley can see that two sentries are posted at the front gate. The closer they get, the harder these men look. Young and wild, with the look of people that fight and kill for their meals each night. One, watching the newcomers, holds a long rifle across his chest. The other stands at a big contraption off to the side of the gate—something that looks like five scattergun barrels on a rotating cylinder. Except they are bigger than scatterguns. Like small cannons, maybe. The man behind the big gun tracks the approaching travelers, the big bores following them steadily.

Rigo raises his hands.

Jay and Huxley mimic the motion.

"That's far enough," The sentry with the rifle calls out. "Just keep your hands where we can see 'em."

Huxley, Jay, and Rigo stop, hands held in the air.

The five-barreled minicannon creaks quietly on its metal hinges, the operator of the thing watching them with narrowed eyes.

"Why are you here?" the sentry with the rifle asks.

Rigo looks back at Huxley with a questioning glance.

Perhaps he is not as familiar with this settlement as it seemed.

Huxley takes a half step forward. "We're looking to do business."

"What kind of business?"

"Trade business."

"You plannin' on causing trouble?"

"No sir, hadn't planned on it."

"See that you don't." The sentry waves them forward. "You say you want to trade. Let's see what you got. And don't waste my time."

The sentry gestures them to a table made of steel legs and a rotting plywood top. The sentry takes a position on the opposite side from them. Behind the table, the rusting scrap-metal walls rise up around the settlement, crowned with sharpened poles and sections of barbed wire and studded with broken glass. A hand-painted sign declares this settlement "BORDERLINE."

The sentry waits expectantly for them.

Huxley isn't quite sure what to do. No one else seems to know either.

The sentry pats the table top. "Jesus Christ, gentlemen. Lay your shit out."

The man from the minicannon speaks up. "They's Wastelanders, Bud. They don't know."

The sentry eyes them, each in turn. "That true? Y'all Wastelanders?"

Again, Huxley isn't sure how to respond. But he gets the sense from how they say it that this somehow makes him of limited intelligence. Which is almost amusing to him. In the old life, under his old name, he'd been a scholar. A teacher. A reader. A lover of learning. These boys probably barely remembered the Old World. They probably hadn't learned as much now, in their burgeoning adulthood, as Huxley had learned by the time he made it out of middle school.

"We come from out west, if that's what you mean," Huxley says. "You'll have to pardon us. This is the first settlement we've seen. We've been in the desert for … a while."

"Well …" the lead sentry leans back a bit. "Idn't that something." He seems sincerely surprised. "Be honest, we don't get many folks come from out west. I mean … the trade caravans and all. But not just a coupla guys walkin'. Y'all seriously never been in a town before?"

Huxley looks at the walls. "No. I come from a farming commune. Seen a few outposts here and there. But nothing in the desert."

"What brings you so far east?"

Huxley senses Jay stiffen beside them. They are in an unknown situation right now. They haven't been in a settlement this far east. Were they friendly? Were they allied with the slavers?

"Just business. Personal business."

The sentry narrows his eyes a bit. "Hm."

"Out east," Huxley clarifies. "Little farther east than this town, I think."

"You mean the Riverlands?" the sentry balks a bit.

Huxley doesn't know how to respond to that.

"Christ, Bud," the man on the minicannon gripes. "You tryna fuck the man? Check his pockets and let him go."

The lead sentry rolls his eyes. He taps the table. "Anything you have to trade, lay it on the table. If you got enough to make our time worth it, you can go inside. Otherwise, you can pass on. This is a trading town only. No place for hanging out and rabblerousin'."

Huxley and Jay and Rigo look amongst themselves.

Huxley has nothing of value but his knife, and that he is not willing to trade. Jay has the satchel of things he scavenged from the wreckage of the Mexican caravan. He upends this on the table, spreading the items out. It is an assortment of oddities from small, burned-out electronic parts and wiring, to some items of a more homemade nature. Some sorts of ointments and salves.

The sentry pokes through them, unimpressed.

Next, Rigo approaches the table and begins to empty his voluminous pockets. From inside these deep folds he produces several ancient candies, bottle caps, paper clips, intact fuses, batteries, a handful of 9mm rounds, and an old multitool.

The sentry bobbles his head. "Well. It ain't a whole lot. But I suppose it's enough." He motions to the gate. "You can go."

The young man at the minicannon steps from his perch at the helm of the contraption and pulls a metal cord that threads through a pulley system and lifts the heavy gate constructed of numerous layers of rusted steel sheeting.

With the huge, heavy thing creaking and groaning over his head, Huxley steps through into the town of Borderline. The earth has been crushed by thousands of footsteps so that nothing grows, except for skeletal strands of scrub brush along the edges of the shacks and shanties. Everything has been constructed of scrap metal and old wood remnants from stick-built houses.

The main businesses—traders' posts, liquor houses, and whorehouses—are clustered around the roadway that feeds from the gate, a sort of main street that extends just two hundred yards or so into Borderline and ends at the back walls of the town—it is small as Old World towns go, but Huxley supposes that when you have to put a wall around things, you can't make them that big.

The gate falls noisily back into place behind them.

Huxley looks around, standing in the middle of the main drag. It is an odd sensation, being in this place. After so long in the wide open, it is disorienting to be in such close quarters. It feels almost claustrophobic.

To his right, a small shack hangs with various jerkies and fills the air with the smell of charred meat as the shopkeeper stokes the flames of his cookfire, preparing a fresh batch of smoked meats for sale or trade. Beyond the smoke-house lies another shanty where a cruel-looking man pulls a tarp aside and yells inside. Two young girls emerge, scantily clad. Across from these two enterprises, Huxley sees a scrapper, his wares set around him, a store full of nameless goods that Huxley can't even identify, or imagine how they could be used. Next to the scrapper, there is the liquor house, hawking whatever spirits the locals have brewed from whatever fermentables they can come up with out here.

Tucked behind the businesses that line the main drag, there is a collection of shanties where the permanent residents of Borderline make their homes. They are all about ten foot cubes, some with windows cut into their sides, others that have been stacked, one on top of the other, to make a two-story structure. There is a surprising amount of people milling about. Most of them congregate in the center of the main drag of the open-air market, a lot of carts and small stands for traders that have no residence in Borderline, or at least don't own a shopfront.

Huxley eyes the trading posts that seem to have the widest variety of things.

Jay seems distracted by the two young prostitutes. They squirm for atten-tion, doing the best they can to attract the eyes of men entering the town. And succeeding, by the look on Jay's face. It's been a long time since Huxley has been with a woman. But these are not women. They are just girls.

Huxley looks at the man that stands behind them. Their pimp, their owner, or their guard, he's not sure which. Maybe all three. Quietly, to Jay, he says, "You think those girls are slaves?"

Jay tilts his head, seems to reconsider them.

Huxley looks around the place. The cold burn of perceiving it in a dif-ferent light. Maybe this is where slavers go. Little towns like this. Maybe his daughter was sold off to a man like the one that stands outside of the little whorehouse with his two girls.

"What's that now?" the man with the whores calls out. "You have a question about my ladies?"

Huxley looks back to him. He takes a few, slow steps toward him. It is odd how he feels this tension rising in him that he doesn't think the other man even recognizes. Huxley only has a knife, and the man is big, but Huxley knows that he is dangling on the precipice of violence, already imagining what he will do to this man, though he has not even asked the question …

"Those slaves?" Huxley says. His voice is flat. Dry. Without inflection.

The man's face darkens and he spits in the dirt. "Fuck that and fuck the slavers. These is free women." The man points a finger at Huxley. "And best you watch your tongue about shit like that. Chairman Warner can claim these lands all he wants, but the Black Hats don't reach out this far and there's some good people here that've lost loved ones to the slavers." He takes a deep breath. "You buyin' or not?"

Huxley eyes the man, trying to wade through everything he just said. Trying to piece it together. But he understands the last question, even if everything else has gone over his head, so he shakes his head and backs away, mentally pulling himself off that edge of reaction. "No thanks."

The man makes a face at Huxley then looks off to the gate, hoping for other potential patrons.

Huxley looks at Jay, suddenly feeling a little odd standing in the middle of everything. He can feel the townspeople watching him with some passing curiosity. "What the hell was he talking about?"

Jay shakes his head. "No idea."

Rigo doesn't seem to have understood any words at all. He looks utterly lost, nervously hitching up his pants. Like at any moment he might take off running.

"Wastelanders?" a voice calls out from behind them.

Huxley turns toward the sound of the voice. Just a few yards behind them is a scrapper's trade hut. There are two men at the hut. One is an ancient old man with a dirty gray beard smudged with black grease. His prominent underbite continuously gnaws at his toothless gums as though he is always chewing something. His eyes are dark and liquid and appearing to lack anything beyond nominal intelligence. Huxley thinks he might not be all there.

The other is a younger man, who stands there and wipes grime from what looks to Huxley like an old engine component. The young man looks up from his work, his fingers still scouring away beneath an old stained cloth. His eyes are on Huxley, an interested smile on his lips.

Huxley raises his eyebrows in question, as though to ask, *Were you talking to me?*

The young man sets the component down and waves them over, leaning on his display table with both hands.

Huxley walks up to the booth and takes a quick glance at the wares on the table. There are glass bottles, old electrical components that Huxley cannot fathom a use for, mirrors, a few picture frames with faded photos of strangers inside them. There is a stack of old books in the corner, their pages yellowed and torn. Several pairs of shoes hang from their laces, ranging from very old and worn to nearly new. Tools are displayed prominently upon a table in the same way a jeweler displays his wares. But there is also food, water, and what look like homemade knives.

The old man gives him a flicker of eye contact, and then a weathered, blackened finger begins to poke through a tray of metal components. He mumbles something and tilts his head, as though he is relaxing upon his own shoulder. His jaw keeps chewing.

Huxley looks back to the young man.

"Y'all Wastelanders?" he says, looking between them. "That's what Bud said."

"Word travels fast," Huxley says, plainly.

The man shrugs. "Don't get Wastelanders that often. And Trigger's right," he nods toward the owner of the whorehouse. "I know you didn't mean nothin' by it, but we don't deal with the slavers. They don't mess with Borderline 'cause of the walls and the guards, but they've been known to hit some smaller groups." The man scoffs. "They tell us we're a part of the Riverlands, but that don't mean nothing to the slavers. If they don't get a good haul from the Wastelands, they'll just as soon fill their wagons with our people."

Huxley works his jaw. "You're gonna have to help me out here. We don't get much news out west."

The man hesitates for a second, then smiles, as though he is realizing something. "Holy shit. Y'all have no idea what we're talking about, do you?"

"We're from farming communes," Jay interjects, with a little irritation in his voice. "We keep to ourselves."

"Huh." The scrapper rubs his nose with a knuckle. "Well then."

"What's the Riverlands?" Huxley asks.

"You're looking at it. Technically."

"Not many rivers around here."

"Nope. Riverlands started out east. 'Tween the Mississippi and the Red River. We never even heard of it. Then one day, a Black Hat comes into town and tells us we're a part of the Riverlands. This is, oh, maybe five years ago. We says, 'The fuck is the Riverlands?' He says, 'The Riverlands is civilization.' Run by the Council. Which is run by Chairman Warner. And they up and decided that they own everything west of the Mississippi. We tell the Black Hat to go fuck himself, and off he goes. But every once in a while one rolls through, says the same shit as the last one. And every time we tell 'em to fuck off." The scrapper shakes his head. "Doesn't seem to make much difference, either way."

"What is a Black Hat?"

"They work for the council. They hunt down outlaws and kill 'em. No trial. No judge. They call it 'serving warrants.' Nobody gets locked up. Ain't no jails. Black Hats come to serve a warrant, they just put you in the ground." The scrapper shrugs again. "Least, that's what I hear. Like I said, only Black Hats I see roll through and tell us we're part of the Riverlands, and then move on."

Huxley smirks. "Why do they call them Black Hats?"

The scrapper smiles back. "'Cause they wear black hats."

"Lot of folks wear black hats."

The scrapper shakes his head. "Not these ones. They're the wide-brimmed ones. Boonie hats. Old military hats. If you ain't a Black Hat and you get caught wearin' one ... they'll put you down just as quick as a common criminal."

Huxley leans on the table a bit. "And the slavers. Is that where they go? Do they go to the Riverlands?"

The scrapper straightens a bit, his eyes narrowing. "Well, now that's a good question. We're told that slaving is illegal. Black Hats claim to hunt down slavers. But I never seen it. No one that's ever been taken by a slaver ever comes back. And all I know is that they go east. Everybody says they go east. So, yeah ... I guess it's somewhere in the Riverlands. Maybe even out past the Riverlands.

Hell, maybe there's a port, and they sail through the Gulf of Mexico. Who the hell knows?"

Huxley forces his gaze down to the table, processing what he's been told while he pretends to look over the things offered for trade. He doesn't really register what he is looking at. He is picturing mysterious men in black hats, and some council that claims to be running everything, though they seem not to have much of a civilizing affect this far west. And of course, the slavers. The woman with the black braid. The man with the scorpion tattoo. Going east. To nobody-seemed-to-know-where.

Huxley grinds his teeth.

He is overwhelmed in that instant, and he almost has to grip the table. He has the sensation that none of this is real. His barley fields were real. His wife was real. His daughter was real.

And then there is some horrible nightmare of endless desert and low-lying scrub, and terror, and living like an animal in the Wastelands.

And then he comes out on the other side, and this is waiting here, and he can't really tell whether he's still dreaming or not.

What do I feel?

I feel very confused.

"You okay?"

Huxley looks up at the scrapper. "Yes. Fine. Just … taking it in."

The scrapper sniffs, looks between the men standing at his display table. These rare Wastelanders. "Well … heard you were looking to trade. Anything in mind?"

"Guns," Huxley says, quietly. "We need guns."

The scrapper purses his lips. "Guns. Of course." He clears a portion of the table. "What've you got?"

Huxley, Jay, and Rigo all look amongst each other again.

"Come on," Huxley says, motioning for everyone to put their items on the table. "Let's pool everything together."

Jay and Rigo empty their satchels on the tabletop.

"Hmmm …" the scrapper pokes through the items, seeming to mentally calculate what they're worth. He grimaces, as though it is coming up short and it pains him.

Huxley points to the 9mm cartridges. "Those bullets have to be worth something, right? You can't find them anywhere. And the batteries …"

The scrapper wobbles his head back and forth. "Well … when's the last time you seen anyone with a cartridge gun besides a .22?"

Huxley doesn't answer. The last time he saw anyone use a cartridge gun was maybe two years after the skyfire.

"You got any .22s?" the scrapper asks.

Huxley shakes his head.

The scrapper grunts to himself and continues poking through the pile. His fingers flit past the couple of fuses, uninterested. Then he double-takes and seizes one from the table, holding it up to the light and inspecting the filament. Realization dawns on him that these fuses are intact. He grabs the others off the table and inspects them as well.

He turns narrowed eyes to Rigo. "Where'd you find these?"

Rigo looks confused. "Qué? No comprendo, amigo."

The scrapper points to the fuses that he cradles in one hand. "Dónde?"

"Dónde?" Rigo repeats.

The scrapper nods. "Dónde? Dónde you find these?"

Rigo seems uncertain with his answer. "Al túnel?"

"What? A tunnel?" The scrapper looks to Huxley. "What did he say?"

Huxley shrugs. "I don't speak Spanish."

But Rigo is nodding. "Yes. Yes. Tunnel. De los coches al túnel."

The scrapper keeps staring at them for a long moment, and he seems unwilling to let them leave his hand. He closes his fingers around them and continues to rifle through the pile with his other hand. He separates a few more odds and ends that he seems interested in, but still isn't happy.

"I'm sorry there's just not enough for a gun here."

"That's all we got," Huxley says.

The scrapper looks at him.

Huxley shifts his weight. "Alright, let's talk water and food." He points to a collection of plastic bottles of water. "Are those bottles still sealed?"

The scrapper snatches one up and sets it before Huxley. "Sealed as the day it came out of the factory. Perfect, clear, purified water, my friend."

Huxley takes up the bottle and closely inspects the cap. He can see the tiny burn marks in the plastic where the enterprising scrapper has resealed the bottle ring to its cap. It doesn't mean the water is bad, but it certainly isn't factory-fresh. Huxley sets the water bottle back on the table and regards the scrapper with a skeptical eye.

"Bullshit."

The scrapper's jaw works. "You calling me a liar?"

Huxley shrugs. "Maybe you didn't know. In any case, those bottles have been resealed."

The scrapper takes the bottle back and pretends to be shocked as he looks at the cap, though Huxley knows he is the one that resealed it. "I will not be trading with the man that brought these in ever again. Clearly he is not an honest trader. I apologize for the misinformation. But the water looks just as pure." The scrapper shrugs. "The fuses and the duct tape."

Huxley nods toward his clenched fist. "What you want those fuses for anyway?"

The scrapper withdraws the hand protectively. "Something I'm building."

Huxley smiles. "You know you'll never find an unblown fuse without some serious traveling."

The scrapper doesn't answer.

"Let me see your guns." Huxley taps the table with his fingertip. "Just out of curiosity."

The scrapper breathes in and out slowly. "What you planning to shoot? Small game? Or something bigger?"

"Bigger."

The scrapper ducks into his shack and returns a moment later with a firearm cobbled from parts. The barrel is short and wide and made of some ordinary pipe, about an inch in diameter and three feet long. It is attached unceremoniously by rusted metal bands to a chunk of wood that the scrapper has carved down into a rudimentary stock. A bulky looking trigger and ignition system takes up the back end.

"I build pretty decent scatterguns," the scrapper says proudly. "Actually built that one out front. The *scattergatling*. That's what I call it." He sets the scattergun down on the table. "This'n takes about thirty revolutions on the crank, but the coils'll stay hot for about a minute. It'll shoot pretty much anything you put down the barrel. Great weapon for a traveler such as yourself. I can give you a pound of my own powder mix to go with it."

Huxley takes a sidelong glance at Jay. The other man is biting his lip. He looks at Huxley and nods. He wants the scattergun.

"Okay," Huxley says. "And you say there's not enough here?"

The scrapper looks pained again. "Well … no. Just not quite enough. I'd be taking a loss. You could barely afford the gun, let alone the powder and wadding."

Huxley senses there's room to wiggle here. He thrusts his hand out. "Then we'll take our business elsewhere. I'll have those fuses back now."

The scrapper pretends not to care. He hesitates for a brief moment before pouring the fuses back into Huxley's hand. Huxley and Rigo then begin gathering up the items from the table. Rigo doesn't seem to really know what's going on, but he follows Huxley's lead. Huxley places the fuses on the tabletop for the scrapper to look at while they gather up the other items.

Huxley is about to sweep the fuses off the table when the scrapper's hand shoots out and grabs his wrist.

The two men stare at each other in silence for a moment.

"Fine," the scrapper says, under his breath. "You're fucking killing me. But I want the fuses, the wiring, the multitool, and the duct tape. I want all of it. Except for the batteries and the cartridges. You can keep that shit."

Huxley's jaw bunches. "I'll give you all of that. But I want the powder and wadding for the rifle, too. And the water."

"Fucking bandit!" the scrapper cries.

Huxley shrugs. "That's the offer."

The scrapper bares his teeth. "Fuck me. I can't do the water. That's too much. You're crazy. But I'll do the gun and the powder and the wadding. And I can give you a tip." He holds up a finger. "A tip that will help you get some food and water. But that's as much as I'll do. You're robbing me as it is. Fucking Wastelanders."

"What's the tip?"

The scrapper extends his hand. "Deal first."

Huxley looks at Jay and Rigo. Jay presses a finger against his lips in thoughtful repose and nods silently. Rigo is staring off at the whores. He realizes that Huxley is looking at him and holds up one of his thumbs and says, "Está bien."

Huxley takes the scrapper's hand and shakes it once. "Deal. What's the info?"

The scrapper begins to gather the items he has traded for. His eyes flicker across the way to the smokehouse. "Barry, the guy that runs the smokehouse?

He's got an old Luger 9mm. He'll give you plenty of food for those cartridges."

Huxley eyes the man suspiciously. "Why didn't you take the cartridges to trade with him?"

The scrapper smiles slyly. "I knocked his daughter up and now he won't barter with me."

The scrapper puts a pound of powder on the table in an old, plastic Coke bottle. He grabs an old paperback book and waves it in the air, saying "That's your wadding," and then slaps it down on the table. Huxley gathers the powder and the wadding and shoves them into Jay's satchel. The scattergun is equipped with a nylon strap secured in two points by nails driven into the wooden stock. Huxley slings the weapon onto his back.

Rigo scoops back his batteries and 9mm cartridges.

The scrapper gives a heavy sigh. "Now y'all get out of here. Go rob someone else."

At the smokehouse, Barry trades them three pounds of salt beef and fills their water skin for the eight cartridges from Rigo's pockets. Huxley leaves one of the pounds of salt beef on the smokehouse counter, and puts the other two in Jay's satchel. Huxley takes the remaining pound and carves it into three equal parts. Jay and Rigo each grab a part.

Still standing in front of the smokehouse, Huxley rips into his piece. It's salty, and hard. It is really meant to be cooked with water to rehydrate it, but it can be eaten like jerky in a pinch. And Huxley is hungry. The ribs and loins from the oxen the previous night have only gone so far to temper his starvation. He wants bread, but it doesn't seem like they get much grain, and he doesn't have much else to trade for it.

Jay gnaws on a piece. "Think it's actually beef?" he says quietly.

Huxley eyes his piece, still chewing. It could be dog. Probably was. Huxley hadn't seen any cattle around here. But he doesn't really care. He's eaten worse than dog. Far, far worse. He shrugs and keeps eating.

Rigo is tearing at his piece with abandon. The question of the meat is either lost or unimportant to him.

Over the sound of his own loud chewing, Huxley hears the gate rattling open again. He turns and sees three men entering. The first thing he notices about the men is how they smile and grin. They toss jokes back and forth with the sentries. They are well known here. They seem genuinely happy. And perhaps it has to do with the heavy satchels they are carrying—trade goods, Huxley assumes. Each of them carries a huge, reinforced canvas sack, and Huxley can tell by the way the men carry them that they are heavy. Just by sheer quantity of goods, these men could have the run of Borderline.

Huxley snorts and shakes his head.

Jay leans in close, saying exactly what Huxley was thinking. "You think they came by all that loot honestly?"

"Not a chance," Huxley mumbles. He looks at Rigo.

Rigo is frozen in place. His dark eyes have gone wide, showing the whites all around. A piece of half-chewed salt beef hangs in his mouth. He is staring at the three men as they enter Borderline. His hands are shaking. The salt beef falls out of his mouth and onto the dusty ground.

"Los lobos," he says.

CHAPTER 8

Los lobos.

The slavers.

Huxley makes the connection quickly and rips his eyes away from the three men as they walk through the gate and into Borderline. He is staring at the counter, but their faces are burning in his eyes. He cannot believe what he has just seen. The way they smile. The way they joke. All the while holding their satchels, weighed down with the belongings of people they've robbed and murdered.

Huxley forces himself to breathe.

What do I feel?

I feel like I want them to bleed.

Huxley has the presence of mind to elbow Rigo in the ribs to get him to snap out of it. "Don't stare," he hisses. In his mind he is thinking, *What do you do? What do you do right now? They're right here. They're right behind you.*

Huxley can hear the sound of their boots in the dirt behind him. It is like having his back to dangerous animals. But no, they aren't the most dangerous animals. *He* is. Because those slavers, those sadistic killers ... they took everything from him and left him with nothing. And a desperate man with nothing to lose is the most dangerous animal alive.

Huxley is belly-up to the smokehouse counter, but he turns his head, discreetly, and looks at the three slavers. They are heading for the whorehouse. Still grinning. So pleased with themselves. So insolent. Huxley thinks of the jawbones clattering from the poles. The wagon is not here. Just these three. Here to sell and trade the loot. Borderline doesn't like slavers, but the slavers can always act like traders, leave their wagon out in the desert somewhere.

There is a sickness to it. To steal and kidnap from these people. And then turn around and trade and sell them back the things you took from them. All the while, their families and loved ones lie in chains somewhere out there, listening to the jawbones of dead relatives whispering to them from death.

Huxley feels like he might grind his teeth to dust. Every nerve in his body seems to be buzzing. His skin prickles as he looks at them. He leans against the counter of the smokehouse. His fingers holding on to the edge of it, painful, the knuckles crying out with white, bloodless skin.

He feels Jay stir beside him.

"Those motherfuckers," Jay whispers under his breath. "Here. Right in front of me."

The salty tang of the meat's aftertaste is going sour in Huxley's mouth. He can't seem to produce the saliva to swallow. He watches as one of the slavers-disguised-as-traders takes hold of one of the young prostitutes by the whorehouse and pulls her in close. She giggles in poorly feigned pleasure, but Huxley can see that her eyes are devoid of feeling. But these men do not care. They want their pound of flesh, and they have the payment to please the whoremaster.

Huxley looks sharply at Rigo. "You sure about this?"

For all his dark complexion, Rigo has gone white. But his cheeks are burning red. "Los lobos," he says again, but this time with less fear, and more rage. He wants it. He wants the blood. Just like Huxley. Just like Jay.

Jay seems unsteady. Antsy. "They're right there. Right there. And they don't even know. They don't *know*."

"They don't know what?" Huxley hisses at him.

Jay fixes him with a wild-eyed look. "They don't know that we want to kill them."

The keeper of the smokehouse has stayed quiet, acting like he isn't registering anything that they're saying. Until Jay says this last bit. Then old Barry straightens pretty quick. He looks between the men at his counter, his countenance wary.

"Now, gentlemen, y'all go easy now," he says, but something that he sees in their eyes makes his voice shake. He tries to hold up a placating hand. "You got an issue with them boys that just walked in, you should take it to the guards, okay?"

Huxley is almost leaning across the counter, like he's about to lump Barry in with the slavers. "You know who they are?"

"They's traders, from the—"

"They're fucking slavers," Huxley snaps.

Barry is shaking. His eyes are shooting back and forth. His voice gets real quiet. "But ... the guards ..."

Jay looks like he's about to reach across the counter for Barry. "You think the guards are gonna do shit to these guys? You're dreamin'. Because they bring goods to this little trading town and nobody has the balls to question where they came from."

The three slavers enter the whorehouse. Huxley's mind is fire and ash. Like his dreams. Like his nightmares. Borderline isn't the end of the nightmares. It's just the beginning of new ones. Unfamiliar ones. At least in the desert, it was a simple nightmare. Here, it seems things have grown complicated.

Like an echo rising from the bottom of a deep well in the wilderness, he thinks of his own wife and daughter.

A tremor works its way through Huxley.

Time to stop hiding, old boy.

You're a desperate man with nothing left to live for.

Huxley's brain is on fire. It is a strange, intoxicating feeling. He has been so cautious, so careful, always trying to gain those miles, not letting anything sway him from his course ... and now, just to put it all aside, to admit to himself that all is lost and that there is nothing left but blood and death, to plunge into it so heartlessly, so mindlessly ...

It feels good.

Huxley pulls the scattergun from his back and smacks it harshly on the countertop.

Barry looks terrified. "I'll call the guards."

Huxley looks at the man that just spoke, as though he is a child that has spoken out of turn. He holds the man's gaze while he yanks out the bottle of powder that he got from the scrapper. "You call who you want. But know this ..." he leans over and speaks quietly. "You know what they are now. You call the guards on me, you're just helping the slavers. And I'll kill a man for that. So maybe it'd be best if you just took cover and minded your own fucking business."

Barry raises his hands and backs away further into his hovel, seeing the imminent violence like dark storm clouds rolling in on gale winds.

Huxley looks back to the whorehouse. The tarp is still swinging after the last slaver went in to purchase his pleasure. Eyes fixed on that piece of blue plastic, swaying in the wind, Huxley stands the scattergun up in the dirt and pours a heavy charge from the bottle of gunpowder. A page from the paperback to tamp it down.

He points to Rigo's pockets. "Batteries."

Rigo hesitates, but produces the items from his coat pocket. The collection of batteries includes several AA and a few D-cell batteries. Huxley snatches one of the D-cell batteries from Rigo's palm and it slides easily down the barrel of the scattergun. Huxley rips another page from the paperback novel as wadding and crams it down firmly in the barrel. Then he winds the crank on the side of the weapon until the copper filament is glowing red-hot.

"Qué vas a hacer?" Rigo says.

Huxley nods toward the whorehouse. "Come with me."

"Hokay."

Huxley can barely even think straight. But this is good. This is better. He is so tired of running. He is so exhausted of sneaking around. Live or die in the next few seconds—it makes no difference to him. To be *moving*, to be grabbing his fear by the jugular and making it submit to him … it is like feeling the inertia breaking at the top of a hill, before you roll down the other side. It is acceleration. It is mindless. And he doesn't want to stop. Not now. Forward is the only way.

Huxley stalks toward the simple structure. The fat man in charge of the two prostitutes is inside, and to Huxley, intoxicated by the fearlessness of his own actions, the whoremaster is just an obstruction between him and the object of his hatred. Huxley is unthinking, unseeing, unfeeling. He is base, primal, and he is hot and cold all at once. He is alive and he is dead. He is everything and he is nothing.

He bursts through the tarp into the whorehouse. He can't see the whoremaster, doesn't know where he went. There is one, large, main room. Two doorways lead to smaller rooms, both shrouded by tarp. Huxley goes left. No reason at all. That's just the decision that he makes. He sweeps through the tarp doorway without a conscious thought, oblivious to his companions and whether they are following him.

Into the room.

His eyes adjust to darkness.

A man. A girl. A bed.

The girl, on her knees before the man. She's naked. He's clothed, but his pants are down. The whole room smells of body odor and sweat and spit. The girl doesn't notice when he enters, but the man does. He jerks and looks indignantly at Huxley.

"What the fuck ...?"

Huxley raises the scattergun without a second thought. The huge bore of the muzzle levels out at the man and there is a brief moment when Huxley sees the realization crashing across his face, and Huxley imagines the victims of this man, the women raped, the men tortured, the children murdered and sold into slavery.

Make him bleed.

There is a great flash of light and a thick burst of gunsmoke like a thunderhead rolling down suddenly out of the sky. The D-cell battery rockets out of the barrel and cleaves the slaver's face into two bloody halves. The body pitches backward.

The naked girl screams.

Huxley turns around and finds Rigo staring wide-eyed. The Mexican utters something in Spanish and makes the sign of the cross over his face and chest. Huxley turns back to the man and the screaming girl. This slaver has a gunbelt still strapped to his pants, which are down under his buttocks, and in that gunbelt is a holstered revolver.

There are shouts from outside.

Where's Jay? Where'd he go?

He rushes past the screaming girl. She crab walks backward on the floor, up onto the filthy mattress. Trying to get away from Huxley. She doesn't understand. She doesn't get what just happened. She doesn't know who the man was, or who Huxley is.

Huxley grabs hold of the man he has just murdered. The body is still twitching. He snatches the gunbelt from the man's pants. Huxley can hear shouting behind him. He doesn't attempt to affix the gunbelt to himself, but removes the revolver and tosses the belt to Rigo.

One of the other slavers bursts through the doorway. He's bare-chested, holding another revolver, identical to the one in Huxley's hand. He cries out as he sees the body on the ground—a friend perhaps—and his cry pleases Huxley. It sounds good to him.

Huxley snaps the hammer back on his revolver and pulls the trigger.

The big revolver bucks and jumps in his grip, like a jackrabbit trying to escape.

The shot goes wide, punching a wide hole in the steel wall.

The slaver in the doorway cringes away, firing his revolver reflexively. The powder billows and the fire belches. The lead ball smacks cleanly through the head of the whore. Her screaming is silenced and she falls backward, legs bent oddly and spread crudely.

Huxley hurtles himself forward. He doesn't know what else to do, except to get close. Suddenly Rigo is there too, and they both slam into the slaver at the same time. The three bodies tumble to the wall, then to the ground. Rigo has attached himself to the slaver's wrist, struggling for the man's revolver as the slaver grunts and groans and tries to hang on.

Huxley plants the muzzle of his revolver deep into the slaver's belly and fires. The man's belly rips open with the force, and things spill out. Rigo slips in the gore once, but recovers and snatches the revolver from the man's weakening grip.

There are screams from outside the room, from the main, center room. Huxley lurches to his feet. He is standing in a cloud of gunsmoke. The room smells like bowels now, and blood, and acrid sulfurous fumes. Rigo is on his feet, fumbling with the revolver, but getting it cocked.

Huxley doesn't look down at the mess he's created. He doesn't care. He wants the blood.

He steps over the dead slaver and pushes the tarp out of the way.

In the center room, the last slaver is lying dead on his belly. Jay is mounted on the man's back. He is holding a third revolver, but he's got it like a club and Huxley can see hair and bone and blood on the curved grip of it. And when he looks down he can see that there isn't much left of the slaver's head. Jay's eyes are wild and strange. He is baring his teeth like an angered animal, and there are speckles of red all over his pale skin. He looks up at Huxley, and a little bit of humanity returns to him.

His voice is a husky croak as he rises unsteadily to his feet. "We should go."

CHAPTER 9

Huxley bursts out of the whorehouse into bright, almost blinding daylight. He doesn't have time to wait for his eyes to adjust. He turns in the direction of the gate and starts running. He's got a revolver in one hand, a satchel of stolen goods in the other, and a scattergun on his back. Gunsmoke and the smell of death trail after him.

Out of the corner of his eye, he can see townspeople scurrying, some standing and staring in shock. But none of them move to intervene.

Up ahead, the gate is rising again. It had closed behind the slavers, but the guards had heard the shooting from inside. They are coming. They are going to fight.

The gate is about chest level now.

Huxley can only see one sentry—the other must be cranking the gate.

Rigo points his own revolver at the one standing there, just as the gate rises enough for them to lock eyes. The sentry has his rifle up to his shoulder. Rigo stutters to a stop, kicking up dust, and he aims and fires, catching the sentry in the shoulder and spinning him.

Before the sentry can recover, Jay hits him, ripping the rifle out of his hands and sending it skittering across the ground. He punches the man in the gut and shoots him in the head as he doubles over.

Too bad. We didn't have a choice.

They were dealing with slavers.

They knew. They had to know.

Huxley turns the corner, just outside the gate, sees the other sentry standing there, hand still on the cable that raises the gate. Huxley points his revolver at the sentry, finger on the trigger.

"Where'd the three men come from?" he yells.

"What?" the young sentry yells, terrified. His eyes are going back and forth between the man that Jay has just killed and Huxley. He is completely confused.

Huxley shoves the revolver barrel into the young man's face, nearly touching his nose. "The three men who just came in here with these bags of goods. Where'd they come from? What direction?"

The young man raises his hands up with his palms spread. The gate clatters down as he releases the cable. The guard closes his eyes. Like he is expecting the shot to take him. "They came from the south," he quavers. "From the south."

Huxley growls deep in his throat, and he does not know himself. "You move from that spot before me and my men are out of sight, I swear to God in heaven I'll shoot you dead, boy."

"I won't move! I swear I won't!"

Huxley pulls himself away from the sentry. Rigo and Jay are already running for a group of horses strung up in a row along a trough. They weren't there before. Must have been the slavers', Huxley assumes, and so he has no issue with taking them. Huxley keeps the young man covered with the revolver while Rigo and Jay untie the horses.

From inside the town of Borderline, people are beginning to scream and shout.

Jay swings into a saddle, a little awkwardly. "We gotta go, Hux!"

Rigo pulls two horses over, one for Huxley. The Mexican shakes his revolver at the sentry, gesturing to the ground. "Abajo, pendejo! Down!"

The sentry flattens himself into the dirt.

Huxley slings quickly into the strap of the canvas satchel and he can feel it pressing the scattergun into his back. He feels cumbersome and weighed down. But he grabs the pommel of the saddle and swings in. His experience with horses is extremely limited. But he does what he's been taught, and what he's seen others do.

Rigo mounts his own ride smoothly, like he's ridden horses all his life.

Someone fires a shot and a clatter of projectiles rips up the dirt below Huxley's horse. He spins to look over his shoulder, sees gunports being flung open on the side of the walls and big bore scatterguns being thrust out.

"Let's go!" Jay shouts again.

Huxley doesn't know how to make the horse go fast, but it seems like Rigo does. Huxley copies the caravanner. He hunches down low, heels the horse in the side, and barks a syllable into its ear. The horse nearly throws him, but then suddenly he is hurtling away, like he's lit the fuse on a rocket.

After months of trudging through the desert, the horse's sprint feels blisteringly fast.

Rigo is ahead of him, Jay by his side.

Huxley squints to keep the dust out of his eyes, but he can taste it in his mouth.

Go. Just go.

More shots from behind.

The horses keep running, the men glued to their saddles like they are just barely clinging to these mad beasts.

Huxley cranes to look over his shoulder. Behind them, Borderline is already shrinking, disappearing into the dust. He can see the young sentry coming up off the ground, betraying his promise. Huxley watches him run and jump behind the five-barreled weapon. It swings in their direction.

Huxley doesn't know if he can make the beast ride any faster—everything is already a dangerous blur—so he just tucks himself as close to the horse's body as he can make himself, feeling the horn of the saddle pressing into his chest, the long hairs of the animal's mane streaking across his face. The animal is heaving, huffing, churning.

It is frightening and exhilarating.

In the increasing distance behind them, the weapon at the gate goes off with an earth-shattering boom. But Huxley, Jay, and Rigo are too far for the weapon to be effective. And they just keep going. Following Rigo.

Rigo steers them smartly toward a draw. Very briefly it makes them each an easily targeted silhouette, as it raises them up and backlights them with the sky, but they are quickly on the other side and racing down, the berm now between them and the settlement.

They race on. Rigo shows no sign of stopping.

They crest another rise, go down the other side. Run along the ravine created by two hills and enter a shallow arroyo. Huxley's buttocks and legs are burning, straining to keep himself tense over the saddle. His arms and shoulders are aching. And the horse seems like it's beginning to flag.

He looks behind them again.

Just rolling hills of low brush. He has no idea where they are, or where Borderline is behind them. He knows that they've been running for …

Shit … how long?

"Rigo!" he calls out, standing up painfully in the saddle and pulling the reins back.

Rigo looks back over his shoulder at Huxley and pulls back on his own reins. The three riders slow out of a gallop, then canter, and then stop.

All three riders are gasping for breath, right along with their horses.

Huxley slumps into his saddle, his back cramping, his mouth dry.

Jay keeps looking behind them. "You think they're following us?"

Huxley shakes his head. "I don't know."

The horse underneath him fidgets and whinnies.

Jay is staring, holding uncomfortable eye contact with Huxley.

"What?" Huxley says between breaths.

Laughter bubbles out of Jay. It is a mad laugh. Almost a wheeze. His eyes glimmer darkly in his pink, peeling face. It seems there is no humor in the laugh. It is the laugh that you cry out to challenge the universe. It is the laugh that comes out of you in the face of death.

"What the hell's wrong with you?" Huxley mumbles.

Jay chokes the laughter off. "Nothing," he says, staring off into an unnamed distance. "Just … fuck them, you know? Fuck those slavers. Fuck the town. They're all in bed together."

Huxley feels a little hollow. "Yeah. Well. We don't know that."

"Where do we go now?" Jay asks. "He said the slavers came out of the south. We could go after them. They're three men down."

"It's still three on seven," Huxley says, shaking his head. "Still not smart. And you heard the scrapper. They still go east. They just stop in these way-points." He looks at Jay. "I don't think the town was in on it. They seemed to hate slavers. And if they were in on it, why would the slavers have to come in and act like regular traders?"

Jay doesn't seem to care too much. "Town's fucked either way. That bitch with the black braid will eventually come looking for her boys. And when she finds out what happened …" Jay whistles. "It ain't gonna be pretty, brother. Ain't gonna be pretty for Borderline."

"Or they'll come after us," Huxley says. "We should loop around. Get back on that road. Keep heading east." Huxley turns to Rigo and points off toward the coming night. "Rigo. East?"

Rigo seems a little taken aback. "South," he says. "Los lobos. Slavers. We go south."

Huxley swipes a quick hand over his beard, holding Rigo's eyes with his. "Rigo, it's still three to seven. You understand three to seven? Too dangerous right now. Look at me." Huxley makes his face sincere as possible. "We will get them. Okay? We will get them. I promise you."

He spurs his horse before Rigo can answer.

They find a small outcropping of stone that will hide them, and they stop there to make camp. By then it is dark. They build a small fire, and like thieves, they huddle around it and inspect the contents of the slaver's satchels in the ruddy glow of the flames.

There is salvage in the form of tools, books, metal scrap, household chemicals, and tightly rolled animal pelts. There is also a coffee can that contains a stash of .22 caliber ammunition, which is as good a currency as any. They also find a stash of gold coins.

Huxley picks up one of the coins and inspects it. It is not something minted in the Old World, he can tell that straight off the bat. The circle of it is crude, the stamping uneven. One side looks like a cross, dividing the coin into four parts. These lines are deeply struck into the coin so that only a thin layer of gold remains there.

"It's like pieces of eight," Huxley says. He tests his theory by taking the coin in his fingers and snapping it into two halves without much effort.

"Why'd you break it?" Jay asks.

"Pieces of eight," Huxley repeats. "Old Spanish coins. You could break them into pieces. Like change for a dollar."

Jay looks at the collection of coinage. "So ... these are old Spanish coins someone found?"

Huxley shakes his head. "Nah. Too new." He flips the halved coin over and looks at the back. He puts the two pieces together, squinting to read the striking on the back. "'The Great Council of the Riverland Nations,'" he reads aloud.

"No shit," Jay says. "Riverland coins."

Huxley grunts and tosses the halved coin back into the sack that it came from, like he doesn't want to touch it anymore. "Come on. Let's get some rest."

The following day they ride east and find a new road, or maybe just another portion of the same one, and where there are roads, there will eventually be towns. It is in the hot, afternoon hours when the three of them are exhausted again that they happen upon the settlement of New Amarillo.

It seems like a stroke of luck to come across a town so soon after another, but then he realizes that they must be reaching some semblance of civilization, where perhaps there are not great stretches of wilderness between everything.

Huxley guides his companions into that place, never once thinking that he should've given the place a wide berth.

CHAPTER 10

They ride into the settlement of New Amarillo like desert ghosts, pale with dust and crusted with mud and stiff with dried sweat and salt deposits. This settlement has no walls, but it is large enough that it doesn't need one—it would take an army of slavers to sack this town. Men with guns and red cloth tied about their upper arms walk the streets in pairs and they watch the three men warily though not aggressively as they enter the town.

It is similar in its arrangement to Borderline, but here the buildings seem more permanent, some even made of stone and mortar. Most are simple adobe, but they are also made with scraps from Old World constructions, and Huxley can tell that this settlement did not exist before the skyfire.

Huxley stops in the dirt street and regards a pair of the red-marked guards who stand at the door of a squat, wide building.

"Help you?" one of them asks.

"Is there a place to room for the night?"

The guard nods and takes a step toward them. He looks Huxley up and down with a suspicious eye, but then points off down the main street to a building constructed of an adobe base and a wood and metal second story. The windows glow with lamplight and several horses are hitched at the front of the building.

"Inn and tavern down there. Josie's the lady that runs it." The guard hooks his thumbs into his belt. "Y'all peaceable folks?"

Huxley takes a second to answer. He wonders if the guard noticed. "Of course."

The guard's discerning eye tracks over the filthy group in front of him. "You folks wouldn't be plannin' on causin' any trouble, would you?"

Huxley shakes his head and dust sifts off of his beard. "No, sir. We're just traveling through."

The guard nods to them. "Alright now."

The riders work their way down the street and dismount in front of the tavern. As they're about to hitch their horses, a young boy wanders up to them.

"I can take your horses, Mister."

Huxley looks back and forth between Rigo and Jay. Neither man gives an indication of whether they trust the young boy.

The kid takes a dirty old baseball cap off his head and scratches the back of his neck with the bill. "Mister, we ain't got no walls around here. Guards do a good job, but if you're plannin' on staying overnight and you leave 'em on the hitching post, there's a chance they might not be here when you wake up."

Huxley wipes grime off his face with grimier hands. "Well ... where you gonna take them?"

"We got a stable around back. Got enough room for all three."

"You work for the tavern?"

"Josie's my mom," the kid says dismissively.

"Okay." Huxley says. "What do you want for a room and three stables?"

"Coin or barter?" the kid asks.

Huxley doesn't want to show the coins he has. There is something about having them that makes him feel like it will call attention. And he doesn't want attention. He wants a bed to sleep in, out of the elements for the night, maybe a hot meal, and then to be gone and never remembered. "Barter," he says. "How far will .22 ammo get me around here?"

The kid purses his lips and sizes the men up. "Take fifty rounds for the three of you and your horses. That's per night."

Huxley makes a face. They hadn't counted the .22 cartridges in his satchel, but he thought there were approximately a hundred. He snorts and spits in the dirt. "Tell you what, kid. I think ten for each man and his horse is a good number. Brings us up to thirty."

The kid chews the inside of his lip, giving Huxley a funny look. His eyes track over Huxley's companions for a second, seeming to count them up. But then he just nods, briskly. "Yeah, alright. Deal."

Huxley pulls his satchel off the horse and reaches in, feeling his way around the different items until he finds the old coffee can. He pulls it free and counts out thirty cartridges and places them in the kid's cupped hands. The kid scrutinizes them, and then nods, shoving them into a little pouch tied to his belt. He takes the reins of the horses and the men remove their possessions, then the boy guides the horses around back.

Josie greets them at the front door. She is a plain woman with a stocky build and sandy hair she keeps in a tight braid. She has a large smile full of badly kept teeth and she welcomes them in with a wave of her thick arms.

"Malcolm already take your horses?"

Huxley nods. "He did."

"Good." Josie makes her way toward them.

Behind her, there is a roughhewn counter with several large clay jugs that Huxley assumes are full of homemade wine and spirits. The tavern area is cramped, containing only the bar and a few tables with chairs around them. Two men sit at the bar, and one solitary man sits secluded at one of the tables, pulled into a dark corner like a spider in a web.

"What you boys looking for? Food? A place to stay?" Josie asks when she is before them.

Huxley looks down at her. "A room. Some beds. Food, if you have enough."

"Sure do," she says cheerfully, and draws them into the tavern. "Have a seat. I'll get some food in you and get your room ready while you eat."

They take a table and Josie disappears into what they can only assume is a kitchen area. When she returns, it is with a platter of what appears to be deer or antelope meat and some potatoes. She sets the platter before the three men and they eat until they have finished the entire plate and can fit no more in their mouths. She takes the three men to their room, a drafty space on the second floor where cracks in the walls between the boards and the sheets of corrugated steel let a dim glow of lantern light across the wall in stippling patterns.

Exhausted from their ride and fuller in their bellies than they have felt in months, the three men collapse on the dirty mattresses that lay unadorned on the floor and they are quickly asleep.

CHAPTER 11

Huxley wakes the next morning to the sound of a horse stamping up to the hitching station directly outside and below their room. Lying on his back and staring at the ceiling with an old blanket wrapped around him in the cold room, Huxley sees the gray sky through the cracks in the walls and roof and knows that it is dawn.

Below the room, he hears muffled voices.

A child's voice and the voice of a young man.

This is the first bed he's slept in since his own bed in his own house. He doesn't want to get out of it. He wants to stay there, stay warm, stay comfortable, imagine that things are better. But there is something about the voices below that makes it impossible for him to close his eyes again.

Huxley rolls in his mattress, and the old springs inside it creak and pop. He leans against the weathered boards and panels and presses his head against the crack there, where his right eye is illuminated in a vertical slash of diffused light. He can see down into the dusty street below where all the green things have been trampled to death by feet and hooves, leaving only a fine powder of dirt.

Below their room, the front door of Josie's tavern is shielded by an overhanging piece of corrugated steel that makes an awning. Beyond this, Huxley can barely see the horse and Josie's boy, but he can clearly see the rider as he swings from the worn saddle and kicks his legs about, working blood back into them. It is a filthy man with sandy hair, his face mottled by a mix of ash, soot, and dust from the road. His hair is shaggy and unkempt and beneath a layer of that same white dust, Huxley can see where the dirt has clung to and darkened around a crusted head wound, the blood now black and sunbaked, the hair stuck in a clumpy rat's nest near his temple.

It is the sentry from the gates of Borderline.

The one Huxley left alive.

The sentry is now leaning tiredly against the horse. His voice is like dried branches crackling in a fire. "Get me some water, boy," he says.

"You need me to put your horse up, Mister?"

"No. I just need some goddamned water."

"Well ... what've you got to trade?"

"I ain't got nothin' to trade with you."

"I can't just give away water, Mister! My mom'd ..."

The sentry from Borderline pulls out an old cartridge pistol, maybe the very same one that once belonged to Barry from the smokehouse. He doesn't point it at the boy, but lets it dangle loosely in his hand, a warning to the boy that he is not to be messed with.

Huxley can feel his whole body tighten like a compressed spring.

The sentry's voice is low now. "Just get me some water. And then I'll be on my way."

"Dammit ..." Huxley rolls off of his mattress and leaves the thick blanket behind and the smell of old skin and sweat trapped in that fabric. The cold air in the room coils around him and makes every muscle tense.

He snatches up his revolver and, dressed only in filthy jeans, bursts through the bedroom door and rushes down the rickety steps to the main level, his feet still clumsy with sleep.

When he reaches the front door of the tavern, he finds it partially open. Through the narrow doorway, he can see the sentry in profile, pistol held down at his side. Huxley pulls the hammer back on the revolver until it snicks into position and then eases through the opening in the door so that only his arm and half of his body protrudes through the door. The revolver is held out level and he aims for the sentry's head.

"Don't you fucking move," Huxley says.

The sentry looks at Huxley, his own sidearm still hanging, pointing at the ground. "Hey, there's no need :.."

Huxley emerges fully from the door. The dawn air is even colder now and he can feel his skin tighten around him with gooseflesh. He keeps the big revolver pointed at the younger man. "You're right. There's no need."

The sentry's eyes narrow. "Hey …"

He's going to recognize me …

Between the two men, Josie's boy backs up a few steps, his eyes wide, and his hands up in surrender.

The sentry's index finger titters outside the trigger guard of his pistol. "You the guy that shot up them slavers yesterday? Shot 'em dead right in the whorehouse?"

Huxley shakes his head slowly. "No."

The sentry continues to stare, his lips drawn in tight as though they are in the process of imploding. He considers Huxley's denial, but eventually nods his head. "Yeah. You're the guy."

Huxley tries to deny it again, but all he can manage is another shake of his head.

The sentry doesn't move. He doesn't aggress, and he doesn't retreat. "You know they came in after you, a woman, her and about seven other slavers. Shot ten good men. Coupla women and children. They lit a fire before they left and it burned half the damn town. Probably another dozen people died in that. I don't know who else got out."

Huxley clenches his jaw. "That wasn't my doing," he says.

The sentry doesn't respond.

Huxley's arm begins to tire from holding the pistol up.

After a long moment of silence, Huxley raises his chin a bit. "Boy …"

Josie's boy looks at Huxley. "Yessir?"

"Get the man some water. Have your mother make up some food. I'll pay for it."

The boy doesn't wait to even respond or acknowledge. He is simply gone in a flash, his footsteps crunching rapidly through the dirt.

Huxley slowly lowers his pistol. "No need for any violence between us."

Still the sentry does not respond, but he very slowly sticks the pistol back in his waistband. With his eyes still affixed on Huxley, he hitches his sweating horse outside the tavern and follows Huxley inside.

Just inside the doorway, Rigo and Jay stand, watching and waiting. Rigo's hand hovers over the holstered revolver at his side and Jay is holding the scattergun. Huxley can see the copper filament glowing hotly. Huxley motions with his head toward one of the tables and he takes a seat himself. The other two men follow suit.

Still standing and staring at the three of them, the sentry is hesitant to join them. From the back of the tavern, they can hear the opening and closing of an old wooden door. Josie emerges, flustered and pasting her hair back behind her ears, her eyes still puffy from sleep. Her eyes flick worriedly to the men at the table but instantly look away, as if resting her gaze upon them for too long would bring swift punishment. She disappears into the kitchen and they can hear the clank of cookware. The boy emerges a moment later, scared, carrying a large glass jar full of water, the vestiges of an old label still clinging to it like the skin on a mummified corpse.

He offers the jar of water to the sentry who takes it, staring at Josie's boy the entire time with a hollow sort of gaze that reveals very little of what he is thinking. The sentry drinks from the jar, slowly, with restraint, and his eyes stay on the boy the whole time. The boy steps away, never turning his back on the men until he is almost to the bar, at which point he spins and scampers into the kitchen where his mother scolds him quietly.

The sentry drinks until the water is gone. Huxley, Rigo, and Jay watch him in silence, just the sound of the water going down his throat. Then the sentry puts the jar down on the table and regards each of them in turn, his face still as blank as before. Then he sits.

Everyone at the table relaxes a bit.

Huxley keeps his hand near the butt of his revolver. "What's your name?"

The sentry stares at the empty jar. "Gordon."

"I'm sorry about your town, Gordon." Huxley struggles for appropriate words. He lies. "We had no idea they would come back like that."

Gordon sniffs. "Well ..." He trails off into silence.

"Did anyone else make it out?"

"I don't know." Gordon looks up and his eyes are sharp and hot. "Town's probably burned to cinders now."

Josie emerges from the kitchen and she carries two metal trays, one with a few slabs of cold deer meat and one with dense biscuits made of lard and some coarsely milled grain. She sets the trays down and waits only until the boy has returned with a pitcher of water for all of them, and then the two of them hurry back into the kitchen.

Gordon stares at the food for a while. Huxley, Jay, and Rigo wait.

"Are you hungry?" Huxley asks.

"Don't matter," Gordon says. Slowly, he reaches forward and takes one of the dense biscuits, breaking it apart in his hand and staring at it. Then he lifts a piece to his mouth and bites a chunk, as though every movement is a struggle. He chews without relish.

Huxley scratches his neck absently.

Rigo is the first to shake off the tension and take a plate for himself. He loads it with biscuits and chunks of meat and begins to eat. He seems to ignore the rest of them. His partial understanding of the language is only partly to blame. Huxley knows that Rigo must recognize Gordon. But for all his smiley outward face, Rigo is as callous as the rest of them. Gordon's tragedy will not affect his appetite.

Huxley and Jay watch Rigo eat. Then they turn back to Gordon.

The filthy young man is still chewing that one bite. His eyes are on the tabletop, but Huxley doesn't think that's what he's seeing. He's probably seeing Borderline, crumbled into ashes, blackened skeletons from friends and loved ones.

Was there someone there that he cared about? A lover perhaps? Hell, he was young but this wasn't the Old World. Someone Gordon's age could easily have a family. Maybe they were lying in the ashes behind him.

Maybe he's in the same boat as the rest of us.

Gordon taps the wooden tabletop twice with his finger. "You know she's out there. Camped out just past Dry Gulch."

"Don't know where Dry Gulch is," Huxley says.

"Maybe two or three miles south of here," Gordon says.

Still going east, Huxley thinks. *Borderline was just a stopover.*

Huxley puts his elbows on the table. "You guys kill any of them when they came to town?"

"I got one," Gordon says defensively.

"Anyone else get another one?"

"I don't know."

Huxley looks at Jay. Neither man speaks, but they each know what the other is thinking. Leaving Borderline, it had been three on seven. Now, worst-case scenario, it would be four on six. And if they took them by surprise ...

Huxley makes a face. "Still not smart," he says, more to Jay than anyone else at the table. "We don't have the lay of the land. Chances are they'll see us coming.

Maybe if we wait. Maybe if we catch them while they're asleep. But not during the day."

Gordon leans forward. "We must've got more than that. And there's gotta be some wounded. That's the only reason I can think of that they'd stay camped during the day." Gordon licks his lips nervously. "I'm goin' after her."

Huxley considers what Gordon's said. One down, according to Gordon. And they are camping. Which would make sense if they were licking wounds. He looks up at Gordon. "They'll kill you."

"Maybe," Gordon says with a shrug. "It don't matter anyhow."

"How long has it been since you slept?"

A shrug. "I slept some in the saddle."

"Sleep first," Huxley suggests. "Then figure out what you're going to do."

Gordon suddenly points at Huxley, his tired, haunted eyes narrowing. He drops his pointing hand to the table with a slap and shakes his head. "Why'd you shoot 'em?"

There is silence around the table. Huxley looks to Rigo, who is just finishing his meal. Rigo's eyes dart back and forth between Huxley and Gordon, showing that he is following more than he lets on. He wisely lets the language barrier make people think he is less intelligent. But he knows exactly what he's doing.

Huxley then looks to Jay. The other man is leaning back in his chair, arms crossed over his chest, regarding the younger man sitting across from them with the expression of an adult dealing with a petulant child. Jay doesn't speak. Huxley looks into those cold gray eyes for a few beats.

Why did we shoot them?

Because we could. Because we want them to hurt. Because we want to take from them, like they took from us. We can't run anymore. So now we bite.

"What's it matter to you?" Huxley says, quietly.

Gordon leans away, flicks the crumbs of his biscuit away from him on the tabletop. "I just thought … thought there must've been a reason. But maybe you're just killers. Maybe y'all just like gunfights."

Huxley feels the question hanging in the air, the accusation. He feels the burning in his chest, what is becoming a familiar warmth. It rises in him like lava flow. Continues searing away anything organic, anything so useless as human emotion. It leaves behind only volcanic rock. And when it cools, it is cold, and it is sharp as broken glass. That is the world his mind has become.

Huxley rises partially from his seat, but only to scoot it closer. He scoots it around the big, wooden spool that serves as their table, and he pulls it in very close to Gordon. So close that Gordon is visibly discomfited. Huxley leans one elbow on the table and he posts one hand on the back of Gordon's chair. His face is very close to Gordon's. He studies the other man. The way he will not look Huxley straight in the eye now. Like a dog who knows he's met the alpha.

Huxley speaks evenly. Just above a whisper. "And if we are killers? What difference does it make? Maybe it takes one to kill one." Huxley opens his arms slightly, showing his chest, as though he is baring his heart. "Look at me, Gordon. I have nothing. I'm just a ghost. I don't even fucking exist. I had things, one time. I had a wife. I had a daughter. I lived in a commune and I grew and tended barley." He tilts his head, studies the youth of Gordon's face. "You're young. You barely remember the Old World. But I was there. I lost all of that too. But I made it to the other side with my wife and my child, and I built another life, and I was happy there in my simple little life. But then even that got taken away from me. The slavers came, and they took everything, and they left me with nothing. And now they've come for *your* life, Gordon, and they've taken everything from you. Now *you* have nothing, just like *I* have nothing. So, you know. You know exactly why I killed them."

Huxley stands up, looking down at the younger man. "You want our help?"

Gordon is staring up at him. "Yes."

"Then it's not over when they're dead," Huxley says.

Gordon's brow creases in the center, confused.

"Where do the slavers go, Gordon? Do you know the answer to that?"

"East. They go east."

"Yes. And we're going to go where they go. We're going to go to their doorstep, like they came to ours. And we're going to make them bleed." He lowers his voice just a bit. "Is that what you want?"

Gordon nods, once, his lips tightening.

Huxley looks at Rigo and Jay.

Rigo puts his revolver on the table, friendliness gone from his face. "Los lobos," he says coldly. "Make them bleed."

Jay only smiles, a slow, steady smile. When all you can feel is hatred, only the promise of blood sets your mind at ease.

Huxley looks at Gordon. "You sleep. We'll get more bullets."

CHAPTER 12

The sky is darkening. Clouds have come in from the south, a thin layer all around, and bigger ones are coming, fat-bellied with rain.

They left their horses about a quarter-mile back, at the bottom of a ridge that runs the length of what Gordon calls Dry Gulch. Here, the vegetation is slightly thicker, slightly lusher. It is still dry, but it seems a far cry from desert. There are things actually alive out here.

Huxley lies at the crest of the ridge overlooking Dry Gulch. He peers over the edge, just the top of his head and his eyes visible. He can smell the plants crushed under him, a fresh, herbaceous scent, and feel the coolness of the dirt. The wind is heavy with moisture as it blows those storm clouds in and races up from the bottom of the ridge, howling over the top like a wildcat in the distance.

At the bottom of the gulch, perhaps a hundred feet below them and a half mile away, the slavers' wagon stands. It is surrounded by five horses. The oxen are free from their yokes and are staked close by, eating the sparse vegetation. The horses are hobbled. The wagon itself provides a lean-to, the tarps that covered its bed now extended out to either side, making a roof for the slavers to shelter under. A single campfire is burning off to the side of the wagon. At the wagon's back end, the slavers' poles rise up like the masts of a ship without sails.

Huxley can see the jawbones at the top, moving in the gusting wind.

He wonders if it is his imagination that he can hear their teeth chattering together. As though the ghosts of the previous owners have much to say.

The wagon is empty.

Where are the slaves?

"How many?" A quiet whisper beside him.

Huxley glances to his left, where Jay is lying, not quite cresting the rise. To Huxley's right, Gordon and Rigo lie, just a little farther down from the ridge. Only Huxley is poking his head up. One head is less likely to be seen. The others wait in tense silence.

Huxley redirects his attention down into the gulch. He can see four men, plus the woman with the black braid. One of the men is laid out. He is obviously wounded. Huxley can make out white bandages stained red, wrapped around a large portion of his right leg. He is lying as close to the fire as possible while still being under the tarpaulin roof.

Suffer, Huxley wills pain onto the man. *Suffer and die.*

His belly is full of cold, dark thoughts. Things grown in lightless places. Things that feast on the leavings of pain and terror. And that is all that Huxley has left. Just the residual *leavings* of those human feelings. There is a fear in him, but it has nothing to do with death or what might become of his body. It has everything to do with the fact that those dark things in him are in control, and he sometimes wonders where they are taking him.

Huxley sidles back away from the ridge, down below the crest. He scoots himself through the dirt and grasses over to where Gordon and Rigo are lying, and he can hear Jay coming along beside him.

"There are five of them," Huxley says, whispering over the wind. "Four men, and the woman with the black braid. One of the men is wounded. I don't think he can fight."

Gordon is nodding, his eyes wide, feverish. "We can take them. Let's take them."

Huxley makes a knife out of his hand and jabs all four fingers into Gordon's sternum. "Shut up. You do what I tell you to do, you understand that? We wait. We wait for the rain. Then we hit them hard, and we hit them fast." He looks at each man in turn, first Gordon, then Jay, then Rigo. "Everyone dies."

"Mi familia?" Rigo asks abruptly.

Huxley looks the other man in the eye and shakes his head. "They're gone, Rigo. All the slaves are gone. I don't know where they went."

Rigo doesn't have much of an outward reaction. He turns his head slightly so that all Huxley can see is the man's cloudy, drooping eye. He is holding dirt between his fingers. He crushes it, rolls it around his fingertips, almost like he's fascinated by it. He doesn't weep. Doesn't get angry. He only nods one time.

Huxley can feel his heart now. It's slamming his chest. But it isn't fear that drives it. Oh, how familiar that feeling had been to him. When the beating of his chest was like that of the prey animal, running at the scent of the predator. But things change.

He has changed.

His heart beats blood, and that's what it wants.

What is this feeling? He can't quite describe it.

It is the same feeling he had when he loaded that scattergun at the smoke-house counter. When he strode into that whorehouse and took the lives of men. It is the feeling of knowing there will be violence. It is a rush. And when you have no fear of what might happen to you, the feeling of impending release dominates everything else.

They reach the bottom of the ridge where their own horses are hobbled. They check their guns. Their loads. They free the horses' legs and they mount.

Huxley stares at the crest of the ridge above them. He waits for the rain.

He thinks of Charity. He thinks of Nadine.

This is for you. This is for what they did to you.

These aren't the same people, but it didn't matter. The slavers would bleed. Eventually Huxley would find out where the slavers go, and when he did, he would find the man with the scorpion tattoo, and he would put an end to him.

Huxley closes his eyes and he tries to picture his wife.

He seems to be able to remember the details in and of themselves, but he can't put them all together. He knows she had blue eyes, but he can't remember how they looked. He knows she had a big smile, but he can't picture her mouth. He can't remember her laugh. Or her smell. Or her taste.

He can remember the color of her hair, because it was the color of the barley fields.

But that is it.

Why can't I remember you?

The rain hits them in a rush. A few fat drops, and then a huge gale of it, thundering down the ridge at them like a great, gray curtain, only slightly translucent. None of them wait a second longer. The longer they wait, the muddier the ridge will become and it will be hazardous to climb, and to descend. Now. Now is the time.

He pushes away his memories of Charity.

Gordon cannot be held back. It is like the rain has spurred his horse. He launches forward. Rigo follows, then Jay, and then Huxley. The four of them race up the hillside, reins in one hand, revolvers in the other. Their horses churn for the top. Here is that feeling, that feeling that he thought of when he was standing at the smokehouse counter. The feeling of reaching the top, of rolling over, of broken inertia, no longer fighting gravity but going with it, letting it plunge you down, down, down …

In the downpour, the slavers do not hear the hoofbeats until it is too late.

Huxley fixes on the wounded man laid out under the awning. The other men are scurrying about, trying to keep the rain out of their shelter, oblivious to what is racing down the ridge at them. But the wounded man is staring out, and he is watching them come. He stares right back at Huxley and his eyes are wide and his mouth is working, his weak arms trying to point.

Huxley pulls up his horse as they reach the bottom of Dry Gulch.

As his horse's hooves stamp through dirt turning to mud, the slavers finally realize they are there.

The wounded man shouts out. Weapons are drawn.

Huxley extends his revolver and fires the first shot. The lead ball catches the wounded man in the throat, spurting blood, and then the world shrinks down to chaotic seconds.

Powder blooms in sharp, gray flashes. Huxley's horse folds underneath him. He is pitched over into the mud.

Horses scream.

Men scream.

And a woman …

Huxley opens his eyes, blinks through the muddy water flowing into them.

Jay and one of the slavers are fighting on the ground beside him. Jay manages to mount the slaver, just as Huxley pulls himself out of the mud, spitting dirt and rainwater. Each of them has the other's gun hand, and they are trying to torque their wrists to get enough angle to shoot each other.

Huxley pushes his revolver out and shoots the slaver in the head.

He staggers to his feet, gasping for air.

Another gun blast to Huxley's left, this one deep and throaty.

Huxley turns and sees Rigo standing there, the scattergun raised, and out in the rainwashed gulch, a figure topples into the dirt.

Rigo looks back over his shoulder at Huxley. He is soaked with rain and blood. Gunsmoke sits in the wet air like low-slung fog and it stings in their throats as they breathe it. Dying horses paw at the ground, like they can outrun what has been given to them.

That is it.

It is over as quickly as it began.

Huxley is left there, soaked and heaving air, clutching his revolver and wondering, *Is that it?*

From the other side of the wagon, Huxley hears a grunt and a swear. The sound of someone slamming up against the side of the wagon, and then feet scuffling in the dirt. Huxley cocks his revolver and runs to the other side of the wagon, Jay hot on his heels.

Gordon is holding the woman with the black braid down on the ground, straddling her back and wrenching her hands behind her as he wraps that long coil of hair tightly around her neck and pulls on it like a grotesque set of reins.

"Don't kill her," Jay barks.

Huxley looks at the pale man. Fragments of brain and bone are still clinging to the side of his face. He is staring at the woman with his pale gray eyes, his nearly white hair matted down in the rain.

Gordon stops choking the woman and she breathes in ragged gasps. He looks at the rope lying in the dirt to his side. "This bitch needs to die."

Jay nods. "Tie her up. She'll get what's coming to her."

Huxley stares at her. He wishes he could come up with some pity. He wishes he could put a staying hand on Jay and Gordon, to tell them "no." He wishes he had enough of himself left. But they took that away from him. They took his decency along with everything else. And for this woman? For this woman, Huxley has nothing.

Over the sound of the driving rain, Huxley hears the moaning of a man preparing to die. He walks very slowly around the side of the wagon and feels the soft squish of the mud underneath his shoes, the rain gathering in his hair and running down his back and soaking through his clothes. He holds his revolver down at his side and it dangles loosely in his grip.

Less than twenty-five yards out from the wagon he can see the hump of the man that Rigo had hit with the scattergun, sloshing through the wet dirt on his hands and knees, making slow and pointed progress away from them, leaving only a slimy trail of reddened muck behind him.

Huxley is at the back of the wagon. He looks up at the slavers' poles. Sees the jaws sitting there. He reminds himself where those jaws came from. Why they are there. Who these people are. He reminds himself that he is a ghost. He does not exist. He cannot exist. Because he is nothing. That is why he *feels* nothing.

In the back of the wagon, there is a crowbar. Huxley has seen it used once before. The hook of it is encrusted with gore, the double-pronged tip filed down to a jagged edge. Huxley slides his revolver into the wet leather of his holster and takes the crowbar with a firm two-handed grip. He looks out at the crawling man who is now rolling about in the mired plains, the sounds of his pain becoming weaker. Water gathers in Huxley's greasy hair and trails along his face, each clump of dark hair creating a tiny river of dirty water that flows into his blinking eyes and tastes salty on his tongue. He spits it out.

He walks after the wounded man. The man sees him coming, and tries to crawl again, but he knows it is over. He rolls onto his back, looks up at Huxley and then up into the rain and he becomes silent. The slaver's eyes are like emotionless glass orbs. Blood trails thinly from his lips, and when he opens his mouth, his teeth are stained with it.

"Do what you're going to do," the slaver says.

"How many others did you do this to?"

"Plenty." The slaver grimaces as pain racks his body. "More than I can count."

Huxley puts the pointed hook against the underside of the man's jaw. "Where do slavers go?"

The slaver coughs, spits blood. "What are you talking about?"

"Where do the slavers go?" Huxley says louder. "Where do you take the slaves?"

The slaver blinks, then starts to laugh. It is a gurgling rasp. He leans his head back into the muddy ground. The rain lashes his face, scouring away the blood that comes out of his mouth as he laughs. "You," he wheezes. "You fucking Wastelanders. What? Did we take one of your family? Is that what you're after?" his smile fades. "We're just the middlemen. We're just providing a service that's desired. We're not the ones castrating your sons and fucking your daughters ..."

Huxley grunts like he's been punched. The words hit him hard and he doesn't think. He doesn't think about any other information he can get out of this man. The rage takes him. He kicks the crowbar with the toe of his boot, plunging it up into the slaver's mouth, hooking the jaw.

He screams at the man, wordlessly, senselessly. Then he kicks him over onto his side, the crowbar still in him, and he stomps down on the side of his head, and he rips back with the crowbar. Things pop and pull free. The slaver struggles and squirms, screams into the mud, but Huxley keeps his boot hard down on the man's head.

He waits for the man beneath him to stop moving, and then he staggers back, dropping the crowbar and staring down at what he's done. What the slavers have done to others. *An eye for an eye*, Huxley tells himself, feeling suddenly sick to his stomach. *A jaw for a jaw.*

He looks up, breathing rapid, shallow breaths.

Jay and Rigo and Gordon are watching him.

The woman with the black braid is strung up to the side of the wagon, weeping.

How is she weeping? What right does she have?

Huxley looks back at those men and he realizes that he doesn't know them. He feels suddenly alone, the sensation of being so utterly lost that it nearly takes his knees out from under him. He doesn't know these men. They are not his friends. They are not his family.

Your family and friends are dead.

He turns away from them, trying to hide his shaking hands.

He does not even know himself.

He wants to think of the barley fields again. He wants to think of his wife, of his daughter. But he is covered in blood. He cannot touch those things. He is too filthy. He is too stained. They are a hallowed place, and he dares not step foot there. Not after today.

I can't think about you anymore, he tells their memories. *I can't hold on to you.*

Huxley begins to walk into the plains, the rain slashing down on him. He strips off his jacket, then his shirt, and he leaves it there clinging wetly to a scrub brush as he walks past, now barechested. He opens himself to the rain, lets it wash away the dirt and blood. His chest is heaving. He walks like this until his skin is clean and then he stops and stares up at the angered heavens, black and roiling. Fists clenched so hard that the nails dig into his own flesh, he opens his mouth wide and he screams into the wilderness, but the noise of it is lost in the storm.

PART 2

CRUELTY

His twelve-year-old daughter was sitting on an upturned log. She had a piece of paper laid across her lap. She would draw on anything she could find, but if you wanted a fine drawing, if you wanted the thing that she was known for, then the price was that you find her a piece of paper. This one was large and Huxley—the man he was before he took that Wasteland name—thought that it was a blank cover page ripped from some sort of large book, maybe an atlas or something.

Across from her sat the man who had given her the paper. He was middle-aged, maybe slightly older than Huxley himself. Worse for wear, his long, dusty beard and tattered clothes all covered in a layer of dirt. A rough character. The kind that made Huxley nervous for his daughter.

He didn't want her too close to this man.

But there was a certain pathetic desperation in the man's eyes that kept Huxley from moving in and stopping the interaction between them.

Besides, two of the community guards were standing behind the man, machetes in hand.

He had been caught ripping half-ripe vegetables from one of the community fields. Stealing, essentially.

They'd offered him an opportunity to pay back what he took with labor. He'd refused, stubbornly. He'd said he was just fine on his own. Said he didn't need anybody else. So he'd been marked and banished and told that if he was ever seen again, he would be killed on sight.

That was the fairest way to do it.

But while he was being marked, he'd happened to see Nadine.

Huxley had been standing with her at the time. They'd been rubbernecking, as was almost the entire commune. It was a farming commune and it was quiet for the most part. Banishings were a little dark, but they were also something to watch. And all the men tended to crowd around, holding their farm implements threateningly so that the man being banished knew that it would be best for him to cooperate.

This time though, the man who had stolen from them completely ignored Huxley and the sickle in his hands. He had looked right at Nadine with an intensity that immediately made Huxley put his arm around his daughter.

"Hey!" the man had called out, pulling his hand away even as they finished marking him. He half stood up, but the guards with the machetes sat him back down. He pointed at her. "Are you the picture girl? Are you the one that draws the pictures?"

Nadine stepped forward.

Huxley put a restraining hand on her shoulder. "Whoa, Nadine. We don't know this guy."

Nadine looked back at her father with a quirk of an eyebrow. "I barely know any of the people I draw for." Then, as stubborn as her old man, she looked at the banished man and called out, "Yes. I draw the pictures."

The man seemed almost stunned for a moment. Like he couldn't believe it. His outstretched hand, finger still pointing at her, trembled just slightly and he retracted it, as though embarrassed. His hands clutched at the satchel at his side— it looked nearly empty.

"I've heard about you," the man said. "From others. On the road."

Huxley took another step forward to hover behind Nadine, ready to strike out with the sickle if the man did anything strange.

"I've seen what you do," the man said. "I've seen the pictures." Now his gaze tore away from her and he looked to the guards. "Please. I know you don't owe me. I won't never come back. But I brought paper. It's in my bag. I brought her paper—it's good paper. Real good paper. Let her draw for me. Please. Then I'll go. You'll never see me again."

One of the guards made a face, then looked to Huxley. "Are you okay with this?"

"No," Huxley said.

"Yes," Nadine called out, slightly louder. "I'll draw him a picture."

Before Huxley could stop her, she'd already crossed and was standing in front of the man, looking up at him like she was seeing things no one else could see. She held out a hand to the man. "Give me the paper, and I'll draw you the picture."

The man looked at the guards to either side.

The guard that had spoken put a hand on the man's shoulder. They'd already searched the satchel when they'd picked the man up. They knew it didn't have anything dangerous in it. "Go ahead," the guard said with a shrug.

Then the grizzled man reached into his satchel and pulled out the big piece of clean, white paper, torn a little roughly on one end, a little dog-eared on the corners. But otherwise, a fine piece of paper. And large.

So then, just a few minutes later, Huxley was standing off to the side—because Nadine didn't like anyone watching over her shoulder while she drew—and he waited while she sat across from the stranger and drew him a gift.

"What did she like to do?" Nadine asked as she worked, keeping her eyes on the drawing, her hands skimming over the page expertly with her pieces of charcoal, making lines here, smudging things there. The amount of detail she was able to render with a piece of burned stick astounded Huxley. How much life she could breathe into those drawings.

The man sat there, still looking so hopeful. "She … uh … she gardened a lot. And she loved to take pictures of the plants. The flowers and stuff. Hang prints of them all over the house. She loved the color."

Nadine glanced up at the man, then back at the paper. She smiled softly. "Would you call her a happy person? Did she smile a lot?"

There were tears in the man's eyes. He wiped at them quickly. "Yes. She was always smiling."

There were more questions, more answers. All about this woman. Huxley didn't know who this woman had been to the man. He didn't know what had happened to her. He only knew that she was dead.

Another thirty minutes passed with Nadine drawing and the man sitting, waiting, expectant. There were periods of time when Nadine would go quiet as she drew. Sometimes she would close her eyes, like she was picturing something. She would just sit there, motionless, breathing with her eyes closed for a while. Then she'd continue. Huxley didn't know what she was doing. She never talked about it. Huxley had once asked her how she drew the pictures so well, but she'd only shrugged. Perhaps she did not even understand it herself. It was just a talent. A very strange, beautiful talent.

When she was done, she folded the paper in half—very gently—and she handed it over to the man. She did this because she didn't want anyone but him to see the picture. She was very private about it for some reason. Huxley couldn't see the picture himself. In fact, he'd only seen one or two of the dozens she'd done. They were all secretively handed to the person she drew them for.

The man opened the folded paper.

He stared.

Here, Huxley would always feel nervous for Nadine. He had this fear that the person would react badly. That maybe they would be disappointed and they would lash out at Nadine. But this man, like all the others, just stared at his picture, tears coming to his eyes again. He stared for a long time. Then he folded the picture. He reached out and very gently took Nadine's hand.

Huxley took a half step forward, his hand tightening on his sickle.

But the man simply kissed her charcoal-stained hand and then stood, sniffing. He nodded to her wordlessly, and then tucked the picture away in his jacket and turned to the guards, ready to be taken away and never return.

Huxley stood over his daughter as the man was escorted out of the commune. He put his hand on his daughter's shoulder, relieved that the tension was gone. Relieved that the stranger was leaving. He was a little exasperated with Nadine. Couldn't really help himself. She insisted on doing that stuff for people who were strangers, and therefore possibly dangerous. He hated it, but she would resent him if he restrained her. She found a certain purpose in it that Huxley didn't understand but didn't want to take away from her.

"I wish you wouldn't do that," he said, softly. "Not with people we don't know. Guy could've been dangerous."

"He was fine," she said matter-of-factly. "I could tell."

"Oh, you could tell?" Huxley rolled his eyes.

Nadine looked up at him. A picture of Charity from twenty years ago. "You know, people aren't as different as they act like they are. I know I don't remember the Old World, but it seems to me like everyone lost someone they love. Even the bad people, the strangers. Everyone lost someone. They all have that in common. I think people forget about that."

CHAPTER 1

They found him in a shallow cave, a boy, olive-skinned and dark-haired, a wretched thing. He was huddled in a dark corner, as if the cave were a womb and nature was the whore that had birthed this forgotten runt. He growled and spit at them like a wild animal cornered until they lured him out with food. A man and a woman, him with a sad expression behind his eyes, and her with disgust and loathing.

By the light of a fire, the man that he would come to know as Father saw the boy's sharp bones and ridges, tanned hide stretched taut over a skeleton. His tattered pants stained with shit and blood from dysentery. And Father took pity on him.

The woman did not want him. She lived in barren grief of her nine-year-old daughter, dead only a week prior. And this untamed thing was no replacement for the child of her own flesh, this thing born of the wilderness and suckled by violence and want. A bastard child of the new world that not even the Wastelands would accept.

Years have passed since they found him in the cave.

The boy is now ten, a full year older than their daughter had ever been.

What happened to his parents, or how he came to be in that cave are questions without answers. The child has no recollection of what came before. There is only Father and Mother and a deep pit in the back of his mind at the bottom of which lies the truth, but he is unable or unwilling to drag it up into the light.

In everything, the child tries to impress Father and Mother. He believes they will discard him if he becomes a burden, and always the imagined threat of abandonment hangs heavy from a frail rope. Time and tears have corroded the sharp edges of the loss of their daughter, and Mother has grown to accept him in her own stunted way. But often he will catch her staring at him as though he is a stranger in her house.

For a long time she refused to allow Father to take him scavenging into the outlying sections of cities, telling Father he was not ready and that it was unsafe. But she has looked at him with that odd, unfamiliar look more times than usual lately, and when Father asked again, she said nothing.

Now the child and Father kneel in the early morning light, stooped in the cold shade of a shinnery oak that stands lonesome and barren in a landscape of sand and harsh grass turned a pallorous white. The grass crunches quietly under their feet as they shift slowly back and forth. Dried remnants of it cling to their shoes.

Their clothes are tattered and torn and mended time and time again so that each article of clothing is a patchwork of other items. Dust and sun-bleaching and washing have caused the clothing to achieve a color as flat and gray-brown as the landscape around them. They both carry canvas satchels slung upon their shoulders, but the boy is small, even for his age and his satchel nearly reaches his knees, even with the strap tightened as far as it will go.

Before them, the land stretches out flat and then dips into a slight cavity, wherein rows of mobile homes stand dirty and beleaguered by time and wind and rot.

They have been sitting there for almost an hour, and the child is growing restless.

He squirms in his low position and pokes at the dirt with a long jab of hickory, the end sharpened and fire-hardened into a spear.

Father places a hand on his shoulder. "Stay still."

The child sighs and whispers loudly: "What are we waiting for?"

"We always wait, and we watch. How long do we watch?"

"An hour."

"And how long is an hour?"

The child's voice is rote. "When the sun's risen one handwidth over the horizon."

"That's right." A slight smile plays across Father's lips. "And what are we watching for?"

"People."

"And …?"

The child bites his lower lip, his gaze casting about as though the answer is hidden in the nearby scrub brush.

"Is it cold out right now?" Father asks.

"Yes."

"And what do people do when they're cold?"

"They build fires …" The child's eyes come alight. "Smoke. We're looking for smoke."

"That's right. Smoke from fires, and steam, because when a bunch of people are together in a small space, sometimes you can see the steam above them."

"Okay … so how much longer?"

"Well," Father takes a glance at the eastern sky, his face washed golden in the sunlight. "Why don't you check the sun?"

The child holds his little arm up, hand crooked in at the wrist so it appears he is reading his own palm. He squints at the sun and tilts his head, slightly. Then he drops his arm. "Looks like an hour to me."

"Okay. Have we seen anyone?"

"No."

"So is it safe?"

"Yes."

Father looks at him sternly. "No."

"But …"

"It's never safe, Lowell." Father sticks his thumb in the strap of his satchel and hitches it up. "We go in, but never think to yourself that it's safe, because it never is. Be wary of everything."

Lowell the child nods very seriously and stands up.

With nothing further to say, they set off toward the abandoned mobile homes to see what can be found. The Father's eyes are apprehensive, the eyes of an antelope moving alone through the wilderness, a herd animal with no herd to surround him. He has done well enough in scavenging to procure himself a revolver, which he carries in his waistband, but he has never used it and secretly fears being forced to.

Lowell's eyes are much different. They are intense, but calm. Aware, but not wary. He is a thing born of these wild, desperate times and he knows nothing of the times that came before. The new world, with all of its violence and brutality, is all he has ever known. He does not fear it but rather accepts it for what it is, unable to compare it to the gentler times before.

Their feet make whispering crunches as they move through the brittle grass, toward the old trailer park. Cold air stings Lowell's nose and it begins to run. He sniffs and wipes it on the sleeve of his jacket. The base of his little spear drags across the ground and he holds it higher, along the line of his hunched body.

Father glances down at him. "Lowell ... there might be some scary things in the trailers."

"Like what?"

"Dead people," Father says quietly. "But I don't want you to be afraid of them, okay? Dead people can't hurt you."

"I know." Lowell nods matter-of-factly. "I've seen dead people before."

"When?"

A long pause. Lowell can't really say when. "Before, I guess."

They reach the edge of the trailer park, which sits in a slight depression in the earth and is surrounded by old posts where fencing was once stretched between, but now stand silent and nearly petrified in the arid desert wind. The two figures, tall and short, slip between two posts and then crouch down at the lip of the depression.

Another few moments of quiet observation pass before Father decides to proceed.

He slides down the six-foot embankment, feet first, and then draws the aging revolver and holds it in close to his body. Lowell follows, the dirt and rocks stirred by his descent clipping and clattering down to the ground, the loudest sound in the desert at that hour.

They make their way toward the nearest trailer, an old single-wide with smoke-black staining around the glassless windows and a charred and caved-in roof. Father approaches the front door first, finger on the trigger of the revolver. The door hangs ajar and stirs in the gusts of wind that whip through the park, revealing in halting glances a scene of destruction on the inside. Father stands there at the door for a while, listening, but no sound comes from inside.

He pushes the door open and enters.

Everything inside is black as coal and smells of soot. The destruction of this trailer happened long ago, and from the ashes of what is left inside, scrub brush and creeping vines have grown. An old bird's nest hangs dilapidated from the inside of a cupboard corner. The plastic and vinyl components lay morphed and bubbled, deformed by the long-ago heat. The remains of a person lay jumbled in a corner, just black bones in tattered clothes, one limb indistinguishable from the next.

Father takes it in with a wrinkled nose and then looks down at Lowell, who still stands at the entryway. The child stands calmly, his spear held at the ready. His eyes move ceaselessly back and forth, but if he is distraught by what they have found inside this trailer then he gives no indication.

With Lowell in tow, Father steps to the human remains and pokes at them with his boot. They stir and crumble like a delicate sculpture made of sand, the solid bones clatter quietly against each other. A mouse flees from inside what was once a person's chest cavity and skirts along the base of the wall and then disappears into a rift in the floor.

The old body holds nothing of value and they move on.

The kitchen is bare of anything passable as food. They proceed to the bedroom. The bed is small and the covers sunken in and covered by creeping tendrils of some plant. The sheets and spread are unsalvageable, as the roots have delved deep into the cloth and left it pocked and pitted as though eaten through by moths.

The nightstand holds a single lamp, which Father retrieves and carefully removes the glass orb, now blackened with smoke. He wipes away the grime with his thumb and holds the bulb up, inspecting the filament. Unsurprisingly, it hangs charred and loose and rattles inside the thin sphere. Father places the bulb gently back on the nightstand.

The small closet holds a limited selection, mostly rotted shirts that nearly fall from their hangers when they are stirred. But there is a pair of sneakers on the floor, and save for a spider huddled in the toe of one of them, they are in a salvageable condition. Father evicts the little black squatter with a stick and inspects it cautiously. A red hourglass shows on its shiny abdomen as it squirms lazily away from him. He crushes it underfoot.

The sneakers are placed in his satchel.

"Not much here," Father says. "Let's keep going."

The next two trailers hold nothing for them to scavenge, though they are better preserved than the first. Muddy shoe prints mark where others have already been and Father shows his disappointment in the grim set of his lips.

Where others have been, there is not likely to be good salvage. And it is increasingly difficult to find places where others have not been.

On the third trailer, a growl warns them away from the door.

Father halts on the front steps. Like the others, the door to this trailer is open enough to see inside, and he peers into the dark belly to see what has issued this noise.

"What is it?" Lowell asks.

Father shakes his head. He doesn't know.

With the long barrel of the revolver, he pushes the door open. The sunlight is at their backs here and it seeps into the dim interior as though the darkness is a viscous fluid not easily moved. Father's shadow stands tense and ready across the floor among a pile of ancient trash mingled with bones from small animals, their rib cages delicate and spindly like the teeth of a fine comb.

The growl comes again, but it seems to come from the trailer itself, and not from any particular direction. Father moves through the doorway, and Lowell follows, his spear at the ready. The living room area is clear, a big-screen TV toppled in the middle with some dry lichen clinging to its sides and brown tendrils thrusting up from the vent slots in the back.

Through the living room and into the kitchen. The growling becomes constant, menacing, and now is accompanied by yips and yawls so diminutive they might have been borne on the wind from some location far away. But the noises come from the bedroom beyond.

They slip through the open doorway.

The source of the noise huddles in the closet amid tatters of old clothes fluffed to a sort of nest. There is a tawny bitch, some wild dog, a mix of breeds gone feral. She lies on her side, ears erect and neck distended so that her jowls tighten as she growls. Her swollen teats are suckled by a brood of squirming pups that jostle for a chance to feed and make high-pitched noises when they are denied.

Father lowers his revolver. "It's a dog."

"Is it friendly?" Lowell asks, stepping to his father's side.

"I don't think so …"

Lowell lunges forward so quickly that Father cannot stay him and he plunges his hickory spear into the dog with a sharp thrust, taking it straight through the chest. The dog yelps and jumps, casting her young aside with panicked legs and tries to bite the spear, but Lowell holds it firmly in place. As the litter scrambles about, crying, the mother weakens and gradually dies, her tail curling up as though in a last attempt to encircle her young.

Lowell withdraws the spear when he is certain that the dog is dead.

He turns to look at Father and smiles anxiously. "We haven't had meat in a while. Do you think Mother will be pleased?"

Father swallows, his words catching in his throat until he can work enough saliva into his mouth to speak them. "Yes. Mother will be pleased."

Lowell's smile falters. "Are you angry with me?"

"No."

Lowell's gaze becomes despondent.

Father places a hand on his shoulder. "I'm not angry with you, Lowell."

Staring at the pups, Lowell asks, "Should we keep the puppies?"

Father looks at them for a long time, then shakes his head. "No. They're too young to be weaned."

"What does that mean?"

"It means they'll die without milk from their mother."

"Oh."

"Why don't you wait in the living room."

"But …"

"Go wait in the living room," Father says more sternly.

Lowell leaves the bedroom and hears the door swing closed behind him, a tumble of empty cans marking its movement across the floor as it clears a swath of debris. The child stands in the kitchen, both hands on his spear, leaning on it as it points toward the ceiling.

In the bedroom, Father takes each tiny pup, their fur soft as down and hot with life, takes them by the back legs and swings them sharply against the floor to break their necks. They strike the ground with hollow thuds and their high-pitched whines cease.

In the kitchen, the child winces at the sound. His eyes are burning, tears coming to them, not for grief over the dogs, but because he fears he's done something wrong, that finally he's done that bad thing that will cause him to be abandoned. Father said he wasn't mad, but Lowell could tell he wasn't happy. Lowell was only trying to help. He was only trying to get meat for them, and he knew that Father wouldn't want to fire his gun because it was so loud …

He blinks away the tears, hoping that Father and Mother will still keep him. Hoping that the meat from the dog will convince them to let him stay. He stares up at his spear and watches as a single drop of blood meanders down the shaft of his spear toward his dirty hands, growing smaller as it travels, and he does not take his eyes off of it until the din of the anxious litter has fallen silent.

CHAPTER 2

Lowell doesn't cry when Father makes him skin the bitch. He just kind of goes still inside. His eyes have a half-lidded, uncaring quality, like he's gone into a place where he can't be affected by things. Father has seen him go here before. It seems like this is where he goes when there is death or blood around. Some holdover from those mysterious times when he was just a child in the Wastelands, by himself.

His hands shake a bit, but Father helps him. Father's hands are cold, but they are very steady when they grab his firmly and help guide the knife. Lowell is amazed at the resilience of animal skin. It takes a lot of effort to get it through.

"Her skin is tough," Lowell says, wonderingly. "It doesn't cut like people skin."

Father gives him a long look, then turns back to their work. "Well ... it ain't skin, it's hide. People have skin, and it's delicate. Animals have hide, and it's tough."

He helps Lowell work the blade from the dog's anus, carefully between her swollen teats. They nick one of the milk glands and white liquid bubbles over the meat. Lowell looks at Father with an expression that says, *I've done something wrong.* Father had clearly told him not to accidentally cut the dog's innards, that it might spoil the meat.

Father shakes his head. "It's okay. Keep going. Milk ain't gonna hurt nothing."

Lowell continues working the blade, careful to keep the tip away from the dog's guts.

After Lowell had killed the bitch, and Father had dispatched the last of the litter of helpless puppies—mercy, though it didn't seem like it—he'd come out into the main area of the dilapidated trailer and he'd held Lowell firmly by the shoulders. He explained what Lowell had to do, and why.

"Sometimes you have to kill. Maybe it's an animal, or maybe it's a person. But each time you kill, you have to bear the consequences. If you kill a man, you have to bury him. If you kill an animal, you have to skin and eat it. If you don't bear the consequences, then you'll kill without respect or thought, and that is very dangerous."

The work goes on, pulling the skin, heaving the gut-sack out onto the ground. Severing the trachea. Cutting around the anus, so now all the innards can be separated from the meat and bones that are left. The knife blade trembles in his hand as he works. It always shakes, every time, but Lowell does the work anyway. Father regards his son with some mix of curiosity and concern.

Sometimes Father forgets about Lowell's past. These days when he seems both child and strange adult are a grim reminder that Father and Mother don't really know the person they've adopted. It seems sometimes that the child barely knows himself.

The shakes have gone from Lowell's hand, and now he works with the knife to cut through the tendons of the hip and pulls the rear quarters from the hip bone with a soggy crunch.

It is moments like these that Mother would have looked at Lowell like a stranger.

Father gently takes the knife. "I'll finish it up. You did good."

The boy nods and takes a step back, but he hovers over Father's shoulder and watches, blank-faced, as the gory work is done. They pack the meat into a bit of tarpaulin to keep the blood from soaking through Father's satchel and then they set out for home. They cannot continue to scavenge as he fears the meat will spoil, and they cannot build a fire to cook it because it would take too much time and possibly draw attention.

Their home is set far into the dry, desertlike plains, because that is the safest place now—away from the highways, away from the roads where people travel and slavers pass. It takes them three hours to hike it, and they do not stop until they reach their destination, neither the man nor the child. Lowell handles the march stoically.

The home is an old streamline trailer, the bright aluminum paneling faded with a caking of dust so that it camouflages itself into the surrounding countryside. It sits nestled into a cavity made in the hollow of a jumble of boulders, each one nearly twice the size of the trailer. This is how they found it, years ago. No sign as to how it got there.

The door in the side of the trailer swings open and Mother steps out, a tall woman, and very slender so her cheekbones appear very prominent, almost severe. She is dressed in an old pair of khaki pants fitted for a man and several sizes too large so that the waist is cinched in with a belt. She wears a similarly sized denim shirt, tucked in, and the rolled-up sleeves reveal that her arms, skinny like the rest of her, show the tough cordage of hard work.

A smile from her is rare indeed, both for him and Father. But she favors them with one now, as she usually does when Father returns.

Father smiles back and waves.

As they near, she steps down and greets them. "Your pack looks full."

"It is." Father puts his hand around the boy's shoulders. "Lowell here caught us some meat."

Mother looks down at him and smiles brightly, so he knows that he has done well. "Really? Well, thank you very much, Lowell!"

The boy beams.

Father slips a hand into the strap of Lowell's pack and relieves him of it. "How about you go get us some water?"

Still feeling very proud of himself, Lowell takes to the task quickly. As Father and Mother disappear inside the trailer, Lowell takes an old plastic pail from where it sits near the rickety steps to the trailer's door. He inspects the sides and bottom and inside, checking for scorpions or brown recluses or black widows, all of which could kill him in a heartbeat, Father had told him once.

When he finds the pail arachnid-free, he takes it toward a dark hole amidst the boulders. Father has to squirm into this spot, but Lowell accesses it easily, his small frame fitting inside the narrow opening without his shoulders touching either side. In the dim hollow, the scent of water is the cleanest thing he has smelled all day. A glistening wet patch trickles from a fissure in the rock and gathers in a sandy-bottomed pool. He dips the pail into the pool and fills it. Lowell doesn't know how much water this small spring provides each day, but he knows that it is more than they are able to use in a day.

Once he asked Father why they didn't barter the water off.

"Because," Father had replied very seriously. "If anyone ever found out we had water, they'd kill us for it."

CHAPTER 3

Dawn has crept up on Huxley like a spurned dog.

Jay and Rigo and Gordon sleep fastly. Huxley watches them, wondering how sleep came so sweetly to them. For himself, it eluded him all night until frustration and anger forced him to give up trying. He sits on a clump of dirt, unrested, feeling twitchy and wakeful. His body aches for sleep, but his mind will not allow it.

Last night …

He shakes his head at the thought. What about it? What about last night? The things that were done? To the man who Huxley showed what it was like to have his jaw taken? To the woman who was shown what it was like to be the victim of wild men in the throes of bloodlust?

Huxley doesn't let it touch him.

He doesn't *dare* let it touch him.

To give into it, to acknowledge it, to look it in the face and to wonder what was wrong with him … that would only make him weak. It would only make him hesitate. And what does he have to live for? Nothing. That much he'd already determined. Jay had put into words the feeling that Huxley had known for a long, long time. He has nothing left to live for, and so he has no hope. And without hope, there is no fear. Reprisal, consequences, both for his body and his soul—they mean nothing to him. Good has become evil, and evil good.

Guilt and shame are useless. He holds his anger in his chest, like you might hold your head above water and wait for the floods to recede. He will not change what he has done. He will just harden himself to it. He will throw away all thoughts of goodness. He will throw away his gentle memories. He will be the animal that they made him become.

This is their doing.

Not his.

Huxley accepts the new day, calcified and bone dry in his soul.

This is the path you have chosen. And now you are hurtling down it. You've crested that hill, and it is all momentum now. You cannot be stopped. You can only plunge ahead. If you try to stop yourself, if you try to slow yourself, you will only succeed in tearing yourself to pieces.

Beside him, Jay comes awake as the sun glimmers against his face, the light setting the fine blonde hairs of his eyelids and brows alight. His pale eyes open, but he doesn't move, staying motionless on his side with his hands folded beneath his head, a strangely beatific pose. The acceptance that Huxley has only just found seems something that Jay has made peace with long ago. His near-colorless eyes land on Huxley and they linger there with curiosity.

Huxley looks away, into the sun. "Sleep well?"

Jay only grunts and rises into a sitting position.

Huxley looks at the wagon that hulks beside them. Bullet holes pock through the graying board walls. One of the two oxen hangs dead in its yoke, a bloody chunk of flesh missing from its hindquarters. The other stands indifferent, chewing its cud. The wagon itself is empty, but it still smells of people. It still smells like a latrine.

"You think they sold them already?" Huxley asks.

"I don't think they attacked Borderline with them in the wagon," Jay says. "So maybe they'd pawned them off before those three ever walked into the whorehouse. Who knows where they are." Jay's fingers start up again. "Maybe there's a ... stash house or something."

Huxley pictures that. All the slaves stuffed into a little shack, tied and bound and waiting in thirst and starvation for the slavers to return. Except that they wouldn't. And Huxley had not asked them where all those slaves had been taken to. He'd taken the one man's jaw in a fit of rage, and the woman with the black braid refused to say anything. She just wept and told them to get it over with.

"Ain't shit we can do about it now," Huxley says quietly, rising to his aching feet. He wishes he'd been able to sleep. He looks to the wagon, glances up those long poles with the jawbones on top. He stares at them for a while.

"We should leave them on," Jay says.

Huxley sneers in distaste. "Why the hell would I leave them on?"

"So people will think we're slavers. Then they won't mess with us."

Huxley gives it the minimum consideration possible, then walks over to the back of the wagon and yanks the pole from its brackets and lets it fall. The sound of it hitting the ground reverberates through the pole and clatters through the dead teeth, loud and sacrilegious in the silent morning air. Then he walks to the other side and does the same thing with the other pole.

He stands there and stares at them laying on the ground. He considers it for a time, then makes another decision. He hefts them up and slides them into the back of the wagon. He cringes as his hands glide over dried gore that, over the years, has dripped down from fresh jaws and hardened at the base of the poles.

Rigo and Gordon are now awake. Huxley supposes the noise of the poles hitting the ground was enough to stir them. They are standing near their makeshift beds—the ones stolen from the slavers—and regarding him with bleary eyes, but still curious.

Huxley motions to the poles, still wrinkling his nose with disgust. "Proof," he says.

It is only then that he forces his eyes out into the surrounding scrub brush where the bodies of the slavers have been laid out, away from the campsite. Huxley has noticed the shadows of buzzards beginning to circle, but he is surprised that coyotes never came in the night. Not like they did at the Mexicans' caravan.

The four men are clothed, bloody.

The woman is naked.

Hold your head above the water, Huxley tells himself. *Keep breathing.*

"Gather the dead," he tells the others. "Put them in the wagon."

Gordon scratches his head, looking at the bodies. "Why?"

Huxley gives him a sharp glance. "Because I said so. And because we're taking them to New Amarillo. We're gonna ditch this shit there so that town knows these fucks are dead and they ain't coming for them. Let New Amarillo bury them."

Jay makes a dubious noise.

Huxley looks at him. "Problem?"

Jay looks at the bodies. "That might bring more attention."

But Gordon and Rigo are already moving toward the bodies.

"No," Gordon says. "No problem."

"And put some clothes back on the woman," Huxley says.

They load the wagon with the dead, piled in beside their slavers poles. Huxley looks out into the low brush surrounding them. He cannot see much of the man he killed. Just his leg. He wonders if he should take this body, but decides against it. The rest have been shot and killed. This one had his jaw taken. Huxley does not want to show that to whoever will be taking these bodies at New Amarillo. He doesn't want to answer questions about it.

The horses that are still alive, they string up in a chain that trails the wagon. The dead animals—an ox and a few horses—are stripped haphazardly and the meat piled in the back of the wagon, away from the rest of the dead, as though the human corpses would spoil the food. Gordon and Rigo ride horses, but Huxley and Jay take positions on the bench seat of the wagon, and Huxley takes the reins. The load is light, and the ox moves them along without much trouble, even though it is only one now.

In the rocking, swaying of the wagon, in the bright sunshine that thaws him from the chill of the night before, Huxley holds to the reins, but he finds his eyes heavy. He drifts in that odd state between asleep and awake, the movement of the wagon simultaneously relaxing him, and then jolting him up out of unconsciousness, so that he bobs in the shallow end.

He does not like this place in his mind.

He has no control over what comes for him.

Nadine . . .

My sweet girl.

Memories and dreams meld, and they are dangerous in their perceived realism as the Texas landscape rumbles by and is lost in the visions that take over his brain for short periods. He sees his girl. Of course, he cannot see the details, he can't seem to get those back, all the little things that made her *her*. It is the same with his daughter as it is with his wife. The small things are lost. But the broad strokes are there. Like he is looking through dark glass at her.

Him and her.

Him and his daughter.

His sweet girl. His Nadine.

Standing outside and looking up at a night sky full of stars …

He is jolted out of his memories by the tires passing over a rut. He jerks a bit, taking a sharp breath in. Had he been asleep? He doesn't think he had been. Gone is the night sky. Gone is the cold air. Gone is the warmth of his daughter holding to him. Gone is the hope for a better future.

Replacing all of this is more empty landscape.

To his left, a man he barely knows, with pale gray eyes that sometimes seem soulless. To his right are two other men that he knows even less. A Mexican who he almost killed for stealing water. And another man he almost killed because … because he *could*.

He looks down at his hands. Hard hands. Holding reins. He can see the darkness of blood, the way it sits in the fine lines of his knuckles, the way it crusts in the tiny valleys of his unique handprint. Sitting like black dirt beneath his fingernails. Crusting his cuticles. He would not touch his daughter with these hands.

He takes a glance behind him.

His periphery sees the bodies, the haphazard way they are strewn on top of each other. Flies swarm around them, and around the piles of meat stripped from the dead animals. The slavers' poles still lay there with their dismantled jawbones still tethered.

He looks forward again.

She would not recognize me, he tells himself. *Wild man with a beard that touches his chest. Wild man with murder in his eyes. Stranger who calls himself Huxley and murders and encourages others to murder. Man with blood on his hands. Who are you?*

No one she knows.

She would not recognize you.

They arrive back in New Amarillo by noon.

Even with the pikes and their grotesque ornaments removed, the wagon is still reminiscent of slavers, and the group receives stares as they stop their small column just inside the ring of adobe-and-scrap constructed buildings that makes up the settlement's southern perimeter. Those who stare do so quickly and then move on. But they also garner the attention of the guards, a red-banded man appearing around this corner, two around that corner.

Huxley steers the lone ox off to the side, stopping the wagon just beside the wooden boardwalks where one of the red-banded guards is standing, hand lazily draped over a scattergun. The guard stretches himself up and forward a bit, peering into the bed of the wagon. Huxley watches him. His eyes narrow slightly, then he realizes what he's looking at, and he looks at Huxley.

"The hell is this?" the guard says, settling back on his heels.

His feet spread, ever-so-slightly. Grip on the scattergun a little more firm.

Huxley holds up his hands to show he's not going to fight.

Off to the side, Rigo and Gordon are sitting in their saddles, relaxed, or tired. They don't raise their hands. Neither does Jay. He regards the red-banded man with an expression that dares. *Crank that scattergun*, Huxley can almost hear the other man thinking. *I fucking dare you.*

"They're dead bodies," Huxley says without humor or sarcasm.

"I can see that." The guard's eyes flit here and there, to each person in Huxley's little group of killers, and then over their shoulders to the opposite boardwalk where Huxley knows there are more guards gathering. "Where'd they come from?"

Huxley spits into the dirt. "Slavers."

"Slavers?"

"Yeah." Huxley lowers his hands. "I'd like to speak to your boss … head guard … whatever."

The guard's eyes go off to the side.

Huxley follows his gaze.

A man is standing behind the wagon. He has one foot up on the boardwalk, one down in the dirt. He is a middle-aged man with the slightest paunch to his gut, but everything else seems wiry. He wears a white cowboy hat turned dingy beige, and a single revolver in fine leather holster at his side.

The man smiles at Huxley. "Can you believe they wanted to call me a 'Public Safety Officer'?" He laughs, his hands settling back to his waistband. His gunbelt, actually. "I told 'em, 'Hell no. You can call me Captain of the Guard or you can find someone else.'"

Huxley looks into the man's eyes. He judges him. Senses that he is also being judged. Then he fixates on the dingy Stetson. "Nice hat," Huxley remarks without enthusiasm.

The man's smile broadens. He looks up at it shading his eyes. "Yeah. I'm partial to them. Besides, you know folks seem to respect a man in a hat. Not sure why. They just do."

"Interesting." Huxley turns fully in his seat so he's not cranking his neck to speak to the captain. He nods at the cargo in his bed. "Bodies."

"I see that."

"Slavers."

"So I gather."

"You want them?"

"Not particularly."

Huxley grunts, half-amused at the situation. A quick glance around reveals that there are now five red-banded guards surrounding them.

Jay lets out a little chuckle. "I told you this was a bad idea," he says in a quiet sing-song voice.

Gordon shifts in his saddle, glaring at the captain. He points to the bodies in the wagon. "These fucks is the ones that hit Borderline. Don't know if you heard about that yet."

The captain's smile falters a bit. "I hadn't heard that news. How'd you hear about it?"

"'Cause I was there," Gordon snaps back. "I was one of the sentries."

The captain's pleasant demeanor is completely gone now. "Well shit. Y'all had decent walls. What the fuck happened?"

Gordon's eyes twitch just slightly toward Huxley and Jay, but he seems to remember himself. He seems to remember where he stands. "Some boys I don't know got into a shoot-out with some other boys I don't know. Turns out some of the boys that got shot was slavers. They were posing as traders to come swap some of the shit they stole during raids. Got recognized by some of the folks they raided from and gunned down in the whorehouse." Gordon rubs his eyebrows and Huxley sees his hand shaking just a bit. "Rest of the slavers didn't appreciate it. Came for a reckoning. We told them the guys that shot their men had already left off and they should do the same. Slavers didn't like that answer. Shot us up and lit the place on fire. Half of it was burned by the time I made it out."

The captain nods slowly. He looks to Huxley and Jay. "And you gentlemen? Y'all from Borderline as well?"

Gordon answers for them. "They was traveling through at the time. Helped us fight. Agreed to meet up here."

One of the red-banded guards spoke up. "Yeah, I saw you boys coupla nights ago."

A few other guards confirm that Huxley and his little group had been spotted before.

Gordon nods. "Yup. Met up at Josie's and went after them."

The captain eyes the bodies again, this time with a different understanding. "Heard you pulled a gun on Josie's boy."

Gordon licks his lips, settles back into his saddle a bit. "I was in a state. I apologize."

The captain shrugs. "Understandable. Wasn't her or her boy that made a fuss about it. Someone else seen it through a window and mentioned it to me, but as I gather, all's well that ends well. Josie got paid for her trouble and y'all moved on." He shoves himself off the boardwalk and walks over to the bed of the wagon. He looks over the contents more closely now. "You boys did all this by yourselves, huh? Took on a crew of slavers. Then you bring 'em to me. Dead as dogs and their slavers' poles stacked in the back with 'em. Jawbones and all." He removes his hat, itches his brow, the settles it back on his head. "Well, shit. Where's the slaves? Did they not have any slaves?"

"They did," Huxley says. "But by the time we caught up to them, they didn't. Off-loaded them somewhere. Had to be somewhere close."

The captain considers this for a long time, staring down at the bodies.

Huxley clears his throat. "We thought you'd want to know that they weren't out there anymore. We took care of it. If you don't have someone to bury them, then we'll drop them off the side of the road and continue on …"

The captain makes a face. "No, no, no. Last thing we need is for another crew to happen by them while they're still recognizable and start terrorizing my areas. They can be a spiteful bunch. As I'm sure you realize." He tips his hat back a bit and squints up at Huxley. "No, we'll bury them for you gents. Let them be forgotten about. But you guys …"

He trails off.

Huxley feels a tingle working through him. His fingers itch for the revolver in his waistband.

The captain wags a finger, looking across Huxley's gathered group. "… You guys. I might be able to solve the mystery of where these slaves have gone."

CHAPTER 4

The captain points to a group of his guards. "Y'all come take care of these bodies, will you?" He walks around to the front of the wagon and holds out a hand to Huxley. "Captain Tim," he says. "Elected town peacekeeper, so I'm told." He says it with a practiced tone of self-deprecation. As though he's not proud of his title. Huxley can tell that he is.

Huxley stares at the hand for a brief moment. It's been so long since someone offered a handshake that Huxley actually wonders what the hell the hand is for, and then remembers. He takes it with some hesitation and gives it a single pump.

"Huxley," he says.

"Alright then, Huxley. You and your boys want a hot meal?"

Huxley actually just wants to be going. But Tim has pressed a button, and he seems to know he has. Somehow the captain senses that he has Huxley on the hook, and now he's casually letting out the line. Huxley wants to know where the slaves went. Because if he can figure out where the slaves went, then he might figure out where the *slavers* go. And that is the question. Because even though the woman with the black braid is lying dead in his cart, Huxley still has unfinished business.

He wants to hurt the slavers in general.

But one in particular.

Besides, hot food would be nice. "Sure," Huxley says.

"Well, come on then."

Huxley and Jay make their way down off the wagon. They both keep their satchels with them. Captain Tim seems to take note, but he only smiles at their precaution and says nothing. Rigo and Gordon find a hitching post and they leave their horses there, also taking their own bags of goods. There is little trust established at this moment. Simply two groups of men—Huxley's and Captain Tim's—that are, for the moment, not going to harm each other.

A parley of sorts.

Tim walks them down the boardwalk to a building just like every other structure—adobe on the bottom, and wood on top. A metal chimney rises out of the roof and pours white smoke. The entire street immediately around the structure smells like charred meat and spices. In the Old World, Huxley would have found the smells cloying. Now they are probably the best he's smelled in some time.

A few guards tag along, but at the entrance, Tim dismisses them. Only he and Huxley's group enter. The interior bears the same smell as outside, only stronger, nearly tangible as though it could be tasted simply by taking mouthfuls of air. The interior is dim and smoky, light coming in from multiple places where the scrap walls don't meet up, and from unglassed windows. Even with all the open spaces, the area is warm almost to the point of stuffiness.

There is only a single wooden table made from what looked like old shiplap boards, surrounded by stools made of semipolished logs. In the center of the single-room structure, a man tends a gigantic cast-iron pot that sits atop a ring of stones holding in the glow of a fire. He is old and balding, and though he isn't fat, it's clear he's better fed than most everyone else.

Huxley remembers a similar set-up in his old farming commune. The purpose was not to be a restaurant, but more of a community kitchen. In his farming community, and the few others he'd come into contact with since then, the work was hard and the hours were long. If there wasn't a man to feed the workers, then the workers found other communes to work in. Plus, they labored from sunup to sundown—they had no time to gather and prepare their own meals. Huxley imagined it was much the same with these outposts and towns in the Wastelands.

Well, not the Wastelands anymore, he reminds himself. *We're in the Riverlands now. Whatever the hell that means.*

Tim greets the man at the pot with a wave. "Food for these gentlemen, please. And I'll take some myself."

Huxley and his companions follow Tim's lead and sit themselves at the table. Huxley finds himself directly across from Tim, with Jay to one side, and Rigo and Gordon on the other. The food comes nearly before they had finished settling onto their stools. Tin plates bearing some sort of stew or chili, heavy with beans, though there appears to be a generous amount of meat in it as well.

Jay, Rigo, and Gordon attack their food, but Huxley is more reserved.

He eyes the captain on the other side of the table. "This is very kind. Thank you."

Tim smiles. "Enjoy your food. We'll talk afterward."

Huxley humors his host by eating half of it before he stops and clears his throat loudly. "You mentioned the slaves. Where they might be."

That same smile. "I think we can finish our food …"

"I think we should talk."

The sound of flatware ticking on the tin plates slows to a steady rhythm as Rigo and Gordon glance warily in Huxley's direction. Jay is almost instantly disinterested in his food and more attuned to the conversation and the sudden tension between Huxley and Tim. He holds his fork with one hand, the end of it stabbed down into the center of his plate, while the other hand drops off of the table and into his lap.

Tim's expression does not change, though it dries up some. Then he takes one more bite and leans back from the table, tapping the side of the plate with his own fork. "Fair enough, fair enough. You seem to be very business minded, so let's get right down to business."

Huxley's lips draw out into a thin line.

Tim continues: "I've got a bit of a problem here in New Amarillo." His eyes fall to the fork as he spins it around in his fingers. "My problem is with a group of slavers that have decided to make a little outpost out past Firelight Bluff, a ways to the south of here. They call themselves the Reapers, or some such nonsense. I'd like to trivialize it but I won't." He looks Huxley in the eyes. "They were most likely where your own group of slavers took their load before y'all caught up with them. Hell, the slavers you took out may have been a part of the Reapers. But even if they weren't, I know these slavers." He leans back a bit. "They stick together. They work together. Some groups are the takers: they go out and make the raids. Other groups transport them. Others sell them. There's no league, but there might as well be."

Huxley finds himself leaning forward, looking at the other man intensely. "How do you know so much about the slavers?"

Captain Tim smiles thinly and assesses Huxley for a moment. "Well, you'll have to not hold it against me … but, once upon a time I was a Black Hat."

Gordon makes a noise from the other end of the table.

Huxley purses his lips, thoughtfully. "A Black Hat."

Captain Tim nods. "Black Hat Bitwell … Timothy Bitwell is my name. I actually worked with none other than Black Hat Davies." Tim barks laughter.

Huxley raises an eyebrow.

Tim stifles his laughter. "Oh. You gentlemen …" he seems to realize something. "You're Wastelanders, aren't you?"

No answer, which is answer enough.

"You've never heard of Black Hat Davies? Black *Heart* Davies, as we called him?"

Huxley shakes his head once. "Not familiar."

"Ah. Well." Tim shakes his head. "Raging maniac, that one. Burned down an entire church full of people because he thought they was hiding a fugitive inside. Never did recover a body, but he claimed the warrant was served. That's when he earned his name."

"And you were his partner."

"Not then. Before."

"So what brought you out here?"

Captain Tim's eyes go dark. Walls go up. His smile stiffens and then falls away. "Tell you what, Mr. Huxley. Let's agree right now that if you don't ask me why I'm here, I won't inquire about why a Wastelander has traveled across the desert to get here."

Huxley grinds his teeth. "Fair enough. Let me ask you a different question."

Tim waits.

"If you know so much about them, tell me … where do the slavers go?"

The two men regard each other in silence for a moment. Each man is a stone statue. Each the other's thoughts a mystery. Each trying harder to hide their own truths, than to spot the lie in the other.

"I'll tell you what," Tim says. "You help me out and I'll tell you what you want to know. I'll tell you *exactly* where the slavers go."

For a moment Huxley is infuriated that this information is something to be bartered for. But he swallows that down like a big, bitter pill. Then he nods. "Fine. What do you need help with?"

"This outpost of slavers," Tim starts, a bit cautiously. "They've been hitting little places that New Amarillo has ... a vested interest in. They wouldn't dare hit New Amarillo itself, but they're getting a little liberal with their raids." He sighs. "Once upon a time, it was understood that you went out beyond the desert for that shit—no offense."

Huxley seethes, feels his body stiff as a board. His jaw locked.

Beside him, Jay drops his fork and sucks his teeth, glaring at Captain Tim.

Tim raises his hands. "I spoke out of turn. It isn't that I wish that upon anyone. I don't. But what I'm trying to say is ... what I'm trying to say is that we used to be *ignored*. And we liked to be ignored. And now, for whatever reason, they're starting to hit us out here. Even though the Riverlands keep telling us we're a part of them, we're under their protection, blah blah blah. Slavers ain't got the memo."

Jay's voice is rigid. "Maybe it's because they've damn near bled the Wastelands dry. Maybe they've murdered and kidnapped everyone out west."

Tim regards Huxley and his group, all silent now. Even Rigo seems to understand enough to dislike Captain Tim. "Look. I get it. I'm a Black Hat—or I was. You don't like me. But you boys ... you got a chip on your shoulder and it looks like slavers to me. So here's an opportunity for you. We're on the same team. Different reasons, but the same goal. We want the slavers gone."

Huxley clasps his hands together. "You want us to help you take down this slaver outpost."

Tim nods without hesitation. "Yes. That's exactly it."

"You're the captain of the guard," Huxley says coolly. "Stop them."

"I've got six men besides myself. The Reapers have eight that I know of—not including whoever y'all had your run-in with. Add to that, the men I have are young and green, never been in nothin' but a drunken fistfight, and the slavers are all practiced fighters and killers ... I'm sure you see my problem."

"And you think we're going to solve that problem."

"Well," Tim puts the fork down and rubs his hands together. "You did well enough against that other group of slavers."

"We attacked them by surprise, during a rainstorm."

"What about at night?"

"Excuse me?"

"If your men and my men worked together and attacked them at night, do you not think we would take them?" Tim lowers his voice. "I'm sure I don't need to remind you who these people are. Complete shit. Scum of the earth. Murderers. Kidnappers. They're taking children and selling them into slavery. And wasn't it Mark Twain that said, 'All it takes for evil to triumph is for good men to do nothing'?"

"Edmund Burke," Huxley corrects. "Not Mark Twain."

"Oh. Well the point still stands."

Huxley feels his neck beginning to itch. He rubs it. Scratches it. Lowers his hand deliberately.

Here was a man asking them to help him take out slavers. Possibly the slavers that the woman in the black braid dropped their slaves off with before they went after Borderline, who knew. But in Huxley's mind, none of that truly mattered. He kept asking himself, *If you walk away from Captain Tim right now, won't you just go hunt them down anyway?*

And the answer was yes. He would.

Gordon speaks up, somewhat demure. "I wanna do it."

Huxley glances at him, then at Rigo. The Mexican has followed enough of the conversation to know that they are talking about slavers. Outside of that, it doesn't seem like he cares much, but he points his fork toward Huxley and speaks his broken English.

"If Huxley go ... I go."

Huxley is surprised. Rigo says this as though Huxley has done something to earn Rigo's loyalty. He's not sure what it is, but he accepts it. He doesn't suppose he can do anything else with it. It is a sudden and almost uncomfortable realization that he has taken the reins of this group without even knowing it. He was speaking for them, striking deals for them, and he hadn't even realized it.

Was I in charge of them last night?

It didn't feel like I was. But what if everything they did was because I let them do it?

Huxley pushes that thought away. It isn't useful to him right then. *She didn't deserve mercy. None of them did. They deserved everything they got, and I refuse to feel remorse for it. It will only make me weak. I am not weak. I am strong. That is why I am alive.*

But did Captain Tim know who they were?

Probably not.

He'll find out, though.

"Fine," Huxley says. "We'll help. Only if you do it tonight. And then I want to know where the slavers go."

CHAPTER 5

Lowell moves half-naked through patches of dark and light. The midnight shadows are deep and black, and they interrupt the endless stretches of sand and dust that shimmer like struck silver in the glow of a bald-faced moon. The sky above him is cloudless and perfect, a host of stars so bright and clustered that his fingertip cannot trace through the spaces between them.

Father had once told him, on a night much like this one, that in the Old World they hadn't been able to see the stars. Father had said that even in the places where they thought they could see so many stars, there were only half as many as they could see now.

"Are there more stars nowadays?" Lowell had wondered.

"No," Father shook his head. "It's the same stars that have always been there. We just covered them up."

"Why?"

"Because we didn't need them anymore." Father's voice grew sad. "We didn't need them to show us the way, or to make us feel less alone at night. We had everything figured out."

Lowell does not know what Father meant by that.

Lowell doesn't have anything figured out.

The world is still a mystery to him.

Now, walking in the dark and light, he wears only a worn-out pair of underwear. The rest of him is exposed to the air, to the moonlight, the stark coldness, the wildness of it all. He spreads his arms, feels the wind across his chest, pulling the warmth out of him. He breathes the night air and regards his spread arms with curiosity, seeing the way they reflect the light of the moon. His skin seems to glow against the muted backdrop of the desert all around him.

He does not know what draws him out on nights like tonight. Some unquenchable desire to wander, some deep-seated quirk in his soul that makes him unable to sleep and to want the cool darkness on him. Without it he grows restless and fidgets in his bed until eventually he sneaks out, silently and without waking Father or Mother.

This was his life for a long time, before they found him. And though he does not recall many specific memories of those times, he remembers the night. The safety of darkness. The light of the moon was the only light he would ever need because the sun was hot and the sun brought out the worst people, and it shined on him so that they could see him and chase him …

Lowell shudders at the precipice of a memory and mentally retreats.

He picks his way through desert scrub and sharp stones, his feet never having lost the calluses he developed when he was alone. Each footfall is just a whisper of shifting sand. He has no destination, but strides carefully around the outcropping of boulders that his home is nestled into. By now he is on the opposite side of the boulders from the trailer and he stops again to breathe deeply and to enjoy the night air.

It is there in the stillness that he hears the noise.

He does not react immediately, but rather inclines his ear.

The noise is coming from the boulders.

What is it?

Water. Splashing. Like the lapping of an animal.

Lowell hunches slightly, his form becoming strangely predatory for such a small and skeletal thing. He wishes for his spear, because he knows how dangerous the night can be and suddenly he wishes the trailer was not so far away. Images of coyotes fill his mind, their toothy muzzles covered in blood after a fresh kill.

Maybe he should call for Father.

But what would Father think?

What would *Mother* think?

To catch him wandering around in the middle of the night, nearly naked.

He realizes how very strange this would appear to them, and how upset Father and Mother would be if they were there to see him.

More than the fear of coyotes, the fear of their disapproval suddenly causes a cold sweat to break out on his back.

It was stupid of him to wander off into the darkness. He should have laid down in his bed and closed his eyes and counted as high as he could count, just like Mother had taught him to do when he couldn't sleep. It didn't work as well as his walks for soothing his mind, but it also didn't have coyotes and he rarely got past a hundred before falling asleep.

If he continues in the direction he had been walking, he will pass in front of the small cave that leads to the spring and he will be forced to encounter whatever is taking water there. He would have to go back the other way …

As he turns to make his way back, another noise stops him.

A sigh.

The sound of someone taking a breath after a deep draught of water.

Not the kind of sound a coyote makes.

The lapping continues for another moment, followed by another sigh of satisfaction, this one slightly quieter.

Lowell fidgets with indecision.

If he calls for Father, he will be in trouble. But there shouldn't be anyone else using their water. Father had made it very clear that the spring was to be a secret, and the thought of some stranger putting his filthy face into their spring makes Lowell angry.

But the only other option is to confront the person alone.

Lowell first turns back toward the trailer. The safe direction. He should bite the bullet and tell Father. But then he hesitates, thinking again of their paralyzing disapproval, and he turns back in the direction of the spring.

He finds himself staring across a short distance at a man.

The two beings regard each other tensely, the boy with raging fear that squeezes the muscle of his heart so hard it seems that blood will begin to leak from him with the pressure of it. The man seems just as frozen, but with a cringing sort of hesitance, as though he fears the boy will scream or sound some other alarm. But there is also some confusion in his gaze. This skinny wretch, standing stock-still in the desert, dripping with translucent moonlight and wearing only underwear—a picture the man cannot make sense of.

Lowell judges the distance between them, and he judges the man he is looking at. The two are separated by less than twenty feet. The man is younger than Father, but still old in Lowell's mind. He has a mop of tangled, curly hair atop his head, dreadlocked in places and parted down the middle so that it frames his face like the man is peering out from behind a curtain of vines. He has a puckered, sour-looking mouth and his eyes flit around nervously. Lowell knows the man is not large compared to other men, but he is still larger than Lowell.

After a long moment's silence that stretches as each waits for the other to do or say something, Lowell breaks the night air with a harsh whisper. "What are you doing, Mister?"

The man holds up a placating hand. He looks around with a grimace. "What about yourself, kid? Wandering around … naked in the desert … what the hell are you thinking? It's almost freezing out!"

"I'm fine."

"Do you live near here?"

"I live in the trailer right there."

The man glances in the direction of the trailer. "All by yourself?"

Lowell shivers, the first time the night has seemed too cold. "N-no."

The man looks at him with a half smile and narrowed eyes. "Really? So … you have parents?"

"I'm gonna yell for them if you don't leave."

The half smile morphs into a grimace. "Relax, kid. I ain't done nothin' wrong."

"You drank our water."

"I was dyin' of thirst, kid." The man wipes at the corners of his mouth. "You gonna let a man die of thirst?"

"You're not supposed to drink other people's water."

"I don't see a fuckin' sign on it," the whisper is a vicious snap.

Lowell trembles, tenses for flight.

"Look," both hands now, raised up, trying to show how harmless he is. "Sorry, kid. I'm tired, and I'm hungry, and I've been on the road all day. My name's Don. What's your name?"

"How'd you find us?"

"I just told you my name, kid. Aren't you gonna tell me yours?"

The boy considers this for a time. Then: "Lowell."

"Lowell, can you come a little closer so we don't have to whisper so loudly?"

"No."

"I won't hurt you."

"I think you will."

"If you really thought that you would've called for your parents by now, right?" Don cocks his head. "Unless you don't really have any parents. Unless you're really all alone out here."

Lowell sticks his chin out. "Maybe I'm just not scared of you."

"If you ain't scared then come here."

Lowell takes one hesitant step, followed by another. The man smiles and shakes his head and it seems a challenge, so Lowell takes a few more steps until he is standing just outside of the man's reach. Don looks him up and down and then nods.

"Alright then. You're a brave little fucker."

"You should go," Lowell says, and he is proud of how firm his voice sounds.

Seeming not to hear him, Don scratches the side of his head. "You got a nice little spring of water. Bet it spits up more than you can drink in a day, huh?"

Lowell closes his mouth.

"Bet you got food in that trailer."

Silence.

"Yeah." Don seems sure of himself. "You got food. Look, kid, I ain't a bad man, but I'm hungry, okay? I ain't eaten anything in almost three days now. Man could do some nasty things for food when he gets that hungry, you hear me?"

"We don't have any food for you."

"Look, kid …"

"I'm gonna scream!"

The man is fast—faster than Lowell expected—and he crosses the short distance between them in a flash. There is the sound of his sharp intake of breath and also of steel drawing from leather, and then his hands are upon Lowell, hard and rough. His neck is clamped between fingers like iron and just as cold, and he feels the sharp point of a metal blade against the side of his face.

"You shut the fuck up!" the man hisses in Lowell's ear. "You make a fuckin' sound and I swear to God I'll cut you up into a thousand pieces, you understand me?"

Rather than speed up, Lowell's heart seems to have seized in his chest, along with everything else. He cannot breathe, he cannot move, he cannot think. All he can feel is the grip and the point of the knife and the wet warmth flowing down his leg.

"I didn't want to do this, you little runt! You made me do this! You could have just given me what I wanted and I would have been on my way! I'm not a bad guy! I'm not a bad guy! I'm just hungry, okay?"

"Okay … okay …" panicked breaths, anything to soothe his attacker.

"I just want some food."

"You can have the food."

"Who's in the trailer?"

"Mother and Father."

"Do they have any weapons?"

"Yes."

Don shakes him hard. "Well? What kind?"

Lowell closes his eyes, feels tears wriggle down his cheeks, warm at first and then quickly turning cold. "Knives … and a gun … Father has a gun."

"Like a rifle?"

"No. It's a pistol."

"Okay." Don takes a deep breath, sounding almost as nervous as Lowell is. His breath smells of dead things and his sweat is a warm draft of rank in the cold night air. "Okay. Okay. We can figure this out …"

A new voice breaks into the darkness, causing Lowell's eyes to snap open.

"I've got a gun …" Father's voice wavers and it is the least confident Lowell has ever heard it. "Just let him go. Please."

Still holding on to Lowell like a shield, Don spins toward the sound of the voice and there is Father, backlit by the moon, almost nothing more than a silhouette except for the arm extended out and the dull shine of light on the barrel of the revolver that he points in their direction. Lowell is immediately afraid that Father will shoot them both. He knows that Father does not shoot the revolver—in fact he cannot remember ever seeing him shoot it—and he points it without confidence and with a wavering grip.

Don seems to sense this weakness. "You gonna shoot me while I'm holding your son?"

"Yes," Father says, and even Lowell cannot tell if he is lying or not. "Please, just let him go."

"You'll shoot me."

"I'll shoot you if you don't let him go."

"No," Don shakes his head, now glancing about desperately. "If I let him go, you're gonna shoot me."

"I don't want to shoot you," Father pleads. "You can walk away. No one needs to get hurt."

Don continues to shake his head, but doesn't respond. He is slowly inching away, still clutching the boy, while Father keeps taking halting steps forward, perhaps in a hope that a shorter distance will provide a clearer shot.

"Don't kill me," Don says, now sounding plaintive. "I'll leave, I swear it. I'm not a bad guy. I swear I'm not a bad guy."

"Just let him go," Father repeats.

Don breaks. He releases the boy and shoves him toward the other man, and then turns and runs into the desert as fast as his feet will carry him.

Lowell stumbles after being shoved from behind, then looks up at Father, who stands as still as the boulders around them, his arm still outstretched, watching the man disappear into the wastelands. Father's eyes are wide and unsteady and they glisten with tears in the sterling light. His hand begins to tremble and then his entire body. Eventually, the revolver sinks down so that it points to the ground.

Father's haunted eyes fall to the pale form before him.

His voice quakes with relief, or anger, or both. "What were you doing, Lowell?"

The child bursts into tears. "I was only walking!"

Father drops the revolver in the dirt, bends down and seizes his son by the shoulders, the boy's skin cold to the touch. "Why would you walk around in the middle of the night? Jesus Christ, Lowell! You don't even have any clothes on!"

"I don't know!" The syllables are a miserable sob of noise. "I'm sorry! I'm sorry!"

"What the hell were you thinking?" Father shakes him.

"I'm sorry!" Lowell wails. "Please don't leave me! Please …"

"What?"

"Don't leave me by myself! I know I was wrong, but I didn't mean for you or Mother to get hurt, and I know she gets angry at me sometimes and that she doesn't want me here, but please don't kick me out! I won't do it again, I promise!"

Father stares at the boy, his mouth hanging open.

Words fail him, and there is only the sound of Lowell's desperate crying. Finally, he hugs the boy to him, wraps his arms around the cold, frail body that shakes with fright and chill. "We're not gonna leave you, Lowell. We're never gonna leave you."

CHAPTER 6

They move in a single-file line up a slight slope, a rocky incline full of fist-sized stones that clatter noisily when they are disturbed. Tim and four of his six guards in the lead, followed by Huxley and his small band. Two of Tim's six had been left behind in New Amarillo as protection for the town.

When they set out from the bottom of the slope where they hobbled their horses, the moon had glared meanly down at them, but now a thin veil of gray cloud cover has drawn over its face so that it shows through only meekly. Even with the slight cloud cover, there is light enough for the men to pick their way up the hill.

Ahead, Tim stops and kneels down. He looks briefly from side to side and then turns to the rest of them and motions for them to join him. Hunching over as though they are already under fire, and moving as quietly as possible, the line compacts into a jumble of heavy-breathing men with Tim in the center.

The captain looks to Huxley. "Their place is right up over the top of this hill."

Huxley eyes the distance, guesses it is about fifty yards.

"It's a big house," Tim continues. "We're gonna come in on the side of it. We'll watch the front door, and Huxley, you and your men will watch the back door. Anyone comes out that back door, they die—that's very, very important, Huxley. No one gets away."

Huxley rubs his beard. "What about any slaves inside?"

Tim shakes his head. "We've done recon on this house. They don't keep slaves here. Not sure where they do keep them. If we have any live ones afterward, we'll certainly question them." He puts his hand on Huxley's shoulder.

Huxley wants to shrug away from it, but resists the urge. "Listen. After the first round of shooting cools off, me and my men are gonna rush the house. Y'all gotta stay outside. If you come in the back door, things might get confusing and I don't want our groups popping shots at each other. Plus, when we go in, someone might come out and I need you to keep that person from getting away. Remember who these people are. Don't wait to shoot. They won't."

Huxley looks at him with a little irritation. Captain Tim might have some experience as a Black Hat, but he wasn't one anymore. He was a tired has-been, and by his own admission, his men were just boys full of piss and vinegar. Huxley and Jay had been across the Wastelands. They'd survived. They'd killed. And they were capable—Huxley had no doubt in himself or the three men with him.

Huxley resented Tim's patronizing nature, but so much the better. Stand guard at the back door, cap anyone that comes out. Seemed simple enough. And then Huxley would have his information and be on his way. His concern wasn't for himself, but rather for the has-been captain.

Huxley put his own hand on Tim's shoulder and squeezed, hoping to impart a sense of sarcasm in his touch, in the overly sincere way he did it. "You just make sure you stay alive."

Tim smirks. "Worried about me?"

"No." Huxley faces forward. "Worried about whether you're gonna survive long enough to tell me what you promised to tell me."

Tim wheezes a laugh and shakes his head. "Don't you worry. I still got a few tricks."

Huxley nods. He looks to his side, where the men that have somehow become *his men* are crouched down. He is about to ask them if they're ready, but they all have revolvers drawn, faces pinched down into focus, fire in their eyes.

Huxley feels the same surge working through him.

Kill them. Kill them all.

"We're ready," Huxley says, quietly.

"Alright," Tim turns away from them. "Huxley, take your boys out to the left. We'll head toward the right a bit."

The group breaks apart, spreading out into a loose line. The rocks around their feet begin to shrink until the ground becomes a compacted loam, full of small pebbles. It starts to level out into a plateau. As it does, the eaves of an old ranch house come into view. An Old World house, still left standing in shockingly good condition.

Coming in from the side of the house, Huxley can see the old and weathered clapboards of the wood siding. The windows are covered with graying plywood and the place seems dark and abandoned. Is there even anyone inside? Do they live here, or just operate out of here at their leisure? Or perhaps they were asleep. Huxley judges it is close to around ten o'clock at night.

Behind the house, in the same direction that Huxley and his group are heading toward, the plateau stretches to what seems like the far horizon. There are perhaps a dozen yards of clear space immediately off the back of the ranch house, but the rest of the ground is populated by what looks like an endless number of tall stalks, standing long and reedy, about knee-high.

As Huxley moves closer to this field, he sees that each stalk is topped by a pale bulb. In the ambient light coming from the moon and stars, diffused by the thin clouds, the bulbs of the plants seem wet and glistening. Huxley pictures them as a field of eyeballs standing on those stalks, watching him, and when the wind blows it seems like they are blinking at him, uncomprehending.

Huxley works his way through the field of plants, toward the back of the house, wondering what the hell they are, and it isn't until he and his little group stops, maybe twenty-five yards off the back of the house, that he takes just a moment to look down and see what it is all around him.

It was difficult to identify them with the flower petals removed.

Poppies.

He reaches out and touches one of the bulbs, feels the cut mark in the side of it, feels the sticky resin oozing out of it.

Opium poppies …

His gut tightens, just a bit.

A clamor of explosions wipes away all thoughts, like a thunderbolt has struck the ground. Huxley can feel the concussions in his chest even from where he is. The guards' overcharged scatterguns blare out, their muzzles stabbing bright pink and red into billows of smoke, strobing the night air.

Pieces of wood fly from the house as the scattershot rips through the clapboards.

Huxley can barely see the shapes of the guards in the dull light, but he can see their movement, and he can see the scatterguns being tossed to the ground in favor of their revolvers as they move quickly toward the old ranch house in a quiet, wordless rush.

The first of the guards reaches the front door and kicks it. There is the sound of cracking wood, followed by the thump of a gunshot, muffled from inside the house, and the guard reels backward, losing his footing and toppling into the dirt. Two guards behind him flinch, extending out their revolvers and firing reflexively into the front of the house.

Huxley considers shooting, but doesn't want to miss and hit Tim's men. He has his hammer pulled back, but he stays there, crouched in the field of poppies, waiting for someone to come out of the back of the house.

From inside the house, someone screams, long and loud and terrible. It sounds like a woman.

The bitch with the black braid was a slaver, too. So is this one. Have no pity on her.

The guards are in the house now. Glass breaks, and a woman shrieks again. Another gunshot.

The back door flies open. A man bursts out, taking the back stairs two at a time. He is clutching something to his chest …

As synchronized as a firing line, Huxley, Jay, Rigo, and Gordon fire their weapons at the man. Huxley sees chunks of his arms and legs and head fly off of him in a bloody spew. His momentum carries him forward another few paces, but he is dead, dead before his body even knows it, and he falls to the ground atop whatever he had clutched to his chest in flight.

Huxley and his men move to the back door of the ranch house.

Tim's instructions were damn clear—don't go in the house.

But Huxley sees a lone figure through a dark window, just the flit of a shape. For some reason, he is almost positive that it is one of the slavers. He sees a pale face in the back window, and then it is gone, huddled somewhere in that back room, right there at the back door.

One of the slavers. He's hiding. He's lying in wait …

The thought comes to Huxley in visuals: the slaver huddling there in that back room with some sort of weapon, one of Captain Tim's men coming in, then the slaver jumps out and shoots them in the back of the head, or slits their throat …

WOLVES

What if it's Tim who goes in there?

Potbellied has-been'll get himself murdered. And then no one tells me where the slavers go.

"Dammit," Huxley blurts, and sprints for the back door. "Watch my back," he calls out to his three companions behind him.

Huxley swings through the back door, which is still hanging ajar. He is in a kitchen, all semblance of modernity stripped from it. The electric range has been replaced with a cast-iron contraption. The empty space below the counter where a dishwasher used to reside houses only a bucket full of stagnant-looking water. Candlelight illuminates the scene just barely, the tiny flames guttering and threatening to blow out in the wind that flows freely from the open front door and out the open back. In the weak light, Huxley registers two things.

The first is a wooden table, crudely constructed, and a pile of yellowish powder in the center.

The second is a wide-eyed man clutching a carving knife, huddling behind that table.

Before Huxley can react, the man launches himself forward with a wild and inhuman cry of rage, his carving knife held above him and the long blade pointed down, aimed for Huxley's chest. In the man's eyes is a lunatic flash, and in a moment he knows that it was eyes like this that stared down at his wife when she was brutalized mercilessly.

It was animals like this that deserved to die.

Huxley pulls his trigger reflexively as the man charges him. The gunshot goes off, the bullet hitting the man in the gut, but it's not enough. The man collides with Huxley, driving him backward into the old, rotted Formica countertop. Huxley grunts, feels the man's hands grappling for the revolver as he tries to get it cocked again. The carving knife is squirming around, the tip and the edge slicing little bits of Huxley, catching his flesh, but the manic man is too focused on the gun in Huxley's hand to actually try using the knife, and he is starting to understand that he's just been gutshot.

Bleed, you fuck!

Huxley roars at him, knees him in the gut, right where the bullet went in. The man doubles over with a strangled cry, but is still latched onto Huxley's gun-arm. Huxley elbows the man's knife-wielding arm away from him for a split second so he can dive to his waistband with his left hand. He draws out his own knife and sticks the man.

Once in the gut, right above the sopping bullet wound.

The man shrieks and stumbles backward.

Huxley sticks him again, in the upper ribs, then slashes at his neck, two quick movements aimed at both carotids, but the man holds up his hand in defense and the knife blade nicks off bone.

But now Huxley's gun arm is free.

He pulls the hammer back, thrusts the gun in the other man's face and scatters his brains on the back wall. The man topples, the life coming out of him with a sigh and then a gurgle.

Huxley steps back, breathing hard.

From further in the house, the sound of fighting has ceased amid a stench of gunpowder that the wind seems to find difficult to scrub away. Footsteps still pound back and forth, and there is the sound of furniture moving and things being dropped, as though the guards are ransacking the house.

Tim suddenly appears in the doorway that leads from the kitchen into the rest of the house. He looks sternly at Huxley, but then down at the body on the floor. He sniffs, like he is enjoying the cloud of gunsmoke that hazes the kitchen.

"Well," Tim says. "You got him." Back to Huxley. "You wanna step outside, like I asked? I almost capped you when I came through the door. That's what I'm talking about. That's why you never go in the back door."

Huxley's heart is hammering. He is on that downhill slope again. He is tingling, rushing, unstoppable. He wants to fight. He wants to kill. Those are the things, the only things, that make sense to him anymore. And in this state, he looks at Tim with murder in his eyes.

I probably saved your life, he is about to say, but Tim turns around and vanishes back into the house before the words can get out of Huxley's mouth.

He chokes them off into a grumbled curse.

Jay steps in, looking around. "What the hell happened?"

Huxley points to the body on the floor.

Jay regards it without much thought, and then his eyes track to the crude wooden table and the pile of yellowish powder on top of it. Jay stares at it with a discerning eye. His jaw opens, like he wants to say something, but then he bites down on his tongue, as though restricting himself.

"I know," Huxley says, glancing at the pile of powder again.

Jay spits into the corner of the kitchen. "I think Captain Tim might not be tellin' us the whole truth and nothing but the truth."

Huxley moves to the door, peering over the man's shoulders at the waves of pale green stalks, and their paler green heads. They bob in the breeze. About five yards into the field of poppies, the man that had tried to escape lays sprawled, motionless. It looks odd the way his body is so still, and the poppies around him are swaying about in the wind. It only draws your eye to it more. It's difficult for some reason to look away.

Rigo and Gordon are standing beside the man. Gordon bends down and pulls at the man's shoulder, trying to see what it is that he was trying to carry out of the house. Huxley watches Gordon's reaction. When he sees it, Gordon just withdraws his hand and stands up, kind of stiffly. He turns and looks at Huxley.

"Hey … you should look at this."

Huxley steps forward, off the back steps and into the dirt. The dead body points westward, the legs crossed. No shoes on the dead man's feet. He seems strangely bare for a slaver. His clothing is loose fitting and homespun. It is a poor man's clothing. Not a slaver's clothing.

His clothing means nothing, Huxley tells himself as he approaches.

Rigo kneels on the body's left side, holding the right shoulder so that the limp body remains in its twisted position, revealing what lies under it. Gordon stands to the right of the body, pointing with a single finger.

An infant lies in the dirt, chest to chest with the dead man. He cannot see the face because a blanket shrouds the infant's head. Below the hem of the blanket, the white arms and white legs lay loose and spread, the tiny fingers partially curled, but relaxed, motionless. Though it shows no outward signs of injury, it does not move, and the chest does not rise and fall. It has either been crushed by the weight of the man, or smothered by him.

"I don't …" Gordon's voice shakes a bit. "I don't get it."

Huxley almost laughs, but can't quite. "There's nothing to get," he snaps.

With that he spins back toward the house, takes the back stairs in a single heated stride and bursts through what remains of the back door. Knife and revolver still in hand, he steps over the body of the man in the kitchen and moves through the doorway, deeper into the house. He is in a dark hall that runs the length of the house, an opening on the right and another on the left. Pictures on the walls. Bullet holes sprouting from the woodwork. Gunsmoke still shifting like restless ghosts on the ceiling.

From deeper in the house, he hears the sound of a woman crying.

He can hear Tim's voice, too. Deep and harsh.

Huxley moves down the hallway, unsure what he intends to do when he gets to where he's going. Unsure of what he's gotten himself into. The front door lies straight ahead, still hanging open, and one of the guards standing on the front deck, rifling through the pockets of a body.

At the end of the hall Huxley looks right, finds the opening leads into a living area where dirty old mattresses and sheets lay bloody and still holding the forms of people shot dead before they could rise from their beds. He turns left and finds another hallway.

The guard at the front door takes no notice of him as he continues to loot the body.

Down this new hallway, Huxley can hear the voices. The desperate woman. And a very angry Captain Tim. He moves down the hall, feeling the blood on the handle of his knife, feeling the heft of his revolver.

Is this the solution for everything? He glances down at his bloody blade and then answers his own question: *What else is there?*

He passes more doors. A bedroom, a bathroom, a linen closet.

At the end of the hallway, he turns left and finds himself at the entrance to a large bedroom lit from the glow of a single oil lantern. He stands in the doorway and tries to assess what he is looking at.

The one remaining guard stands lackadaisically with his shoulder against a wall and his back turned toward Huxley. A woman kneels in the middle of the floor. Tim has a fistful of her hair, forcing her head to be cranked to one side. She weeps hysterically, her eyes fixated on a form that lies in a dark corner of the room. Huxley can only make out the naked legs of it. It is a man. The woman bleeds profusely from her nose and it mixes with snot and tears and flows into her mouth so that when she sobs and splutters the spray is a mix of all these fluids.

Tim stands before her, face hard and edged like a hatchet. He holds her hair with his left fist, and his revolver in his right fist, the hammer back and his finger on the trigger. He does not seem to notice Huxley standing in the doorway, nor does the woman, or the guard.

He twists her hair again, causing her to cry out. "Where the fuck is it? Where do you keep it?"

She sobs, tries to speak, but he backhands her and she crumples to the ground.

He bends over at the waist so that his face is close to hers. "I told you. Didn't I tell you? I told you that you could work *with* me, or you could work *against* me. I warned you. Didn't I?" He seizes her by the throat. "Didn't I fucking warn you?"

Her eyelids flutter closed, red-stained teeth bared. "Yes," she chokes out.

Tim makes a disgusted noise and shoves her to the ground where she coughs and curls into a ball. His voice is softer now. "It doesn't matter anyway. We'll find it." He puts his hands on his hips and shakes his head. "You know, Theresa, this makes me sad. It really does. We could've had something good. We could've had a mutually beneficial relationship. But you decided that you wanted to do things your own way. Even after I *repeatedly* explained the situation—and the consequences—to you. Now *this* has happened. And your husband, and your brothers, and your little baby girl are all dead. Because of you."

She moans, wordlessly.

"Yes." Tim nudges her with his foot. "You just remember that, in the little time that you have left. You just remember whose fault this is. *You* did this. It's *your* fault."

A sound like a wounded animal escapes her lips. "I wanna die ..."

Tim sniffs. "I know you do, honey."

Then he levels the revolver at her and fires.

Huxley doesn't see the aftermath of the shot in the puff of white smoke from the revolver, but he sees how still her form becomes and knows she is no more. He must have made a sound when Tim shot her, because both Tim and the guard suddenly look in his direction.

Tim seems annoyed. "I thought I told you to get out of the house."

Huxley stares at the other man, unmoving. "What the fuck are you doing?"

"What needed to be done, Huxley. These are bad people—very bad people."

"They're fucking opium farmers," Huxley snaps back. He points his knife at

Tim. "You used me and my guys to take off an opium farm."

Tim's eyes become very suddenly flat and dark, like nuggets of coal. "I would be very cautious about fucking with me, Huxley. As a point of reference, I encourage you to look around." He folds his arms so that the revolver is held very pointedly across his chest. "While it's inspiring to find an outlaw with a conscience, I think it's best that you leave this house immediately and wait for us outside."

"I'm not an outlaw," Huxley grinds.

Tim smiles patronizingly. "Of course not."

He looks between Tim and the guard. They both have revolvers, held in the hand, and the hammers cocked back and ready. Whether they are loaded or empty could be debated. Huxley considers his odds. The problem is that they are as ready now as he is. They are tensed, fingers on triggers. If Huxley raises his revolver, he'll take one, but then the other will take him.

"Tell me what I want to know," Huxley says, quietly.

Tim's face remains impassive. "I'll talk to you outside, Mr. Huxley. And you best start thinking about doing what I ask."

Huxley lets out a bark of laughter. "Do what you ask? Okay, Captain Tim. I'll do what you ask." Then Huxley backs out of the doorway.

They watch him go but don't make a move.

In the hallway, the sensation becomes worse, almost uncontrollable, like the reflex to pull your hand away from a hot object. He wants to lash out. It begins in his gut and radiates out like the feeling of phantom limbs moving into violent action, only to look down and find himself still locked in place.

He walks down the hallway, toward the open front door. It seems the only thing that he can see. His blood rushing about his head, forcing the field of his vision down and causing the edges to dance and darkle. His thoughts follow the same track and become singular.

I should kill him. I should.

Again the question: *Is this the solution for everything?*

And again the same answer: *What else is there?*

A man steps in front of him.

The guard.

The man smiles, obscenely. "Did you at least get some before they shot her?"

Huxley's eyes narrow. "What?"

"You get some pussy?"

The next thing Huxley is aware of, he is standing over the man, trying to pull his knife out of the man's temple where it's wedged, and not quite sure how it got there. The guard convulses on the ground. His mouth hangs open wide, his tongue lolling out, his hands contorted into weird and strenuous shapes. A nasally groan escapes his open mouth.

Frustrated, Huxley finally puts his shoe against the man's face and rips the blade hard. There is a scrape and crunch, and the knife is free of the man's skull.

Huxley looks down and spits on the body.

He looks behind him. The hallway is empty.

He steps over the dead body and moves quickly for the back door. Outside, he finds the others still standing over the body of the man they had slaughtered—had been *tricked* into slaughtering. They look up as they see him coming, and they tense because they can see the wild rage in his face, the quick movement in his step.

Huxley pushes past them, grabbing Jay's jacket as he goes and towing him along behind him as they head for the rocky slope at the bottom of which waits their horses. "We have to go," Huxley says sharply. "We have to go now."

CHAPTER 7

They clatter down the scree slope in a near panic. Any moment could be the moment that Tim and his men come after them, start winging shots at them in the dark. And any one of those shots could find Huxley's heart, or his brain, or hell, just about any part of him, and things would go downhill real quick.

They make it to their horses at the bottom of the slope. Huxley is acutely aware of the fact that his revolvers are mostly empty, and probably everyone else's as well. He runs to the horses of Tim and his men and begins unhobbling them, then swatting them on the ass to get them to run. The others join in, working quickly, getting all the horses out of there.

Not much time now.

As the last horse gives a perturbed snort and gallops off in a cloud of dust, Huxley looks at the dark, moonlit faces of his companions, his chest heaving. "Does anyone have a loaded gun?"

They trade glances. But no one does.

"Shit."

"Should we load?" Gordon asks.

"Fuck no," Huxley stalks to his horse and swings into the saddle with a grunt. "We need to get the fuck out of here. The sooner we can put Tim and New Amarillo behind us, the better."

The others scramble into their saddles as Huxley's own horse, sensing the sweat and anxiety, begins to whinny and turn circles, wanting to leave just about as much as Huxley himself. It takes another twenty seconds, but each one feels like it's forcibly removed from Huxley's chest.

Then they are speeding through the dark. Cold, dark, night wind against their faces.

Huxley keeps looking over his shoulder, waiting to see Captain Tim and his men coming after them, shooting at them, waiting to see the muzzle flares and the puffs of smoke caught in the moonlight, but there is nothing behind them but dark desert.

Huxley doesn't know how far they ride, but they go until the horses demand a break, then they walk them, and then they run them again. And it must be sometime well after midnight when they finally stop, the men breathless, the beasts heaving and snorting and lathered.

"Do you think we've gone far enough?" Huxley says, looking behind them into the darkness.

Gordon, Rigo, and Jay all follow his gaze.

"I don't know," Jay says. "I don't know how far we've gone."

"Twenty miles?" Gordon offers, unsure. "Thirty?"

Huxley has no clue.

"And what direction are we headed?"

Huxley looks at the sky, as though he can read stars, which he can't. "Uh … east. I hope."

"If we could find a waterway to cross," Jay suggests. "Maybe we could break the trail."

"But who knows how long that's going to take?" Huxley says, spitting a wad of gummy saliva. "We don't even know if they got their horses. We don't even know if they're tracking us right now. In the dark. Wouldn't that be dangerous for them?"

Gordon speaks up. "It's your call, boss."

Boss.

Huxley looks at the man's face, his skin blue in the moonlight.

"Alright," he says. "We'll camp here. No fire. No nothing. Just hit the sack and try to get a few hours of sleep. We'll head out at first sign of dawn."

The group gets out of their saddles, and they hobble their horses amid grunts and groans and muted curses. In the dim moonlight, they fumble their way through reloading their revolvers. Then they collapse into the dirt with blankets as their only shelter, their bodies huddled close together.

Huxley will be able to see the dawn coming, he thinks. Because he doubts he'll be able to sleep.

But then he does.

CHAPTER 8

Huxley's eyes open, his veins and arteries throbbing rapidly, and he doesn't know what has jolted him awake. Above him the sky is stark black and cold, and the Milky Way is a band of dust tossed in the air that hangs indefinitely. There is no sound but the great empty sound of open spaces, which, in this moment, seems overpowering.

He exhales, watches his breath, illuminated by starlight.

He turns toward the others. Jay is lying down, but his head is turned toward Huxley and his eyes are open wide, glistening and oddly pale.

Huxley whispers, "Did you hear something?"

And the night explodes.

The air around him flares with smoke, stabbed through with red muzzle flashes. Dirt scatters into his mouth and eyes as bullets strike the ground around him. Chips of stone sting his face.

He throws his blanket off and snatches up his revolver. Without conscious thought or effort, he begins to scramble away from the camp, firing at the muzzle flashes that leap out of the darkness at him. He fires, works the hammer back, fires again.

He looks behind him as he runs. He sees Gordon trying to get to his feet, searching through his blankets for his weapon. A fusillade of gunshots rips him to pieces and he collapses back into his bed.

Huxley stands straight up, not having any conceivable reason for doing so other than panic. "Jay!" He shouts. "Jay!"

He is tackled from the side, laid out flat into the cold dirt.

A hand covers his mouth, cold and clammy. "Shut up!"

It is Jay.

The younger man holds him down to the ground and neither moves while the gunshots continue on, then slowly slacken, and eventually are silenced. As the last boom echoes back to them from across the plains, Huxley works his mouth free of Jay's hands, feels the sweat go cold as it dries around his mouth.

"What …? Who …?"

"Ssh!" Jay elbows him in the ribs. "Start crawling."

They roll onto their bellies and begin squirming slowly in an unknown direction. The cold prickles their skin, but after a while they can't feel it from the effort of the crawling. They can hear voices coming from the campsite, loud and angry, and the beat of horses' hooves traveling back and forth. They crawl for a long time, and it seems the voices never grow quieter with distance. It seems they are always just out of sight.

They find a depression in the dirt, an old path that water flows through during the rainy seasons. They breathe heavily and have to stop to rest often. Huxley forces himself to breathe through his nose as he fears the huff of his breath in the cold air will give him away.

They follow the depression down a hill that grows steeper as they go, the depression becoming a trench, the walls of it rising over them until the ground flattens and becomes muddy. They stop there, coated in mud and desperately exhausted. Huxley tries to hear between the beats of his own heart.

No hoofbeats.

No voices.

"Get up," Jay says, already slogging to his feet.

Huxley follows. The world spins uncontrollably around him, but Jay's voice seems utterly calm, even cold. Maybe before it would have bothered him to see Jay so unaffected, but now it is a steady thing to grasp in the middle of this maelstrom.

They jog at first, but slow to a walk. They move to the side of the gulch where the dirt is harder and drier. Their saliva dried on their tongues, and eventually the chill begins to set into their skin, their muscles, and finally their bones until they are both shivering with their arms wrapped around their chest.

It is not until this point that Huxley notices the pain in his right thigh. It began as a dull ache while they were crawling and he thought it was a bruise, but as they ran and now walk, and as his body grows colder, the pain grows sharper and more severe until it shoots up his body with every step. For a while he limps along, not saying anything, but after about an hour, he stops in his tracks.

"Wait," he holds up a hand to Jay's back.

"We can't wait."

"I think I've been shot."

Jay spins. "What?"

Huxley sinks to the ground and places his dirt-covered fingers against his right thigh, feels the sharp tenderness just inside a gash in his pant leg. It is a long wound, mirroring the shape of the tear in his pants where the bullet slashed through him.

Jay walks to him and crouches down, peering at the leg. "Shit!"

"It's not bad."

"Everything is bad when you're out here!" Jay hisses. "Is it bleeding?"

Huxley touches it. The wound is impacted with dirt, but he can feel the slick edges of it where wet blood is escaping. "It's bleeding, but not much."

"Good." Jay looks around. "We need to find some water to wash it with. Bandage it." He offers his hand. "We should keep moving. They'll be tracking us."

Huxley takes the hand and Jay hauls him to his feet.

They move on through the gulch, knowing that it will eventually lead them to water, but not knowing what direction it is taking them. Huxley's mind wanders to and fro through his life's history, but always comes back to the pain in his leg that continues to grow. His mind travels back to a classroom, bright and warm in the sun which shoots through a bank of windows and hangs there in the center of the glass like it was placed there as an ornament. The smell of the school—a strangely familiar mix of floor wax and chalkboards and coffee, but mostly of that heavy industrial paint that was slathered on the walls, a smell that was not overpowering, but that never seemed to lessen over the years.

Then he is there in the gulch again, dark and cold and smelling of dank earth. Pain shooting up his leg with each step, the hard grip of Jay's hand around his midsection, the fingers digging into his ribs. A skyward glance reveals no change in the sky. How long have they walked the trench? An hour? Possibly more? The passage of the day is marked by the sun, but Huxley doesn't know how to read the stars outside of their simple constellations, and to him night is a big blank period and in the time between light it seems the turning of the earth keeps no schedule, and that the sun will only rise again when it feels good and ready.

He curses the sky and wonders if this is the beginning of delirium, or just exhaustion.

Pain brings him back again. He hobbles, curses the world and everything in it, and keeps hauling each foot out of the marshy ground and planting it in front of him, shoes caked with mud, pant legs hanging heavy with it. He closes his eyes and tries to picture his little girl, tries to see the brightness of her eyes and the purity of her smile, tries to recreate in himself that indescribable feeling of belonging.

But the pieces will not come together.

"They're gone," he whispers to the black air in front of him. "They're gone."

Jay looks at him. "What's that?"

Huxley stares back, wide-eyed and slack-mouthed, but he doesn't speak. *All the good people are gone*, he thinks. *We killed them all. And now the only people left are the animals like me.*

"No room," Huxley mumbles to himself, looking away from Jay. "No room for weakness."

It loops in his mind as they walk.

It becomes a mantra.

A creed.

And in the endless repetitions, at some point in time, the sky begins to gray and dawn comes lumbering over the horizon slow and leisurely, ignorant of the injured and frozen men still winding their way through a muddy arroyo. The bed of the gulch grows muddier and promises water.

They eventually find it, beginning with just an inch of standing water and then connecting to a shallower but wider streambed where a thin brook flows. They scan around them in the growing light but don't see any pursuit, so they kneel down at the brook and stick their faces into the water. It is almost ice-cold and stings their faces, but it soothes their tongues.

"We should take a look at your wound," Jay says.

Huxley gives him a glance. "I'll take care of it."

He pulls the knife from his belt—the only object besides his pistol that still remains in his possession. He cuts away the tattered fabric of his pant leg, exposing the dirt- and blood-encrusted wound. Despite the cold air, a single fly appears and begins to buzz desperately around it, as though it has starved in this desert just as much as they have and is panicked to sink itself into Huxley's open flesh. Huxley splashes the cold water onto the wound, rinsing it of dirt and grime as best he can. The mud gives way to the pale skin of his leg, red and raw around the wound. Moistened, the split in his leg begins to leak blood again.

"How is it?" Jay asks.

"It'll be fine," comes Huxley's lukewarm answer.

He cuts a strip from the bottom of his shirt and uses this as a bandage to tie around the wound. It does little to stop the steady flow of blood, but Huxley is less concerned with blood loss than he is with more crap getting into the wound.

They drink again until they can hear the liquid sloshing around in their stomachs, and then they stand.

In the stillness of the dawn light, the reality of their situation seems to hit them both at the same time, and it hits hard. They are in worse shape now than when they had first encountered each other. Now they are hunted, and wounded.

"Do you have anything?" Huxley asks.

Jay shakes his head, but holds up his revolver. "Just grabbed this. What about you?"

"Same." Huxley didn't even have time to grab the gunbelt and holster. He only has the revolver.

"Have any bullets left in it?"

Huxley eyes the unspent percussion caps set against the cylinder. "Two shots."

"I have three," Jay says. "Where are we going?"

"East."

CHAPTER 9

Eventually, and without conferring with each other, their course steers them back toward the road and they find it only when their heels strike hard pavement. By then, the morning frost is long gone and a dry wind whips at them, not cool enough to be cold, or warm enough to thaw them, but dry enough that it leeches the moisture from their lips and their faces become raw and chapped.

At night, they camp in a clump of trees, this time taking the time to gather wood and build a fire before it gets dark, but they still huddle together, sharing their own body heat for warmth as the fire dwindles in the night.

"We're fine," Huxley mumbles into the darkness.

Shivering slightly, Jay's eyes gaze out at the orange coals of the fire, and they do not reveal his thoughts.

"We had food and water yesterday." Huxley sniffs against a runny nose. "We're good for a few days."

"Yeah," Jay offers quietly.

Huxley feels the prodding pain in his leg. But he tells himself it's not so bad. Could have been far worse.

"We'll be okay," Huxley insists. "We'll make it."

They wake the next morning, and unsurprisingly, Huxley feels worse than before. Dehydration has taken the form of a headache now, and his mouth feels like a dusty hole in his face. He grabs a small stick off the ground and breaks it into small sections, popping one of them into his mouth. He chews it, trying to at least get some saliva to moisten his parched tongue.

The trick works—at least for now.

There is no camp to break down.

They move along, knowing that they must find water today, or they will likely be too weak to find it tomorrow.

And then they will die.

I've been there before, he thinks. *I know what it's like to almost die of thirst. This is old news. I'll push my way through it. Just keep putting one foot in front of the other.*

They wander east at first, then northeast, hoping to run into a road that will take them to some town that might have pity on the filthy, dangerous-looking mongrels of men that they are. They bog themselves in thickets and brambles and it slows their progress, but by midmorning they find another road—perhaps the same one they left the day before—and they plod on.

They stop to rest more frequently now, and a quick pace sets his heart to racing and his head to feeling fuzzy. He knows that his body is dying its slow death yet again, but perhaps the most telling sign of all is his lack of anxiety at the coming reality. For all his anger the day before, and all the fire to survive, he feels almost fatalistic now, as though this is simply the lot he has drawn and there is no changing it.

One of the times they stop seems like perhaps it will be the last. It is around midday. They stop for a time, just standing in the middle of the road. Once it had been blacktop, and it would have been too hot to stand on, but now it is covered in dusty-looking dirt and scrub, and it is just as cool as the rest of the dry plains around them.

Huxley stands there for a time, his feet straddling a length of the yellow highway lanes that had once been visible and are now scoured away or covered. A double yellow line, he sees. Do not cross, is the meaning, and yet he has a foot on either side.

He wants to sit, but sitting will take effort. Finally, his exhaustion drives him to the ground and he sits exactly where he had stood. As he bends his legs, the wound in his thigh complains, just barely. It's getting easier to ignore it now. He wonders if that is a good sign. He stares down at the dusty and sparse grasses around him, the blacktop that once was, the tiny section of yellow road lines that used to represent an intrinsic order to things.

He looks to his left, but Jay is still standing, looking out at the horizon that they've been chasing. His lips hang partially open, untouched by moisture.

The skin peels and dries. Jay seems either not to notice, or not to care.

"Fuck it," Huxley says, a dry, windy sound, the consonants made soft, like stones that have been sandblasted into smoothness.

Jay says something in reply, but Huxley cannot hear him.

"What?"

Jay turns slightly, his cracked lips closing as he tries to work enough moisture into himself to be heard. Finally, the pathetic, peeled things part again and he speaks a little louder. "Someone's coming."

Huxley draws himself up, just enough to gain himself a full view of the roadway that stretches out ahead of them. It ripples and boils, though the day is not that hot, it doesn't seem. It feels hotter than it is, Huxley suspects. Because he's an engine with no coolant in it. He pants through the dry cave of his mouth as he struggles up onto his knees. An engine running hot, no lubrication, no coolant. It's going to seize up and die.

Out in the shimmering mess of distance, Huxley can see the watery shape moving along the path of the road, along the edge, as though he is some pedestrian from the Old World, staying out of traffic, and perhaps hoping that someone will stop and pick him up, give him a ride to the next city over.

Huxley can see only that one shape.

One lone figure. Out in these wild places all by himself.

"You think he has water?" Huxley asks.

"Hard to live without it," Jay responds.

Huxley looks up at him. "Maybe we don't kill him. Maybe we ask him nicely."

"Are you asking me or telling me?"

Huxley feels his tired chest tighten, and he wants to do violence to Jay. But the exhaustion, the dryness of his mouth, the effort it takes just to get words out. It makes him just shake his head once and look back out at the approaching figure. "Telling."

Jay shrugs. "Okay."

They do not move to meet the man, but stay where they are, resting, as he draws closer.

The man had been so far away when they first caught sight of him it takes nearly twenty minutes for him to reach them. When he draws within a hundred yards of them, he is walking with his head down, staring at his shoes as they traverse yard after yard of barrenness. But he finally looks up and he sees them, and he stops.

Huxley and Jay make no overt move. Neither do they raise their hands in peace.

He is still a bit of a distance from them. If he were to run, they would have no hope of catching him. At this distance, they can just barely see his eyes, shifting around. After a long moment, he continues walking forward, but more cautiously this time. He stops at about fifty yards from them, looking hard at the landscape all around them, clearly trying to discern whether an ambush has been laid for him, perhaps a group of outlaws hiding in the low scrub brush. There are some rocks and brush around them, but they are sparse and no movement or noise comes from them, so the man turns his gaze back on the two strangers in the road, one sitting, the other standing.

"Hello," the man calls out.

Huxley inspects him at this closer range. He is a smaller man, slight of build. His head is a mess of curly hair long turned to dreadlocks. His features are pointed and all pinched into the center like a weasel. He has the same dark, glistening eyes as a weasel, too. An animal that is aggressive, but knows its size and is smart enough not to test it. The man is dressed in the usual garb you might expect someone to be wearing on these roads: an old pair of tan Dickies that have been patched and repatched probably a dozen times; a few raggedy T-shirts; and a hooded jacket made of some denim material that looks so caked with dirt and grime it seems like a dark sheen on the fabric, the original color a mystery. He carries a small satchel, white braided rope across his chest. Huxley can see no weapons, though the grimy jacket the man wears covers his midsection.

Huxley raises his hand. "Hello, stranger."

"Just passing by," the stranger says. "I don't want trouble."

His dark, glittering weasel eyes say differently. Here is a man who thrives on trouble.

"Do you have water?" Huxley asks.

The stranger considers this. "Maybe."

Huxley feels hope, then irritation, then black, bald anger. "Maybe? What the fuck does that mean?" His hand slips to his waist where the revolver is shoved into his belt line. How many rounds does he have left in the cylinder? Two? One?

The movement is not lost on the stranger. He takes a step back and raises his hands. "Easy now, partner. I ain't tryin' to fuck with you. Happens to be the true answer to that question. 'Do I have water' you ask, and the right answer is 'maybe.' Maybe I have water."

Beside him, Jay makes a dry, chuckling noise that devolves into a strange little growl.

Huxley grinds his teeth together. He can feel the grit of dust between them, but his mouth is dry to the point that he cannot taste anymore. "Explain."

The stranger holds his hands up, walking toward them at a relaxed, leisurely pace. When he has displayed his palms, shown that he means no harm, he moves slowly to his satchel, which he pulls around to the front and opens at the drawstring top.

Huxley watches the stranger's hand disappear inside, and he slips his whole hand onto the grip of the revolver, his finger sliding past his belt and into the trigger guard, his thumb already on the hammer.

The stranger looks back up, holds eye contact with Huxley, and then slowly withdraws what appears to be an ancient plastic bottle. Green tinted. Like it once contained a lemon-lime soda. There is liquid inside. Perhaps half-full. The stranger sloshes it around to demonstrate, then he uncaps the bottle and takes a long swig of it. Huxley's mouth wants to water, but it is incapable.

The stranger then takes the bottle down and caps it. There is still maybe a fourth of a bottle of water left. The stranger leans down and slides it under-handed across the ground. The bottle skitters along the dusty pavement and comes to a stop on the ground next to Huxley.

Huxley eyes the bottle. Then eyes the stranger. Doesn't want to take his hand off the revolver in his waistband. But thirst is a powerful driving force. Finally he reaches forward with his non-gun hand and snatches up the bottle. He struggles to get the cap undone with a single hand, succeeds, and then sniffs the contents.

It smells surprisingly clean.

Huxley doesn't hesitate. He takes a mouthful, then swallows.

It's lukewarm, but it tastes clean and sweet and in that moment it makes Huxley almost giddy to taste water on his lips again. He wants to down what little there is left in the bottle, but he restrains himself at great effort and passes the bottle to Jay.

The stranger smiles. "You got a piece tucked up in your drawers, or you just acting like it?"

Huxley draws the big revolver out and rests it on his thigh, visible to the stranger.

The stranger's smile doesn't falter. He steps closer. "You got bullets for that thing?"

Huxley nods. "Some."

"Because I can take you to water, my friend. More water than you'll be able to drink. A spring, that's where that water came from. That's why it tastes so good. Ain't no rainwater been sitting in a muddy ditch for months. Pure, perfect spring water is what I'm talking about. And I can take you to it."

"But there's someone already there," Huxley says, just a matter of fact.

The stranger's tongue plays across his top teeth, making him look even more weasel-like. "Yeah, that's the size of it. But they're greedy fucks, my man. That little bottle I had to take by force. There's just a few of them, guarding more water than they need. Ten times more than they need. A hundred times, even. But they horde it all to themselves. They sell it, I think. Sell it to people that are about to die of thirst, rather than trying to help. That's what these people do. Three of them, I think. Three of them, running the show like they're a fucking army. But we could take them if we did it right. We could. Enough water for days. Months, even. Forever. Who knows how much water that spring can spit up?"

Thirst has been known to drive a man mad. Things that are required for survival often do, if a person is pushed long enough without them. The proposition seems strangely familiar to Huxley, but without water it's like the contact points of his brain have been corroded and he cannot even remember the lessons of just a few days gone past. All he knows is the sweet water drying on his lips, and that he might have more, and that without it he will die.

And he refuses to die. This world will not get the best of him.

He will not be one of the weak ones.

"Okay, stranger," Huxley says. "What's your name?"

"Name's Don," he says, closing the distance with an outstretched hand. "Good to meet a friend on this road."

CHAPTER 10

The night calls to Lowell, as it always does. Black and deep and cool. Inside the trailer the air grows thick with his own breath and the breath of Father and Mother. They sleep peacefully. Lowell is the only one that can hear the call of the night.

Tonight, he resists. As he had the night before, and the night before that. For three nights he has sat in the confines of a small, metal box, smelling the smells of himself and Father and Mother, their breath stale and acrid in the still air. Outside, the wind is cold, and it moves, and it is alive. He needs it on him. The stillness inside the trailer is maddening.

But he cannot go. Not after what had happened.

Mother had wanted him beaten. Father had refused. So instead, Mother glared at him and refused to talk to him. In the quiet rooms of the trailer, where Mother and Father were separated from Lowell, but from which Lowell could hear every word that they said, Mother spoke to Father in hushed tones and called him "creepy," and "an animal."

These words terrify him. It terrifies him that Mother might convince Father that Lowell should not be there with them, and then Father will tell Lowell that he has to go back out into the world. Father has sworn he won't do that, but Lowell knows that people's words are only kept when it's convenient for them.

He cannot go out. He must be a good child.

He must stay inside, even when the air in the trailer seems to have run out. Even when his muscles ache to work, when his skin wants the moonlight and cold wind on it.

Stay inside, Animal Child, Lowell chides himself bitterly. *Act like a boy. Act like you should. Go to sleep. It's late and tomorrow you're going to be tired unless you sleep. Sleep now.*

He closes his eyes.

His heart beats on harder.

This is not normal. You are not normal. Mother doesn't think so. Father won't say it, but he doesn't think so either. They both know that you're an Animal Child. Even if you try to hide it. You'll never be normal. You'll never be like their own child.

But I'm alive, and their own child is dead.

Why wouldn't they want a live child over a dead one?

His eyes are open again. He doesn't remember opening them. They seem to have drifted open without his knowledge, much like a normal child's eyes might drift closed to fall asleep. He is staring at the ceiling. The dome of shiny metal. The rivets holding everything together. Dark spots that he knows are rust, even though they seemed like smudges of blood in the darkness.

He thinks about dogs and whelps and spears and everything trying to *live*. Everything struggling to *survive*.

His eyes track around in the darkness, though it is not so dark to him. The moon insists on lighting everything. A big, square patch of it is coming through the window, illuminating the inside of the trailer. The moon wants him to be up, too. The moon wants him to look.

He leans up and turns in his bed, very quietly, so that Mother and Father won't hear him. He is very good at doing things quietly. The window that the moon is trying to squeeze all its light through is behind him, at the head of the pile of blankets that he calls his bed. When he leans up and twists and looks up, he can see the sky above him. But the moon hasn't risen high enough for him to see it from his spot on the floor. It teases him. He knows it is out there, but it can't be seen.

The sky is clear and cold and the stars want him to come out into the night, just like the moon. They're all old friends, hanging in his window, trying to get him to disobey Mother and Father.

He looks across the trailer at them. The metal construction is too small to hold individual rooms. Mother and Father are squeezed into a bed, Father propped up on pillows, and Mother propped up on Father's chest, or on his arm. That is how they fall asleep. Come later in the night, they will have tossed and turned and twisted away from each other, as though they'd been arguing with each other in their dreams, but for now they are peaceful. Mother snores, softly. Father always sleeps silently, to the point that Lowell wonders sometimes if he is in fact sleeping. Sometimes when he looks at Father, he can't tell whether Father's eyes are completely shut or not.

He was a "light sleeper," Lowell had heard Mother say.

Which, perhaps, is why Lowell is still alive.

Still, neither of them has stirred since he moved. He does not think he has disturbed them. And he wants badly to look out the window. He will not go out into the night. Not now. Not after what happened. But he wants to look. Is that so bad? It will calm him, he knows. And it's not really disobeying. Not really.

In the center of the room, the brazier, constructed of an old piece of scrap that Father calls a "grill" ticks and pops quietly as its embers burn down, a tiny tendril of smoke reaching up from the coals. It drifts upward, upward, and escapes through the hole in the ceiling. Lowell watches it go, thinking, *The smoke can be free, but I can't …*

He pulls the blanket off of him, very carefully. He keeps checking to see if Father has awakened, but everyone still sleeps. Father's even, quiet breathing. Mother's steady snoring. The sound of nothing without but the plains, which can be eerily still, particularly when autumn and winter start coming on.

There are the stars.

There is the moon, only a few handwidths above the horizon.

There are the rocks that hide the spring that keeps them alive.

There are the cold, silent plains, stretching out in their enormity.

And … what else? For a long moment he stares, nose touching the glass of the window, feeling the chill of it. He stares out and wonders if he is dreaming. Normally, he would not wait so long to react, but for some reason his heart has not started to pound, and it seems his mind and his body are not connecting the dots. So, of course, he must be dreaming.

Still, he turns away from the window, and when he does that, he smells again the smells of the trailer, the smells of sleep and breath and musty air and dirty clothes and unwashed skin and he knows that this cannot be a dream. Because you can never smell in dreams.

He walks stiffly to Father's side, but fears to wake him. For some reason, that fear is bigger than the fear of what lays outside.

Now his heart is catching up. The sweat is breaking out on his palms. His breath coming faster.

Father senses someone watching him, or maybe hears Lowell's breathing and wakes from his light sleep. He jerks a bit to find Lowell there at the side of the bed, staring at him with a ghostly face, mouth open, chest rising and falling oddly quick. Father blinks a few times, as though he wonders if the image will go away, then he frowns, and Lowell fears he is in trouble, but that should not be his concern right now.

"Lowell," Father says thickly. "What are you doing? What's wrong?"

Lowell points to the window and whispers, "There are men outside."

Father doesn't hesitate. He rips the blanket off and is out of bed in an almost drunken lurch, the sleep still clogging his neural pathways. But his big revolver is in his hand already, finger on the trigger, thumb on the hammer. He bolts to the window, but stops himself short, conscience and caution making their way through the muddle of sleep and sudden panic.

On the bed, Mother has come upright, clutching the blanket, her face bordering on angry. That is her default setting for a rude awakening, but she can see how Father is leaning up against the side of the trailer, just next to the window, the way he holds the revolver tensely in his hands as he slides, slides, slides so slowly so that just a sliver of his face is peeking out of the window.

"What?" Mother demands, her voice a husky whisper. "What's out there?"

Lowell knows what Father is seeing.

It was not so much the shapes of the men themselves, but the bright moon casting an ink-black shadow underneath them and Lowell had seen them moving stealthily across the starkly pale landscape, around the big boulders where their spring was kept.

Father's breath is coming harder now. Fogging the window next to his face.

Mother is out of bed. Rummaging underneath the mattress.

Lowell doesn't know what to do with himself. He wants to find his spear, but he is unsure whether that will anger Father and Mother or not. He keeps looking between them, wondering what is going to happen, wondering what they want him to do.

Mother comes out from underneath the mattress with a big bore scattergun. One that Lowell didn't know that they had. He realizes that they must have kept it a secret from him. He does not have time to wonder why, does not have time to fully think about how frightened Mother is of him sometimes, how she did not want him to know that they had it in the house, or where it was hidden.

Father puts his back to the wall. "They're coming around the rocks," he says, dipping his head toward his right.

Mother takes her eyes off her scattergun for a brief moment as she pulls out a small bottle of powder and charges the contraption. "What are you gonna do?"

Father thinks about it for a moment, but not too long. His lean face shows the strain of fears that stretch the cordage of his being so tight. And he looks at Mother with longing, and Lowell can see in his eyes the wish for more time.

It's okay. It's okay. Everything is going to turn out okay.

Lowell realizes his heart hurts in his chest, it is beating so hard. "What do I do?" he whimpers. "What do you want me to do?"

Father reaches out and puts a hard hand on his shoulder. "Stay in here. Do what Mother says."

Then he pushes through the door to the trailer and gently closes it behind him.

Lowell watches him go, the edges of his vision sparkling as his body fills with adrenaline and his blood pressure spikes, bringing everything in his world down to a pin-point, tunnel-vision view. He turns his head in Mother's direction, and he sees her in the darkness, the little portal-like view that he has of her, the little cropped image that is all his eyes can manage to focus on at that moment. She is staring at the door as it closes behind Father, her mouth hanging open with an unspoken protest, her eyes brimming with tears. The look she gives that closing door is just the same as Father had given her. The wish for more time.

Lowell's mind is panicked. *IT'S GONNA BE OKAY! WE'RE NOT ... WE CAN'T ...*

Mother holds a dozen ball bearings in a cloth pouch. She empties them into the scattergun. Lowell listens to them skitter down the barrel and rest against their bed of gunpowder at the bottom. Then she uses the cloth itself as the wadding, ramming it down with a thin, wooden rod until it is all packed tightly inside.

"What do you want me to do?" Lowell asks again.

Mother looks at him. She looks at him with surprise, like she had forgotten he was there. Like she turned and found him there, once again a stranger in her house. The moment passes in a flash, but it is not lost on Lowell. Then she shoulders the scattergun and looks over Lowell's shoulder.

"You need to hide," she says.

"But ... but ..."

Mother grabs him firmly by the collar of his old shirt, tearing it a bit as she twists the fabric up in her fist. "Lowell!" she hisses, her eyes flashing angry again. "Do what I say!"

She tries to turn him toward the back of the trailer, but then they are both frozen by what they hear. A gunshot. The loud, sudden *snap-BOOM* of a ball-and-cap pistol going off. Then just the sound of the echo crackling back. Nothing else at all for a long moment.

Lowell and Mother look at each other, eyes wide, mouths open, sucking in cold, musty air.

Snap-BOOM!

This time someone cries out, and a second gun answers the first, and this time the light of the muzzle flash illuminates the interior of the trailer for the briefest of moments. Something strikes the side of the trailer, punching a neat, clean hole through the siding and whistling through, causing Lowell and Mother both to duck.

Two voices are screaming.

One in pain, another in anger.

Lowell cannot tell which is Father.

Mother pushes him to the back of the trailer. "Go," she says, her voice shaking. "Go, go, go, Lowell. Hide. Hide and don't come out until I tell you to."

CHAPTER 11

Lowell stumbles through to the back as the sound of men's voices and the angry belching of black powder fill his ears and tumble through his brain, lighting things on fire as they go, a mudslide unearthing things that seemed to have been buried for geological ages. For the first time in a long time he feels helpless, defenseless, small, infantile. He can only run, only hide, find the dark place, find the place that no one else could find. Stay there. Befriend the dark. Live at night. Embrace the fear like a hunted animal does, at no time able to close his eyes, always watching, always knowing that this might be the time that his life is suddenly snuffed out. The reality of the situation, the fact that it is everlasting, that there is no coming back from the place it puts you, no ghosts, no after, just a rotting patch of meat left on the desert floor, soon to desiccate and disappear.

He is spinning, rolling, caught in a current he can't get out of.

He finds the water closet with his hands, pulls himself inside and struggles with the door. The sliders are rusted and gummed up. The door is never closed, because the toilet is never used for its intended purpose—Father had to explain to him what it was for and Lowell had crinkled his brow, not quite getting it. Now the toilet bowl is filled with dirt and herbs are growing in it.

Lowell fumbles with the tiny latch that is used as a door handle. It clicks and clacks in his fingers as outside the metal hull of the trailer he can hear the sounds of fighting drawing closer. Finally the casters break free of the rusted tracks and the water closet door slams shut. Lowell backs up until he is sitting on the toilet seat, his rear end in the dirt, crushing the herbs. He is in complete darkness here. He smells mint and basil. The smells of Mother's cooking.

He is shaking uncontrollably. "Help me," he whispers to no one in particular. "Help me."

A gunshot, very close outside of the trailer. A man curses loudly, sounding like he is just on the other side.

In the darkness, a crease of light becomes apparent along the seam of the water closet door. Through the crack, Lowell can see his bed, the covers thrown over, the window above it pouring in blue moonlight. Lowell leans to his left, breathless and tense. The soft soil of the herb bed shifts underneath him. The skinny image that he can see through the door pans, little bit by little bit, until he can see Mother. He can see the back of her. Her elbow. Her hair swept back. Her ear. Once, she turns sharply to the sound of a noise outside the trailer, and Lowell can see her dark eyes, intense and fearful. Then she turns back again and faces the door. He can tell that she is standing in front of it, with the scattergun leveled, held at her side. Waiting.

Lowell wonders if she is shaking as much as he is.

Something hits the outside wall, just behind him.

Lowell jumps off his seat, puts his back up to the wall, sucking in herb-scented air. He cannot seem to breathe fast enough. Every time he gets a breath in his chest, it expels, almost against his will, and he has to take another. He has not felt this way since ... since ...

There is a man on the other side of the wall.

Two men. Struggling.

Lowell hears their sounds of desperation. Grunts and groans. Noises like two wild animals locked in combat. One of them slams up against the trailer again. The sound of feet scuffling in the dirt outside. Curses strained out between clenched teeth. Something clatters, metal on metal.

One of them is Father.

And one of them is not.

There are words in the animal noises, but Lowell cannot make sense of them, as though they are spoken in a different language. He stares at the dark wall, seeing nothing, and seeing everything in his mind's eye. Seeing everything and more, his imagination creating horrible things that may or may not be real.

"Father," he whimpers.

Outside, the inflection of a voice changes.

"Ah!" it is high-pitched, panicked. "No, no! Ah! Ah! Stop!"

The last noise is a high-pitched mewl. Something that does not sound like it should have come from a man. Something that should have come from an animal, a dog perhaps, a bitch with swollen teats lurking in the dark corner of a trailer, the sound that bitch would make when a wooden spear was thrust through her ...

No ... no ... please ...

Outside, a body drops.

Shuffling feet. Muffled curses.

Lowell just keeps picturing the bitch in his mind. He cannot stop seeing her in the darkness. Because now he knows how she must have felt. Hiding. Hoping that the intruders would go away. Hiding and hoping not to be found, hoping just to be left alone, to be allowed to live, to survive, for just another short time ...

The sound of the trailer door rattling.

Mother is whispering to herself, but Lowell cannot hear what she is saying.

The *zzz-hiss* of the scattergun's element being charged.

"Hey!" a man's voice, unfamiliar.

BOOM!

The scattergun shakes the walls.

Outside, men yelp and curse.

Inside, Mother weeps, her sobs suddenly wrenched loudly from her, the crashing of her gun the storm surge that broke her levies.

Through the crack in the door, Lowell watches as she upends the scattergun, homemade buttstock to the floor, and gropes around for her powder and another charge of ball bearings, or anything that will fit down the monstrous barrel that she might fire at the men outside of the trailer. That single shot has left a haze like a bank of fog crawling slowly through the room, and he watches Mother move through it.

"You *fuck*!" a monster's voice from outside, raspy and angry.

The crack of a pistol.

Lowell can actually hear the lead ball punching through the trailer, and then Mother screams out and falls to the ground. His heart seizes in his chest and he wants to tear through the door, but he finds that he cannot move. He can only wait, like that bitch dog and her whelps, hiding in that dark corner ...

Mother's body on the ground, thrashing around, clawing away from the door. And then the door bursts open, violently, with the sound of a boot smashing into the thin vinyl, and the hinges creaking wildly. Moonlight pours in, caught in the haze of gunpowder, and he can see the shadows of men that are not Father.

"You bitch!" the monster says, and he falls upon Mother as she tries to get away, screaming. "Did I get you? Did I fucking get you?"

Through the tiny crack, Lowell watches the scene unfold. Mother flailing her arms and legs as the man that had spoken grabs at her and pins her down. He yells obscenities to her and then language seems to flee him. Mother keeps pleading, but the man is not hearing. Lowell knows that Mother has been hit by a bullet, but he cannot see where. Maybe it's not bad. Maybe she won't die. Maybe she will live.

He realizes that he is crying only when the slit-image blurs. And he is almost thankful that it does, because he does not want to see, and yet he cannot stop himself from seeing. He cannot look away, or close his eyes. The image blurs and blurs and drips and becomes liquid, but the sounds are still so very real and tangible. The sound of heavy breathing. Mother saying repeatedly, "No! No! No, please!" The sound of clothes being rent. A harsh slap. And Mother's words become a slurry of pain and grief, and the breathing quickens.

This isn't happening. This isn't real.

It's real. It's so real. It's happening.

It's happening again.

Again.

You're cursed.

You ARE a curse.

Mother and Father are being killed because of you.

Time and terror swirl into incoherence. He blinks. Very slowly. Very deliberately. The watery image clears. He sees Mother. A dark shape atop her, wild blond dreadlocks tossing as it moves over her. He sees Mother's breasts, laid bare and pale in the moonlight, and her face, turned in his direction, looking right at him, right at Lowell, seeing him, though her eyes seem vacant, her face blank and empty.

"Mama," Lowell says and he does not know why he calls her that, except that he has used that word before, not for this woman that he calls Mother, but for another, a long time ago. One that he had lost, much as he knows she will be lost as well. "Mama, I'm sorry."

But Mother only stares on.

"I'm so sorry," Lowell wretches the words out of himself. "So sorry, so sorry …"

The man on top of Mother stops his movement, and Mother's body lays still, no longer rocked to and fro. She lays there, limp and lifeless. In the sudden quiet, Lowell can hear the man's heavy breathing, how hard he has exerted himself, and Lowell can hear the blood rushing through his own veins, like it has all turned into a clatter of marbles. He stares at Mother's empty eyes and he looks at the still and unmoving shadow that is cast not only over her, but over the man that has taken her.

A horrible feeling unearths itself in him. The cataclysm of death rips the fault lines apart, and pounds the earth down low, and this jagged, ugly thing comes sprouting from the upturned soil of his mind, veined in dark and built of rage and fear, so much fear, and hate for everyone and everything that exists, the hate that makes him want to kill it all, but the fear always staying him, telling him to hide, hide, *stay in the dark!*

She's dead! Mother's dead! Father's dead! They're all dead!

The feeling expresses itself in a sound that rips out of his throat, completely without his control. He could not feel or hear the sound that he made, but it is short and sharp and filled with the ungodly things that he has been a witness to, both in this life and in the past.

The man who lays atop Mother's body comes up from the ground, fumbling to get himself back into his pants, fumbling for his weapon, and for the first time, Lowell can see his face. It is a pinched, weasel face. One that he knows because it has kept rattling around in his brain since the night at the spring, and now it flashes across the back of his eyelids like lightning and he falls off the toilet with a yelp of terror.

"Motherfucker …" the man with the weasel face starts to rise, but this time, through the narrow slit in the door, Lowell sees a shadow fall over the man. It is quick—one second sprawled across both the weasel-faced man and Mother, and then there is a hand, large, and a long arm, and it grabs a hold of the weasel-faced man's shoulder and shoves him roughly back to the ground.

A voice, thick with disgust. "You sit the fuck down. Focus on getting your pants back up."

A body fills the crack in the doorway.

Lowell lifts his eyes, up and up, a very tall man, and he looks at a face shrouded in darkness, but just the barest of light reflecting off two wet, cold eyes as they look straight down at him.

Before Lowell can move, before he can even think to move, those long arms and strong hands punch through the crack and rip the flimsy watercloset door straight from its hinges. Lowell cries out and tries to back up more, but there is no place else to go. Just spilled soil and crushed herbs. But even as Lowell scrambles, the tall man outside of the door doesn't make another move toward him. Lowell has seen the revolver in the tall man's hands, held at the hip. But as Lowell screams and sobs and claws at the walls, the tall man simply lowers the revolver, then shoves it in his waistband.

"Aw, you gotta be fuckin' kidding me," the weasel-faced man says. "The kid again?"

The tall man looks over at him sharply. "That's why you clear the place before you start …" the rest of the words trail off in a sound that is like a dog's growl.

The weasel-face man looks down at what he has done, as though he does not comprehend. As though only a great fool would consider his actions wrong. "What? Her? She fucking *shot* me. Stupid bitch. Grazed my arm."

The tall man stares at the weasel-faced man a moment longer, then turns his gaze back on Lowell, but Lowell cannot stop crying now. It is coming out of him in big uncontrollable sobs. He keeps trying to ask what has happened to Father, what has happened to Mother, though he knows the answer to both questions. But no matter how hard he tries to force the words up his throat, they just come out in groans and bleats. He can hardly catch his breath.

The tall man's jaw clenches tightly. He looks down at the child in front of him and his nose twitches slightly, as though he's smelled something distasteful. "Calm down. Stop crying."

Lowell tries, but only because he is afraid of being killed if he doesn't. He manages to close his mouth, but the sounds still go on behind his sealed lips, like an argument behind a slammed door.

The tall man reaches out with one hand, the one not resting on the butt of his pistol, and he grabs the boy by the chin, squeezing Lowell's cheeks hard and shocking the grief out of him at least for a moment. "Shut up. Just stop. You're alive. Be thankful."

Lowell's chest hitches noisily.

The weasel-faced man starts toward them, hitching up his pants. "Here, let me …"

Lowell blinks and the revolver is no longer in the tall man's waistband. He has drawn it and it is leveled between the eyes of the weasel-faced man. The tall man holds it oddly, almost awkwardly, but the intent is not awkward. The intent leaves no room for discussion. It is cold and clear, like a winter night.

"You back off," the tall man says. "And take the woman outside with you while you're at it. And don't do anything else. She's dead for God's sake."

The weasel-faced man eyes the gun barrel, but he is already moving backward, his hands up. "Alright, alright. Christ Almighty. It ain't gotta be like that, Mr. Huxley."

The tall man keeps the revolver pointed at weasel-face until he has slunk out of sight. Lowell looks past Mr. Huxley and can see Mother's hand, small and delicate in all this roughness, lying against the ground with the fingers so carefully curled, as though she is asleep. But her fingers are bloody, and her fingernails are torn away from clawing at the floor. And then there is the sound of the weasel-faced man's grumbling effort, and the sound of a weight being dragged, and Mother's hand disappears from sight.

Lowell feels it like a hole in his chest.

Mr. Huxley lowers the revolver again. He seems to remember that he is still holding the kid's face. His hand relaxes and falls back to his side. He stares down, judging, measuring, and Lowell does not like that look one bit.

"You done crying?"

Lowell cannot talk yet. He fears that if he opens his mouth, the sobbing will come again. So he just nods, though his chest still hitches.

Mr. Huxley's thumb plays over the hammer of the revolver in his hand. Lowell watches it, then watches Mr. Huxley's eyes.

Finally, Mr. Huxley puts the gun back into his waistband. He looks out. Then looks back in again. Then down at Lowell. Tired, for a flash. Then stern. "What's your name?"

Lowell's mouth moves, once, twice, and on the third time he manages to speak: "Low." He isn't sure why he wasn't able to finish his name. It just seemed to stop there, like the other syllable has been lost, left behind with the rest of him, buried in the rubble. When those dark things rose from their buried places, they destroyed everything around them, it seems.

"Low," Mr. Huxley speaks quietly. "That your mother and father?"

Lowell closes his eyes because he cannot bear the world. He feels the tears gush out of him. He sobs, feels snot running over his upper lip. He sniffs and wipes at it and tries to control himself, if for nothing, than for the fear he has of this man. So he manages another nod.

Yes, they were mine. Mother and Father.

"Look at me," the man's voice says in the darkness. It is strangely flat.

Lowell opens his eyes. Once again the world is blurry, but he blinks all of that away. He looks up as he feels the wetness clinging to his eyelashes begin to chill. The man stares down at him, and Lowell does not know this look that he bears. It is nothing, it seems, and yet it is everything. It is a tired rage, if there could be such a thing. And a panicked depression. Cruel compassion. Two opposing creatures vying for control.

Mr. Huxley works spit around in his mouth. His thumb is hovering over the hammer of his revolver again. "Do you want to live?" he asks, as plain as can be. An honest question, seeking an honest answer.

At first Lowell does not know what he wants, but then he realizes that he must want to live, because he is terrified that if he says "no," Mr. Huxley will gun him down dead, just like Mother and Father. If he is afraid of death, then that must mean that he wants life, right?

"Yes," he says. "I want to live."

Mr. Huxley does something odd. He kneels down in front of Lowell and puts his hands on Lowell's shoulders, gently. This is a touch that seems out of place, when only moments ago the man had gripped the boy by the jaw, hard enough that Lowell could still feel the burn where Mr. Huxley's fingers had been. But even though it seems out of place, Lowell can tell that Mr. Huxley has spoken to children before.

"Wipe your face," Mr. Huxley says. "Clean your nose. Wipe your eyes."

Sniffling, Lowell does it.

Mr. Huxley speaks sternly, but not without compassion. "Stop crying, Low. Stop crying and wipe your tears away. Take everything and bury it way down deep, okay? That's what you have to do. Bury all that stuff really deep."

Lowell takes a breath and shoves it all down, deep inside the empty crater where those other things had been. He gathers all the bad things, from the past, and from the present, and he returns them to the empty grave that they had abandoned, and he crams them down so they will all fit into such a small soul and he covers them up as best he can. And when he releases that breath his eyes are dry, his chest is still.

Mr. Huxley takes Lowell's face in his hands, gentler this time, and looks into his eyes, judging them for a time. He seems doubtful, but then he nods once. "If you want to live, you can't be weak. Weak people die, Low. You have to be strong. That's the last time you're ever going to cry, okay? Figure out something else if you feel those emotions. Figure out some way to make yourself feel better. Turn it into anger. That's fine. You can use that. But you don't ever cry again. Okay?"

"Okay."

Mr. Huxley stands up, and looks outside. Then he reaches out his hand to Lowell, palm up, and it hangs there in the air, an invitation waiting for a response.

Not knowing what else to do, Lowell takes his hand and steps out.

PART 3

THE RIVERLANDS

Him and her.

They stood just outside of the cottage that he had built. It was night. It was cold. Winter. The clearest skies, when there were so many stars that it seemed there was more light in the sky than there was darkness. Huxley would point to shapes in the sky and draw the constellations for her. He would tell her what they were. What their names meant.

Then they were quiet for a while, as though respecting what was displayed for them.

She was five years old, then. Precocious. Talkative. Beginning to look more like her mother every day. Surprising Huxley with the things she would say.

They'd only just come to the commune. The Old World still haunted them, but it seemed those things were in the past now. Here, they were far away from the turmoil of the cities, of the population centers that lit up like matches to gasoline after the skyfire. Here they were removed from all of that. Here there was hope again, and Huxley—or at least, who he was before he took that name—allowed himself to feel like maybe everything would be okay.

She leaned against him. "I love you, Daddy."

One of those moments. The ones that made him think, I should try to remember this. She will not love me like this forever. One day she will not have so much faith in me. One day I will do something to spoil how she feels about me. So hold onto this, so you can remember it later.

"You know what?" he said to her, squeezing her tiny frame. "I love you too. In fact, Daddy loves you bigger than the moon."

This was a game they would play. Each profession of love had to be bigger and more outlandish than the last.

She smiled at the game. "Well, I love you bigger than the world."

"I love you bigger than the sky. Huh? What do you think about that?"

"The sky's not bigger than the world," she stated, matter-of-factly.

"Oh, yes it is. Way bigger. A bajillion times bigger."

She thought for a minute, then pointed at the Milky Way, which he has just taught her about, just explained how huge it truly is. "I love you bigger than that."

"Hm. That's pretty big," he said. "But I'm gonna win this. I love you more than all the stars in the sky. And tomorrow night's sky. And the night after that. And the night after that. All of them. See? I win. Daddy loves you best. You can't beat Daddy."

"Okay," she said.

Remember this, *he told himself.*

And he did. For years afterward as they grew and settled in this little commune, he would tell her just before she went to sleep. He would say, "I love you more than all the stars in the sky."

CHAPTER 1

The night is dark and long. Huxley stands in the doorway of the trailer, looking out at the sandy, grassy landscape that stretches out in front of him, the plains dry and pale as a dead man's skin. He cannot see very far. Clouds have come in, and they are thickening, first blotting out the stars, and now the moon is just a subtle glow behind them.

He can see far enough to recognize the humps of the bodies. They were dragged just a few yards away from the trailer. Grooves in the sand mark the paths where their heels had scraped. Two of these paths zigzag away from the trailer, like sidewinder trails, and there at the very edge of his vision, two dark lumps in the earth.

Mother and Father, the boy inside had called them.

Screamed for them.

Though Huxley doubts they truly are his parents. This boy ... he is an orphan. And those people that he called Mother and Father were not like him, Huxley can tell it immediately. Besides, the boy is dark, and the two adults are both light skinned.

Huxley stares at those forms for a long time. His belly feels heavy and bloated with the water he drank. He feels nauseous when he looks at the bodies, when he thinks about how he killed them for the water, but then he tells himself that he did not murder them, not in cold blood. The man had fought them. He had forced their hand.

And the woman ...

Huxley looks over his shoulder, back behind him and into the trailer.

By the dim red glow of a smoldering fire, he can see two figures. One is Jay, still awake. He sits there against the wall, his face and body turned to the brazier that burns warmly. But Jay's eyes are looking right back at Huxley, matching the intensity of his gaze.

The other figure is Don. The man who is all but a stranger to them at this point. The man who led them here. The man who'd raped a dead woman. And Huxley hadn't done a damn thing to stop him. Not because he wasn't thinking about it, but because he couldn't decide if he hated the woman. Couldn't decide if he cared to pull Don off of her, if it was worth the effort and conflict, because she'd fought back along with her husband and nearly killed one of them, and that made her an enemy, right?

Huxley is a man of reason. Or at least he was, in his past life, under his old name. But still, he likes to think he considers the world around him with a realistic eye. For all his rage and his anger, he knows that the man and the woman who inhabited this trailer were not his enemies. He knows this. And because of this, he feels a pang of guilt for their deaths.

But the other part of him knows that if he had not had the water, he would have died. And they would not have given him the water. He would have had to take it.

How do you know? Did you ask?

He bares his teeth at his own self-reproach.

I make myself weak. I tear myself down.

He needed to remember what he was. He was just an animal now. He was the most dangerous animal alive. And he would do whatever needed to be done, just to make them bleed. He could have been a good man, once upon a time. But that died along with his wife. It died on a long desert road when he realized there was no possible way that his daughter was still alive. It died along with all of his hopes.

That woman was her husband's responsibility, and he failed because he was weak. And now he is dead. And now his wife is raped and murdered. And that is the way of the world now. That dead man out there knew it just as well as Huxley did when he pulled out his revolver and chose to fight. He knew the consequences. And he would have spit on Huxley's body had he managed to kill him.

"Come in and close the door," Jay says quietly.

Huxley looks at his partner, not sure if he wants to come inside. There is a lot to think about. There is a lot rolling around inside of him that he hasn't figured out. But he is trying. Oh, he is trying.

Jay leans forward and waves with a single hand. "Come on. You're letting all the warm air out."

Huxley gives one last look over to the dark mounds of the bodies, and then he turns back inside and closes the door behind him. It creaks on its hinges and latches flimsily. The air inside still feels cold, but it is somehow stifling. In the reddish glow, he can see the haze of smoke, and the air tastes and smells thickly of it.

The fire is in a homemade brazier of sorts. There is no chimney, but only a small hole in the roof, patched over with screen to let the smoke out and keep critters from getting in. The coals had been almost burned out by the time they'd hauled the bodies from the trailer, but a few more pieces from the collection of sun-kilned wood outside brought it back to life.

While they'd worked, Huxley had watched the strange boy warily. The boy—Low, apparently—had backed himself into a corner of the trailer where he still sat even now, with his knees pulled up to his chest and his arms hugging them tight. Over the tops of his bony, scuffed-up knees, he had stared at Don. He had not taken his eyes off the man, even when Don had fallen fast asleep.

And Huxley knew that look.

The spirit that it came from was a violent one, intimate to Huxley's own soul.

With his back to the door, Huxley regards the boy for a long time.

I know you, he thinks about the boy. *I know what you're thinking right now. I know how your brain is working. I can see the same things inside of you that are inside of me—fear and anger. Rage that eats away until all you want to do is strike out.*

Is Huxley that person now? Does he cause fear in people?

He doesn't want to think about that. It will only weaken him. And he cannot afford to be weak.

He steps across the filthy floor to the wall where he intends to make his bed for the night. His footsteps sound loud and hollow on the floors. His bones creak and complain as he lowers himself into a sitting position against the back wall of the trailer. He looks into the burning coals for a while, then sniffs loudly.

"Boy," he says.

The boy named Low does not respond.

"Low," Huxley says, looking at him.

This time he sees the boy's eyes jag toward him, flashing in the firelight. They seem dry, though, so perhaps the boy has taken that much advice from him. Is there any purpose for this boy to live? And is it up to Huxley to make such decisions? What fallen state is he in that usefulness was the primary reason to let someone live, let alone whether to kill them?

Perhaps it is not up to him.

Still looking at the fire, but knowing that he has the boy's attention, Huxley pulls the revolver from his waistband and holds it to his chest. He has already reloaded the empty chambers and wiped thick grease across the openings to seal them. He feels the warmth of the metal that has sat against his skin, feels the heft of it. It has become a comfortable thing to him.

"I bet you're thinking about slitting my throat," Huxley says. "I don't begrudge you that. I really don't. I would want to kill me, if I were you. I would want to kill every one of us. But even though I know that's what's going through your head, I'm not gonna kill you. Unless you make me. You sneak up on me in the middle of the night, I will put a bullet into you. You understand that?"

Low stares, and then nods, only fractionally.

Huxley looks back to the fire, sidles lower, more comfortable. Crosses his feet in front of him.

Does he actually mean what he says? Maybe. It's hard to tell sometimes, between what you say to protect yourself, to manipulate those around you, and what you say because it is the truth. The truth is ... the truth is that Huxley let Low live because he couldn't bear it. He couldn't bear to kill him. He couldn't let a man rape this boy's mother in front of his eyes and then take the boy's life. Why he has decided to draw the line there, he doesn't know. But he recalls the moment very clearly when he realized there was a child in the room, the instant that he knew it, he felt some paternal pull, some responsibility to protect this child, like he had failed to protect his own. And it reminded him. It tore him away from the present, and threw him back into the past. It forced him to remember who he was.

And as soon as he saw the boy, as soon as he saw how Don was just going to murder everyone in the trailer, he had the very real fear that if he allowed it to happen, he wouldn't be himself anymore. The boy's death would be the straw that broke the camel's back. Huxley would break. He would become someone else. His previous life would cease to exist, and he would *forget*.

He would forget that he'd been a good man once. He'd forget that he'd been educated. That he'd been a father, a husband, he had loved and been loved, and he had hoped and held those hopes and loves close to him. For all that has happened between now and then, he still knows that.

But he feels somehow certain that if the boy was to die, if his life was to end, whether from Huxley's actions, or because he didn't act, then all memory of his true self would suddenly be stricken from him, and he would really and truly be the person that he feared he was. Not a man that did what he had to do because he had nothing left. But a man that did evil, and did it because he himself was evil.

It is a strange mental place.

But that is the reason why the boy is still alive.

That is the reason why Huxley will not let him die.

The boy speaks for the first time since saying his name: "What if I leave?"

His voice is young, unseasoned, and yet somehow it is hard, even in its youth.

"What if you leave?" Huxley repeats. "If you leave, then you'll die. Out there alone. In the sand and the brush. Bit by snakes or scorpions, or maybe just dying from dehydration or starvation. You'll die, I guarantee you that. And if you don't, you'll get picked up by slavers and then you'll wish you were dead." Huxley shakes his head, slowly. "There isn't anything out there for you."

There's nothing in this world for you now.

Except for me. I could be your friend.

I could help you. I could make sure that you survive.

I need to make sure that you survive.

Neither of them say anything else, and Huxley closes his eyes, though it seems that sleep will never come to him, and that dawn is only a few short hours away, threatening to take what little sleep he might get. Still, he closes his eyes, and at least in the relative silence, there is some sort of peace.

When Huxley dreams, he is in his cottage, the one he built at the northeastern corner of the barley fields. But this cottage is not the one that he remembers from dreams past. This one is dark and it smells of cold and mildew. The walls are burned and charred, the floor is just dirt and ashes. The only light that illuminates the scene is that of a cold moon, seeping in through the broken door.

He hears a quiet scrape behind him and turns, but there is nothing. What he sees is a different cottage behind him. This one is smoke-filled and somehow modern, somehow factory-made, and he knows it is not really a cottage, but the trailer. He sees three figures, the glow from the coals in the brazier giving off an oddly strong tone of red, like a brothel light. On the ground, his wife is naked. Charity. She is splayed and dead, and Don is on top of her, thrusting. He watches Huxley the whole time.

Huxley wants to scream, but he doesn't have the voice.

He wants to move, but he is frozen instead.

The third figure is in the corner of the room, a dark ghost, small, and clothed in tatters. It is the boy named Low, but it is not. At the same time that it is Low, it is the little girl from the barley field, the one that huddled beside him under a vast night sky. The one that he told how much he loved.

More than all the stars in the sky.

Nadine.

Now her eyes are horror-stricken and her lip trembles as she watches this man, this beast, this stranger, clambering over top of the woman on the floor.

Her mother.

My wife.

My daughter.

Charity. Nadine.

He recoils, and it all turns to dust at the sound of a creaking hinge.

He wakes to a wash of cold air and the trailer door latching back into place.

Huxley sits upright, feeling the blood drain from his head and face with the suddenness of it. He still holds his revolver, and his thumb moves to the hammer but doesn't pull it back yet. The interior of the trailer is dark—no more glow from the brazier. The coals have burned out. Through one of the trailer windows, Huxley can see the sky, and it is a dull black, washed out by the coming dawn.

To his left, he can just barely see the forms of Don and Jay. Neither seems to have stirred.

To his right, there is nothing but empty blackness, where before there had been the strange child.

Huxley realizes that his heart is pounding in his chest, his skin flushed, but his forehead, neck, and back are damp from where a cold sweat has broken out. *Just a dream,* he tells himself. *Just a dream.*

But he keeps staring into the darkness where the child used to be. He keeps picturing the girl, the little girl, *his* little girl, standing there and watching. Watching the horror. Watching the atrocity. Watching the world crumble down around her as men turned to animals and all things good and honest became prey.

What was Huxley now?

A man is not a man to himself, but he is who he is for the people around him. With nothing but the imperative of survival, all men cast aside such cumbersome things as character and honor and morality. Alone in the wild, a man can be anything, as long as he lives. But introduce a woman or a child, and a man must be something more.

Who was this child that called himself Low?

He was only the offspring of two dead people.

Adopted by two more people, who then died, just like the first ones.

Huxley isn't weak like they were. That's why he's still alive, and they are dead. He can teach this boy how to be strong. He can teach this boy how to survive, in ways that he never showed Nadine, because he *just didn't know.* He can help this boy. And if Low went out there, if Low died …

I'll forget who I was.

Never mind who I am. That ship has sailed.

But who I was? Now, there is something to cling to.

I was an educated man. Loved by my wife. Loved by my daughter. I was a good person.

He leans forward from his bedroll, then climbs slowly to his feet. The sounds of Don and Jay's breathing stays slow and steady. They are still asleep. He steps over a jumble of blankets that had clustered at his feet while he kicked at them in his dreams—not his blankets, but the blankets of the people they had killed. The floor creaks underneath him, but it is the only sound, and still Jay and Don sleep.

He goes to the door. He can feel the cold air rushing around the flimsy seal that it creates, seeping into the trailer and drawing the warm air out. These lands take everything from you, whether they need it or not. Sometimes it seems like a vacuum.

Huxley pushes the door and it opens, unlatched. The cold takes him. He steps out onto the little metal stairs and then down onto dirt, packed hard enough to be concrete. The door hisses closed behind him.

Coming from the almost perfect dark of the trailer, the outside seems bright and clear. The moon has long ago sunk across the horizon, but the clouds have been scoured away, and the eastern sky has already begun to blush, the stars fizzling out in the path of the sun.

The boy, Low, stands between the two mounds that had been dragged away from the trailer. Huxley can tell at first sight that the bodies had been disturbed—and not by Low. The clothing has been ripped away, bellies opened and soft tissue stripped. Jackals and coyotes and rats do not wait long.

Low stands between the two ravaged bodies, kneeling down to the ground, clutching what Huxley realizes is a spear. The boy has nothing else on his person. Just the clothes he wears and the spear he holds. He is bent over, the spear seeming to be the only thing keeping him from falling over. His shoulders shake violently, but he doesn't make a sound.

Huxley approaches, and when he is about halfway to Low, the boy straightens and turns, hearing Huxley's footsteps. He holds the spear in both hands, brandished with the point hovering in the air before him, extended out toward Huxley like an accusing finger.

"You stay away from me," Low says shakily. "I'll stab you. I will."

Huxley believes him. He stops and holds up his hands. "What are you doing, Low?"

Low makes a strangled noise and glances down at the two bodies next to him, then back up. Huxley looks at the bodies too, but he doesn't feel what the boy feels. They are only bodies to him. They are not people anymore, and when they were, they'd been troublesome. Huxley feels bad about the woman, but the man had fought them.

Why are you like this?

Because I have to be.

The point of the spear wavers and dips a bit. "I'm going," the boy says, resolutely.

Huxley wrinkles his nose. "Don't be stupid, kid."

"You killed them."

"I killed your father. I didn't kill your mother."

"It doesn't matter."

"It does. And be honest, Low, were they really your parents?" Huxley lowers his hands, slowly, and they find their way into his jacket pockets. Through the cloth he can feel the grip of his revolver, still stuffed into his waistband. "Did they understand you, Low? Yes, they fed you. They gave you a roof over your head. But think, kid. Because I can see things inside of you. I can see hardness. Strength. You're not the same as them. You're more like us." Huxley sniffs, snorts, then spits. He feels filthy saying these things to the child, but he can't think of any other way to convince the boy to stay. These horrible things are where his mind goes now. It's who he is. "Did they understand you, Low? Or were they afraid of you?"

The spear is shaking. Low's entire body is shaking. Even from ten feet away, Huxley can see the tears in his eyes, glistening, and then falling down his cheeks.

Huxley's brow furrows. "Stop crying, Low. I told you about that."

Low bares his teeth, sheer willpower cutting off his grief. "She was Mother."

"Yes, she was Mother. The woman that you called mother. The woman who you wanted to be your mother. But she wasn't." Huxley shakes his head. "The world is full of people like you, Low. Children born to weak parents that couldn't survive. Left alone. Orphaned. Adopted by some others along the way, out of pity or a sense of duty, who knows. But they were foolish to adopt you when they knew that they were not strong enough to keep themselves alive. But you're stronger than all of them, Low. I know this. Do you know how I know?"

Low shook his head, eyes wide and watching. An impressionable child.

"Because you're still alive. They're all dead, and you're still alive."

Low looks at them, the spear pointed down now. "They're all I remember."

Huxley kneels down next to the boy and addresses him, eye to eye. "I'm not afraid of you, Low," he says quietly. "I can see what's inside of you. And it doesn't scare me. Because I know exactly what's inside of you. I know how it feels to be that angry, to have that much sitting inside of your heart. You want to do to the world what it's done to you. You want to lash out but you feel like you're not strong enough. I know how you're feeling, because I've felt it too. I still feel it, sometimes. But you know what I've learned?"

Low looks up at him, waiting.

Huxley stands up and looks down at the boy. "If you're strong, you don't have to be afraid. And we're strong together. So we can lash out at this world, because that's what this world deserves. It's taken everything from me, just like it's taken everything from you. And we can do it because we're strong." Huxley looks off to the sunrise. "I know you, Low. And I'm not afraid of who you are. You can be who you are. I want you to be who you are. Who you are is who you need to be to survive. That's good." Huxley nods toward the glow in the sky. "We're heading east. To the Riverlands. You can go off by yourself and die, or you can stick with us, be strong, and live. The choice is yours."

Low closes his eyes for a time, as though he cannot bear to look at the bodies anymore, their rent clothing and the foul smell of them, the way their insides are trailed off in random directions where the night creatures have grabbed what they could and run. When he opens his eyes again, they are dry and calm.

Huxley can appreciate that. It shows a fortitude that was rare in someone Low's age.

Huxley jerks his head back to the trailer. "Come back inside. We'll leave soon enough."

When he walks back in, the boy follows after him.

CHAPTER 2

In the dawn blush, Huxley and Don work their way through the trailer's kitchen, rifling for containers that might hold water. Jay tends to the fire in the brazier while Low hauls in old, sun-seasoned wood, stacking small cords next to the brazier. Jay watches the boy, but neither of them speak to each other.

Don is not so reserved with Huxley. He rattles and clanks through old and dented pots and pans, looking for a water container with a sealable lid. "So, tell me, Mr. Huxley, why you headin' east? Seems like a long trip, and you seem pretty dead-set on goin'."

Huxley stands on tiptoes to rummage the top cabinet in the cramped kitchen. "I'm curious. About the Riverlands," he says. *I'm curious where the slavers are going, obviously somewhere in the Riverlands. Obviously someone is buying the slaves. I want to know who. And I want the man with the scorpion tattoo.*

"The Riverlands, huh?" There is a smile and a laugh in Don's voice.

Huxley stops and turns to him, tapping a pot lid on the Formica countertop. "Yeah. The Riverland Nations."

Don returns to the search. "Well, technically you are already in the Riverlands. Or a province of them, anyway. Council claims to own pretty much everything west of the Mississippi, though they got no way to enforce that past the Red River. But, you know … on *paper* …"

Huxley keeps tapping the pot lid on the countertop, louder now. He is wondering what it would do to Don's face. He doesn't like the man. "You come from out east?"

Don comes up with a moldy-looking, plastic half-gallon jug, which he waggles in the air, proudly. He sets it on the countertop. "Yeah, used to live out there. Was a *leal subject* to Councilman Grafter. But ..." Don shrugs. "... you know how it gets, sometimes."

Tap. Tap. Tap.

His neck is itching.

"No," Huxley says. "I don't."

Don regards him steadily for a moment, then goes back to the cabinets. "Well, my brother got into a little scrape at a bar. Got a little extra friendly with one of the tavern girls, after hours, that sort of thing. She set her grievance before Councilman Grafter and he signed a death warrant and sent the Black Hats after him." Don laughs. "A bar bitch! She had to've been a piece on the side for Grafter. Can't imagine why else he would give a fuck about a bar bitch. Anyway. Maybe I was mixed up in the whole thing. And the Black Hats like to kill the man as well as his associates, so when I heard about the warrant on my brother, I decided to head out into the Wastelands until this shit blows over. Or they catch and execute my brother, one of the two."

Huxley looks down at the pot lid. "Black Hats spend a lot of time chasing down random criminals. Can't seem to get a handle on the slavers, though."

Don gives him an odd look. "How's that?"

Huxley feels stiff. The way Don is looking at him, like he just said something completely ridiculous. Like a child whose understanding of the world is very naïve. It flushes the back of Huxley's neck and suddenly he is not so sure. "I was just saying. It doesn't seem like the Black Hats do a good job of controlling the slavers."

Don blinks a few times, mystified. Then suddenly, inexplicably, he starts laughing.

Huxley grinds his teeth at the other man's braying. He glances around, almost self-conscious, but Jay has stepped outside and there is no one else in the trailer. No one else there to see Huxley if he were to ram the pot lid into Don's face, maybe into his throat, using the edge of it to crush his larynx and stifle that laughter.

"What?" Huxley snaps, loudly through Don's breathless humor.

"You fucking Wastelanders," Don cackles, as though Huxley has told the best joke. As though people from the Wastelands have the very best senses of humor. "You don't get it, do you?"

Huxley's teeth hurt. His jaw aches.

Kill him. He's a rotten thing anyway ...

But Huxley is on the precipice of an understanding. He can feel it, uncomfortable, hurtling at him. But he needs to know. He needs to find out what he doesn't get. He needs to control his irrational anger for a moment and let Don talk, let the fool spill his guts.

"Let me explain," Don forces his laughter down. He uses his hands on the countertop, pointing to random points on the surface to illustrate an invisible hierarchy. "The Riverland Nations is run by the Great Council. The Great Council is led by Chairman Warner and twenty-some-odd councilmen who own big pieces of land in Louisiana and Mississippi. The Black Hats work for the councilmen. And the councilmen are the ones that buy the slaves. Of course the Black Hats don't go after the slavers!" Don guffaws again. "You really didn't know that? You're this far east and you didn't *know that*?"

Huxley almost lunges for Don. Killing the messenger. Killing this spawn of the Riverlands, this piece of shit, this being who holds everyone else in such low, dispensable regard. Was this how everyone in the Riverlands was? Was the whole damn place filled with creatures like this?

I'll kill them all.

"You Wastelanders," Don says, somewhat more serious, because he can see the rage bubbling up in Huxley. "You're just fodder for the Riverlands. How did you think they rebuilt a society?"

Huxley can't speak for a moment. *Where do the slavers go?* The words are on the tip of his tongue ...

Jay bursts into the trailer. "Someone's coming."

Huxley just stares at him for a moment. He doesn't know what to do. The words *someone is coming* make it into his brain, but they just kind of roll around in the back. He keeps thinking to himself, keeps picturing it now, an accurate picture ...

The people they call "Wastelanders." Simple people in their isolated little farming communes. Just trying to scratch a life out of the dirt. Naïve. Ignorant to the fact that others were gathering power and looking at them greedily.

They were far away. They were removed. They were not "Riverlanders," they were just "Wastelanders," just savages really.

But I was just like you, Huxley thinks. *I taught English to your children.*

All I wanted was to live. I just wanted to live and to farm. To be left alone to enjoy what time I had left in this miserable world with my wife and my daughter.

But none of that mattered. They would come anyway; they would come for those people out beyond the desert. People like Huxley and his family. Because they could. And there was nothing to stop them.

It's not fair, Huxley thinks, and feels like a child for it, though it is as true as anything he's ever thought. It wasn't fair. It was the highest inequity imaginable.

"Huxley!" Jay says sharply, bringing him back to the real world. "You hear me? Someone's coming!"

Huxley slaps the lid down on the countertop and squeezes through the narrow opening and into the tiny living space where they'd slept the night before. Who was coming? More Riverlanders? More of those corrupt beings?

I'll kill them all, he thinks again, but he forces himself to be rational.

Think first. Kill if you need to.

Jay is standing in the open door of the trailer, staring at something in the distance. Low is there with a load of thin wood under one arm, the other holding the door open. Huxley looks down at the body of the door and he can see the holes in the flimsy sheet metal where Low's mother had fired a single shot from a scattergun, and Don had answered back.

Badly done …

Huxley brings his eyes up and squints into the eastern sky. The red blush has turned to pinks and golds. It looks like the sky will be cloudless this morning. It is hard to stare into the sun as it crests that overwhelming flat and expansive landscape, but Huxley can see the object of their attention, not by the object itself, but by the small trail of dust it leaves rising behind it on the road.

"Wagon," Jay says. "Got to be a wagon."

Don is rubbing his face. "Fuck, man. Are they coming here?" He turns his gaze on Low. "Hey, fucker! Who is that? Who the hell is that coming? You set off a signal last night? Who are those people in the wagon? You tell me or I'll take your eyes out!"

Huxley takes a hold of the man's chest by seizing a fistful of his jacket, then he pulls him off balance and shoves him into the wall, still holding him there with one hand while the other pulls his revolver, but keeps it pointed low to the ground.

"I told you once, Don. Don't threaten the boy. I won't warn you a third time." Huxley shakes his head. He takes in a breath through clenched teeth and stares down into Don's dark little soul. Very quietly he says, "Don't try my patience."

"Huxley," Jay says, demanding attention.

Huxley turns to Low, revolver still in hand. He doesn't brandish it at the boy, but Low stares at it anyway. "Low, you need to tell us who's coming. Even if you're not sure who it is. We don't want them to know that we're here. If we can make it so these people get out of here without us having to shoot them, that's what we'd like to do."

Low looks horrified. "No, don't shoot them. Please don't." The words tumble out of him so quickly he forgets about his bundle of sticks and it clatters to the floor. "It's just Mr. Crofter. Maybe his wife too, but they only come by to check on us and make sure we're doing okay. Mr. Crofter lost his kids, so he tries to look after us and make sure we're safe, make sure that I'm okay. He brings me sweet meat from the market when he can afford a few pieces. Please don't hurt him. He didn't do nothing wrong. If he don't see you, he won't say nothing. Please. He's nice. He's a nice man. Don't hurt him."

Huxley blinks rapidly, processing the information. "Is he going to the market right now? To a town?"

Low grabs his head, his fingers clawing into his hair. "I don't ... yes, I guess so."

"Is there a sheriff in that town?"

"I don't know!" Low seems on the verge of tears again, but he is holding them back. Either out of conscious effort, or perhaps because he has nothing left inside of him. "Please, don't hurt him. Don't do it. He'll go away. You don't need to hurt him."

In his distress, Low has let go of the door and it has swung closed, though not latched. Huxley leans into the door and looks out the small glass window pane to the eastern horizon where the smudge of road-dust has grown slightly bigger, and now there is a dark shape growing, taking on the dimensions and form of a small wagon and a single horse.

"Okay. Okay." Huxley scratches his neck, thinking for a moment. He scratches until it hurts, and then he turns back to Low. "Here's what you're going to do. You're going to walk out to him. We're going to stay in here. You're going to tell him that your mother and father are very sick and that you're tending to them." Huxley reaches into his pocket and draws out a faded piece of cloth. "Tie this around your face. Tell him that what they have is contagious and not to come close." Huxley pushes the piece of cloth into Low's hands. "You need to be convincing, Low. Convince him to go away, or we're going to have to hurt him. Him and whoever is with him. Do you understand that?"

Low nods, looking scared. "Yes."

"Do you understand what you need to do?"

"Yes."

Huxley folds the cloth in half to form a triangle. "Turn around." As Low does it, Huxley glances out the window again, sees the approaching shape. It's clear now. One man on a wagon drawn by a single horse. The wagon is an old chassis—what had been a small, compact car—built up with what looked like wood. They were moving at a good clip. They would be there any second now.

With Low's back to him, Huxley ties the cloth around the boy's face, then double-knots it. "Okay. You're ready." The thoughts storm through his mind: *What reason does this boy have to lie for you? Wouldn't it be quicker if he just told the man that he was being held, then jumped in the wagon and drove away? We have no horses. We would not be able to catch them.*

Huxley looks across at Jay, sees the man's cold blue eyes. Somehow, Jay gives him the answer without speaking. *Because the boy thinks that we'll just gun them both down if they make a run for it. He doesn't know that I won't shoot him …*

Huxley pulls his own revolver from his waistband. Checks the chambers. They are loaded and ready. He pulls the hammer back, watches the cylinder rotate and *snick* into place. He holds the revolver close to his torso, then steps back away from the door and waves for Jay and Don to do the same. They melt away into shadows turning from blue to gray to orange as tiny facets of the dawn's light seep through cracks and openings in the trailer. The brazier gives off stifling heat, but still they can see their own breath.

Huxley waves at Low with the barrel of his revolver. "Go now."

The boy's hands tremble as they take the door and unlatch it, pushing it open.

The townsman will know. He'll see the shake in Low's hands. He'll see the fear in his eyes.

Maybe he'll believe it's fever …

The door swings shut on its hinges, the hydraulic cylinder in the upper corner barely putting up any resistance. It bangs closed noisily, much more noisily than the night before. Low had crept out and he'd been quiet save for the sound of the latch. He was a sneak, this young man. He was more than just a scared, mourning child. There were other things underneath that surface. Things the boy was trying to hide, trying to deny their power over him.

From the shadows inside the trailer, Huxley leans out, just slightly. Most of his body is hidden behind a floor-to-ceiling cabinet that marks the beginning of the kitchen area of the trailer. Only half of his face sticks out, a single eye peering out of the darkness, staring into the dawn light, watching what unfolds.

The sky is yellow now, the sun sitting above the horizon line. Despite the added light, the landscape looks darker. It is backlit by the rising sun, and it makes things harder to see in detail, but he can get the gist of them from the movement of the shapes.

Low stands in the middle of what might be considered the "yard" of the trailer. A dusty expanse with boot prints belonging to the family, and many more belonging to people that the townsman would not know. But he would not notice such things, Huxley thought. Or *hoped.*

Off to the right, in amongst the dry scrub grasses, there are the corpses.

Huxley's heart hammers in his chest as he stares at the corpses.

They are side by side, like they are holding hands and staring up at the sky to talk about shapes in the clouds. Two young lovers on a grassy hillside in some park, a long time ago and in a place so far away from Huxley that he does not remember the name. They are barely concealed. There is some dry brush around them, and their rags are the color of the desert. But they are not camouflaged, and they are only a few short paces from the dusty road that leads to the trailer.

He will see them, Huxley tells himself, gripping his revolver hard.

He won't. He can't. He'll be focused on the boy. The half-light will make them hard to see. The brush and the rags will conceal them …

On a whim, Huxley dips his knees and cranes his neck, looking skyward first through the window, and then bending back to look up through the hole in the roof that serves as their chimney. A dark shape swoops across that small opening, then another, or perhaps the same one.

Huxley grinds his teeth furiously, feeling the pit of his stomach like a hollow, heavy hole that seems to be expanding, eating him up inside. Those were carrion birds. They'd smelled the dead and had come for their meal.

He'll see the carrion birds. He has to see them.

Everyone sees those birds. Everyone looks for them.

One did not simply travel without an eye to the sky to see where the birds were hovering over death. They were a sign from nature that warned wise men away, warned them to take a different path, warned them that the path they were on was headed for death and danger.

Too late now. Too late to do anything about it.

Huxley leans hard against the cabinet, feels the coolness of the fake wood against his face, the scratch of his beard, the sweat breaking over his brow. *I shouldn't sweat. I shouldn't worry. It's not for me to die today. I'm not weak. The townsman is weak. He's riding alone into an area hovered over by carrion birds. He's making stupid choices. The world won't miss him. If he sees the bodies, or if he notices the birds, it means nothing to me.*

If he has to die, I will kill him.

Low stands, very still in the dawn, in the middle of the yard. Now Huxley can hear the *clip-clop* of the horse's hooves on the hard-packed trail, the subtle grind of the tires as they pass over rocks and gravel and course sand. The entire wagon creaks as though it is held together precariously by just a few nails or bolts.

Huxley can see the man much clearer now. He holds a scattergun in his lap, two revolvers in fine leather holsters on his legs. His face is shadowed by a wide-brimmed straw hat that has seen better days, but Huxley can still see the gray that traces through his beard. An older man. Not old as old used to be, but old in the way that men grow old and survive only by the skin of their teeth. The only men that grew truly old were those that had children to lean on. But Mr. Crofter's children had died, according to Low.

In the yard, Low waves, haltingly.

He doesn't look natural.

Huxley looks across the doorway and into the shadows where Jay and Don are hunched next to each other. He looks at Jay first, but Jay is staying quiet. He is staying quiet often enough to cause Huxley to wonder. Up to this point, he had been so vocal, pushing his opinion on every issue. Now he seems to be just sitting back and watching.

Beside Jay, Don is shaking his head and baring his teeth. "That fucking kid," he mumbles, looking back and forth between Low in the yard and Huxley behind the cabinet. "He's gonna get us killed. This was a dumbshit idea to begin with. Shouldn't have even let him live."

Huxley turns his focus outward again. "Ssh."

The old man and his wagon have slowed now and are pulling into the yard. Huxley watches his face carefully, watches to see where the eyes go, what expressions he makes, whether the truth is apparent to this man or whether he is tricked.

Low waves at him, more aggressively this time, a gesture that says to keep his distance. "Mr. Crofter!" he calls out. "Mr. Crofter, stay there! We've got the sickness!"

Crofter reins up and lifts his head so that he can see past his low-hanging straw brim. He has a pair of squinty eyes, suspicious either by nature or what he has seen, Huxley can't be sure. The horse comes to a stop, stamping little marks into the dusty yard, about fifteen feet from Low. The wagon creaks as it rolls back and then catches on the horse harness.

"Wha's'at, Lowell?" The man calls out, inclining an ear. "Couldn't hear yah. What're you doin' out in the yard with yer face covered up? Wha's wrong, son?"

Low steps forward, his eyes glancing about. Huxley prays that he will not look directly at them, and that at least is a prayer that is answered. Low clears his throat and speaks again, his voice a little firmer than last time, a little more sure of himself as he repeats the lie.

"Mother and Father have the sickness. I'm taking care of them, but it's catching. Didn't want you to get too close."

Crofter leans back in his bench seat, concern scribbled over his features. "Oh, well … Son, that's no good news. What type of sickness?"

Huxley can watch the boy's thoughts scrambling about in his brain. He can see it in the way the boy's fingers twitch and his knees knock around, locking and unlocking as though in his mind he is running. He hopes that to Crofter, Low just seems like a fidgety boy.

Maybe he's not fidgety normally. Maybe that will just raise Crofter's suspicions.

"I don't know," Low finally says. "But they're real sick. Mother caught it from Father."

"And you haven't got it yet?"

"No, sir."

"Well, you should come to town with me then, get Doc Watson and bring him back here. Ain't got much to trade at market today, so the day won't be that much of a loss. I don't mind making the trip. Specially for good folks such as yourselves."

"Uh …" Low seems trapped, his feet shuffling around like he's looking for a way out.

Inside the trailer, Don is cursing under his breath, even as Huxley's heart is throbbing in his chest. He wonders why his body is sending these signals through him, telling him to be scared. He should not be scared of a single old man on a wagon. The man should be scared of them. They are three, and he is one. He will not win that contest, no matter what.

This is the way of the world.

I am not weak. I will not be weak.

"This kid's gonna blow it," Don hisses. "We should just shoot this motherfucker and get it over with."

"Shut up," Huxley bites back under his breath. "Stop talking."

Outside in the yard, Crofter leans forward and puts an elbow on his knee, for the first time perhaps sensing that something is off. "Son, if your parents are down sick like that, then they should be checked out. Could be the flu, or it could be something worse. Doc Watson should look at them." Crofter glances to the trailer. "Can they not even get up to come talk to me?"

"No," Low says hollowly. "They can't get up."

"Well, if they can't get up, that'd be pretty serious."

"They'll be fine."

Crofter looks at the boy, then at the trailer again.

Huxley cringes, thinking, *He knows, he knows, he knows that something is wrong.*

Crofter's hand scoots up to lay on the butt of his scattergun. Huxley

WOLVES

watches it. "Well, mayhaps I should walk up and holler at 'em through the door. At least that way they know that help is comin'."

"No," Low says abruptly, then seems to rush to find a reasonable justification. "They're sleeping. They should sleep. Don't wake them."

"You're acting strange, son."

Low is suddenly stock-still where before he had been fidgety. "No. I'm not strange."

Crofter's hand is fully gripping the scattergun now.

"Hux," Don whispers. "We need to do it."

But Huxley is shaking his head. *It's gonna eat me alive.*

No, you need to do it. You're just being weak.

Stop. Stop being weak.

Crofter's finger is hovering near the trigger, his thumb hooked on the crank, the scattergun held in both hands, but still across his lap, still not completely threatening. "Lowell. What's wrong? Has something happened? You know that you can tell me. It's okay to tell me if something happened."

Low stands in the yard, struck dumb and mute.

Huxley watches the old man's eyes pass over the trailer, lingering on the front door and the window, looking into the darkness. Huxley knows that Crofter can't see him, but he feels the man's eyes on him anyway. It makes sweat break out on his palm and the grip of his revolver becomes slick in his hands. His finger wants to touch the cold, steel trigger.

"Hux." This time it is Jay that speaks.

Huxley looks at his companion. "Just wait. There's still a chance."

CHAPTER 3

In the middle of the yard, Lowell stands stock-still, trying not to shake. Boots dusty. Clothing dirty. His face feels stiff and cold. The rag over his nose and mouth smells like a strange man's sweat and his own breath, hot and sour, clinging to his lips and nostrils. He has nothing in his hands, but he wishes for something, anything. Here and now, he feels naked. Defenseless.

He looks up at the old man who is now standing on the wagon. Mr. Crofter's scattergun is held in both hands, but down at his side, not pointed at anything in particular. His eyes are directed at the house, squinting as though with concentration he can see through the dull aluminum walls and view what lies inside.

Strangers, Lowell thinks. *Dangerous men.*

"Please," Lowell says, his voice very quiet.

Mr. Crofter looks down at him, for the first time, those squinting eyes showing some fear. "Lowell, what happened?"

Lowell shakes his head, ever so slightly, and he hopes for his sake and for the sake of Mr. Crofter that his words are too quiet to be heard, that they are lost and carried away by the steady winds that gust through the flat plains, whistling and moaning in the collection of boulders where the spring of water lays like dragon's gold, lusted after and dangerous to touch, killing all those that come into contact with it.

"Please, Mr. Crofter," Lowell says, so very quietly. "You should go. Please, just go."

Crofter leans over, catching the cue from Lowell to be quiet. He mumbles, just loud enough for Lowell to hear, "Who's inside there?"

Lowell feels his whole body trembling. His limbs feel like dead weights hung about his torso. His chest is on fire. His head buzzes uncontrollably. It is difficult to see, to think, to feel anything but fear. He knows what will happen if Mr. Crofter does not go away, please, *please, just go away, you don't know what's inside, you don't know …*

"There's bad men," Lowell whispers. "There's bad men inside and they're gonna kill you."

Crofter looks back up to the trailer, his eyes wide, and he starts to raise his scattergun, starts to crank the element, *zzzzz …*

Too late.

Lowell hears the door slamming open behind him, and he flinches. Up on the bench seat of his wagon, Crofter's whole body locks, stiffens, his mouth coming open in a wordless cry, teeth bared. Lowell turns and looks to see who has come out of the trailer, but as he turns, in that tiny split second, it is already done.

Lowell hears the *snap-BOOM* and something rips through Crofter's gut, causing the old man to grunt like he's been punched hard. Almost on reflex, the scattergun in the old man's hands goes off, a giant plume of smoke and a belch of flame and the sound of a hundred tiny projectiles clattering and pinging across the trailer.

Lowell ducks as he turns. Hits the ground on one knee, his hands up around his face as though to cover his ears. He can see the trailer now, the door still hanging open. It is the man, Don, who stands in the doorway, revolver held out before him, barrel pointed up as he snicks back the hammer for a second shot.

It is Father's revolver. He stole it from Father after they killed him.

"No!" Lowell screams.

Crofter drops the scattergun. It clatters noisily onto the deck of his wagon, and then over and onto the ground. His knees tremble unsteadily, one hand on his gut, turning red, and the other groping for his holstered revolver. "You sonofabitch," Crofter whispers, weakly. He gets his hand on the butt of his revolver.

Don levels another shot at him, squeezes off the trigger. He disappears behind a cloud of gray, shot through brilliantly with morning light. Crofter cries out as the second lead ball careens through him, this time through his upper chest, collapsing lungs and rupturing arteries. He falls to one knee, still trying to yank his revolver from its holster, his cry turned to a ragged groan. And then the third shot comes, this one striking him in the cheek, spilling him backward over his own bench seat and silencing him.

Lowell huddles on the ground.

The horse harnessed to the wagon is pulling in different directions but not really going anywhere, whickering in a quiet, scared sort of way. The horse is familiar with the sound of gunfire and it is not fully panicking, but it smells the blood and knows the danger. Its owner and rider is sprawled across the bench seat, chest slaked in blood, brain matter dripping from his head and into the back of the wagon. One of Crofter's feet twitches, the toe pointing at the trailer, then at the sky, then at the trailer again, like an accusation.

"Goddamnit!" Don shouts out.

Lowell looks at him, numbness and shock settling over him like a cold, white cloud. A chunk of Crofter's scattershot has ripped into Don's shoulder and the man is turning in circles like a dog chasing his tail, his weak hand holding the revolver and flailing it about while his strong hand tries to find and extract the piece of whatever it was that found his flesh.

"You said," Lowell mumbles, but he knows it isn't loud enough for any of them to hear. "You said you weren't going to kill him."

Lowell's gaze falls to dust and gravel and dead grass. He stares at the tiny contours of the ground in front of him, the grooves that his own feet and shoes have dug into the soft, dry dirt. The imprint of the soles of his shoes. He stares at it and sees blood and bone and murder. He stares at it and feels nothing. Nothing save for some peripheral sense of falling, sliding down, losing ground, going backward.

He knew the world was like this.

He had experienced it before.

How could he have ever allowed himself to believe that goodness was alive again? Mother and Father did not love him. They had only pitied him. Father more so than Mother. But regardless of their own loss, regardless of his strangeness and his savagery when they pulled him from that cave, they had taken him in and given him food and shelter and clothes to cover his skin. They had shown compassion, and he had believed that the world was capable of it.

But then they'd been killed.

I let them trick me, he thinks. *I was stupid, and I let them trick me.*

Dead, dead, dead. Everybody is dead.

He does not lift his eyes, but he hears the words spoken in the dusty yard as gunsmoke settles and the horse steadily calms itself.

"What the fuck was that?" Huxley's voice, though his voice is not as edged as his words might imply. As though he wants to care, but couldn't find the gumption.

Don is matter-of-fact. "He knew. He fucking knew."

Huxley swears. "We could have taken him captive."

"And done what? Tied him up and taken him with us?" Don makes a derisive noise. "If he was alive, he was gonna find a way to get to a town and tell a sheriff, and then they would've been on us."

"There's already a captain of the guard after us," Huxley says flatly. "Why not a sheriff?"

"What? What captain? What for?"

Huxley doesn't respond to Don.

Lowell hears boots crunching on dust and gravel. He is sitting on his heels, knees in the cold dirt, hands splayed across his thighs. He appears almost restive, and perhaps in a way he is. His soul is not in the turmoil that it should have been. Something inside of him, something that was supposed to be processing all of this, was broken.

This time, he looks up.

Huxley stands there, revolver in hand, the barrel hanging low and tapping out a slow, thoughtful rhythm against the side of Huxley's leg. He is looking at the wagon, the horse, the dead man. His lips compressed so that they disappear behind his beard and mustache. He sniffs. Spits in the dirt. Then he meets Lowell's gaze.

"Where's the town?" he asks.

Lowell blinks. "What town?"

"The town where this guy goes? Have you ever been there?"

"Yes. Me and Father go … we went … to sell scrap."

"Where is it?"

Lowell looks to the east. "That way. Straight on the wagon road. No turns." He dares to hope that Mr. Huxley is asking these directions because he intends to leave Lowell there and move on by themselves. His heart beats fast with his desperation. Then he wonders if he wants Mr. Huxley to leave.

Of course I want him to leave. He's evil.

But he's like you, Animal Child. And you're like him.

And if Mr. Huxley left, then it would be just Lowell again, in the wilderness, all by himself. And he would die. Just like Mr. Huxley said he would. Maybe he would survive for a time … but eventually …

"How far?" Mr. Huxley asks.

Lowell thinks about handwidths and horizons. He and Father would leave at dawn and the sun would be two handwidths above the horizon when they got there. "Two hours, I think," Lowell says. "Maybe a little faster on the wagon. I don't know." He is suddenly unsure of himself. All the things he knew, all the things that Father had taught him, they seem far away and unreal now that he is no longer there. Like maybe they were foolish things that he had dreamt up in his sleep.

Goodness is not real. Why would any of it be real?

I am an orphan again.

I am lost again.

Mr. Huxley is speaking.

Lowell blinks again.

"Low?" Huxley says, repeating himself. "Can you take us there?"

CHAPTER 4

"Red Water Landing is barely even a town," Don gripes as he sways in the cramped back end of the wagon. "It's just a dock in the middle of the Red River."

"You been?" Huxley asks from the bench seat where he handles the reins awkwardly and mostly lets the horse walk down the wagon trail on its own. Underneath him, the small, one-man bench seat is still dark with blood. But when he is sitting on it, he cannot see it. He pretends that it isn't there.

"I been through that way a time or two," Don says. "I promise, it's not much to see."

"We're not going to see things," Huxley says. "We're going to cross the river. Right? That's how you said we get to the Riverlands."

"Yeah, yeah. Going to the Riverlands," Don mumbles. Then louder, "What's a Wastelander trying to do in the Riverlands anyway?"

Jay speaks up suddenly. His voice is thoughtful. "I heard what you were saying about the Riverlands. About the slavers. The councilmen."

A pause. "Yeah? What of it?"

Jay sighs, chuckles darkly. "Let's be real honest with each other, shall we?"

Huxley doesn't stop him. He just faces forward. And remembers everything Don said. Don, who was also a Riverlander. One of *them*. One of the people perpetuating this cycle that they'd established, that the stupid, dumbshit Wastelanders didn't even know they were a part of. Don was right. They were just fodder for the Riverlands. They were just cattle. Livestock to be harvested when the need arose.

Jay's voice takes on an antagonistic tone. "We savages from the Wastelands don't know much. I really appreciate you educating us so well. And it just so happens, maybe we're here in the Riverlands because we want to kill some slavers."

Nothing from Don.

Huxley cranes his neck to look around, finds Don just sitting there, looking uncomfortable, while Jay smiles at him, pale eyes fixed on the other man. The way a snake might hold a conversation with a rat. Then, very quickly, the humor in Jay's eyes fades to nothing.

Huxley turns back to the road.

Jay continues, icily: "You see, we're not just fodder, Don. We're people. And we had families. And we had loved ones. The slavers came and took all of that. Something I doubt you can really comprehend. But suffice it to say that we're going into the Riverlands because we want them to know we'll bite back. And after what you just told us ... well ... seems like our opportunities have really branched out."

Don is off-balance. "What the fuck you mean by that?"

Jay presses, prods. "I mean you're all dirty. You're all filthy. So now it's just a matter of seeing how many we can put in the ground before they catch up to us."

In the front, Huxley shifts in his seat.

Do I agree with that?

Kill them all, he thought when Don had told him. But he'd been angry. Now, after being able to cool off some, he knew that not everybody in the Riverlands was evil. There would be farmers. There would be workers who weren't slaves. It wasn't the populace that was the enemy. It was the councilmen. The people who purchased the slaves, for whatever purpose. To build, possibly.

But the words from that slaver—just before Huxley had taken his jaw—still make his heart sink in his chest. *Castrating your sons and fucking your daughters*, he'd said. And he must have been talking about the councilmen. Maybe they used the slaves to build too, but a decade of slavery could've boomed their newfangled economy. Maybe now it was just about money.

Still, he didn't agree with Jay.

But he kept his mouth shut. For now.

"You got a death wish," Don says, petulantly. "Riverlands'll chew you up and spit you out."

"Then why are you still on this wagon?" Huxley asks, almost hoping the man will simply agree and then jump off the wagon and walk away.

"Hell, I dunno." Don sounds briefly wistful. "Same reason I went along with my brother, I guess. I tend to just go with the flow. Got a gypsy soul, my mom used to say. But don't worry. I'll sure as hell jump ship before you catch me up into anything real bad. Hope you're not offended by that. Nothing personal. I just like living."

Huxley grinds his teeth. "I won't take it personal."

The motley group rides on in silence.

Don's impression of Red Water Landing was uncharitable, Huxley thinks. As they top a rise and the town comes into view, Huxley judges that it is about as big as New Amarillo, as far as its sprawl. But it seems more densely populated, the buildings grown up on themselves, one stacked on another. It almost looks like a city from Huxley's slight vantage. A simple wall surrounds it, only eight feet high or so. Different materials for different sections. Some of it is stone. Some of it is wooden poles stuck into the earth with sharpened tips. Some of it is chain-link fencing with barbed or razor wire across the top.

The town sits nestled against the river, and from this viewpoint it seems that the eastern side of the burg simply falls into the water. Beyond the clamor of stacked buildings, the Red River moves slowly by, the color of it more brown than red. A breeze rolls up to them from the river valley and it carries with it all the smells of Red Water Landing—smoke, latrines, cattle, and the odd fishy smell of the river itself.

Huxley twitches the reins back a bit, and the horse slows, shaking its mane as though it is irritated at having to be slowed. Huxley feels exposed on the top of the hill leading down to Red Water Landing, but they are still a ways off from the gates and if there are guards posted, he hopes they do not notice them yet.

Hopefully they wouldn't recognize the horse.

Or the wagon.

Or see the blood on it.

Huxley turns around and sees Low sitting between Don and Jay with his hands clasped between his knees and his shoulders slumped against the burden of the world and the life that it gave him. *Like a turtle in its shell.*

"Low, is this the town?"

Low raises his eyes, then cranes his neck. He looks down the road. Assesses what he is seeing. His lips are downturned at the edges. His nose wrinkled like he smells something bad. Which he does: Red Water Landing, if it is the right town.

"Yeah," Low finally mumbles. "That's it."

"You tellin' the truth?" Don demands, jutting his face very near the boys.

Completely unnecessary. Don knows the boy is telling the truth. The boy had said it was Red Water Landing, and Don had claimed to be familiar. You would think he would recognize it at sight, and Huxley believes that he does. But he seems to want to goad the boy.

Low turns to meet the man's gaze. Something flashes through the boy's eyes, all those things that Huxley recognized the previous night. They are dark things that slip behind the mask of the boy's face like swift shadows in the woods.

"Yes," Low says. And then he turns back forward.

Don sneers, apparently dissatisfied that the boy did not quake. On the other side of Low, Jay watches the man with a certain sort of eerie stillness. Like he is already picturing Don's death. Wondering what his insides would look like if they were piled on the ground. Maybe wondering what facial expression Don would make if he were to be opened up ...

Who's thinking about it? Me or Jay?

Huxley's neck smarts and he pulls his fingers away from scratching, finding his nails slightly red with blood. *Damn.* "Will anyone there recognize this wagon? Or the horse?"

Low thinks, then shrugs. "I don't know. There are a lot of wagons and horses."

Huxley grimaces and shifts in his seat, suddenly uncomfortable. For a moment, he thinks he can feel the wet blood that stains the bench, seeping through the seat of his pants.

"Don't go to the market," Low adds.

"What's that?" Huxley looks back again.

Low leans forward, his jaw working like he's rethinking what he had just said. Perhaps he wants them to be caught. Perhaps he thinks it would be best if they wandered into the wrong area, or if they were recognized by someone. Then he would watch the city guards surround them. And he would watch with those cold angry eyes as Huxley, Jay, and Don were strung up, and he might even laugh as their necks snapped and their feet kicked.

But I'm your friend, Huxley thinks. *I know you don't know it yet. But I'm your friend and I'm going to keep you alive, because otherwise I'll forget. I'll forget about who I was before I became … this.*

Low finds his words again. "Don't go to the market," he says, more subdued this time. The sound of his voice is the sound of a final decision. He leans back and looks off into the gathering woods that are beginning to crowd in the sides of the wagon trail as they draw closer to the river basin. "Everybody in the market knows Mr. Crofter. And some of them know me. They might recognize the horse or the wagon."

Huxley nods and faces forward again, wondering if it is all a trap. The boy seems smart enough. Wily enough.

Huxley flicks the reins and the horse picks up the pace. The ride with a harnessed horse is significantly easier than horseback, Huxley has decided, even if he is still getting the hang of it. And the horse seems more docile, perhaps older than the ones that Huxley had stolen from Captain Tim back in New Amarillo.

As the wagon descends the hill toward Red Water Landing, the boy speaks from the back again, his voice flat and without inflection: "It's Lowell," he says. "Not 'Low.'"

Huxley raises an eyebrow, then nods. "Okay, Lowell," he says, loud enough to be heard in the back. "Lowell it is. And we don't go near the market."

He hears no response, so he assumes that the boy concurs.

As they approach the front gates, Huxley can feel his legs getting jittery. He aches for the revolver that sits in his waistband, but he knows that to take it would only serve to draw more attention to him. He feels eyes on him already, though he tells himself it is only paranoia. He feels like he is walking into a lions' den, disguised in a costume mane and tail, hoping that it will fool the real beasts around him.

There are guards at the front gate where the wagon trail ends, but they seem to be relaxed about who enters the city. One leans up against a post, his eyes half-closed as he enjoys the heat radiating from a burning barrel. The other guard is distracted by a young woman with a huge duffel bag, though he seems to care little for what is inside the duffel. They banter back and forth. Huxley watches her touch his arm.

Maybe they won't notice me.

When they are within fifty feet of the gate, the woman with the duffel looks back over her shoulder and sees them approaching, and she hikes the duffel further onto her shoulders and gives the guard a nice smile, and then walks away.

Huxley swears under his breath.

The two guards straighten at their posts and look at Huxley, the wagon, the horse, and the ragged crew in the back. Huxley immediately takes note of their weapons—both of them are carrying long rifles. Those are not common. Whoever was in charge of Red Water Landing was not skimping on arms.

One of the guards—the amorous one—steps forward to block their path, his hand upraised.

This is normal, Huxley tells himself, even while his chest starts to burn like an overheating engine, the piston of his heart suddenly throttling up. *They probably stop all the wagons coming through here.*

"We should've approached on foot," Jay says from the back.

Huxley jags a glance behind him to his companion. "Too late now."

But even as the words leave his mouth, he's wondering what the hell they had planned to do with the wagon? They couldn't take it across the river with them, could they? Or was there a ferry that could haul them across? They could leave the wagon in a quiet corner of the town, but that ran the risk of being noticed, and people would want to know why you were leaving a perfectly good wagon just sitting with a horse attached to it.

Find somebody to sell it to. Somebody not in the market.

Huxley pulls the reins to stop the horse and wagon at the gate.

The guard seems to be looking hard at the horse and wagon, then up at Huxley.

He doesn't recognize it. Who the hell would recognize a damn brown horse? Or a wooden wagon? They all look alike. There's no way he knows.

"Whose cart is this?" the guard says, his brow furrowed.

Fuck.

Huxley's throat dries very suddenly. "What?" he manages.

The guard looks up, irritated. "The horse and wagon. Whose is it?"

"Mine and my partner's," Huxley says, the lie coming out suddenly. He throws a thumb behind him, indicating Jay. "My business partner."

The guard peers into the back, looking at the passengers, crammed shoulder to shoulder. Huxley turns in his bench seat and looks at them. Don has become very still, as though he somehow hopes not to be noticed. But he watches the guards from under his eyebrows, a strange look on his face, like a man ready to jump into action.

Please don't, you idiot, Huxley curses him in his head. He'd jumped the gun with Mr. Crofter. There was a strong chance he might do the same with these two guards. All he had to do was sit there and keep his mouth shut. No reason to fail at something so simple.

Lowell, on the other hand, does not seem to care at all. If he has any intention of diming them out to the guards, Huxley can't see it on his face. Lowell stares blankly off at the riverside town, his face a mask of apathy. Huxley can't figure out what he's looking at. Probably nothing. Probably he is seeing memories from his own head.

Jay is sitting, comfortably, with one elbow on a knee, the other cocked up onto his side. He seems almost jovial. He smiles brightly for the guards and flicks the inquisitive one a quick salute. "Gentlemen," Jay says fluidly. "Name's Marcus." he lies, and then motions to Don and Lowell. "This is Mike and his boy, apprenticing with us. Heading east at the council's request. Apparently somebody got a bug up their ass about electricity, and it just so happens I was an electrical engineer back in the Old World."

The guard looks at them both dubiously and opens his mouth, as though to ask another question.

Jay quickly raises a finger. "Copper wire and a magnet," he says abruptly.

"What?" the guard seems confused.

"You pass a magnet in front of a coil of copper wire and you get electricity. Didja know that?"

"No."

"Well, now you do." Jay smiles, then spits into the dirt. "Electricity ain't all that complicated. Couple windmills passing some big magnets around some big coils of copper wiring and you got yourself a generator. You look young—you know what a generator is?"

The guard looks irritated again.

"It's a machine we used to have back in the Old World. Had an engine in it and it would make electricity for us. Turn on lightbulbs and whatnot. You ever imagined such a thing? How old are you?"

The guard takes a marginal step back and waves them through. "Just go," he says, boredly. "Good luck with all that."

"Alright now," Jay says cheerfully.

Huxley buzzes, his stomach in knots. He snaps the reins quickly, not waiting to give the guard a chance to rethink it. They pass through the flimsy gates of the town and then they are inside Red Water Landing. The streets are dirt, pounded and compacted over the years, to nearly a cement-like consistency. Most of the buildings are wattle and daub, particularly on the second stories. The first story of the buildings, or at least the foundation, looks to be an even mix between stacked stone and timber.

The old road that led them here becomes the main street of the town and it bisects Red Water Landing in a perfectly straight line, as wide as four of their wagons put abreast, and it descends steadily to the river. Even from just inside the gates, Huxley can see the docks that he'd not been able to see before. Only a single boat is berthed.

"Go right," a small voice says behind him.

Huxley looks over his shoulder at Lowell. "Right?"

Lowell nods. "Straight is the market. You'll want to go around. Far to the right. Follow the wall. It'll take you around the market to the docks."

A few residents of the town are walking around along the main street, heading to or from the market, carrying some items that Huxley recognizes, and others that he does not. A mule and a single-axle cart, laden with what looks like drums of river water, struggles up the inclined street, led by a man with a whip.

No one seems to give them a second glance.

Huxley steers the wagon onto the street that follows the wall. The horse plods along steadily. The street is a narrow one, but well used. Their horse's hooves clop steadily down the hard-packed dirt. Pedestrians push to either side to allow the wagon to pass—there is only enough room for one wagon. Huxley hopes they don't come face-to-face with another, or he would have to back the wagon. He'd create a traffic snarl. He'd call attention to himself. Not to mention he had no idea how to back a wagon, or if it could even be done.

As they proceed, they glimpse the main street through flashes as they pass by other narrow streets and alleys that cleave across this quarter of the city to the main drag. The streets are all oriented in a straight-edged grid, very little curve to any of the roads, save the one they are on that follows the wall.

At a point, Huxley sees what he can only assume is the market. The glimpses that he gets are no longer of a wide street, but instead of carts and stalls and a hundred different colors blazoned boldly in dyed fabric that stretches over each vendor's stall. Huxley can hear the criers in the market, yelling out catches and deals and whatever things they have to hawk that day.

Huxley does no more than glance into the back of the wagon but when he turns back, a hooded figure has appeared in front of their single yoked horse and has put a hand to the mantle, steering it off to the side.

"Whoa, hey!" Huxley drops the reins and grabs for a pistol, but doesn't want to pull it. There are people on these side streets and he doesn't want to call attention to himself. Nor does he want to yell. So he hisses at the man, "Get your fucking hands off my horse!"

The man keeps his head down so that the hood completely covers his face and he ignores Huxley's order like he didn't hear or didn't care, take your pick. He is moving quickly, guiding the horse toward the mouth of an alley that cuts from the street that follows the wall back toward the main drag. He is moving with purpose.

Leading us into an alley.

An ambush.

"What's going on, Hux?" Jay says from the back.

"What the fuck?" Huxley snaps, and rises, partially, his eyes flitting about, looking for the ambush, but there are only townsfolk milling about, carrying on with their business. He gets a few dirty glances for raising his voice, but that's about it. "Hey!" he hollers at the man in front of him. "Hey!"

I'm gonna have to shoot this sonofabitch …

And then they are in the alley and the man sweeps his hood back off of his face. Brown skin. Wide eyes. One is dark, the other is cloudy and drooping. He is motioning to them to get off the wagon, and pointing around the corner, back onto the street they just came from.

"Ándele!" Rigo hisses at them. "Black Hats! Black Hats!"

CHAPTER 5

Huxley stands frozen for a few beats. "Rigo?"

That's all he can think to say.

Rigo becomes more animated, gesturing rapidly around the corner and speaking so fast Huxley can barely even make out the few English words scattered in with the Spanish.

Don is standing up in the back, nearly beside himself. "Did he say Black Hats? What the fuck is he talking about? Who the fuck is this guy? You know this guy?"

Huxley turns quickly on Don. "Could you just shut the fuck up for once?"

Rigo has not stopped rattling on.

In the wagon, Jay is standing up now, revolver in hand, looking back toward the corner.

Huxley throws the reins down and jumps from the wagon. The landing on hard-packed dirt makes his knees tingle. "Rigo," he has to reach out to put hands on the man, make sure that he's real. "Rigo, I don't understand a word you're saying! Slow down! Are there Black Hats?"

A voice from the wagon, small, and matter-of-fact: "He said there's a Black Hat and a captain here in town."

Huxley looks around, still holding Rigo by the shoulder.

Lowell stands there in the wagon, looking at Huxley. "He said they've been going around telling everyone that they're looking for you. And that you're wanted for murder. Of a guardsman. And some farmers. Flower farmers, or something like that."

Huxley's brain feels like it's on fire. He realizes his mouth is hanging open.

There are Black Hats here. After him. After *him*. Well, of course they would be after him. They wouldn't bother going after slavers. They're part of the system. Part of the Riverlands. Part of the whole corrupted thing. But after *him?* For murder? The guardsman—yes, Huxley killed him, and yes, it was about as cold-blooded as could be. But just the fact that they'd also charged him with the murder of the poppy farmers …

How dare they?

Rigo is pointing up at Lowell, eyebrows raised. "Se habla Español?"

Lowell just nods, seeming momentarily as bewildered as the rest of them. "I guess," he says.

Like he didn't remember that he spoke it.

Jay is at the corner of the building, peeking out. "Shit, Huxley, you better see this."

Huxley releases his grip on Rigo. Is he happy to see the man again? Yes, he is, but it's covered up by the sudden panic of the moment, him trying to wade through a million dissident things and make them all come together in a way that makes sense.

He stalks quickly to the corner. The building is stacked stone on the base, wattle and daub for the rest. It smells of mildew and dirt. Wood smoke. Yesterday's fish. A woman in the second story opens shutters made of reeds and glares down at him.

"You can't park that shit in the alley!"

Huxley points up at her so she knows that he is talking to her. "I'll fucking kill you. Go back inside."

The woman, startled at his response, ducks back inside and pulls the shutters closed. He can faintly hear her yelling to someone inside the house.

"What the fuck …?" Don is still looking around, distraught, just a little more confused than the rest of them, just a few more dots unconnected in his picture.

At the corner of the building, Huxley leans out, just letting one eye make that corner.

Two men on horseback, floating high above the rest of the people who are traveling on foot. They are speaking to a shop owner and they don't see the little sliver of Huxley's face peering around the corner. One has a black hat, the other a dingy, white cowboy hat.

A Black Hat.

And Captain Tim.

"Shit, shit, shit." Huxley pushes himself off the wall and moves quickly to the wagon. "Out, out!" he barks at Lowell, but the kid is already clambering down. Huxley reaches in and grabs a few satchels—useful things stolen from Lowell's trailer, a little bit of food, a little bit of water, a small collection of Riverland gold coins. There are two satchels, and he throws one to Don simply because he is the closest person, and slings the other one on his shoulder.

Huxley skirts down the alley. Rigo is already jogging along and he slows to let Huxley catch up. "Glad you're alive, Rigo," he says almost as an afterthought.

"Is hokay," Rigo says hurriedly. "We go."

Huxley looks at the boy, trailing behind their little group. "Lowell, cover your face."

The boy has a wide scarf around his neck that can be pulled up to form a hood over his head. He looks at Huxley, unsure, but he slowly puts his hood up.

"We have to go into the market," Huxley explains. "We can't keep going on that road along the wall. And we can't have the wagon or you seen in the market. So we'll just skirt the edges. Just skirt the edges and everything will be okay. No one will recognize you if you're with us and you have your hood pulled up. Right?"

Lowell considers it, pulling the hood closer around his face. Then he just shrugs. "I don't know," he says.

As they near the mouth of the alley, Huxley slows his pace. He doesn't want to run through the market. Running will only draw attention. He needs to move at the same semibusy pace as everyone else.

Huxley holds his hand close to his midsection, the fingers resting on the grip of his revolver, still not drawing it just yet. Jay has tucked his away as well. They move into the market, skirting the edges, trying not to be noticed. Many-colored awnings and loud people trying to gain attention and arguing over the prices of things that people used to throw away. Busy place. Safe place. Everyone too preoccupied to notice a few men and a boy passing through.

Don has shouldered his way up to Huxley. "I don't know what the fuck's going on, but I'm out."

Huxley doesn't hesitate. He puts all his effort into looking casual, even smiles nicely for a lady as he passes by her. He reaches out with his left arm and grabs a tight hold of Don's elbow, like a child being towed by his mother. Huxley's left hand gets a firmer grip on one of his revolvers.

"Why? So you can dime us out to the Black Hats?" Huxley says quietly as they move through the market.

"What?" Don seems genuinely taken aback. But Don is scum, and Huxley wouldn't put it past him to be able to lie so smoothly. "Of course not! I just don't want to get shot with the rest of you idiots! I'm done! I told you I would duck if things got dicey ..."

"Well, it's too damn late," Huxley says. "You try to run, I'll gun you down in the street and deal with the consequences."

"You wouldn't."

"You don't think so, fucking Riverlander? You think I give a fuck about you or anyone else in here? I'll shoot my way out until I'm out of bullets and I'll die a happy man. Test me."

They are Jay's words, coming out of Huxley's mouth. But whether or not he believes them, they appear to give Don pause. And Huxley doesn't want the man getting away. Because he knows that's exactly what he will do. He will try to cut a deal with the Black Hat to save his own neck. That's just the kind of person Don is. And to him, Huxley is just a *Wastelander*. Just an ignorant savage.

"Stick around," Huxley says, faking an amiable tone for the benefit of those passing by. "When there's no Black Hats for you to run to, you can leave with my blessing."

"Fuck me ..." Don moans. "You're gonna be the death of me."

Ahead of them, the road dips down into the river. The dock, a long, cobbled-together thing that looks on the verge of collapsing into the waters, juts out creakily over the swift-moving brownness, and from their current vantage, seems to extend halfway across the river.

There is still only the one boat.

A large flatboat, Huxley can see now. Huge logs for its hull. Weathered planking for the deck. A big, square box in the middle where the quarters would be. Stations along the sides and back for oarsmen. No sail or other mode of speeding it along is visible. This one is simply carried by the flow, or pushed by oars to get it back upstream. The deck is crowded with people. People sitting, people laying. A few men standing, with rifles or scatterguns.

As they draw closer, Huxley can see what it is and his stomach drops like an anchor.

Along the cabin, slavers' poles have been erected, their grisly ornaments clattering with the motion of the water underneath the decks.

A slave barge.

I'm fucked at every turn!

The five of them make their way down the main street to the docks. Here the street is steeper. Huxley keeps glancing back behind them to see if they are pursued or followed. He does not see Captain Tim. He does not see the man wearing the black hat.

Not seeing them does nothing to extinguish the urgency burning in his legs, in his gut. The desire to suddenly be rid of this small town.

Huxley glances up and down alleys. To his right, as they pass by a long, narrow lane, he can see people moving along the street that follows the wall. And then he sees them again at the next alley, and the next after that. Like they are shadowing him. A man with a handcart. A woman with two wooden cages, stuffed with wriggling, angry chickens.

They reach the docks, and here at the edge of the worn, wooden planking, Huxley stops, his breathing elevated from their quick strides down the hill to the river. He takes another glance behind them, then a glance to the flatboat in front of them, rising and dipping slowly in the undulating river water. He stares at the slavers' poles around the cabin. The mess of bodies about the deck, and noticing for the first time that they are chained together in groups of four.

Why? Why a slave barge?

"Now's not the time, Huxley," Jay's voice says, quiet and practical as he too stares out at the barge. "Not the time to worry about who owns the boat. It's a boat and we need to get across the river. That's all there is to it."

"It's a slave barge," Huxley says, like the words are putrid on his tongue.

This time Don answers. "Yes it is. And it's the only boat on the dock. If you're real lucky and you blow the captain real nice, he might let you run his oars for him. The few slavers I've known are real assholes and they tend to not care about other people's problems."

"Huxley," Jay says again, this time more insistent. "We need to go."

Huxley looks over at Jay.

We have to go. We have to.

Huxley turns, holding his meager pack of provisions at his side, his fingers still gripping his revolver, and thinking, *I will not give them my guns. I will not disarm myself for this slave master or captain. They are slavers. If you let them disarm you, they will put you in chains, or more likely they'll just kill you—they've no use for a middle-aged man with no skills besides teaching. They do not care. This is dangerous, murky water you are treading in. Be careful of the things you can't see through the silt. Go carefully, and keep your weapons ready.*

Huxley heads down the pier, the others in tow.

The slave barge is berthed at the last spot on the docks and it seems that Huxley has arrived in the nick of time. Whatever business was to be conducted here at Red Water Landing, the slave barge is finished and already crewmen are untying their lines from the dock. Teams of slaves are taking up the massive oars—four to a single oar.

Huxley jogs the rest of the way to where the gangway is still attached to the dock. As he approaches, one of the slavers, a man armed with a fine, muzzle-loading rifle, steps onto the gangway, his rifle held low, but ready.

"Whoa there, friend," the man says, his smile a lie below lizard's eyes. "You can't just come walking aboard the *Misery*. We're not a public water taxi."

Huxley holds one hand up, but the other remains close to his revolver. This does not go unnoticed by the slaver. "I need passage on this ship," Huxley doesn't want to sound desperate because he knows that it will come down to bargaining, and he does not want to lose his bargaining position. "For me and my friends. Can you let me on, or do I need to speak to the master?"

The man with the lizard's eyes chews thoughtfully on the inside of his lip, but anything he had planned to say is cut off when a big, wide man lands a hard hand on the slaver's shoulder and peers down the gangway at Huxley and his unfortunate crew.

"Some dock waifs trying to stow away?" The big man asks.

"Something like that," Lizard Eyes replies.

Huxley takes another glance over his shoulder. The way is still clear. No Black Hats behind them. But for how much longer? "No stowaways. We can pay for our passage." He is thinking of the meager stash of gold they'd found from looting Lowell's trailer, and he doubts it would pay for all their passages. "Where are you headed now?"

Where do slavers go?

The big man takes his meaty hand from his compatriot's shoulder and rubs his belly obscenely with it, though his face remains pensive, considering the group he has before him, and why he should even be talking to them. Of course he would be swayed by money. Money is all the slavers care about.

"*Misery* is headed for Shreveport. Now. And you're going to make us late. River's running low and we're overburdened with forty head as it is. The longer I sit here, the longer the dry season keeps running this river lower. Strong chance of running aground and having to waste time digging ourselves out of a sandbar. Probably will lose two or three head to that, I can imagine. So now you're costing me time *and* money. I should tell you to fuck off."

You should, but you haven't.

"Shreveport," Don mumbles under his breath. The word is dirty, the way he says it. "Nothing there but niggers and outlaws."

Well, we should fit in well.

To the slave master, Huxley inclines his head, hopes that the slave master can't see his pulse throbbing in his neck. "Shreveport," he says, casually enough. "Is that where all the slavers take their hauls?"

"Most," the master says, though now he is looking at Huxley differently. He points a finger at Huxley, and begins to wag it. Then he steps onto the gangway and begins to descend, a knowing half smile spreading across thin, greasy lips. "You. I know you."

Huxley looks away, feeling his face beginning to burn as the man gets closer to him. It is difficult. It is so difficult to stand in front of this man with two loaded revolvers in his waistband … and do nothing.

"You don't know me."

"Yeah. Yeah, I do." The master reaches the bottom of the gangway, his reptilian friend hovering behind him. The master reaches into a pocket in his jacket and withdraws a thick-looking piece of paper. He unfolds it and holds it up officiously. The sun catches the paper the way the master is holding it, and Huxley can see what is written on the other side, though he sees it imprecisely.

A drawing. A drawing of a face.

"The spitting image," the master says with a whistle. "Usually these drawings are terrible, but this one bears a striking resemblance." The master looks at Huxley, then turns the paper around to display it to him.

Huxley is staring at an ink drawing of himself. He feels his heart spasm in his chest. The breath catches. He stares, and cannot believe it, but it is there, just as plain as day, no matter how surreal it seems. The drawing is not perfect—they've missed him in the eyes—but the likeness is unmistakable.

In the back of his mind: *Nadine could've drawn better than that …*

A WANTED poster, he thinks, but there is text below it, and it does not offer a reward to anyone else to catch Huxley. The instructions are written boldly below his picture, and they are very clear, and they twist his insides up as he reads them.

GIVE THIS MAN NO QUARTER. HE GOES BY "HUXLEY." HE IS SOUGHT BY THE BLACK HATS OF THE RIVERLAND NATIONS, TO BE EXECUTED FOR CRIMES AGAINST THE NATIONS. ANYONE FOUND HELPING THIS MAN WILL ALSO BE EXECUTED AS A PARTNER IN HIS CRIMES. STAY AWAY AND OFFER NO HELP.

It's says nothing of Jay, nothing of Rigo, nothing of Gordon.

It's only me that is marked for death. And anyone found with me.

This isn't right. This isn't right. It was Captain Tim who was wrong. He was the murderer. He was the torturer. He was the evil one, not me. I wouldn't go along. I was framed. I'm innocent. This can't be. I'm not a murderer. I'm not a criminal at all …

"Shocked you speechless, huh?" The master folds the paper up and puts it away. "Being marked for death by the Black Devils will do that. Those boys don't fuck around, I can tell you that. So now we have an issue. You have become very dangerous cargo to be caught with. A Black Hat himself gave me this little drawing of you, so I can't even say that I didn't know. If he finds you with me, he'll definitely kill me. And if he learns of it after the fact, he'll probably still take an eye or a limb. That's Riverland justice."

What about you? Huxley wonders. *What about all the atrocities that you've committed? What about all the stolen lives chained to your boat? Why are you not wanted by the Black Hats?*

The master continues: "Luckily for you, I had a cousin who was once killed by the Black Hats, so I have no special love for them. In fact, you wouldn't be the first man I've hidden from them. But you would be the first man that I've hidden from a Black Hat that's about five hundred yards away."

Huxley looks over his shoulder again, chest on fire. In the market, he can see two figures on horseback, skirting the crowd. White cowboy hat. Black boonie hat. He turns back, feeling lightheaded. Now it is desperate. And now the master knows that they are desperate. Huxley's options have slipped away. Now the only thing he can do is either make the deal, or surrender himself to the Black Hat. Which will mean his life, and the life of Jay, Rigo, Don, and Lowell.

The master smiles. "I'm a man who's known to take risks, but it must be worth the reward. And I don't think you'll like the terms of my reward."

"Name the price," Huxley says resolutely.

The master smacks his lips. "How much gold do you have between the lot of you?"

Huxley tries to sound confident. "Seven pieces."

The master makes a raspberry noise, condescension thick in his voice. "Hardly worth it. Of course you don't have enough gold. You're Wastelanders. You trade in beads and knickknacks." He looks at Lowell. "The boy, then."

"What? No!" Huxley blurts before thinking.

Lowell steps back, looking alarmed.

"Is he family?" the master says with a chuckle. "Is he kin to you? No? Then why do you care? Young, strong man like him will get a good price at the auction—enough to pay for the rest of you. We'll even run the cost up high so only councilmen will be able to afford him, and then he'll live a good life as a councilman's porter or something. He'll be warm and safe and well fed. You'll never have to worry about him. He'll be happier than he is running with you, and less likely to get a bullet in the brain when you're all caught by the Black Hats." The master looks up toward the market. "Ah. Here comes your friend now. Might want to make your decision quickly."

You can't do this. You will not do this.

Huxley glances up toward the market, where the two men on horseback are descending out of the mash of people. The townsfolk and marketeers move out of the way of the horses, making a lane for them. He sees them and then he looks down at Lowell, but he doesn't see the boy. Again, his memories plague him and he sees the girl ...

Not just the girl. Your *girl.*
Your daughter.
Nadine. My sweet girl.

He closes his eyes, wishing for calm, wishing for the good memories, but they are gone, destroyed, whisked away like sandcastles in a rising tide. There is nothing in his mind but blood and smoke and fire, and through all of that he can only see a dying woman, covered in blood, crying out for her child.

Our child.

Because it had all been ripped away. By a man just like the man that stands before him now. It had all been destroyed, Huxley's entire life, his entire being, by a man that made his coin in living flesh, bought and sold and traded to the highest bidder, like any soulless inanimate object. A man just like this one, who stands before him demanding this boy, demanding this unfortunate creature that Huxley has found, and orphaned, and adopted, and for some reason clings to like the ghost of his old one.

My child.

Huxley looks again to the market, his mind scrambling about for answers. There isn't much time. He senses the moment receding. He senses the decision on the part of the slave master being made, the doors closing. And then he will be stuck. And in this place where he will be stuck, there is only death. The Black Hat will kill not only Huxley, but everyone that is with him, including Lowell.

Sell Lowell and save yourself?

Or save your soul and sentence everyone to death?

There's a third option here …

Huxley snaps his teeth together, as though he is biting down on the idea, not letting it flee from him. It's a bitter fruit, but even a bitter fruit can sustain you, though it might turn your stomach. "Fine," he blurts out quickly, very conscious of how close Captain Tim and the Black Hat are coming.

Perhaps close enough to recognize him.

The slave master sticks out his hand with a smirk. "Deal?"

"Deal," Huxley says, the word coming out like a cough.

"No," Lowell backs up another step, his hands coming up, terror in his eyes, maybe some disbelief that strikes down to the core of Huxley, but doesn't strike hard enough to make Huxley take back the deal that he has just made. Besides, he has shaken hands. A gentlemen's accord.

"Please," begs Lowell. "Don't do this, Mr. Huxley …"

Don grabs the boy before he can retreat much farther. His hands close around the boy's arm and he pushes Lowell toward the slave master's henchman, the man with the lizard eyes. "Don't run off the dock, now," Don says. "Get on the boat, boy. The man's right. You'll be safer as a slave than runnin' around with these jackasses."

Lizard Eyes grabs Lowell and hauls him up the gangway, roughly.

The boy looks over his shoulder, stumbling along in shock. His eyes locked with Huxley's the whole way.

Don't be weak, Huxley tells himself. *The strong will survive.*

The slave master is not wasting time. He steps out of their way and waves them up the gangway. "Well, get on the boat, Mr. Huxley. Don't want that Black Devil recognizing you and putting my sweet *Misery* to the torch."

CHAPTER 6

The gangway is pulled up almost the instant Huxley's feet leave it, and the big slaver's barge is already pushing off from its berthing. Teams of slaves take hold of the giant oars and use them to brace against the side of the dock and guide the big, flat-bodied boat away from the pier and out into the flow of the Red River.

Descending the hill to the docks, Captain Tim and the Black Hat who had joined his company stop their horses and gaze out at the slave barge, their eyes shaded by the brims of the hats. Huxley stands there, wanting to look away for fear that they will recognize him even at this distance, but he keeps watching them, wondering what they are going to do. Raise an alarm? Order the boat to return to the dock so the Black Hat could inspect its cargo?

A hand on his shoulder.

The slave master pushes him toward the big box in the center of the barge, along with Jay, Don, and Rigo. "Might behoove you to get the fuck indoors. Those gentlemen seem to be taking a special interest in you." The slave master shuffles them along, trying to get them into the cabins, but trying not to look like he is hiding anything.

Huxley looks up at the structure of cabins looming above, worm-eaten and moldered in places and otherwise dilapidated. An ancient houseboat that has been expanded and built onto with whatever materials were at hand. Even as he approaches it, Huxley can smell the unpleasant odor from it. The smell of unwashed people. The smell of them being held in tight quarters like cattle in a car.

This was a bad idea, Huxley thinks, his stomach souring. *He's just going to put us all in the cages with all the other slaves and he's going to beat us into submission and then sell us to whoever will pay in Shreveport.*

Huxley looks around for Lowell, but he has disappeared.

Like he was never there.

This is what the slavers do. They swallow people whole. And now I'm walking freely into their mouth.

The doors to the cabin structure are thrust open and then Huxley, Jay, Rigo, and Don are inside. The doors close behind them with a slam, like the closing of a jail cell, and in the breathless silence that follows, Huxley listens for a door locking, but there is none. He reaches for the door handle, to test if it is locked.

"Don't," Don says. "I wouldn't push this guy."

Huxley grinds his teeth and pulls his hand back.

They are in a large room. One long hall, with iron and wooden bars to either side. It reeks of filth. Piss and shit. Huxley can only imagine the disease. It is dimly lit by oil lanterns hanging at intervals of ten or fifteen feet. They swing back and forth with the slight pitch and yaw of the boat on the water, casting shadows this way and that, the movement of the boat exaggerated by the lanterns and making Huxley dizzy, though when he closes his eyes he can feel that they are barely moving. There is a brazier in the center of the room, but it is not burning.

The smell of the room makes it feel like it is stuffed to the brim with living misery, but in the swinging lantern light, Huxley can see past the iron and wood bars to the long holding areas inside, the metal rings mounted to the walls to secure these groups of slaves chained together at the ankles. The entire hall is empty. All of the slaves on this boat are outside, tending to work.

Why have deckhands that you have to pay when you can just make your slaves do it for you? It takes no training to pull an oar. Huxley suspected that the heavy chains he'd seen on the groups of slaves also served to deter them from trying to jump overboard. Even if you were a strong enough swimmer to handle the weight of the chains, one had to wonder about the others that you were chained to, and whether they were strong enough to swim as well, or if they would just pull you down into the silty river bottom.

Huxley moves quickly through an open cell door. The ground underneath his feet is wooden, but it is slick and moldy. He can see daylight pouring through cracks in the walls and he presses himself to one of these openings, his nose against the cobbled-together wood, peering with one eye into the slat of light coming through.

He sees the dock. The streets of Red Water Landing.

He searches for the two men on horseback, but they are gone.

Huxley's hands are splayed against the wood. It is cold and feels slightly damp. They ball into fists as he stands there, peering out. He realizes that the silence in this place is not so silent. He can clearly hear the orders of the slavers being shouted, the grunt of the slaves handling the oars, the lap of water slapping the underside of the barge. The *Misery* is drifting away from the dock now, too far even to be touched by one of the massively long oars. Now, some of the teams are dipping the long oars down into the river, pushing off of the bottom like a pole boat, while other teams are seating their oars into large, brass oar locks.

Red Water Landing slides away from them, more and more of it coming into view as it shrinks and begins to drift as the current catches the slave barge, headed south and east.

Still, Huxley cannot see Captain Tim or the Black Hat.

He has the discomfiting thought that they are on the boat with them at that moment.

Huxley pulls himself away from the wall, his hands still bound into fists at his side, and he looks about the dark interior of the cabins. He looks about it like a man that fears he will never leave it. "What are we doing here?" he says, looking to Jay. "This was a mistake. Was this a mistake?" Huxley shakes his head vehemently. "It was a fucking mistake. I shouldn't have … I shouldn't have let them take the kid."

Jay is leaning casually against a wall of rusted iron bars. He seems not to care. He works spittle around in his mouth and he spits onto the dirty floor where an unknown myriad of diseases are mingling and growing. Maybe some form of plague that will begin in the belly of a slave barge and kill half the populace before the year is out.

But Jay still seems to have very little to say.

Rigo stands in the center of the room, regarding Huxley with his good eye, his hands held at waist level, the fingers picking at each other. What is he thinking? Is he judging Huxley?

Finally, Rigo breaks eye contact and looks away with a heavy-sounding sigh.

"You did the right thing," Don says. "We're alive. That's what matters."

"The boy trusted me."

"He was a kid," Don snaps back. "He was probably gonna die anyway. Sooner rather than later." He fixes Huxley with a hard stare. "You want to explain why the Black Hats are after you? I think you've been very evasive about that. But I'd like to know. I think I deserve to know."

"Deserve to know?" Huxley's eyebrows quirk up, then clamp down. "You're a murdering psychopath. You deserve to die."

Don seems completely unperturbed by that assessment. "And yet you're the fugitive from justice who just sold your newly adopted sidekick for a ride down the river." Don snorts. "I've killed, yes. I've murdered. And I have yet to feel bad about any of it, so maybe there is something wrong in my head. But at least I know who I am. You, on the other hand, are confused. You don't even know who or what you are. I've never seen a man fight himself so hard."

Huxley regards the other man for a long moment, the shadows on their faces casting about at extreme angles like they are standing on a planet where the sun rises and sets every few seconds. How fast that planet would need to spin. Out of control. Spinning out of control.

Breathe. This isn't lost. You did all of this for a reason. And your plan is not lost.

"I didn't sell the boy," Huxley says, his voice becoming quiet. He glances around the lonesome, empty darkness for prying eyes and ears but there are none. "And I've been wrongly accused by Captain Tim. The man is dirt. He's framing me for some shit he tried to pull, but I wouldn't let him. He already got one of us. Guy named Gordon."

Don eyes him up and down, like he is trying to determine the truth of what Huxley has told him. He does not let on whether he believes Huxley or not, but he finally shrugs. "Fine. That can be your story. Might even be true. No one knows 'cept you yourself." He points a finger at Huxley. "But you sold the boy. That much is true. Don't put that off on no one else."

Huxley smacks the finger out of the way. "I didn't sell him," he hisses. "We're going to get him back."

Don raises his eyebrows. "Oh? Are we?"

Huxley turns away from the man, tired of looking at his face. He seeks Jay out in the gloom. The other man is standing a little straighter now, looking at Huxley with some interest. Huxley goes to him in the darkness, reaching out and pulling Rigo in by the sleeve. He stands next to his companions and looks over his shoulder, casting a few words at Don. "We need to talk quietly."

Don hesitates for a time, then looks around, and finally takes the two long steps to join Huxley, Jay, and Rigo. He leans in and the four men huddle together, conspirators in the gloom.

"I won't do this," Huxley says, his voice barely more than a whisper, but all the ire and hatred coming out nonetheless. "I won't sell someone to the slavers. I won't do it, no matter what. I made the deal because that was what we needed right then and there. Now we're on the boat, and we need to figure out how this ends. But I can tell you right now, I've no intention of playing nice with slavers." He looks at Jay. "How many slavers on the boat with us?"

Don makes a thoughtful noise and begins to answer, but Huxley holds up a finger to silence him. He gives the other man a glare, but holds back a tongue-lashing.

Jay looks between the two men, then rubs his hands together, staring at them as he does. His pale skin appears dusky with the dirt and soot that coat them, as do his hair and face.

"Six, by my count," Jay says. "Including the slave master."

"I saw a few long guns," Huxley observes. "A few scatterguns."

Jay nods. "They're more likely to use the scatterguns on the deck. Long guns for escaped slaves. A few of them had revolvers, but not many."

Huxley rubs his face. "Do you think they plan to disarm us?"

"I imagine they would have done so already. In any case, if they try, we simply refuse."

"What happens when we refuse?"

Jay shrugs. "We'll have to cross that bridge when we come to it. What's your plan here, Hux? Spring the boy and make a swim for the eastern shore? Is that the big plan here? Because I don't think we'll reach the shore."

"I'm not getting off this boat," Huxley says. "We're going to Shreveport. And when we get there, we'll own this boat."

"You plan to take the boat?" Don nearly coughs.

Huxley looks at him and nods. "I do."

"Don't fuck with slavers," he is shaking his head. "You just don't do it. That's how your jaw becomes an ornament ..."

Huxley grabs the man by the face and slams him into a rack of wooden bars that creak and rattle treacherously. He digs his fingers into the other man's face, feeling the man's teeth through his flesh, thinks about ripping the jaw off then and there. "This jaw?" he says. "This precious jaw right there? You fucking coward. Well, let me explain something to you, Don. You're just a fucking drifter. Me? I'm a calamity. I'm a goddamn plague. You led me to water and that kept me alive, and for that reason I'm choosing not to kill you. But you're hanging by a thread here. These slavers? They're just men. They're just flesh and bone, like you and me. And flesh and bone dies when you shoot it. I've taken out slavers before, and I'll do it again, do you understand me? And if I have even an inkling that you are going to betray me, I'll just flat out kill you. And trust and believe when I tell you that the slavers will kill you, too. They'll use you to betray me, but in the end your jaw will hang from those pikes outside, just like mine. So what's it going to be, drifter? Are you going to help me or should I gut you right now?"

For once, Don's insolence has fled him.

Perhaps it is the Black Hats who seek Huxley, perhaps it is the mysterious nature of his crimes, or perhaps it is something that he sees in Huxley's eyes that stirs some primal fear in him, but Don's eyes are no longer those of a jackal, but those of cornered prey. He believes that Huxley will kill him.

Huxley is thinking about it.

If he shoots Don dead, the slavers will not care and likely Huxley can make up a story to cozy himself with the slavers and put them further off their guard. In the moment, standing there with Don's head rammed back against the wooden bars and Huxley's hand gripping hot and tight on the handle of his revolver, Huxley thinks that maybe he should just kill the man and get it over with. Maybe it would be best.

Don's hands pat rapidly at Huxley's shoulders, lightly, like fluttering birds.

Weak, you are weak, you worthless drifter. You are weak and I can smell it on you.

"Okay, man," Don says, his voice shaking. "Just … Jesus Christ, just calm down."

The answer is unsatisfactory. Huxley slams his head against the bars again. "Are you going to help me?"

Don winces as his head bounces off the wood. "Christ! Yes, I'll help you. I won't betray you. I promise."

Huxley removes the pressure from Don's face, but keeps his hand on the man's jaw. He looks him in the eyes when he speaks, so that Don can know the truth of it. "No matter what, if this goes bad, your jaw is hanging with mine. Do you understand that?"

Don nods. "Yes. I understand."

CHAPTER 7

When Red Water Landing is nearly a half an hour out of sight by Huxley's estimation, the door to the big cabin opens, spearing light into the gloom and silhouetting the stout form of the slave master. When the light hits them, Huxley, Jay, Rigo, and Don squint accusingly at it. They stand at the door to one of the long holding cells.

The slave master laughs at them. "Don't look so angry. Did you think I'd trapped you in here?"

Huxley's jaw muscles clench rapidly as he steps forward, his hands resting on the handles of his revolvers. "The thought had crossed my mind."

"The door was unlocked," the slave master swings a step aside and motions them out. "But I'm glad you stayed in the cabin as instructed. The Black Hats have been known to travel in groups. Who knows where this one's friends were hiding? Maybe along the riverbank."

Huxley walks to the door and eyes the slave master before stepping through and onto the deck. He immediately scans the flat expanse of weathered boards, looking into the groups of slaves that are tending the oars. He looks for Lowell, but can't see him.

"Where's the boy?" Huxley asks as Don and Jay edge past him and into the sunlight. Rigo is still standing behind Huxley, looking around the slave cabin but then he too steps through, head down, back out into the light.

The slave master lets the door shut behind him as he steps away. "He's in the crew's quarters, being fitted for chains. Can't leave one like that to chance. He's got a spark in him, that one. Be a shame if he tried to escape. I would have to kill him. And that's like killing money, which I hate to do. Besides, if

I have to kill him, then I'll have to toss you gentlemen overboard! Ha! He is your ticket, after all."

Huxley continues to look around, taking stock of the other slaves being shipped to Shreveport for sale. Many of them are dressed in tatters and Huxley can see the marks on them, mostly on their backs—those that are bare—but some of their faces are bruised or striped with healing scars as well.

"Your slaves are pretty beat up," Huxley says, and his voice seems like it is easily lost in the breeze that blows downriver with them.

The slave master grunts. "Those are the difficult ones—and a lot of them are difficult. A good slaver breaks his slaves before he brings them to market." He smiles, enthusiastically. "You wouldn't let me sell you an untamed mustang as a horse. Why buy a slave that might try to slit your throat in the middle of the night?"

"I imagine that would be a constant danger."

The slave master shrugs and begins walking leisurely toward the front of the barge, Huxley following. "Freedom is not as special as the beliefs of the Old World would have you think. It's much easier to be a slave. Once we break them down and keep them miserable, they're purchased by some rich councilman, or another clan leader out in the Nations, and treated like a member of the household. Well … sometimes they are. If a boy goes to serve a woman, chances are he'll be castrated when his balls drop. Unless the councilman's lady is into that sort of thing. And the girls? Well …" he laughs as he reaches the edge of the boat and looks over the water. "Simple psychology, I suppose. By the time I'm done with them, the people that buy them look like benevolent angels. It's all part of the game. But that's why I'm in business where so many others have failed." He looks at Huxley, guardedly. "I realize that I know your name, but you don't know mine. How rude. Master Bristow, they call me. You can call me that too."

I won't call you master.

"Okay," Huxley says, looking down the river where the ruddy water twists and turns into the distance. To either side, the banks creep by seemingly slow, but Huxley can see that the water is moving quite fast. "How long to Shreveport?"

"Four days, in good water," Master Bristow says, hooking thumbs into his belt. "Four or five, depending on whether we get stuck in the mud, and how many times we get stuck. The *Misery* has a shallow draft, but the sandbars are a bit treacherous in the southern stretch." Bristow turns and folds his hands over his wide torso, a stance of repose. He regards Huxley long and carefully. "I told you before that I've hidden men from the Black Hats. I fuck them over any chance I can get. But you ... there's something about you that I don't like."

Huxley stands very still, wondering if this is the moment when Bristow will try to take their weapons by force. Bristow's eyes scan up and down Huxley, lingering a moment on the two revolvers stuck into his waistband.

"The Black Hats," Bristow says. "Why are they hunting you?"

"I was falsely accused," Huxley says, thinking about the man in the hallway, Captain Tim's man, the one whose head Huxley had punched through with a knife.

Bristow gives a smile with very little humor in it. "Aren't we all? What's the accusation?"

Huxley sniffs, spits over the side and into the river. "Murder, I suppose."

"Hm." Bristow nods, slowly, thoughtfully. "It's a very serious thing to have the Black Hats hunting you. And, frankly, you can tell me all you want that you were falsely accused, and maybe you were. Maybe you were falsely accused for that one crime that they're hunting you for, but I can see that you're not innocent. I can see it in your eyes, Mr. Huxley. You're a dangerous one. I feel like you're trouble."

Huxley's teeth are ratcheted together so that they hurt. "So what are you going to do?"

"Well ..." Bristow makes an unpleasant face. "Unfortunately, I'm not a fair-weather Easterling. Or a savage Wastelander, like yourself. I'm a man of the Riverland Nations, and around here, when you shake a man's hand, it means something. I won't go back on my word. I'll transport you to Shreveport. But once we pull into port, the second you step off of my boat, that promise is concluded. I will have fulfilled my obligation, and if you so much as look at me from that point on, I'll gun you down dead on the docks." Bristow gives this a moment, as though he is reviewing his own words to make sure that they are accurate. He seems satisfied that they are, and he nods. "Until then, keep yourselves on your best behavior. You can break the peace of my promise just as easily as I can, and then the Black Hats will find you floating on the river like a bloated gray bobber. This is my boat, and on my boat, I am god. And I will smite anyone that challenges that. Understood?"

"Understood," Huxley says, managing to keep his voice calm.

"Good." Bristow makes an expansive gesture. "Ground rules, then. First of all, no fraternization with the slaves. Don't even talk to them. You can sleep on the decks when we put them in the cabin at night. If you have to shit or piss, do it over the backside of the boat. Don't interrupt my men in their work or try to befriend them. They are not your friends. Do not, in any way, shape, or form, undermine my authority, or the authority of my men. That is very important. Lastly, if we're accosted by another boat, report directly to me. There's a place in my cabin that I can put you in case we're boarded. If you violate any of my rules, then my obligation to you is over. Very important that you are clear on all those rules."

"Very clear," Huxley says.

"Then I'll leave you to yourselves." Bristow nods curtly, and then strides off, surprisingly light on his feet for such a large man.

Huxley watches him go, standing there at the front of the flatboat. The big slave master hollers an order to a team of slaves and the slaver watching them, a dark-skinned man with a scattergun and two pistols, both holstered on his right side, a giant bowie knife on his left.

They're well armed, for sure. But so are all the slavers, and we've dealt with them before.

Huxley looks sidelong at Don. *Well, Jay and Rigo and myself have dealt with them. I'm not so sure about Don.*

They are relatively alone, and the occasional shouted order of the slavers, the grunts and groans of effort from the teams of slaves as they pull the oars, the sloshing of the river underneath them, and the wind that scours the deck and causes the dried jawbones to clatter atop the slavers' poles, all these noises will drown out their voices. Huxley is sure that they cannot be heard when Don leans in close to him and speaks in a level tone.

"What are we going to do?" Don's voice is filled with nerves, boiling over. "There's six of them, and they're armed to the teeth." He is shaking his head. "This is a bad idea. Bad idea."

Huxley looks away from Don and finds Jay, standing next to him, his brow knit in question. Huxley pushes Don gently away from him with the back of his forearm, a dismissive gesture, and Huxley does not care whether it is insulting or not. Don makes a little noise of displeasure, but says nothing.

"Can you give us a minute?" Huxley says, gesturing between himself and his two actual companions.

Don's eyebrows squinch down into angry little jags. "Fine."

He turns and walks ten feet away.

Huxley and Jay turn, Rigo following, and they walk another ten feet. They speak quietly.

"Don is a problem," Jay says.

"He's weak and I don't trust him," Huxley nods.

"All flame and gunsmoke when it's a family of three armed with sticks and an ancient revolver, but when it's actual men with real guns, all of the sudden it's a bad idea to act." Jay shakes his head, looking over his shoulder at the other man. "He's a coward. That much fear in a man … it makes them unpredictable."

"But who does he fear more?" Huxley asks. "Me or the slavers?"

Jay shakes his head. "Hard to tell." Then he fixes Huxley with an evaluating look. "Why are we really going to Shreveport?"

Huxley feels the heat of the question on his neck like hot coals being held an inch away from his skin. He dislikes the question. It pulls away protective layers that Huxley has spent time building up. It reveals things that he does not want revealed.

"Because that's where the slavers go," Huxley responds, shortly.

"Yes, that's where the slavers go," Jay echoes, quietly. "But you have other reasons for going where the slavers go. I don't think you and I are on the same page here." Jay folds his arms across his chest. "I want to kill every single one of them. And here? In the Riverlands?" he laughs. "You can't miss! But you … you want to go to Shreveport. Right into the belly of the beast. Because you're looking for someone."

Huxley makes a noise in the back of his throat, as though he is trying to discredit Jay, but can't find the words. He's picturing scorpions.

"So, who are you looking for in Shreveport?"

Huxley looks away, jaw working without words.

"Huxley," Jay pries. "Who are you looking for in Shreveport? There are plenty of places to cross the Red River, by ferry or by bridge. We take this barge, we can run it aground anywhere we want. We don't have to go to Shreveport."

Huxley looks up at him sharply. "No. We're going." He holds up a finger. "Leave it alone. Focus on the matter at hand, please. Focus on how we're going to get Lowell back."

Jay watches him for another long moment, then looks away, smacking his lips loudly. "Well, that's easy. We kill the slavers and free the slaves. It's simple enough."

"They outnumber us almost two-to-one."

"It's a fight with a man twice as big as you," Jay says. "You don't shy away from the fight. You circle and you wait for an opening and you take advantage of it when it comes. That's all we have to do. Circle and wait. Watch for our opening."

"We only have a few days."

"Big men's weaknesses are easy to find. They trust in their size." Jay looks around them. "These men, the slavers, Bristow ... they trust in their numbers and all the weapons that they have strapped to them. But there will be a point when there'll be a level playing field. Soon. Sometime soon. And then we move. Quickly."

"Without hesitation."

Jay nods.

Huxley nods along with him.

Maybe Rigo speaks more English than he lets on, or maybe he doesn't. Either way, he looks at Huxley, his hands gripping Huxley's shoulder tightly. "Los lobos," he says quietly. "Make them bleed."

CHAPTER 8

Misery floats southward, and on its weathered decking Huxley and the three others keep to themselves, huddled in the fore of the big square flatboat. At midday, the slavers allow their charges to break from manning the oars. They are given food, and Huxley and his two companions dip into their own meager provisions. Afterward, the slaves are ushered into the expansive, shit-smelling cave of their cabins. Their chains clink solemnly as they go in teams of threes and fours, always a careful grouping, Huxley realizes. Any adult males are linked with women or children. To keep them cautious. Complacent. No grouping has two adults in it. There are a lot of children, Huxley observes. Some about Lowell's age. Some slightly older, nearing adulthood. A few that are very young—six or seven, by Huxley's guess.

They file into the cabins with downcast eyes, save for a few who take cautious, almost accusatory glances in the direction of Huxley and his group, but none of them make eye contact with him. The ones with the scars, their faces are full of bitterness and spite, but the fight has gone out of them, like all that is left of their fire is cold, pale ash.

Bristow's right, Huxley realizes as he watches them. *They're not even thinking about freedom anymore. They're just hoping their next master will be kind to them. They're down to their last bit of hope, like a skin with only a few mouthfuls of water left in it, and miles of desert left to go.*

Oh, I've been there. I've been to that point where hope dies.

Huxley looks away from the sight of them. He still has not seen Lowell.

Without the crews to man the oars, the barge drifts with the river, Lizard Eyes manning the rudder and steering them away from the banks as the river pulls them on its gradually winding course, mostly south, sometimes to the southwest, sometimes to the southeast. Ahead of them, the midday skies are darkening and the wind is beginning to howl.

Jay sits with his arms around his knees, his face uplifted to the sky, eyes closed, smelling the air.

Huxley watches him for a time.

Perhaps he senses being watched, or perhaps his eyes are not truly closed. Jay takes a big breath of the dank river air and smiles, face still uplifted. His voice is very quiet. "Storm's a-comin'."

By the afternoon, the dark clouds on the horizon have become dark skies. In places along the river bank where the trees are clear and the banks are shallow and flat, Huxley can see the rain lashing down a few miles from them and coming closer, an ominous gray haze that marches toward them. It still seems to be a mile or so from them when the first few fat drops start to slap the deck boards around them, tiny icy spots on their skin. Huxley grits his teeth, not wanting to get wet, but knowing there is no way to avoid it.

"Unusual for this season," a big voice says.

Huxley turns where he is sitting and finds Bristow there, pulling on a long, leather duster, something of a storm coat, Huxley supposes. It is black, or at least was black once. Now it seems more a grayish green. Bristow is looking out at the skies, but then he looks down at Huxley with a frown.

"Not sure if that's a good omen or a bad omen," the master says. "But I'm pretty sure it's an omen about you." Then he laughs, a short sharp bark. "The storm will surge the river, so we won't have to worry about the sandbars. But the current might try to slam us into one of the banks. You men might want to hold onto something. It's going to be a wet, miserable night, but this is the *Misery*, so I suppose that's quite fitting."

Bristow laughs again, and turns away from them, calling over his shoulder, "Don't get accidentally thrown overboard!"

A few minutes later, the rain hits in force. Giant gales of it that come out of the sky like falling curtains and scatter themselves over the deck and over the men and turn the big red-brown mess of the river stretching before them into a great, gray snake. Huxley, Jay, Rigo, and Don huddle in the cold rain, cursing and wishing they were anyplace else, as the slavers pull teams of slaves from the cabins to man the oars. The rain is cold and the slaves are poorly dressed for it, as are Huxley and his companions. But Bristow and his slavers have no obligation to see that Huxley or his group remains in good health, while losing a slave to pneumonia would be money out of their pockets. Huxley can see one of the slavers starting the big brass brazier that sits in the middle of the slave cages, and billows of thick gray smoke begin to rise out of the metal chimney.

Huxley wishes fervently for the fire, but Bristow doesn't want them inside. He doesn't want them fraternizing with the slaves.

After the first onslaught of rain, the wind all but stops, but by now the river has begun to creep over its banks and it is moving fast and hard carrying them around corners with an uncomfortable speed as Lizard Eyes bares his teeth and works the rudder around the curves of the river and the teams of slaves groan at the oars, slamming them back and forth, first the right side of the barge, and then the left, lashing at the water around them.

One of the slavers stands at the port side of the barge as they work it into a starboard turn. He is a large man, entirely shrouded by a brown poncho that glistens wetly in the lashing rain so that Huxley cannot tell what it is made out of. He cannot see anything of the man's face, and even his arms are hidden in his poncho. But he can hear his voice, shouting orders to the oar team.

"Pull. Pull. Break. You! Get on the end and leverage that fucking thing! Pull. Pull."

The slave that he'd addressed, a young man, slides down to the end of the oar, his chains extended tight with the others, who are all smaller children. The oar rattles and creaks in its brass lock. Each stroke pushes the big barge a little more to the right, but not quite fast enough for the river.

"Pull that shit faster! Pull! Pull!"

The bank looms up at their right side, the river pushing them into it.

The slaver in the poncho moves rapidly. A hand emerges from under his poncho and he pulls a pin from the oarlock, freeing the long wooden oar. Then he points to the bank as the slaves pull the oar loose. "Brace it on the bank! Brace it hard! Hold that shit!"

The slaver himself grabs hold of the end of the oar, along with the young man. All the slaves instinctively spread their feet, getting their base and balance as they raise the oar up so that it protrudes sideways out from the barge, leveled at the encroaching bank.

"Push off!" the slaver shouts. "Push off!" and he rams the head of the oar into the rising mud of the bank, the slave team around him following suit, so that the flat blade of the oar disappears into the red clay wall. "Push!" the slaver yells. "Push!"

Misery groans underneath them, the current pushing her underbelly in one direction, the slaves with the oar pushing her topside in the opposite. The bank keeps reaching for them, the river keeps pushing, but everything slows, slows, and gradually stops, amid the silence of the other slave teams, and the grunts and straining effort of the team with the oar embedded into the bank.

The slaver is no longer yelling.

They are all pushing. They cannot push any harder.

Then suddenly, they are off the bank. The river catches them back into its current, the momentum of the big river barge overcome. The barge tries to yaw in the water, but Lizard Eyes leans into his rudder and straightens her out again.

The slaver at the oar steps away from it. "Pull her out. Don't lose that fucking oar."

The team strains backward now, back into the ship as the big bulk is caught in the current and carrying them away. They stagger as the barge starts to move downstream again, the head of the oar caught securely in the bank and not wanting to free itself. The team of slaves stumbles and is suddenly dragged, all four of them, five feet toward the aft. A few of them cry out, but none of them let go, because they know if they lose the oar, they will pay.

The slaver is shouting again. "Pull the fucking oar out!"

The slaves begin to yank, panicked, as the deck of the barge begins to dwindle under their feet, the oar dragging them closer to the edge. They scrunch together at the end of the oar, leaning back, yelling with the effort. The oar is working free, Huxley can see, and it comes free very suddenly, knocking the entire group to the deck at the slaver's feet. All but one—the young man, who is the biggest of the four. He loses his footing and slips.

His legs hit the water, the chain attached to his ankle yanking at the next slave in line, a small, wisp of a boy, and pulling him toward the edge. The older slave panics, doesn't think, and reaches out for anything to hold on to. He catches the ankle of the small boy, the one who does not have a chain and manacle around it. The small boy is no support. They both begin to slide off, the small boy suddenly screaming, a high-pitched wail.

The remaining two slaves—a boy and a girl—cling desperately to the cracks in the decking.

The glistening black poncho is suddenly over top of the slaves, the hood sweeping back to reveal a hard, blocky face and long, wet tangles of black hair. The slaver's arm emerges out of his poncho, holding what looks like a tomahawk in his hand, and for a second Huxley thinks he is going to use it to give the boys in the water something to hold to.

Then he rears back and strikes the chain.

Sparks fly off.

Someone yelps out a scream.

Another strike, and this time the sound of the chain breaking, a harsh, final sound.

The young man and the wispy boy, nothing left to tether them, plunge into the cold, silty river.

The slaver's other hand rises out of his poncho, this time with a revolver.

In the river, to the port side of the barge, the two slaves flail in the water, their heads and arms barely above the rain-lashed surface, liquid in their mouths, slipping down their throats so that they can't scream for help or mercy, only choke and gag on the muddy water as chains and currents pull them under.

The slaver on the deck aims his revolver and fires once.

The young man's head snaps back, red and purple and white, and then sinks.

The slaver cocks his revolver again and lets out a second shot, very quickly aimed. The smaller boy, Huxley cannot see where he is struck by the lead ball, but he can see his body jerk and stiffen and then he too sinks.

Within seconds, both are gone.

The slaver with the poncho retracts his hands, both the tomahawk and the revolver disappearing again. His face remains out, cold and hard, staring at the rushing water in front of him. Behind him, the remaining boy and girl from that team of slaves cling to the deck and they both sob loudly, though Huxley cannot tell if it is from relief or terror or sadness.

The slaver swears loudly at the water and then flips his hood up again to shield his head from the driving rain. He turns and scoops the two children up, one in each arm. He does not carry them gently, nor does he handle them roughly. He does it with indifference, as though they are sacks of grain. He takes them quickly to the cabin, kicking the door open with his foot then setting them down inside.

Huxley watches through the open door as the slaver manning the brazier comes away from his warm place at the fire and takes possession of the boy and the girl.

"Lost two to the river," the slaver in the poncho says. "Need another team to man the port oar. Now. Quickly."

The slaver inside says nothing, but acknowledges with a nod and hurries the two children back into the cages. He selects another team—this one a man, two boys, and a small woman, and unchains them from their spot on the wall.

At the portside, two other slavers sink the oar back into its lock and man it while they wait for the new team to be dispatched into the driving rain.

The slaver with the poncho turns. The open shadow of his hood seems to be looking at Huxley, who stares back through the rain. Inside of that hood, all that Huxley can see is the man's lips, just a grim, thin slash across a grizzled face.

Huxley stares into the darkness, knowing that it is staring back.

"Better to lose two than four," the slaver's voice says, matter-of-factly. "And it's better to be shot dead than drowned in cold mud. Wouldn't you agree?"

Huxley remains silent.

The thin lips smirk at him underneath that hood.

With a strange, musical tone to his voice, Jay says again, "Storm's a-comin'."

CHAPTER 9

The rain only lasts for an hour or so, but the river has already swelled, and it continues to rush, bloated, pushing them between the banks. Huddled close together, the companions at the fore of the slave barge are soaked to the bone and shivering. After the downpour, the temperature drops, and autumn nightfall is coming fast.

The storm clouds, although wrung dry of rain, still hover over them and block out the stars and moon, so that the night is dark as ink. Lanterns are lit at the corners of the barge, and around the slave cages, and the smaller structure that sits adjacent to it, the crew's quarters. The flames flicker and writhe and cast yellow light around them in dappled circles. Beyond the dimly lit decking, the river is just an impression, sometimes an undulation in the water catching the reflection of the lanterns and glistening briefly, like phosphorescent fish swimming close to the surface, and then disappearing down below again. Beyond the dark river, the land is infinite black and nonexistent. They might as well be floating through empty space in some bizarre dreamscape.

The river is a constant noise beneath them, heard more often than it can be seen. It rushes and trickles and burbles beneath them and along its banks. The slaves' oars splash the water for a time, adding to the sensation of reality and substance, but once it is full dark the lanterns lit at the fore of the ship are not bright enough to truly pierce the gloom, and the need for slow, steady progress becomes apparent. The wet and shivering teams of slaves are brought in to warm themselves by the brazier in the slave cages. When the door opens for them, it does not seem as dark and dank and miserable as it had before. The brazier flames almost cheerfully, and it is so warm inside that billows of steam roll out when the door is opened, and continue to leak from the cracks in the walls after it is closed again.

Still, the slaves inside are quiet.

Without the oar teams, the barge simply drifts, carried on by the river, which has significantly slowed, Huxley feels, though in the dark it is hard to be certain. Interesting that Bristow complained so much about time, but now wasn't running the oar teams, Huxley thought. Maybe it was all just to drive the bargain.

A slaver strides the foredeck between the two front-most lanterns, sometimes hanging off the boat to peer beyond the lanterns and try to catch a glimpse of the bank. He calls out sometimes to the slaver manning the rudder—no longer Lizard Eyes, but another. "Port," he calls, or "starboard," and sometimes qualifies it with a "hard" or "steady." Huxley cannot see what causes him to make these calls, but they do not hit a riverbank, or even scrape against the downed trees that Huxley knows line the bank like half-submerged skeletons in the dark. These men all know this river well, and even in the dark and gloom, they are able to navigate it.

Can we navigate as well as them? Or would we only run this thing aground?

The miserable foursome shivers and curses, unable to sleep.

Gradually, steadily, like a thief in the night, the world around them becomes closer, denser, wetter. The lanterns begin to give off halos. Huxley blinks through the darkness as he looks at them, thinking his own eyes are hazy.

"Fog," one of the slavers calls out. "Fog rolling in."

Beside him, pressed close to him, Huxley feels Jay stir. He looks over at the other man and sees Jay's cold blue eyes, just dark little orbs in the night, staring pointedly back at him.

The slaver at the fore makes a grumbling sound as the fog thickens, thickens, very quickly into a murky soup of cold, damp air. From where Huxley sits on the deck, he can barely see the man hanging off the front lantern post, trying to see into the darkness. The lantern itself cannot be seen—just the yellow glow from the flame.

The slaver hanging off the fore of the barge makes another sound of displeasure and swings back onto the deck, the shape of his body just a darkness in the pale, corpse-like gloom. "Fuck my life," the slaver mumbles as he strides past Huxley a few paces and then stops, his hands raised up to his mouth to project his voice as he shouts: "Fog! Too thick! Can't see shit!"

"Mother*fuck* …" is the muted reply from the opposite end of the boat.

The fog thickens by the second. The lanterns become dimmer, more distant. The shape of the slaver standing only a few paces from Huxley darkens again, until it is barely visible. The fog is thick and blanketing, and it muffles the sounds of the world all around them. The boat no longer creaks. The river no longer gurgles and rushes. Everything is very still in the fog. Cold, wet, and still.

A sound makes it through the thickening haze. The sound of a wooden door opening and closing. Huxley turns to look behind him, but he cannot see the slave cages or the crew's quarters. He can see the demure glow of the lanterns that are hung on these structures, but even these seem to dance and move in ways that they should not, like will-o'-the-wisps.

Huxley can hear the slave master's voice, deeper, more commanding, projecting itself across the deck. He utters a string of curses. Someone—the rudder man, Huxley presumes—says something that's not quite audible. Bristow's voice responds with more curses.

"Reno! You can't see anything?" Bristow's voice booms through the mist.

The slaver beside them calls back, "Naw, can't see shit!"

"Well, fuck it," Bristow's voice is more resigned. "Drop the poles and anchors. Let me know as soon as the fog clears out."

The slaver standing close to them grumbles underneath his breath, a disembodied voice hovering in the air off to Huxley's left. "I fucking *hate* this river. I fucking hate this *river*. Just want some fucking pussy. Can't get no fucking pussy 'cause I'm sitting in the fucking fog. I fucking *hate this river.*"

More voices mumble from the other end of the ship. Beside them, the slaver's breathy murmurs dwindle, the sound of his boots on the decking fading as he walks away from them. A few voices go back and forth. The words cannot be heard, but the tone is obvious. Bored men, delegating the orders they'd received. Then there is the loud sound of heavy wood on wood, a huge splash, coming from underneath the barge. Huxley feels the boat jerk underneath them, the wood groaning loudly. Another sound of some huge wooden thing dropping into the water, and then another, and finally a fourth. More orders are called out, the words hidden in the mist. From the starboard and port sides, simultaneously, the sound of metal, another large splash, and the sound of heavy chains clanking away as what Huxley assumes are the anchors sink down and embed themselves in the river silt.

The barge twitches and groans like a felled beast in its death throes. First it goes this way, then that, caught in every direction by something that stops it, and then finally it lies still, as though resigned to its death, its stillness, and it rests.

Muted voices back behind them, joking now that the stress of finding their way through the fog is done. The sound of Bristow guffawing at something. Then wooden doors to the crew's quarters opening and closing.

Huxley realizes his heart is pounding hard. In the cold, in the mist, he still shivers. But his hot blood is coursing now. He can feel it in his chest, the feathery, electric feeling of something impending, something bloody and violent.

He looks at Jay.

Jay looks back. "Not quite."

"What are you talking about?" Don whispers from where he is huddled at Huxley's right side. "We can't see shit in this. I hope ... I think ..."

Huxley turns to him, matching the low level of Don's voice. "It's not even midnight. We have time. The fog won't clear until daybreak."

"What do you mean we have time?"

Huxley pushes his face closer to Don, his voice straining a bit with sudden anger. "Don't do that, Don. Don't play games with me. This is the best chance we're going to get—the best chance you have of not having your jaw strung up with those others. We're gonna take it. And when I say 'Go,' we're going to go. We're going to do this."

Don shivers and looks terrified.

How could one man change so extremely from one conflict to another?

Because he's a coward. He knew he could beat the man and his wife in the trailer, especially with me and Jay. Now we're outnumbered and outgunned, so suddenly, he's not so vicious.

Huxley sucks on his teeth and regards the man to his right. "Are you weak, Don?"

Don closes his eyes and buries his face in his arms. "No," his voice says, from the folds of his coat. "I'm not weak."

Huxley sneers and looks away. *I think you are. I think you're weak. I think Lowell has more strength than you. Lowell deserves to be with us more than you do. He's more of a man than you. His chances of surviving out there are much better. You, Don? You're just dead weight.*

The hours creep by in cold silence. It is difficult for Huxley to gauge the passing time while he sits on the deck of the slave barge, surrounded by white mist, barely able to see five feet in front of him. His pounding heart turns to steady rage. In his mind, he tries to picture her face …

Charity.

Wife. Mother.

Why can't I remember you?

Think. Think about what she looked like.

But all he has is words: She had hair the same color as the sun in the barley fields. She had blue eyes that were bluer in the middle, and they sparkled when she smiled. A big smile. Beautiful mouth. She'd been a joyful person. A wonderful person. The best person he knew …

He can say these things.

He can recite the facts about her, and yet in his mind's eye, he cannot piece them together to be a complete picture. He cannot remember, aside from thin impressions of all these disparate features, what his wife had looked like.

He knows that she'd smelled a certain way.

But he's been so long amid his own stink, and the smell of smoke, and the smell of blood, that he cannot remember her scent.

He knows that she had laughed, that he had liked the sound of her laugh. It had made him laugh as well when she thought something was truly hilarious and her eyes would water and her nostrils would flare.

But he's been so long in the company of men with rough voices, he's heard so many dying screams and shouts of rage, that he cannot remember her laughter.

He is losing her. She is falling away from him, like she was a puzzle and every day he woke up and more pieces had been removed. He could tell what the picture of the puzzle had once been, but the picture itself was not there.

You have lost her. She's gone.

Your daughter too.

Stop trying to breathe them back to life. It only makes you weak.

But he wants to remember. He wants to remember who he was.

Huxley opens his eyes to the dark, still draped with the innards of clouds.

The sound of boot heels on the deck, a slow pace, around the edge of the barge. The lanterns are still lit, distant yellow orbs that dance with the sway of the boat. Seeing them sway gives him a sense of losing his balance. He looks away from them, in the direction of the boot heels as they draw closer.

Clump. Clump. Clump.

A handheld lantern, a softer glow than the others, swaying through the air, becoming more defined as it nears them. A single flame in a glass box. Then the arm of the man holding it. Then the general shape of him, and then the man himself, standing there, looking down at them.

It is the man in the hooded poncho.

The lantern light illuminates his face queerly in the dark, causing his rocky features to look extreme, like sunset on a stone monolith. Huxley cannot tell if the man is grinning, or grimacing. His eyes are shadowed pits of black mud, with only the slightest winkle of reflected fire in them.

"Shitty night to be stuck on the deck, that's for sure," he grumbles. He nods in the general direction of the slave cages. "Ol' Bristow's gone down for the night. Into half a jar of shine. If you'd like to go stand by the brazier to warm yourselves, Bristow won't hear of it from me."

Without waiting for a response, the slaver turns away from them and continues his rounds through the mist.

Huxley watches him disappear. Dissolving, just as he had seemed to form, until again he is just the sound of boot heels and the sway of lantern light. The muffled sound of the river. The breathiness of the fog as it hangs on them and swirls all around them. The lantern, now a little yellow orb, hanging in some indeterminate distance.

Jay rises, very slowly, from Huxley's side. His wet clothes barely make a sound. His eyes are locked on the dancing orb of light somewhere at the fore of the ship. Huxley cranes his head to watch him. But he doesn't say anything. Doesn't ask any questions. And neither does Don. For the moment, they keep their mouths shut.

Jay moves like a cat, prowling. Focused on the objective. And when he does move, it is quick, and quiet. His boots don't make a sound but perhaps the barest rubber squeak on the wet wooden planks of the deck. Then, he too disappears into the mist.

Huxley and Rigo both watch the lantern light.

Beside them, Don fidgets nervously.

The lantern light is the only thing that is real to them in that moment.

It sways and dances, almost antagonistically. Like a little lighted lure, baiting this way and that while the angler creeps after it but doesn't strike.

Then the little yellow light vanishes.

There is the very faint sound of something hitting the water. If Huxley hadn't been so focused on the lantern light and seen it disappear, he might not have even noticed it, or would have chalked it up to the river gurgling under the flatboat. But now, he feels it in how his heart suddenly starts slamming. Not fast, but hard. Almost painfully hard.

He rises to his feet.

Rigo rises beside him, knowing that it is time without having to be told. He draws two revolvers.

Don stumbles to his own feet, still shivering, still not quite knowing what is happening.

"Uh ... hello?" Don says into the darkness displayed before them, a panorama of nothingness, not even the lantern to give them a point of reference.

Huxley nudges him with an elbow. "Quiet."

In that quiet, Huxley can no longer hear the boot heels striking the deck of the barge. Instead, there is just the unassuming little sound of rubber soles on wet wood, quietly but quickly approaching.

Jay is less than ten feet in front of them before Huxley even sees him. He comes striding out of the mists, walking quickly and confidently. It is hard to see the details of him, but his pale skin and almost-white hair stand out in the gloom. They are splashed with gore.

"Oh my God ..." Don moans out a whisper.

"Quiet!" Huxley hisses again.

Jay's pistols are still tucked into his holsters. But he holds his own knife which glistens wetly. And a tomahawk. The one that had belonged to the slaver in the poncho. He has another revolver, this one stuffed into the front of his waistband. He hands the tomahawk to Huxley.

Huxley feels the heft and balance of it. The handle is wet. It smells of blood.

It feels right in his hands. It feels like justice.

"Come on," Huxley says, turning his back to the darkness that spans out across the Red River and faces the rest of the barge, where the lanterns on the slave cages and crew quarters are still lit like beacons. "Stay with me," he whispers, and starts walking in that direction.

He feels rather than hears the other three fall in behind him.

He walks through the mist and it feels like his heart is burning so hot that it will sizzle the mist away in his path. The slave cages loom in the darkness like a great ship in and of itself. As he nears it, he can see the glow of lantern light and the hot-burning brazier through the cracks of the wooden slats. There is no one posted outside. On this ship, the slave master is god, and the slavers are his demigods. Their authority cannot be questioned. Their security is infallible. They conduct themselves as though they are safe, because they believe that their confidence will make it so.

But it won't. It won't. Nothing can make you safe. I am your reckoning. I am the toll you must pay for the path your life has taken. I am vengeance and justice.

He knocks on the door and the sound of his knuckles striking wood seems to shatter the night around them. He hears the grumbling of the man inside, a single slaver, armed to the teeth, Huxley is sure, to watch over the broken souls of men and children huddling in their broken bodies and hoping for a kind master at the other end of this trip down the river.

The door opens. The slaver looks at them, clearly expecting someone else. He seems confused.

"You're not supposed to …" he starts.

Huxley splits the slaver's skull open with the tomahawk. The rough-hewn iron makes a strange *thunk* as it splits hair and bone and brain. Almost like chopping wet and rotted wood. The slaver's knees lock, his body spasms, and he falls backward, blood squirting from his nose and ears. Huxley yanks the tomahawk from his head and the body hits the wooden decking.

The slaves inside their cages look on, and seeing their faces in the red glow of the brazier, Huxley cannot tell if they are hopeful or terrified. Some of them are staring at Huxley and the men behind him, and some of them are staring at the slaver that lies crumpled and twitching on the floor, one hand still opening and closing.

Huxley looks down at the tomahawk. He readjusts his grip.

"Jesus Christ," Don mutters. "What do we do with all these slaves? Did you think about that?"

"I did," Huxley says, plainly. He looks up at the slaves, taking a step deeper into the slave cages. Everything he can feel is running together now. It's all a vicious tidewater, and he is riding it, riding it on a delicate raft. He finds a young boy, not much older than Lowell himself, pressed up against a set of iron bars, his hands clutching them.

Huxley looks at him while he speaks. "If you want your freedom, you'll stay quiet."

The boy points to himself, surprised that he is being personally addressed.

Huxley scans the faces, now addressing everyone. "All of you. Stay quiet."

He steps back, over the limbs of the dead slaver that now lies still and cooling. He lifts a finger to his lips, presses it there, indicating the need for silence, and then he closes the door behind him as he leaves.

In the cold again, Jay whispers, "They'll think we're trying to steal them."

Huxley nods. "Maybe. But they'll hope that we're not."

And hope makes people do stupid things.

Huxley turns away from the slave cages and begins walking with the boarded walls to his left, around the structure toward the crew's quarters, where he might find this Master Bristow, this purveyor of *Misery*. Where he might find Lowell, whom he had never intended to leave for the slavers.

They make it to the corner of the slave cages before someone inside begins to scream.

"Help! Someone help! They're trying to kill the master! They're trying to kill Master Bristow!"

CHAPTER 10

Huxley freezes there at the corner of the cabin.

Inside the slave cages, the voice is still yelling—a man's voice, Huxley is almost positive.

"Well, shit," Jay growls, sliding his knife away and pulling out his revolvers.

Rigo flattens himself against the wall, revolvers held up and ready.

Huxley's hands wrench down on the tomahawk. He sees it splitting skulls. He doesn't know who the hell is screaming in the slave cages, but he wants to split their skull open too. Bristow had been right apparently: some of these creatures can't even comprehend their own freedom.

"What do we do now?" Don whines. "What do we do?"

Around the corner, shouts of alarm are being raised. The sound of running feet on wooden boards. The sound of the doors to the crew's quarters slamming open.

Huxley switches the tomahawk to his left hand, pulls one of his revolvers with the right. "We fight. We kill. You know what to do."

Huxley pulls himself away from the wall—it is a false sense of security, he knows. It is only thin wooden slats, and the gaps between might give him away. He holds the tomahawk at the ready as the foggy night fills with shouts and bellowed commands, the sound of the crew stirring to life, making for weapons.

The danger of it is lost on Huxley. In the moment, he can only see blood and fire. He wants to destroy. To maim. To mutilate. There is nothing else. Perhaps this isn't justice. Perhaps it is only vengefulness. But such high-minded things escape him in this moment. He only knows his weapons, and what he wants them to do.

Boot steps clatter down the side of the slave cages.

Huxley extends the revolver out, stepping out in front of the others.

A man's face turns the corner of the gloom—Lizard Eyes, perhaps? His eyes land on Huxley, but by then it is too late. He tries to level a scattergun, but Huxley is already aimed and ready. He pulls the trigger and the hammer falls. Smoke and flame belch out, briefly turning the gray-white mists around them to amber and gold.

The man staggers, choking. The lead ball caught him in his throat. He tries to shout, but only sprays blood. One hand goes up to the wound, his scattergun forgotten for a moment. Huxley sees the weakness in him and it is like fuel to his fire. It only spurs him on. He cannot be stopped now.

The man with the hole in his throat stumbles forward another step. Huxley strides in quickly and lands the tomahawk on the side of his head, cleaving the top half of his cranium off and killing him instantly.

Abruptly, muzzle flashes pierce the fog all around them. Guns blazing. The sound of scattershot pebbling over the decking.

Huxley feels something nick his side.

He has no time for it. He aims for the blossom of a muzzle flash and he fires, once, then twice.

He registers that Jay is off to the side, both revolvers brandished as he moves through the mist along the slave cages, punching out with this weapon or the other and firing a shot at some target that Huxley cannot see.

Huxley himself is suddenly moving through the mist, his feet pounding the decking like they are doing their own thinking.

Bristow. I need to find Bristow.

Shapes in the darkness.

He strikes out at them with the tomahawk. One parries his stroke, and then Huxley puts the barrel of his revolver under the other man's chin and the top of the man's head pops, smoke coming out of his mouth as he falls.

Another comes, and Huxley shoots him in the gut. The slaver crumples against the side of the slave cages, screaming as he clutches at the fire in his guts. Huxley scoops the scattergun up from the ground and leaves the man who had carried it to die his slow, agonizing death.

Huxley fumbles with his weapons. He stops at the beginning of the crew quarters, both hands filled, and now the scattergun in his arms. It is loaded, the filament still hot and glowing red. Huxley jams his revolver back in his waistband, the barrel warm against his groin like some horrible lover that he cannot leave. He slides the tomahawk through his belt. He holds the rough-hewn stock of the scattergun at hip level and moves toward the crew quarters, winding up the filament a little more to make sure it is hot enough.

The door is hanging open, just barely.

Huxley noses it with the muzzle.

The door bursts open.

Huxley senses the force of another man at the other end of his gun. The barrel is being pressed suddenly skyward. He sees the shape, backlit by the glow of a fire—a big man, thick in the shoulders, thick in the hips. Fat, perhaps, but powerful, and Huxley cannot get the muzzle of the scattergun back down. Simply out of reflex, he pulls the trigger. The gun fires, a gigantic, enveloping *boom* and then it is being ripped from his hands. The cloud of gunsmoke hangs there, mixed with the mist, and Master Bristow pummels through it, the scattergun in his hands, and for a moment, Huxley thinks that the man will use it to try to beat him to death.

He manages to get one of his revolvers out.

But Bristow throws the scattergun aside and rushes headlong into Huxley. The weight and simple mass of the man cannot be resisted. Huxley feels the air going out of him as the slave master hits him. Huxley is tipped backward, the world upended, and it seems to him that he is in the air for a long time. And then his back hits the decking hard, and he feels sharp pains and dull pains, and the sensation of things cracking inside of him.

Hard, iron hands on his neck, rough like sandpaper.

Hot, rank breath in his face, like a furnace wind cutting through the dank fog. "I fucking knew you would do this! I knew you had no honor, you piece of shit! You couldn't resist, could you? I'm gonna fucking squeeze the life out of you! Gonna squeeze it right out of you!"

Huxley feels his windpipe closing under the pressure of those hands.

He realizes the revolver has been knocked from his grip when he fell.

The stars in his vision clear momentarily, now replaced with black at the edges that wants to creep in, but still, in the center of his vision, he can see Bristow's face, all fury and rage and darkness, his teeth bared, spittle clumped white at the corners of his mouth like he is a rabid dog.

A rabid dog. That's all you are.

I am not weak.

I will survive this thing, this slave master, this human filth …

Huxley ignores the hands around his neck. The moment is strange because he can think so clearly in it, where it seemed impossible to him before. In that moment, with oxygen in his system running out, and pain in his body screaming at him, and the sensation that his larynx is going to collapse, he knows for certain that he will never be able to pry those hands from around his neck. So he ignores them. He moves to a different option.

Bristow is so incensed, he cannot feel Huxley's hands scrambling for the other revolver in his belt. Huxley's fingers quest across his belt line, his waist-line, searching for the cold wooden grip, that curved, hard combination of metal and wood.

Where? Where? It's gone. Where did it go?

Then he feels it, jabbing in his back.

Must have shifted positions on him.

Now it is pinned beneath him.

He tries to roll his body, to hitch himself up enough that he can get his hand underneath him and draw that second revolver, but Bristow is a big man, and straddled completely atop of Huxley, choking the life out of him, bearing all his weight down. He can't roll. He can't get to that gun.

Not now! Not this!

The blackness is advancing across his vision now, swallowing him like the fog had swallowed the slave barge. He can see almost nothing, except for Bristow's eyes, the cold, dark eyes, just barely visible in the night, like they have some inner glow of hellfire.

Is this how it ends?

Failed?

Weak?

Then the pressure on his neck is gone.

Air floods his lungs, so cold that it feels hot.

The black retreats from his eyes.

He sees, but does not immediately understand.

Bristow backpedaling. Two hands that are not his own are clutching the sides of his face, the fingers sinking into his eye sockets. The big slave master is bellowing like a beast in combat. He is rearing back, trying to reach ineffectively to whoever is behind him.

Rigo.

Rigo, clinging to the big man's back with a manic look of terror and ferocity on his face.

Bristow slams himself back against the wall of the crew quarters. Rigo yelps, but he doesn't let go. He's latched on like a fighting dog to another's jugular, refusing to release. Those fingers, formed into claws, sinking into Bristow's eye sockets, scraping red lines through his flesh.

Huxley stumbles to his feet.

Bristow thrashes about, still trying to slam Rigo back into the wall, trying to get the smaller man to release the hold on his face. His hands and arms are up, reaching for Rigo, trying to unlatch him. Exposing himself. Exposing his whole great, wobbling midsection.

Huxley's feet feel like wooden trunks underneath him—dull, and insensate. But he takes one staggering step forward, pulling air through his swollen throat. He yanks the tomahawk from his belt and takes a single swipe that strikes Bristow in his midsection, opening his abdomen from hip to hip.

Bristow curls inward with an odd, unmanly scream, and Rigo releases him. The large man doubles over, hands going to his stomach as he falls to his knees, trying to keep things from tumbling out. He hits the ground and pitches face-first onto the deck, still screaming.

Huxley plants the blade of the tomahawk in the back of the man's head, silencing him.

Die. Die like the dog you are.

He stares down at the dead man, then up at the rest of the slave barge, breathing hard, smelling the smells of death and sulfurous gunsmoke. In the fog, all across the dark deck, men are crying out. Some of them are the slaves, and they are scared. One or two are slavers, crying out in agony as they die. Huxley feels no horror at what he's done. He feels a burgeoning sense of vindication, an undeniable sense of satisfaction. And it is this sensation, and only this, that gives him pause.

He is baring his teeth as he breathes hard through his swollen throat, and the air feels like hot rage, and he wonders how much his face looks like he is grinning in that moment.

They wouldn't recognize you, the little thought needles at him.

But they are dead. And I am alive.

I am avenging them. They would understand.

They would have to.

Because it's too late. Too late to turn back now.

"Did we get them all?" Huxley asks, feeling his own pain beginning to make it through the veil of adrenaline.

Rigo looks up at Huxley like he doesn't recognize him for a moment. Then he shrugs and nods toward the crew quarters where the door still hangs open.

Huxley touches his side and absentmindedly notices it is wet.

I've been hit. Shot or cut. Not sure which.

Am I okay?

I'm still standing, so I think I'm okay.

He brandishes the tomahawk and takes out the fully loaded revolver he'd been trying to grasp around his back.

Huxley and Rigo move to the open door of the crew quarters. Huxley uses the blade of his tomahawk to pull it open the rest of the way. It bangs loudly against the back wall. Inside the quarters, it is light enough to see clearly. Two oil lanterns hang from the ceiling, rocking back and forth. A heavy brazier of some dubious construction sits in the middle of the room filled with red embers. It sends up tendrils of smoke that wander up to the ceiling and slip out a small ventilation hole.

It is stiflingly warm inside the crew quarters. As he steps closer to it, the heat from the brazier tightens the skin around his face. He feels sickly and out of sorts for some reason. Unsure of himself like a small part of his old mind, his weak mind, is trying to reassert itself, trying to tell himself that he does not have to be an animal, that he can still be civilized, but he knows that is not true. There are no more civilized people left in the world. They have all been murdered by the animals.

The room is one big square. There are bunks on the walls, simple affairs that are lashed in place with ropes and pieces of wood, the bedding made of old wool blankets that look half-eaten away. Everything is tossed about, a scene of disorder and panic that lies still while their recent inhabitants die screaming outside, or are already dead.

Most of them are already dead.

Except, perhaps the man that Huxley gut-shot.

He is probably the one still loudly clinging to life.

Huxley steps past the brazier, feeling sick again, but this time it is different. Not sick with the things he has done—this time he actually feels faint. He scans the room, feeling a clammy sweat break out across his forehead, his nose, his upper lip. Things seem watery and unsteady to him.

"Lowell?" he says, his hand going again to his side, this time pressing into the wetness there, finding the hole in his jacket. He feels the wound underneath, ragged and moist, and it smarts from his touch, the salt of his skin.

Where's Lowell? Did they hurt him? Did they kill him?

Maybe he was hit with a stray round.

He remembers his hallucination the previous night, the boy standing there, but in Huxley's mind, he saw the girl …

Huxley clears his throat, then spits. Blinks rapidly.

If I lose him, I will forget …

"Lowell!" he says again, louder.

This time there is a stirring from the back of the room. The shadows underneath the bunks are deep, but Huxley can see the movement in them. First it squirms, and then it slides out, very slowly, very cautiously. The boy is looking around the room, his eyes wide. On his wrists are manacles, chained together, and bolted to the wall nearest to the bunk he'd emerged from.

Relief nearly knocks Huxley to his knees.

You know this is not your kid. He's not your daughter. You have not found or saved your daughter. Only a boy who is no blood of yours.

But despite this cold voice in the background of his mind, Huxley moves quickly to Lowell. "Are you okay?" Huxley grabs the boy's manacled hands, inspecting the lock on them, but there is none. They are simply bolted on tight. "Are you hurt?"

Lowell looks up at him. His eyes are strange to Huxley. They search him like they do not believe his sincerity. They hope, as though they want to be cut free, but they hesitate like any freedom given by Huxley could just as soon be taken away.

Huxley takes the boy by the shoulders and looks him in the eyes. "I wasn't going to let them have you, Lowell. I had to get on the boat somehow. We had to get out of there somehow. Or the Black Hat would have killed us all.

You included, just because you were with me. We needed to get on this boat, and selling you was the only way to do it. I never intended to leave you. I was just waiting for the right time. Okay? Just waiting for the right time."

Lowell looks shell-shocked, like he is trying to comprehend what he's heard.

"Do you believe me?" Huxley asks, feeling the room begin to spin again. He leans heavily on the boy.

Lowell doesn't seem to notice. He nods his head once.

Huxley gets to work with fumbling fingers, to undo the bolt and security clasp that hold the manacles in place. They are positioned in a way that is difficult for anyone to get to, let alone the person whose hands are manacled. Still, it must have been a temporary solution. The other shackles and manacles he had seen were all riveted.

"You have to trust me, Lowell," Huxley says as he works. He feels his tongue getting thick in his mouth. He is extremely thirsty.

This time, the words find their way into the strange machinations of Lowell's brain. His accusing and assessing eyes relent, look briefly ashamed, and then drop to the floor. "Thank you, Mr. Huxley."

Huxley manages to get the bolt of the manacles out and drops the whole thing to the floor. He reaches into his right side and draws the knife out that he keeps there. He flips the handle around so that he is holding it by the sharp blade, and he pushes the handle into Lowell's hands.

"Take this," Huxley says. "Take it. I'll get you a gun later, but for now, you take this. Okay?"

Lowell closes his hand around the bone grip, staring at the blade. "Okay."

"You're a man now." Huxley takes the boy by the shoulders, grasps him hard, trying to make him understand how important this is. How important it is that he learns to be violent. Because Huxley is suddenly terrified that he will not be able to protect the child. He'd never taught Nadine how to be violent. He wonders if she would be alive today if he had. He'd never taught her how to be strong. "Listen to me, Lowell. Those people that you call your mother and father? They weren't. They adopted you. Your real mother and father are dead, Lowell. Probably killed by slavers."

There is no way for Huxley to know this, but the boy needs to harden himself to what they are doing, what they will continue to do. He needs to direct his anger. It is just as likely as any other explanation. The boy spoke Spanish, and

Huxley could see that maybe his family had been a part of a caravan. He has some Caucasian in him, but the olive skin and dark hair and eyes are likely Hispanic. Maybe they'd been hit by the slavers like Rigo's family.

"The people you called Mother and Father wanted you to be different than what you are. They wanted you to keep all that stuff inside of you. They were frightened of you. Because they didn't know if they could control you."

Huxley watches the boy's chin, quivering, but no tears come to his eyes. "Let it out, Lowell. You have to be strong. You have to be violent. That's how you survive. You know this. I can see that you know it. I can see that you can be violent but they've tried to stifle that in you. Let it out."

Lowell hesitates again, but then nods. "Okay."

"Stay in here and watch this room. If anyone tries to come in here and mess with you, scream loud and start working them with the knife. You understand?"

"A man don't need to scream for help," Lowell says, his voice flat.

"A man is smart enough to know when he's smaller than everyone else. And he knows who his friends are. I'm your friend, Lowell. That's me. Your only friend in the world." Huxley points his finger at the boy as he backs up toward the door. "No man is an island unto himself. You know what that means?"

Lowell shakes his head.

"It means a smart man doesn't try to go it alone. You call if you need help."

"Okay."

Huxley turns to the door. Don is there now, with Rigo, just inside of it. Don is looking at the boy and the look on his face does not escape Huxley. It is half a sneer, half a smile.

Huxley stops abreast of Don and looks hard at him. "Why don't you come with me?"

Don keeps staring at the boy. "Yeah. Sure."

Then he turns and follows Huxley and Rigo out.

Out of the crew quarters, the cold air braces him, but only momentarily. Then the faintness comes back, the darkness clawing away the reality at the edges of his vision. His sense of balance seems precarious, oddly enough.

How much blood? How much blood did I lose?

He touches his side again. Warm and hot. The blood still flowing.

"They got you good in the side," Don observes with a snarky tone.

"I'm fine," Huxley mumbles. There are other things on his mind. Other things that must be done. *I need to focus on that. Focus on the anger. Don't let that go. That's your lifesaver. Hold on to it.*

"The fucker …" Huxley mumbles to himself as he makes it to the corner of the slave cages. "… the bastard …"

Huxley turns the corner. The world sways, swoons. Huxley holds on to the gap in the slave cages' walls that he's able to get his fingers through to keep him from falling. There is the door to the slave cages. There are two bodies there. Dead men leaking blood across the deck. Jay stands over them with two smoking guns, smiling up at the dark sky, like he's seen something strange and beautiful in the fog.

"Where is he?" Huxley demands.

Jay looks down from the skies and meets Huxley's gaze. Then he shrugs and points one of his revolvers into the slave cages, almost lazily. "Somewhere in there." His eyes scan over Huxley and he frowns. "Seems you've sprung a leak."

Huxley grunts, steps over the bodies on the ground, then goes through the door into the heat and smoke and stench of the slave cages. He brandishes one revolver and thumbs back the hammer, inspecting the cylinder by lantern light and ensuring that there is an unused cap on the nipple. He cannot remember how many shots he has fired.

One good round, he says, seeing the cap. *One is all I need.*

"Who yelled?" Huxley demands.

There is a long and total silence.

He raises his voice. "Who the *fuck* yelled?"

Again, there are only the eyes of young men and women, and numerous boys and girls, glancing around at each other, knowing, but not knowing whether to say so. Huxley watches them for a moment and thinks, *not too late to turn away from this course.*

But if he'd betrayed Huxley once, he'd do it again.

Huxley gestures about the room with his revolver. "Every one of you is free now. Everyone but the one who dimed us out to the slavers. Your captors. The people who mistreated you. Every one of you gets a second chance from this point forward. Except that one. That one I'm going to kill." Huxley gives a moment, working more saliva into his mouth. He knows that his words are slurring together, that he must be swaying on his feet. He wishes he could appear strong, but perhaps that is not in the cards right now. At this moment, he only needs to handle the problem.

"You can tell me who it was," Huxley says, in a much quieter voice, so that the sound of the river lapping at the bottom of the barge almost overtakes him. "Or I can start on one side of the room and see how far I get before I run out of lead. Maybe I'll get that sonofabitch just by pure chance."

"It was him," a small voice says.

Huxley snaps his head to his left, scans, sees a young girl standing against the bars, pointing, one single, scrawny arm, tipped with one single, wiry finger, a little needle that gauges out a man who stands against the back wall, his arms hugged around himself, his eyes full of terror. He is a sad thing, a skinny thing, as they all are. He is perhaps twenty years of age, maybe a little younger. Black hair that shoots out on all sides in a tangled mess. Sunken cheeks. Dark, tremulous eyes.

He raises his head up, but strangely, he does not deny the accusation.

Huxley walks to the cage, the pain in his side now asserting itself and causing his gait to hitch.

As Huxley approaches, the man begins to shake his head. "You're idiots. You're all fucking idiots. You can't stop the slavers. You can't steal from them! We were headed for rich households, I heard Master Bristow say it! All of you young ones, you would have been stewards and playmates for councilmen's children. Now you're *free*." The man laughs bitterly. "Free to do what? Wander around in the Wastelands? An orphan? Starve to death on a city street? That's the only life for any of you now, because you're not going to make it out in the wilds. On a fucking city street begging for scraps, when you could have been fed and clothed and kept by councilmen."

Huxley reaches the bars—these ones made of wooden beams—and he braces himself against them with one hand, staring through to the man that speaks.

The man meets his eyes. Fear, yes. But bitterness and resignation as well.

He shakes his head. "You can't beat the slavers, you idiot."

Huxley shoots the man in the chest.

There is a collective cry and the rest of the slaves jump away, like water pulsing outward when a stone hits a still pond.

The man with the dark wild hair jerks back into the wall and his legs go out from under him, collapsing to the ground.

Huxley watches in numb silence.

A single cough from the man, blood splattering out of his mouth. His chest strains for breath, hitching up and down several times, and then quite suddenly it is still. The man's mouth, wide open, as though in his last moment he thought that if he opened his mouth wide enough he might get some air into his lungs. His eyes, staring right back at Huxley. For a moment, fear leaves them and it is just that anger, like the slave is determined to *will* himself through the hole in his chest. But when his chest gives out, the fear returns to his eyes, and it stays there until they fade.

He dies on the stinking, filthy floor, still staring at Huxley.

Peripherally, Huxley hears something hit the floor.

He looks down and realizes that he has dropped his revolver.

Raven wings beat and batten at his eyes, covering them in darkness. But there are colors there, too. The brightest, sparkling white he's ever seen. Rich, deep purple. Red as bright as arterial blood, with which Huxley is uncomfortably familiar. He tries to blink to clear his vision, and he can see, like looking through a keyhole. He can see his revolver lying on the ground. He bends to pick it up.

Then he falls and feels nothing.

CHAPTER 11

He is not dead, he doesn't think.

Well ... maybe.

Maybe this is heaven or hell or purgatory or the sea of glass.

Wouldn't that be nice? Wouldn't that be peaceful? A sea of glass?

Glass shards, ripping him to shreds.

Everything has an evil side.

"Just like you," a voice says, cataclysmic in its familiarity.

"No, no, no," Huxley says. He can feel his mouth moving, but he cannot hear his words. He sees nothing. Around him is only darkness. "You're dead. You're gone."

"Everything has an evil side, doesn't it?"

He screams. He is terrified, though he doesn't know why. He is terrified by things that speak to him from beyond the grave. He forces his eyes open and when he does, he smells wood smoke and sees everything around him is on fire, burning brightly in places, charred black in others. Ash is falling from the sky, a great open sky as though the roof of whatever wooden structure he is inside has been burned away and the slate clouds over his head are just one giant smudge of soot.

He is lying on his back, on a bed of some sort. Or perhaps an altar. It feels hard, like stone. This registers with him, oddly enough, and he thinks again, *this cannot be real. This is a dream, or a nightmare, or I am dead, and the great mystery is being answered.*

What comes after?

Fire and soot and ash.

Terror.

A woman is standing over him. The source of the voice that he recognizes so well.

Charity.

The sight of her fills him with sudden and unabashed panic. Because he is covered in blood. She can see his sins. She can see *into* him. She knows everything that he has done from this day back to the day he lost her. He cannot hide it all from her. And in his dream state, though the perfect details of her memory are still foggy and hard to see, her eyes are very poignant. And in them he can see that she is ashamed.

No, no, no …

Huxley is weeping. Like he has not in a long time. His sobs are silent in his own ears, but he can feel them shaking his body, he can feel the tears, hot in his eyes and cold on his cheeks.

"You don't understand," he tries to plead.

"What have you become?" She reaches out a hand and touches his face, her own eyes filled with sadness as she looks down at him. He wants that hand to be real so badly, but he knows that it is not, it cannot be, because he buried her a very long time ago, and the wounds that had led her to the grave are nowhere on her body, no evidence of that violent day that tore her away from him.

"I don't want to be here," he tells her, sobbing. "I don't want to be here anymore. Please, just take me with you. I just want to be with you again. Wherever you are. Just take me with you."

She only shakes her head. "All the things you've done …"

"For you!" Huxley cries out. "For Nadine!"

Still shaking her head. "I barely recognize you anymore."

"Don't leave me here!"

But she is gone.

In her place is Jay.

There is no more fire. Now the world is coated in a soft layer of ash, and it is ice cold. Cold enough for Huxley to see his breath, though he cannot see Jay's. Cold enough to trick the mind into thinking that all this whiteness around them is snow, until you see that it is gray and not white. It is dirty, not clean. And Jay is there. Standing over him, and he is bloody too, but it is not his own blood. He is bathed to the elbows in other people's blood. His chest and face are smeared with it. And he grins, his white teeth like blazes through the crimson.

"The weak die," he says. "But the strong live."

Huxley opens his eyes, and he is awake this time, and this time he knows that it is real. It is real because he can feel the cold and the pain, a hot poker in his side. He only sees dimly, reality shrouded by his black dreams, but there is someone there that he doesn't recognize, and their hands are at his side, and for a flash Huxley thinks that they are trying to crawl inside his open wound.

Huxley jerks upright, snatching a thin wrist and wrenching it away from him. His other hand gropes about his waist for his knife, realizes that it is gone, then tries for one of his revolvers. He feels the wood and steel handle and he yanks it free, not sure if this is the one that is empty, but he doesn't care. He levels the long-barreled handgun at his attacker, thumbing back the hammer, taking ragged breaths.

"Who are you?" he demands. "Don't fucking touch me!"

Nightmares and realities swirl and eddy. But his vision clears enough to see the face that is staring back at him. It is a young woman—one of the slaves, he assumes—long of face, with a tangled mess of brown hair, and dark eyes that look back at him, not with terror, but with a calm like a slow-moving pool that gathers at the side of a fast river.

That, above all else, stays him from pulling the trigger.

The calmness in her eyes. Like she knows him. Like she knew that this would happen. He did not surprise her. She is not shocked.

His hand is still clenched around one of her wrists, and he looks at her hand, the way it lays limp in his grip, the way he has her wrist torqued, causing the fingers to splay out all in one direction. Where his fingers sink into her skin, her flesh turns white. But the rest of her hands are covered in blood.

My blood, he realizes.

It must be painful for her but she doesn't react to it. She ignores the big bore of the gun barrel just inches from her face, the delicate balance of pressure from that finger twitching on the trigger—just an ounce or so more and her head would be caved in. She ignores all of that, and she raises the hand that she still has free. She shows Huxley her open palm. And then, very gently, she pushes the muzzle of his revolver away from her face.

"Mr. Huxley, my name is Brie," she says evenly. "I'm trying to help you."

Huxley feels his heart, knocking against his chest plate, heavy like solid iron. His lungs burn with the desire to breathe. He sucks in air, feels the coldness in his chest, pushes the air out, sucks more in. He breathes rapidly for a moment, feeling panic trying to take hold of him, he looks around for something solid to cling to.

What he finds is Jay.

Standing where Huxley had not seen him before.

Jay nods to him, but says nothing.

"What happened?" Huxley croaks at Jay.

It is Brie who answers, now beginning to twist her wrist away from him, not suddenly, but slowly, getting the point across to his tattered mind that she is trying to extricate herself. He realizes his grip is still latched onto her like a vice. He loosens his grip, then releases it altogether as she speaks again, her voice so calm in that moment that it salves him.

"You've been shot. Scattergun, I think." She rubs her wrist, then looks at him again, not seeming to take offense. "You got four holes in you. Two chunks of something still inside of you—the other two were through-and-through. I don't think they hit any of your organs, but you bled a lot and we need to get projectiles out of you before they cause an infection."

Huxley closes his eyes tightly. "You digging your fingers around inside of me is going to cause an infection."

"Maybe," she admits. "But if the projectiles are lead ball, leaving them in will give you lead poisoning. I can poultice an infection. I can't solve heavy metal poisoning."

Huxley slows his heaving chest, forcing himself to breathe through his nose. "Who are you?"

"My name's Brie."

"I know your name is Brie." Huxley opens his eyes and flashes an angry look at her. "I mean how do you know this shit and where did you come from?"

Brie, for the first time, looks slightly unsettled, but it is a mild look that passes over her face and then is gone. "I'm one of the slaves. My settlement got raided. Small, pioneering settlement. I was the daughter of the resident healer."

"How old are you?"

"Twenty."

Huxley looks her up and down with a critical eye. Her form is much like her face—long and thin and unfortunate. She wears a heavy brown tunic of sorts and if she had any beauty to her figure, it was hidden from him. He meets her eyes again. "You're a little old for a female slave."

She sniffs. "And not quite pretty enough?" She bends back to his side, addressing his burning wound with her thin, bloody fingers. "No, I wasn't taken for pleasure," she says, and she says the word in a way that is both relieved and resentful. "Medicine is a valuable field. Even a novice can get a good price." She shrugs. "So I'm told."

"You're not a slave anymore," Huxley says, trying to relax and let her work. Every time she touches his wound it feels like a branding iron.

She furrows her brow and takes hold of a thin metal shank. "Am I not?"

"Are the slavers dead?" Huxley says through gritted teeth.

Brie glances at him, her look inscrutable, and then she pries her fingers into one of his wounds and slips the metal shank in. Huxley does his best not to cry out, but every muscle in his body locks down against the pain and it takes everything he has not to smack her away from him. The sound comes out of him in ragged scream, muffled behind his clamped lips.

It feels like she is being intentionally rough as she jabs around inside of him.

He looks down, closes his eyes and prays for it to be over.

She's just trying to hurt you! God knows what she's doing! She doesn't know what she's doing!

He is about to wrench away from her when he feels the odd sensation of something being *scooped* from inside of him, and he hears the sound of something small and weighty hitting the wooden deck.

"Holy *fuck*!" he gasps, leaning away from her and looking down at the ground.

Brie bends to pick up what has dropped.

She holds it up, pinched between her thumb and forefinger.

A lead ball.

"Good thing I'm getting them out of you," she says flatly.

Huxley collapses back onto the bunk that is serving as his operating table. He takes a few breaths, then reiterates his question. "Are the slavers dead?"

"Yes," Brie says. "They're dead."

"Then why wouldn't you be free?"

She rolls the bloody ball between her fingers. "Dead slavers isn't all it takes to be free."

"What else does it take?"

Brie sniffs and drops the lead ball into a little tin can that contains a brown liquid that Huxley can smell from where he is—whiskey. "We're on a slave barge, in the middle of a river, in the middle of the Riverlands. Chances are, most of us will be rounded up soon after we leave the barge. Particularly if we dock at Shreveport." She takes up the thin shank of metal again, but she pauses as she bends to his side. Almost as an afterthought, not even looking at Huxley, she asks, "Who's Charity?"

He turns at her sharply, suddenly the pain in his side forgotten. He raises his hand toward her but manages to catch himself before he touches her. She doesn't flinch or shrink away from the sudden, violent movement toward her. But her eyes look down at his hand and her expression seems to realize that she is treading on thin ice. She looks into his eyes and there is an unspoken apology of sorts there. But also a knowing.

Huxley wants to hurt her. He wants to strike at her. He has no explanation for why. The same reason you strike an inanimate object that has inadvertently caused you pain. It is a simple reaction. But the fact that she is a person, a young woman, and she is trying to help him, it stays his hand.

He cannot keep the fury out of his voice, though. It shakes when he speaks, as quietly as he can, so that it comes out in a husky whisper. "Don't ever talk about her."

Brie stares back at him for a moment, then nods, just once.

Huxley falls back into his bunk.

Brie bends to her agonizing work.

Huxley can see Jay, standing in the room, watching him carefully, hearing the question that Brie had just asked, seeing Huxley's reaction. *I must have said her name when I was asleep. He would have heard me. He knows. Just like Brie knows.*

He closes his eyes as he feels the tears coming to them. He covers his face with his hand. He forces himself to remain still while Brie works, and the pain permeates through him, but he is distracted by what aches in his mind.

The next lead ball takes more effort to remove from his side. Gradually, the pain turns from something sharp and pointed to something dull and throbbing, but still extreme. It makes the entire left side of his body ache. The back of his neck prickles with gooseflesh and sweat breaks out across his skin. His toes and the soles of his feet tingle unpleasantly as his nerves fire to exhaustion.

When she is finished, she drops the second lead ball into the tin can with its twin. Then she takes time to poultice the wound, and to bandage it, though Huxley is dubious of the bandages. Nothing is clean. Nothing is sterile. Hopefully she boiled the cloth beforehand. If not, the ensuing infection would be a painful bill to pay.

She does all of this without speaking. She does not look up at Huxley until she has tied the bandage off around his waist. Then she does look up at him, and she holds his gaze for a long and uncomfortable moment.

She has something else she wants to say.

But instead, she picks up the instruments that she had used, and she stands up and walks out.

Huxley hears her footfalls on the wooden planking as she walks back to the slave cages.

The crew's quarters are silent for a time. Huxley can hear the river below them, around them. It seems monotonous and hypnotic all at once. He is exhausted, through and through, and daylight seems on the verge of breaking. Or perhaps it is his hopeful imagination. Sometimes he looks through the cracks and seems to see the deep blue sky of a coming dawn. But then he looks again and sees only blackness.

After a time, he hears a quiet rustle of clothing, and two very slow steps on the decking.

Huxley keeps looking at the ceiling, because he knows who it is.

A hand on his leg.

Jay's voice, quietly assured of itself: "Tell me."

Huxley tilts his neck, stares at the other man's cold blue eyes, so very opposite from his own.

So very different. And yet the same.

A good man turned bad.

His own thought angers him. *I'm not bad. I've had to do bad things, that's all. Necessary evils.*

Huxley reaches his hand up to his face to rub it, but notices how badly it shakes in the air. Jay notices it too. Huxley grimaces and then plants his hand onto his beard to hide its instability. His fingers rake through the greasy, tangled mess of hair. He swallows and finds his tongue dry and his throat raw-feeling.

"Is there anything to drink?" he asks.

Jay looks behind him to a few jugs stacked in a corner. "Water and whiskey. Take your pick."

He yearns for the whiskey, but knows it will only hurt him more. "Water."

Jay turns and lackadaisically takes one of the water jugs from the floor, along with what looks like an old, plastic children's cup. It is blue. Huxley can see some sort of design on it. Jay pours it full of water and hands it over to Huxley.

Huxley takes the water down in two gulps. It tastes metallic and earthy at once, but it is cold in his throat, and wets the dry parts of him. He holds the cup for a moment longer, looking at the design. Stuffed teddy bears holding balloons, smiling happily, ignorantly. Most of their images had been worn out to nothing, but a few remained, and in their slight reliefs, dirt and grime had gathered.

Huxley puts the water cup on the floor, refusing to think about who might have owned this cup so many years ago. Perhaps no one had owned this cup. Maybe it'd been found in a raided supermarket, back before they'd been stripped down to nothing—even the wood and metal framing taken.

"Speak," Jay says, quietly, commandingly.

Huxley turns away from Jay. He faces the brazier. The embers are burning out.

What do you say? Sometimes it seems like he is waiting for inspiration to speak. For the right words. But there were no *right words*. There was just ... the past. The past was the truth. It was history recorded, if not on paper, then in his head. And there was nothing here but to spill it, to let it out of him, to tell Jay what he'd not told anyone else in the past eighteen months.

He did not know Brie. She had not earned the truth from him.

But Jay ...

Well ... Jay was Jay.

Huxley isn't even sure what that means, but he finds himself taking a breath, and then he is speaking.

"Charity was my wife," he says with the suddenness of someone making a decision to confess everything. "Nadine was my daughter. I ..." he hesitates, then starts again. "Do you ever feel like you've lived three lives? I do. I think about it sometimes. Who I was. Before the skyfire. And then after. And then now. Except that now's not really a life. It's just … a nightmare." He shakes his head. "Two lives. Two *good* lives, anyway. One bad."

Huxley smiles faintly, going far back. "In the Old World I was a school teacher. I taught English. Made kids read all the old books. We lived in a little house, in a little neighborhood. We had problems, but …" he thinks back to the things that were so major back then. Things that could bring you to the tip of divorce. Like money. Money, of all things. "We made it through. Charity got pregnant, and we stayed together and things were a little tough, but not so bad now that I look back. It was really … It just wasn't that bad. We had Nadine. She was a beautiful girl. I called her my sweet girl, because she was kind, like her mother. You could tell it from the day she was born." He smiles fully, then lets it fade. "I got to see her grow up to just past her second birthday in a normal world. And then the skyfire hit and everything went to shit, and we were running. But you know what's odd?"

Huxley looks at Jay. "It was good. Looking back, it was good. We were scared at the time. But looking back, I think we were relatively safe. We got out of the city fast enough that I think we were never really caught in any bad situations. And we were just … kind of nomadic for a time. It had its own hardships, but we were together and all the bullshit from the Old World was burned up. It was strange. We made love like we actually loved each other. And we did. I think we'd forgotten, but we remembered. That was the key. It was hard, but it made you remember who you were."

Huxley looks at his grimy hands again. Steadier now. Bloody.

"Whose hands are these?" he asks, quietly. "I don't know these hands. Mine never had another man's blood on them. They were never cut by another man's knife. Never blackened by gunpowder. Chalk. They had chalk on them. They were clean. I was clean. Clean-shaven. Healthy layer of fat—I drank a lot of wine." He laughs, as though he's said something ridiculous. "Wine," he mutters disdainfully, more to himself than Jay.

Huxley clasps his hands together, as though to hide his bloody, calloused, gun-blacked palms from his sight. "We found a commune. This was maybe two years after the skyfire. Nadine was four. She was good. She was a good kid. I remember just watching her. Just watching her walking along with us and thinking how good she was. She never complained. Always kind. She was her mother's daughter.

"The commune was small when we found it. Just a couple of other families that were trying to get together in the middle of nowhere, away from everyone else. Trying to make something. Grow some food. Live out some semblance of a life. And we stayed. And the commune grew. We had a dozen families. A bunch of kids. We had a school, but by then I was busy with farming, so I didn't teach unless I really needed to. I grew barley. Big fields of it. I built a cottage for me and Charity and Nadine. We lived there for nine years. And it was good." Huxley takes a deep shaky breath. "Those were the two lives I lived that were good."

Huxley's voice becomes low, almost trancelike, his gaze absent, faraway, as he pictures old, horrible things. "I was in the fields when I saw it. The smoke, rising up over the commune. I stood there for a minute, thinking about it, thinking about what was happening, and I was absolutely terrified. I wonder what that minute cost me now. That one minute of inaction. Maybe it cost me everything. But when I finally got my wits back, I ran, all the way back to the commune. But when I got there, they were still there. They'd set fire to every standing structure. They'd taken everything there was to take. Killed the men. And now they were raping the women, while their children watched and screamed. When they were done, they'd stab them in the gut. Birth control, one of them called it, and they laughed. They stabbed them just one time, not to kill them immediately, but to make sure they'd never make it out. So that they died slow deaths."

He looks at Jay, desperation in his eyes. "Why? Why do that, Jay? If you're gonna kill them, then kill them. But why wound them so they die so slow?"

Jay has no answer—why would he?

But he has a question: "Where were you?"

Huxley blinks rapidly, then looks away again. "Watching. Hiding and watching. Too scared to do anything about it. There were more than a dozen of them, and only one of me. I would have died. But still … I just sat there and watched. I watched them go around and take the jaws from the men. All the while the women wailing in pain. The children screaming in terror. I couldn't see where Nadine was. They had a wagon and it was filled with the kids. But I couldn't see where she was.

"Then they left. And so many of the women were still alive. They were still screaming, still crawling, and everything was burning around them, some of them couldn't crawl fast enough and they were being burned alive. I didn't know what to do. I couldn't help all of them. I couldn't help *any* of them. I was blank. I had nothing."

Huxley opens his hands and finally looks at his palms. They are dark hands. He stares into them like one might stare into a crystal ball. "I found Charity on the doorstep of our cottage. It was a shack, really. They'd dragged her out and done the same to her as they'd done to everyone else. She was holding her stomach. I could see she was bleeding. I went to her. I wish I'd had something to say, but I had nothing. I was sitting there on my knees." He looks at Jay, like he is asking for forgiveness. "I was weak. That's why they're gone."

Jay considers this for a time. "How long ago was this?"

"Eighteen months. A year and a half." Huxley hates himself for it. "I tried to go after them, straight out of the commune. But ... I caught something." He laughs, a dry wheeze at the ridiculousness of it all. "Something in the water or food I ate when I was going after them. I was eating anything I could get my hands on. Drinking from stagnant puddles. It was something in my gut. I knew I wasn't going to make it across the desert. I found another commune. Barely alive. And they kept me from dying, but they demanded I help with the harvest to pay for the care they'd given me. They were smaller than my commune had been. They didn't have enough people. And by the time I got my strength back and paid them off ..."

Huxley trails off.

Jay fixes him with a stare. "That's too long, Huxley. You know it's too long."

Huxley frowns at him. He doesn't understand why Jay would say that. Has he been listening to anything Huxley has said? Does he even care?

"Your daughter is ..." Jay sighs. "It would be hopeless to try to find her."

Huxley comes up a bit, leaning on an elbow. "I know that, Jay! I'm not an idiot. I know it's been too long, you don't need to tell me." He leans back down again. "I'm not looking for my daughter."

Jay spreads his hands. "Relax, Huxley. Don't attack me on this. I'm not the enemy. But we're going to Shreveport for a reason. And it's your reason. I'm trying to understand it. I'm trying. Help me out here."

If you're going to tell him the truth, tell him the whole truth. He knows most of it anyway.

Huxley continues. "Just before she died, Charity said that it was a man with a scorpion tattoo. He was the one that killed her. He was the one that took my daughter. I know that I can't find her, I know I can't bring my wife back from the dead, and I'm not trying." Huxley has to restrain himself from raising his voice. "I'm not trying to do that. But if this man is still alive, then I intend to find him, Jay. And I'm going to kill him."

Jay frowns down at Huxley for a few moments, then looks away. "I understand. I'm here for the same reason as you, Huxley. The same exact reasons. But I don't want a man. I don't care about the man. I want them all. I want to terrify them. I want to make them feel what I felt—what you felt when you saw the smoke coming out of your commune." Huxley watches the muscles in Jay's face clench and unclench, a vein in his temple becoming more prominent. "Blood and death, Huxley. That's all there is once we step off this boat. Just blood and death."

Huxley lies back again, staring at the ceiling. The only sounds in the cabin for a time are the steady lapping of the river, and the creaking and groaning of the old wooden barge rocking away in its berth.

"Don't talk about this," Huxley says finally. "Don't tell anyone what I've told you."

CHAPTER 12

It is in the predawn hours when Huxley wakes again. He opens his eyes to see the brazier dark and cold, but the light through the cracks is that deep blue-black of a morning just shortly over the horizon. He knows that something has stirred him, but he is half in and half out of sleep, and strange dreams of terror and love and bloodlust still color everything he sees, and the pain in his side is hot and excruciating. He is cold, but sweat dots his brow, chilly and greasy.

Jay is not in the room.

And yet, Huxley is not alone.

His eyes track to the door, and there he sees what caused him to wake.

A dark, smallish shadow standing there with the closed door to its back.

"Lowell?" Huxley says in a dry, thin whisper.

There is something in Lowell's hands, and for a half second, Huxley feels fear. But it is a low flame, and it blows out in the midst of everything else. Huxley is so full of other, darker fears, that it seems he has no room for more. Besides, why should he fear this child?

The wild is in his eyes.

Lowell steps carefully away from the door, his footsteps almost inaudible, his steps chosen and placed, padded like a cat. He is a stealthy creature when he wants to be. Huxley can see that Lowell's arms are glistening like he is wearing wet sleeves. And the object that he holds, long and thin ...

The knife I gave him.

He stands in front of Huxley now, at the side of his bunk.

Huxley looks the kid up and down. Wild-eyed waif. Fearful urchin. Dangerous creature.

Blood. He's covered in blood.

Is this a dream?

"What are you doing?" Huxley asks, as his own hand strays to the revolver that still lies in his waistband.

Huxley has been so focused on the blood and the knife, that he hasn't looked up into Lowell's eyes until that second, and he sees the tears in them, just a thin layer, which the child quickly blinks away. He is silent though, his mouth seeming to be clamped shut.

Huxley considers asking his question again, or perhaps asking whose blood is on Lowell's hands, but then Lowell sinks down to the ground, not as though he is fainting, but a controlled crumpling, and he curls into a ball at the side of Huxley's bunk.

Huxley leans over the side of the bunk and looks down at the child. Bloody and strange, Lowell holds the knife to his chest as though it brings him comfort. Both hands clasped around the handle, the blade glimmering weakly in the light of the coming dawn. Very still, and very silent, Lowell closes his eyes and seems to be instantly asleep.

Huxley stares at the child for a time before exhaustion takes him under again.

His dreams continue as though he never left them. They wait on the other side of his consciousness with open arms and then they drag him down, they smother him. He falls into them, and they are the same as before, but now the strange child is standing before him, bathed in blood, with a bloody knife in his hand, and he is trying to push it into Huxley's chest.

Huxley has his hand on Lowell's, staying him, but the boy seems incredibly strong. The tip of the knife is inching slowly to his chest.

"Why are you doing this?" Huxley's voice is a weak whisper.

The boy only stares on with those wild eyes of his, pressing the knife closer.

Then the knife slips and slices into Huxley's side.

Huxley wakes up, reaching for his wounded side and feeling someone else's fingers there. Anger and fear make him come fully awake. He grasps two of the fingers in his fist and pulls them away from his side.

It is Brie, standing over him with a look of consternation and concern on her long face.

Huxley groans, feeling the ache of his wounds overcome his sudden reactions. "You again."

"Just checking the wound," she says, shaking her fingers away from his grip. "Seeing if it looks inflamed."

"Infected, you mean?"

"Yes." She leans down and peels the bit of bandaging back to inspect those little holes in his flesh that could cause such problems. She makes a face like she's not happy. "Well. It could be better, but it could be much worse. Little bit of reddening around them. How do you feel? Feverish at all?"

Huxley takes a few breaths to see how he feels, then shakes his head.

Brie nods. She seems to be coming down to something in her mind.

"What is it?" Huxley asks, seeing her expression.

"You feel good enough to walk?"

Huxley glances over at the bunk beside him, sees that Jay is now awake, watching the two of them. Huxley turns back to Brie and nods, swinging his legs out of bed with significant effort and pain.

"Yeah," he strains to get the words out without making them sound like lies. "I can walk."

His legs are fine. But each step engages the muscles in his side where lead balls had so recently been lodged. He walks carefully, but glances down at the base of his bed. Lowell is huddled there like a lost dog, awake and watchful, but not moving from his spot. There is something like guilt in his eyes, and Huxley notes that his hands are still reddened, though he wiped the majority of the blood off on his pants and shirt where they left dark brown stains.

Lowell watches him.

Neither says a word.

Jay climbs out of bed and follows behind, not waiting for an invitation, and certainly not expecting one. Brie leads them outside of the crew quarters, out onto the decking, where a clear morning is breaking, sharp as a knife, with no trace of the fog from the previous night, and not a cloud apparent in the blue sky.

Brie shrugs her shoulders against a slight autumn chill. She leads them around the mass of the slave cages that takes up the majority of the barge, past the doors that lead in, and to the starboard corner, where, slumped against a pile of ropes and a set of oars, Don lies.

Huxley stands there, looking at the man for a minute, not quite computing what he is seeing.

Don is dead. That becomes apparent almost immediately. His skin is milky white. His eyes glazed. His neck and chest are dark red, almost black. Someone has opened his throat with two cuts, the first shallow and hesitating, and the second strong, deep, and running from ear to ear.

"Hm," Jay grunts from where he has appeared beside Huxley. "That's interesting."

Brie watches Huxley carefully. "We found him like this, not ten minutes ago. It was none of us. I'm the only one that's unchained. And it wasn't me. I was in with the others all night. I swear by that. You can ask anyone in there."

Huxley nods, slowly. "No. I believe you."

He looks back toward the slave cages and sees Lowell there, standing at the corner. The two of them lock eyes for a brief moment, and then Lowell turns to duck away.

"Lowell," Huxley calls out, keeping his voice calm.

He watches the corner of the slave cages for a long moment.

Lowell turns the corner again. He stands hesitantly, but also with a certain posture, as though he has been caught, but he is challenging Huxley to do something about it. *Why would I?* he thinks. *This is what I told you to do. I told you to let it out. And Don ... Don kept pushing you.*

He motions Lowell over—just a quick wave of his hand.

The boy takes his steps slowly, judgingly at first. But then his strides lengthen, quicken, and he is standing before Huxley, watching him very carefully. Like something that could very easily destroy you, but you remain calm simply because ... you don't think it will.

A moment of silence lengthens between them.

Just the water on the underside of the barge.

Huxley asks, "You kill him?"

Lowell glances down at the body. His expression is unknowable.

"Did you?" Huxley presses.

Lowell straightens. "Yes."

"Why?"

"Because he would've killed me," Lowell says, taking the words slowly. "And because he killed Mother."

Huxley can't do anything but nod. He can't be angry. He looks to Jay, who just shrugs. Then to Brie, who evaluates the boy carefully. Then to the body, the blood long stopped pumping. Killed sometime in the night. Just before he entered Huxley's cabin, covered in blood. Don's blood.

Finally he looks at the boy. "Why are you cowering then? Like you're in trouble?"

Lowell is silent.

Huxley bends at the waist, down so that his eyes are on a level with Lowell's. "This is dirty business, Lowell." He remembers Jay's own words. "There's nothing ahead of us but blood and death. You need to be able to handle that. You need to understand it." Huxley straightens, looking this time to Brie. "You need to understand it too."

Brie seems a bit surprised at the sudden switch.

Huxley gestures to the slave cages. "You said you were the only one unchained?"

She nods.

"What are you going to do when this ship lands in Shreveport?" he asks her. "What are all the slaves in there going to do? If I pull those chains off, what happens? Do they go home?"

"Home?" she lets out a black chuckle. "We don't have homes anymore, Mr. Huxley." Her face goes bitter. "The slavers destroyed them along with everything else. No. If you pull the chains off … I'm not sure what they'll do. They've got no place to go. And I'm no different. Some of us might be able to sneak in as freemen and find work—those of us old enough to have a skill. I'm sure I could."

Huxley is nodding as she talks.

She stops and eyes him. "What are you doing? You and your men?"

"You don't want that."

"Maybe I do." There's a glimmer in her eyes that he hadn't seen before. A hardness. "Maybe I want what you want. Maybe I don't want to make nice with these people."

"And what about the rest of the slaves? How many are like the man I shot last night? How many don't even want to be free? How many are going to run back to the slavers as soon as we dock?"

"A few," Brie concedes. "But more won't."

"Half of them are kids," Huxley says.

"They're not much younger than him," she points to Lowell. "There are three that are very young, but what else would you have them do? They have no parents. No caretakers. You either leave them for the slavers or you take them in. There isn't another option."

"Take them in?" Huxley scoffs. "I don't think you understand what we're doing."

"No, I do understand. I'm not slow. You have a vendetta. So do I." Her voice pitches up a notch. "You know, you're not the only one that watched slavers murder their family. I did too. I want to hurt them just as much as you do. But I also don't want to leave these others behind. We can figure it out. *I* can figure it out."

Huxley spits on the deck between their feet. He looks into her eyes and takes the measure of her. Wonders how serious she is. Does it matter? Does any of it matter? He doesn't know that it does. He cannot leave the slaves, not without at least giving them the choice. You cannot battle something with every fiber of your being but turn a blind eye to the wastage that it leaves behind. That must be taken into account too.

"Come with me," he says. Then he stalks toward the slave cages. Brie hesitates for two of his long strides, but then jogs to catch up. By the time she is with him, Huxley has reached the door and thrown it open. He steps into the center and he hears the small voices around him, the whispers and the gasps, wondering if he has come to murder another of them.

I don't even recognize you anymore.

"Look at me," he nearly shouts, though everyone already is. "This is what you will be. Either that, or a slave. You're being given the choice. You can choose to stay behind when we land in Shreveport. You'll stay in your chains as we leave. You'll eventually be found. You'll be sold. If you are a male, they might castrate you to be a slave for their wives. If you're a female, you might be sold to a brothel, or raped at the pleasure of the councilman who buys you. But you will live. Probably. And you will be fed. They will give you a place to sleep. And you'll probably avoid dying a violent death."

Huxley spreads his arms. "I am your other option. I am not a good option. I will not make your life any better. It will be a trade. One for the other. You will give up safety and comfort. You will be cold. You will probably go hungry.

Some of you will die. But you will gain blood, if that's what you want. You will kill slavers, and you will terrorize the very people that preyed on you and your family. But listen to me when I tell you … do not romanticize this. There is nothing good here. There is nothing noble down my path. It is exactly what it is—bloody revenge. You will have blood on your hands, and you will wonder if your family members that were slaughtered by the slavers would even recognize you if they survived to see what you have become. And it will tear you apart inside. But you'll have blood. And you will be free. For however long you live.

"Those are your choices, as bluntly as I can put them, as simple as I can make them for you. I don't care what you choose, but remember what I told you." He turns to Brie. "We should land in Shreveport in two days. They have until then to make a decision. Release the ones that want to come with us. Leave the other ones chained up for their masters."

And then he walks out.

PART 4

———

BLOOD AND DEATH

They huddled in the back of the station wagon. Him and his wife and his daughter. Behind them were three weeks of disaster and a smoldering city they could no longer see. They'd crossed many horizons since they left that city behind. They were somewhere in the Sierra Nevada mountains, parked out of the way, as far off the meandering mountain road as the station wagon could get them. The night was cold and they couldn't run the car for warmth. There was less than a quarter tank of gas left. All their gas cans were empty. And they hadn't seen a gas station with any fuel left in its underground tanks in four days.

They were lucky they even had a vehicle. This car had been at the basement level of a parking garage. It was the only reason it was still running, and it was the only reason they'd managed to get out of the city. Many people had not.

He and Charity had one blanket to share, and Nadine lay nestled between them, asleep with the hard unconsciousness of a two-year-old. They were very lucky that she slept so well. But the days had been long and exhausting. When the sun went down, she passed out and didn't wake up until dawn.

He and Charity, though … they would lie awake at night, exhaustion creeping in, but their fears keeping them wide-eyed and awake.

How did all of this happen?

How did it come to this?

He and his family, crammed in a station wagon with barely any gas left in the tank, almost no food left, and just a few bottles of water to sustain them until … until … what? What was his plan? What was his endpoint here?

He didn't know. He was just running.

He looked at Charity. It was dark, but there was a moon that night and he could see his wife's face.

She was actually smiling, looking down at Nadine.

He wanted to ask her why she was smiling. But why break into her pleasant thoughts, if she was able to have them? She was strong. She had surprised him. He thought that all of this would break her, but it seemed to have done more of a number on him than her. She had taken it in stride, it seemed.

He stared at her and felt an ache in his chest.

He reached out and put his hand against her face, then pulled her into him, gently. He kissed her fiercely over their daughter. When he pulled away, Charity looked at him, her eyes searching his for a measure of what he was thinking.

"If I ever lose you ..." he began.

Charity interrupted him. "Stop. Stop thinking about that. Look at our daughter."

He looked down at her. It was astounding to watch a two-year-old sleep. They were immune to the world. And she didn't really process what was happening. This was just a long car ride, in which she got to play around in the back of the station wagon with noisy toys whose batteries were dying. She had no concept of what they were without. She didn't think about their near-empty gas tank, or their dwindling food and water. She just slept. Tight and comfortable between Mommy and Daddy.

Charity touched his face in a way that she did to get his attention, to make sure that he was listening, to let him know she had something to say.

He looked at her again.

"We're here," she said. "We're here, and we're gonna be okay. Okay?"

"Okay."

"We're together," she said, pointedly. "And you're not gonna lose us."

CHAPTER 1

Shreveport looms, a dark smudge at the bottom of the sky. There's the smell that always comes with human habitation in groups, but it is the visual of the city that strikes Huxley as he stands at the front of the slave barge and looks down the river to where it appears that the water ends in nothingness, a small black hole at the end of the world.

The late afternoon sun melts tiredly against a skein of darkness that seems to hover over the city. When he looks closely and squints, he can see all the individual pillars of smoke, some large, and some small, rising up into that grayish smog. Thousands of fires belching smoke into the sky, turning the clouds all around a sort of brackish tint, like dirt and dust. A fire in every home, in every business, all of them burning at once against the autumn chill. It has been a very long time since he's seen an actual city. He is not happy to see one again.

Brie stands next to him, the scattergun that she claimed resting on her shoulder. Her face is slightly pinched as she looks out at the city that continues to expand before them, swallowing their horizons.

"They took me in Nevada," she says. "Not Bristow. He's a middleman. He bought me from a group of raiders. But still, I've been around these slavers since Nevada. Since March, actually. What month is it now?"

"October," Huxley replies, wincing slightly as he shifts his balance and feels a throb from the wound in his side. "I think."

Brie sniffs and wipes her nose. "The raiders killed everyone in my settlement except me and two boys, but the boys got sold off in a town, two stops before the raiders met with Bristow. They didn't even know that I had medicine skills. They were going to kill me if I didn't sell quickly as a bedslave, which they didn't think I would. And they probably weren't wrong." She snorts and shakes her head. "Bristow was smart enough to ask them if I had any skills, and I answered for myself, and he bought me on the spot for the cost of a bedslave—significantly cheaper than you might buy a healer. So everyone left happy. Even me. I didn't have to be raped *or* killed. Lucky me."

Huxley shifts uncomfortably, eyeing her.

She seems to realize that he is looking at her strangely. She nods toward Shreveport. "All of that to say, I've been with Bristow for a while. Learned some things about this place. Just from listening. Asking a few questions here and there, when I could. I can tell you about Shreveport. I can even show you some maps. They're in Bristow's things."

"Okay," Huxley prompts.

"Shreveport's run by a warlord, I can tell you that. Some guy named Overman. The slavers always called him the 'Nigger King.' Apparently, he's not beholden to the chairman of the Riverland Nations, or any of the other councilmen. He and Shreveport are their own little state, but the Riverlands need him for slaves and cattle, and he's got no money or power without the Riverlands buying his two main exports."

Huxley thinks of his daughter being treated like a sack of grain. An export. Something to be tallied and bought and sold and traded. He feels black and heavy inside. Like volcanic rock—dark and encrusted on the surface, and boiling hot below.

"Where do the slaves go?" Huxley asks, his voice quiet.

"The slaves themselves?" Brie touches the wooden stock of the scattergun, worn smooth by rough handling. She strokes it, almost lovingly. "Most are put up at least once at auction. Apparently Shreveport is where you get the best price, but many of the lower councilmen and clan leaders can't make the trip to Shreveport. They get the 'second runnings': the slavers take all the slaves they couldn't sell at a Shreveport auction and take them toward the Mississippi to various points. I don't know about these towns. But they're easier for the less wealthy and powerful slave buyers to get to."

She takes a moment to judge how her words have affected him. "I don't tell you this to upset you. I know you're looking for someone."

Huxley jags a glance at her. "I'm not looking for a slave."

"Oh. I thought ..."

"I'm looking for a slaver," he says, hollowly, realizing for perhaps the first time the forlorn hope of this endeavor. To find one man. One man in a hostile country. Difficult. But maybe not impossible. "A man with a scorpion tattoo on his neck. I'd like to find him."

Brie grimaces. "Tall order. I told you about Overman because I heard that part of his treaty with the Riverlands is that he work closely and cooperate with the Black Hats."

Huxley doesn't give her much of a reaction, though his stomach flip-flops.

"We all saw when you convinced Bristow to take you aboard," she says, looking out at the city, from which individual buildings and the docks could not be seen. "We heard the conversation. We know that you're wanted by the Black Hats."

She looks behind her and Huxley follows her gaze to the open doors of the former slave cages.

Of the forty slaves, only eleven have chosen to be free.

They are kids, Huxley tells himself. *Don't judge them harshly.*

"The ones that stay," she says. "When they're found, they'll tell the slavers everything, hoping to be treated well. They'll tell them who you are, what happened on the boat, and what you're doing in the Riverlands. What *we're* doing. And then it will become a big problem. The Black Hats will be enlisted to find you. Towns will know about you. There will be a bounty on your head, most likely." She takes a deep breath. "Unless we cut their throats and pitch them in the river right now."

Huxley's eyes widen just a bit, shocked to hear the suggestion come from her. "Jesus Christ."

She frowns. "You killed that other slave for diming you out. What's the difference?"

And Huxley wonders to himself if he shouldn't just do it. If they are in league with the slavers, then they're just as bad as the slavers, right? Shouldn't they be dispatched just as mercilessly? But no, there is a difference. He can feel it. Even he cannot rationalize his way around it.

"The difference is that they're not a direct threat," Huxley says. "We'll be out of the city by the time they can spill their guts. Let them live. Let them go to their masters."

Brie nods. "Then I wouldn't stay in Shreveport for long."

Huxley grunts and looks down the river.

"I wouldn't go into the city at all, if I were you," Brie continues, carefully.

"Thank you for the advice. I'll judge for myself."

She shrugs and turns to leave him, as though she predicted this would be his response.

Huxley turns and touches her shoulder, stopping her.

"What?" she asks.

"The ones that are with me … they trust you?"

Brie considers it for a moment. "Yes."

"You're gonna show me these maps of the city you claim Bristow has. We're going to figure out how to get out of that shithole. And you—you're going to take the freed slaves. You and Rigo will act like slavers, and you're going to get them out of the city. We'll choose a place outside to meet up again."

"Okay," she blinks, like she is memorizing the instructions.

He looks at her, his eyes narrowing. "Do you know who I am?"

Her head pulls back a bit, confused. "Who you are …?"

He turns fully, squaring his shoulders to her. "Do you know who I am? Do you know how I think? Do you know what you're getting yourself into? Do they?"

The confusion fades from her face and her eyes do a circuit over him. They soften with something almost like … pity. Almost like she feels bad that he has not made peace with who he is. But she knows, and she is the same, and she has made peace with herself. Could she be that hard? Could the things in her be truly as bad?

"You're an angry man," she says. "You have nothing left in this world but hate and a gun. You'll use your life up to inflict pain on the rest of them for taking everything from you." Her brows furrow, creating a crease right in the center. "You think any of us are different? You think any of us have anything left in this world? No." She shakes her head sadly. "We've had the hate, Mr. Huxley. We've had it for a long time. It kept us warm on cold nights. It was cool water in the desert. It helped us survive with our minds intact so that we didn't break like all the others that did. We've had the hate, Mr. Huxley. Now you've given us the guns."

CHAPTER 2

Huxley takes the steps up from the docks two at a time, a steady pace, but he cannot deny his desire to be away from the slave barge. At the top step he stops and turns, glancing over his shoulder again at the hulking flatboat *Misery*, as it lies at berth in the North Docks of Shreveport. All around it are similar boats, in similar sizes, their cargo both human and cattle. The boats are prickly with slavers' poles, and the docks are swarming with slavers. There is little to no control over what comes and goes at the Shreveport docks. Which means that Huxley and all of the freed slaves were able to dock without question or inspection.

At the end of the pier that jutted out from the crumbling concrete of the riverside, Huxley scans the crowd and sees a trail of young men and women dressed in brown and tan tunics. Some of them are armed, others are not. A girl with a long face carries a scattergun and leads the way, while Rigo follows in the back, the two of them acting as best they can like they are the slavers in control of this string of slaves. They move quickly, not stopping, and head out of the docks and toward the nearest exit out of Shreveport. His side smarts with every step, but he keeps his wound hidden and his expression blank. This was not the place to show weakness. Beside him, Jay watches the column disappear into the streets of the city. All along the riverside, the crumbling decay of the city that had been is evident. In some places, it is "revived," after a fashion. In others it remains decrepit and burned out. The buildings that have been reclaimed are bolstered by large timbers, others by pieces of steel and scrap. Nothing has any sameness to it.

Everything is a different version of decline and reclamation.

Huxley lifts a strip of cloth to his face and holds it there at the bridge of his nose. The purpose is twofold—to relieve himself of the incredible stench of the place, and to hide his face. First and foremost, the smell is overpowering, like a physical being that hovers invisible and chokes the oxygen out of the air. Fires burn all around them belching smoke, and they are all cooking something different—strong stews, beers, liquors, roasting meat. Under the smoke and spice there is the smell of raw sewage in the streets.

Not "sewage," Huxley thinks. *That would imply that it came from a sewer.*

Looking around, he can see it, like a slurry, on the sides and gutters of the streets, concentrated near drain pipes, piles of shit with swarming flies. Every so often, an old man or a young boy who are probably slaves, shoveling those piles of shit into the open drains for the rain to carry away during the next storm.

All around them there is some wretched form of life: drunks, fighters, whores, homeless, criers trying their best to sell what they have cooking in pots and grills or what they have dragged with nets from the sewage-polluted waters of the Red River. It is the market of Red Water Landing, but without concern for rule of law. In Shreveport, money and fear of violence are the only laws that seem to exist. There are guards posted here and there—at least they are what Huxley assumes are guards. They're armed with revolvers and wear white bands around their upper arms, and they seem to watch the people carefully. But it also seems that there is very little they are interested in stopping. Prostitutes are clearly of no concern, nor panhandlers. Even the fights they simply watch with disinterest.

Huxley and Jay continue on from the docks. They are on a wide street, crowded on both sides with shops and taverns and storefronts that have been cobbled together, sprouting from the side of the existing Old World buildings like tumors. Huxley scans them all, still keeping the cloth pulled up over his face. There are plenty of fliers posted on the outside of these things, but none of them bear his face. No wanted posters.

"Any idea where you're going?" Jay says, keeping pace with Huxley.

Huxley continues to glance around. "No. Not really."

"Maybe we should ask someone."

Huxley stops again in the middle of the street. A group of slavers shoulder roughly past them, but seem to take no offense to their stopping in the middle of everything. Everyone is moving about their business, whatever that business might be. There are brothels to be patronized and alcohols to be consumed. No time to fuss with two men standing in the middle of the road.

Huxley looks about one more time, seeing if any eyes have fallen on them, but they are largely ignored. This place is a place where a man could very easily disappear. Be forgotten. Forever.

He looks at Jay. "Who the hell do I ask?"

"Wandering aimlessly will call more attention to ourselves," Jay states.

Huxley shakes his head, exasperated. This place has a suffocating nature to it. Especially for those that don't belong. He is surrounded by men that would kill him outright if they knew who he was, or what he'd done. It sets his teeth to grinding and his muscles contract all across his body.

Another circumspection.

And there, a sign.

A handwritten sign, held by an ancient old man, skin black as charcoal and a beard white like bleached bones. Not a hair on his head. The man sits on a stool to the side of the road, snugged in between two shops hawking unknown merchandise.

INFO 4 TRADE

The old man seems to be staring right at Huxley.

Huxley stares back for a time, but the old man gives no indication that he cares. He does not beckon Huxley to him, or change his facial expression. The prolonged eye contact seems to be utterly lost on this old man.

"Infuhmation," the old man calls out suddenly. "Infuhmation for trade."

Huxley glances about again, and again finds the street unaware of his existence. All except for the old man with the sign. Huxley looks at Jay. His companion squints with a discerning eye at the old man with the sign, but after a moment, he can't seem to come up with an objection, so he shrugs.

"Might as well," Jay says, gesturing toward the man.

Huxley moves slowly through the lanes of people until he reaches the curb and steps up onto it, perhaps five or ten feet from where the old man sits.

Standing up close to him, Huxley realizes just how old the man is. His skin sags like ancient leather. There is nothing under it but bones, old tendons, and swollen joints. One leg is propped on the stool, but the other is not there. Just an empty pant leg that drapes across the rough-hewn rungs of the homemade stool.

The man never breaks eye contact.

Suspicious, Huxley sways to the left and to the right.

The old man's eyes don't track.

They are dark and bloodshot and Huxley realizes they are not staring at him. They are not staring at anything.

The old man's eyebrows furrow. "Who's'at?" he says roughly. "You wah' some infuhmation?"

"He's blind," Jay says.

The old man's mouth takes a downturn. "No shit I'm blind. Don't matter. Ol' Reggie sees e'rything." A slight smile tweaks the man's mouth. The corners are crusted in parts, pasty white froth on the inside edges. "Ol' Reggie *knows* e'rything." He turns his head slightly to the side. "Jerry! Jerry! Who's 'is gen'lman?"

The man at the neighboring booth leans over with a flash of annoyance, but eyes Huxley up and down. "Some fuckin' guy," the man says. "Never seen 'im before."

"Ahhhh," Ol' Reggie trails off into a chuckle, his mouth gaping open in his face and revealing only two mangled brown teeth, one on the top, and one on the bottom, and both on opposite sides. His voice attains a quiet sort of introspection. "So ... some li'l lost sheep tryin' to fin' his way through the big, bad forest, huh?"

Huxley glances between Reggie and the man he called Jerry.

Jerry shrugs, rolls his eyes, and returns to his own business.

"C'mere." Reggie waves Huxley forward, setting his sign down on the ground. "C'mere, little sheep. How can I help you get through the forest?"

Huxley smirks. *Little sheep.* But he steps forward, intentionally scuffs his feet on the dirty concrete sidewalk so that Reggie knows he's there. "I'm looking for someone."

The little smug smile fades off of Reggie's face like the last glimmers of sunlight at dusk. His blind eyes stare up at nothing, but his face shows an understanding all its own. Almost as though he had recognized Huxley's voice.

Do you know me? Huxley is suddenly alarmed. *Do I know you?*

But of course, the man is a stranger. There is no way he could know Huxley.

Reggie's lips compress and he looks suddenly very cautious. Almost frightened. "So," he says slowly. "You're no little lost sheep after all. Are you?"

Huxley pauses, thinking about a trap. But Reggie is only one blind man. And no one else around them seems to care, or listen, or watch. "What makes you say that?"

The old man's bushy white eyebrows furrow together. "My, but what big teeth you have."

Huxley's face darkens.

He feels a tug at his shoulder.

"C'mon," Jay says. "This guy's a waste of time."

Huxley sneers down at the blind man and begins to turn, but Ol' Reggie reaches out and grabs Huxley by the wrist.

"You said you're looking for someone."

Huxley's voice takes a warning tone. "You got a very accurate grab for a blind man." His voice goes quiet, so that only Reggie can hear him. "Maybe you take your hands off me before I open you up right here on the street."

Reggie immediately releases him. He wags a finger at Huxley. "Someone, you say? You're looking for someone?" His hand waggles back and forth in the air. "Jus' so happens, I know someone. Maybe it's the same someone."

"How much?" Huxley reaches for a leather pouch filled heavy with gold coins taken from the *Misery*. The sacking of the slave barge had at least been lucrative.

Reggie holds up one of his gnarled old hands, his nearly toothless mouth working slowly.

Huxley hesitates, his hands touching the strings of the pouch.

"No," Reggie says, finally, waving his hand once. "No payment for this. You see, I lied when I said that Ol' Reggie sees e'rything. 'Cause I'm blind. Cain't see shit. But oh, I can hear. And your eyes can tell you lies, but the truth always rings clear like a bell. So what I really should say, is Ol' Reggie *hears* everything. And I can hear inside of you, Mr. Man. I can hear the truth. And I says to myself, 'Don't take no money from this man, but give 'im what he wants and speed 'im on his way and stay on his good side.'"

Huxley compresses his lips, picking through Reggie's odd words. "You want nothing?"

Reggie shakes his head once. His expression is grave, his eyebrows raising up. "I jus' want you to get what you came for and move along. And never have a reason to be mad at Ol' Reggie. That's what I want."

Huxley's tongue rubs the front of his teeth. He can feel the grime on them. Taste the foulness of his own breath. What did he sound like to this old man? What did he smell like to him? Something frightening. Something unsettling. The scent of danger. Like the scent of a predator in the nose of prey.

He hears inside of you …

"Let's just ask and go," Jay grumbles.

"Yes," Reggie gestures with a hand. "Ask about this someone that you're looking for. And then go."

Huxley spits on the sidewalk at his feet. "I'm looking for a slaver."

Reggie snorts. "Well, you're in Shreveport, my friend. Look around you."

"A particular slaver."

Reggie bows his head and closes his blind eyes. "A'course, a'course. Someone that's done you wrong. M-hm. And you want to know where to find this partic'lar slaver. But I says to myself, 'Don't this Mr. Man know that these slavers get around? Here today and gone tomorrow? Ain't no tellin' where this one partic'lar slaver has gotten off to.' Maybe it might help to narrow it down a bit."

Huxley trades a glance with Jay. The risk is there, but there is no reward without risk. He cannot find the man he is looking for without asking around. Yes, it might call attention to him. Yes, word might get back that Huxley is looking for the man. But by the same token, he cannot simply divine where the man is. He must be told. By someone.

Huxley turns his attention back to Reggie. "He's got a scorpion tattoo on his neck. That's all I can tell you."

Reggie's bony index finger hovers in the air, quivering. "All you can tell me? Or all that you're *willin'* to tell me?"

"It's all I know."

"M-hm." The bony finger retracts, folds up into Reggie's fist. The ancient old man raises his head, opens his bloodshot, blind eyes, and turns his old, leathern face down the street, further away from the docks, further into Shreveport. "Haven't heard his voice in a while. But last I did, he was the number one customer over at Big Josie's tavern. Maybe you go ask around up there. And maybe you don't ever say nothin' about me, you hear, Mr. Man? That's a part of the deal. That's what you agreed to."

"Yeah," Huxley nods, following Reggie's gaze down the road. "I never talked to you. Where's Big Josie's place?"

Reggie picks up his sign again and sets it on his lap, as though clearing their accounts and indicating that he is done. He straightens and fixes his blind gaze out into the passing throngs. Under his breath, he says, "Two blocks down and make a right. First door on the left. And now we're done. Now you leave me be."

Huxley looks at the man a moment longer, wondering if he should not deposit something quietly at the man's feet. But then he thinks, *Fuck this shriveled old man. He said he doesn't want anything from me but to be left alone. So I'll give him what he wants.*

Huxley turns away and steps down off the curb.

Ol' Reggie's voice calls out, stopping Huxley in his tracks.

"Full moon tonight," the blind man says, loudly.

Huxley turns and looks over his shoulder.

Again, the blind eyes seem to be staring right back at him.

For some unknown reason, he feels his heart hammering in his chest. Not the anger this time. But a nervousness with no clear subject, no clear focus. Just a cloud of apprehension hovering there in the back of his mind, vaporous and unsubstantiated.

"What did you say?" Huxley asks, though he heard the words clearly enough.

A big, two-toothed grin spreads across Reggie's mouth. Rather than answer, he lifts his face to the sky and lets out a long, mournful howl: "Ah-*whoooooooooooooooooooo*." And then Ol' Reggie dips his head back down and looks out into the crowd, his face blank, his eyes blank, as though Huxley is already forgotten. "Infuhmation," the old man cries to the passing throngs. "Infuhmation for trade. Whatchoo need to know? Ol' Reggie sees e'rything. Ol' Reggie *knows* e'rything."

Then the crowd seems to catch them like a current, and they drift away down the road, Huxley and Jay, until they cannot see the strange old blind man anymore.

Down the street, two blocks.

They hunch their shoulders against a brisk wind that Huxley wishes would scour away the smell of Shreveport that is turning his stomach. Or maybe it is the unsettling feeling he has growing inside of him. Maybe that's what is making him queasy. He just keeps thinking about those blind, bloodshot eyes. Those bony fingers. Those two brown teeth.

My, what big teeth you have …

Down the street, two blocks, and then a right-hand turn.

Another street, just like the previous one.

The first door on the left is nondescript, just a wooden ensemble pushed in about twenty feet from the corner of the building that houses it. The building is an old brick construction. The top windows are broken, some of them boarded over with rotting boards that look ready to fall from the nails that keep them in place. Four stories down and onto someone's head. A bunch of tiny widow makers just waiting to drop.

The first story and second story are alive, where the upper stories are dead. The glass is still broken and boarded in many of these lower windows, but behind them there is lamplight glowing, and the ground floor looks busy. It is midday, and the tavern—if it is indeed Big Josie's tavern—still receives a steady stream of in-and-out traffic.

Huxley and Jay watch it for a while, wondering who is going in, and who is coming out. The big front door creaks open and bangs on its stopper. A drunken man steps out, bleary-eyed, into the world of Shreveport. Another customer steps in, swinging the door wide. It is in these little glimpses that Huxley can see inside.

The interior looks poorly lit. A good place to sit and drink and forget your miserable life. There is noise, but it isn't raucous. Just a steady bubble of conversation, and every once in a while a loud laugh. Busy barmaids and lazy patrons that only move to bring their drinks to their mouths.

"Nice, quiet, dark place," Jay observes. "Maybe we won't be noticed too much."

"I'd assume a lot of travelers come through here," Huxley says, without the confidence he'd hoped to display. "I'm sure new faces aren't that big of a deal."

"New faces asking questions, though …"

"Well." Huxley steps out into the street and begins crossing. "We'll just step carefully."

"Hux," Jay calls.

Huxley stops and turns. Jay is still standing on the sidewalk. The other man looks around a little cautiously, then nods his head toward the tavern. "Go ahead. I'll stay here. Watch the outside. That way we both don't get trapped in there."

Huxley rubs his nose. "You seem pretty sure that something bad is going to happen."

Jay shrugs. Looks away.

Huxley turns back toward the tavern and puts one step in front of the other. There's not much else he can do. He doesn't enjoy the idea of being alone in this strange place.

Huxley allows the cloth over his face to drop as he steps up to the sidewalk in front of the tavern. He does not think whoever is in charge of it will appreciate him coming through with his face covered like a bandit. The smells of the street hadn't been blocked out anyway—only muted and mixed with the smell of his own stale breath under the cloth. But now they resurge, strong and assertive, making his nose curl.

He reaches the door behind a group of three that enters the tavern loudly, slamming the door on its rusty hinges and calling out to the barmaids as soon as they step foot through the door. Huxley slides in behind them, close to the last man, like he is a part of their group, and then he slips to the side.

The inside smells better than the outside. The odors here are just as strong, and some have an unpleasant aspect to them, but none of them are raw sewage so that is an improvement. Inside, it is wood smoke and tobacco smoke and burning tallow and lard-fueled lamps. Stale sweat and the rank stench of unwashed men. Old ales that have been spilled and dried on the floors and on the tabletops. But also better things, like rosewater blooming in the wake of the barmaids as they hurry past.

He stares after them, pausing for a moment as he slides along the back wall.

Watching the way their hips move under their dresses—simple things, though colorfully spun, and belted at the waist to hint at those things the shapeless fabric hid. Low slits in the front to reveal smallish breasts on all but the oldest barmaid, also the shortest and thickest built, whose enormous breasts bulge out proudly from the open top.

Huxley's brain is sparking with primal thoughts. He's been so long in the company of stinking men and misery that he'd almost forgotten what it was like to look at a woman, to see the way her body moves, the soft scent of them underneath everything else. It's been so long since he's seen them without fear in their eyes. He is a stranger to them. They do not know what he's done. They don't fear him.

It's nice.

He chooses a table and sits.

The table is small, and situated on the back wall of the place, near to a burning fireplace. The fireplace pours out sweltering heat, large logs simmering and smoking on the ends, their centers burning hot. The seat is a small stool with no back. The table is big enough for two, but it is only Huxley.

There are several others inside of the tavern that are sitting at tables, either alone, or with one or two companions. But it appears that the majority of the in-and-out traffic has been for the brief use of rooms, and the barmaids, who apparently also serve as a brothel.

The short, thick barmaid with the enormous breasts swings up to his table, hand on her hip, the air immediately smelling of rosewater. She is pretty, her face shining and pleasant, though her eyes scheme and that cannot be hidden. Plump, but still well formed. An inviting figure. She smiles for him, revealing some white teeth, and a few silver ones on the side.

"How is it, fella?" she says. Her voice is strong, but sweet in a way. "I'm Josie. Haven't seen you around here before."

"Big Josie?" Huxley asks.

"I look big to you?" She lays a hand to her chest and bats her eyes in shock. It is a well-practiced response to a common question.

Huxley smiles, just slightly. "You look nice."

As he says it he pictures her, with her skirts hiked up to the belt at her waist and her top ripped violently down to expose her breasts, and himself behind her, pinning her down onto the table …

Can you hear the truth inside of me, Josie? Does it ring clear for you like a bell?

If she hears it, she gives no response to it.

Still smiling, she touches his shoulder. "We've got dark ale and light ale, and shine for a price. Meat pies if you're hungry. Or, if you're in the mood for something a little more lively, we have some rooms in the back." She leans in close and says in a conspiratorial tone, "But I warn you, I'm not on the menu."

Huxley just keeps smiling back at her.

Pinned down to the table …

But she's not on the "menu."

The "menu," she says. So aptly put.

Huxley reaches into the pouch at his side and discreetly withdraws two gold pieces, which he sets on the table. "Just a drink. Dark ale. Please."

Josie swipes up the gold pieces and eyes them suspiciously. Huxley doesn't know the going rate for a drink, but he imagines that two gold pieces is far beyond the asking price. "You want me to keep them coming all night?" she asks.

"Just one, please." Huxley folds his hands on the tabletop. "The rest is for your discretion."

Josie eyes him for several breaths. Then looks at the gold pieces in her hands. Probably worth a meal and a room for the night, if Huxley were to take a guess. Finally, she pockets it with a look on her face that seems to say, *what's the worst that could happen?*

She leans over, close to him, her substantial chest swinging and almost touching the tabletop. Huxley doesn't try to hide his gaze. He locks his fingers together on the table, as though to restrain himself. Then he sniffs and finds her eyes, which seem amused by his self-control.

"I'm looking for a man that frequents your establishment."

"For drink … or women?" she asks, her lips hanging open on the last word, her tongue glistening right behind them.

Huxley shakes his head. "Don't know."

"Can you describe him?"

"He's a slaver," Huxley says, meting out the information slowly, and judging Josie's reaction after each piece. If she is loyal to the slavers at all, she doesn't show it, just keeps waiting for the next piece of description. "And he's got a scorpion tattoo on his neck."

Josie raises an eyebrow at him. She leans away, like she's suddenly been put off. "Well, isn't that a goddamned coincidence," she remarks with a hand on her hip. "Looks like one of your buddies beat you to the punch. Maybe you should just talk to him."

She turns away and starts toward the bar on the other side of the room.

Huxley sits frozen, though he has the sudden urge to jump out of his seat. He is still trying to sort through what she has just said, trying to make sense of it, when he hears her grumble under her breath, halfway to the bar now, "Goddamn Black Hats."

Another couple of heartbeats …

Black Hats. Black Hats here …

He wants to make a run for the door, but suddenly, he wonders if it will only call attention to him. He stares at the men gathered at the bar, as Josie sidles behind it. There are three of them. None of them are wearing black hats.

You should get out. You should get out now.

Stupid whore!

He rises from his table as calmly as he dares. His hand slides to the revolver at his side. A fresh load in each chamber, he'd made sure of that before he left the slave barge.

At the bar, Josie leans close to one of the men and whispers something to him.

Huxley watches the man perk up a bit.

Get out. Get out now.

He starts moving for the door.

The man at the bar twists in his seat. He is hunched over the bar, and it is only his eyes that Huxley can see, peeking over his own shoulder. Huxley looks away, trying not to hold eye contact. Eye contact could make you look guilty. He had to pretend that he wasn't worried about this man.

Just get out.

The man rises from his seat at the bar.

Huxley slides his hand to his waistband and closes his fingers around the grip of one of his revolvers, his finger finding the trigger, his thumb finding the hammer. The man at the bar is lean, weathered. Older. *Don't make me kill you, old man, just go back to your drink.*

Where's Jay when I need him?

Huxley faces the door, the light around the door, the way out of this shithole. He wants to run, but for some reason, it doesn't feel right. He keeps walking for it. It's close, just a few paces away. He keeps his right hand on his revolver, his left coming up to push the door open.

"Huxley." The voice is calm and cold and right behind him.

And Huxley stops.

In that split second, he thinks about turning and shooting, but then he pictures a weapon leveled at his head. A wrong move could get him a lead ball through his skull.

What do you do? What do you do right now?

Huxley doesn't turn, but he glances over his shoulder.

He sees no big bore pointed at his head. Just the man, standing there about a pace away.

The others at the bar are watching. The conversation has died down to a sudden silence.

A little closer, Huxley can see more detail about the man.

Not so much old as *worn*. His skin sallow, marked by years of hard use.

Turn and shoot him. Gun him down and then run.

"I see you got your hand on your weapon," the quiet voice says. It is confident, as though this man knows the beginning from the end. He already has seen how this plays out. "But I ain't got nothing in my hands."

Doesn't matter. Kill him anyway.

How do you know he's even a Black Hat?

"You aren't wearing a black hat," Huxley says, his voice coming out hoarse.

But of course he's a Black Hat. How else would he know Huxley's name? How else would he recognize him in this land where Huxley has never been?

The man just stands there, stock-still, his lips a thin, grim line on his face. The shadows from the lantern at the door make his cheeks and eyes look sunken. Cruel.

"Sit back down at the table and we talk," the man says. "Or you can walk through that door. And you won't leave Shreveport alive."

Huxley turns now to face the man. His hand still lingering on his revolver. Every nerve in his body firing. *Goddamnit, Jay. Where are you when I need you?* To the man with the weathered face, he says, "You think I'm here alone?"

"I didn't figure you were." One eyebrow comes up. "Do you think I am?"

Huxley grinds his teeth together.

The man gestures languidly back to the table Huxley had just abandoned. "Sit. And we talk."

Huxley peers into the shadows where the man's eyes should be, trying to ascertain truth from trickery. "What are we going to talk about?"

The man fixes him with a serious look. "Life and death. Nothing more, nothing less."

CHAPTER 3

Very slowly, the pair walks back to the little table next to the smoky fireplace. They walk beside each other, perhaps an arm's length apart, neither wanting to go in front of the other. Out of the corner of their eyes, they watch each other, and everyone in the bar watches them as they make this long but tiny journey with slow, steady steps, each one planted with the realization that the other man might turn on him in an instant.

Huxley has pulled his hand away from his revolver, but his thumb still sits on his belt, inches away.

The other man's hands might be empty, but he is not without weapons, Huxley notes. Underneath a thick jacket of canvas, the man has a trench knife on one hip, and on the other, only visible when he steps with his right foot and the jacket swings open a bit, Huxley can see a holstered sidearm.

Not a revolver.

An actual cartridge pistol.

Huxley reaches the seat that is probably still warm from him sitting on it, and turns to face the man. Enemy? Perhaps. It didn't feel terribly friendly at this point.

The man pulls out the other stool and sits, gesturing for Huxley to do the same, as though he owns both the table and the chairs. Huxley takes his seat. He sits stiffly, with his back erect, both feet on the floor, and his hands in his lap.

The man scoots his chair in, props his elbows on the table and shows his hands, wiggling his fingers for effect. "Generally speaking, when two men who might kill each other are trying to parley, they talk with their hands on the table."

Keeping his eyes on the man across from him, Huxley slowly extracts his hands from under the table, disliking how far they are from his weapons now, but at least both men are equally disadvantaged. *Except he has a cartridge pistol. He'll get rounds off long before I can even pull the hammer back. Unless his doesn't work. Unless he keeps it for show.*

Around them, the rest of the men in the tavern seem to realize that it will not come to a fight—not just yet anyway—and they slowly turn back to their conversations with each other, or staring down into the head of their ales. Josie comes from behind the counter, carrying two clay tankards with a very unsure look on her face. She is not predisposed to feeling off-balance, Huxley can tell.

She sets the tankards in front of the men at the table and doesn't speak a word. Before she turns, she glances at Huxley, and there seems to be some sort of an apology there. *You should be sorry, you backstabbing bitch,* Huxley glares at her as she walks away. *You took my gold and then sold me out.*

The man across from him takes his tankard and raises it to his lips, taking a long, slow sip as he watches Huxley over the rim of the cup. He sets it down and wipes a thin layer of froth from his lips. Just keeps his eyes on Huxley.

Huxley takes a swallow of his own ale. It's bitter and sweet and spicy all at once. Good, but it cloys at his tongue. Or perhaps it is just the situation that he now finds himself in. He looks for the door. It stands there, closed, the outside world inaccessible.

Walk out the door and you won't leave Shreveport alive.

Huxley rubs the cool, soft surface of the tankard. "How do you know who I am?"

"Word travels fast for wanted men," the man says. "Your warrants were posted here just yesterday. And now here you are."

Huxley is very stiff, sitting on his stool. He looks at the man's uncovered head. "Where's your hat then?"

The man grunts and opens his jacket. He reaches into the inner pocket and withdraws a big chunk of weathered black cloth which he then plops on the table between them. It unfurls when it strikes the wooden top and Huxley can see what it is.

"You *are* a Black Hat," Huxley stares at the boonie hat, the color now more of a charcoal from sun and weather and sweat.

"I've been called worse." A smile twitches the corners of the man's thin lips, but then disappears quickly. "Some of the others wear theirs around town, and that's fine, but I find that Shreveport's promises of cooperation with the Black Hats only go so far as its leadership. But the leadership can't help me track a man down. The smallfolk can, but they know they'll get their throats cut if they're seen talking to a man in a black boonie hat." He shrugs, takes another sip of ale. "I could compel them. But that's not my style."

"That's very forward thinking of you."

"Very *old* thinking of me." The Black Hat looks around, a moment of wistfulness passing over his face. "It's amazing what a decade will do."

"Why aren't you killing me?" Huxley says, unable to restrain the question any longer. It blurts out and then he wishes he could suck it back in, but it's already been said, cannot be unsaid.

The Black Hat drums his fingers against the side of his tankard. He looks at Huxley. Then down into the murk of his ale. "I should be. That's true enough. But in my somewhat substantial time hunting people down and killing them in the name of justice, I've learned that sometimes being a little slow to pull the trigger can turn out to be advantageous."

"You want money?" Huxley snorts. This was not the hardcore manhunter he'd been expecting from a Black Hat. But maybe this one was just a poser. Maybe he just played the part so he could threaten people and then coerce valuables out of them.

Huxley gets his answer in the form of a dark glare from the other man.

"No, I don't want your money. Try to bribe me again and I will end this straightaway." The Black Hat leans back in his seat, appearing to take a moment to harness his anger. "Do you believe me, Mr. Huxley?"

Huxley does believe him. He nods.

The Black Hat lays his hands flat on the table. "I'll cut to the chase since I don't think either of us wants to be sitting here at this table. If I wanted you dead, I'd've just followed you out into the street and done it in the back of the head. It's not a duel. I'm not looking for a gun battle or an honorable fight. You're a walking dead man. My job is to put you down. I'd slit your throat in your sleep, if that was the best way to do it. Doesn't matter how it gets done, as long as it gets done. Except that you're not my quarry."

Huxley's stomach is roiling. He feels suddenly queasy. "Your quarry?"

The Black Hat shakes his head. "No, you're not. Secondarily, from Josie's little case of mistaken identity, I gather that you and I might be looking for the same person."

"Who are you looking for?" Huxley's mouth feels numb around the words.

"Nathaniel Cartwright. He's a slaver. He's got a lot of tattoos. One on his neck."

"A scorpion," Huxley mumbles.

"Yes." That wan smile again, coming and going almost instantaneously. "The difference is that I'm looking for him because that's what I've been charged to do. In all honesty, I never hold a grudge against a man I'm sent to kill. The grudge is on the behalf of the councilmen and the chairman that I serve. Me? I'm just a means to an end. And I'm okay with that. But you ..." he wags a finger at Huxley. "Here you are in the armpit of what is left of America, looking for a man that I also happen to be looking for. Why?"

Huxley feels a tremble that starts in his legs and goes up through the small of his back and into his shoulders. He hides it as best he can. It isn't fear. It's simply ... strangeness. A dark, grisly sort of excitement, perhaps. It doesn't feel distinctively negative, but neither does it feel good.

Huxley's voice is almost a whisper when he tries to speak, so he clears his throat and says it again, more forcefully. "He took something that belonged to me."

The Black Hat nods slowly. "Yes. He has a habit of doing that."

"Why did the council send you after him?"

The Black Hat tilts his head slightly, but then shrugs. "It's fairly common knowledge, so you might as well know. He attacked a caravan under my sworn councilman's banners. Killed several of his men and made off with his daughter and a few other household members. The councilman's daughter and the others were recovered alive, but Mr. Cartwright escaped. And there were allegations of rape."

Of course.

Huxley snorts. "So it's perfectly okay for slavers to rape and pillage out in the Wastelands, but God help us if they do it here in the Riverlands. Is that right?"

The Black Hat nods. "Yes, that's about the size of it. The Wastelands are part of the Riverland Nations in name only. The claim on that territory exists only on paper. Nobody owns the Wastelands. They simply are what they are. They send us out there in pairs, as though two of us might corral the whole, giant fuck-upedness that is the Wastelands. Two men for the entire southwest. It's just a gesture. Nothing more. There's no expectation that the lawlessness will actually be curbed. So, yes. Pretty much anything goes in the Wastelands. But here between the rivers, we have rules for a reason. People travel under councilmen's banners so that they can get safely from point A to point B. Without that ability to travel, there is no trade, no economy, no government."

"And yet you support the slave trade. The very thing that keeps the Wastelands lawless."

"I don't support the slave trade," the Black Hat corrects. "I serve at the pleasure of the council. And they support the slave trade."

"You're a part of the same system."

The Black Hat nods. "I am. I understand this. I've made my peace with it. Because, the truth is, Mr. Huxley, everything is built by slaves. Slaves, violence, and coercion. Subjugation. Indentured servants. However you want to term it. Without computers and machines to do everything for us, human misery is the only way to get anything done. You think I'm wrong?" The Black Hat shakes his head. "You sound educated when you speak. Think back, Mr. Huxley. Think back to every civilization that ever was, and ask yourself, 'Where did it come from?' Capitalism and free trade? No. Every civilization that ever was or will be was built on a bedrock of slavery, in one form or another. Slaves, violence, and coercion. I promise you, Mr. Huxley, that is the way of humanity. I dislike it. I find it distasteful. But disliking something doesn't make it untrue. And I like to maintain an honest relationship with myself. What about you?"

Huxley grabs his dark ale and drinks a heavy draft that tingles the back of his dry tongue and settles in his stomach with an almost uncomfortable warmth. Why bother with this man? He clearly had his own opinions. And nothing that a wanted man was going to tell him would change that. This was not an opportunity for the airing of grievances.

Huxley glances for the door again.

"You look like you want to leave," the Black Hat says. "I won't keep you much longer. So let's get down to the facts, as they say. You know why Nathaniel Cartwright is a wanted man. And then there's you. And apparently, you have your own reasons for wanting to find Nathaniel Cartwright. I don't know what you plan to do with the man once you find him, though I imagine just from looking at you, that it isn't pleasant. On top of all of that, you're a wanted man yourself. And here's the kicker: I'm very familiar with the affiant of your case, Captain Tim of New Amarillo. And I can only imagine his affidavit is a stretch at the very least, and most likely an outright lie. So now I see an opportunity that does not interfere with the operation of my moral compass, which, as wayward as it sometimes points me, I still do try to follow."

The Black Hat props his elbows on the table and holds up a single index finger. "I'm going to give you one day. I'm going to tell you everything I know about Nathaniel Cartwright and where he is, and the minute you walk out that door, the clock starts. You get one day, and then I'm coming for you and Nathaniel both. And I will find you. This is what I do. This is what I've been doing for the last decade of my life, and I'm quite good at it. So you have a one-day head start on me. And you're going to go find Nathaniel. And when you find him, you're going to deal with the business you have with him, and then you are going to leave him for me—dead or alive, it doesn't matter to me, as long as I can clear his warrant. And then I will have to kill you as well, but at least you will have a chance to do what you came all this way to do."

Huxley looks away, blinking, looks at the flames spewing out from between the logs on the fireplace, breathes in the oaky smell of smoke coming off of it. "He took something ..." Huxley has to stop, take a slow swallow, and breathe. "He took something from me ..."

Fire. Smoke. Everything burned to ashes.

Charity.

Nadine.

"... I just want to talk to him about it," Huxley finishes, his voice quiet.

The dubious expression on the Black Hat's face turns into something like a look of pity, though it is just a hint, as though it was a tiny drop of that substance, one of the very few that the Black Hat still had left. Huxley avoided his gaze.

The Black Hat takes a deep breath. "You must've loved that person very much, whoever they were. To come all this way … I know how love can turn to anger. When it's taken away from you unexpectedly." The Black Hat says the last part a bit harshly, reliving some old memory of his own. He clears his throat. "But I'm not in the business of mercy, you understand. Warrants for execution were signed for both you and this man. There's nothing that can be changed about that. And you cannot escape us for very long, Mr. Huxley. Especially between the rivers. We're numerous, and so are our eyes and ears. If you intend to get far, if you intend to find this man and whatever or whoever he took from you, then my deal is the best chance you have of actually accomplishing that. Bitter as it might taste to you."

Huxley stares into the fire, feeling the heat of it contracting the skin on his face. He looks back sharply. "If I'm a dead man anyway, then why not just kill you right here and be on my way? I've been wrongly accused. I might as well earn my death warrant."

The Black Hat shrugs as though the threat is inconsequential. "You could try. Maybe you'd be the first one to succeed. But probably not. You don't live ten years in this job by being slow on the draw." The Black Hat rubs the thumb and forefinger of his right hand together, lightly, seemingly unconsciously. It does not escape Huxley that this is the man's apparent gun hand, and that index finger would be the one to pull the trigger. "Besides," the man continues. "Even if you're the one to get me, what'll you do then? You going to continue to ask around about this man? You, the stranger in a strange land where everyone you meet views you with suspicion and is actively protecting the man you want to find?" the Black Hat shakes his head. "I doubt you'd get far. More likely an enterprising young man that wants to be a part of Nathaniel's crew will cap you in the back of the head when you aren't looking and take your jaw as a trophy to get his foot in the door. Best-case scenario you waste away entire days and get no answers while Nathaniel Cartwright goes deeper and deeper into hiding. Farther away from your grasp. And days are valuable in this business, Mr. Huxley. That's why I'm only giving you one."

A pall of silence falls between the two men.

Huxley looks back to the fire, fixates on the bed of red-hot coals burning beneath everything else. "Where is he?"

For a moment, all Huxley sees are the red embers and the smoke pouring from the fireplace. There is a sudden realization. The realization of death, the endpoint in his life, not in some far-distant, unknown future, but something that was fast approaching. But before that, a chance. A chance to find the man with the scorpion tattoo, Nathaniel Cartwright—though it felt odd for him to have a name now. For so long, for so many miles, through the deserts and the pain and the struggle, the man with the scorpion tattoo was just some mindless beast that prowled the shadows of his mind, snatching away bits and pieces of who he was, feeding on the memories of the people that Huxley had loved.

Now he was a name. He was a man. And other men wanted to be a part of his crew. And he'd done these things, not only to Huxley, but he'd done them to other people as well. Nathaniel Cartwright was a natural disaster, something that left destruction in its wake, moved of its own volition, and could not be stopped.

Until I find him, Huxley thinks.

Huxley realizes that the Black Hat hasn't answered. His strict and weathered features are furrowed, a look of focused concentration, as though he is trying to determine how sure Huxley is, how capable, and whether he truly wants to go down this road.

Huxley straightens and puts both his hands on the table. "Where is he?" Huxley repeats.

The Black Hat nods, seemingly convinced. He grabs his tankard and turns it up, draining it in three quick gulps. Then he sets it down and sucks in a breath through his teeth. "There's a string of small trading outposts and towns from here to the Mississippi, called the Slavers' Trail. Five different places between here and Vicksburg, each with a slave market catering to lower clan leaders and councilmen that don't want to travel here to Shreveport. Mr. Cartwright's warrant was issued exactly a week ago. I don't know whether he got wind of it when he hobbled back into town after being run off from his little incident with the councilman's daughter. But from what I hear, he, his crew, and a group of fifteen slaves fresh off a barge lit out for the Slavers' Trail four days ago." The Black Hat stands without ceremony and looks around briefly. "My best guess is a day per stop, with a day's travel between. Which puts him on the road today to the third town on the Trail. That'd be Monroe. Unless he sold his slaves already. I would guess he's making quick sales for gold so he can take it either into the Eastern Democratic States, or west into the Wastelands. Either case, he won't be sticking around the Riverlands for long. So I suggest you not waste time."

Huxley stands. "I won't. Can I leave now?"

The Black Hat begins to button his jacket closed. "No, you sit here for a minute. Let me leave. Then you can go."

"I'd like to know your name," Huxley blurts.

The Black Hat's fingers slow down as they close the last button. He glances up at Huxley with curiosity, and then frowns at the button as he hooks it through the buttonhole and straightens his jacket. "Why?"

Huxley considers it for a moment, because he isn't really sure why he'd asked the question. It seems inconsequential. A Black Hat was a Black Hat, according to what everyone said. An emotionless, dispassionate wraith that slunk around in the shadows like the bogeyman, snatching up and executing falsely accused men and anyone that dared show those fugitives any kindness. Perhaps it was the fact that this Black Hat seemed more like a person that Huxley wanted his name.

But Huxley chooses a different reason. "I'd like to know the name of the man that promises to kill me."

The Black Hat bobs his head back and forth, as though admitting that Huxley has a valid point. "I suppose that's reasonable. I'll tell you what. A name for a name. Mine for yours."

Huxley frowns. "My name's Huxley."

The Black Hat let's out a bark of laughter. "No. That's a chosen name. I've heard all kinds before—from the somewhat stupid to the downright insane—though I've never heard someone choose a name for themselves that made them sound like an old doorman." The Black Hat subdues his chuckles. "I'll tell you what. You don't have to tell me your name. Just tell me why you chose 'Huxley.'"

The sound of the Black Hat's chuckling makes it all very surreal to Huxley in that moment. The pure insanity of his current situation becomes apparent to him, like suddenly being able to see the other side of an optical illusion. In that moment the Old World and who he was exists in his mind, side by side with the new one, and the Black Hat's laughter is like a soundtrack to the grisly parody of the whole damn thing.

I barely even recognize you anymore.

He sees himself walking into a classroom. Studious. Glasses. Combed hair. A sweater-vest under a tweed suit. How scholarly he must have looked to those high school students. For what? What was he trying to accomplish? What was he trying to portray? That he was smarter than they were? That they should worship him because he had made the collegiate pilgrimage of the learned and come back enlightened?

It was all just fluff. Worthless bullshit.

Not a goddamn thing he'd ever learned or taught in any school had equipped him to feed his family in the world after the skyfire. Nothing prepared him to be able to defend them. He had taken the raw land of his natural, violent instincts, and he had pruned them into a garden of flowers with no legitimate use but to look pretty for a casual observer. And then someone had come along and they'd burned that to the ground. Nathaniel Cartwright had come along. And he had reduced Huxley to ashes and dust.

But nature abhors a vacuum, and the earth does not stay scorched forever. The native plants reclaim themselves as time goes by, harder and crueler and more twisted in their growth than ever before.

You're right, darling. You'd barely recognize me anymore.

But this new me, this ugly, tangled patch of briars, it would've kept you safe.

Huxley sticks his thumbs into his belt, his palm covering the hammer and handle of the revolver that protrudes from his waistband. He stands up straight. He raises his head like a proud man, as though to show that he has accepted what was, and what has become. "I was an English teacher. I chose Huxley because of Aldous Huxley. The author."

"I'm familiar," the Black Hat smiles with one side of his mouth. He scoots the chair out from behind his legs and pulls a warm knit hat over his head—not the black hat. He looks to the door, briefly, as though he would prefer to be leaving through it. "Back before the skyfire, I was a sheriff here in Louisiana. Guess that's not such a stretch, is it?" the man's eyes flick to Huxley and in them is almost a prayer for absolution, but that is fleeting. The man's face goes dark again, flat and impassive like stone. "Sheriff Jim Davies. But then things changed. And I had to change with it. Just like you did. Now my old name and my old title are things of the past. Some of the men still call me Black Hat Davies. Most everyone else in this godforsaken country calls me Black Heart Davies." And then he smiles a hopeless, empty smile. "But some names are earned, not chosen. Aren't they?"

Black Heart Davies doesn't wait for an answer. He turns and strides out of the door and is gone in a cloud of yellow, failing sunlight and a gust of cold air that stinks of the filth of Shreveport.

CHAPTER 4

Huxley follows quickly. He pushes through the door, slamming it on the wooden stopper like everyone else.

All around him is Shreveport. The stink of it. The sight of it. Alive, but falling apart at the same time. Bustling and almost industrious it seems at first glance, but then you see that everyone leers and stumbles drunkenly and their bustle is in fact only hustle. Shreveport is decay masked as progress.

Huxley moves out of the way of the door and lets it swing closed behind him. He looks to his right and finds Jay standing there with his back against the wall of the tavern. Jay notices Huxley and straightens, his eyebrows raised with question.

Huxley continues looking all around, scanning through the crowd. But Black Heart Davies has disappeared so quickly Huxley wonders if the whole encounter had been a figment of his imagination.

"Did you see the man?" Huxley demands from Jay. "The one that came out right before me. Did you see him?"

For two beats of his heart, Huxley thinks that Jay is going to look at him confused, having never seen this man, and that if he went back into Josie's tavern, none of the patrons would know what the hell he was talking about. He was mad. Sick in the head. Hallucinating as his mind went wild with grief and tension.

But Jay nods quickly. "Yeah. Is there a problem? Who was he?"

"Did you see where he went?"

Jay looks out into all the bodies moving through the streets, then shakes his head. "I wasn't watching where he went," Jay says, somewhat defensively. "I figured if he had left the tavern he wasn't a threat to you."

Huxley brushes past Jay, heading toward the main drag where they'd come from. "He's a fuckin' Black Hat."

"A Black Hat?"

Huxley looks pointedly at Jay as he walks. "Black Heart Davies. You remember that story? Captain Tim's old partner that burned the damn church down to get one fugitive? Yeah. That guy. That was him."

Jay looks over their shoulder, and then he lets out a mad bark of laughter. "Ha! You must be joking."

Huxley spins on his partner. "No, I'm not fucking joking! He was a fucking Black Hat, and he said his name was Jim Davies, but everyone knows him as Black Heart Davies."

"Then why aren't you dead?"

Huxley looks around, then walks quickly down the street, motioning Jay to follow. He speaks in a slightly lower voice, but he still has to be loud enough to be heard over the voices and shouts and criers all around them. "He's after the man with the scorpion tattoo—Nathaniel Cartwright is his name. But he figures it'd be easier just to let me handle it. Then he's going to kill me anyway. But he's giving me a one-day head start. And he told me where to start looking for Cartwright."

Jay is shaking his head. "That's a horrible deal."

"Yeah, well …" Huxley turns right onto the main drag, still heading away from the docks. Heading to the north side of the town. "It's the deal that I got."

"Where are we going?"

"We're getting out of here. As quickly as possible," Huxley speaks as though he's thinking on the fly. From the corner of his eyes, he can see Jay remaining circumspect, scanning around them and behind them. "We need to meet up with the others. Then we need to go to Monroe. And we need to go fast. That's where Cartwright is. Or at least where he'll be for the next day."

"We're gonna need horses," Jay says, somewhat distractedly as he looks behind them. "Ain't gonna chase a man across the Riverlands on foot."

"I know." Huxley feels the enormity, the impossibility of everything, just stacking up over his head, like an unbalanced tower that he keeps adding to and knows that it is only a matter of time before it collapses on top of him, crushing him in the dust and rubble. "We'll figure it out."

"You mean we'll steal them."

"Or buy them," Huxley says.

Jay looks back around. "By the way, two very angry men are following us," he says, as though nothing is wrong. "Not sure if they're friends of yours. One's short, wearing green. The other's tall, wearing black. Keeping pace with us about twenty yards behind."

Huxley feels a skitter up his spine, the feeling of something unpleasant hovering behind him. He turns as casually as he can and hazards a glance behind. The two men are hard to miss. They are staring straight back at Huxley. Glaring at him in a way that says they do not care if they are noticed or not. He recalls what Black Heart Davies had said about men that want to get in good with Nathaniel Cartwright—how they'd shoot him in the back of the head and take his jaw to get their foot in the door.

That's who you're dealing with.

Huxley looks straight ahead, that jittery feeling working all the way up to his scalp, where it tingles, and then dissipates. When the momentary rush is gone, there is just the itch, the heaviness, the teeth-grinding feeling of imminent conflict.

"They're from the tavern," he says, flatly.

"Yeah, I figured. Who are they?"

"Friends of Cartwright's, would be my guess," Huxley says, and in a flash, the words he spoke become images in his brain. Those two men trailing them, standing by Cartwright, laughing, drinking, carousing. Going with him on raiding parties. Killing whole villages. Raping women and girls. Holding them down for each other. Executing most of the survivors. Torturing others for sport.

Just like all the other slavers, like the woman with the black braid, whatever the hell her name was. She and her crew. And Bristow. And his crewman that shoots a young man and a boy because he can't be bothered to save them.

Those are the kind of men that are behind you.

Huxley can barely think now. He is buzzing, ticking.

I want to kill them.

You wanted to kill the others, too, he argues with himself.

They all deserve to die.

It'll never be enough.

It doesn't matter.

Huxley feels himself, elementally. Something that cannot be stopped, but only steered a little bit to either side, giving the illusion of control. In these moments, sometimes it feels better to give in to it. Sometimes trying to stop it will only cause the whole thing to swerve and crash into pieces. Sometimes it is best to accept it, to focus on it, to let it carry you.

"This alley here to the right," Huxley says. "Dip into it. And get ready to fight."

"In the middle of town?" Jay says, but he is not truly resisting. Huxley can hear it in the other man's voice, almost a giddiness. Almost excited. "In the middle of the day?"

Huxley doesn't respond.

They hit the corner of the alley and duck into it.

Huxley draws both his revolvers, cocked back.

The two men appear at the mouth of the alley. Huxley stares, identifying them, looking them in their faces, making sure they are the ones.

A passing thought about whether they mean to harm Huxley and Jay, but the looks on their faces say everything that needs to be said. And their hands are at their waistbands as they turn the corner, one man drawing a large hunting knife, the other a revolver.

Is that it? Is that all you brought?

The feeling is exultant.

Huxley pulls both his triggers and the alleyway is suddenly mired in whitish-gray smoke. There is a clatter of gunfire—more than just Huxley's two rounds. The clouds of gunsmoke screen the two pairs of men from each other. There are shouts of fear and surprise.

Huxley feels the old masonry wall to his left explode, feels the shards of brick sharply against the side of his face. He thumbs the hammers on his revolvers back, watches the wind catch the cloud of gunsmoke, lift it away just enough for Huxley to see their legs, and he lets his revolvers loose, winging the rounds just above the pairs of legs that he can see through the haze.

The thought is singular and determined: *You have to see them to kill them. You have to see them. You have to see them. Then kill them. Kill them kill them kill them.*

Hammers back again. Moving without thinking, moving forward.

The wind again, catching the gunsmoke.

Two, then three big steps forward.

A shape in the clearing gunsmoke. A man. It doesn't matter who, or which. The man is there. He is bad. He must be killed.

Huxley is still driving forward and is nearly on top of the man.

Now he can see him. Now he can see the whites of his eyes as he fumbles with his revolver, both hands clasped onto it. It is the shorter man. Small, stubby fingers. Hard to work with. Numb and stiff with fear. He is not the elemental force that Huxley is. Not his equal. Because Huxley is not afraid. He is bloodthirsty.

Out of pure reflex, Huxley strikes out with the revolver in his right hand, the big, heavy piece of metal clobbering the short man in the face, smearing his nose across his face in a billow of red. Then he shoves the barrel of the other revolver into the short man's chest and blows his heart to pieces.

The man crumples, almost melts to the ground.

Kill them.

But Huxley is not finished. He spins around in this strange world he has created, a world of winding tendrils of smoke that smell of sulfur and saltpeter and charcoal. He extracts his own legs from the tumble of limbs that the short, dead man has created, and he looks for the other man.

Kill them both. They both have to die.

The other man is leaning on the corner of the alleyway, clutching his Bowie knife, apparently somehow unaware that this was going to be a gunfight. He sees Huxley coming at him through the smoke and he raises the bowie knife and yells, though it is high-pitched, half fear and half rage. Huxley guns him down—one, then two lead balls into his torso.

The man's yell is silenced, but he spills backward, into the street, trying desperately to get away. Huxley just keeps yanking those hammers back, keeps pulling those triggers. Plume after plume of smoke. Projectiles punching through the man as he crawls backward and finds his voice again, screaming wordlessly for mercy, but Huxley has none to give him.

Huxley empties both revolvers before registering that the man is dead.

Dead in the middle of the street. Huxley standing over him with a smoking gun in each hand, sucking in acrid smoke through his teeth, feeling the burn of it, a beautiful smell, a taste, like retribution.

From behind him the shout, "Huxley! Look out!"

Huxley looks up, sees two men with white armbands and brandished revolvers. Out of pure reaction he snicks back the hammers of his revolvers before realizing there isn't a single bullet left to be fired in either one.

"Drop it!" one of them shouts, raising his revolver.

Huxley doesn't want to turn, doesn't want to take flight. He wants to fight. He wants to barrel forward, to kill, to make them bleed. But he has nothing to resist them with.

He hears Jay's revolver bark off to his right, sees the plume of dirty smoke go jutting out from the corner of his eye. The two guards with their white armbands flinch and separate suddenly, both diving out of the path of the bullet, and raising their revolvers as they go.

Huxley seizes the opportunity to turn and run.

Jay stands at the side of the alley with his revolver outstretched, hammering out the last two rounds in the cylinder, and then turns as Huxley flies past him and falls in behind. Huxley can't see him, but he can hear Jay's rapid, hard footfalls across the dirty, cracked pavement of the alley, counter-rhythm to his own.

Ahead of them, nothing but a brick wall.

Gunshots from behind them. Something whines past his ear, smashes the brick wall that looms in front of them.

A door to the right. Metal, but a rotted wooden frame around it, and crumbling masonry.

"The door!" Huxley shouts, knowing there is no other way out of the alley.

He hits it hard, putting his shoulder into it. There is the sound of old wood rending and the resistance against his shoulder is suddenly gone, and he is falling through the doorway into darkness.

Not darkness.

Dim, red lamplight.

He tumbles, head over heels, then skids to a stop amid the splinters of a doorjamb, in the middle of a carpeted room. The carpet smells ungodly.

Huxley staggers to his feet, blinking rapidly, looking around and trying to assess his situation in the dimly lit room. The pain in his wounded side hits him suddenly, like it had been saving up all this time to remind him that it was there in one big blast. It nearly doubles him over, but he stays standing, gasping.

Jay stumbles in behind him, holding his smoking revolver, looking wild and excited, sweating and out of breath.

Huxley recovers enough from the pain to realize there are others in the room. Three men and four women, and not a bit of clothes between them—except for one heavy-set redheaded woman who still wears an old lace bra. They are seated on couches, in various acts and positions, frozen like a photograph.

"The fuck …" one of the men starts to rise from the filthy couch, and that breaks the moment.

Huxley lurches forward, going for the man that had spoken, for the gunbelt that hangs next to him on the arm of the couch. He kicks the man in the chest before he can rise fully, sprawling him back into the couch and sending the thick redhead squealing like a frightened sow.

Huxley snatches a pistol out of the gunbelt.

An old, single-shot muzzleloader.

"Hey!" a shout from behind him.

Huxley spins, sees a guard just coming into the room, his gun up …

And then Jay hits him hard from behind, coming out of the shadows of the doorframe, using his revolver like a club and bashing the guard's brains in until the man has collapsed onto the foul carpet, twitching and gurgling.

All the women in the room are screaming.

A couple of the men, too.

Jay leaps up from the body. "Help me get him in!"

Huxley leans down, helps Jay drag the body in and slam the door closed, and then he spins back on the naked men, hoping that one of them hasn't gone for a weapon and been more successful than the last guy. "Where's the other guard, Jay?"

Jay is breathless. "He must've gone through the front of the building."

One of the men leaps up from the couch, his chest puffed up, though his erection has gone flaccid. "You know who the fuck I am?"

Huxley shoots the man in the chest with the muzzleloader. There is a flash of smoke and a belch of flame. He actually hears the lead ball striking the man's chest and it sounds like a wet smack. When he lowers the gun, the man is writhing on the couch with a huge hole in the very center of his chest, squirting out streams of arterial blood.

"You're a fucking dead man!" Huxley yells, then drops the now-useless muzzleloader. He turns to the other side of the room where the other men are sitting, along with their hired lovers. They have their hands up, eyes wide, not wanting what their friend got.

Jay holds his empty revolver in one hand, the guard's nearly empty revolver in the other, and he keeps that one trained on the two men. "Your guns. Real gently. Toss them over."

Both of the men have their gunbelts hung on the side of the couches that they are occupying, and they both reach with one hand, very slowly, and pull the guns from their holsters, holding them with two fingers, like a soiled linen, and then toss them to the floor.

"Your horses," Huxley says. "Where are they?"

"We ain't got horses," one of the men says thickly. "Well, we got two, but they's hitched to the wagon outside. Mister, I don't want to end up like Mikey on the floor over there, but I gotta tell you, man-to-man, you don't wanna take that wagon. And it ain't me you gotta worry about."

"I'm not worried about anybody," Huxley says, swiping up one of the revolvers from the ground. He checks the cylinder, sees that it is fully loaded. He pulls the hammer back, shoving his empty revolvers back into his waistband. "We're taking the fucking wagon."

The concerned man is shaking his head. "Everything in that wagon belongs to the Nigger King. He'll pull off your balls when he finds you."

Huxley squints at the man. "I wonder what he'd think if he heard you call him that."

The man swallows. "Oh Jesus. *Overman*. They belong to *Overman*."

"Well, that just makes it even better, doesn't it?" Huxley looks to Jay and nods, pointing for the door that Huxley assumes leads into the front of the brothel, or tavern, or whatever business this is. "Let's get the fuck out." To the still-breathing two, he waves the revolver. "Now you boys just sit tight right there and don't move. That'd be a bad mistake."

Jay catches his arm. "Let's go out the back. If the other guard went around, he'll be on the other side of that door."

Huxley doesn't have time to think it through. Any action is better than no action at all.

Jay opens the door, peaks out.

Huxley keeps his revolver trained on the men on the couches, but glances over his shoulder at Jay. "Is it clear? Can we go?"

"Yeah." Jay reaches back and smacks Huxley on the shoulder as though to spur him. "Come on."

The two of them slip through the door, Huxley keeping his revolver on the men and their whores until the very last second, then he turns and sprints down the alley. It still smells of gunsmoke. At the mouth of the alley, strangers have gathered around the two bodies and they look up to see Huxley and Jay running at them, weapons in hand. Most of them jump back. One stays a half second longer, as though considering challenging them, but no one wants to just throw themselves on the tracks in front of a hurtling locomotive.

My, what big teeth you have …

"Everyone get the fuck back!" Jay shouts at them, waving his weapon.

Around the corner and onto the main drag.

There, in front of the whorehouse they have just come out of, there is a wagon hitched to a team of two horses. It is guarded by a single young man.

Too old to be called a boy, but not by much.

He stands at the side of the wagon, a scattergun in his hand, looking toward the main door of the whorehouse. The front door has been flung open, and a steady stream of people are exiting, whores and patrons alike, some of them dressed, some of them not.

Huxley and Jay cut through the flow of people, making a line for the wagon.

At the last second the young man guarding the wagon looks in their direction, sees their eyes fixated on him, sees the weapons in their hands.

But by then it's too late.

Huxley smashes him with his revolver, right across the temple, sending the man sprawling onto the ground with a little cry of surprise and pain. Huxley kicks the scattergun out of his hands and jumps atop the wagon.

The young man writhes on the ground, clutching his face. He rolls onto his back, looking up at Huxley, and Huxley can see that he has broken the bones on the side of the man's face, the eye already swelling and bloodshot. "I can't see!" the man is screaming. "I can't see!"

Price of doing business.

Huxley grabs up the reins of the wagon as Jay bounds onto the great wooden contraption with him. Jay points his pistol at the crowd around them.

"All you fucks get back!" he bellows. "Everyone look at the fucking ground! I'll shoot the next motherfucker that looks at me!" And for good measure, he fires a shot, though Huxley can't tell if it was aimed at anyone or not.

The horses whinny and stamp in their harnesses, but they are not strangers to violence. Huxley yanks the reins, swinging the horses in a tight turn and pulling them onto the main drag, people trying desperately to get out of their way. Leather reins in his hands, clumsy as his fingers work around the revolvers he refuses to holster.

The other guard with the white armband emerges from the whorehouse, weapon up.

Huxley wings a shot at him, but doesn't have time to see if he hit. He faces forward and snaps the reins, hunching over as he anticipates the crack of incoming rounds. He glances over his shoulder, but the guard is not in the doorway anymore.

The horses churn forward, their shod hooves striking loudly against the old pavement, the wagon wheels spinning faster and the momentum beginning to build, the whole heavy burden speeding up as they charge down the street.

North. Out of the city.

Up ahead of them, two guards stand at the side of the street, but they seem unsure of what to do.

Huxley and Jay and the stolen wagon roar past them. They don't make a move to intercept.

They crest a hill—that long, steady rise that leads away from the river-bank—and Huxley can see the gate ahead of them, guards standing about it, but they have no way of knowing that this wagon is anything more than a fast-moving delivery. Huxley and Jay don't even look at the guards as they pass. Huxley just keeps snapping the reins, yelling at the two horses to go faster.

The wagon bursts out of the northern gate of Shreveport. The sound of the wind. The sound of the hooves on concrete. The sound of Huxley's own breathing. And …

Huxley looks to his right and realizes that Jay is laughing.

Laughing hysterically.

His eyes are bright and dark at once, they are catching the light of the sunset and they look like burning coals, like something made of fire. And it scares Huxley for the briefest of moments until he feels that same manic laughter rising in his own throat, and he can't keep it down, he can't deny the reckless, cathartic, violent joy of it all.

You showed them, Huxley's mind bubbles over. *You fucking showed them.*

And he begins to laugh with Jay.

CHAPTER 5

Lowell's mind is a scattered mess. Every thought inconsistent with the last. He is fighting with himself, even while he maintains a calm demeanor.

They have moved quickly through the edges of the city. The man named Rigo and the woman named Brie, they are the oldest among them. They carry the guns openly. Rigo walks in front, Brie in the back. Between them, a column of eleven of the slaves from the barge, plus Lowell. Chained together, but only for show—their manacles are not bolted. But the feel of the iron on Lowell's wrists is peripheral to what is going on in his mind. They pass guards at the gate, and maybe they give Rigo and Brie an odd look, maybe they seem suspicious of all these slaves walking when they are generally carried on wagons, but they say nothing, and they allow them to pass without question. None of this even registers with Lowell. He is elsewhere.

He is picturing the man, Don, drunk off the liquor stores he found stashed in the crew quarters, and the way he had looked at Lowell. The fear that Lowell had felt, but also the rage. This memory is followed by one from before: the memory of Don on Mother, even as she died. The way her body moved only because he was moving it. Like a dead animal. Like the dead dog that he'd skinned.

A glimpse, a piercing glare in his mind, some recollection of *before*, the *before* that came before Mother and Father ...

A woman. Her hair is dark, almost black. She has a tan complexion. The same coloring as Rigo. He can barely see the blood pouring out of her head, except for when it trickles across her brown skin. She is looking at him with terror in her eyes and she is holding his face in hers so that he can feel the callouses on her hands, her longish fingernails biting into his skin.

She speaks in Spanish. Even the memory is in Spanish.

The language that he didn't know he spoke.

"Run, Lowell. Run away from these men. Don't ever let them catch you."

He pulls back from that memory, recoils from it. Hurls himself into another. Very recent. So recent he can still feel the stickiness of the blood caught in the webbing of his fingers ...

Don. Lowell's left hand pulling his head back, his drunken head, loose with alcohol and the bitter stinking breath that pours out of him. The knife is in Lowell's right hand. The knife that Mr. Huxley had given him. And he is terrified, but he put it to work, one cut, not knowing how it would feel, remembering the bitch in the trailer that he'd skinned and thinking it would be so hard, but then remembering how human skin is so soft. He doesn't know how he knows that. He can't remember. But he feels it again when the blade goes in, just slides in so easily that it surprises him, makes his cut short and hesitating.

I know this feeling. I don't know how I know. But I do.

He cuts again, angry this time. This one goes deep. He can feel the easy parting of the flesh, the hard resistance of the windpipe, the gush of blood. The sound that Don made—he remembers that very clearly ...

"Stop here."

A voice in Spanish again.

Lowell looks up, out of the world of memories and into the world of the present. The here and the now. Rigo had spoken in Spanish. He understood it perfectly. The language slides into his mind with surprising ease, just like knives go into people's skin oh-so easily.

Lowell looks around. They have stopped. The stinking city of Shreveport is gone. They are on a road, but it is not a big road. This one is some overgrown side road, surrounded by houses. More houses than Lowell has ever seen. Everything is dilapidated and falling apart. Nature here is more insistent than on the other side of the Red River where Lowell comes from. Everything here is green. It climbs over houses and old cars. It reclaims what it owned before.

The girl named Brie is going down the line of slaves, pulling manacles off their hands. Rigo has a big, heavy satchel and he sets this on the ground and upends it. What topples out is a collection of edged weapons, revolvers, and scatterguns. Brie has a similar pack. They'd taken all the weapons they could carry from the slave barge.

Rigo kneels over the weapons. He grabs two revolvers, but he already has two revolvers strapped to his person. He looks up at Lowell and nods his head. "You. Boy. You speak Spanish?" he says in their shared language.

"Yes."

"Come here," Rigo waves him over. The man's face seems like it's built to be kind. But his one good eye tells Lowell something else. Just speaking the language, just being around Rigo, it pulls all those old memories from *before* up a bit more from where they went, deep inside of Lowell. He still can't access them at will, but like the image of the Mexican woman who told him to run, he is remembering more frequently now. Little bits and pieces. He doesn't want to remember. Every time he remembers he feels angrier.

Lowell goes to Rigo, stands over him.

Squatting, Rigo has to look up at Lowell just a bit. His one good eye is expressive. The other just hollow and dead. But that one good eye ... it can be cold. Or it can be kind. He looks at Lowell like a friend, and for some reason Lowell is filled with relief. "Where'd you learn Spanish?"

Lowell shakes his head. "I don't know."

"You can't remember?"

"I don't remember things from before."

Rigo nods, slowly. "Okay. You wouldn't be the first." He pushes one of the revolvers into Lowell's hands. "That's for you. You know how to work it?"

Lowell looks at it. He remembers Father's revolver. But Father never shot it. Never reloaded it. Lowell didn't know much about them. He shakes his head. "I don't think so."

Rigo hastily points at the parts. "You pull the hammer back, then you pull the trigger. It's that simple. You got six shots. It's already loaded. I'll teach you how to reload it later, okay? If you need it now, it's pull the hammer back, then pull the trigger. Understand?"

Lowell nods. "I understand."

Beside Rigo, Brie has knelt down to help distribute the weapons.

Rigo gives her a glance over his shoulder, then rises, taking Lowell by the shoulder and pulling him away from the others.

When they are a few yards from the others, Rigo asks him, "Where'd you come from?"

"I was … I was in my home," Lowell says, a little unsteadily. "Then they came."

"Huxley, you mean?" Rigo raises an eyebrow.

"Yes. They killed Mother and Father."

Rigo's gaze intensifies a bit. He lowers his chin, holding eye contact with Lowell. "Listen to me. All of that's done and over with now, okay? You can't go back. No one can go back." He puts his hands to his chest. "I can't go back either. I lost people too. But this thing? This thing that we're doing?" His lips pinch together a bit, a stern look. "This is what needs to be done. Okay? These people out here. These so-called Riverlanders … they're bad people Lowell. I don't know your history and I don't know where you came from, but I'd bet money they were the ones that hurt your other family—the ones that taught you Spanish. I bet they were traders, just like my family. I bet they got attacked by slavers, just like my family. And somehow you got away. Just like I got away."

Run, Lowell. Run away from these men. Don't ever let them catch you.

"You and me, we're like brothers," Rigo says, his eye softening. "These people we're after … those are the ones that destroy everything. I don't know what happened to that family you can't remember. I wasn't there. I had my own problems to deal with. But I will tell you this: Huxley saved you for a reason. He saw something in you. Maybe he saw in you what he saw in me. Maybe that's why we're both here." He slaps Lowell's shoulder. "Trust Huxley, okay?"

Lowell nods. "Okay."

Trust Huxley, Lowell says. *Trust him because he knows who you are. He knows what's inside of you.*

Lowell feels a strange sense, a feeling he hadn't felt in a very long time. A feeling of familiarity. A feeling of … belonging to something. He wasn't weird to Rigo. He wasn't weird to Huxley. He wasn't just an Animal Child to them. With Huxley and Rigo and Brie, Lowell was normal.

They were all alike.

They were all Animal Children.

CHAPTER 6

Several miles north of Shreveport, Huxley takes a sharp left turn into an old abandoned neighborhood—or at least what he hopes will be abandoned. All of the burning rage has left him. The insane, roaring laughter has died in his chest. It's all compressed down into black coal now.

They are lucky that the lantern hanging on the side of the wagon was already lit. It will not be long now before they are in complete dark and it is the only light they have. It is not much, but it is enough to splash some dull yellow over what is in front of them, and make navigation a little easier.

When they are deep into the abandoned neighborhood, Huxley pulls the reins and stops the two horses. They whinny and snort at him and then clomp to a halt. The wagon shifts and rocks beneath him. All around them, the neighborhood stands in rotted ruin, everything being taken over by vegetation. Nature is a patient native. It always gives way, but in persistence, always wins in the end.

Huxley leans forward, putting his elbows on his knees and he hangs his head and takes one giant breath and then heaves it out.

Jay sits beside him in the wagon, his leg propped up. He tilts his head and regards Huxley with a very small measure of concern. "You alright there, brother?"

Huxley's heart is skipping, jumping around in his chest. Over an hour has passed since the shoot-out. His body doesn't seem to realize that. It is strange. He's never had this reaction before. He has the sensation of losing ground, sliding down a very slippery slope with no handholds to work his way back up.

Why? Why do I feel this way?

What is it? What is it that I'm feeling?

He remembers his fever dream. Remembers the feeling of it so clearly. The panic that he'd felt when Charity was looking at him, telling him that she did not even recognize him anymore. And he'd told her that he didn't want to be here anymore. He just wanted to be with her. With Nadine.

I just want to go home.

But you have no home.

There are moments when you realize your utter powerlessness in life. It is an almost paralyzing moment when you realize there is no backing out. There is no escape. You can kid yourself into ignoring it, but eventually the realization will hit you, and it carries with it the sensation of being trapped, of claustrophobia. No way out.

Huxley remembers reading years ago about people trapped in tunnels. How, in their desperation, they would press themselves forward, forcing their bodies into tight spaces, so tight that they couldn't even move backward and the only option was to keep pressing forward and hope, hope to God that there is an opening that will set you free ...

That is what Huxley feels.

He raises his head, taking in more air.

Keep your head above the water.

He steadies himself. There is nothing to be done about it. He is here. This is now. Give in to it.

The feeling begins to fade, gradually, like a momentary sickness.

Beside him, Jay lets out a long sigh. "You thinking about them?"

Huxley runs a hand over his face, then looks at Jay. "About who?"

Jay's cold eyes are taking him in. "I heard you in the slave cages yesterday. Talking to the slaves. You think about them. And you think about how they wouldn't recognize who you are now. You worry about it. Is that true? Is that what you're thinking about?"

Huxley doesn't answer. He just faces forward again.

Jay stretches his back, languidly, and pulls his revolver. Huxley eyes the other man, but it is obvious that Jay is not intending to use it. The other man just inspects the gun, points it at a few random objects. He is just giving his hands something to do. He aims down the barrel at an old, rusted mailbox, squints one eye, and says quietly, "You gotta throw them away."

Throw them away, Huxley echoes in his mind.

Jay lowers the revolver into his lap, runs a thumb over the worn wooden grips. "Throw them away, brother. It's the only way. If you don't, it'll kill you. I know. I've been there. But you can't bring them back. They're dead as dead can be. So why do we try to hold on to to their corpses?" Jay shrugs at his own question. "Human nature I suppose. Misguided love." He looks at Huxley. "Throw them away. Forget about them. They have no bearing on the world now. They cannot affect you. You have to take their power away. Forget that you loved them. Forget that they ever meant anything to you. If you don't then you'll keep worrying about what they would think about you. But the reality of the situation is that they're dead and they *can't* think about you. And if they were alive, you wouldn't be who you are. You wouldn't have become this person. You are this person because they were taken from you. And that's why you do what you do."

That's wrong, Huxley wants to say, but even as his conscious mind rebels against the concept—*That's my wife, my daughter, I can't forget about them!*—he does the horrible thing that Jay tells him to do, and just for a moment, he imagines that they never were. That he never loved them. That they had no power over him. He throws them away.

And he feels nothing.

Nothing at all.

And isn't that better than the pain?

"We've got no room for that stuff now," Jay says. "No room for love. There's too much hate. And maybe it'll send us straight to hell when we die, but it's the only way anything will ever get done. It's the only way we're going to make them bleed."

It's the only way.

A sound to their right. The snap of a twig.

Huxley's revolver is suddenly in his hand and pointing off to where the noise came from.

"Easy now," a voice says. "It's me."

Brie steps out from between two abandoned houses, covered in rot and mold and ancient graffiti. She holds a scattergun, the barrel pointed at the ground. She smiles at them, her long face impossibly improved by it.

"Fancy seeing you here."

Huxley lowers his revolver. "Is everybody with you?"

She nods. "Hiding in the woods behind the neighborhood."

Huxley stands up and shoves the revolver in his waistband. He looks around, assessing the situation. The wagon wasn't going to fit back in the woods. It might fit back behind one of the houses or old buildings, but he doesn't want to camp tonight. He wants to keep going until the sun comes back up. And when he does stop, he doesn't want to be on this same road. It would be wiser to take a few turns before settling down.

Can't stay here. Can't stay anywhere around here.

"Go get everyone," Huxley says. "We need to move on."

Brie seems a bit unsure. "We're off the road ..."

"We need to move," Huxley says again, more firmly. "We got a wagon and two horses that have plenty of miles left in them before they need to rest. Go get the others. We'll get everyone in the wagon."

Brie looks dubiously at the wagon. "There's already stuff in the back. What is it?"

Huxley looks at the cargo. "I don't know. We just took it."

"You took it?" she asks. "From who?"

Huxley spits off the side of the wagon. "Overman."

Brie judges him to determine if it is a poor joke, and gradually realizes he is serious. "Well. Now we'll have the Black Hats, the slavers, *and* Overman's goons after us. You weren't joking. This isn't going to be an easy road."

Huxley grabs the lantern from where it hangs on the side of the wagon and pulls himself over the bench seat into the cargo bed as Brie approaches. Jay stands on the bench and looks down at the contents of the bed, while Brie pulls herself up onto one of the rear tires. The yellow lantern light flickers over a bed full of hastily constructed wooden crates. Shallow and long. At least a dozen of them.

Brie whistles quietly. "I don't know what's in those. But I think Overman might want them back."

"Well, that's not gonna happen." Huxley pries at one of the box lids with his fingers, but they are held in place by thick tacks. He mutters a curse and then reaches for his knife, but remembers he gave it to Lowell. He looks around for something else to use.

"This might help," Jay says, reaching into the back and unearthing a rusty crowbar. He holds it out to Huxley.

Huxley swipes the crowbar and starts working it in between the box and the lid and prying upward. Boards creak and crack. He moves the crowbar along, loosening the lid little by little until it is barely hanging on. Then he stands back up fully and kicks the lid twice. It tumbles off in a clatter.

Huxley leans over the exposed box and brushes away a coating of straw that has been used to cushion the contents.

Still standing on the bench of the wagon, Jay claps his hands together. "My oh my. We chose the right wagon to hijack, didn't we?"

In the crate, lain side by side, are five rifles. Beyond the fact that they are rifles, Huxley cannot determine. He bends and picks one up. He can tell immediately from the intimidating heft of the rifle, and the crudeness of its construction that it is newly manufactured and not from the Old World. But this is no crank-charged scattergun, or even one of the old muzzle-loading percussion rifles. In place of the hot-wire and crank that Huxley expected, there is a cast-iron lever and a breech.

"Holy shit," Huxley says. "These are goddamn cartridge rifles."

"What?" Jay comes over the bench and into the cargo bed.

"Cartridge rifles," Huxley repeats. "At least these five are."

Jay looks around. "Where are the cartridges?"

Huxley grips the rifle like it might fly out of his hands and disappear. But he looks around, swinging the lantern around in his other hand, the light washing and swaying back and forth in the cargo bed. In the corner of the bed, just behind Jay, Huxley sees a set of smaller boxes, these ones cubes.

He rattles the lantern in that direction. "Check those boxes."

Jay turns, sees what Huxley sees, and bends to start working at these smaller crates. As he works the lid off the one, Huxley turns to Brie. "Go and get the others out of the woods."

Brie nods once, then hops down off the back tire and jogs back into the woods.

Huxley's attention is drawn back by the sound of splintering wood and tacks popping free. Jay hunches over the small, cube-like crate, staring down. His shoulders shake and Huxley wonders what he is doing, but then he hears the laugh.

"It's our lucky day, brother." Jay spins aside on one foot and displays the contents of the smaller crate. Inside, cushioned on beds of coarse sawdust, are rows upon rows of little brass cylinders, with silver centers.

Huxley steps over the lid he had removed from the rifle crate and bends over Jay, plucking one of the little brass objects from its snug packing in the sawdust. It is a short, fat cartridge with a big, conical bullet on the end. The bottom of the casing is lipped to fit in a breech, and the center is bored out to receive a primer that looks identical to the caps from his revolver.

"They're manufacturing this shit now," Jay says, and his voice is almost rapturous. "Progress, Huxley. That's fucking progress."

Huxley ignores him. He levers the breech block open on the ugly rifle in his hands. He looks at it suspiciously for a moment, then at the cartridge, wondering how secure these things were, how well they were made. Just by sight and touch, they did not seem to be very well manufactured. Still, the draw of the concept moves Huxley's hand and extinguishes most of his fears.

He puts the cartridge in the breech. It fits tightly so that he has to press on the back with his thumb to get it slip into place. But it does slip into place. It fits. Then he pulls the lever back into place and watches the breech slip closed, the lever locking with a surprisingly confident *click*.

"I can't believe that shit works," Jay says, almost giddy. "Breechloaders. You know what kind of leaps and bounds this is over everyone else?"

"We don't know if it works until we fire it," Huxley says. "And I'm not gonna fire it here." Huxley breaks from his nearly trancelike stare at the rifle in his hands. He sets the loaded rifle off to the side, thinking a mile a minute now. "Help me unload these crates. Get all the crates open and get everything they have out."

"Okay …" Jay seems unsure.

Huxley points behind one of the houses. "Except for the cartridge boxes. Leave those. But the rest of this wood … let's pile it on that house and start a fire."

"We don't …"

Huxley waves him off, stooping to pull the other four rifles from the opened crate. "I know, I know! We're not sticking around. We're gonna light the fire to draw people off. If anyone is coming for us out of Shreveport, they'll see the fire and figure it's us. They'll slow down and take time to sneak up on us. Might give us a half hour or so lead on them. Or at least make up for the time we've lost here."

Jay is nodding now. "Okay. Yeah. Good idea."

The two of them move quickly, ripping lids off of crates. Six crates in all, each with five of the same breechloading rifles sitting in them. They unpack the rifles, stacking them on one side of the wagon while they noisily toss the empty wooden boxes over the side. They are just finishing the last crate when Brie returns with a string of semifamiliar faces, Rigo taking up the rear.

Lowell stands next to Brie, looking up at Huxley and Jay and the wagon-load of rifles stacked to one side. Huxley can see a revolver in his waistband that hadn't been there before.

They had the hate, Huxley remembers. *I gave them the guns.*

Huxley points to the discarded crates. "Everyone grab those boxes and stack them up against that house."

They make quick work of it. Huxley watches them. Kids, really, but they range. Some are younger than others. Some are older. Maybe even old enough to get a rifle. How the hell should Huxley know?

He catches Brie and motions her up into the wagon. She climbs up, glancing back and forth between the rifles and him. Huxley takes one up, shows it to her in the dim light of his lantern, opening and closing the breech.

"You know how to work one of these?" he asks.

She gives him a half smile. "Do you?"

Huxley looks at the rifle in his hands. "Just what I've read in books. Never seen one before. But I guess the concept is pretty simple." He points to the open breech, the chamber a hole in the center of it. "It's a cartridge gun. Like they used to have way back in the day. A long time before the Old World. Like an old buffalo rifle. You put the cartridge in the chamber. Close the breech. Like this. Hammer back. And then you shoot."

She inclines herself over the breech, brushing hair back as it hangs in her face. Huxley can smell her sweat and stink from being on the road all day. He is sure that he smells much worse. They all probably do. He had hoped in the back of his mind to afford the time for a bath, but hadn't anticipated being run out of Shreveport so quickly.

"Okay," she says. "I got it."

Huxley hands her the rifle. "How many of yours do you think can handle one of these?"

"How many of mine?"

"Your people."

She looks up at him oddly. "Not just mine. But I'd say maybe … most of them."

Huxley looks at the pile of rifles. They have more than enough to go around. "Give them to whoever you think can handle one. And then get everyone on this wagon. We're leaving as soon as I light that fire."

She doesn't ask him why he is lighting a fire, and he doesn't give her a chance. He slips over the side of the wagon and stalks to the house where the slaves have stacked up the broken crates.

"Is this good?" one of them asks.

The way it is said. Almost pleading with Huxley. Almost desperate to please him.

Or afraid that they've angered me.

Huxley frowns at the speaker, a teenage boy. Slightly older than Lowell. "Yes, it's fine. Go to the wagon."

When the slaves have left him, Huxley stoops to the pile of wood, grimacing at the pain it causes in his side. He scoops up the straw and wood shavings that had been inside of the crates and stacks it up underneath all of that dry, brittle wood. He pours a charge of gunpowder to make it light easier and strikes a flint into it. The sparks fly and after a few tries, the gunpowder ignites in a hissing flash and a plume of white smoke. He leans away from it, squinting. The straw and wood shavings catch quickly and it takes no encouragement from him. The boxes are old, dried wood. They go up like they are dipped in tar.

He makes his way back to the wagon with urgency in his step, absently holding his side. He can still feel the heat of the fire at his back as it spreads hungrily. Everyone is packed into the wagon, and the horses do not seem happy about their load, but then, they have not even begun to tow it.

Give it time, boys. You'll like it even less.

Brie and Lowell sit on one side of the wagon, Rigo on the other. Jay is sitting in the front bench seat, a new, breech-loading rifle in his lap, and he looks pleased.

Huxley pulls himself up into his seat and grabs up the reins. He snaps them and the wagon groans and creaks back into motion, the pair of horses chuffing their displeasure at the load. With the fire burning, consuming the house behind them, and sending up a huge pillar of smoke, they leave the abandoned neighborhood for the main road east. Plunging themselves into the Riverlands.

East, where the slavers go.

CHAPTER 7

They come across the small ranch, visible from the crest of a hill about a mile to the west of it. Stakes driven into the ground with less than a few inches between create the fence, and corralled inside, Huxley can see several horses. A large stable. A barn of faded scrap wood that is stuffed with what looks like hay. A small cottage built of stone and timber sits just outside the fences. Smoke pours from the squat little chimney. A banner is displayed on the canted flagpole—some image of yellow and green that Huxley cannot make out and suspects he wouldn't recognize anyway.

Huxley eyes the little cottage and the ranch, the fresh horses inside. He tries to clear his throat but finds it gummed up and dry. He grabs a water skin and sips from it very conscientiously. He swishes the cold water around in his mouth, then swallows.

He is exhausted. The effort of anything seems too much for him. His hands feel frozen around the reins, and the horses look no better than he does. They are close to blown. Or maybe they are blown already, just barely hauling the heavy wagon on. They've had little to no fodder in the day since Shreveport— only whatever they could graze on while Huxley and his group took turns sleeping in the warmth of the day. None of them has had food but what they had been able to carry in their hands off the slave barge. And no human or beast has had more than two hours of rest since they fled Shreveport. Brie has put a fresh poultice on his side, but it is only to keep from infection and does nothing for pain. And pain he is learning to deal with.

But we have good rifles, Huxley thinks, finally clearing his throat.

He blinks, and even that feels hard and sluggish. His eyelids don't want to come open again. "How many do you think there are?" he asks Jay who is sitting next to him.

Brie leans in from the back where the rest of them are dozing off fitfully, jounced awake by every pothole in this long road. She looks at the little ranch with a calculating eye, as though the question was posed to her.

"People or horses?" Jay asks, rubbing life back into his face. His eyes are squinty and bloodshot.

"Both." Huxley leans on his elbows.

"It's a horse swap," Brie announces. "Councilmen's business only."

Huxley grunts, as though Brie has said something darkly amusing. "Of course."

Jay stretches his back. "I'd guess about a dozen horses."

"Probably just a family to tend to them," Brie says. "A man and a woman, at least. Maybe some kids. Maybe they're old, maybe they're not. But we could take them."

"We could take them?" Huxley asks, though the conviction of his question—the shock of it—is lackluster. He wants to believe that he wasn't thinking about just riding in and wiping out this family for the horses that he so desperately needs, but it seems he cannot lie to himself.

"Easily." Brie nods.

Huxley snorts, then spits off to the side. "We'll try to pay for what we take. But we need the horses. And I won't be negotiating. Have everyone loaded up and ready. In case things go badly."

Brie passes it along to the others in the back of the wagon, and then Huxley spurs the tired duo of horses on down the mild slope of the hill toward the ranch. Behind them, the sun is just barely above the horizon, and as they descend the hill, the shadows swallow them up. Dusk is here again, a reminder that they need sleep, and also that there are many, many miles to cross and time is running out. This day is at an end.

Which means it has been over one day since they left Shreveport.

Black Heart Davies is after me now. He'll be on my trail, all the mercy used up.

He's just a man, Huxley tells himself, but he feels the weight of that one man on his head, the feeling a field rat might get when a hawk's shadow passes over him.

Forward is the only way.

They emerge from the shadow of the hill into tame, ochre sunlight. It is cold and ineffectual. It does not warm and it barely provides light, skewing everything into the same odd hues of orange and gray, a messy palette where shapes are hard to see. Onto the dirt drive, a man steps in their path, holding a long gun similar to the ones they *procured* from Overman.

The man is middle-aged, it seems, but gone almost completely gray. He is a big man, and he holds the rifle in his grip, not exactly pointing it at them, but not holding it in a welcoming way either. Huxley pulls the reins back and the horses readily stop, huffing plumes of steam from their giant, flared nostrils, happy to no longer be pulling their load.

The man with the rifle stands resolutely and eyes them up and down. "What's your purpose here?" he challenges.

Huxley looks over top of the man's head at the little cottage behind him. The smoking chimney. The two dark windows that face them on the front of it. There is no one else that Huxley can see. The rancher talks big for a man by himself.

Tiredly, Huxley addresses the man. "My horses are blown. I'd like to trade them for fresh ones. And I need some additional horses to be saddled. For riders."

The ranch keeper looks Huxley over again, his face all but a complete sneer. Then he looks at the ragged group that fills the back of the wagon. Huxley knows that it has not escaped the man that they are all holding rifles, but the man does not budge.

"Where are your markings?" the man asks.

Huxley's exhausted mind tries to work through the question. "Our markings?"

"Your sigils. You have no banner," the ranch keeper says, almost as though he is making up his mind. "No banner. No councilman's protection. These horses are for council's business only. You should move along."

The words float through the air, slipping into Huxley's ears and bouncing around, swallowed by the caverns of his mind. Like stones down a well, they skitter and scatter down and stir things sleeping in the darkness. All the while, Huxley stares at the other man, and nothing about his face changes, no tremble on his lip or twitch of his eyebrows.

The beard around Huxley's neck begins to itch again.

Huxley's finger creeps up, but fastens itself to his collar.

"Council's business?" he asks quietly.

So quietly that the ranch keeper leans forward a bit, eyes squinting as he tries harder to hear.

A horse whinnies loudly, tossing its head around as though it smells something foul on the wind.

Huxley's finger finds the spot in his beard that itches. His fingernails scrape at the dirty flesh. It stings raw and he withdraws his hand, then leans forward, elbows on his rifle. "Council's business, I asked. Just what is 'council's business'?"

The ranch keeper leans back, licks his lips. "Well …"

"Running slaves to and fro?" Huxley says, his voice coldly calm. "Ripping children from their mothers? Sons and daughters from their fathers? Castrating the boys? Raping the girls? Is that the sort of councilman's business you're talking about?"

The ranch keeper opens his mouth to argue.

Huxley stands up, throwing down the reins of the horses. He towers over the man in the road, who suddenly seems smaller, and by the look on his face, feels it too. Huxley has his revolver in his hand, but he doesn't point it, doesn't cock it. Just stares this little man down.

"Fuck this guy," Jay says from beside Huxley. The pale man leans forward, his rifle resting across his lap, almost lazily. "That's a nice house you have behind you, my friend. I had a house once." Jay's voice gets quiet and breathy. "I bet you got a nice little family up in there. You know I had a family one time? I did. So did my friends. We all had nice little families. You know what happened to them?"

"I-I …"

Huxley interrupts him with a shout: "Do you know what happened to them!" Silence.

Jay taps his finger steadily on the frame of his rifle. "Councilman's business. That's what happened to them."

The ranch keeper is clutching his own gun now, nervous. If he had strength to show, he would have shown it now. He is exactly what they thought he was. One lonely man, perhaps with a wife and child huddled in the cottage behind them, praying that the words of protection blessed over them by some councilman is enough to keep them safe, despite all signs pointing to the opposite.

Huxley spits in the dirt between them.

The ranch keeper stumbles over his words. "Listen … I'm not a slaver. I don't do that stuff. I just … I just give them fresh horses …"

"You sit here," Huxley interrupts. "In the middle of nowhere, on this so-called Slavers' Trail. Just you. And a dozen or so horses. And no one robs you." Huxley snorts. "Is that the power of a councilman's banner? Is that how much fear they wield? That you feel that you and your family are safe here, just resting under the threat that if anyone takes anything from you, they'll piss off a councilman? Those banners hanging on your ranch house … is that all the protection you need?"

Nothing. Stammering.

Jay tilts his head, just slightly as he speaks, like a curious dog. "What if we don't give a fuck about your banners? What if we're not afraid of your councilman?"

"You … you should be!" he stutters, powerless.

Huxley reaches into the satchel at his feet and pulls out the sack of crude gold coins—melted and cast with Riverland Nations stamps. It is enough gold to pay for twice the horses that the ranch keeper even cares for. Huxley throws the entire sack of gold onto the ground where he just spat. The leather pouch loosens and spills as it strikes, scattering little golden disks across the hard-packed dirt.

The ranch keeper stares at it, then up at Huxley, not quite sure what to do.

"What the fuck?" Jay says to Huxley. "Don't give him the gold …"

"Shut up," Huxley cuts him off with a hand. He stands there in silence for a moment, then speaks to the ranch keeper in low tones: "Take the gold."

The ranch keeper is visibly shaking. But he draws himself up and raises his chin.

Just take the money, Huxley thinks, trying to will it into reality. *Just take it and let me on my way.*

"I am an official of the Riverland Nations, appointed by the Great Council," the ranch keeper announces in a loud, but quavering voice. "Deputized by Councilman Barkley. I will not be bribed by outlaws. This is Barkley land that you're standing on, and I'll extend you the kindness of warning you that Councilman Barkley doesn't take to outlaws. Leave now and I'll forget about you. Continue trying to take what isn't yours and Councilman Barkley's men, and his Black Hats, will hunt you down and have your skins hanging on the side of the road by the end of the week."

Huxley is shaking his head, his teeth clenched together. He points to the coins on the ground. "Just take the fucking money," he hisses. "For yourself and your family. So they don't have to watch you die. So we don't have to murder them in their own house."

The man raises his rifle in unsteady hands. "You ... you're all under arrest!"

A plume of gray smoke erupts from beside Huxley. He watches the ranch keeper stumble backward, blood spinning in ribbons out of his chest. His rifle swings wildly and goes off, the round zipping off to Huxley's left. He hits the ground, dead as a sack of rocks.

Huxley looks to his right. Jay is standing there, levering open the breech of his rifle, smoke pouring out of it. He inserts another cartridge and snaps the breech closed. "That man," he announces loudly. "Was a part of the slave trade. He deserved to die. He's taken from people like us and our families long enough. I'm done with these people feeding off of us. I'm done with these people."

Huxley stares at the body.

What do I feel?

But he refuses to think about Charity, about Nadine, and what they would think of him. So when he looks at the body he feels ... nothing. He raises his eyes to the cottage, but speaks to everyone standing behind him. "Everything he has is yours. Restitution for what's been stolen. Take what you want. You have ten minutes before I burn that house to the ground. Take what you want and get out."

Huxley can feel the wagon shaking as the occupants hop down out of it. Some of them are running for the house, rifles held up to their shoulders, aware there might be others inside. Some of them seem eager, but some of them seem hesitant. The eager ones spur on the hesitant ones, and they become a wave. A mob. A riot, small in scale, but with the same sense of general anonymity. Out here in the middle of nowhere, there is no one to witness the sharing of their sins. No one but God himself, and in these wildlings' hearts and souls, they have forgotten that such an entity exists.

"Come on," Brie's voice speaks from behind him.

Huxley turns, thinking that she is talking to him. But he sees that she is standing up in front of Lowell, her hand extended while Lowell keeps his seat on the side of the wagon. At first he is staring at Brie, and it seems he is about to take her hand and go with her. But a gunshot snaps his attention to the house. Then there is screaming—a woman screaming. And another gunshot. And another. And each one makes Lowell flinch, and each flinch seems to sink him further into his seat.

Brie takes him by the face and forces him to look at her. "Don't feel bad for them, Lowell. They're bad, bad people. They deserve what they get. Do you trust me? Do you think I know what I'm talking about?"

Lowell stares up at her, eyes glistening. But he nods.

"Then come with me," she smiles, disarmingly, and there is something horrible and beautiful about it as the screaming and shouting crescendos within the cottage. Someone pleading for their life. And others, not sure what to do with the person pleading, an argument being set forth, voices shouting at each other. Huxley cannot hear the words, but he can imagine the context of the situation.

Is this justice?

Is this right?

To kill, or to show mercy?

They stand in a world of conflicting magnetic fields, and the needles of each of their moral compasses simply spins and spins and spins and never seems to point one way or another.

"Come on," Brie insists, taking Lowell by the hand.

And Lowell stands up.

From the direction of the cottage, there is the sound of a final argument, and then a gunshot. A moment of panicked shouting. Then silence. Lowell does not seem to notice any of this as Brie walks him to the back of the wagon. The two of them jump down and make their way to the cottage.

Now in the wagon, there are only Jay and Huxley, and Rigo, who is silent in the back.

Jay takes in a great breath, like he is smelling and tasting the air. He lets it out slowly, languorously. He watches the backs of Brie and Lowell as they make their way toward the cottage. There is no more arguing coming from inside of the cottage. Now there is only the sound of pillage—things breaking and being overturned, everything rifled about in search of whatever might offer some immediate value.

"Are you going in?" Jay asks.

Like it's a backyard party.

Huxley just stares, the cold making his eyes water. "No."

Jay sniffs, makes a grunting noise of realization. "That one. Brie."

"What about her?"

"She's either your best friend or your worst enemy."

Huxley doesn't respond. He just stares at the little cottage with all the criminal sounds coming from inside. He stares at it for a long time and tries to feel something bad, something self-recriminating, but there's nothing. Only a dark, sludgy sort of satisfaction.

Finally, Huxley stands up from the wagon's bench. "Come on. Help me burn this place to the ground."

As the cottage goes up in a giant pyre that reaches fifty feet into the dusky-dark sky, Huxley and Jay and Rigo, Brie and Lowell and the whole ragtag assortment of freed slaves, stand outside, a safe distance away, and they watch the fire consume it entirely, the heat washing over their faces, burning away whatever sins they committed inside.

Huxley doesn't know what happened inside. He didn't go in to look.

In the orange glow that is more powerful and hotter by far than the setting sun that is no longer to be seen, Huxley looks around at these young, grim faces. Some of them are weeping for the things that they did, or the things that they witnessed inside. Some just look on blankly, seeming untouched by it all. Still others pass around a bottle of liquor that they found in the house—several bottles, actually—and they shout at the sky and howl at the fire, and they seem something unstoppable, a wave that Huxley is riding.

They had the hate. I gave them the guns.

Just like Brie promised.

Just like Brie herself.

A healer and killer, all at once.

He finds her face in the line of people standing at the edge of heat and firelight. She is smiling brightly, her eyes twinkling merrily as she passes a bottle to the next person in line, and she holds hands with Lowell around this great, joyful bonfire. And Lowell smiles uncertainly, his lips wet from liquor, his eyes glazed.

They take the horses and string them all onto the same lead, which is affixed to the back of the wagon. They finagle the harnesses from the two blown horses and they replace them with fresh horses from the ranch. They find saddles and saddle blankets that smell of horses and sweat and the outdoors. They set everything aside, and then they eat the food they had taken from the ranch keeper and his family, and they drink his liquor, and they sleep in the glowing warmth of the burning cottage.

CHAPTER 8

They encounter a rider as they approach the town of Minden.

The day is full of cold wind and clouds that rush from south to north across the sky, like they are in a hurry to get somewhere. They darken as the day goes on, first a few wisps, and then the sky around them starts to blot out with more, and by late morning there is no sky to be seen.

They are heading east. The rider is heading west.

Neither party seems to react much as they see each other from a half mile off.

Huxley keeps the wagon moving, all the freed slaves either resting in the back with their horses strung in a line behind it, or riding. Some of them sleep in the saddle. Some of them are alert and hard-looking, their expressions much sharper than their youth should allow.

"Just one," Jay observes as the rider draws closer and it is clear that no one is following behind him. "One lonely little man."

Huxley just keeps the wagon moving, thinking, *If we don't react to him, he probably won't react to us ...*

As the rider draws up abreast of them, Jay puts a hand on Huxley's, forcing him to pull the reins back and stop the wagon. At the same time, he partially stands from the wagon bench, looking at the rider. "Hello there, friend!"

Shit.

The other rider stops, looking up at Jay curiously, his eyes searching for some sort of recognition, but of course, he doesn't know Jay. Politely, he says, "Hello there."

Huxley gives Jay a sidelong glance. "Jay …"

Jay ignores him. "Weather looks bad today, friend." Jay is holding his rifle, but it is cradled in his arms, the barrel pointing down. The perception of nonthreatening.

The rider looks skyward. He is young, Huxley realizes. He has a full, reddish beard that hides much of his youth. "Yup." He looks back down, a slight frown on his face. "Something I can help you gentlemen with?"

Jay smiles, very charmingly. "Where you headed?"

The man fidgets, just very slightly in the saddle. "I don't believe that's any of your business."

"Oh, you know. The Slavers' Trail is my business," Jay says, and his voice is cheerful, but his words carry a warning. "Let me ask you, friend … you on council's business right now?"

The rider frowns and points to the sigils that are prominently displayed on his saddle. "On business for Councilman Barkley and under protection," the man's voice is almost haughty.

Huxley hates him in that moment, and he can't explain why.

Jay grins at the other man, his eyes twinkling. "Interesting."

Then he raises his rifle and shoots the man in the heart.

Huxley jerks and almost comes to his feet, almost grabs his revolver—but what would be the point?

The gray smoke washes over him.

The rider topples from the saddle, dead.

The gunshot echoes back to them, just one time, and then it is silent. Just the wind in the trees, unmoved by what has happened.

Now Huxley does stand up. "What the fuck?" he hisses.

Jay reloads his rifle and sits down. "Councilman's business doesn't pay." When his rifle is reloaded, he looks into the back of the wagon and singles out one of the freed slaves, a teenage girl with an expression on her face as though she's been shocked by what she's seen. "You. Take his gold, his guns, and any provisions. Leave the sigils on his body. And leave him in the road."

The girl stares back.

Huxley doesn't even know her name.

Beside them on her horse, Brie clears her throat. "Now, hold on …"

Jay raises his arms in plaintive innocence and Brie trails off.

"What?" he says. "I didn't tell her she had to do it by herself."

The girl whose name Huxley can't recall—or never learned in the first place—slides down off the wagon, ending any further discussion. Two of the younger guys accompany her.

"There you go," Jay says quietly, rubbing the gunblack from his rifle's muzzle. "All's well."

CHAPTER 9

They skip over Minden altogether. Huxley weighs the costs and benefits. He doesn't think that Cartwright or any of his men would be sticking around the first stop on the Slavers' Trail. It just didn't make sense—too close to Shreveport. Too close to home for Cartwright. He was on the run, and he needed distance. Huxley intended to go into some towns and ask about Nathaniel Cartwright, but Minden seemed like a waste of his time. Too much risk. Not enough reward.

They have enough stolen provisions to last them a few days. They make camp in an abandoned neighborhood a few miles off the Slavers' Trail, and in a place that Huxley judges to be about halfway between Minden and the next town, Ruston.

Jay volunteers for watch, along with two of the boys. They wander off into the night, away from the campfire.

Huxley sleeps, but he wakes in the middle of the night to gunfire.

It is distant. A muted, popping sound.

He sits upright. He strains to listen. He can only hear the sound of everyone's steady breathing around him. No one else has been stirred by the gunfire. Was it a figment of his imagination? Was it a part of a nightmare that he just couldn't remember he was having?

Distantly, maybe just wind, the sound of a scream.

Huxley looks around, but no one stirs.

You're imagining it.

But he should check on Jay and the others.

He takes his rifle and his pistol. He slides out of their campsite, quieter than he expected he would be. He slips through houses and overgrown natural areas turning back into forest. He stops and listens for a while, and he hears voices, and one of those voices is Jay. He continues through the wooded neighborhood, stopping and listening every once in a while. As he gets closer, he hones in on the noise of voices, and he is almost positive that one of them is Jay. And he does not sound angry, or under duress. He sounds happy.

There is laughter.

Huxley pushes through a dense patch of briars, cutting his legs and arms, but emerges on the other side to a lone, narrow, two-lane road and a glimmer of firelight from a lantern. It is a tiny stage scene in the middle of black emptiness.

There is a single horse, bearing a very small wagon. Not really even a wagon. More of a cart. The horse seems unperturbed. The cart has a few large plastic drums in it. The lantern is sitting on one.

Beside the cart, Jay has punctured the side of one of the plastic barrels with his knife, and Huxley can smell the sweet, yeasty smell as liquid pours out. Jay is bending his face to the arc of the stream and drinking it deeply. He switches spots with one of the boys that went with him for the night watch, and the boy bends, gulping down the liquid. The third boy is on the ground, rummaging through the pockets of a dead man who lies facedown.

Jay finally notices Huxley standing there. "Whoa! You fuckin' snuck up on me!" he points to the barrel. "Ale! Fucking barrels of it! You want some?"

Huxley is staring at the dead body, at the boy, probably no older than thirteen, looting the pockets, pulling items out and inspecting them by the dim firelight. Tossing some away. Keeping others. Huxley drags his eyes back to Jay.

"What are you doing?" Huxley demands.

Jay smacks his lips. Ale is dribbling down his chin. He wipes it away. Huxley can't really see his eyes in the lantern light. But he does see Jay tilt his head in that way that he seems to do. "It's blood and death, brother. It's what you wanted. Remember?"

Huxley points his gun at the dead body. "And what did this guy do, huh? More council's business?"

"Fuck no," the boy looting his pockets says. "He ain't even got a sigil."

"Then why the fuck did you kill him?" Huxley can feel his volume rising.

Everyone stops. Jay looks at him. The boy next to Jay stops slurping the ale that is pouring out. The boy standing at Huxley's feet stops looting the body and cranes his neck to look up at Huxley. The two boys … they seem confused. Very confused. Almost like they want to say, "Wait … we thought this was what you wanted!"

Is this what you wanted?

Just the sound of the ale, splashing onto the ground, creating a puddle.

To answer Huxley's question, Jay simply shrugs. "I wanted his beer."

Huxley's jaw works. No more words forthcoming.

Jay pushes himself off the cart and steeples his fingers in front of him. It is an odd stance. Like a teacher speaking to his pupil. "Why don't you go back to sleep, Hux? You're tired. Leave the night watch to the night watch. Okay, brother?"

All three of them. Just staring at Huxley. Staring at him like … like …

Like I'm the one who's wrong. Like I'm the one who's fucked up.

What can you say? What *do* you say?

Huxley turns around and heads back into the brush, thinking, *What the hell is happening? What did I start?*

They had the hatred. You gave them the guns.

Behind him, he hears Jay's voice calling out after him, "Blood and death, Huxley. That's all it is."

CHAPTER 10

On the road to Ruston they happen upon a group of slavers. Five slavers with a wagonload of eight slaves in chains, mostly girls and women. Huxley sees the slavers' poles and their trophies of jaws from a long way off, and there is no stopping his rabid group, and he does not even try.

He doesn't want to try.

The slavers feel safe here in the Riverlands, and they are unprepared to fight.

All five slavers are slaughtered. One woman dies in the crossfire, and a girl. A second girl is wounded. Huxley tells himself that it was the slavers' bullets that caught these innocents. The women don't weep for their loss—maybe they barely know each other. And they don't seem to react at all when Huxley's freed slaves begin to pull the jaws from the bodies of the slavers. They leave the jawless bodies there at the side of the wagon with the slavers' poles and the broken chains inside, so that anyone who found this massacre would know exactly what happened, and fear would strike them.

They would not feel so safe in their Riverlands anymore.

The women and girls are given the choice—run away, or grab a gun and fight. Two of the girls stay. The rest flee.

They loot the slavers' provisions, money, and guns. These are given to the girls.

They leave the blood-washed roadway behind them. Huxley decides to skip Ruston as well, and head straight for Monroe, the last suspected location of Nathaniel Cartwright.

CHAPTER 11

He is a small man, sitting in the corner of the tavern. Small, but in an odd way that makes him appear larger than he is. His body seems to be an optical illusion—stretched and thin to give the appearance of height, but if an average man were to stand next to him, they would find him a head-and-a-half shorter than themselves. Sitting down, the illusion remains unseen.

The man is simply called Niner. That is what everyone in Nathaniel Cartwright's gang has called him since the day he joined them five years ago. No one he's ever introduced himself to has batted an eye at the name—the missing index finger on his left hand is obvious at a glance and offers sufficient explanation.

Rain hammers the roof of the tavern.

For now.

In a few moments, it will abate, and then start again, as it has been doing for the past few hours. It came in on the dusk, riding the tails of a strong wind that shook the eaves and made the man slightly uncomfortable about the structural integrity of the tavern. But the wind left and the rain followed, and now it slams the roof, drips through weathered cedar shingles, and plops on the dirty plank floors in several places.

This tavern is the only drinking establishment in a little settlement that sits on the outskirts of an abandoned city. They call the city abandoned, but it is not really abandoned, as nothing ever truly is. It is rife with gangs and outlaws, as so many "abandoned" places are. What they should call it is *uncivilized*. That would be closer to the truth.

The settlement shares its name with that of the former city: Monroe. It is less of a settlement and more of a town, Niner supposes. And it is not really separate. It is simply new growth. Like a shoot coming off of an old, dead stump. The old Monroe is referred to as Old Town, by the locals, and it is generally avoided. It is a place for desperate ones. The sick and the damned, and the fugitives from the Black Hats.

But here in the new version of Monroe, everyone feels just so safe and secure. This is a slavers' town, the third in the string of cities leading to Vicksburg, known as the Slavers' Trail. Sometimes it surprises the man how peaceful these slavers' towns can be. Their trade, their livelihood, it exists out of violence and pillaging. But these towns are where the money is to be made, and so they remain peaceful, and they prosper.

You don't shit where you eat. Every slaver knows that.

Except for Wild Nate. He seems to shit where he pleases.

Niner sips from the clay tankard that has been placed in front of him. *Little beer*, they call it. Just enough grain to create just enough alcohol to make it sanitary. It costs a quarter of the price of regular ale, and mostly just tastes like water with some sort of sour bread in it. But it makes the tavern keeper happy that Niner is at least paying for something while he sits there in the dark corner, day after day. And sipping slowly from the little beer keeps his head clear, which is important.

From the little spot he has claimed for himself, he can see the entire tavern. Which is not much. No extravagant filigrees or brass chandeliers or girls painted in dazzling makeup with their breasts pouring out of corsets. Nothing like he remembers from the old Western movies. This place has none of that wild charm to it. This is all made of weathered wood and metal sheeting. The main source of decorations is old hubcaps. The bar is just a box. The bottles of spirits are mismatched and labeled with grease pencils to differentiate the types, though there are only a few. The ales are stored in big, blue plastic drums. The smell of the place is stale and abysmal. The only whore that hangs around is a sad little creature with two hungry mouths to feed back in some hovel a block from the tavern. She used to be some mistress of a councilman, a slave, but then freed in exchange for her silence. But she'd been a slave for the better part of her life. Niner isn't sure if her attempts to live free had simply failed miserably, or if prostitution was as far as her imagination could take her.

The tavern keeper is young. Eddie is his name. It had been an old man that kept the tavern up until a year ago when he died after a bad flu swept through the town. The young man is his son. He is a good guy. Little antsy about payment, where his father had been a bit more forgiving. But that is why Niner always has his tankard of little beer. The tavern keeper stands at his post, drinking a glass of his own abominable cider wine. He occupies himself by reading old paperback books that are barely held together with twine. He looks up at the ceiling every time the rain begins to pour again, he mumbles something at it under his breath, and then returns to his reading.

The whore—Jocelyn—sits impatiently at a table on the opposite side of the tavern, watching the door and waiting for the next customer, probably cursing the rain herself. Sometimes it drives people into the tavern. Sometimes it keeps them away. Tonight looks like a night when business is going to be slow. Jocelyn ignores Niner for the most part. She has tried three times to accost him, but he has neither words nor money for her. He won't even buy her a drink. She has pretty features, in a mousy sort of way, but her breath was unusually foul from a set of rotting teeth somewhere in the back of her mouth. Besides, the man had never been fond of whores. He'd known plenty of men who'd suffered rotten dicks after displaying a lack of self-control.

So, Eddie the tavern keeper stands behind his box of a bar, and he reads his tattered manuscripts, and occasionally curses the rain.

And Jocelyn the whore fidgets at her table on the opposite side of the tavern and stares at the doors.

And Niner sits quietly, hour after hour, taking small, measured sips of his little beer.

Sometime around what he estimates to be eight o'clock in the evening, during a lull in the pounding rain, he hears the sound of men's boots slapping the planks outside and the growl of their voices as they work their way up out of the mud and shake off their wet clothes. He looks at the doors as they swing open, curious, but he recognizes the two figures that enter.

So does Jocelyn.

She comes up out of her chair and sashays over with a broad smile of her rotting teeth. "Hey, baby. Didn't wanna stay home tonight?"

The first man shucks off his sodden leather overcoat and tosses it over a chair. Then he hooks an arm around Jocelyn's waist and pulls her close. "Oh, you know I couldn't stay away. Not on a shitty night like tonight. Eddie! Where are your customers?"

Eddie already has two small glass cups on the top of his bar. He smiles. "Guess it's too wet for them."

The second man edges past the first. He also takes his overcoat off and tosses it on top of the other man's. The first man—the one with his arm around Jocelyn—casts his glance to the dark corner of the room. "Well, hi there, Niner!" his voice is filled with a cheerful sort of sarcasm. "What brings you here today?" He laughs.

He is well aware of why Niner is here.

Niner holds up his tankard. "Philly. Staying dry?"

"Trying to," Philly says, guiding himself and Jocelyn to the bar. "Failing miserably. What a shitty night. Ain't nobody comin' to call in this weather. I'm guessin' the next few caravans scheduled for this week are gonna be delayed. Roads are gonna be nasty. I sure as hell wouldn't want to travel on them. And I been hearin' shit about some band of outlaws knockin' over my caravans. Ridiculous," he sighs, exasperated. "Whole world's gone to shit."

The second man—Slope, as Niner recalls, though he has no idea why—gives Niner a cool glance as he follows Philly and Jocelyn to the bar. Slope doesn't talk much. Niner gives him a nod and receives one back. Slope isn't hostile toward him—he treats everyone with that same chilliness.

Philly and Slope take seats at the bar. Jocelyn stays standing, attached to Philly.

Eddie holds up a bottle. "Whiskey, gentlemen?"

"Ayup," Philly nods, then looks at Jocelyn. "What about you, darling?"

"That sounds just fine for me."

"Three, then," Philly says with a smile.

He either doesn't notice or doesn't care about Jocelyn's rotting mouth.

Eddie pours the drinks. One, two, three, careful not to spill any. The spirit is precious.

Outside, the rain has all but stopped. For the moment. The two leaks in the roof continue on, though, slowing as they dry out. Fat drops plopping onto wet wooden planks with a surprisingly sharp *slap*. Niner watches the leak closest to him. Watches the big silver drops catching the light of lanterns and fire, then crashing into the ground like fine china.

Philly takes a sip of his whiskey, then turns, glass still in hand. "So how long you gotta stick around this place? Not that I'm tryin' to get rid of you. Just seems like you're gonna end up being bored out of your mind."

Niner runs his still-existing index finger over the rim of his tankard. "No offense, Philly. Loose lips sink ships."

Philly, an outgoing person by nature, has trouble letting go of conversations sometimes. "If Nate wants to know which Black Hat's after him, I'd be more'n happy to keep an eye out myself. They know he's a slaver, so chances are I'll be the one they come questioning. I'll tell 'em he went north and send word along." Philly is smiling brightly. "Black Hats ain't got no friends around here."

No, the Black Hats don't have many friends. But it's no secret that you'll take a piece of gold over your own goddamn mother.

Niner keeps the thought to himself. He forces a smile. "I trust you, Philly. But you know how Nate is. If I caught up with him and told him that I delegated my job to you … hell, he'd probably cut me open on the spot."

Philly laughs. "Yeah, he just might. Well … here's to Wild Nate. Hope he makes it. Wherever he's going."

Niner raises his tankard marginally and takes a sip.

Eddie gives him a look of consternation. "You've been nursing that thing for a goddamn hour. You done with it yet?"

Philly turns back around, emptying his whiskey glass. "Come on, Eddie. Give the guy a break. It's not like you got a line of paying customers waiting to get in."

Niner looks into his tankard. "Almost done, Eddie. Almost done."

Eddie rolls his eyes and refills Philly's whiskey.

Another half hour rolls by. Philly is in his cups, draining the whiskey faster now. He is getting handsy with Jocelyn who giggles girlishly as he paws at her breasts, nuzzles her neck, and squeezes her ass. Niner wonders to himself if Philly can hear how contrived Jocelyn's laughter is, or if, much like her breath, he just doesn't care.

Slope doesn't drink as much. He's only on his third whiskey. He sits with his back to the bar, eyes on the door most of the time, though he glances in

Niner's direction every once in a while, like all the years of good business between them doesn't mean anything, and that he suspects Niner might be up to something. Which, if Niner is honest with himself, is probably a good way to approach the slave trade. A good way to survive. People could be quite treacherous, but it was always for money.

It's not personal, it's business.

That old phrase. A carryover. That sentiment will never die.

The rain starts up again. Gradually at first, and then hard and insistent. The steady dripping of the leaks in the roof speed up, and then turn into steady little waterfalls.

Eddie looks at the leaks with extreme annoyance. Then at the roof itself. "Motherfuck," he gripes at the roof.

Philly follows his glare. "Shit, man. When you gonna get your roof fixed? No wonder you ain't got no customers."

Eddie just mumbles something under his breath.

Philly laughs.

Jocelyn giggles.

Slope doesn't seem to care.

Niner doesn't register the presence of new guests until the door swings open. The rain is loud and thunderous now, and it hid the sound of their boots in the mud outside, and on the planks of the doorstep. At first the swinging door hides who is there, and Niner wonders who the hell comes out in a deluge like this just for some shitty whiskey?

A drunk, that's who.

Or a Black Hat.

All four people at the bar raise their eyes to the door, smiles on their lips— all except Slope. Eddie is hopeful to make some money. So is Jocelyn. And Philly sees every new customer as a potential drinking buddy.

The door closes with a slam.

There are two men standing there.

One is very tall, though Niner can see nothing of his features because of how his body is angled. He is wearing a leather poncho and hood. The other man is short. Dark skinned. He turns first to the right, scanning the room, then to the left, and he catches sight of Niner. He also wears a hood, which shades his face, but Niner can see that he is Latino. Mexican, by Niner's guess.

The two stand there at the entryway, dripping.

The smiles of those at the bar don't disappear, but they are tempered by the sudden strangeness that follows a few long moments of awkward stillness.

Philly spreads his arms. "Jesus Christ, gents! Don't just stand there dripping on the floor! Come on in and grab some fucking whiskey!"

Neither of the men move.

The Mexican leans into the tall man just slightly and murmurs something. The tall man turns his head to look over his left shoulder at the corner where Niner is sitting. Niner sees only a sliver of the man's face—gaunt cheeks, a sharp nose, a scraggly beard. A single eye that looks Niner up and down and gauges him coldly.

That's no Black Hat.

Still, Niner doesn't feel relieved. He can feel his gut winding up.

He notices that neither of the newcomers' hands are visible. They are both hidden in their ponchos.

Now, the smiles at the bar begin to falter.

Eddie: "Can I help you with something? You guys need ..." he swallows, obviously uncomfortable. "Need a room or anything?"

The tall man takes his cold eye off Niner and faces the bar. Now he is just a wet, black poncho. Like a picture of a ghost. *Or Death.*

"We want to buy slaves," the tall man says. His voice reminds Niner of the Wastelands—dry and dead.

Philly glances between the two newcomers and Slope, a nervous grin still twitching away at his face, his slightly glazed eyes wondering if he was drunker than he felt, or if indeed this entire situation wasn't making sense. Slope's expression stays suspicious, and Philly seems to take some comfort from that.

While the slave seller and the two newcomers are staring at each other, Niner drops his right hand off the table and onto his right thigh, just above where his revolver is holstered.

Philly stands up from his stool at the bar. "Gentlemen, if it were any other time but right now—late in a rainy, disgusting evening—I would be more than happy to broker a deal. Unfortunately, the bad weather is delaying some of the caravans that were planned to arrive today." He opens his arms, apologetically. "I have nothing to sell you right now. But you're welcome to have a drink. My friend Eddie here can put you in a room, and perhaps the weather will clear up in the morning and we'll see some of the wagons that were due today."

The tall man and the Mexican exchange a glance that lasts a moment. Neither speaks. The tall man wipes a drop of rainwater from his face. Clears his throat. "So you're the man to talk to about slaves? You're the ... uh ... *broker?*"

"That's exactly what I am!" A smarmy smile and an outstretched hand. "Philly Thomas. And you are?"

"Your caravans won't be coming."

There is stillness.

All parties frozen in their poses. Philly's is the most extravagant, with his salesman's smile and his outstretched hand hanging there unreceived in the air. Slope with his right elbow on the bar top, his hand hanging close to his holstered revolver. Eddie standing stiffly behind his bar, looking like he is struggling with whether to cut and run or make a grab for the scattergun he keeps behind the counter. And poor little Jocelyn, completely unaware of the tension rippling around the room, caught in the middle of everything.

A drop from the ceiling and a drop from the tall man's coat hit the ground at the same time, a simultaneous, wet *plap*.

"Excuse me?" Philly says, dumbly.

In a flash, the tall man's poncho flies open, a revolver swinging up in his right hand, the snick of a hammer coming back. The flap of the poncho sweeps droplets of water through the air that scatter across Niner's tabletop.

The tall man levels his revolver at Philly and shouts, "Nobody move!"

Slope is already moving, his revolver half out of its holster.

The Mexican produces a rifle from under his poncho and fires from the waist, a giant boom in the enclosed space.

Slope's chest bursts, spraying the ground and Jocelyn with blood.

She screams and ducks away from Slope's falling body.

Both Philly and Eddie cry out in fear, raising their hands.

Slope's body hits the ground, but he is still trying to pull the revolver out, his teeth bared in pain and rabid determination. The tall man has another revolver, this one in his left hand, which he fires twice in rapid succession. The first strikes the bar top, sending up wooden splinters, the second strikes Slope in the forehead, killing him instantly.

Niner grabs the handle of his own revolver.

One quick movement and the tall man's left-handed revolver is pointing directly at his face.

Niner freezes.

Two eyes now, looking at him from under the soaked poncho hood, the thin slash of the man's mouth nearly completely covered by the beard and mustache, but you could intuit the cruelty in it.

"Don't," the tall man says.

Jocelyn is still screaming.

Eddie is cursing over and over. "Holy fuck! Holy *fuck!*"

Philly just keeps staring at Slope's dead body, saying, "Whoa! Whoa!" Like these two violent strangers are a team of horses that might be reined in with a pull and a strong word.

The Mexican opens a lever on his rifle and reloads it.

The tall man has his left-hand revolver pointed at Niner, the right-hand revolver at Philly, and incidentally at Jocelyn, who is clinging to him and still wailing.

The tall man stabs the air with the barrel of the revolver. "Shut that bitch up!" he shouts to be heard over her.

Philly snaps out of his trancelike stare at Slope and snakes an arm around Jocelyn, clamping his hand over her mouth. "Quiet, honey. Quiet, quiet, quiet." He looks at the tall man. "What do you want?"

"You," the tall man says. "You're coming with us."

Philly pushes Jocelyn gently away from him, keeps his hands up, palms out. "Easy, man. You don't want to do this. I've got friends."

"Do you think they can stop me from killing you right now?" the tall man asks, almost earnestly.

Philly is silent. He knows his powerful friends can't help him.

"Come with me. If you fight or resist, I'll kill everyone in this tavern. Then I'll kill every man, woman, and child in this godforsaken town of yours. I'll burn it to ashes. In fact, I should do that anyway. But I'll show them mercy. If you cooperate."

"Just two guys?" Philly says, nervous, but a bit dubious. "You're gonna wipe out a whole town?"

"More than two," the tall man says. "And in the rain? Late at night? Not so hard. We could probably just slit everyone's throats in their beds. Might not even have to fire a shot. Stop talking and come with me or I'll take your knees off and drag you. One way or another. Makes no difference to me."

"Okay. Jesus-fucking-Christ. I'm coming."

The Mexican, his rifle reloaded, strides to the bar top. "Whiskey," he says.

Eddie is confused. Then his shaking hands point to the whiskey bottle.

"Whiskey," the Mexican repeats.

Eddie grabs the bottle from the bar top and offers it over.

The Mexican grabs the bottle, tucks it away somewhere in his poncho. "Gracias."

The tall man takes a hold of Philly, spins him around so he's facing the bar and grasps him by the collar with his right hand, the revolver still in it, the barrel rapping on the back of Philly's head as a constant reminder. The tall man turns and fixes Niner with that stare again.

"You just stay right where you are."

Then the tall man and the Mexican open the door and drag Philly out into the pouring rain and darkness.

The door slams closed behind them.

Jocelyn erupts, her hands flapping around, not sure what to do with herself.

Eddie yells out a curse and finally grabs the scattergun from behind the counter, as though it'll do him any good at this point. He crosses around the counter to where Slope is lying crumpled against the bar. He shakes the man, calls his name.

Eddie looks at Niner, grim-faced. "He's dead."

Niner comes up out of his seat. "No shit he's dead! He's got a hole in his head, you dumb fuck!" Niner draws his revolver, clutching it in white knuckles as he storms around his little table, jostling it and causing his tankard of little beer to spill out, frothing onto the wood plank floors. He moves quickly to the door.

"What are you gonna do?" Eddie gasps, standing up, hugging his scattergun.

Niner puts his hand on the doorknob and glances over his shoulder. "I'm gonna see who the hell these people are. Get behind the counter. And get Jocelyn, too. And Jesus Christ, Jocelyn, could you calm down? Stop screamin'. I can't hear a goddamned thing."

Eddie takes her by the shoulders, quite tenderly, actually, and leads her back behind the counter, murmuring comfort to her while she sobs and wipes tears and blood from her face. Niner watches them, waits until they are hidden, then he turns back to the door. He can't hear anything outside except for the rain, and then, the sound of a horse whinnying, but it could've been anybody's horse.

He opens the door slightly, tries to peek out, but his vision is hampered by the light of the bar. The tavern itself is dim, but compared to the blackness without, it is blinding. He can't see out into the dark rain. He grits his teeth and swears under his breath, then yanks the door all the way open and strides out into the night, still under the tavern's awning and out of the rain.

"Whoa there," a voice calls out from the darkness.

A woman's voice. Almost cheery, but with a hint of warning to it.

Niner is extremely conscious of the revolver he still holds in his hand, hanging at his side, barrel pointed at the planks he is standing on. He blinks rapidly, scouring away the light from inside the tavern. As his eyes struggle to adjust, things begin to take shape in the darkness.

Horses. At least a dozen of them. Standing in the middle of the street.

And there, in the center of them all, a wagon. In the back of the wagon, Niner can see a shape that he thinks is the Mexican, and it is tying rope around another shape, which he assumes is Philly. Another shape, tall and lanky, stands at the driver's bench, seeming to look straight at him.

"Hey there, Mister," the voice calls again.

Close by.

His eyes focus on the horse and rider closest to him.

By the light of the single lantern hanging under the awning of the tavern, the little flame guttering around in the wind and rain, he can make out the barest details of a piebald roan and its rider. A smallish shape, dressed in an oversize coat and a wide-brimmed hat that droops in the rain.

The rider's head lifts up and the dim lantern light plays across a woman's face, long and homely, smiling broadly at him, her teeth a brilliant white in the gloom.

A rifle, leveled at him.

"Why don't you hop back inside?" she says in a voice that sounds cheerful, but is hewn out of cold rock. "Nothing much to see. And besides, it's a frightful night to be caught outside."

Slowly, Niner backs away, into the doorway, and closes the door on the frightful night.

CHAPTER 12

They ride hard eastward in the driving rain.

What do I feel right now? What do I feel?

Mystery. Void. Nothingness.

Maybe some satisfaction.

Huxley is soaked through completely, even the leather overcoat cannot keep him dry. He had shivered, but now his entire body is clenched against it, his jaw aching as his teeth grind together. He cannot feel his hands holding the reins. He just jerks his arms awkwardly to snap the reins when he needs to, barks out an order to the horses that spurs them on, little tricks and calls he's learned from Rigo who is much more of a horseman.

They are cold and wet too.

A half an hour outside of Monroe, Huxley yanks back on the reins and pulls the brake lever. The horses trundle to a stop, each of them issuing stout fogs of breath from their nostrils. The dozen or so riders that flank him—some more adept at piloting their horses than others—pull themselves to a stop. Their horses stamp the ground, almost impatient to continue on. There is no light, save for the lonely oil lantern that flickers at Huxley's side. It barely illuminates the road before them, and mostly the horses just follow the worn path of their own accord.

Huxley looks around him. The riders are watching him.

Brie, one of the more proficient riders, stays front and center of them. She holds her rifle casually across her lap. Huxley thinks there is more to her history than she has said. She is not just the daughter of some village healer.

There were other things that went wrong besides just being captured by slavers. Her hatred burns too hot.

Who knows what they did to her. To her family. To her village.

"Why are we stopping?" Brie asks.

From his spot, hunched over on the bench next to Huxley, Jay peers out of the hood he's drawn around him to shield himself from the cold rain. "Yes. Why are we stopping?"

Huxley doesn't answer. He stands up from the bench, his legs sore and stiff in the cold. He looks into the back of the wagon. Rigo is there, and Lowell. Both of them are sitting, hunched much like Jay, with their rifles pointed at the man who is bound and gagged.

"Stand him up," Huxley says.

Rigo and Lowell bend down and drag the man up to his feet. He makes a pathetic whimpering sound and tries to say something, but the words are unintelligible through his gag. Huxley looks carefully at Rigo, and then at Lowell. Rigo simply looks to Huxley, waiting for further direction. He is not bothered. And Lowell ... his eyes are dead. His eyes say, *I don't care what happens next.*

That's good, Huxley thinks. *It's better that way.*

Better to feel nothing than everything.

"Move him to the edge of the wagon," Huxley says, gesturing.

The bound man is trembling. Cold or fear. Perhaps both. Tears in his eyes, or maybe just rain.

Rigo and Lowell hook their arms through the bound man's and drag him backward, wordlessly but noisily protesting, back to the edge of the wagon where it drops off into mud and old, cracked concrete.

Huxley grabs the lantern from Jay and holds it up, casting its yellowish illumination over the wagon. He steps over the bench and into the cargo bed. Two strides. He stands in front of the bound man, the lantern swinging between their faces so they can see each other.

The bound man's face is terrified.

Huxley's face is ... nothing.

He reaches up and hooks his index finger around the cloth gag, yanks it roughly out of the man's mouth. Like a stopper yanked from a keg, the words start bubbling out of him.

"I don't know what the fuck you want! I don't even know! Just tell me what you want! I can help you! Just promise that you'll let me go! You don't want to hurt me. I'm a nice guy. I am. I just do my work and then I go home. I don't hurt anybody. What's this about? Did Barkley send you? Is it about that big fucking nigger? I didn't find out about him being crazy until after the auction, I swear to God. What am I supposed to do? Have a full medical history of every slave I sell?"

Huxley holds a finger to his lips. "Ssh."

"What do you want? Tell me what you want. If you're from Barkley, I promise, I'll get him a good deal next time. I pay for my mistakes. I mean, I don't think I was responsible, but in the interest of keeping a good customer, I sure as hell will cut him a deal! Philly Thomas never cheats anybody. I'm an honest businessman, I swear to God! Does he want me to pay him back? Fuck, I'll pay him back for it. I'll pay him back with interest, how's that?"

Huxley grabs the man by the face. "Quiet, I said."

"Okay," the man whispers. "Okay."

"Philly Thomas. That's your name?"

The man gives a shaky nod, Huxley's fingers still clamped onto his cheeks. "Uh-huh."

"You broker the slave auctions."

"Yes."

"You broker the buying and selling of people's lives. You're the middleman in this whole system. It's you. Encouraging the buyer. Encouraging the seller. Giving these motherfuckers a pat on the back as you wish them luck and happy hunting when they go out past the rivers and into the Wastelands to grab another couple of lives."

"I … I …"

"Let me ask you a question." Huxley bends the man's head, his grip harder and harder into his face, so that the man winces and groans. "Have you ever been to the Wastelands, Mr. Philly Thomas? Have you ever watched these slavers do their work? Their *honest* work? Have you ever seen the bodies all naked and stacked up like cordwood, covered in each other's piss and shit, while these filthy savages rape mothers just feet away from their dead infants? Have you seen them play their games? Have you seen what passes for amusement in the Wastelands? It all amounts to murder. Rape and murder, every bit of it. And you stand here in front of me telling me that you're an *honest* man, and that you do *honest* work, and that you've never, ever hurt anybody."

Philly Thomas is weeping now. There is no mistaking it for rain.

"You see these faces?" Huxley jerks his head to force him to look at the riders that have crowded around the back of the wagon. "Look at them. Look at their eyes. Know who they are. You'd be selling them right now, if it weren't for me. And do you know what they are? Do you?"

"I don't know," Philly cries, closing his eyes.

"They're ghosts, Philly. They're the ghosts of dead families. They're the ghosts of villages that were just trying to build something. Did you ever think you'd see them in the Riverlands? Did you think they'd never come to haunt you? Did you think you could just keep stealing and never have to answer for any of it?"

"Are you going to kill me?" Philly sobs, opening his eyes wide. "Is that what this is? Revenge?"

Huxley pushes his head away in disgust, releasing him.

"Oh my God, you're going to kill me." Philly starts to wail.

"No," Huxley says. "I'm not."

Philly stifles himself for a moment. "You're not?"

"No. I'm looking for a man."

"Okay," Philly looks suddenly hopeful. "Okay, okay. I know lots of people. Just tell me who he is ... wait ... if I tell you about him do you promise not to kill me?"

Huxley sniffs, snorts, spits off the side of the wagon. "Sure."

"Okay. Who are you looking for?"

"Nathaniel Cartwright."

"Nathaniel Cartwright?" Philly looks horrified.

"He just came through Monroe, didn't he? Don't lie to me."

Philly is thinking hard. "He did, he did. But he's on the run. You know that, don't you? The Black Hats are after him. You guys aren't ...? No. Obviously you're not Black Hats."

"How long ago did he leave?"

"Three days ago. I haven't seen or heard from him since."

"Where is he going?"

Philly looks pained. "The guy at the bar, the other guy that was sitting in the corner, that's one of his guys. Niner's his name. Wild Nate left him to see who was coming after him. You should've grabbed *him*."

Anger flashes over Huxley's face. "Well it's a bit late now, huh?"

Brie interjects from where she sits on horseback. "Should we go back and get him?"

Philly nods emphatically. "Yes. He'll know way more than I do."

Huxley glares at him. "Well, then you're not much use to me are you?" Then he turns to Brie. "And we can't go back. The town'll be on high alert, if they aren't already sending a party after us. We've gotta keep moving forward."

"Forward to where?" Brie demands. "If we don't know where Cartwright is, where the hell are we going?" Then she fixes a savage look on Philly and hoists her rifle. "And what do you think we should do with you in the meantime, huh, Big Guy? What should we do with a useless fucking slaver?"

Huxley lets out a noise like an angered dog. "Kill him."

Philly gasps. "But you said ..."

"I said I wouldn't kill you if you told me what I wanted to know. You didn't tell me what I wanted to know. You're useless. And you're a slaver. You're already dead to me. All that remains is pulling the trigger."

Philly jerks around, looking for a sympathetic face, and finding none. Everyone is hollow.

"Wait! Wait!" Philly stammers. "Now ... I can't say for sure, okay? But I overheard some things."

"Bullshit," Brie says. "He's lying. Just trying to save his hide."

"No, no, no!" Philly shakes his head. "I'm telling the truth."

Jay kicks a foot up onto the back of the bench and rests his elbows on his knee. "Just kill this motherfucker so we can find a place to sleep."

Huxley clenches his jaw. Wipes dripping rain off of his nose. "Speak. Speak for your life, Philly. Make it good. Convince me."

"Okay," Philly nods rapidly. "Like I said, like I said ... uh ... I overheard them talking. Wild Nate and some of his crew. I acted like I didn't know, but I kind of have to know, you know? I have to know everything. It's what the Black Hats expect when they come rolling through. They drop me a few coins, I give them info on where people are, you know? So I try to listen. So, right before Wild Nate leaves town, I hear him talking with some of his crew in the back room at the tavern. And I already know that he's in trouble. Word travels fast. He wasn't even supposed to be in Monroe, but me and him go way back …" Philly seems to realize he might not want to align himself with Nathaniel Cartwright. "Well, I mean … we're not friends or anything. But … but … you know, I try to do people favors when I can. So he's not even supposed to be in Monroe, but I let him come in and … and … well, fuck, you already know what I do for a living. I know it's not right, okay? I know that. But I have to eat, too. Everyone has to make a living. So I helped broker his auction. And the councilmen, shit, most of them don't care. They're always half a step from going to war with each other anyway, so they'll buy from Wild Nate, even if they know he's wanted for kidnapping another councilman's daughter. They don't give a fuck …"

Huxley crosses his arms over his chest, buries his cold fingers in his warm armpits. "Philly. You're talking too much. I need you tell me where Nathaniel Cartwright—or Wild Nate, or whatever it is you call him—I need to know where he is."

"I'm sorry." Philly takes a breath. "I was getting there. I overheard him talking to his guys. He's only got a few slaves left. In fact, he may have just …" Philly looks around cautiously and lowers his voice. "He may have just killed them off. They weren't selling. Not for three towns. And they were weighing him down. Anyway, he's probably already in Vicksburg. But that's the thing, that's the thing … he's not coming back through. And that's what I heard him talking about. He and his whole crew are going to cross the Mississippi to defect."

"Defect?" Huxley asks, confused.

"To the Democratic States," Philly says, matter-of-factly. "Once he's over there, he's as good as gone. The whole eastern borderline, about a hundred miles east of the Mississippi? It's a fucking warzone. I wouldn't go over there. I mean … how bad do you want this guy?"

Huxley seems deep in thought until Philly's last question sinks in and registers with him. He snaps his head up and stares at the man standing in front of him. Like you would stare at someone who has lulled you into a moment of complacency, and you then wake up and remember that you find their existence repugnant.

Huxley looks at Lowell. "Lowell. Do you want to do something?"

Lowell seems unsure. But those eyes …

He nods.

Huxley looks back up at Philly, makes sure he has eye contact before speaking again. "Shoot this man in the leg."

"What?!" Philly is shocked for half a second, then starts to struggle. "No! No! Absolutely not! You can't shoot me! I told you everything I know!"

Lowell steps back away from the man, leveling his rifle, but not quite bringing it up to aim. He is hesitating, Huxley can see it. Huxley stands there, looking at Lowell, wondering if he is wrong. Wondering how much of this Lowell is feeling. But the more you feel, the less you feel. Wasn't that the conundrum?

Huxley keeps telling himself, *He needs to do this. This is necessary.*

"Lowell," he says again, slowly and sternly. "Shoot him in the leg."

Lowell looks at the man standing in front of him. The boy's expression is inscrutable. Then he looks at Huxley. Then he looks at Rigo, who is standing just behind Philly, holding the slaver in place. They lock eyes for a moment. Then Rigo nods.

All the while, Philly keeps protesting, jerking against Rigo.

Lowell looks back at Philly. "You're an evil man. I won't enjoy shooting you. But I have to."

"No you don't! You don't!"

Lowell, wide-eyed, points the barrel of his rifle at the man's leg and fires.

Philly screams, his leg buckling as the bullet punches through, and he topples off the edge of the wagon and into the muddy road.

Huxley follows him down, drawing his buck knife and cutting through Philly's bindings as he wails in pain and tries to speak.

Philly finally finds his words: "You said you weren't going to kill me!" he screams in Huxley's face.

Huxley finishes cutting through the bindings around Philly's wrists and straightens, still holding the buck knife, in case Philly decides to try something squirrelly. "I didn't kill you, Philly Thomas. You're still alive. For now. That's the mercy that you get, you understand? Your life is in God's hands now. Maybe you'll be able to crawl back to Monroe before you bleed out. Maybe not. Either way, this is where I leave you."

Then Huxley swings himself back into the wagon, while Philly Thomas lies squirming and moaning on the ground, crying out for additional mercy that he will not receive, begging for them not to leave him, as though he fears the dark more than his wound. And maybe he is right to fear the dark. There are things that roam around in it. Things that can smell wounded animals from miles away.

Huxley ignores the cries and the pleading.

There is nothing. I feel nothing.

He sits on the bench and takes up the cold leather strands of the reins and he snaps them, urges the horses on, further through the sodden blackness, Jay hunched next to him with the lantern, Rigo and Lowell in the back, and followed by an entourage of ghosts on horseback.

CHAPTER 13

The following day the rain clears and leaves the countryside wet and cool, but the sun comes out, golden, and it seems for the first time like autumn. Huxley can smell it in the oaky scent of the air, the crispness of it, the slight turn in the color of the leaves. A feeling that pulls him back to childhood memories and classrooms, and first days of school. So very far away from where he is now.

Now Huxley sits in the shotgun position of a wagon, his hands clenched tight around a breech-loading rifle, peering out at the very farthest point in the road that he can see. This particular stretch of highway seems abandoned.

There are old towns that they come across, small communities that have come and gone, died out like stars, the way people coalesce and then explode and move on to another area. The safety of numbers is the gravity that pulls them together. The violence of living in close quarters is the fission that scatters them apart.

Jay has taken the reins. He hums quietly, as he had done on the road through the Wastelands. The same, simple melody he hummed in the Wastelands, over and over. The wagon rocks and rumbles along to it. It rings some bell in Huxley's mind, as it did before. Some old country voice, yodeling along with an out-of-tune guitar: *O-oh Jesus, please ...*

Sometime around midday they come to a section of road that has been almost completely swallowed by dirt, and it is here that Huxley comes out of his seat, gripping his rifle hard and looking over the tops of the horses as they bob their heads along.

He gives Jay's shoulder a light push. "Stop-stop-stop."

Jay glances up at Huxley with something like annoyance but hauls back on the reins and pulls the brake lever.

Huxley stumbles slightly as the horses rapidly slow to a stop.

"What's the problem?" Jay says, standing with Huxley, one hand holding the reins, the other on the grip of his revolver.

"Tracks," Huxley says, pointing with his free left hand.

All before them where the dirt has swept over the road it is disturbed. Numerous half-moon marks have ripped through the soft black earth, the curvatures of them heading in the very same direction as Huxley.

Jay looks down at them. "Horse tracks?"

Huxley nods. "I think so."

"How many horses?"

Huxley gives him a look of irritation. "I'm not a fucking tracker." Still, he scrutinizes the marks again, hissing through clenched teeth. "Maybe three? I can't really tell. More than two, I'm pretty sure."

By now, Lowell and Rigo have moved up to the front of the wagon and are looking down at the mess of dirt in front of them. Brie and a few of her former slaves have pulled their horses abreast of the wagon. Everyone is judging the tracks like a portent read in scattered bones.

"They're heading east," Huxley says. "And there's no way those tracks were made before the rain. These have to be recent. I mean, *real* recent."

"Somebody passed us last night," Brie says with a solemn sort of certainty.

Huxley nods again, scratching at his beard. "Somebody out of Monroe."

Jay waggles a finger at the mess of dirt. "I would call that *several* somebodies."

"You think they're setting up an ambush?" Brie asks, leaning over the pommel of her saddle.

Huxley grimaces, giving it a moment's thought, but then shakes his head. "If they were going to ambush us, then why not hit us while we're sleeping? We didn't even post a guard."

God that was stupid …

Brie doesn't look convinced. "They may have overlooked us. If they passed us when it was still raining. Rain and dark? Probably didn't notice us."

"A dozen horses tied to a gas pump?" Huxley taps the butt of his rifle on the floor of the wagon. "Uh-uh. These guys were hauling. Look at how the dirt's all turned up. Whether they noticed us or not is a moot point—they weren't coming to stop us. There's only a few of them. I think they're running to send word to the next town."

Brie wets her lips, wipes them dry. "Close the gates—the barbarians are coming? Something like that?"

"We need to catch them," Huxley says suddenly.

"There's no way to tell when they came through or how far ahead they are," Jay points out.

Huxley gestures at the road. "Black Heart Davies said it was a day's ride between towns on the Slavers' Trail. You can't run a horse much harder than we've been doing without stopping to rest it or swap it out." He looks at Brie, who seems the resident equestrian.

She bobbles her head, not quite sure. "Maybe there's another horse ranch on the way. One where they can swap the horses out."

"Or they had to stop and rest them. Even for just a bit." Huxley bites his lip, almost eagerly. "Hell, they might be a mile in front of us. Either way ... either way we might be able to catch them. We have to at least try. We *have* to try."

Brie looks ahead at the road. "Okay. We'll try."

Huxley turns back to look behind him. He spots the three smallest of the ex-slaves, younger boys. Huxley points at them. "You three. Yes! You, you, and you. Get off your horses. Get off and come sit in the wagon. I need your horses. Now."

The three of them seem confused, worried. They look to Brie.

Huxley kicks the bench of the wagon. "Now!" he bellows at them, climbing over the wagon bench, gesturing wildly. "Off your fucking horses! You think this is a fucking game? Quit looking at Brie. I'm telling you to get off the fucking horses!"

"Hey!" Brie says, but Huxley can hear there is uncertainty in the exclamation.

Huxley points his finger at her. "You shut the fuck up. I told you how things were going to be. Those boys don't need a goddamned mother, they need to grow the fuck up before they die. You're not doing them any favors." He turns back to the three boys. "And you boys need to toughen up before things go real bad for you. Now get down or I'm gonna throw you off."

Brie bares her teeth, just briefly—her lower lip pulled tight, showing her white bottom teeth. She takes a deep breath and maybe finds some nugget of truth in everything that Huxley has just said to her. She breaks eye contact with him and looks hard at the three kids.

"Do what he says," she snaps.

The three of them, biting lips and looking scared, dismount and scurry into the back of the wagon.

Huxley slides down off of the wagon and vaults himself out of the mud and onto horseback. "Rigo, stay here. Jay, Lowell, you're coming with me."

Brie fixes him with an odd look.

Huxley tilts his head. "Another problem?"

Brie shakes her head. "Forget it. Let's go."

Lowell and Jay come down off of the wagon and mount horses. For the first time, Huxley sees something very different in Lowell's face, in his eyes. There is the fear—of course there is—and the same wildness that Huxley sees in him every day. But now there is something else added to the mixture. Something in the way that he leans forward in his saddle, the way he grips his rifle surely, but loosely, the way his eyes are affixed forward.

Perhaps he has been convinced by Huxley's speech. Perhaps he wishes to impress Huxley. Or more likely, Brie. Perhaps that wild fire inside of him is blazing out of control and he is spiraling down, standing in the smoke and flames and giving up his soul to what is coming. And Huxley knows that feeling. He knows it very well.

They ride hard eastward, Huxley in the lead, with Jay and Lowell and Brie and the remaining riders of her ex-slaves trailing. Huxley keeps his eyes on the road before him, the dirt and mud and fallen leaves flying by in a blur of earthy browns and black mud from the night before. He keeps his eyes on the tracks and they keep extending in front of them, and he keeps waiting for the tail end of the riders from Monroe to come into view.

Just before a bridge, he sees ahead the tracks veer sharply off to the right, down a shallow slope toward the river that the bridge spans. Huxley doesn't point, doesn't communicate with the others. He assumes that they have seen what he has seen.

They're watering the horses, Huxley thinks. *They've probably blown them running all night and into the day.*

He does not want this to make him happy, but it does.

Perhaps happy is too light of a word. There is nothing light about what he feels. But he feels the thrill of closing with quarry, dark and violent, and in his mind's eye he watches them crumble in front of him, cut down by rifle fire, their bodies torn apart by bullets.

You do not know these men. You do not know what they're riding for.

They're from Monroe. They have to die.

He reaches the point in the road where the tracks veer off onto the embankment. He can see down through the trees and underbrush, a path cut through the forest by countless riders who have rested and watered their horses here. Like a tunnel of trees, he sees straight down it and he puts his eyes on three riders, their horses looking up from the river, ears alert, water still dripping from their mouths, while the men scramble, fear in their eyes.

Huxley dismounts his own horse—the path is narrow and will force him and his riders into a funnel. But the trees are all around them …

One of the men at the river shouts and yanks his horse by the reins, leading it into the shallow foot waters and then swinging up into the saddle. He's wearing a faded red shirt, and it tickles something in the back of Huxley's mind, makes him think, *Get him! You have to get him!*

The other two men yank revolvers from holsters and dip behind their horses, using the big broadsides of the animals as cover.

Huxley tracks the man on horseback as his horse plunges into the river, quickly going deeper, up to the horse's neck, the man clinging to the beast while it paws its hooves at the water. It is deep, but it is slow-moving at this point in the river, and the horse is making progress across.

Huxley fires a shot that breaks wide, splashing a gout of water up just a foot or two from the swimming horse and its cringing rider.

There are other gunshots around him, and peripherally Huxley sees the bullets are striking the horses at the riverbank, sending them stumbling and rearing and whinnying and screaming, their riders trying to avoid being shot, or being trampled or crushed.

Brie is there, behind a large tree, slamming a fresh cartridge into the breech of her rifle while other ex-slaves flank out to the right, firing their rifles and stopping behind thick tree trunks to reload as they quickly work their way down the embankment.

Huxley looks back to the fleeing rider and sees that the horse is halfway to the opposite bank. He yanks the lever of his breech open, fumbles with a cartridge.

He is looking up to try to find where his horse has gone, and down to make sure he seats the cartridge. His horse is there, stamping its way across the road, trying to get away from the gunshots, but trained enough to not simply bolt.

Huxley gets the rifle reloaded. He runs for the horse and swings himself up into the saddle, as fluidly as though he'd been on horseback his whole life. He snatches up the reins with one hand and whips the horse around, facing east again, toward the bridge.

Lowell and Jay are still at the top of the embankment, Lowell still on his horse, aiming his rifle down at the riverbank.

Huxley spurs his horse and points with his rifle. "There's one getting away!" he shouts. "One getting away!"

The horse lurches into a gallop, headlong toward the bridge.

Huxley pulls the horse close to the guardrail of the old bridge, hears the hooves thundering on it. He looks over the edge, and the swimming horse has pawed itself nearly to the opposite shore, where the bank is clear and a trail shoots up and off of it, disappearing into the woods.

He's going to hit that trail. And then I won't be able to get him.

Huxley hazards a glance behind him and sees that Lowell is not in sight, and neither is Jay. They either did not hear him, or were too engaged in the fight at the riverbank to pull away.

Huxley reaches the opposite side of the bridge just as the escaping horse and rider struggle out of the muddy riverbank and onto dry land, the horse slipping on crumbling dirt a few times, but then finding purchase. Still, the rider clings to his saddle, getting low, and he doesn't look up.

Huxley yanks his horse to a stop. The horse lets out a panicked noise and starts to rear back, but Huxley slides himself off the saddle, hits the ground, stumbles, and then comes up, rifle still in hand.

Don't let him get away! Don't let him get away!

Huxley posts himself to the guardrail, his elbows skinning on the old, rough concrete. Propped there, he takes a half a second to breathe, to sight, to put the bead on the end of his barrel on the fleeing rider as the horse tears across the bank toward the trail that leads through the woods.

He fires.

Watches the dirt to the right of the running horse explode.

Harmless.

This time the rider looks back, and Huxley sees the man's face hovering over the end of his rifle barrel, and there is something passingly familiar about him, but in the moment it is lost.

Huxley levers the breech and grabs at a fresh cartridge, but already he knows it is pointless. The horse and rider disappear onto the trail that leads away from the riverbank.

Huxley watches him go, the brass cartridge impotently clutched between his fingers.

He kicks the guardrail in frustration. Kicks it again. Screams at the world. And only at that point does he realize that there are no more gunshots coming from the opposite riverbank, only the shouting of men, which turns into the screaming of men, which is an odd sound, and it braces him like being thrown into ice water.

He looks to the riverbank and he sees blood in the water. One horse is half in, and half out of the river, its legs still pawing at the soft dirt and mud as it pumps its blood out from a half-dozen holes. But the screaming of the men—that is something Huxley cannot see. It is just inside the woods, and he can see movement, but not what is happening.

Huxley pulls himself into his saddle again, but he knows that these screaming voices are not any of his own. Because he can hear the yelling of the ex-slaves, Brie's voice high above the rest of them.

He feels stiff. Suddenly afraid of what he might see.

Fear is weakness, he tells himself, swallowing the sick feeling that is growing inside of him.

His horse canters to the opposite side of the bridge where the screaming has abated to a single man's moans, and the voices of everyone else have turned to the distinct sound of jeers.

Huxley stands at the top of the embankment, and he looks down the slope, down the little narrow trail, to the clearing just beside the riverbank. There, gathered in a circle, are the ex-slaves, and Lowell and Jay. In the middle of them all lie two men. One is dead, the front of his body an apron of blood from gunshot wounds. The other man is alive, shot in the leg, and he writhes. But his hand is not on his leg. It is holding his head.

Both men—the dead and the live one—have been scalped.

Bright red blood is pouring from where the skin over his skull is missing.

It covers his face like a mask, and when he cries out, he splutters blood in a spray. Huxley sees all these things as though he is standing right there amongst the others, he sees them with extraordinary clarity, though he is twenty yards away, at the top of the embankment.

The ex-slaves gathered around are watching the man. Some of them are yelling at him. Others are kicking dirt in his face which coats his open wound, melds with the blood and becomes a red mud that cakes his head.

Jay is standing there, watching, with a knife in one bloody hand, and a scalp dangling from the other. In that moment, Jay takes Huxley back to the Wastelands, back to the woman with the black braid, who watched while her slavers committed atrocities, watched as they raped and murdered their way across the southwest.

Maybe that's you.

Maybe you're the woman with the braid. Standing up here at the top of this embankment, doing nothing but watching …

"It's not the same," he whispers to himself. "These men are bad men."

Although there is no possible way that Jay heard Huxley's voice, he looks up from the man on the ground and makes eye contact with Huxley. His expression is a mystery. His mouth is something that could be a grimace, or possibly a smirk. But his eyes … his eyes are satisfied. They seem to say over the distance between he and Huxley, *My work is done. My task is complete.*

From the circle of ex-slaves, Lowell moves into the center where the man's desperate squirming is beginning to slow. He holds a revolver in his right hand and he extends it toward the man on the ground, and he fires a single shot that ends the man's life.

Very slowly he lowers the revolver, staring at the two dead men.

Huxley can see what is dangling in Lowell's other hand.

It is the second scalp.

CHAPTER 14

Huxley and his group of riders, gun-blacked and bloody, make their way back westward until they meet up with Rigo and the wagon. Leading the procession of horses, Huxley looks from Rigo to the three children who he kicked off the horses. He wants them to look him in the eye so he can communicate to them without words, but none of them are willing to meet his gaze. He wants to tell them that they need to be stronger. He wants to tell them that if they keep being weak, they'll die.

Lost causes, he tells himself, and strikes them from his mind. *They're useless. Just mouths to feed.*

They are simply there.

Let them be. For now.

They would eventually die, but that's not Huxley's problem. That's for Brie to figure out. Huxley has one problem, and one problem only—and that is Nathaniel Cartwright. After him … after him …

It didn't matter what was after him.

Focus on the now.

"What do we do now?" Brie asks, leaning forward, crossed arms on her pommel.

"We continue on," Huxley replies. He thinks about taking his place back on the wagon, but then decides he prefers the horse. The wagon is slow and cumbersome. The horse lets him move freely.

"What about the one that got away?" Lowell speaks up, his voice deadpan.

Huxley looks at him, somewhat surprised. It is the first time Lowell has joined in these conversations.

"He'll alert Delhi," Huxley says, looking east. "That's for sure. They'll know we're coming."

Jay chimes in, inspecting the weathered leather of his saddle. "They'll be waiting for us. A lot of them."

Huxley nods, thinking. "But they'll be on the lookout for a group. Not a single rider."

"You can't go alone," Lowell blurts.

Huxley raises his eyebrows. "I can't go in a group either. Alone is safer. Alone, I might have a chance to get in and ask around. Maybe find out if Cartwright came through."

"It doesn't matter if he came through or not," Brie said. "That fuck from Monroe told you Cartwright was going to Vicksburg. Why not just go around Delhi and Tallulah and go straight to Vicksburg?"

Huxley shakes his head. "No, that fuck from Monroe said he was going to the Eastern Democratic States. So, by your logic, why not just cross the Mississippi and head straight for there?"

Brie shrugs. "Yeah. Why not?"

"Because we don't know how much shit Philly was feeding us," Huxley says. "Cartwright could be anywhere between here and there. Shit, he could've gone north for all we know. I can't say for sure that Philly was lying, but I sure as hell am not going to travel halfway across the Riverlands without stopping and asking questions in places that Cartwright might've been."

Brie rubs the back of her neck. "Whatever. It's your skin."

"Yeah, it is," Huxley says. "We'll find a place for you guys to wait. An old house or something. Out of the way. Away from the main road here. Then I'll go in alone and figure out our next step." Huxley looks around at the gathered faces, rough and young. "Besides, I think everyone could use a rest."

With nothing further to say, they ride out, continuing east. They pass the bridge. No one looks over the side of the bridge, where the dead horses are floating in the water, or down the embankment where the two scalped bodies are lying motionless.

Brie rides alongside the wagon, keeping conversation with the younger kids to distract them while they pass over the bridge.

She should let them see it, Huxley thinks. *Let them get used to it.*

The sun is nearly touching the trees and Huxley estimates they are only ten or so miles out of Delhi, when they find a road that seems less traveled than the one they are on, but clear enough, carved out of the forest. He cannot tell if it is a preexisting road, or one that was made out of nothing. If there is blacktop there, it is buried under a decade of fallen leaves turned to dirt.

But the dirt is full of weeds, indicating a road not welltraveled, and there are no fresh marks. No hoofprints, no wagon wheel marks, not even a boot print from a traveler on foot. The abandonment of the road, the closeness of the trees, it makes Huxley feel edgy and he holds to his rifle and scans the woods carefully. But logically … logically it is a good place.

They follow this road and about a mile in they locate the remnants of an old brick mailbox.

Huxley stops at it, looks down at it from horseback. "This must've been an actual road if it has a mailbox. Not just some path cut through the woods."

Lowell is beside him, looking up and down the road. "Is that a good thing?"

Huxley squints into the trees behind the mailbox. "Well … it means there's probably a house back there."

The only evidence of a passageway through the woods—what once may have been a driveway—is a strand of new-growth pines, all standing about seven or eight feet tall, while everything else around them towers thirty and forty feet high.

"We gonna be able to get back there?" Lowell asks.

Huxley gives the strand of new pines a calculating look. "I bet the wagon will be able to roll right over those skinny little things."

And it does. The slender two-inch saplings simply bend as the wagon rolls over them, the horses slightly hesitant and irritated as the saplings pop back up and smack the harnesses with a *whoosh-thwack* sound. But when the wagon has traveled down the driveway, all the trees stand back up to their original positions and it is like no one had ever passed through them.

When the whole group has made it through to the other side, they find a brick house. A ranch. On one side the roof is caved in where half of an oak tree has fallen into it. But the rest of the house seems surprisingly intact. The windows are unbroken, though they are nearly entirely covered by green mold. There is no graffiti on it. All around the base of the house, weeds and saplings have started to grow, nearly half as high as the walls of the house itself. To either side of the door, two holly bushes left to their own devices have grown into monstrous hedges, nearly hiding the door, which, miraculously, is not ripped off its hinges.

Huxley looks back behind him at the forest, and he can barely see where they have made it through. Only someone deliberately looking would notice it. A casual passerby would just keep on traveling with no hint of the band of people a hundred yards into the woods.

"This is good," Huxley says. "This is perfect."

Huxley stays on horseback while the others dismount and make their way inside. Jay stays beside him. Lowell jumps down from his horse, but loiters nearby, not sure whether to go in or stay with Huxley. After all the ex-slaves have gone inside, Brie comes out again, rifle swinging loosely in her hands. She stops in front of Huxley's horse.

"You still plan on going into Delhi?"

Huxley nods.

"If you insist on going," she glances behind them. "We could use some food."

"We're out already?" Huxley mumbles.

"We've been out since last night," she says. "You told us to only take what we could carry, and we've been on the road for days now."

Huxley rubs his finger under his nose, then smooths his mustache and beard. "I'll get what I can. One guy buying food for a dozen might look suspicious."

"One guy asking around about Nathaniel Cartwright will look suspicious," she shoots back. "I don't think buying food will be the thing that gives you away."

Lowell speaks up from where he stands, hands still hooked to the reins of his horse. "We should go with you. Me and Rigo."

Huxley shakes his head. "No. You should stay here. Make sure everyone is safe inside that house." He looks at Lowell sternly. "I don't want to hear anything else about it. And don't let me catch you following me."

Lowell looks displeased, but turns away.

Huxley makes it to the road before realizing that Jay has followed behind him. Huxley stops his horse and lets the man catch up. "Go back to the house, Jay. They know us. They know us from here all the way to the Wastelands. We walk in together, we might as well turn ourselves in to the nearest Black Hat."

Jay keeps his eyes on the road ahead. "I didn't ask you to wait up for me. Go on. Go do your business. I'll hang back."

Huxley stares at him, jaw clenching and unclenching.

Jay looks at him. "You're wasting time. And you know you can't get rid of me."

Huxley spurs his horse, mumbling, "Yeah. I know that."

Huxley takes his horse up to a gallop for a while, the miles slipping by quickly as the road stretches toward Delhi and the sun sets. Whatever shops might sell food will probably not be open much later than sundown. He should go there first. Then, if he needs to, he can ask around at the local tavern.

Cartwright and his men need food, too. Maybe the guy who sells me supplies will know something. Then I can just get in and get out. No muss, no fuss.

Whatever happens, he does not want it to be Monroe again. He does not want to drag someone out by their collar and leave a string of bodies behind him. It was effective—as Jay had promised it would be—but for once, Huxley wants to avoid drawing attention to himself. He would like to make it back to their hideout without a posse in pursuit.

Just go in, keep your head down, and don't look too obvious.

The sky is a splash of orange and black, like magma has been thrown across it. He passes through the dilapidated wreckage of the old suburbs that surrounded Delhi. Up ahead, what has become Delhi "proper" stands low and sprawling, the walls lit up by the setting sun behind him.

The gates are open. Surprisingly.

But it's obvious that bad news has come recently.

There are a dozen guards at the gates. The front four are obviously guardsmen by trade—they wear something that might be considered a uniform, and they wear armbands. But the rest that crowd behind them and clutter the catwalk that overlooks the gate are just townspeople with scatterguns, old homemade muskets, a few bows, a crossbow.

They look scared.

They look nervous.

Like everyone's on a hair trigger. And that's bad for him.

They'll know who I am. They'll be able to see it. They'll see it like Ol' Reggie saw what was inside me. He saw the thing lurking in me and he knew, even though he was blind . . .

"Stop!" a voice calls out.

Huxley pulls the horse to a stop. He's about fifty yards from the gate. He hazards a glance behind him, hoping and praying that Jay will not be there.

But the road behind him is empty.

"State your business," the voice calls out.

Huxley looks forward again, and can see that he is being addressed by one of the regular guardsmen. He considers running for a second or two. But at this distance his odds are dead even that someone would get him with a bullet or an arrow.

Stick it out. Act normal. See how it goes.

Huxley clears his throat. "I'm here for food," he calls back. "Just trying to buy food before the market closes. I don't plan to stay the night. Just want to buy food and leave. I have gold, or I can trade. Whichever you prefer."

"The market closes in twenty minutes," comes the answer.

Huxley bites his lip. "Then I guess I better hurry."

There is some hesitation, a brief discussion amongst the actual guardsmen. The volunteers huddle around them, eavesdropping.

Finally, the speaker for the guardsman calls out again: "Put your hands up above your head and approach slowly. I'll tell you when to stop."

He raises his hands up and then he nudges the sides of his horse gently. The beast plods forward at a steady, rocking pace. Now, he feels the dozen weapons aimed at him. Twitchy fingers hovering over questionable triggers. Everyone looking at him with suspicion.

He nears the gate, now within ten yards or so.

The speaker for the guards steps forward, standing in the middle of the road and holds out a hand, a scattergun in the other. "That's far enough. Stop right there."

Huxley stops the horse. He doesn't want to reach down and grab the reins, so he says, "Whoa," and that seems to do the trick.

The guard looks up at him, peering with discerning eyes.

He knows me. He recognizes me.

"Who are you?" the guard asks.

Huxley knows that any name he gives them will reek of a lie, so he tells them the truth: "Just a traveler. Looking for some food."

The guard is not happy with the answer, but he doesn't press—he knows as well as Huxley that people, particularly transients, don't like to announce their names. "Where'd you come from?"

"West," Huxley says, carefully.

You're being too evasive. Someone is going to realize what's happening.

"You must've come through Monroe," the guard says.

"Three days ago," Huxley says, the lie coming out fluidly enough.

"Three days?" he questions. "Monroe is only a day's ride from here."

"I stopped to hunt the woods in between."

The guard looks at Huxley's paltry belongings. "Don't look like you were too successful."

"Two squirrels and a rabbit," Huxley says. "Those I ate. Haven't seen hide nor hair of a deer. Not in two months."

The guard smiles. "You must be an unlucky man. They're all through these woods. At least, when you don't have a gun in your hand."

Huxley forces a smile of his own. It feels wooden and brittle. "Perhaps I should take up the bow. Maybe it's the gunpowder they smell."

The guard nods. "I've thought the same." He looks back behind him, seeming much more at ease. "Market's straight through on the main stretch. If you want to buy anything, you better hurry. Most of the stalls are closing down now. General store might still be open, though."

Huxley has to take a steady breath to keep himself under control. He nods to the guard. "Thanks. Don't keep the gate open on my account."

"We will," the guard says, a little tiredly. "So make it quick."

Huxley spurs his horse. "I will."

He gets about ten feet from the gate when the guard calls out again, "Hey, wait!"

Huxley stops. Hand touching the grip of his revolver. Heart stopping in his chest, and then hammering at double-time. He turns back to the gate. Looks at the guard who stands there, still in the middle of the road.

"Yeah?" Huxley says, his voice almost a croak.

They know, they know, they know …

The guard squints at him again. His little beady rat eyes. "You pass any group of travelers? Maybe about a dozen of them? A wagon and a bunch of horses? Anything like that ring a bell?"

Huxley looks skyward, pretending to think. "Uh … no, I don't believe I did. Seemed like the road was fairly empty." *Give him something, something, deflect!* "I did see some wagon tracks, but never the wagon itself. Didn't pay it much mind. Why? You looking for someone?"

The guard shrugs. "No, but they might be looking for us. You see a group of people like I just described, you turn around and go the other direction, you hear? That's a bad bunch. Been looting and murdering all the way from Shreveport. Some wild men from the Wastelands I hear. Goddamned savages."

Huxley nods stiffly. His knuckles ache from the grip he has on the reins. "I'll keep an eye out."

"Best you do," the guard says. "Best you do."

CHAPTER 15

As the guard predicted, there are only a few stalls open in the market by the time that Huxley arrives, his chest still thready and feeling raw. He keeps waiting for the guards to reappear, to have realized their mistake, and to arrest him, or to simply shoot him down. At any point in time, around any dark corner, Black Heart Davies could be waiting for him, his revolver out and ready to be fired.

Time's up, Huxley thinks. *That's what he'd tell me before he put a bullet in my brain.*

And I'm no closer to finding Cartwright than I was a few days ago.

Time's up, and I've wasted it all.

None of the stands that are open are selling things Huxley wants. He bypasses them all, keeping his head down, trying to blend in, that difficult balancing act between being casual and looking like you're trying too hard to be casual.

The general store is a little wooden construction, something like a barn, tucked in the middle of all the closed stands, the carts empty for the night, all their wares sealed up and carried away by the vendors. But from the inside of the general store, lamplight still glows. By now the streets of Delhi are dark, and out beyond the market, Huxley can hear the tavern warming up for the night, all the miserable field hands and cattle drivers and slave runners gathering for booze and women and to hopefully forget about their lives.

Huxley presses into the general store.

A bell above the door chimes, a lonely, tinny sound.

There are shelves all around him, a collection of wooden slats and posts, crammed full of random assortments of objects. Old rusty things that have become useful again. New things made from other old rusty things. New things forged fresh that don't have a spot of rust on them. Food. Booze. Gunpowder. Lead balls. Lead ingots, to mold your own.

"We're closed," someone says. An old man, judging by the voice. Gruff and irritable.

Huxley peers around a shelf of goods, sees the shopkeeper standing at the counter, an old man, but big. Hands underneath the counter. Resting on something that Huxley can't see. The two men catch eyes for a moment.

Huxley points a thumb behind him. "Your door's not locked."

The shopkeeper presses his lips together so they flatten out in front of his face. His white eyebrows are furrowed over dark eyes. He is broadly built, and tall as well. A thick neck that hides his jawline. Sloped shoulders that press against a stained button-up shirt. Perhaps not as old as Huxley had thought, but his hair is completely white, and his features weathered enough to give that first impression. Older than Huxley, for sure. Perhaps in his early fifties.

The shopkeeper watches him, something more than just normal caution in his face. But Huxley is now focused on the counter behind which the shopkeeper's hands are hidden. Huxley nods toward it. "You got a scattergun pointed at me right now, sir?"

The shopkeeper sticks out his chin. "Might be I do."

"Any reason why?"

"You go through the gate?"

"I did. Answered all their questions."

The shopkeeper makes a *harrumph* noise. "Come here."

"You planning on shooting me?"

"You planning on robbing me?"

"No. I have money."

The shopkeeper pulls the scattergun out from behind the counter, lays the big barrel on top, keeps his hand on it, finger on the trigger. "You don't rob me, I won't shoot you. Lay your money down. Right on the counter. And get it slowly. You touch either of those pistols and I'll let this thing eat."

Huxley very slowly reaches for the satchel of coins. He pulls it out, holds it up delicately between his thumb and forefinger as he takes two steps to the countertop. "You treat all your customers this way?"

The shopkeeper takes a long look at him, up and down, but it does nothing to cool him down. He seems to get more irritated. "Jesus H. Christ," he mumbles. "What jackass let you through?"

Huxley isn't sure he's supposed to actually answer. He lays the satchel of coins on the counter. "I think …" he finds his throat has gone dry. He works some saliva into his mouth and swallows it, keeps glancing down at the big bore of the scattergun. "I think there's some mistake."

"Fuck you," the shopkeeper says, dismissively. "I know who the fuck you are."

Huxley stiffens, all attempt at humor or deflection or deception leaves him. Now he stares at the barrel of the scattergun, and then at the shopkeeper, and he wonders if he can get his revolvers out before it blows a hole in his belly.

"I just want to buy food," Huxley says, quietly.

The shopkeeper works his jaw. He knows who he is dealing with, and that realization carries with it a significant gravity, which seems to just be dawning on the man. There is a second thought behind the shopkeeper's eyes, a painful hesitation, like he is thinking maybe he should not be pointing a gun at Huxley, that maybe Huxley was the wrong person to mess with …

The shopkeeper shifts nervously, eyes glancing around. "Now … now you listen to me, okay? I don't want any trouble from you. Nor your crew. I know what the slavers have done to your kind, okay? That ain't me. I just run a shop. You ain't got an issue with me or my family. I hope you don't want any trouble either."

"I just want food," Huxley says again, quietly, trying to be nonthreatening.

"Well …" the shopkeeper adjusts his grip on the gun. "Here's the deal: I'm going to keep this here gun on you. You're going to get what you need from the shelves. You're going to give me the appropriate amount of gold pieces from your pouch—no more, 'cause I ain't a crook—and then you're going to leave. I'm going to forget that you came in here. And you're going to forget that I held a gun to you. And you're going to pass by Delhi. And you're never going to bother us again. Do we have a deal?"

Slowly, Huxley nods. "Deal."

The shopkeeper nods toward his store. "Then get to gettin'."

Huxley backs away from the counter a step, then turns away to face the shelves. For a brief moment, he thinks about snatching his revolvers and gunning the shopkeeper down. If he dove out of the way as he spun on the shopkeeper, chances are the scattergun wouldn't catch him.

No.

That was Jay talking.

There was no need for that here. If the shopkeeper meant to raise the alarm, he would've done it already. He only wanted to close his shop and go to his home. Maybe he had a wife. Maybe he had children. He wanted to be allowed to continue with them. And Huxley didn't want to gun him down, not really. He didn't want to run from the town like an animal. He wanted to pay for his goods like a normal person and then leave, no shots fired, no blood spilled.

But he's one of THEM.

He's a part of the SYSTEM.

Huxley closes his eyes. *He's just a damn shopkeeper.*

So Huxley opens his eyes and he goes to a shelf directly in front of him that he can see has food provisions on it. He isn't going to shop around. He doesn't think the old man wants him to do that. And he doesn't want the scattergun on him any longer than necessary. He grabs items without really paying attention to what they are, catching labels only in the periphery of his conscious.

Beans.

Millet.

Dried corn.

A chunk of salt beef.

He takes what he can carry in his arms and in his satchel and he hauls it to the counter. The shopkeeper looks over the things, tallying them in his mind.

"Eight gold pieces. And that's rounding down."

Huxley opens the satchel and takes out the requested eight pieces. As he does, his eye floats away from the shopkeeper and his scattergun for the first time, and he sees some of the other things that have been arrayed on the counter for sale. Funny, how these things used to be stationed at the counter as *impulse buys*. Huxley cannot imagine anyone buying anything on impulse anymore.

But then his eyes fall on one of the objects for sale.

A battered tin can, in which are sticks of charcoal pencils.

Huxley stares at the pencils and a silence grows.

The shopkeeper shifts, uncomfortably, and the barrel of the scattergun scrapes an inch or two across the counter.

Slowly, so he doesn't spook the shopkeeper, Huxley reaches out and takes three of the sticks of charcoal from the tin can and lays them gently beside the other supplies. He looks up at the shopkeeper, who is watching Huxley with an odd expression. He is curious. Somewhat taken aback. What brigand or thief needs a charcoal pencil?

"Do you have paper?" Huxley asks.

The shopkeeper clacks his teeth together. "I do."

They share a moment of expectant silence.

"Will you sell it to me?"

The shopkeeper's eyes stray off to the side, as though he is trying to look behind him. "I'd have to get it. And I don't want to take this gun off you. I don't trust you."

Huxley lays both his hands flat on the countertop. "Please," he says with all the earnestness he can muster. "Three pieces is all I need. I'll give you another gold piece for the lot."

The shopkeeper hesitates for a long time, but Huxley can tell he is thinking.

"Who's it for?" the older man asks. "You draw?"

"No." Huxley shakes his head. "It's not for me."

The shopkeeper lets out a laborious breath. Then, holding the scattergun with one hand, he reaches back behind him, feels around a shelf, keeping his eyes on Huxley. His fingers float over and around a ream of tallow-colored cloth paper. They finally touch the paper, and he deftly counts out three pages. He brings them over. Slides them gently onto the counter.

Huxley pulls out another gold piece, places it with the other eight.

The shopkeeper takes the gold in one hand, slides them into a pants pocket. "Anything else you need?" his voice is almost polite.

Huxley shakes his head and gathers his items.

The shopkeeper watches for a moment. "You don't seem like a bad man to me."

Huxley pauses in the middle of stuffing the sack of millet into his satchel. "No?"

The man across the counter leans back an inch or two, seeming partially relaxed for the first time, though he doesn't take the gun off of Huxley.

"You just got a devil on your back. I know a thing or two about that." The shopkeeper looks very serious for a second or so. "It'll end up eating you alive. It's best to let it go."

Huxley clears his throat and stuffs the rest of his purchased items into his satchel. When he is done, he leaves his hands up on the counter and faces the shopkeeper. "Maybe you're right. But I have to ask ... have you seen Nathaniel Cartwright come through here?"

The shopkeeper considers this for a long time.

Huxley is about to turn around and walk away.

The shopkeeper takes a sharp breath. "Look. I've got no part in your fight with him, whatever it's for. And I ain't gonna dime him out, because eventually that'll come back on me. It always does when it comes to Wild Nate. But I will tell you this ... if I were hunting Nathaniel Cartwright, I'd take into account that he's not a man who runs and hides."

Huxley raises his eyebrows.

"Hunting bears ain't like hunting deers," the shopkeeper says. "When you hunt a bear, you take into account that it's probably hunting you back."

Huxley just nods. Taps the counter twice. "Thank you."

The shopkeeper sniffs, then nods toward the door. "Don't come back."

"I won't," Huxley says, turning for the door. "You've got my word, whatever it's worth."

If the shopkeeper expresses his faith or distrust of the promises of a murderer and a thief, Huxley doesn't hear them. He pushes through the shop door and out into fast-falling darkness, a windy chill gusting down the main street.

Huxley mounts his horse, stiffly, looking over his shoulder, wondering how much of what the shopkeeper said was truth, and how much was the myth and legend that surrounds a certain stature of outlaw. In all the dangerous shadows, now there was more than just a posse from Monroe or Black Heart Davies to worry about. Now there was also a man with a scorpion tattoo. A man who had a reputation for not running and hiding. A man that everyone seemed to know as "Wild Nate."

But they don't know me. They don't know where I came from, what I've been through.

Perhaps Wild Nate is not as wild as they think he is.

Perhaps he knows that there is something much more dangerous than him out there.

Jay's old words rattle through Huxley's head, and they warm him like a fire when the cold darkness surrounds him: "Desperate men with nothing to live for are the most dangerous animals alive."

You made me who I am, Nathaniel Cartwright, Wild Nate, man with the scorpion tattoo.

You made me a desperate man. You took away everything I had to live for.

You created this monster. And now it's coming after you.

Huxley rides out of Delhi. The guards at the gate give him a nod and a tip of the hat. They holler out warnings to Huxley to beware of the Wastelanders, oh how dangerous they are, especially in the dark.

CHAPTER 16

About a mile from Delhi, on the dark road, just barely illuminated by the stars and a rising moon, Huxley sees his companion coming out of the woods. There is a rustle and he knows that someone is there, but there is no fear in him, because he knows that it is only Jay.

He sidles up next to Huxley and rides abreast. He looks at Huxley carefully in the darkness, assessing everything. "You seem fairly relaxed. I assume you got in and out without having to kill anyone?"

Huxley looks at him, tired. Tired of him being there. "No. I didn't have to kill anyone."

"Well …" Jay adjusts his seat in the saddle. "Good for you."

The place where they camped is difficult to find in the darkness, but luckily Brie assigned a watch, and just as Huxley is about to pass the driveway by, one of them steps out of the trees, rifle in hand, and gives them a short whistle.

Huxley looks over his shoulder, sees the young man standing there.

"We must be well hidden," the young man smiles.

"Must be," Huxley says.

The young man melts back into the forest and Huxley and Jay follow the row of low-growth pines back to the clearing where the little brick ranch sits, its backyard a clutter of horses. They leave their horses and go in the front door.

Most everyone has gathered near to where the roof has caved in, because that is where the fire has been constructed. A large pot that had been taken from the slave barge is sitting on some coals while a smaller fire burns behind it and is vented out the hole in the roof, dispersed nicely by the fallen tree that protrudes through the ceiling.

The ex-slaves are huddled close to the fire and each other for warmth, sharing blankets and body heat. Brie is crouched down next to the pot, speaking in low tones with Lowell, when they both notice that Huxley and Jay have walked in.

Brie points to the pot sitting on the coals. "We found some water. There's a creek about a mile south of here."

"Good," Huxley says. He drops his satchel next to her. "There's food."

She rummages through the satchel, taking stock of what Huxley has purchased. She comes to the three sheets of cloth paper gently folded against the side of the satchel, the pieces of charcoal enclosed inside. She frowns at them, and then looks up at Huxley with a question on her face.

Huxley takes them from her, almost with a flush of embarrassment.

"What are those for?" she asks.

"Nothing," he replies quickly.

He holds the paper behind his back and waits while Brie returns to the satchel. She selects the salt beef and the millet, and returns the rest of the items to the satchel. She slides it back to Huxley. Then, holding the salt beef and the sack of millet, she looks up at him again.

"Thank you," she said. "You didn't have to do this."

"Yeah, I did." Huxley takes his satchel, the papers and charcoal still grasped in his other hand, furtively, almost, and he turns away from her. He doesn't want her thanks. It makes him feel small. It drives something into his heart that threatens to crack what he thought couldn't be broken anymore.

He puts the satchel in a corner of the room and he stands there for a moment, looking around at the ex-slaves. He sees the three youngest ones, huddled together, watching Brie work by the light of the fire, mixing the millet into the boiling water, carving off little pieces of the salt beef.

Huxley sits. Puts his back up against the wall.

He holds the paper and charcoal in both hands, in his lap. He stares at them.

He thinks about his little girl, her tiny hands, the fast, erratic way they moved across papers and canvases and boards—anything that could be drawn on. The way the pictures came to life out of lines that made no sense to him.

But she could always see the picture. She always knew where to put all those little lines and marks and then all of a sudden, there would be something there.

I love you more than every single star in the sky.

Huxley blinks rapidly. He looks up at Brie and Lowell, but they are focused on the pot and the fire. He looks over to the three younger kids, and he sees that one of them is looking at him. When he makes eye contact, the kid looks away, still scared of him. Terrified, in fact.

Huxley feels a pang that he immediately stuffs away.

Useless feelings. Useless emotions.

He waits until the child looks up again, knowing that he will, and then Huxley waves him over. "Come here," Huxley says, and realizes it sounds a bit stern. So he softens his voice a bit. "It's okay. Come here. I want to show you something."

Now Brie has looked up from her cooking. Lowell, too. She looks cautiously between Huxley and the three children sitting by the fire. Like she isn't so sure about Huxley, but doesn't want to piss him off even more than before. She makes a quick judgment from Huxley's apparent mood, and then seems to acquiesce.

The children watch her, like they are waiting to see what she thinks.

She gives them a look that seems to say, *Go at your own risk*, then turns very deliberately back to the pot, though Huxley can see her eyes glancing back in his direction every so often.

I'm not going to hurt them, Huxley thinks, resentfully. *Even I have my limits.*

The first child stands up, slump-shouldered and nervous-looking. The other two follow him. They walk, shoulder-to-shoulder, taking those small steps that children take when they are certain that they are in trouble. They stop five feet from Huxley, which seems to him too far, so he waves them closer, which gains him another few inches.

"Seriously," he says. "I'm not gonna hurt you. I have something for you. For all three of you."

Fear and piqued interest. They shuffle forward so their feet are almost touching his. They peer at what he has in his hand.

He opens the papers toward the three of them. The charcoal sticks inside.

"What is it?" One of the boys asks.

"It's a paper and pencil," Huxley says. He feels this old voice, unused for so long, the voice of a father speaking to children. He hates it. It feels awkward in his mouth. He feels embarrassed by it. But in the same moment, it comes out so readily. The way the inflections go up. A way to imbue excitement and interest. "You ever had a paper and a pencil? You ever draw?"

The three of them look amongst themselves.

The one that seemed the bravest—the one who had already spoken—scratches at his head. "We used to draw in the dirt. With sticks. Is it the same?"

"It's kind of the same." Huxley takes one of the charcoal pencils and flattens one of the pieces of paper against his leg. "Let me show you how it works. What's your name?"

"Bryce," the kid says, fidgeting.

"How do you spell that?"

"I don't know."

Of course you don't. Huxley nods and puts the charcoal pencil against the upper left corner of the page. He writes "BRYCE" in bold letters. He points to it. "See? I just wrote your name. That's your name right there. B-R-Y-C-E. That's how you spell it." Then Huxley hands him the paper and pencil. "That's yours. It's got your name on it. You can draw whatever you want."

"Okay," Bryce says. The ghost of a smile plays across his lips, and then is gone.

Huxley looks at the other two boys. "What're your names?"

"Christian," one says.

"Paul," the other blurts.

"Christian and Paul." Huxley writes the names on the other two pieces of paper. "There. Those are your names. This one's yours. This one's yours. You can draw whatever you want."

The two kids, Christian and Paul, they take the pieces of paper and the charcoal pencils as Huxley hands them over. They look at their names written out, just scribbles without comprehension. But the way that they hold the pencil and paper ... they are happy to own something.

Walking close together in a jumble of footsteps, they retreat back to the fire.

Huxley watches them go, his hands clasped in front of his mouth, his lips pressed together. He watches them and he feels a growing heaviness inside of him, a tension in his throat, in his chest, like the great weight of his soul is pulling at the tethers that hold him together, the cordage, and it is straining under the load.

Out of the corner of his eyes, he can see Brie looking at him. He cannot tell from his periphery how she is looking at him—maybe with thanks, maybe with suspicion. He doesn't look back at her. That will only add more weight to him. And he cannot take that right now.

This was stupid, he tells himself. *A waste of a gold coin. And a waste of three young lives, to boot. They don't need kindness. They need hardness. They need to learn …*

Huxley rises from his spot on the floor and he quickly exits through the front door and into the cold night air. The diffused smell of the wood smoke plays with his nose, plays with his memories, a smell of hearth and home. But it does not come from a hearth, and this is not his home.

He feels his chest hitching as he makes it into the darkness outside of the house. Away from everyone that can see him, away from the eyes that will judge him. He can feel it growing in him like a swelling wave, like a sudden sickness.

In the darkness, hidden by the pines, he drops to his knees and cries for everything that is lost.

CHAPTER 17

The chill of the night gives way to an unseasonable warmth. Huxley watches the sun coming up above the trees, chasing away the cold, and there is a wind blowing from the south, warm southern air coming in off the gulf. All around them are trees, trees, trees. The forest chokes the road and it has narrowed it significantly, so that the roots of some of the nearest trees are pushing up chunks of ancient blacktop out of the dirt. In areas, the road is low grasses and Huxley begins to wonder how frequently this stretch of the Slavers' Trail is traveled, and if there is a reason for that.

They've gone around Delhi. As promised.

Every once in a while, he sees an old, washed-out hoofprint from a horse, but the edges are worn away by age and rain and the settling of the dirt it's pressed into. He tries to judge their age, but he really has no idea what he's doing. He has spotted the track, that should be something. He feels confident that the print couldn't be recent. Not *too* recent.

Jay rides alongside him on the right, peaceful in the growing heat, almost seeming to enjoy himself. He always did seem like that. Like he was one pleasant thought away from letting out a soft chuckle. Like none of this could touch him. Like none of it was real.

How do I be like you? Huxley would sometimes ask himself. But the thought would come unbidden, and immediately afterward he would chastise himself: *You don't want to be like Jay. That's not something you should want.*

The sun is reaching about the peak of its arc now, seeming to hover there in the sky, not really gaining altitude, not really falling. Like a thrown ball, that moment when it appears to just hang.

Brie rides up beside him on the left, a light sheen of sweat on her brow. "Odd weather."

Huxley looks up at the sun, dazzling his eyes. He blinks away the sunspots. "It is Louisiana. Was."

"Yeah. Was." Brie adjusts herself in the saddle. "How close are we to Tallulah?" she asks.

Huxley shrugs. "Black Heart Davies said a day's ride between the towns. So I'm guessing sometime around dark."

There is a long pause while Brie watches him.

"What?" he asks.

She looks away. "I thought those boys didn't need a mother," she says, quietly vindicated. "I thought you said they needed to toughen up."

Huxley scratches his beard. "They do."

"Well then what was all that last night?"

Huxley doesn't look at her. Prefers to look at the road. He doesn't answer.

Brie presses. "What was with the paper and pencil?"

He spits off to the side. "You know …" he shakes his head, working for control. "I'm not … I don't like it. You know that right?"

Brie glances at him, unsure of what he's talking about.

"I don't like this," he says again. "I don't enjoy these kids having to do these things. I don't get anything out of it. It doesn't make me happy. I hope you know that."

She sniffs and considers. "I guess … Yes."

"I just wish that they'd learn. I want them to be hard." He looks at Brie, plaintively for a half second, then turns away. "I wish my daughter had been harder. I wish I'd taught her how. Maybe she'd be alive now."

"Maybe. Maybe not."

Huxley says nothing for a minute. Then, "She drew."

Brie looks at him, assessing him differently.

"My daughter," he clarifies. "Nadine. She drew."

Brie looks down at her saddle for a while.

Huxley looks straight ahead, grinding his teeth against the pain in his chest.

"Thank you," Brie says, very quietly.

Huxley doesn't acknowledge. He acts like the conversation had never happened.

In the quiet of the road, in the monotony of the horse's steps, Rigo suddenly calls out: "Oye!"

Huxley looks at Rigo, who is standing at his bench seat on the wagon now, both reins in one hand, pointing with the other. Huxley snaps his eyes to where Rigo is pointing—down the road.

At the very end of where Huxley can see, where the road seems to turn into the forest like some strange optical illusion—the dead end that never truly ends—there is a man. A horse. The horse is standing there in the middle of the road, the man standing next to the horse. One hand up on the saddle, like he wants to jump in, but has been waiting.

Waiting …

Faded red shirt.

The same red shirt as the man that swam his horse through the river and got away.

"It's him," Huxley blurts. "The guy, the one that got away!"

Recognition seems to dawn on Brie's face as well.

Huxley realizes that the wagon and all the riders have stopped.

Jay is nearly standing in his stirrups. "We should go get him!" he urges. "Grab his ass before he gets to Cartwright!"

Huxley almost kicks his heels into the sides of his horse, but he stays himself at the last second. The horse feels his legs tense and seems to jump at the start, but Huxley pulls back the reins.

Something's not right here …

The man in the red shirt has vaulted himself into the saddle now. He looks over his shoulder at them as he puts the spurs to his horse, and even from this distance, Huxley can see his eyes, and they look scared, but everything else seems stiff and false.

Why was he just standing in the middle of the road?

"Huxley!" Jay says, slightly louder this time. "Let's fucking go!"

"Whoa, whoa!" Brie shouts.

Huxley whips his head to his left, glaring at her. "What?"

To his right, Huxley can hear Jay's horse stamping its feet. Jay is growling under his breath, "Come on, Huxley, he's gonna get away! He's getting away!"

Brie points down the road, but her eyes are locked with Huxley's. "You're gonna run off after this guy? It could be a trap!"

"You see me going after him?" Huxley snaps.

"Hux!" Jay is nearly shouting now, the bloodlust evident in his voice. "He's gonna get away! We've got a chance!"

Brie shakes her head. "Don't do it."

"Fuck that," Jay bites back. "You gonna listen to this bitch? I'm goin' after him. I'll bring his scalp back."

"Jay!" Huxley calls after him.

It's too late. Jay has already made up his mind. He turns his horse and jams his heels into the beast's flanks. The horse snorts and leaps forward, clattering down the roadway after the man in the red shirt.

"Shit!" Huxley can't let him go off by himself. He starts urging his horse forward, looking back over his shoulder at Brie and shouting, "You stay right here! Don't move!"

He rides hard, hunched in his saddle, peering down the road just over the top of the horse's head as it bobs up and down with each rapid stride, the mane flying in Huxley's face, but he feels like he is holding on for dear life.

Ahead of him, Jay roars down the roadway and shows no sign of slowing down.

What are you doing, Jay? Why are you doing this?

He just can't stop himself. He can never fucking stop himself.

The road meanders out into another curve, another turn, a straightaway, a hill—going up, then coming down. He pushes the horse, keeps spurring it on, yelling in its ear to keep going. He's gaining a little ground on Jay, but it doesn't seem like enough. Jay is leading him down the road, still riding recklessly ahead.

Think about it! Think before you act!

Why was the man just standing in the middle of the road?

Huxley feels the squeeze in his stomach, the sensation, that tiny little moment in time when you put your foot out for a step and realize that you miscalculated, the step is not there—the quarter second or so when your mind tells you, *You fucked up, you're gonna fall, you're gonna hurt yourself, here we go …*

The road flies by underneath them. He keeps looking ahead, wondering if the man in the red shirt is going to appear. He's a little closer to Jay, but then he wonders what the hell he's going to do to get Jay to stop pursuing? And then he wonders, *What if we just catch the guy?*

What if we catch him?

What if we can kill him?

You should kill him …

That is not his thinking. That is Jay's thinking. Reckless. Foolhardy. Giving into rage rather than thinking his way through it. That is not him. He is better than that.

He comes abreast of Jay's horse and reaches out quickly, before Jay can steer away, and he grabs a hold of the reins, pulling it back just a bit to slow it. He totters there, unbalanced, half of him stretched out and the space between their horses widening as the confused animals pull away from each other and make sharp noises of distress. Huxley regains some of his balance and pulls back on his own reins, the horses slowing now to a stop in the road.

Jay wrestles his reins out of Huxley's hand, then spins on him, wide-eyed. "What are you doing?" he demands.

Huxley looks past Jay to the empty road. "This is wrong!"

"Wrong?" Jay is breathless. "Fucking *wrong*? This is right! That man is going to get to Tallulah and he's going to tell everyone there, just like he did in Delhi. Except for one of these times, they're going to get the gumption up to send a posse out to meet us, if they haven't done it already! I hate to break it to you, brother, but we've been pillaging their shit pretty good all along the Slavers' Trail, and they can't be real happy about it!"

"And whose fault is that?" Huxley almost screams. "I didn't kill the ranch keeper! I didn't kill the random motherfucker on the side of the road! I didn't kill a man for his cart of beer! That was you! It was fucking *you*!" Huxley flails his arms, wants to strike Jay, wants that conflict, feels it brewing in him like it is imminent. "I'm not even talking about the morality of it, you fuck! I'm talking about this being a trap!"

"A trap?" Jay seems flabbergasted, like he hadn't considered that.

Of course you hadn't!

"Why do you think he was sitting in the middle of the road?" Huxley demands. "Jesus Christ, Jay! You're fucking reckless!"

Jay starts looking around, eyes wide, suddenly realizing their situation.

Huxley spins his horse around. He looks behind him. "He had to have gone off the road somewhere we didn't see him. He's in these woods somewhere. Somewhere behind us."

The anger, the frustration, growing.

This isn't me, this isn't who I am.

I'm not this person. I'm not this desperate man at the end of his rope. I'm not you, Jay. I'm not you and I never will be!

He turns on Jay. "Why the fuck was he in the middle of the road?"

Jay raises his hands, mirroring Huxley's sudden anger. "How the fuck should I know?"

Huxley stabs the air with his rifle. "Because he wanted us to see him, that's why! Because he wanted us to chase him!"

"Why are you getting angry at me?"

"Because what did you think was going to happen when you randomly start killing people, Jay?" Huxley is struggling. Struggling to keep control of himself. "We could've been in and out, could've found the man we were looking for, without ever having called attention to ourselves. But you had to fucking kill everyone we came across! You're fucking everything up!"

Jay points at him. "This guy? This Cartwright guy? The man with the tattoo? That's *your* mission, brother! Not mine. I told you what I was here for. I told you I was here for blood and death. I told you I was going to kill every one of them that I could."

Huxley cannot deny it, so he deflects. "I'm so tired of your mouth!" he grinds out. "You're reckless! You don't *think*! You just wanna kill, kill, kill, you're so wrapped up in your fucking vengeance that you just never STOP AND THINK!"

"Look who's standing in the middle of the road with me!" Jay's face is only inches from Huxley's, their stirruped feet tapping together, the flanks of their horses brushing.

They are galaxies colliding, stars igniting, compression, gravity, momentum—powerful, undeniable forces swirling around each other.

"Everything we've done we've done *together*!" Jay shouts at him. "I never forced you to do anything, and if you ever took my advice on anything, it's because deep down inside, you *agreed* with me! Deep down inside, you wanted those things to happen just as much as I did!"

That's not me! Huxley's mind is railing. *That's not who I am!*

"I'm not you!" Huxley screams. He lets go of his reins and he is about to reach across to grab whatever of Jay's face or head or neck that he can take in his hands and drag him to the ground where he intends to beat him into submission, or maybe to kill him …

And that's when they hear the gunfire.

CHAPTER 18

Huxley jolts, then freezes. The sound of the gunfire like a static shock. It crackles and rolls, suddenly, and then is answered in force. It is distant. Coming from behind them. Back west.

Back toward the wagon.

The feeling of the misstep, this time worse, this time a plummeting.

He swears under his breath, the sound coming out as a noise of panic. He wheels his horse around, Jay forgotten, and he kicks the horse hard. It bolts, back down the road that they'd come from. The hooves hammer out on dirt and bare patches of old concrete.

Behind him, he hears a voice: "Huxley! Wait!"

He doesn't wait. His mind is a shower of sparks, gears grinding. He has no conscious thoughts, nothing that comes out in words. All the pages of his mind that describe him have been burned away to ashes and husks and all that is left is this feeling of impenetrable dread, a suffocating blanket.

One thing in his mind, one nightmare, filling his brain: Lowell and Brie, side by side, bullets punching through them, dozens of bullet holes, and blood flying out of them in ribbons as they spin to the ground, eyes already dead.

Huxley denies it with an animal cry.

He is terrified. He knows how this ends. He has been here before, running toward the sound of the gunfire and knowing that he can never make it in time, no matter how fast he runs. And this memory, it drags him out of the present, and it also plays right along with the present, they are just mirrors of each other …

He is running.

In his hand is a sickle.

All around him are half-harvested fields of barley. The ground is dry, the air is warm. His feet crunch through gritty, rocky loam. His breath is harsh and arid in his throat. The sun is in his face. He tries to squint past it to the commune, but he can see nothing except the primitive, stick-woven fence that surrounds it, and great pillars of gray smoke rising up from inside.

The gunshots. The screaming.

The sound of women and children. Pain and terror.

Not again. Not again. Please, God, have mercy on me, not again!

The road flies underneath him. The sweat of his horse is lathering at the sides of the saddle.

Huxley looks up, sees the road, the bend in it, and he knows that the wagon is just around this curve in the road. But now he registers silence between the beating of his horse's hooves.

No gunshots.

No screams.

The wagon comes into view. Not very far at all. He can see how the wagon is angled off to the side, to the shoulder of the road. The two horses harnessed to it are slumped, one dead on the ground, the other pawing away its last breaths.

And there are mounds, strewn all over the road.

Huxley knows what they are. He knows what a massacre looks like.

The air comes out of his lungs. He tries to leave the saddle while the horse still gallops. The confused horse slows to an unsteady trot while Huxley's feet dangle, then touch the concrete. He tries to find purchase, tries to move his numb legs, but they just pull out from under him and he falls flat on his face, busting it on the concrete. It is a numb feeling. It sends sparkles of white light through his vision and he tastes blood and feels chunks of his own broken teeth swimming across his tongue.

He gasps, cries out, but not from physical pain.

Not again ... not again ...

He hears hooves behind him, hears Jay's voice. "Huxley!"

He ignores it. He drags himself to his feet, spitting blood and fragments of teeth. He still grips his rifle in skinned, bleeding knuckles. He draws his revolver with his weak hand. At first he cannot rip his eyes off the wreckage in front of him, but then he becomes aware of the forest all around them and he scans. His gait is plodding and unsteady and he swings his weapons around at the trees like a drunken man looking for a fight.

"Lowell," he slurs, his tongue thick and painful. He might have bit it when he slammed into the ground. "Lowell! Rigo!"

Nothing stirs. No one responds.

The wounded horse, still lashed to the wagon, lets out a horrific sound.

Down the road, two horses stand, riderless, one of them with a bleeding hole in its rump and its leg poised oddly beside it. They stare at the yelling man behind them as he staggers through the bodies.

There amongst the dead, Huxley looks down at his feet.

What do I feel?

Is it nothing? Or is it everything?

The ex-slaves surround him. Young, sallow faces looking skyward, or planted facedown in the dirty ground. There are others, other men that he doesn't recognize. But there are only a few. Only a few that got caught. Huxley feels like he is wandering amongst their bodies and he isn't sure why he is doing it. To see if any of them are alive?

What do I feel?

"Lowell?" he calls out again. But again, there is only the screaming of the dying horse. "Rigo!"

Huxley finds him before he gets an answer from the man.

Rigo is propped up against one of the wagon wheels where he has dragged himself. Huxley can see the trail of his blood, from the middle of the road over to the wheel. His stomach is a mess. He clutches it, his eyes closed, mouth open, face inclined to heaven with his chest heaving rapid, shallow breaths.

"Rigo," Huxley takes two quick strides and then kneels next to the man.

Rigo must not have heard Huxley's other calls, because he startles when Huxley touches him. His eyes come open, strained and bloodshot, and for a moment, recoils from Huxley.

"Los lobos," Rigo mutters, weakly pushing Huxley's hand away. "Diablos y lobos. Ave Maria Purisima."

"Rigo," Huxley says, pushing the other man's defensive hands down. "It's me. It's Huxley. It's okay."

It's not okay. It's not okay at all.

Rigo blinks a few times, fear in his eyes, but also recognition. "Husley," he says, weakly. "No más, hokay? No more now."

Huxley glances at Rigo's wound and knows there is nothing that he can do for the man. The amount of blood already spilled has put Rigo's life out of reach. "Rigo. Rigo, where is Lowell?"

"Todos muertos," Rigo mumbles, his chin dropping to his chest, jumbling his words even more. His brown skin has turned to sweat-slicked ash. "No more. Tired. No more dead." Rigo puts his bloody hands to his chest, a gesture of self-recrimination. He meets Huxley's eyes, and his own are watery with tears, and he lapses back into Spanish. "No soy malo. Ave María purísima. No soy malo."

"I didn't … I didn't see their bodies," Huxley says, not knowing what to do, not knowing what to say. "Did they get away? Are they still alive? Lowell and Brie?"

Rigo falls to sobbing, his words now unintelligible, but taking on a certain litany, the rhythm of a prayer. Huxley keeps hearing those words—Ave María purísima—mixed in with the rest that he cannot decipher. He understands none of it. He shakes Rigo gently, trying to get him to snap out of it for just one more second, trying to get him to tell him something, but Rigo's eyes are battened shut and his words come weaker between his jagged inhalations.

"Huxley." Jay's voice behind him again.

He ignores it and stands. He shakes his head, his eyes wide and blank as he stares at Rigo. He leans forward, almost falling, and braces himself on the side of the wagon, his revolver clattering on the wood. His fingers feel numb and unwieldy. He's not sure why that is.

Why is this happening? Why does any of this happen?

He tears his eyes off of Rigo—there is nothing that he can do for the man. His gaze lands in the back of the wagon. Three small bodies, smaller than the rest, huddled close together, heads held down, though it didn't save them. They are still in their positions of hiding, and the wooden sides of the wagon are splintered around them, bored out by lead balls. Their blood soaks into the dry wood.

They are all facing down, but Christian's head is turned just slightly. A bullet entered the top of his head. Passing down through him, it warped his features, just slightly on the left side of his face, so that his eye bulges out a bit and his cheek looks swollen.

His hands are curled together underneath him, holding onto an unfired rifle. His fingers are stained black. Huxley stares at them, remembering how his own daughter's fingers would look so much the same after hours upon hours of scribbling and sketching with those chunks of charcoal.

He tries for words, but has nothing.

His mouth opens and the air comes out in a groan.

He sags into the side of the wagon, his face against the cold barrel of his own revolver, his lips touching the cylinder. He can smell the axle grease in the unspent bores. The stink of gunpowder. His breath is hot against the cold metal, fogging it. Wet against his lips. Like kissing someone dead and succumbed to rigor mortis.

He looks at the three boys.

Christian looks back, with that one, slightly bulged eye.

Not this. Not this. Not again.

What do I feel?

I feel everything. And it's bad. It's all bad.

A piece of parchment sticks out of one of the boy's pockets. Huxley reaches out with trembling fingers and he takes it, very gently. It slides out of the pocket and unfurls a bit. A piece of charcoal falls out. The parchment is blood stained in the corner, but not badly. At the top of the paper, "Christian" is spelled in Huxley's own steady hand, and beside it a half-dozen times, it has been copied in a hesitating, shaking hand.

Huxley folds the paper back. He pockets it. Pockets the charcoal piece.

He realizes that Rigo is no longer making sounds. Huxley doesn't look. He doesn't need to look. He is very familiar with the sound of death. The three boys in the back of the wagon are making it now, louder than all the silences he'd ever heard.

Todos muertos. Huxley didn't speak Spanish, but he'd learned enough in passing to understand that. *All dead. They're all dead.*

A hand on his shoulder, very soft.

Huxley jerks like he's been electrocuted, and then spins.

Jay takes a step back, his eyes making a quick circuit—Huxley's face, then his revolver, then his rifle, then back to his face. His own revolver is in his hands, but he doesn't seem prepared to use it. Is Huxley? Have they fallen so far? Have they burrowed so deep?

Huxley takes up the step that Jay relented. He doesn't point the revolver at the man, but he wags it in the air. "You." The word comes out softly, seeming not to be the accusation that it absolutely is. In a single word, everything shifts to Jay. In the span of time it takes for Huxley's mouth to form it, he reels back through memories, through nights and days filled with cold and terror and blood. Darkness. Murder. Cruelty.

For what?

What do I feel?

All of the angry parts.

Jay shakes his head once. His expression wants to be exasperated, but he can't manage it.

Huxley takes another step. The rifle slides out of his grip, thumps on the ground. The forest, the danger, the dead bodies, all of it has been forgotten. He is inside of himself now, deep down in the center of him, and now there is only Jay. Everything else has faded away.

"Why are you here?" Huxley asks him, his voice still soft. "Why did you come here? With me, I mean. Why are you with me? What is your purpose? Is this it? Does this satisfy you? Does this … *fulfill* you?"

"Huxley …" Jay murmurs, uncertainly.

Huxley cuts him off. "You should be smiling, Jay. Why aren't you smiling? This is all you ever wanted."

"I didn't …" Jay falters, showing weakness for once.

"Blood and death." Huxley's words growing sharp. "Destruction. Abandon. You've come to eat the world. You consume, that's what you do. That's all you do. You just consume everything. You burn it all up."

"I tried to help you."

"You destroyed me. You ate me alive."

"You're ridiculous," Jay snaps back. "You're insane. You wanted my help. You *needed* my help." He sticks his chin out in that challenging way that he does and he braces his hands against his chest, the barrel of his own revolver touching his heart. "I saved you."

"You saved me?" Huxley almost coughs. "You *saved me?*"

"Without me, you'd be a pile of roadkill out on some Wasteland road."

Jay chuffs. "You were weak, Huxley. You were fucking weak and you would have never survived. Think about how I found you! Think about how you were! Wandering around in the middle of the desert, almost dead from dehydration. No purpose in your life."

"I had purpose."

"I *gave* you purpose."

"My daughter was my purpose!" Huxley suddenly yells. "She should've *always* been my purpose!"

Jay lets out a snarl. "Your daughter is dead! I gave you a new purpose. A *different* purpose."

"I didn't need that purpose. That was you. That was *your* purpose. You just wanted to massacre them. You just wanted to kill. Blood and death, right? That's all you wanted, and you said as much but I was a fool and I didn't listen."

Jay points at him. "Because you wanted it too! You still do."

Huxley shakes his head. "You weaseled your way into my head, Jay. You embedded yourself in there and you twisted everything up. I didn't want this. I didn't want any of this. All I wanted was to find my daughter. I don't need you. I don't need your *purpose.*"

"You need me," Jay says. "You'll die without me."

"There are things worse than dying, Jay." Huxley takes another step forward. Jay takes another step back. "That's where you got me. That's where you hooked me. You had me so scared. You had me so terrified of dying, of *not surviving,* that I thought I had to keep you around. Survive, you keep saying. Survive. Don't be weak. But you're the weak one. You're the one that's so terrified of death. That's why you're weak. You know what's worse than death, Jay? Do you know?"

Jay's face is clamping down, gearing up for a battle.

Both of them can feel it. Imminent. Like pressure dropping in front of a rain storm.

Huxley puts the barrel of his revolver to his own cheek, using it like an extension of his index finger, using it to point at himself. "This. Becoming this. Becoming something that my wife and daughter wouldn't even recognize. And then turning around and *throwing them away* just so I don't have to feel the guilt for it. That's far worse."

"Horse shit. You want to live."

"I do. But not the way that you want me to live. I don't need any of that. And I don't need you."

"Put your gun down," Jay hisses.

Huxley drops it on the ground. "I don't need the gun, Jay. I'm going to strangle you to death."

I'm going to reach down and I'm going to pull up everything you ever planted in me, Jay. I'm going to reach down and pull it all up right by the roots.

Jay scoffs, brazenly. "I taught you how to be bold, Huxley. You were running scared before I came along. And now you think you can take me?"

Without another word, Huxley throws himself into Jay. The smaller man topples backward, twisting as he goes. They hit the ground, rolling, skidding. Heels scuffing through the dirt to the concrete underneath. Jay tries to hook an arm around Huxley's neck, but Huxley pulls back, swings a leg over top of him and mounts him, squeezing his legs together hard, trapping Jay there.

Strange how the body moves.

Strange how it seems to know how to kill, once that channel has been opened.

Jay swings hard for Huxley's gut with one hand, the other pushing up, the heel of his palm against Huxley's chin. Huxley blocks the blow with an elbow, but feels his teeth clack together and his head snap back. He sweeps Jay's arms out of the way and plunges both his hands down toward Jay's throat. Jay deflects one hand, but the other gets its fingers around his neck. Then he tries to pry them away, and Huxley gets his other hand there.

Both hands around Jay's neck now, and he starts to squeeze, gritting his teeth, feeling the blood pressure in his head building until it sparkles his vision and makes him think the vessels in his face are going to burst with the effort of bearing down so hard on Jay.

Jay tries to buck his hips, tries to toss Huxley off of him, but Huxley refuses to budge. He is clamped down. If he has to give every ounce of his energy to kill Jay, he will do it. He will kill himself to kill Jay.

It's over. It's done. You're done. You're finished.

Leave me! Leave me be!

Jay is trying to speak to him, but his throat is being crushed shut. All that comes out are gagging noises.

"Leave me be!" Huxley realizes he is shouting. He watches his spittle fleck over Jay's purpling face. "Leave me be!"

And then, somehow, Huxley is on his back. There is a splitting pain in his skull. His vision is dark, but coming back. He is on his back, and he is looking up at the sky and he realizes that something has hit him hard in the back of the head. There is a man standing over him, and he thinks for a moment that it is Jay, but no … this man is darker. His skin is darker, his hair is darker. His features are swimming into focus.

Huxley coughs. His throat aches.

The man over top of him is looking at him with mud-brown eyes. Looking at him with some sort of wonder and disgust. Almost amused. He has a cruel face. A scar across his lips, down to his chin, and it twists his mouth into a sneer, but Huxley thinks this man would have a sneer regardless of the scar. The world itself is disdainful to this man.

He is a psychopath. That is clear from the second he meets Huxley's eyes.

He stands up to his full height.

Huxley's perception is widening out a bit and he registers the fact that there are other men around him. But this man … this man is standing in the middle of them, standing over top of Huxley, and he is holding a rifle, a breechloader just like the ones that Huxley stole from Shreveport, and Huxley thinks maybe the butt of that rifle is what struck him in the head.

The man with the scar is still looking at him, holding the rifle up, ready to deliver another blow. He shakes his head at Huxley. His voice is a thickly southern drawl. "I guess the stories about you are true." He lets out a single bark of laughter. "You are a bat-shit-crazy motherfucker."

Then he rears back to deliver the strike.

Huxley sees the tattoo on his neck.

The buttstock slams into his face.

The image hovers in the darkness of unconsciousness.

A scorpion.

PART 5

THE TALLY

CHAPTER 1

Lowell drags her through the woods. She is slightly taller than him, and she has the weight of an adult, Lowell realizes, though she seems skinny. Brie moans as he drags her another ten feet, and then stops so he can gasp for air. Her arms and hands are clutching her side and her leg. Everything is slaked in blood. She is going pale.

How much blood? How much blood has she lost? How much blood can she lose without dying?

Brie closes her eyes.

Lowell, breathing hard, lungs on fire, leg muscles breaking down from hauling her nearly a mile, he reaches forward quickly and slaps her a few times in the face. "Brie!" he whispers. He isn't sure why he is whispering—if the men find them it won't be because of his voice, it will be because of her loud groaning and the sound of him struggling to drag her through the dried leaves all around them.

Brie blinks, looking half-irritated. "What?"

"Don't fall asleep," he says between sucking in air.

She frowns at him. "I'm not ... I'm not fallin' asleep ..." but her voice trails off like she is.

Lowell feels panic rising in him. He feels sick from exertion. Had he really dragged her this far? He reaches over with fumbling hands and shakes her shoulder. She grimaces, flinches at some pain this causes her and lets out an unhappy sound, but doesn't open her eyes.

She's gonna die, he realizes. *She's gonna die if I try to drag her any farther. I have to ... I have to ...*

He looks around, completely lost. *What do I have to do?*

The bleeding. The bleeding is killing her. I have to stop the bleeding.

He is at the bottom of a shallow ravine. Lowell remembers guiding himself into it, trying to get low, trying to get out of sight in case someone is tracking them. He doesn't know. He can't remember if there was anyone following them when he took off into the woods with Brie. He remembers her crouched by the wagon with him, fumbling to get another cartridge into her rifle, and then watching two shots punch through the side of the wagon, ripping her side, her leg. He remembers the look on her face when she realized that she'd been shot. The look of surprise. Dismay. And finally, agony.

He and Rigo stood and started firing into the woods where the shots were coming from. The south side of the road. They couldn't see anything. Just shadows flitting in between trees, strange, ululating calls, a screech and a battle cry all at once. Whooping.

Lowell remembers grabbing Brie, completely panicking and grabbing her by her wounded leg, and then just dragging her into the woods to get away. He wanted to get away so bad, but he couldn't leave her. He wanted to help her, but he couldn't help her there. They had to leave.

The rest was a blur of mud and leaves and breaths that raked his lungs ragged.

Am I far enough away from the road? He wonders. He can't think of how long he's been dragging her through the woods. Can't think of how far. The woods all look the same. He can't see the road. Just trees, trees, and more trees.

"Okay," he says, swallowing air. "Okay, okay. Brie. Brie!"

She squints at him again. "Huh?"

"I'm gonna … I'm gonna stop here, okay?" He looks around. He finds a tree with a thicker base. It seems like a good place. He bends down, ignoring her painful moaning as she realizes she's about to be dragged again.

His legs feel like green wood—stiff and bendy and uncooperative.

He manages to get his hands hooked under her armpits again and he drags backward. The first few steps are horrible, but then the momentum is his and he manages to stumble his way to the base of the thick tree and manhandle Brie so that she is propped up against it. He apologizes while he does it. He knows that it is painful for her.

"You can't die," he says as he works. He is spooked by the oddly assertive tone of his voice. It does not sound like his own voice. It sounds like a man's voice. And he does not feel that way. He feels weak and lost. Men do not feel that way. Mr. Huxley never feels that way. Does he?

"I'm not gonna let you die, okay?"

Her eyes flutter at him. She is having trouble keeping them open, but she is hearing him. She nods once. "Okay, buddy."

It kills him.

She has been kind to me.

She doesn't deserve to die. It isn't fair.

He realizes he is crying, and for once he is glad that her eyes are closed because he does not want her to see his weakness. Rather than sniff and make it audible, he lets the snot run down his nose, lets the tears run down his face. Silently.

Control yourself. Don't be weak.

He pulls her unwilling arm away from her side. He gently pulls apart her coat and lifts up her shirt while she hisses at him. Her stomach is flat like a board, completely devoid of any fat. Her ribs stand out harshly against her pale skin. The wound in her side is bloody, but not the bloodiest thing he has seen. Lowell knows enough about death and blood to know that if the blood isn't pulsing, then it's not as bad as it seems.

"You're okay," he says, preemptively, trying to make himself believe it. Trying to convince himself that the next wound will be just as superficial. *And she's a healer, so she can tell me how to fix her. She can help me make poultices, and that will get rid of the infection. So she won't die. As long as she isn't bleeding to death, and none of her guts were hit by the bullet, then she won't die. It's gonna be okay.*

But still, she is very pale.

Maybe it's just the pain. The sight of her own blood.

But everything that Lowell knows about Brie tells him that she would not fear the sight of her own blood. She would not pale because of pain. She is losing lots of blood. And it must be coming from her leg.

He looks down. The wound is high in the middle of her thigh, maybe a foot or so down from her hip. He tries, oddly modest, to work around the thick fabrics of her pants, but everything is a sopping mess of red. He can't tell what's what.

"Just …" she groans and struggles to lift her hips. "Just take them off."

Lowell hesitates for a moment of misplaced decency, but she is fighting to keep her hips up for him, and he realizes that it doesn't matter. None of that other stuff matters right now. He reaches forward, forcing down the tingling heat in his face as he hooks his fingers in her waistband and pulls the pants down to her knees as gently as he can. She wears some sort of roughspun cotton underpants. These have a hole in them as well, but they are loose and he can easily lift them up to expose the wound.

The blood is pulsing.

"Uh …" Lowell's hands are shaking. He tries to force them still. "What do I do?"

Brie's face is to the sky, eyes closed again. She is in a lot of pain. But maybe that is what's keeping her awake for now. Still, when she speaks, her words are unsteady, slow, and slurred. "Ah … I need … tourn'quet."

"Okay. Tourniquet. How do I do that?"

She tells him how, stumbling through the instructions, and sometimes the instructions don't make sense. A few times she trails off and when he looks up, her eyes are closed. Following as much as he can make sense of, he uses his knife to take a strip of her pants and ties it around her thigh, as far up as it will go.

She mumbles about a stick.

"A stick?" he says. "You need a stick."

She nods, weakly, her mouth hanging open.

Lowell doesn't know what she needs the stick for, but he starts looking for one, scouring along the forest floor within reach of him, but there is nothing but tiny twigs. Would these work? He has no idea. In desperation, he grabs one and is about to hold it up and ask her if it will work, but then he hears a voice.

Distant, echoing through the woods.

"Lowell! Brie!" the voice calls. It sounds ragged. Panic-stricken. "Lowell!"

He looks at Brie. "That's Mr. Huxley."

Brie's eyes are closed, head hanging, jaw slack.

"Brie," Lowell feels his stomach clenching up, his throat tightening. His voice goes up when he says her name again, and then a third time. He reaches forward to touch her and hesitates because he doesn't know what to do. How do you check and see if she is still alive? She seems very still. More still than she should be.

Lowell puts his hand against the side of her face. It is clammy. Cool, but not cold. Sweaty. He slaps her lightly. "Come on, Brie. Come on. Mr. Huxley … that's Mr. Huxley! He can help you! He can fix you, I think. You have to wake up!" He slaps her harder, feeling a tweak of anger at her now. "You have to wake up, Brie! Wake up! Don't be weak! You can't be weak! You have to be strong!"

A snap of twigs. A crunch of leaves.

Lowell is about to turn, but first feels the hand on his neck, hard and harsh, and the cold of a steel revolver barrel against the back of his head.

"She's dead, boy." A voice like rocks and crags and wind in the desert: "Now you come with me."

CHAPTER 2

My head, my head, my head …

The pain is incredible.

He can feel his heart in his chest. It isn't beating so fast, but each pulse is like the revolution of an engine, and it feels like there are cylinders slamming in his head every time his heart palpitates. It is a harsh, knocking sound inside of him. He can hear it against the inside of his eardrums. He can feel it in his swollen-shut sinuses and the feeling of blood pressing at the backs of his eyes as they struggle open.

Stars.

Blackness.

Not a real night sky, though. Just his eyes trying to see again through the haze of concussion. He blinks, squints, tries to fight some of that pressure back down into his body from his head, but it can't be overcome.

An image comes into a view. It doesn't make any sense. An oil lamp hovers in the air. Wooden planks float above his head. Someone's booted feet, as well. They shift about when Huxley moves. The world is upside down.

His shoulders burn. He tries to move his arms, realizes that they are restrained behind his back.

Holy fuck, my head …

The crown of his head is a beating drum. His face is crashing cymbals.

He groans, tries to look down at his feet, but his head is unwieldy and extremely heavy.

None of this makes sense …

He feels hands grab his face and shake him.

He lets out a little bark of pain, then squints through more stars at a face that looks at him. The face is upside down. He is staring at the mouth. Thin-lipped with a scar running through it that causes the lip to curl in a permanent sneer.

Huxley tries to speak, but only lets out a weak cough.

The hand shakes him again, then slaps him across the face—not hard, but almost playfully.

"You're awake," the sneering lips move to the rhythm of the voice. Huxley tries to focus on the face, but it's hard to do.

The face withdraws, but Huxley still hears the voice. That thick southern accent. "Heyo. You sure this is your boy?"

Another face comes into the picture. A head on a big body. Gray hair. Thick arms. Huxley doesn't recognize it at first, because it too is hanging upside down. Huxley tries to twist his head to orient the picture correctly, but the movement is too hard, too painful, and it makes him feel nauseous.

"Yeah," the big, gray-headed man says. "That was the guy in my shop."

The guy in my shop.

Huxley frowns at the gray-headed man. He almost laughs.

It is the shopkeeper.

"You sonofabitch," Huxley mumbles. He's not sure they heard what he said.

"Niner?" the man with the scarred lip says.

Huxley pans his darkling vision over to a third man. He wears a red shirt. Huxley recognizes him as well. A little spike of adrenaline plunges into his gut, but at least it masks the pain in his head and face for a brief moment.

The man in the red shirt—Niner, apparently—crosses his arms and nods without hesitation. "Yeah, Nate. That's him. Hundred percent."

Nate.

Wild Nate.

Nathaniel Cartwright.

The scorpion tattoo on his neck.

Huxley cannot help himself, he feels the laughter in his chest. *This is madness. This is the way of the world. It is insane. And none of it makes sense. None of it is fair. None of it is right. This is no longer earth. This is no longer reality. The skyfire was the end of the world, and this is Hell. God must have hated the world so much that he sent us all straight to Hell.*

Do we deserve any better?

He wheezes out laughter, which turns into a sob, and he chokes it off.

It wasn't all Hell. There was a little patch of green in the Wastelands where he and Charity and Nadine lived for a short time. And there was peace there. That was not Hell. It wasn't Heaven either, but there was peace, and there was love. There was hope.

There is no hope here.

Nathaniel Cartwright bends down and twists his head to get a better look at Huxley. Huxley realizes now that he's been strung up, hanging by his feet from the rafters of an old dilapidated … something. A barn. An old cabin. He isn't sure which. The light from the oil lamp doesn't illuminate much.

"Well," Cartwright says, scratching his chin. The bristly hairs make a rough, sandpaper noise across his palms. "I guess we've found the great and mysterious Huxley."

Cartwright kneels down. His expression is odd to Huxley. While his eyes are cruel to a certain extent, while his lip sneers and he seems disdainful, there is something else there. Almost a pity. And that scares Huxley more than anything else. Here is a man that feels pity, but refuses to let it stop him from doing what he wants.

"Strange," Cartwright says, quietly. "I'd expected … more."

Behind the scenes, Huxley's mind is piecing back together the timeline of memories that had been blown apart by the strikes he'd received to his head. He remembers now, looking up at Cartwright from the ground. He remembers that he was doing something just before that. He'd been trying to kill something … trying to kill *someone* …

"Where's Jay?" he suddenly mumbles.

Cartwright's eyebrows knit and he inclines his right ear just a bit. "What's that?"

Huxley manages to twist his head enough to see another body hanging beside his. Blond hair. Pink, sunburned skin. A lot of blood on the face, though. Beaten pretty badly. Had he done that? Or had it been Cartwright and his men? He tries to determine whether Jay is breathing or not, but he can't hold the straining position long enough to watch for the rise and fall of Jay's breath.

Does it matter? You were trying to kill him.

Huxley looks back at Cartwright, grunts and clears his throat.

Cartwright leans away, as though he expects Huxley to spit the wad of phlegm at him, but Huxley just swallows hard. Cartwright leans back in.

"What do you want?" Huxley croaks.

"What do I want?" Cartwright laughs, glancing over his shoulder at Niner and the shopkeeper. There must be other men that Huxley cannot see, lurking in the darkness. He hears a slight chuckle ripple through them. "You're the one that's been chasing me." Cartwright seems genuinely offended by it. As though he's been wronged. "First the Black Hats ... shit, I thought you was a Black Hat yourself, but clearly that ain't the case. Never seen a Black Hat with an entourage of children. I mean ... what's up with that anyway?" Cartwright shakes his head, waves his last question away as though it's unimportant. "It's a stupid question you asked. What do *I* want? What do *you* want? I know the Black Hats want me 'cause of ... well ..." he smirks. "... I have refined taste in women."

Another few chuckles from the darkness.

"But then there's you," Cartwright continues. "Supposedly some seven-foot-tall wild man from the Wastelands, or a warlord from up north—I've heard both rumors—and you're chasing me around for God knows what reason. Burnin' down towns, that's what I heard. Murdering everyone that ever gave help to me. Single-handedly killing a group of a dozen of the Nigger King's men and then *robbing* him—*fucking robbing him!*—I mean, the list of impressive exploits just goes on and on."

Cartwright frowns deeply and gestures to Huxley with some genuine confusion on his face. "But here I have a half-starved scarecrow, clearly a madman, rolling in the dirt with the corpses of children that he's somehow convinced to be his minions, and now you're hanging in a fucking barn, bleeding." He shakes his head, flabbergasted. "I mean ... I don't get it. I just don't get it. So what the fuck? Why me? Why are you so pissed off at *me*?"

Huxley strains to look over at Jay again. This time, he sees Jay's eyes fluttering.

He's alive.

How do I feel?

Angry, still. He should not be alive.

Huxley closes his eyes.

"Heyo," Cartwright gives him another slap across the face. "Answer my question."

Huxley doesn't open his eyes. He clamps down on them harder. Behind his eyes, his vision is black and red. Darkness and blood. But he reaches down deep inside of him where sacred things are stored, past all the brambles of hatred that Jay sowed in him—that he *let* Jay sow in him—and he looks at the reason why he is here. The reason why he has chased this man halfway across the continent.

Because of a woman and a girl.

Charity and Nadine.

"My wife. My daughter," Huxley says. Then he opens his eyes and looks at Cartwright.

Cartwright can see the fury in Huxley. The impotent rage. Huxley knows he can see it. But as Huxley suspected, Cartwright is not intimidated. He stands up, pursing his thin, scarred lips together and he looks down at Huxley.

"Your wife," the slaver says. Slowly, flatly. "Your daughter."

There is a long moment when neither of them speak.

Niner and the shopkeeper are silent.

The gathered of Cartwright's gang say nothing from the shadows.

Cartwright sniffs loudly. "You're not from around here. I know that straight off. I see the Wastelands in your eyes, that's easy enough. So I must assume that you are from some shithole hovel, tucked away somewhere in the Wastelands. And at some point you lost your wife and daughter to a slaver. One that you fervently believe to be me."

"You killed my wife," Huxley says, and is surprised how emotionless he sounds, when inside of his chest it feels like iron hands are wringing him out like a sponge. "And you took my daughter."

Cartwright frowns at Huxley. "Even if it was me … do you realize how many men's daughters I've taken over the years? Sons? Wives?"

The question is sincere in its incredulity.

Huxley can't stand the coldness of this man.

He closes his eyes. He pictures Nadine by the barley fields. Nadine, looking up at the stars in her childlike wonder. Nadine, drawing pictures for people that had lost everything, to give them a glimpse back into their past, to let them hold on to their humanity a little while longer and remember what it was like to have love.

It seems like everyone has lost someone they love, she'd told him. *I think people forget about that.*

"No," Huxley says, with his eyes still closed. "My daughter was special."

Cartwright shakes his head. "Of course she was. To you. To me, she was just another mouth to feed until I sold her off to whoever was interested in having another female in their household. What happens after that ain't my business. I don't tell the councilmen what to do with the slaves they buy. That's not my problem. All I can promise you is that—and understand that I'm not trying to be an asshole here, I'm just telling you the truth—your daughter was a dime a dozen. I know you think I'll remember her, but I won't. Just another Wastelander girl that I probably sold for about twenty pieces."

Huxley's eyes shoot open as Cartwright speaks and he wishes he could be free of his bindings, just let him down, *Please, God, let me down, let me kill this man …*

"She drew pictures." His voice betrays him, cracking as he speaks. "She drew charcoal pictures for people."

There is more silence.

Cartwright turns away from him.

Huxley stares. He can see the side of the slaver's face, his hand up, touching the scar on his lips. His brow is furrowed.

He knows. He remembers.

Huxley's heart beats twice, and then plummets.

She is dead. He may remember her, but she is dead.

"You remember her," Huxley says.

Cartwright is very still. His finger keeps tracing the line of his scar, across his lips. Down to his chin. Finally, he lifts his face, just slightly, looking at something Huxley cannot see. "I always remember my top earners." He turns, smiles tightly. "She gave a drawing demonstration. Where was that?" he looks up, summoning the memory from thin air. "Shit, I think she was sold in Shreveport. Drew some pretty pictures with some lumps of charcoal and I sold her to the Murphy family for forty-eight pieces."

Huxley blinks several times, trying to clear his brain. "Is she … is she …?"

He can't even say the words.

Cartwright is irritated now. He ignores Huxley. "What the hell were you trying to accomplish? Did you think you were just going to ride into the Riverlands, burn down people's shit, and then walk out the other side alive? You fucking idiot. There's probably more Black Hats after you than there are after me. Not to mention posses. Good God, you've pissed some people off …"

Nathaniel Cartwright's voice becomes background noise.

Nadine.

Everything seems very still. Very quiet.

Nadine.

But I lost everything, I have nothing. That is who I am.

But … what if she was alive?

It is impossible.

Why? Because Jay said it was?

But what if?

What if …?

Nadine.

Cartwright smacks him hard in the face. "Are you even fucking listening to me?"

Huxley doesn't feel the sting in his cheeks. He can hardly feel anything.

He is buzzing. Overflowing.

"Is my daughter still alive?" Huxley asks.

Cartwright squints at him, like he is the most irritating man in the world. "How the hell should I know?"

Then there is a sudden noise.

Like running water … or …

Burning.

Fast burning.

A bright flash.

A momentary strobe in the dark cabin that illuminates everything for just an instant, enough for Huxley to see that the source of the flash is outside. It is outside, and the light slips in through the cracks between the slatboards that make up the shoddily constructed shack …

And then it is gone.

Cartwright spins toward the door, revolver held up. "The fuck was that?"

"Sounded like a powder charge," someone says, their voice tight.

There is stillness, all the empirical data of the moment just kind of hanging there like unpicked fruit, and Huxley plucking it down and looking at it. Because he just did this. He just used gunpowder to set fire to a house …

There is a crackling sound, and it quickly turns to a roar.

There is angry, orange light slipping through the slatboards now, and tendrils of smoke. And it is all around them. Not just at the door, but on every wall. At the base of everything. Completely surrounding them, and the orange glow gets brighter by the second, glowing on the faces of several men who have been sitting in the darkness.

"Fire!" someone cries.

And Huxley keeps thinking, *I know this, I know this, I remember it …*

Cartwright points to someone. "Nobody move! Stay where you are!"

Someone runs for the rickety outline of the door and flings it open before he can really register Cartwright's command. He stands terrified for a brief moment. He looks back over his shoulder at Cartwright, confusion and fear on his face. He doesn't want to be caught in the fire. But he doesn't want to disobey Cartwright.

Cartwright knows something too.

He waves hurriedly to the man standing in the doorway. "Get back inside!"

The man at the door twitches—his neck explodes.

There is the ringing of a gunshot from outside.

Cartwright swears loudly, dives off to the side. He reaches out a hand and grabs the man by the collar, hauling him back inside while someone in the shadows of the hideout kicks the door closed again. The man on the ground, shot in the throat, is kicking in a panic, hands grabbing at his throat, spluttering blood.

Already the fire is licking at the walls, prying at the slats, trying to get in through the murder holes and the windows.

It has them pinned. Surrounded.

If they leave, they will be shot.

If they stay, they will be burned to death.

"Fuck!" Cartwright screams.

Huxley begins to laugh, the raw laughter that comes out of that deep, dark, hopeless place inside of him. The kind of laughter that Jay put in his chest. It starts as a wheeze, drowned out by the yelling men around him and the roar of flames as they grow and grow along the walls outside like burning vines. But his laughter grows with it, louder, into a cackle that spends every bit of air in his lungs and makes his head hurt, but he can't stop laughing at them, these huge, ironic fools.

Cartwright is staring at him, his eyes a little wider than they should be, maybe for once feeling the fear that he was so good at striking into others. Maybe for once feeling his rank fall to a position lower than the top of the food chain. Maybe realizing that he is not the apex predator. Maybe all of the things that he has done are flashing through his brain in that instant and he knows that death is chasing at his heels, and wondering, knowing, that if anything comes after, it will be punishment.

The things you do are never lost. No matter how far into the Wastelands you did them.

"The fuck are you laughing about?" Cartwright screams at him as the man in his arms splutters his last breath, drowning in his own blood.

Huxley gasps, breathless. "It's Black Heart Davies," Huxley says. "He's come for you. He's come for us both."

CHAPTER 3

The shopkeeper is determined. He drops the big scattergun on the ground. He has to hunch over as he strides quickly through the room, everyone yelling at him to get back away from the door, to get down.

They all saw what happened to the other man.

Smoke is filling the room and the shopkeeper has to duck under it, still coughing as he goes.

"I'm not a part of this," he says, perhaps more to convince himself than anyone else. "I'm not one of your crew, Nate! I'm going out to explain myself!"

Cartwright is shaking his head, distracted, scooting himself away from the burning wall while he tries to fish a bandanna from his pocket to filter some of the smoke from his mouth and nose. "It don't matter," he coughs once. "He'll shoot you dead as soon as you step outside."

"I ain't burnin' alive!" the shopkeeper shouts back.

The door is on fire. He kicks it open, flinching away from a shower of embers, then plowing through a screen of smoke and into the night. His voice can be heard, and Huxley can see the silhouette of the man, made indistinct by the billowing smoke, his arms raised high above his head.

"Don't shoot! Don't shoot! I'm coming out!"

Boom.

Boom.

The shopkeeper's silhouette disappears, and so does his voice.

Another voice, belting through the night outside, loud and clear above the crackling and the roaring around them. Huxley knows that voice. He knows exactly who it is, and it dries up the black humor in his chest and he realizes that this is his time too, just as much as it is Cartwright's.

"Come out and take your justice like a man, or burn alive like a coward," the voice calls out. "Choice is yours. By the end of tonight, you'll all be dead anyway."

Panic is coursing through the men inside. The fire is burning their wits away. They are huddling now toward the middle of the shack as the walls start to sprout flame. Huxley can feel it now, the heat on his face, on his back. No one is going to cut him down. No one is going to free him. He does not have the choice that was given to Cartwright. He will die in this fire.

Cartwright holds both of his revolvers now, he fidgets on the floor, unable to get into a position where the heat is not painful. And the smoke is filling the room. They will not last much longer in here. "Davies!" he barks out into the darkness beyond the open door. "There are five of us in here. How many do you have?"

"Just myself," the voice comes back, supremely confident. "But I got about two bullets for each of you. Think I'll use 'em all?"

Cartwright gets his bandanna over his face, muffling a string of curses as he stamps his feet. He pulls the bandanna away, his voice taking out a desperate tone. "We have Huxley!" he coughs. "Let us go and we'll give you Huxley!"

"I know you have Huxley," Davies responds, his tone almost amused. "He ain't my problem. You are. And he's either gonna stay in there and get burned up, or come out and get his justice anyway. So you don't really have a bargaining chip there, Nate. Come on out and take it like a man."

Niner speaks up, holding his rifle, snot and drool and tears coming out of his mouth as he coughs profusely. The words come between coughs. "We can't stay … we'll fight … fight our way out!"

Cartwright is nodding, jerking himself up onto his knees, then his feet, still bent over to avoid the thickest smoke. "Let's go," he waves his revolvers. "Everyone ready?"

They are all ready. They do not want to be burned alive.

There is a flash of time just before they burst out of the door when Huxley can appreciate the simple efficiency of Black Heart Davies' tactic. It is cruel. But it is effective. The smoke weakens the men, fills their eyes with tears. The fire will blind them. And Black Heart Davies will be in the darkness, likely behind a thick tree, and he will pick them off casually as they funnel through the door. Their fire-blinded eyes will never be able to see where he is. They are blind men in a gunfight.

There is a reason they call him Black Heart Davies.

Even as low as Huxley's head is to the floor as he dangles upside down from the rafters, the smoke is still hitting him. His eyes are watering profusely, and his lungs are burning. He tries to take short breaths, tries to avoid that whole big inhale of smoke, but it still burns, and now it burns for oxygen too. He coughs, takes an involuntary breath, coughs again.

What do I feel?

I don't want this.

The smoke is going to choke him. And then the fire will strip the skin from his body, it will bubble him, it will cook him until his blood turns solid and the water separates and runs out of him …

Cartwright's men stand up in halting movements, all of them coughing, bleary-eyed from the sting of smoke, and they stumble for the door, lambs to the slaughter. Their choices shrunken down to two pitiful ends. One seems like a way out if they can fight hard enough, but in reality, it is only an illusion.

There is a fusillade of gunfire from outside.

It should've been satisfying, but the fire is creeping in, and Huxley has only one thought.

Nadine.

He needs to live. Because his daughter is alive. *Might* be alive. And he is here, strung up with no way out, and flames ripping closer to him every second. She is out there. Out there somewhere in the cold, cold night. She wonders what became of her father, perhaps believes that he is already dead.

I'm not! I'm alive!

He twists and manages to catch a glimpse of Jay. The other man is jerking around, trying to yank himself free of the ropes that bind him. They are not coming loose. Huxley didn't think that they would. He catches Huxley's gaze and there is pure panic in his own.

"Help me!" he yelps. "Get me out of here!'

No, Huxley thinks. *I need to be free of you.*

Huxley can feel the heat, the horrible heat. His body is involuntarily jerking around, trying to avoid it, but it is all around him. He is trapped in an oven. It is growing, rapidly, exponentially, every half second that passes is a world of pain worse than the previous.

"Huxley!" Jay is screaming, his voice ragged. "Don't let me die like this! Don't let me die, you sonofabitch!"

Huxley does not want to scream. He does not want to scream because he does not want Black Heart Davies to hear him scream. But the pain is growing so rapidly that it becomes a battle that is fought over endless seconds. He slams his eyes shut against the stinging smoke and heat, feels the tears rush out of his eyes and immediately evaporate on his face.

Oh my God it hurts so bad

He grits his teeth together. When he bares them he can feel the heat of the flame through his teeth. It is a ripping pain now, along his back, and along his forearms. An indescribable pain. He feels his diaphragm bucking in his chest, trying to let out that scream. It ruptures through his throat, scrapes its way up and comes out through his clenched teeth, hissing spittle through them. He tries to hold it back, but the concept of it begins to elude him, why he is trying not to scream is suddenly forgotten in how monumental the pain is.

The fire is gonna burn me alive!

It's gonna eat me alive!

The scream bursts out of him, three quick screams, like they've built up, like the pressure is so great to excise the pain that he cannot contain it. He gasps and screams, gasps and screams, as fast as he can let the pain out, as fast as he can suck in the burning air. His world has become agony. But the screams give him tiny flashes of clarity, little jumps and starts for the bit of his mind that can still think beyond what his nerves are telling him.

Those clear moments flash with blood and tragedy.

Charity, his wife, bloody and broken on the floor.

No, no, no.

Think of something good.

Try to think of something good.

Because these might be his last moments.

These might be his last thoughts.

Just a picture.

Her face lifted up to the sky. Starlight in her eyes. Mouth open in wonder, a slight smile on her lips. A moment of happiness, of peace, when his little girl was just his little girl and he was just Daddy and for a brief moment things were normal, wonderful, beautiful.

"I love you more than all the stars in the sky," he would say.

I'm sorry, sweet girl ...

He is floating in fire.

Then he hits the ground.

Flames. Pain. Burning.

He feels disassembled. His arms are moving free.

He can't make sense of it, but he doesn't try. His skin prickles and feels like it's cracking in the intense heat as he moves, but he pulls his head up and opens his eyes to the burning again. Everything is orange and yellow and white. Everything but that square straight in front of him. That is black. Black and cold. Cold like the ocean. Like quenching water. He wants that black square more than anything else.

Go! Go while you can!

He claws. His feet are still bound together, he can't move them. As he squints through the heat, he manages to catch a glimpse of his wrist and he plants his hand on the plank floors and pulls himself forward. He can't tell if his skin is truly burned or not—everything looks red. On his wrists are smoking threads of rope that have been burned through to ashes. That is his right hand.

He hitches himself forward. Left hand out. That one is not so bad, the rope looks less burned there.

The cold black square. The door.

He focuses on it.

Behind him, there are screams.

Is he still screaming?

No, it's Jay. Jay is screaming. Jay cannot make words any longer. He cannot shout Huxley's name. He can only scream in agony. And the sound is horrible, and perhaps if Huxley was not about to die himself he would have turned around for the man out of sheer pity, but there is something hard inside of him that blocks that thought and he keeps thinking, *I need to be free of him.*

Huxley can feel the air rushing in at him. It feels arctic compared to what is behind and around him.

Just make it to the door!

Huxley cries out again as he drags himself across the planks. He reaches the door and rolls himself through it. He feels hard earth. Dusty dirt. It is cold. The wind is like ice all around him, but it soothes him, cool water on a burn. How badly is he burned? How much of his body is covered in burns? How badly are his lungs scarred? He made it out, but that doesn't mean he will live.

He hears a crumbling sound behind him, the sound of charred timbers beginning to collapse on themselves. He twists through a fog of pain and looks at the shack. It is a lonesome thing, a cube of wood, nearly entirely consumed by flames now. From inside the groaning structure, there is still screaming. Huxley stares into the flames with wide eyes and hazy vision and he lifts his hands to block his ears, but it does nothing. No matter how hard he presses his hands to his ears he can still hear Jay screaming, endlessly, painfully. And then, very suddenly, it goes silent.

Huxley gasps for breath. Coughs hard.

He realizes smoke is still trailing off of his body. Steam, too. His body is so hot that it is steaming in the cool night air. He is singed. The pain begins to center itself, not just an all-over pain now, but beginning to focus itself in certain spots—his right arm and hand, his right leg, the right side of his face.

He rolls to his left, trying to take some pressure off the skin. Everything hurts. The brush of grass and dirt is painful. The wind scouring across him is nearly unbearable. He begins to shake.

But he is exultant.

He is alive.

He curls in on himself, like a pill bug. Clutching his burned arm, wondering how badly his face is burned. He smells the stink of roasted hair. Acrid. Nauseating.

"Mr. Huxley," a voice says.

That voice.

He rips himself out of his pain and cranes his neck. He sees old dusty boots. Tracks them up to the torn and mended pants. And then the muzzle of a pistol. Not a revolver, but a semiautomatic pistol. One of the cartridge pistols of the Old World. Its black slide and muzzle glimmer with the light of the fire behind him. And beyond that muzzle there are two cold eyes, alight with the same fire, a sad line of a mouth, craggy, bony features.

Huxley stares into the black hole hovering over his face and says the only words that mean anything to him in that moment, the ones that have been jarred loose from their ancient, encrusted moorings and drift around endlessly in his head: "I think my daughter is alive."

CHAPTER 4

The muzzle.

The slide. Firelight across it.

Black Heart Davies, looking down the sights with his finger on the trigger. His expression remains unchanged.

But he doesn't shoot.

Huxley feels the cords of his neck tiring from holding his head up. He lets his head fall to the ground. He closes his eyes, because he doesn't want to see the gun anymore, doesn't want to see Black Heart Davies. But mostly because it helps him focus through the pain.

What does he feel?

He feels that he doesn't want to die. He feels that there is something just out of his reach that wasn't there before. His Nadine is *alive*! And *he* is alive! This is something to cling to. This is hope.

Davies' voice in the darkness: "You think you're the first person to try and talk themselves out of their predicament?"

Huxley peels his eyes open to look at the man standing over him. "I don't know. I don't know anything." He strains against the pain in his arm, the burns, strangely enough, giving him cold chills. It's difficult to speak. He has a million thoughts and words rolling through his head, from the eloquent to the baseborn curses, from the high-minded to the violent. Threatening or cajoling. None of it matters.

Nadine. That's what matters.

Nadine. Somewhere. Alive.

It is difficult to speak, but he grinds words out. The only ones that make sense.

"I don't know what you want from me. I don't know what any of you people want from me. You've taken everything. I just … I just …" he realizes he is weeping, fighting the words through his grief. "I just want her back. She's the one thing. I didn't even know I still had her. I thought she was dead. I just want her back."

Davies shakes his head for a moment, seemingly unmoved. And why would he be? Huxley didn't expect him to be moved.

"You know," the Black Hat says. "When I let you go the first time, I had no idea the shitstorm you were going to create for me. Honestly, that was an oversight on my part. I should've been able to tell from our conversation that you weren't just after Cartwright. You were after anybody that had ever sold or bought a slave." Davies' eyes narrow. "This wasn't about Cartwright. This wasn't about revenge against a single man. It was about revenge against the entire system. You wanted to take it all on. And here you are, at the same place as every other man that has ever taken on a system all by himself—at the business end of a gun, trying to talk his way out of dying."

Could he tell him that it was Jay?

Would it matter?

No, it wouldn't. And Black Heart Davies wouldn't care about Jay. To Black Heart Davies, Jay didn't exist, and never would, because he was buried behind Huxley in a burning pile of wood. To Davies, it was Huxley and Huxley alone that committed those things.

And it was me. Because I let it happen.

"I know what I've done." Huxley coughs. "I know what I let happen."

"Realizing you're wrong doesn't scrub everything away," Davies says, slowly. "Atonement must still be made."

Huxley feels suddenly extremely tired. "I'm not trying to run from the things that I've done."

"Then what are you asking me for, if it's not mercy?"

"I don't want your mercy," Huxley struggles to keep his voice even.

"Then what? Are you just clearing your conscience before death?"

What is it? What do I want?

"Time," Huxley blurts. "I want more time."

"Time?" Davies coughs out a single laugh.

Huxley has no trickery anymore. He will not beg or plead because he knows that if he does then Davies will simply end him right then and there. The Black Hat has seen enough men beg and plead to be inoculated against it. All Huxley has is a question.

"Did you ever have children?"

Davies face becomes blank. But Huxley can see the truth flickering behind the man's eyes. There is something there that is not allowed out, some other version of Davies, the same as there is another version of Huxley, forgotten in time, delineated from the present person by some cataclysmic moment.

"Before," is all Davies says.

"What would you do to see them again?"

They stare at each other, and through each other.

They have both lost children. They both know the answer to this question, because there is only one answer.

Just to hold them again. To have just a few moments to blurt out all the things they had wanted to say in the intervening years, all the words and simple things that had to die in their hearts unspoken because the ears to hear them no longer existed, and never would again.

Anything. That is the answer.

Davies knows it.

But then he seems to snap back into himself. That older version, so close to floating up from the depths, just barely visible through the murky waters, now sinks back down to the bottom. Pressed back to where it belongs.

He is Black Heart Davies again.

He adjusts his grip on the pistol and reaches behind him to extract a black sack from somewhere in his coat. Without speaking, he stoops down and places the sack over Huxley's head. And inside his mind Huxley is surprisingly calm, even though his heart is beating like mad.

This is it. This is the end.

No more hope. It was a little too far-gone …

"Put your wrists together in front of you."

Huxley does it, feels the sting of something touching the burned side of his wrist. He hisses in pain. *What is he doing?*

Davies voice again: "This is going to hurt. Hold still." The Black Hat wraps something around Huxley's wrists, binding them together.

Why is he tying me up?

You don't bind someone if you plan to execute them …

But what if you plan to transport them to another Black Hat?

Maybe the one who's assigned to me, the one that was chasing me in Red Water Landing.

A familiar voice of hatred in his mind: *You're not a man to him. You're just a bargaining chip so he can show all his Black Hat buddies that he's still Black Heart Davies, a ruthless man to be feared, the best that they have.*

Davies takes him by the arm—the one that is not so burned—and he picks him up off the ground. A shove to the shoulder. "Start walking forward. I'll tell you when to stop."

They walk for a time. Not too long. At first it is dried leaves Huxley is crunching through. Then it is what feels like rock, or hard-packed dirt. The wind is gusting and it whips his charred clothing around and freezes him and sends needles through his burned arm and leg.

Davies pulls him to a stop.

Huxley can hear the snorting of horses. He can smell them.

"There's a wagon in front of you," Davies says. "Climb up."

Huxley hesitates. "Is it my wagon?"

"Climb up."

Huxley puts his bound hands forward until he feels the deck of the wagon bed. He rolls into the bed, clumsily, trying to avoid the spots of his body that are hurting the worst. He feels Davies' hands on him again, pulling him to the side of the wagon. Then his bound wrists are lashed tightly to the side of the wagon so that he cannot move them more than an inch or so away from the wood.

If it is his wagon, Davies must've hitched new horses to it.

The others were dead. Along with everyone and everything else.

Except Nadine.

Huxley does not ask where they are going.

He figures he will find out soon enough.

What about my daughter? What about her?

The pain in his skin is bad. But now his gut wrenches along with it.

This can't be it. This can't be the end.

The voice of hopelessness, bitterness, quieter now, but still there in the background, telling him that he is tied to a wagon, burned over a good portion of his body, and he has a hood over his head. He is in the custody of Black Heart Davies. And he already knows how this ends.

No. It can't. She's alive.

That only means something to you. The rest of the world continues on.

Huxley can hear Davies climbing up into the bench of the wagon. There is a snap of reins. The wagon starts moving.

A small voice, elsewhere in the wagon: "Mr. Huxley?"

Huxley jerks like he's been stung by something. "Lowell? Lowell is that you?"

He wants to reach out, try to find the boy in all this darkness, but his hands cannot move from where they are lashed.

Lowell's voice comes back again. It is strained. "What happened?"

Huxley can't control the emotion in his own voice. "I don't know, buddy. I'm so sorry. I'm so, so sorry. Where's Brie? Is Brie here? Did she make it with you?"

Lowell doesn't respond to that question.

Huxley hangs his head. "Lowell …"

Nothing else is said between them.

They move on through darkness. Huxley cannot think of how long he had been hanging in that cabin before he came awake, surrounded by Cartwright's men. But it is night, he knows that. The air is cold and windy. His world becomes the rocking, jarring motion of the wagon, and the pain in his wrist and arm and face.

For a time, Huxley tries to figure out where they are going by the motions of the wagon. But it is disorienting.

Should I be trying to escape?

But if he escaped, he would have to leave Lowell. There is no way to communicate with Lowell. Huxley can't plan anything verbally—Davies will hear them. He can't catch the boy's eyes and communicate that way, not with the sack over his face, and probably one over Lowell's face as well. They can't communicate by touch—they are lashed to opposite sides of the wagon.

And he will not leave Lowell.

He can't leave Lowell.

So I have to sit and wait?

Yes, you have to sit and wait.

The pain makes time stretch. The ropes around his burned wrist become the focal point of everything. It is bad enough to turn his stomach. If he had anything in it, he might feel the need to vomit, but he is empty, through and through.

They stop.

The wagon is rocking back and forth, and Huxley hears the sound of Davies' boots climbing down from the bench of the wagon before he even registers that they are stopped. He has spent so much focus on trying to position his hands and wrists in a way that keeps the rope from rubbing the burned area, or even to just limit it for a time and give him a gentle reprieve if only for a few moments.

The sound of boot heels on gravel.

The sack is lifted off of Huxley's head.

It is still dark out. There is a moon shining over top of them, and it casts enough light to see by. Black Hat Davies is there, standing at the side of the wagon with Huxley, his elbows propped up on the boards that Huxley is lashed to. In the ghostly light of the moon, Davies' skin looks paler than before, making Huxley think again of a marble statue, but the face is not smooth like some work of art. It is hacked with chisels and left craggy and sharp.

His eyes catch the moonlight in an eerie way, so that his pupils and the whites of his eyes almost seem the same color, just the dark little dot of his iris floating in the middle of all that icy blue. It unsettles Huxley to see him, but at the same moment, he is glad that the man is there. Because an opportunity to speak is an opportunity to figure out what the hell was happening.

"You look like shit," Davies observes. He reaches out a casual hand and presses the back of his hands against Huxley's forehead. There is nothing tender about it—purely clinical. "You in a lot of pain from that burn?"

Huxley is in enough pain to be sweating in the cold night air. He nods.

Davies looks over the burn on his face. "Some blistering," he says. "Not the worst I've ever seen, but I bet you're hating life. Your face is bad. Burned half your beard off. Your arm ..." Davies peeks down to look at it.

Huxley considers lunging for him, but it would do no good.

"Your arm is worse."

"Where ...?" Huxley blinks through a slew of chills.

"Where are we going?" Davies finishes for him. Then he shakes his head and looks off. He appears to be thinking, and Huxley lets him think. After a few moments, he speaks, steadily. "You don't even know where your daughter is."

"Councilman Murphy," Huxley says. "She was bought by Councilman Murphy."

Davies looks at him as though Huxley has told a joke with an inscrutable punch line. Then he grunts and pushes off of the wagon. He reaches into his coat and pulls out a small metal flask—almost more of a vial than a full flask—with a cork and a leather thong to stop it. He plucks the cork out and pushes the flask into Huxley's face.

Huxley pulls back. He can smell alcohol ... and something else.

"Whiskey laudanum," Davies says. "Trust me."

Huxley purses his lips, but the thought of something for the pain makes him give in. If Davies meant for him to die, then he would have put a bullet in him, or slit his throat if he wanted to save himself a bullet. And there was no other reason to drug Huxley—any so-called truth serum wouldn't do him any good, because Huxley had nothing left to hide.

He leans forward, parting his lips slightly.

Davies puts the flask to Huxley's lips and tips it up, giving Huxley a generous mouthful. It is a foul, hot, bitter mixture that Huxley nearly coughs up. It burns down his throat and has an odd consistency, almost astringent. Davies corks the flask again and puts it back in his jacket.

Huxley coughs against the burn in his throat. "You drink that shit?"

Davies smirks. "You ever broken a bone a hundred miles from the nearest settlement? It's not a fun ride. I keep it for emergencies. But no, I don't make a habit of it."

Huxley is about to ask how long it takes to kick in, but Davies puts the sack over his head again and a moment later Huxley hears him climb back into the wagon's bench and snap the reins. The horses whicker and the wagon starts moving again.

"Mr. Huxley?" Lowell's voice says, quietly. "Are you still there?"

Huxley closes his eyes against the pain. "Yes. I'm here."

He loses track of time. Perhaps it was fifteen minutes, or maybe it was an hour, but he realizes that the pain is gone. No ... not gone. Just blanketed. Just sitting under a warm blanket, like a blanket that has been sitting next to a fire for a good long while. The emptiness in his gut is fuzzy and unmemorable, and bad things seem far away.

There is a moment when his chest feels warm, and all his skin extraordinarily soft, and he tries to think of what it reminds him of, the sensation. And he thinks that it is those perfect spring and fall nights when the air temperature was just so, and the humidity was gone, when he would lie next to Charity, both of them bare-chested, and her skin against his was this very same sensation—not cold, not hot, not sweaty. Just smooth and warm. Perfect.

Perfect …

CHAPTER 5

When Huxley comes to, it is daylight.

It is warm. He can feel it on his face, and he realizes that the sack is no longer over his head. The air is crisp, but not uncomfortably cold. And in the sunlight, he is okay. The pain stretches and yawns, awakening with him.

The burns. I've been burned.

Fuck, my wrist …

He grimaces and feels some portion of the flesh on his face crack, near the corner of his mouth. It makes a painful, brittle sound and he feels wetness oozing out of it. He keeps his eyes clamped closed for another few minutes, wishing like hell for more of Davies' whiskey laudanum, but he won't ask for it. He won't ask for it, and he isn't sure if he wants to take it again if it is offered. He does not want to sleep again. He wants to be free. He wants to figure out how to get out of this situation.

The sunlight blazes on the other side of his eyelids.

He squints through them, dazzled by the early morning.

There is the smell of smoke, but Huxley only registers it when he sees it rising from a meager campfire, over which Black Heart Davies stands in a brooding posture, his back turned to Huxley and the wagon.

He took my hood off, Huxley reasons his way through it, observing that his hands are still bound together, still lashed to the side of the wagon. *But I'm not free.*

He looks to his right and he can see Lowell there, his hands also bound, no hood over his head. Now, in the daylight, with his vision returned to him, Huxley can see the horrible shape the boy is in. He is huddled in the cold with his chin against his chest, the fingers of his bound hands turning blue from lack of circulation. His eyes are pinched shut, like he is straining to sleep, his eyebrows knit. He is covered in blood. Old and brown and scabbed over. It is caked in his fingernails, in his cuticles, in the folds of his knuckles.

Brie. Brie didn't make it.

"Lowell," Huxley says, huskily. He clears his throat.

Lowell's eyes open. He looks across the wagon with a confused glare. The look of someone snatched from sleep that was difficult to find in the first place, someone that views the world as a sudden intrusion and cannot make sense of things just yet. He blinks a few times through his glare, and then his eyes clear as memory and logic come back to him.

Huxley can almost watch the moment when Lowell remembers where he is, and how he came to be there, and everything that had come before. It is like watching his face age a decade in only a few seconds. He goes from a boy to a hard-bitten young man right before Huxley's eyes.

He wonders if any of that bitterness is for him.

Some of it must be.

Lowell's eyes drift to the spot over Huxley's right shoulder.

Huxley turns and finds Davies standing there, as he had in the darkness of the previous night, with his elbows propped up on the side of the wagon. He watches Huxley and the boy with an intense, measuring gauge, as though every twitch and expression that flies between the two is being catalogued and recorded for some mysterious purpose.

"You two," Davies says after a moment, wagging a finger between them. "What is your relationship?"

Friend? Guardian?

Captor, perhaps?

Huxley looks at Lowell because he does not know how Lowell sees him. He does not know where the relationship between them stands in the eyes of this boy-turned-man. Lowell meets his gaze in turn, cold and wild. *You have been bad*, the gaze seems to say. *But you've also been good. You've been cruel. But you've also been kind.*

Rather than put a word or phrase to describe their relationship, Lowell simply tells Davies what has happened. "He and his people killed my parents. But he saved me from being killed. And he kept me alive. Didn't let people kill me, or capture me. He also forced me to be strong. I've had to hurt people. But they were people that needed to be hurt." Lowell looks at him. "He's helped me survive."

Huxley does not know whether the words crush him down or elevate him.

He wants to weep for the boy that never was. Beg forgiveness from the young man that now is. He wants to tell him to leave and never look back. If it hadn't been for Huxley, Lowell wouldn't have needed saving in the first place. Huxley allowed it to happen. Lowell's adopted parents were dead because of Huxley. He had created the problem to begin with.

No, Lowell. I did not save you.

I did teach you how to survive. But at what cost? When does survival outweigh humanity?

But you are young, and I am old. You still have a chance. But I am damned.

Huxley says nothing in response to Lowell's words.

Davies looks between them again, then takes a laborious breath. "Huxley. You've done evil on my watch. You've killed people that didn't need to be killed. No matter what you think about the Riverlands and the council. And your boy here … he's an associate. We don't just kill the man, we kill the associates. Just like Cartwright and his gang. You can't just chop the plant off at the ground. You have to pull it up by the roots."

Yes, you do, Black Heart Davies. I know it better than you think.

"Listen …" Huxley begins.

Davies looks at him sharply. "Huxley would you give your life for this boy? Would you let me put a bullet in your brain so that he could walk?"

Huxley is confused. He looks rapidly back and forth between Davies and Lowell.

Lowell is confused too.

Davies is watching.

"I don't …" Huxley stutters.

"Just answer the question," Davies says. "Looking at everything exactly as it stands right now, will you—*right now*—willingly accept your execution so that this boy can go free?"

This is some sort of trick, Huxley thinks as his mind scrambles for an answer, but there is no endgame that makes sense. Why would Davies even make the offer? He could just as easily shoot them both in the head right where they were sitting in the wagon. Truth be told, he should have already done it, so why are they still alive? Is he delivering them to the Black Hat who's in charge of tracking them? Or is there something else going on here?

It doesn't matter. The question still hangs in the air, requiring an answer.

So how do you choose? Your own flesh and blood, or some strange orphan? His daughter was snatched away from him. But Lowell was orphaned by him. Dragged into a bloody mess. Forced to do things no boy should ever be forced to do. Should he have to pay for that?

But his daughter …

Somewhere, she is being held. Perhaps her masters are kind to her. Or perhaps they are cruel. Maybe she had forgotten about her father, maybe she had given up. Or maybe she lies awake at nights and wonders where he is, and why he has not come for her.

The thought of it wrenches his heart out. He does not need to ask himself what he feels in that moment. It is clear. It is sharp. It rends and crushes all at once. If he were standing it would've brought him to his knees …

"I can't." Huxley shakes his head, feeling the tightness in his throat. The gumminess of the spit in his mouth. "You're asking me to choose between him and my daughter. I can't make that decision."

Davies looks at Huxley with a different expression, as though just now discovering another facet of Huxley that needed to be examined, some surprise aspect that he had overlooked before. He taps an index finger against the side of the wagon a few times, thoughtfully. "And if your daughter was free? What then? What would be your answer then?"

Huxley looks at him.

Well, then there would be no more excuses. Then it would merely be Huxley's life for Lowell's. And Huxley's life is miserable and damned, and Lowell's life has just begun. There is hope for him.

There could be no more excuses.

Now it was a question of right and wrong.

"Yes," Huxley says. "Yes, I would."

"Then you will," Davies says, and Huxley sees that he has a knife in his hand.

For an instant, a thousand questions flash through Huxley's mind.

Davies slides the knife deftly between Huxley's wrists. The blade is sharp and slips through the bonds with a few quick sawing motions. The pain of the rope on his wrist makes Huxley want to cry out, but there is the irrational fear that if he makes a sound, Davies will suddenly remember that Huxley is his prisoner and then he will not free him.

Then the ropes fall away, taking scabbed burns with them.

Huxley looks at Davies, then at his unbound hands. "What are you doing?"

"Atonement," he says, without much inflection. "The way I see it, everyone must pay their tally. I am merely the collector. All the evil that men do in their lives runs up their tally. And if someone does not make them pay for it, then there is no justice. If there is no justice, there is no law. And if there is no law, then we are only animals, hacking away at each other."

Davies moves to the end of the wagon, where the gate hangs open. He gestures to Huxley with a wave of his hand. "Come here."

Huxley exchanges a glance with Lowell, then stands up with some effort, his bones creaking, his muscles protesting. He shuffles uncomfortably to the end of the wagon, then slides awkwardly down from it.

Davies leads him to the fire where there is a small tin can full of some strangely colored liquid, steaming by the fire. Huxley can see leaves and bits of other things floating in the top of it. It gives off an odd, earthy, herbaceous smell.

"Kneel down," Davies says, then pats the outside with his bare fingers a few times to test the heat. The heat is apparently tolerable. He picks up the can. "Hold out your arm."

Huxley hesitates, then he does it.

Davies looks at him, the can poised at a slight angle over Huxley's arm. "This is going to hurt. A lot. I put some laudanum in the mix, so the pain will get dulled after a minute or so, but for a minute, it'll be agony. Grit your teeth and don't move your arm around."

Huxley takes a breath, bites down on it, then cringes.

Davies pours the liquid over the burn. It's not scalding, but it feels like it is. He pours it until the water is mostly gone, then he dips his fingers in and draws out a paste that has formed at the bottom of the tin can, which he spreads over the burned areas, including Huxley's face. Then he wraps it loosely in cloth that Huxley isn't sure is clean. But he doesn't argue.

Davies inspects his work when he is done. "You learn a little bit of this, a little bit of that, when you're on the roads by yourself. That should keep the wound from infection. Hopefully. No promises." He sits back on his haunches and props his elbows on his knees. "You wanna know why I cut you free, why we're talking right now?"

"Atonement," Huxley says. "For yourself?"

Davies considers by looking into the sky. "No, not quite. My time will come to atone for the things I've done. But that time isn't now. No. I was talking about the people that think they'll never have to pay their tally. They think the collector doesn't come to their door."

"The Murphys."

Davies wipes the poultice from his fingers and looks at the fire. "There's some history between the Murphys and me."

Huxley gives silence, letting Davies fill it.

"Not so much with Councilman Murphy himself," Davies continues. "But Mrs. Murphy … she has some dirt on the councilman that I report to. She has blackmailed him somehow and uses him to move me around like a pawn for her own ends. And I resent it." Davies' jaw muscles bunch rapidly. "The burned church. The fact that I burned a whole group to get at one person— that's what the story says. That's the story *I made up*. But the truth is, I didn't know why those people had to die. There were no warrants to be served. I couldn't tell you the name of a single person that died in that church. I suspect the preacher or someone else in the congregation had spoken out against the Murphys in one way or another, because the church was on Murphy land. I never did find out the truth behind it. But I know it was Mrs. Murphy that was behind it. She wanted those people dead for some reason." He rubs his hands together slowly, thoughtfully. "And I did it."

Davies goes quiet for a time, hands still rubbing together.

"What do you want from me?" Huxley asks, slowly and deliberately.

Davies takes a breath, looks up from the fire at Huxley. "I want you to get your daughter back, Mr. Huxley. This councilman's wife is a blight. She's an opium-addled psychopath. If there is any redeeming quality to this system of government the Riverlands has set up, she is ruining it. Their family is wealthy on the backs of slaves, and they have been since the beginning. She wants her husband to be chairman, and she's doing everything in her power to make it that way." Davies interlaces his fingers. "You've shown your rage across the entire Riverlands. You've left a trail of destruction behind you. You demonstrated your anger in a selfish and scattershot way, directing it at the guilty and the innocent alike. Now, direct it at those that deserve it."

Huxley looks at the ground, wondering how much of that rage is still in him.

But anger is a virulent weed. No matter how much you pull up, there are little pieces left behind. Little tendrils that grow back and take over again, if left unchecked. You can never truly be free of it.

"You realize I'll probably be killed," Huxley says hollowly.

Davies raises an eyebrow at him. He speaks gently, like a doctor with a kind bedside manner, explaining a terminal illness. "Your life is already forfeit, Mr. Huxley. Living is not in the cards anymore for you. The only question is, what are you going to do with the remaining few days that you have? And I suspect that if it means your daughter's freedom, you'll find a way."

"And if I find her?" Huxley's voice trembles a little. "If I can free her? Then what?"

Davies stands up. "Your tally will still need to be paid, Huxley. Either by you, or by your boy in the wagon there. Return yourself to me inside of two days and the boy goes free. But if you're not here by the dawn of the third day, I kill him. And then I find you anyway. And this time I don't talk. I just do what I do."

"And what are you getting out of this?" Huxley cannot keep the bitterness from his voice.

Davies shrugs. "I'm unleashing you on House Murphy. What you do there is up to you."

Huxley glares. "I'm not ..." the protest dies in a hiss through his teeth.

Davies snorts a harsh laugh. "You're not *what*? Not a violent man? Bullshit. I'm not a preacher here to tell you that repentance turns your life around. Penitence is just an admission. An acknowledgement. Your near-death experience has not changed you, Huxley. You still have blood on your hands. You may not have wanted any of this shit to happen, you may not have wanted all those deaths to wind up on your shoulders, but they did."

"And the people that burned up in that church?" Huxley asks. "Does the collector ever have to pay his tally?"

"Yes, I do," Davies nods without hesitation. "I take responsibility for what I did, and I'm certain that I will have to pay my own tally someday. And when it comes, I won't flinch away. But it's not my bill that's come up. It's yours. So, what will you take responsibility for?"

Death.

Murder.

Lowell.

My daughter.

"Find a way," Davies says. Then he points east. "Vicksburg Landing is two miles east. You'll need to cross the Mississippi. The Murphy Township is just outside of Old Town Jackson. I'm sure you can figure out the rest."

Huxley raises his hands and looks down at himself as if to demonstrate how empty-handed he is. "I have no money. No weapons."

Davies reaches into his coat and pulls a satchel out of his pocket—a small leather satchel that Huxley is very familiar with. He tosses it and it lands in the dirt at Huxley's feet. The contents jingle loudly, densely.

"Your stolen gold," he says. "I don't want your blood money. Use it for whatever you want to buy. Give the rest away, or sink it in the river, I don't care. But it should be more than enough." Davies looks at the sky. "It's two hours past dawn, Huxley. That means you have less than sixty hours."

Huxley stoops and picks up the satchel of coins. When he stands again, he looks past Davies to the boy that still sits, quietly listening to all of this, in the bed of the wagon. The boy looks back. Huxley nods. And Lowell nods back.

To Davies, Huxley says, "You'll be here?"

Davies points at the ground. "This very spot."

"What about the other Black Hats? What if they're still looking for me?"

Davies smiles without humor, and Huxley can feel the other man's eyes traveling over his face. "You haven't seen what the burn did to your face. I don't think they'll recognize you."

Huxley feels his face smarting, as though in response to the words. He reaches up a finger, but holds back from touching his burned face for fear that it will only hurt more. It hurts, but not near as much as his arm. He hopes that means it is not quite as bad of a burn, but then he realizes that it doesn't matter. It doesn't matter whether or not his skin is burned off. It doesn't matter that he is exposed to infection. It doesn't matter about the pain or the disfigurement.

The end of his time is in sight.

It lies just around the corner, three days from now.

He turns away from Davies and begins putting one foot in front of the other.

My daughter is not dead.

And now there is another fear.

Would she even recognize me?

If he lived long enough to find her, and if he were able to stand in front of her, she would only see a burned and ravenous animal. No trace of the man who had been her father.

But then, that man had failed her.

This new one, as repugnant as he might be, would not fail. And in the end, what his daughter saw in his eyes was not half as important as making sure that she was free, and alive. Maybe he would only be a cruel shadow of what she remembered, but at least she would know that he came for her.

I won't forget about you.

I won't throw you away.

Time is wasting. And the shadows are lengthening.

Facing east, Huxley begins to run.

CHAPTER 6

Vicksburg Landing. Another river-port town, ferries going across the great, wide expanse of brown water. It is like Red Water Landing, but with wider streets and more people. Like Shreveport, but less dilapidated concrete roads and buildings and not so many miscreants walking around. But if you were to close your eyes, it would sound the same. The sound of business. The sound of lives going about in a great big jumble, all ignorant of each other.

Ignorant of what walks among them.

Down the main street Huxley walks. Most of the buildings were constructed when Vicksburg Landing was a little municipality called Delta. Here and there between them he can see the Mississippi. At Vicksburg Landing, the width of the river is not quite so legendary. A sandy shoal comes off the western bank and protrudes out into this little bottleneck almost a quarter of the way across. Small boats tethered to deeply sunken posts on each shore pull small groups of passengers and small loads of goods across purely by muscle, the boaters walking the length of their little crafts with the ropes on their shoulders. Sometimes sitting and pulling the boat along, if the load is not causing the boat to take too much draft.

There is a bridge there also, spanning the entire river. Old World construction. But it is being dismantled. Huxley cannot imagine why, but huge throngs of working crews scurry over it and every so often a blast from dynamite to break the concrete superstructure. It is obvious that the bridge is closed to travelers, and so everyone is relegated to the ferries.

Why the hell would they destroy the bridge?

Huxley walks stiffly down the street. The salve that Davies put on his wounds is numbing some of the pain. But still, people cast glances his way. He doesn't look at them back. He does not want to be noticed beyond their peripheral observation that, *There goes a burned man.*

In another life, another time, the pain might have weakened him to the point of debilitation. But what is it now? Pain. A firing of nerves. They've fired so much over the course of the last year that Huxley finds it easier and easier to ignore them. His pain receptors are collectively crying wolf. Someday, they will tell him of something truly, terribly wrong. But that will be the day that he dies, and until that time, he can continue to put one foot in front of the other. It is the least he can do for his daughter.

It should never have been about Nathaniel Cartwright. It should've always been about you.

No point lamenting things too far gone to retrieve. Now is not the time to lament.

Huxley has nothing. His clothes are burned. His flesh is burned. All he owns in the world that is still whole are his shoes and a satchel of gold. But gold can buy new clothes. It can buy weapons. It can buy bandages.

Gold can even buy a life.

And sometimes, it can buy the things to take that life back.

He goes to a healer first. He is an old man. He asks no questions about Huxley, or where the injuries came from. Huxley would not have given the answers anyway. He gives the old man half a gold piece for clean bandages. He doesn't care about the healing of his face—that is unimportant. He cares about covering the burns so his face is not so memorable. The half piece buys him enough bandage to wrap around the burns on his arm, too. He leaves Davies' salve on them so the skin can't meld to the bandages.

As he gives the old man the half piece, Huxley asks him, "Where is the general store?"

The old man eyes him, as though the request is somehow meaningful. "Two blocks east," his frail voice croaks. "He's got what you need."

Huxley frowns, just slightly. "And what is it that you think I need?"

The healer looks at him smartly, his wrinkled old lips drawn up into a little smirk. "A man with burns wants something for the pain. And yet you only want bandages. The only thing that kills pain so naturally is anger. You're a man that seeks vengeance. And a man must have weapons if he wants vengeance."

Huxley lets out a tiny snort. The old man thinks he is wise, but age does not always bring wisdom.

"Old man," Huxley says, softly, "I've had my fill of vengeance. If they want to give me back what they took from me, I'll just take it and walk away. But … I don't think that's how it's going to happen."

The healer purses his lips. "Weapons are weapons. They do the same thing regardless of why they are carried. Your motivations don't matter."

"They absolutely matter," Huxley says, a bit sharper in his tone now. Then he turns and pushes out of the door before the argument can be pressed any further.

At the general store he finds the shopkeeper the very opposite of the burly one from Delhi. The one that had betrayed him to Nathaniel Cartwright. Huxley stands there in the doorway of the shop, staring at the shopkeeper as he remembers the other one's stupid warning. *Beware of Wild Nate*, he told Huxley, while in his mind he plotted how to turn him over. *You said you didn't want to be involved*, Huxley thinks bitterly. *But then you got yourself involved, and where are you now? Dead in the ground. Not how you thought that one would turn out, huh?*

"Help you?" the shopkeeper asks, his voice bordering on uncomfortable.

Huxley looks at the scene from the shopkeeper's perspective—strange man enters, bandages on his face and arm, clutching a purse of gold and standing in the doorway, staring for a long, awkward moment at the clerk, eyes probably going murderous for a moment.

"Sorry, friend," Huxley shakes off the memory of the shopkeeper from Delhi. "I was trying to remember what I needed. I would've written a list, but as you can see, I'm a little down on the luck right now. Fire burned most of my stuff."

"I'm sorry to hear that," the shopkeeper says, more friendly, but still cautious. He is mousy. Small. A round, bald head. Wiry gray hairs protruding. Large glasses that make his eyes seem buggy. He is lucky to have them though.

Huxley steps up to the counter and lays his satchel on the wooden top. "I'd like to buy a gun. A few guns. And some ball and powder …" Huxley looks up and off into nothingness. "… actually … I've heard rumors about cartridge weapons floating around the area. Would you have any cartridge weapons?"

"Mm," the shopkeeper makes the noise a negative sound. "Yeah, there's some floating around, but ain't nobody got 'em but outlaws. All the legal ones are being sent to the front lines. Arming the councilmen that border the EDS. Anyone got the capability of making them cartridges is …" he waves his fingers, conjuring the correct words from the air. "… *contractually obligated* to send all he has to the front."

Huxley nods, eyes still fixed to the shopkeeper. "Oh, I see."

The shopkeeper's buggy eyes flick toward the satchel of gold on the counter. "Uh … well …" he adjusts his glasses. "How much gold you got?"

Huxley lifts the satchel by its thong, then sets it back down sharply so that the shopkeeper can hear the clank of gold, so he can see the weighty quantity of it. "Plenty," Huxley says.

The shopkeeper's wide, mousy eyes squint down so he seems to be taking stock of Huxley. "Reckon you don't strike me as a councilman's man. And you damn sure ain't no Black Hat. Is you?"

Huxley smiles, plainly. It hurts the burned side of his face. "No. Me and the Black Hats … we don't get along."

"So, a fugitive then, huh?"

Huxley taps the satchel again. "I'm a man with some gold to spend."

The shopkeeper looks at the gold. Then at Huxley. Then over his shoulders at the door. "Alright," he says, suddenly. "Come on then."

He leads Huxley into the back. There is machining work there. Hand-cranked metalworking devices.

There are brass casings lined up near the machining tools. Some large, some small.

Revolver and rifle, Huxley thinks.

The shopkeeper folds his arms, looks at his things with pride. "It's not so hard, if you know what you're doing. And if you have the right tools. Gotta have the right tools. But revolvers? They're simple things."

"You got any to put those cartridges into?" Huxley looks at him.

The shopkeeper gives him a sidelong glance. "Now, let's just be clear. I ain't no traitor or nothing. I work hard for the Riverlands. For the council. It cost me damn near an arm and a leg to start machining this shit. Then, just when I'm about to break even on my investment, the chairman wants it all for his people, and at a damn steep discount. Did I complain? No I didn't. I did my duty. But if I make a few more than my quota and sell them on the side, then is that really breaking the law? I don't think it is."

"How many and what price?" Huxley presses.

Instead of answer, the shopkeeper walks to a table and pushes it out of the way. Then he bends down, uproots a floorboard and pulls out three revolvers and sets them on the table. He waves a proud hand over them. "Bored out the cylinders to take cartridges. Takes me about a week of work to get each done on the side. So I ask a week's wages per."

Huxley looks at the revolvers. They look identical to the ones he had before, but for some minor modifications to the cylinder. "Which is?"

"Fifteen pieces. For each. And the cartridges are separate," he adds quickly. "I can do six for a piece, or a dozen for one and a half. And you won't find these anywhere else. Well … I mean … You'd have to travel a ways. You won't find anyone else in Vicksburg Landing—or Vicksburg proper, for that matter—that has the capability to even make them."

"And they work?"

"Damn right they work," the shopkeeper is miffed. "Same ones I send to the front, and they woulda told me if thems wasn't working."

"Okay," Huxley nods. "I'll buy."

The satchel is emptied, its contents counted. Fifty-six gold pieces, including several that had been halved already, and a few that had been quartered. Huxley buys two of the revolvers. The shopkeeper can only sell him twenty cartridges—there are more, but he is afraid that selling them will impact his quota and raise suspicions. It totals thirty-one and three quarters.

Huxley also buys new clothes. He discards his pants for some new ones. The shopkeeper offers to take them in for him because they are loose, but Huxley buys a leather belt to cinch the waist. He also buys a jacket of some sort. He had seen them worn around. Something like a duster with a hood on it, but made of wool, rather than leather. It is heavy, but it is warm, and the hood is voluminous. When he pulls it up, it does a good job of hiding his face.

He also buys himself a knife to go on his belt, because he'd carried one all this time, and it feels strange to be without it. It's not as nice as his old one with its stainless blade and its bone handle. This one is homemade, it looks like, with a leather-wrapped handle. But it will do for the day or two that Huxley has left on this earth.

Before he discards the old pants, he takes out the piece of parchment and the charcoal piece. He puts them in the inner pocket of the wool jacket.

He loads the two new revolvers with their cartridges and he seats them in his waistband. The shopkeeper tries to sell him a holster, but Huxley doesn't want it. He's grown used to carrying his guns in his waistband. Odd, because he'd never considered himself the type of man to have a preference for the placement of a firearm. But things change, don't they? They are always changing.

The remaining eight cartridges Huxley puts in the pockets of the heavy woolen jacket—four in the right pocket, four in the left. In case one arm is injured, he figures.

He leaves the general store with eighteen-and-a-half gold pieces left.

He hopes it is enough for a ferry ride for one. And then maybe for two.

What do I feel?

Hope, maybe. Not for me. For her.

If I can be hard enough. If I can be strong enough. Then there's hope for her.

But there is also dread. Dread is seeping in, through the urgency. The dread that a doomed man feels when he looks at the gallows and knows that the fresh, tight ropes are being strung just for him, to snap his neck cleanly. He keeps trying to push the fear away from him, but it lives with him now. All he can do is ignore it. Keep brushing it aside and convincing himself that it isn't growing.

He makes his way toward the water. The street bends down a slight bit, then levels out. None of the construction here is Old World. Everything here is "new," in the way that slatboard construction is "new." Insufficient for people a dozen years ago, now the best that can be had. At least this lumber looks fresh, which means someone has managed to rig a mill of some sort, water or steam powered, possibly. Advances are being made. It should make Huxley feel hopeful, but it only makes him feel like something valuable is slipping through his fingers.

I'll never see life return to the way it was. This is the world I will die in.

He begins to notice the number of people in the streets. Not just the fact that they are in the streets, but the fact that they are all going the opposite direction as him, making their way from the riverbanks where the large ferries berth in docks, and the small boats run aground on the sandy shore.

They have the look of tired people. There is not a pack animal to be seen amongst them. They are heavy-laden with things that are not what you would see someone take to market. These are their belongings. Their entire lives, wrapped in moth-eaten blankets and stuffed in old burlap satchels and leather bags, odds and ends strapped to the side of anything that something else can be strapped to.

Refugees.

He keeps his nose down, keeps the hood of his woolen coat shading his face, and he keeps moving. He veers off the road before he reaches the docksides and he takes a set of old timber steps down to the sand where two johnboats without motors sit under the dripping ropes that will pull them across.

The boatman stands to the side, offering no help to his passengers as they gather their things and disembark. More people coming from the opposite side of the river. A flood of them.

Huxley watches a family walk past him, and he holds his breath, as though the man will suddenly stop and turn in fear and scream bloody murder at the sight of Huxley. Bleat like a sheep when it realizes that the wolf is among them.

But they pass by and they do not give Huxley a second look.

Huxley strides to the boat, raises his hand incrementally to garner the boatman's attention. "How much for a crossing?"

The boatman is short, well muscled, but with a paunch hovering over his stomach. His forearms bulge and ripple as he grips the rope. A man that works with his hands, and has worked with his hands his entire life. He is sweating despite the cold wind coming off the water.

"You want to cross to the eastern side?" there is an amused quality to his voice.

"Yes."

"Well, you're a rare prize."

Huxley understands what he means. He has been ferrying people from east to west all day. No one wants to go west to east. The return trip is an unpaid waste of his time, and yet the only way he can make money is to pull himself back to the east bank.

"Why isn't anyone going east?" Huxley asks.

The boatman doesn't want to lose the only west-to-east fare he's had all day. He just shrugs noncommittally, though Huxley can see something like worry behind his eyes. "Cost for a crossing is one-and-a-quarter."

Huxley looks across the water to the city of Vicksburg on the other side. There is nothing obviously wrong. No reason why people would be fleeing that city. But does it really matter? There is nothing that could be said to him now that would keep him on this side of the river. Not even the exorbitant cost of the crossing.

He opens his coin satchel. "Seems steep," he observes.

"Busy day," the boatman says with a sigh. "Everyone else is charging one-and-a-half. You can feel free to check, but I'll be gone by the time you make your way back."

Huxley gives him the whole piece, and a quarter piece, and then climbs on.

The trip across takes less than ten minutes. On the other side, the riverbank is steeper and has no sandy shore. Here there are old wooden docks, and some new ones, that jut out from the muddy banks just far enough for people to be able to climb down onto the boat. The one that Huxley's boat finds is only a few yards off the shore.

The shore is filled with refugees. They stand in one big mass in the center, and trickle out into lines that form at the start of the docks, waiting for another ferry. Refugees, most definitely, but whatever they are fleeing from, they do not seem particularly urgent.

Huxley mutters his thanks to the boatman who says nothing in return. He climbs the dock and moves along it with his head down, shouldering past the families that press in with all their belongings, trying to be next in line.

The boatman calls out behind Huxley, "You four are next? Five? I can't take five. Not unless you ditch your bags. I can come back for one, or for the bags, but that'll cost you extra. Two pieces to cross, *per person*. Three if you want me to come back for your bags."

They want to cross. The boatman knows it. There are far more refugees than there are boatmen. Why cut a deal when you can force them to pay? One piece seems like an expensive trip. Three is robbery. But Huxley looks over his shoulder and sees the family pulling out the necessary gold.

Huxley continues on until he is most of the way through the crowd. He sees a pair of men. One is old, hair white, beard white. The other is young, a boy really. Not much older than Lowell. A grandfather and grandson, perhaps. Or a tradesman and his apprentice. Huxley cannot tell. They don't have anything with them that identifies what they are. But they seem unassuming. Harmless. That is why Huxley stops beside them.

"Why are you going west?" Huxley asks the older man.

The old man has sharp eyes and a jutting chin. Not many teeth left. "You don't know?"

Huxley remains silent. *I wouldn't be asking if I did …*

The old man snorts. "Don't know what rock you just came from under." He throws a thumb over his shoulder. "The EDS armies are pushing east. And it seems like they have help."

"There's a dozen towns that have risen up against the council!" the boy says excitedly. "They're siding with the EDS!"

The old man glares at the younger. "Hey. Don't talk out of your ass. You're exaggerating and you need to think about *the ears.* You don't know who the hell is listening, so you be careful what you say."

The boy mutters an apology.

The old man looks at Huxley again. "There've been rumors about EDS guerrillas, embedded in …" a sharp glance at the boy "… *a few* towns and cities along the border. They all picked last night to start up, and the rumor going around is that our … *honorable* Councilman Murphy's scouts have caught sight of what they think is a large EDS force, moving toward Jackson. Where, as you might suspect, the majority of the guerrilla groups are rising up."

Huxley's heart takes one beat, then stops for a few seconds. His breath is stuck in his chest.

The old man doesn't seem to notice Huxley's reaction. He continues on. "Whole borderlands have turned into a goddamned mess. Most of us are farmers, but I know a lot of these poor bastards are from Jackson. I hear Old Town Jackson is a war zone. Don't know if the main EDS force has got there yet, but the guerilla fighters have taken to the streets with bands of local rebels that apparently have a bone to pick with the Murphys. Not that I ever had a problem with Councilman Murphy or any of his people. Just repeating what I've heard." The old man looks at Huxley. "You alright, son?"

Huxley tries to swallow, but finds his mouth dry. *Jackson is under attack. If Murphy falls, what happens then? What happens to the slaves? What happens during the fighting?*

His window of time abruptly seems smaller.

It's slipping away. It's all slipping away.

He swallows, this time finding some moisture in his mouth.

If it's slipping, then hold on tighter.

He looks at the man. Focused. Intense. "What about the Murphy Township?"

"Eh?" the old man quirks an eyebrow. "What about it?"

"Will it hold? Will they evacuate? Will they run or try to put it under siege? Can it even withstand a siege? And if so, for how long?"

The old man frowns. "Hell, I told you, I'm just a farmer. Ain't got no clue about war or walls or sieges or nothing like that. If you're asking my humble opinion, then I'd say that Councilman Murphy'll hold on to his township until he's dead. I've heard he's stubborn like that. Won't be any evacuation. As for how long it'll hold? Ain't no walls. Just sticks and tires and guns. It'll be a hellacious fight, but I don't think it'll last long. Day or so." He smiles. "Why? You plannin' to vacation in Jackson? Might want to make different plans. Place'll be burned to the ground by the time you get there."

"I hope it does," the boy murmurs.

"Hey!" the old man backhands the boy in the face. "Watch your mouth. I already told you once. *Ears*, Jason. *Fucking ears.*"

The boy looks more irritated than hurt.

"Thank you," Huxley says absently, then turns to walk away. He speaks out loud to himself, his mind running in a million different directions, suddenly lost in the scenarios, in the possible outcomes, in the sudden shifting of everything: "I need a horse."

CHAPTER 7

It is almost evening. The wind has turned into Huxley's face as he rides, as though the Riverlands themselves are trying to beat him back. He hunches into it, his eyes watering at first, and then drying out, his nostrils burning with chill, his mouth gumming and drying. But he keeps going. Nothing has stopped him yet. Not the miles, nor the things and people and elements that have lain between the desert that he came from and this landscape of towns and fields and people.

He is a stone, rolling down the mountain.

There is no stopping until it reaches the bottom.

The horse between his legs is a powerful animal, but it cost him almost every gold piece left in his satchel, all into the hands of the price gouger at a public stable in Vicksburg. "There is war on the horizon," the stablekeeper says to him, defensive of his high prices. "The price of everything is going up."

Huxley had only kept enough to pay for the passage back. And he hoped ... he hoped there would be a passage back. Huxley doesn't squabble. There isn't time for it. And besides, the horse is fast, and that is all that matters. But even this horse, a good horse, and an expensive one, is nearing its limit. Huxley was able to ride for the first half hour out of Vicksburg before stopping to let the horse breathe. He is down to ten-minute increments, but the sky is changing, he notices, and he knows that he is getting closer to Jackson.

The road is now packed with people.

This countryside is crammed with towns and hostels and inns, both newly constructed and made from large houses left over from the Old

World. There are fields, but not the sad, weedy things with twelve-year pines growing sporadically through them like he is used to seeing. These are fresh fields, fresh tilled, some of them with winter wheat sprouting like a green fuzz on the landscape.

These are rich lands. Wealthy owners.

And all these little towns, all these little places where people are living in this relative gentrification, they are emptying out onto the street, a long line of refugees plodding their way westward on the road, fleeing from what is behind them.

What is ahead of Huxley.

Cresting a hill, the horse flags beneath him again and he loosens the reins and lets her walk. And at the very top, he stops, momentarily forgetting himself as he stares across a countryside like none he's ever seen. This is some cataclysmic blending of the Old World and the new. Concrete and steel meeting flame and black powder.

War has come to the Riverlands.

Here at the top of the rise, everything rolls out in front of him. It is like three distinct stages, set adjacent to each other, and each a little farther away from Huxley than the previous. The first is a patchwork of fields. Huxley can see that this is once where suburbs had sprouted up, but all the people that lived in those houses are dead, and their houses were razed to the ground and plowed over. Still, the old neighborhood streets stand as testament to what was there once, little gray lines coursing through everything. The faltering sun glows golden down on this stage, as though it is separate from the others.

The next stage is something that Huxley must assume is the Murphy Township, growing out of the western side of Old Town Jackson. This looks red in the sunlight. There is a wall around the entire thing, and inside there are clusters of houses, new and old, and there are buildings made of redbrick and they seem pristine from this distance. Huxley can feel the pride of this place, the Township on a good day, bustling with business, watched over by its councilman, its namesake. It is massive, expansive, a proclamation of the power and wealth that Councilman Murphy wields.

But this is not a good day for the Murphy Township, and the power and pride of it seems washed out, like watching a great man go pale with fear. It sits in the shadow of the third stage, and this is what looks like Hell. This is what tells Huxley that minor spats are over with and an offensive has begun.

Old Town Jackson is on fire. All of it, as far as Huxley can see. The buildings blaze, their walls black, their windows twinkling with firelight that Huxley can see even from his vantage point five or six miles away. Great gouts of smoke are pouring into the sky, like gravity has been reversed and the city is dripping streams of black, black blood from a thousand different wounds, up into the heavens where they pool and mix with the night that creeps in from the east. The streets flash every so often, and even from this distance Huxley can hear the reports of massive explosions, and he can see the clouds of gray and black smoke mushrooming up from the streets where the flashes came.

The land, the township, the cityscape. Three different stages. All sprawling out, filling Huxley's whole view of the world like they are all that is in it. And that is not far from the truth. The rest of the world is just a distant afterthought. What occurs now, what *matters* now, is what happens in those scenes.

Five or six miles.

Even with the horse almost blown, he could be at the edges of the township in fifteen, maybe twenty minutes. What would happen in that short time? Right now, right at this moment, the Murphy Township stands untouched by the burning city right beside it. But how long would that last?

Not long.

He spurs his horse's flanks before he can think about it again.

You're a stone, rolling down a mountain.

You cannot be stopped.

The horse tears down the side of the hill, grunting and snorting violently, its belly heaving with the giant breaths it takes. Huxley focuses on that. He focuses on the feeling of speed, and he ignores all the faces of the people that watch him as he flies by, all these people fleeing the city, fleeing the township, wondering what madman would willingly enter into that bleeding, broken, burning heart.

The road flattens out. The horse's pace flags again. Huxley doesn't let it slow. He keeps yelling into its ear, spurring it in the sides. A pack of armed men with sigils on their arms watch him pass. Soldiers, perhaps? Huxley cannot tell, but they make no move to stop him. Huxley hopes that if he keeps moving urgently enough, no one will suspect his real business. Perhaps they think ...

It gives Huxley an idea. Half-cocked and spur-of-the-moment.

But better than nothing.

Around him, the fields made from neighborhood plots sprawl out around him, the very same ones that he had seen from the hill. He follows the line of people, not straying from the main road. He figures that they are all coming out of the township, and he notes that they are women and children. The men have likely been conscripted to fight.

If the township is bleeding refugees, then the gates are open.

Please, please, let the gates be open.

The road curves northward and then straightens again. Here the stream of refugees becomes a trickle. The last few leaving the gate, fleeing while men with weapons, bearing the sigils of Councilman Murphy, escort them out, yelling at them to speed up. They are trying to close the gates.

Up ahead, Huxley can see the squat walls of the Murphy Township looming in front of him.

A few stragglers, eking out of the gate.

"Come on," Huxley says to the horse. "Come on!"

When Huxley is still a hundred yards away, he sees what looks like the last family leaving the township. They huddle together as they run and the gates are manned by two guards who wave them past with urgency and then begin to pull the heavy gates closed.

"Wait!" Huxley yells, because he can't think of anything else.

They'll know. They'll know who you are.

But he is a hooded rider with half his face in bandages. How would they know?

The guards at the gate look at him when he yells at them, and they hesitate.

That is all he needs. He doesn't slow his horse, but the horse slows itself, seeing the gates growing in its vision. Instinctively, Huxley ducks as they pass under the catwalk that guards the gates. It is far over his head, but it feels like it will lop it off at the speed he is going.

His pure audacity has shocked them. The two guards stand beside the gates, and they watch him and his horse shoulder through.

"Hey!" one of them yells, but still doesn't make a move.

"Message!" Huxley blurts. *If I act official, they will think it's official.* "Message for the councilman!"

Huxley doesn't stop to talk with them. His shouted explanation is carried behind him and the horse gallops through. He hunches over the nape of the beast's neck, wondering if bullets will start to wing in his direction. He doesn't dare to look back because it might make him look guilty.

There is shouting behind him.

Don't stop. Maybe it's not for you.

He doesn't know where he is going. This is a maze of streets, but he can see something conspicuous ahead of him and he knows, just like any grid of streets, that he can eventually make it there if he keeps it in sight. It is what looks like a tall condominium complex. It overlooks all these dilapidated houses and it has the feel of a castle set amongst the town.

That is where they are. That has to be it.

He winds his way through the streets, left, then right, then left, then right again, trying to keep the tall complex in front of him. Groups of men with rifles watch him gallop past, but they say nothing. If he was not stopped by the guards at the gate, his business must be legitimate.

His ruse is at least partially effective.

How long it can continue, Huxley doesn't know.

He doesn't care. He's the stone on the mountainside.

He will keep going until they try to stop him. And then he will shoot. And he will shoot until he is out of bullets. And then he will stab. And when he cannot stab, he will bite and claw. But he will move forward. Until he is dead. That will be the only thing that stops him.

All around him are houses. Turned into businesses. Turned into brothels. Turned into auction houses. Turned into taverns. What once had been suburbs with quiet streets and joggers and lawnmowers—the picture is so clear in his head—now some strange, mixed-up cityscape, except that it is empty. All the stands, all the stalls, all the businesses are abandoned.

The storm has come, these streets say to Huxley. *The storm is here.*

In front of him, the houses-turned-businesses are suddenly gone. The complex towers up in front of him—not tall by Old World standards, because it is only five or so stories tall. But in a world built with sticks and boards and scrap, anything over two stories seems a skyscraper. It is all dark-hued brick, like it has been painted with old dry blood. The image sticks with him.

There are balconies. Guards on those balconies.

It is surrounded by a wrought iron fence—an affectation of safety when in fact it is only a mild deterrent. Wrought iron fence, wrought iron spikes, and a three-foot-tall section of brick below. A large, gated entrance.

The wrought iron gate is closed.

Barred.

Guarded.

Fuck.

Huxley reins in his horse as he comes close to the gate. "Message for the councilman!"

The guards are alarmed with how quickly he's come upon them.

Two guards. Plus the guards on the balconies.

One of the guards holds his rifle across his chest, a breechloader like the ones that Huxley stole. "What's that now?" he demands. "What are you doing here?"

Huxley waves violently at the complex that towers over them. "A message! I have an *urgent* message for the councilman!"

The guard looks more irritated than anything. "Who from?"

Huxley spits out the first thing that comes to him. "From the chairman." He tries to sound official. "Open the gates, immediately."

The guard looks him up and down.

A hooded man with burn wounds on a blown horse belonging to a public stable.

No sigils. Certainly none to identify himself as a courier from the chairman.

This is bad. This was a bad idea.

The guard reaches his hand out. "Give the message to me. I'll deliver it."

Huxley feels his pulse heavy in his throat. Like his heart is pushing ball bearings instead of blood. His eyes flit up to the balconies, but the balconies are on the front of the complex, and the gate is inset between two of the buildings. The guards on the balconies are not visible.

The guard's hands work rapidly in a *give me* gesture. "The message?"

This was a bad idea.

But it's too late to turn back.

You are a stone rolling down a mountain.

"Sir," the guard's voice bears an edge. "Do you have a message or not?"

"Yes," Huxley meets his eyes. "You can have the message."

He reaches into his wool coat with his right hand. Draws the revolver from his waist and shoots the guard between the eyes. The roar of the weapon is deafening. Much louder than the ball and cap. The cartridge is fast, and powerful, and the projectile is large.

The upper half of the guard's head disappears.

The other guard jumps, watches his friend fall, rather than watching Huxley.

Huxley shoots that man, the first big bullet ripping his pelvis apart. He collapses, screaming. Huxley thumbs the hammer back and puts an end to him with a round to the chest.

The sound of his own thunderous gunshots echoes back to him.

"Shit!" Huxley stands up in the saddle, revolver still in hand. "Shit," he strains the words out. "Shit, shit, shit ..."

There are shouts. From the balconies. From the complex.

How many guards?

More than me. More than I can kill.

What did you do? You reckless fool.

No time. Keep rolling.

He grabs the top of the wrought iron spires, one foot still holding him up in the stirrup to give him extra height. He hauls himself up and rolls his side and his back across the spikes. His heavy wool coat blocks them from piercing him, but they jab mercilessly at his ribs, his wounded side, his spine. And then a piece of his coat catches and twists his body around at the last moment. He flails, falls, six feet to the ground, solidly on his back.

He hears something crack.

Coughs.

Blinks. Stares up at the sky.

Groans, but forces himself up.

His entire body hurts. Old wounds and fresh wounds. Bullet holes and burns. But he can still move. Nothing is stopping him from moving. He manages himself into a sitting position, his revolver still in his hand, the other in his waistband, but threatening to fall out. He shoves it back into place. All around him, his situation takes on a sharp clarity, small details being processed in tiny flashes, and he pieces them together to make the full picture.

They are here, he tells himself quickly. *The Murphys are here because the guards are here.*

The complex around him is five buildings. One on each corner and one in the middle. What had once been parking areas are now covered with dirt and grass, and horses and wagons are hitched to the sides of buildings. He can see the two buildings that frame the main gate—they are to either side—and he can catch a sliver of the other two corners, but the center building blocks most of his view.

The implications of what he sees are obvious.

The four corner buildings are for the servants and the slaves and the soldiers.

The center building is for the councilman and his house.

All around him, cries of alarm are going up. The gunshots have been heard. Men will be coming. Huxley is tempted to flatten himself onto his back and to grab one of the dead guards' rifles, to post up behind him using his corpse as a sandbag and lie there, picking them off as they come. He wants that because it is comfortable. Movement is frightening.

But he is not here to kill guards.

He is here for his daughter.

He lurches to his feet. Somewhere in what could be considered the "court-yard" of this complex, he hears men running. He can see the flicker of lantern light that they are carrying. Huxley stoops down quickly, grunting in pain. Something is cracked or broken in his side. He scoops up one of the guards' rifles. It is already loaded. Huxley stuffs his revolver back into his waistband and grabs a handful of cartridges from the guard's belt.

Time's running out. Don't waste time.

He hobbles to a corner of the building to his right. There is a large wooden planter in which nothing currently grows. He half-crouches behind this and he rests the rifle on the planter and sights down it, aiming for the left side of the center building.

Door. The front door. Is it unlocked?

Only one way to tell.

A guard rounds the left corner.

Huxley fires. The rifle bucks in his shoulder. The guard stops like a gut-punch has halted him, crumples around the hot lead with a grunt. He falls forward and begins to scream.

That will stop the others from hurtling around the corner.

Huxley hurls himself away from the planter and toward the door. His side hurts, but so does his hip. But he can still put one foot in front of the other. He jacks the round from the breech, slams a new one home, aims the rifle at the corner of the building and lets it loose again, breaking off a huge chunk of red brick. Further discouragement.

He makes it to the front door of the center building.

He yanks at it. It's locked.

"Fuck me," he mutters, blinking and squinting through the adrenaline to try and make sense of the barricade in front of him.

He kicks it, feels some give there. So he screams and kicks it again. It flies in, the glass cracking down the center and spidering across.

Someone shouts, to his right.

Huxley slips the rifle to his left hand because he hasn't had a chance to reload it. He snatches the revolver out again and holds it out with a single arm. A man's face appears around the right corner of the building, his face, then his chest, his eyes wide, searching for the threat, a rifle up and ready.

Huxley fires.

The man sees him at the last instant, tries to flinch away.

The flash of powder and smoke reach out and kiss the man's face just before the bullet obliterates it and sends him spinning backward.

Huxley shoves his way through the broken door as a smattering of gunfire lances out, sending bits of dirt and old concrete up in the spot where he'd just stood, and one of the rounds finds the glass of the doors and shatters it completely.

Huxley is inside.

They are outside.

But not for long.

Think! Think!

Run.

Huxley cries out in fear and frustration, twists, and lays eyes upon what he is looking for, recognizing and remembering all at once. "Stairs!" he shouts at the door that is clearly marked. He runs into it, shoulders through it and then spins, slamming the door behind him and fumbling around on the emergency handle for the lock ... the lock ... where is the lock?

There. A tab at the top.

He slams it upward, feels the metal poles slide into their places, securing the door.

A bullet lances through the door with an odd banging sound, leaving a little blossom of metal on Huxley's side. He glances at it—so close to his head—but he is already moving. Up the stairs.

Where am I going?

Where would the Murphys be?

At the highest point in the building.

He slams his feet up the stairs, two at a time, letting the rifle clatter down on a landing—it is just weighing him down—and he uses that free hand to pull himself along the old metal bannister. By the second level, his legs are aching, and the breath is raw and painful in his chest. He can feel spittle flying out of his mouth and onto his lips as he huffs, and he doesn't take the time to wipe it off.

His situation becomes disastrously clear.

I am in a tower. I am running up this tower. There are men below me. And there will be more below me in just a minute. They'll seal the exits, and I'll be trapped in this tower. How are you going to get out? If you even find her, how the fuck are you going to get out?

The only problem is, he cannot stop.

All he can do is hope to God that some miracle happens.

Hope. Cling to that hope.

There has to be hope.

You are not Jay.

He can't stop. He won't stop. His legs become like unwieldy rubber. Down at the bottom of the stairs, there is a horrendous banging noise. They are trying to break through, shouting as they do, and Huxley knows that the doors won't hold forever. They are behind him, and he does not know what is in front of him, but he will find out, he has to find out.

He reaches the top of the stairs, barely able to breathe.

There is a door, marked with a big red "5."

Huxley staggers to it and shoves it open, his revolver cocked and ready.

Men with guns. He watches the muzzles of their rifles flash.

There is a rolling boom.

Huxley tries to dodge, but he feels the bullet rip into him.

CHAPTER 8

I've been shot.

Booming. Crackling. Pounding. Shouting.

Huxley manages to roll himself out of the doorway. He can see the big metal door swinging leisurely closed. His left arm is hanging limp and a pain grips it, somehow both intense and distant. He thinks fleetingly that it is the intensity that makes it distant—his mind can't process it right now.

He looks at it. The blood has barely begun to well just yet. The muscle is pulverized. It is hanging to his body, completely useless and immovable.

The door is still swinging closed. There is the sound of breeches being levered. Huxley must act. There is only one way, and that is to *flow*, to never stop, to keep pressing forward, always forward, not stopping. He does what they do not expect of a dead man.

He rushes through the door, his left arm blinding pain, his right arm pointing that big cartridge revolver out. There are four men. Three of them have rifles, but in that instant, every one of them has their breech hanging open, trying to reload. They scramble for new cartridges and their eyes come up to see this broken, burned, hooded madman hurtling through the door at them.

Behind the three riflemen, the fourth man stands, somehow cold, somehow terrified, and he is not dressed like the others, not standing like the others. He is the one being protected from Huxley.

Councilman …

Huxley punches his revolver out. Takes the shot. In the small room, the sound shatters his eardrums. The center of the three guards screams, pitching backward.

The left drops his cartridge, yelling out something in fear.

The right tries to rush Huxley.

Huxley takes it, pulling his revolver into his body as he thumbs the hammer back and plants the muzzle into the rifleman's belly, even as the man swings his rifle up and catches Huxley under the jaw. Stars dance, but Huxley pulls the trigger. He staggers back into the wall and the man's dead body collapses onto him and then slides down.

Huxley has to breathe through his mouth. Blood and spit dribble out. He's bitten his tongue.

The last rifleman almost has a new cartridge in.

The fourth man, the councilman, he is screaming, "Kill him! Kill him!"

Huxley shrugs off the body of the rifleman that had charged him, pulls the hammer back again.

Click.

Empty.

The rifleman seats his cartridge, slams the breech home.

Huxley hurls the empty revolver at the man's face.

The rifleman grunts as it strikes him square on the nose with an audible crack of breaking bone and cartilage.

Huxley snatches his other revolver out and plows two rounds into the man in quick succession, bursting his chest open.

He shifts the revolver to the councilman who stands, frozen. Now the pain is reaching him, snowballing. He wants to bend. He wants to break. His body wants to crumple under all that pressure. His vision is stars and darkness and only little tiny spots of reality that swirl. He is on the verge of passing out. Willpower is all that keeps him upright.

He tries to speak, but the breath catches, the pain making his stomach clamp down.

He takes a breath.

This is for your daughter. This is so she can have hope.

"You!" Huxley finally manages to shout. "Councilman Murphy!"

The man stares, speechless.

From the stairwell there comes a massive, shattering boom. There is the sound of shouting. Boots slamming up the stairs.

No time for words. No time for anything clever. Huxley has none of that anyway. All he has is violence and momentum.

Huxley waves his revolver at the councilman. "Go to the door. Now. Or I kill you."

"You'll kill me anyway," there is some defiance in the man's eyes now that the shock is fading. "Go fuck yourself. Kill me, and when they get to the top of the stairs they are going to slaughter you."

Huxley shakes his head. "You can live. And so can your wife. If you cooperate. I'm not here to kill you. I'm only here to take back what you stole from me."

Murphy thinks it over and Huxley watches his eyes stray to an adjoining room. *Mrs. Murphy is there. She's hiding in the room.*

"You're not ... are you ... EDS?"

Huxley shakes his head. "I'm nobody. I'm just a piece of trash blown in from the Wastelands." Huxley's voice is without emotion. "You'd have never thought I would get this close to you and I did. You'd be stupid to doubt me now. I can bring you pain. Or I can just leave with what I came for. Now ... do what I tell you."

The councilman's eyes narrow a bit and he moves cautiously at first, but he seems to understand something now, seems to be wrapping his brain around something. He moves quickly to the door, knowing that if the guards reach the top of the stairs, then things will go downhill fast.

"Close the door," Huxley instructs.

The councilman obeys.

"Stand in front of the door. Face it."

The councilman puts his belly to the door. He looks over his shoulder. "What is this?"

Huxley approaches on unsteady feet. He manages to pull the knife from its sheath on his belt, tucking his revolver into the armpit of his broken left arm. "Put your hand up. Palm on the top of the doorframe. Do it."

Even as the councilman complies, putting his right palm on the top of the doorframe, he tries to crane his neck to see what Huxley is doing, why he is approaching so quickly, what the glint of steel is in his hand ...

"What ...?"

Huxley slams the knife into the councilman's hand, spiking it to the top of the door.

The councilman screams, knees wobbling.

Quicker than he thought he could be, Huxley grabs his revolver, reverses his grip to hold it by the barrel, and slams the handle into the base of the knife three times, pounding it in deeper, more securely into the thick frame.

The councilman writhes against the door, but knows that he can't pull away, or the knife will rip his hand into shreds.

Huxley hears the pounding of footsteps coming up the stairwell. He jumps back, putting himself against the wall so that he can see the door to the bedroom and the councilman at the same time. He levels his revolver at the councilman. "If they open the door, it's gonna rip your hand off. And you might want to tell them not to shoot through!"

"Fuck!" Rage and terror grips the man. He is beginning to sweat profusely as blood runs down his arm in sheets. His other hand is clutching the wrist of the one that is posted to the top of the doorframe. He kicks the door viciously and yells raggedly, "Stay outside! Don't fucking come in! Do not come in!"

The footsteps clatter to the top landing.

The councilman is wide-eyed, alternately kicking the door and shouting, "You hear me? Don't come in! Stay the fuck outside, do you hear me? Stay outside! For God's sake don't open this door!"

Huxley swings his revolver over to the bedroom door of the suite. He stares at it, wondering what is behind it. Mrs. Murphy? She must be there. Where else would she be? But who else is in there with her? Are any of her slaves there? Is his daughter there?

What would she think? What would she think of me?

Huxley becomes aware of himself, amid the sound of unsure mumblings from outside in the stairwell, and the councilman's groans of desperation. Huxley is aware of how his ruined arm hangs against him, how the blood has soaked his side. His burns. His bandages. His wild eyes.

She will not know me. I would not know myself.

Huxley realizes that he is leaning his back against the wall more than he should—his knees are growing weak. He tries to moisten his tongue, but it is thick and pasty. "Councilman," he says, unsteadily. "Councilman."

"What?" Panic. Anger. "What do you want?"

"Tell her to come out."

"Tell who?"

"Your wife."

"She's not in there …"

"Councilman!" Huxley raises his voice. "Tell her to come out or I'm going in there after her, do you understand? No one needs to get hurt."

"You spiked my hand to the fucking door!" the man screams.

"You'll live," Huxley says, plainly. "Tell her to come out. We need to talk. All three of us together."

The councilman moans. Finally he turns his head so that he is looking over his shoulder at the door that leads further into the suite. "Trisha," he calls, his voice almost soft. "Trisha, come out here. Come out here, *now*."

There is a long moment of stillness.

The door cracks.

Huxley adjusts the grip on his revolver.

The door swings open slowly.

A woman. Tall. Pale. Beautiful. She wears a dress that seems odd and out of place to Huxley. It is a nice dress, with a floral pattern on it. In the Old World someone would have called it a "house dress" but to Huxley it is one of the nicest garments he's seen in a long time. But it doesn't disguise the woman's hand, the way she has it half-tucked behind a fold of her dress, and Huxley can see the long barrel of her own revolver there.

He looks at her face. The post of his own weapon's sight hovers under her chin, her long, regal neckline. Her hair is a strawberry blondish color, messy as though she's been asleep. And perhaps she has. *Opium-addled*, Black Heart Davies had told him.

And she looks it. For all her beauty, Huxley can see it in her eyes like an animal hunger. Some aspect of her humanity gone. And then Huxley can't tell if that is addiction, or if it is simply cruelty. There is something … off about her. Something that is intrinsically wrong with her that can be sensed, even through the fog of violence, immediately upon laying eyes on her.

Huxley's finger hovers over his trigger. "I see that gun, Mrs. Murphy. Put it down. Slow."

The councilman snarls from the doorway where he is pinned like a live bug in a glass case. "Oh, for fuck's sake, Trish, put the gun down. You can't even see straight to fire the damn thing."

Her eyes cut to her husband and there is a moment of sharp lucidity there that makes Huxley think that all the opium does not addle her as much as some believe. There is a cold, reptilian way she looks at people. Like they are just sacks of meat.

She reminds Huxley of Jay.

She looks back to Huxley. Her voice is strong, husky. "What do you want?"

Huxley winces against the pain in his arm. His own words are ragged syllables. "I want you to put the gun down. No one needs to get hurt. I want to talk. I've come all this way … just to talk."

"To talk?" there is a scoffing note in her voice.

"Trisha!" the councilman bellows. "Put the fucking gun down!"

Her eyes, locked with Huxley's, blink slowly, leisurely, as though none of this situation matters. She smacks her lips one time and looks at her husband again, seeming for the first time to register that he is stuck to the doorframe with a knife. The smallest smirk comes to her lips, and is gone in a flash, but not before it registers with Huxley.

She brings the revolver around, casually, not moving slow like Huxley requested. But he stays his trigger finger. She is doing it to prove a point. She shifts the revolver to her weak hand, reaches back inside the doorway and Huxley can hear the thud of the heavy metal weapon being set onto some wooden piece of furniture just inside the door.

She looks boredly at Huxley. "There, big man. Now talk. What have you traveled all this way to talk about?"

Huxley licks his lips with a dry tongue. "I came for my daughter."

His words are issued, they float out, hang in the air like dissipating smoke. No one seems to care about them. The tall, cruel woman in front of him tilts her head just slightly, eyeing Huxley up and down, looking past the blood and the grime and the heavy wool coat and the bandages.

"Oh my," she says. "Darling, it seems we have a bandit in our midst."

The councilman takes a few rapid breaths. "Jesus, Trisha, you stupid …" he trails off under his struggling breath.

Mrs. Murphy takes a step forward, bringing up a single index finger, which she wags at Huxley. It is as though the gun pointed at her is not making its way through her synapses. She believes herself to be in charge. She is always in charge. People are always afraid of her. Why should now be any different?

"You," she says with some recognizance in her voice. "You must be the mysterious *Huxley*."

He swallows. He wants to pull the trigger. But he needs answers.

"Oh, you are!" she giggles girlishly. "How exciting! Darling! A real live bandit!"

Huxley is befuddled. A million withering things come to mind, but by the time he wrestles them to his mouth, he's forgotten what to say.

"Trisha ..." a warning note in the councilman's voice. "I swear to God ..."

"You swear what?" she snaps at him. "You impotent prick. You're stuck to the wall like the faggot I always knew you were. Your city is falling around you and you're hiding in your fucking home, swishing your skirts." She lets out a bark of laughter. "But here," she motions to Huxley. "Here's a man. Look at him. Look at this man. This man from ... where are you from again? The Wastelands. A Wasteland Wildman. Usually we don't meet your kind. Except in chains. Actually, I misspoke. We've met several of your kind. We *own* several of your kind."

The revolver is getting heavy in Huxley's hand. He keeps having to bring the muzzle back up.

She's stalling. Huxley knows that she's stalling. Because he seems weak. He knows that she's hoping to say something that will make him give up. She's hoping to talk her way out of it, or maybe hoping that Huxley will run out of blood before she runs out of time.

Time is short.

Focus on what you came here for.

"My daughter," he says again.

"Oh, your daughter, your daughter. I'm bored of your daughter. Who even knows who she is? Let's talk about you. That's what's interesting. I get a dozen men's daughters coming through my household over the years, but this is the first time I've had a bandit come into my chambers. It's ... arousing."

"I'm not a bandit," he says quietly. The muzzle droops.

"Oh, but everyone else thinks differently. *Mr. Huxley.*" Another laugh. "The Wolf of the Wastelands, they're calling you. No one knew what the hell you were here for. Just revenge, we figured. Too many of your ... kinfolk or whatever ... taken by our slavers? Who knows? Obviously you held a grudge. You streaked through the Riverlands, murdering, raping, pillaging ..." she smiles, brightly. "Doing all of those things that you hate us so much for."

Huxley blinks. Sweat is getting in his eyes. The room feels sweltering. And then he breaks out in cold chills. The muzzle of his revolver dips a little lower.

Her eyes become cold. "You think you're the first to come after someone? You're not. And none of the others succeeded before you. They all die. But you didn't know that. You were blinded by your hatred because you have a small mind, *Huxley*. Let me tell you something, *Huxley*, you slavering wolf of a man, you fucking murderer, rapist, thief, *bandit* ..." She takes another step forward, gesturing expansively. "Have you looked around, you great, godless oaf? Have you seen what we have? Have you seen what we've built? Fucking civilization! Do you remember how it was? Do you remember the violence after the skyfire? Do you remember how we were all slaves to terror and fear? You couldn't travel. You couldn't farm. You couldn't trade. Do you remember any of that?

"Now look around you! Look at the fields! Look at the crops! Look at the trading posts! The lumber mills! The buildings that we're making! We're starting from the bottom up, but *we've started!* And do you know how we did it? Do you know what makes it all possible? Slaves. Workers. Because people are selfish. Because if you want safety, if you want society, you have to work for it. And no one wants to put in the effort. Everyone just wants to look out for themselves. So someone has to take the reins. Someone has to steer us back on course. Force people to put in the sweat and the labor to make civilization possible." She shakes her head at him in disdain. "You still think like an Old Worlder. You think that slavery was bad because politicians told you it was bad. But all they wanted was a fucking vote. It was all just a big game they were playing—the entire institute of civilization. You think if the cotton gin hadn't been invented they would have done away with slaves?" she shakes her head. "They only rid themselves of slavery when technology made it convenient to do so. But we're back to square one, aren't we? All that technology gone. And the only way to have society, is to bring back the slaves. So that's what we did. That's what we did, and it's *working*. That's what you Wastelanders don't understand. It's *working*. So how much do you hate us now, you small, nearsighted man? How much do you hate us for taking these people as slaves and giving them lives they couldn't dream of in whatever trash heap you came from? The desert? The *desert*? That's the glorious life you resent us taking from them?"

No. It isn't true.

She is evil, Davies said so himself . . .

Mrs. Murphy sneers. "Your daughter, whoever she is, had a better life with us than she could have ever had with you, trapped in that giant sandbox you called home. And she would hate you for dragging her back."

Huxley's muzzle lowers toward the floor. His eyes look down.

Then he shoots her in the foot.

She recoils away from the smoke and flame, and howls out a sound of shock as she looks down at her foot, which is just a splash of gore now. She chokes on her own cries and tries to back up, but her foot seems stuck to the floor and she just falls backward, collapsing into a heap.

"My daughter," Huxley says, louder, clearer, the gunshot bracing him, the smell of gunsmoke reminding him of what he is here for. He takes a step forward. "Would want to be with her father."

"You sonofabitch!" Mrs. Murphy screeches.

Huxley takes another step toward her. "She had a place. *We* had a place. A little house that I built on the northeastern corner of our barley fields." There are tears in his eyes. He doesn't know when they sprung up. "She drew pictures. Beautiful pictures. She had a place. She had a place with *me*."

The door into the stairwell bangs loudly and Councilman Murphy yelps and curses. "I told you to stay outside! Stay! Do not fucking come inside! I'm *ordering* you not to come inside!"

From outside the building there is another loud noise.

An explosion. The sound of men screaming. A smattering of gunshots.

The EDS is breaking through Old Town Jackson. They are coming.

Mrs. Murphy groans, then pants like a dog for a few seconds, looking up at Huxley balefully.

Huxley puts the muzzle in her face. She watches the smoke exit the barrel.

"When I came to the Riverlands I did it for blood and hatred, Mrs. Murphy. I did it for revenge. And I wreaked havoc on your people. I murdered them wholesale and I set loose others who hated you just as much as I did. I gave them weapons and I pointed them in the right direction to take their own revenge. To make you bleed. But all of that is done now. I did not come for you or your husband. I came for my daughter."

"You're just as bad as the men that took your daughter," she hisses, voice seething. "You know that you're just as bad. You know that you're just as *evil*."

Huxley nods. "Yes. I've killed many. But I never enjoyed it. And I won't enjoy killing you. But I will if you force me to. I only want my daughter."

"I don't have your cunt daughter."

Huxley touches the toe of his boot to Mrs. Murphy's ruined foot. She shrieks again. "Don't fuck with me, Mrs. Murphy. The opium won't block out what I'll do to you. I'll smash every bottle you have and teach you about true pain."

For once, there is fear in her eyes.

Huxley bends down slightly. The change in position makes his eyesight darken and sparkle. "Nathaniel Cartwright is dead. But before he died, he told me he sold my daughter to you. He remembered her for her drawings. Said you liked her drawings. Where is she, Mrs. Murphy? Just give her back and I will leave."

She looks up at him through tear-stained eyes. But these tears are like crocodile tears. There is no grief in them. Just the body purging pain out of itself. "I told you, I don't have her. Nathaniel Cartwright was a wild man no different from yourself. The two of you are cut from the same cloth. I refused to buy from him because he was wild. He lied to you, Huxley. And now he's dead," she laughs. "All the blood you shed has left you with no options. You killed the only person who knew where your daughter was. Do you feel like an idiot for being too liberal with that trigger?"

Huxley sways, involuntarily. He feels his right knee wobble.

"My daughter ..."

Mrs. Murphy looks up at him, this time in earnest. There is something behind her cruelty, behind the hunger of her addiction. Something like some forlorn pity. "If I had her, I would give her to you. Not because you deserve it, but because I want you to leave. Just leave. Leave us be! Don't you think you've done enough harm?"

Another explosion from outside, this one closer.

There is an exchange of gunfire that sounds like it is coming from the complex courtyard.

Out in the stairwell, the guards are chattering with each other.

"We need to leave," the councilman groans. He's having a hard time keeping his arms straight up. He wants to wilt but when he gives in, the knife threatens to rip his hand in two. "They're going to storm this place and kill everyone inside. You included, Mr. Huxley."

They're here, Huxley thinks. *The battle is here.*

But it is muted, the realization like someone speaking to him while water is in his ears. The only thing that presides over his mind is a crushing sensation. Nightmare. He is surrounded by worlds of nightmares, and waking from one only delves him into the other. It never ends. The nightmare never, ever ends.

Is this some joke? Is this some cosmic fucking joke?

He stares at her foot, pulsing out red, red blood. He can see the bones. The tendons twitching with every involuntary movement. She was not barefoot. She wore some type of canvas sandal. But the bullet ripped so much of it away. She is shaking now. Paling. Blood pooling under her foot.

"Leave," Mrs. Murphy says, her voice strained. "Just go."

Huxley stutters while he feels himself sinking into the ground. "My ... my daughter ..."

"Leave!" Mrs. Murphy yells shrilly. "Fucking leave us!"

There is the sound of metal scraping across wood.

Mrs. Murphy's pale, sweating face swings toward the doorway of the bedroom. From where she slouches, so close to the doorframe, she can see inside and she is looking at something there. She grimaces at it, apparently displeased.

"No," she says quietly. "Go back inside."

Huxley stares at the side of the doorframe. There is someone there on the other side.

Mrs. Murphy holds out one of her bloody hands to whoever is behind the wall. "Disobedient girl! Give me the gun!"

Whoever is there does not hand the gun over.

The disobedient girl steps into view.

Tall and skinny. Still short because she is not full grown, but tall it seems for her age. Long-limbed and gangly in her adolescence. Hair pulled back, but it is still that same color. Just like her mother's. Eyes still big and round and wondering, though they have changed, they have changed so much. In her hands, the revolver looks huge. The tip of the muzzle extends past her knees.

Huxley feels his legs go out from under him. Everything comes up from every place that he had stuffed it. She is the sight that he cannot take and still be the same. She is the one small weight that he cannot carry with all the other weights, but he will not let her go so he drops everything else.

He cannot let her go, so everything else that he kept buried comes roaring up out of him.

He hits the ground on his knees. His chest feels like it is caving in on him. He would have thought seeing her would be rapture, and in some ways it is, but in other ways it only destroys him. It is the most painful thing. His face contorts and he doesn't even try to hold back the tears, he does not even try to be strong, or appear strong. Everything melts. Everything gives way under the tide.

He can't speak. He can only weep.

My daughter. My daughter.

The girl stares at him while he cries, her eyes wide and uncomprehending. Mrs. Murphy also looks at him, almost pityingly.

Huxley manages to choke out a single word: "Nadine."

The girl looks at Mrs. Murphy, then at Huxley. There is a twitch behind her eyes. Something dark and resistant. She raises the revolver in her small hands and points it at Huxley and says the words he fears more than anything else in the world: "Who is this man?"

CHAPTER 9

Huxley sits in stunned silence that rings like cannon blasts in his ears. If there is a hell, he has found it. This is it, kneeling there broken on a floor, bleeding and beating eagerly at death's door, hoping for absolution and realizing that there is none.

She doesn't know you.

His wife's voice in his mind: *I don't even recognize you anymore.*

Huxley is suddenly, oddly, juvenilely self-conscious of himself. Laid bare in front of the judging eyes of the only person left in the world whose thoughts on him matter. And here, he is nothing. Here, on this most important of scales, he has been weighed and found wanting.

Jay's hateful voice in the back of his mind. *Why would she recognize you, brother? Look at yourself. You're a broken man. You're a killer. You're burned and bandaged and covered in blood like the butcher that you are. Even your eyes cannot be recognized. The eyes are the windows to the soul, brother, and your soul is a black hole that light cannot escape from. You are not her father. You look nothing like her father.*

Huxley has nothing. He is crumbled stones. He could die on the floor right now. He doesn't care. He almost wishes she would shoot him. Almost wishes that she would turn him away, because how does he deserve her? Mrs. Murphy was right. The neatness of this girl's clothes, her clean face, her brushed hair. Perhaps she is better here than she ever was with him.

She didn't need him. He was hatred and pain and destruction.

He was a demon, trying to claw its way into heaven.

Did you really think you belonged? Did you really think you could change?

Penitence doesn't change you, just like Davies said. Huxley was still the same man he was when he'd walked out of that burning commune with nothing left but hatred in his heart. He ruined himself. He went down a road that he knew he couldn't come back from, and he knew that this would happen. He knew what he was doing, and he didn't stop himself.

The people that he loved didn't recognize him anymore.

Mrs. Murphy is looking at Huxley, her half pity turned to a cold smirk. She manages to smirk even through her own pain. "I don't know who he is, my darling. Just some madman come to hurt us. Now give me the revolver."

You are a madman.

Perhaps it is best that she does not recognize you.

But he'd seen her. He'd laid his eyes on her. She is alive. She seemed well fed. Her eyes might be haunted, but how much worse would he make it for her? Perhaps Mrs. Murphy is not as cruel as Davies suggested. Perhaps Nadine is happier here …

"Nadine," he says again, almost involuntarily. Not really addressing her in that moment, but more just saying the name because of the comfort it brings him in this moment.

Mrs. Murphy hisses in pain and snaps her finger. "Girl! Don't listen to this madman. Now, obey your mother and give me the gun."

But Nadine is looking at Huxley. She is looking into his eyes. Very intense. She doesn't move. Her face doesn't soften. And the revolver is still pointing at Huxley. He can see how quickly she is breathing. Is it fear of him? Is he that terrifying?

"How …?" she whispers, then swallows and speaks stronger. Her voice has changed. "How did you know my name?"

He shakes his head, blinking through unrelenting tears, trying to maintain that clear view of her. It'll be the last thing he sees. And that is okay. It is the best he has seen. Even with her expression one of confusion and fear, it is still the best thing he has seen.

"It's me," he mumbles. "It's me."

"He's a liar," Mrs. Murphy's voice has more edge to it now. "Do as I say!"

Nadine raises her voice, to be heard over Mrs. Murphy, and to issue a challenge. But her voice trembles as she speaks, and Huxley can see tears in her own eyes. "Tell me about the place where I lived. Tell me about the fields."

Huxley feels the muzzle of his revolver hit the ground.

He pictures their old home together. It is easy to do when he looks at her. "When the sun set behind the barley fields it was the same color as your hair." He speaks slowly, hopefully. "In the winter, after pruning the fruit trees, I would burn the switches and you would use the charcoal sticks to draw. You could draw beautiful pictures of people's families that they'd lost." He smiles, falteringly. "On clear nights we would look at stars. I would show you constellations. I would tell you that I loved you more than all the stars in the sky."

The words have reached her. Huxley can see that. But the problem is him. He knows it. She wants to see who he is, but it is like he is wearing a mask. She can't see him for who he was, but only for who he has become.

"Nadine, please …" he whispers.

Outside, there are more gunshots and screams as men die.

Mrs. Murphy speaks now, her voice full of venom, her eyes locked on Nadine. "I won't tell you again, girl. Give. The gun. To. Your *mother*!"

Nadine's mouth opens as if to say a word, or to let out a sob, but then there is only stillness and nothingness. The revolver lowers just a bit, no longer pointed at Huxley's face. She looks to her left and stares at Mrs. Murphy. And here Huxley sees that dark thing again.

It is a terrible thing to see. To watch the weaknesses of your own soul somehow manifest in your children. To see that the darkness seems hereditary. The capacity to hate. Because that is what is in Nadine's eyes. Hatred. The same hatred that Huxley felt each time he stood over a man and killed him.

No, Nadine.

It's gonna eat you alive.

She swings the revolver to Mrs. Murphy. "I had a mother," she says, quietly. Then she shoots Mrs. Murphy in the head.

The woman's body tips over, falls to the ground, dead and motionless.

Nadine drops the revolver on the ground. Not disgusted or terrified of what she's just done. But because she is finished with it. Then she looks at Huxley with tears spilling down her cheeks.

The councilman is screaming. Out beyond the door that he is stuck to, there is a gunfight in the stairwell, each report like a cannon blast as it echoes up the enclosed space.

Huxley doesn't care about any of that. He pulls his broken body up off the floor and takes the two steps to stand in front of Nadine. His left arm will not move. His right holds the revolver. He wants to touch her, but he isn't sure she wants to be touched. He isn't sure about anything.

She looks up at him. "I waited for so long."

"I'm so sorry," he breaks.

She lets out a single sob, but even that is controlled, immediately stifled. What has happened to her? What has she seen? What has she been through? Huxley just wants to hold her and protect her, but he cannot, and he doubts she wants him to. There are still years of horror between the two of them, and those experiences create vast gulfs that can't simply be jumped over. Bridges must be built, and that takes time.

Her voice is strained. "I thought you were dead."

He shakes his head. "I wouldn't let them kill me."

She blinks rapidly, suddenly remembering their situation. She looks at the councilman who is still screeching and kicking at the door. Huxley registers that the councilman is terrified of the gun battle on the other side of the door, he is begging to be taken down before someone shoots through the door and kills him. Huxley isn't sure he even cares about his dead wife.

Nadine is suddenly focused. She grabs Huxley by his good arm and pulls him into the bedroom. "This is the penthouse," she says. "It had a private elevator. We still use the shaft to pull things up. Come on."

Huxley lets her guide him through the bedroom and into another area, a sort of lounging area or atrium. There are two sliding brass doors that are propped most of the way open. Beyond them is a dark elevator shaft.

Out in the room he just came from, there is a round of gunfire.

The councilman screams, grunts, and then is quiet.

Someone is pounding at the door.

"Is that the EDS soldiers?" Nadine asks.

"I think it is," Huxley says. "We need to get out of here."

"But ... they're the good guys, right? They're gonna free us."

His revolver is still in his right hand, but he reaches out and touches her shoulder with a few free fingers. "Listen to me. There's no 'good guys' out there, Nadine. There's just men on a warpath. EDS, Riverlands, it makes no difference. Their blood's up and they don't care who we are. We need to get out and we need to not be seen." He looks at her earnestly, hoping against hope that she can see past the blood and bandages and eighteen months of weather-beaten skin, and the hollow wildness in his eyes. "I know you barely know me. I love you so much, but I know that you barely know me and you barely even recognize me. But please trust me. Trust me and I'll get us out of this."

She looks at him. Judging him.

Then she nods. "Okay. Let's go."

She pulls him to the elevator doors. There is a rope and a pulley system attached to the ceiling of the shaft. The rope extends down into darkness. The elevator has been turned into a dumbwaiter of sorts. Nadine looks back at the man that she wants to believe is her father, though she seems like she's still not sure. Her eyes hover on his left arm.

"Can you climb down the rope with that arm?" she asks.

He cannot believe how strong she is. How purposeful she is in the face of all of this. He wants to grab her up and tell her that he loves her, but that is selfish catharsis. That isn't what this is about. This about getting Nadine out of here. Now there is a chance. All other things can wait. All other things can take a back seat.

You have her now. You've proved who you are.

Now banish all the nice stuff back where it came from.

Now be the beast again. The one the Wastelands couldn't kill. That is what she needs from you right now.

"Nadine," Huxley lowers himself just slightly, fighting the pain to look his daughter in the eyes. "You need to know something before we go any further, okay? There's nothing more important to me in the world than getting you out of here. Do you understand that?"

She stares back at him, apparently not sure what to say.

"You're going to see some things," he says. "I'm going to have to kill people. You're going to see me do bad things to people. But that's the only way. Okay?"

She only hesitates for a second. "Okay."

Huxley looks down the shaft. "Where does it go?"

"The first floor lobby," she says.

"There'll be fighting there." He shakes his head. "Can you get off on a floor above?"

"I don't know," she says. "I've never been in the shaft. Usually just pull food back and forth."

There is a huge boom and a crash from the other room.

"They're through," Huxley says. "Go. I'll follow."

She doesn't wait, doesn't hesitate. No need to speak soft things.

She grabs both ropes so the pulley won't fly beneath her and she begins to slide carefully down. Huxley notices for the first time that she is barefoot. Her toes skim along old steel girders and elevator tracks, black with ancient grease. She is gone in two heartbeats.

He is irrationally terrified that he has lost her forever.

From the other room, sounds of men shouting.

Exclamations at what they've found inside the penthouse room.

Huxley isn't sure how he is going to make it down the rope with one arm, but he doesn't have a choice. He stuffs his revolver in his waistband again, knowing as he reaches for the rope that the only way to hold to it tight enough will be to wrap it around his burned forearm.

Don't think about that.

Think about Nadine.

If he stays, he will risk his life to determine if the invading soldiers are offering quarter, but the purposeful, deliberate gunfire outside and in the stairwell sounds like the execution of the wounded and the surrendered. They are not taking prisoners.

Pain it is, then.

He grabs the rope, feels the tension in it from Nadine's weight, working her way down. He wraps his forearm around it. It stings and he clenches himself, hoping it won't be worse. Then he swings himself out, his bad left arm dangling uselessly, and all his weight comes down on that coil of rope around his forearm, and it turns into a branding iron.

He bites his lower lip to keep from crying out.

Tastes blood.

His legs flail a bit until he manages to hook them around the rope. When he has his feet clamped on the rope, they take some pressure off, but then he has to begin sliding himself down. The rope runs its steady course across his seared skin.

Don't think about the pain.

Think about Nadine.

You have her. You finally have her. Don't fail her now.

He descends quickly ten feet and then yanks himself to a stop. Up above him, from inside the penthouse, he can hear rummaging and rattling and course voices calling back to one another. *If they find us in this shaft, they'll just shoot. And they won't miss. We're just fish in a barrel.*

He slips down, keeps slipping down.

He manages to look below him. He can see Nadine there, dangling about twenty feet off the ground. But she's getting there. She's almost there. Huxley has a little farther to go and he can't move as fast. He tells himself to go faster.

Another ten feet for him. Another fifteen.

He glances down again.

Nadine is just above the lobby door. She is trying to swing her leg far enough to catch the lip of the door to the second floor. She is close, but she's missing it by inches. Huxley can feel the rope jerking around underneath him as she tries to get it to swing wider, and he can hear her grunting with effort, trying to get there.

He is sweating. Weak with pain. His grip feels slick and wet. "Come on, baby," he says but isn't sure he managed to say it loud enough for her. He wants to shout encouragement, but he doesn't want the men in the penthouse to hear them.

From up top, someone shouts, "Hey!"

Huxley jerks his head up.

A man's face, floating forty feet above him, looking down. "There's two trying to get away!" he shouts.

Shit.

Huxley tries to slide. His grip loosens and then he can't quite get it back. He is slipping. Ten feet. Fifteen feet. The elevator shaft suddenly rocks and seems to shake on itself and a bullet ricochets down the narrow vertical passage with a threatening, warbling whine.

Below him, Nadine yelps.

Huxley can't grab his pistol. His only good hand is struggling to hold onto the rope.

He slips more. Then completely loses it.

He is plummeting now.

He tries to shout out to Nadine, tries to warn her …

He slams into her, falling uncontrollably now. Their two bodies tangle and hit the ground. The air goes out of Huxley's lungs. He can't breathe, but he's trying wildly to move, because he can feel his daughter underneath him. He's trying to get off of her. Did he hurt her? Did he crush her underneath him? The fall hadn't been that far …

From above, another shout, another bullet winging down the passage at them.

Huxley rolls off of his daughter.

Nadine is lying with her back on the ground staring straight up with a look of shock on her face. Huxley feels his stomach go ice-cold. *Something is wrong! Something is hurt bad!*

He reaches out—no time to check for wounds. The rope has stripped the skin of his right palm away, but at least it still works. It is just pain. He can force himself to work through it. He grabs her by the front of her dress—the clean, plain dress now smudged with dirt and grease. He hauls her to the corner as another gunshot roars at them, this bullet not hitting any of the walls, but coming down straight into the floor in an explosion of dust and concrete.

Huxley shoves Nadine's body under the lip created by the lobby door. It isn't much cover, but it's better than nothing.

She's coughing now.

"Nadine!" he says, shakily. "Are you hit? Are you shot? What's wrong?"

She closes her eyes and grimaces. Seeing the pain in her face is horrible, but it means that she is *feeling*, and that means there isn't shock yet, and that her spine isn't broken. She coughs again, sucks in air and curls up on herself. Her hands are like claws, spidering down her left leg to her calf.

"My leg," she moans. "My leg."

Huxley looks at it. It lays at an odd angle. It's broken.

The door! The door! Get the door open!

Up above, the voice is distant: "They're on the bottom floor! They're gonna get out!"

No more shooting. A brief reprieve.

What's beyond the door?

Who knows?

Huxley jams the fingers of his right hand into the crack in the elevator door and shoves as hard as he can. The door surprises him by coming open easier than he expected. It causes him to lose his balance and stumble, almost stepping on Nadine.

She groans at his feet.

Huxley snatches the revolver up in his burned hand. He points it unsteadily out the half-open elevator door at the lobby beyond. It is a mess of bodies, a haze of gunsmoke still hanging in the air like an early morning fog.

They need to get out. It will only take a few more seconds for the men in the stairwell to come back down to the lobby level and catch up to them. But Nadine can't walk. Not under her own power, and Huxley can't put the revolver out of his hand or he'll have nothing to defend them with.

So he kneels down as close to Nadine as he can get.

"Nadine. Honey. You gotta get up."

"My leg is broken!" she snaps at him.

"I know. You gotta grab my shoulders. Grab my shoulders and hold on tight, okay?"

She pulls her hands from her broken leg and reaches up, tears streaming out of her eyes now. She seizes his shoulders, his coat bunching thickly in her grip. She is grabbing skin and muscle, but he has to let her. He can't think of another way to get them moving.

When she's holding tight, he lifts himself out of his kneeling position.

He strains, but manages to get himself upright.

Nadine wobbles, balancing on one foot, leaning on him.

"We're gonna go to the lobby doors, okay? Straight out. You ready?"

"Okay. Okay." She is panting in pain. "I'm ready."

He shuffles his feet, letting her try to match his rhythm. Out into the lobby. They have to go around the sprawled bodies, because she can't really get over them. There are at least a dozen. Most of them are House Murphy guards. Some of them were dead on the ground. Others were wounded and crawling for safety before their brains were splashed across the tile floor.

War has come, Huxley keeps thinking, just like he thought when he stared out at the hellish, burning ruins of Old Town Jackson. *War has come to the Riverlands.*

He hears a door slamming open behind them.

He knows that it's the stairwell door.

He turns, raising his revolver.

A man stands there with a rifle, half-ready. He doesn't look like a soldier. He's just a man in a homespun shirt of bland off-white and old wool breeches. Maybe one of the people from Jackson and Murphy Township that rose up with the EDS. Just a normal man. Somebody trying to pull his family out of bondage.

Huxley shoots him in the chest, watches him spill backward.

Then he turns quickly and pulls them toward the door. There's no time for Nadine to hop along with him. He puts his gun arm around her and squeezes her tight into his side and simply drags her as best he can through the mire of dead men, speaking softly, "I'm sorry, Nadine, I'm sorry you have to see this."

"Go," she says, voice strained. "Just go."

They make it out of the lobby, and into the courtyard. Here, it is generalized chaos. Those fighting for House Murphy are marked by their armbands. They're backed into firing positions on balconies and in the corners of the complex, blasting away with their breechloading rifles and losing ground by the second. The front gates have been ripped off their hinges and scores upon scores of men and women are pouring in.

These people are like the man inside. They bear no marking. They are dressed normally. Some of them carry weapons of opportunity—machetes, clubs, old scatterguns—but many more have revolvers and rifles of their own. They are expensive things for random commoners to have. And Huxley cannot tell whether these are the Riverlanders that have been armed by the EDS, or whether this is the EDS army itself.

It doesn't matter. Out here, no one is his friend.

He hauls Nadine along with him, along the side of the building, trying to stay between the wall and the giant ornamental planters. Trying to stay unnoticed. Bullets smack the ground around them and gunshots echo across the courtyard, but it doesn't seem like anyone is singling him out. There is so much lead flying around, there are likely more people dying out of pure chance than any cold-blooded intention.

Above chest level, the courtyard is a drifting, swirling cloud of gunsmoke, shot through by sparks and flashes from muzzle blasts and explosions from grenades. Below that, it is just people's bodies shoving about in mass confusion, trying to figure out where their enemy is and shooting at anything they suspect might be it.

Men and women are shouting and screaming.

There are dead and dying littering the courtyard.

A man lying against the side of the building reaches out suddenly, grabbing onto Nadine's broken leg as Huxley drags her past. She cries out more out of fear and kicks the man away from her. Then she wilts in pain. Against the wall, the man begs for help.

Huxley ignores him. Nadine is the only thing that matters now.

You got out of the building, now get out of the complex.

And if you can get out of the complex, then get out of the city.

And then you're home free …

And all of this leads to what?

Don't think about that now.

Just get out of the complex.

Get out of the city.

Sticking to shadows and walls and dragging himself and his daughter through the groaning wounded and bleeding dead, Huxley makes it to the big cement planter beside the gate. His and Nadine's backs are to the wall, half-crouched. Above them, the building shakes and shudders as a firefight rages inside. Shards of glass rain down on them as bullets punch holes through the windows. Bits and pieces of cinders fall from one of the stories of the building that is on fire.

In his arms, Nadine is breathing rapidly against the pain and she is starting to shiver. He isn't sure if it is from the cold, or from the shock of the broken bone. He wishes that he could do something for her, but the only thing to do is get out of there.

Ten yards away from them, the gates hang open, twisted and mangled, the ground blackened by a blast of some sort. Some giant powder charge that blew them open for the invaders. Huxley waits there, trying to catch his breath as the stream of men storming the complex begins to taper off. With this moment's reprieve comes more agony.

Time to move again.

He reaches out to a nearby dead body and takes the revolver in its hand, a ball and cap with three unspent chambers. He stuffs it in his waistband. Then he fumbles around in his pockets, coming up with the four cartridges he put there. He reloads his revolver.

"Are we gonna make it out?" Nadine's voice.

He feels that strange, prickling heat against the back of his scalp.

That feeling of insufficient blood pressure. He ignores it.

"Yes," he tells Nadine. "We're gonna make it out."

He speaks in faith. Because how can he make these promises? He cannot control the wind. He cannot control all the dangerous men that are pillaging the city outside those gates. He can only hope to get around them. And he prays that his body will hold. His body has to hold together for just a little while longer. Until he gets Nadine out of the city … then it can fail.

But what about Lowell?

Fear in his gut.

He finishes loading his revolver and cocks the hammer back. "You ready?"

Nadine nods quickly.

He hauls her up again and they move through the breech, and into the nightmare of the township.

CHAPTER 10

Here in the Murphy Township, the pace has slowed. The frenetic movement of combat, the hardheaded purposefulness of it, is gone. And so begins the sacking of a city. The combatants have bloodied each other, and one side has died or yielded. Now the victors roam about, unsated, wild, and unpredictable.

Mercy is lost in these moments.

Carve a path. Get her out of here.

The city is dark. Clouds of smoke hang above them. They are black, but tinted orange by the fires below them. That is all the illumination that Huxley has. The entire world is either charcoal black or raging fire. He can see the figures of people moving about like demons among the flames. EDS soldiers, or the townspeople themselves, he doesn't know. These townspeople, these rebels, they burned their own homes to the ground in the frenzy. This is war. This is what it looks like when you are down close to the dirt. Down low enough to smell the blood in the gutters.

As they work their way through the darkness, Huxley begins to speak quiet encouragement. He needs it. He needs to say it just as much for himself as for Nadine. He needs to repeat things that make him think they will make it out, because right then, he is disoriented, he feels lost, and it feels like the town is a maze that is collapsing down around him.

Then you will have to climb over the rubble.

"Come on," he says quietly, taking big gulps of air as he exerts himself through his own pain and loss of blood, speaking whispered words on the ragged exhales. "We got this. We can do this. You and me."

He wants to call her the things he used to call her, those terms of endearment still so close to his tongue, so natural feeling in her presence that they threaten to fall out against his will. But she has not called him "Daddy," like she used to. She has not even called him "Father." Or even used his name. He is not sure she wants to be reminded of her relationship to the man that she clings to now. He is not sure that she loves him anymore.

But it doesn't matter if she does. Love him or hate him, or even if she is simply indifferent, it is her *living* that matters. Her *being free* that matters.

He continues to pull her along.

At the mouth of an alley between two larger buildings, Huxley can hear a woman screaming. He can hear other voices talking. He peers around the corner. By the hellish light of burning buildings he can see a woman on the ground, on her hands and knees. A group of both men and women strike her and rip her clothes off of her. She is nearly stripped naked. One of the men is unbuckling his pants. It seems no one cares.

Who are these people? None of them wear uniforms. Huxley doesn't think they are EDS. Were they neighbors once? All townspeople living within arm's reach of each other? How many times did the woman on the ground and the man unbuckling his pants pass each other in the street? How many times did their eyes meet, neither with any knowledge of the things that might happen on this night?

Or perhaps there was always enmity between them. Perhaps the woman was a loyalist. Perhaps a purveyor for the Murphy family. A tax collector. Some other position of the council's power over these other people.

She will be shamed. Raped. Probably murdered.

"Don't look," Huxley says, and then quickly drags Nadine across the mouth of the alley.

She stares anyway as they go, her face looking like it might break. "No," she cries out.

One of the men looks up at them. His eyes catch Huxley's.

Huxley keeps moving. He refuses to stop.

He makes it another block before he hears footsteps behind them.

"Hey!" the voice says, all cocksure, almost hoping for a conflict. A man whose appetite has been whetted by the violence around them. But he doesn't know. How could he know? Who is standing in front of him?

Huxley turns his head to look at the man, but keeps his body faced away so they can't see the weapons he has. He can't tell much about him in the darkness. He can tell that there are three of them. He assumed it was the man in front that spoke, so he looks there.

"Who are you with?" the man challenges. "You're not one of my people, and that bitch there looks like a member of the Murphy household."

Huxley blinks, trying to focus himself. He feels almost outside of his body now. He feels the weight of the pistol in his grip. It is held in his one working arm, which is wrapped around his daughter. They might not have seen that he is armed.

"Leave us be," Huxley says. "We're not the ones you want."

Then, in his daughter's ear, he whispers, "Nadine. Take the gun in my waistband."

Huxley feels Nadine grab the grip of the revolver and draw it slightly it out of his waistband, but not completely.

The challenger steps forward another step and Huxley can see he has a scattergun. "Let the bitch speak for herself. You a part of the Murphy household?"

"She was a slave," Huxley says.

The man laughs. "Their slaves were just as bad. Brainwashed motherfuckers."

Huxley whispers to her, "When I turn, shoot the man on the left."

"You're being seized by the People's Resistance Army." He lifts his scattergun.

"Now," Huxley blurts, and then he turns.

Nadine swings with him, ripping the revolver out of his waistband with both hands.

Huxley points at the man with the scattergun, firing as the glimmer of the revolver barrel connects with the shadowy figure of the man. The man lurches, and the scattergun fires off, still low. The bits and pieces of whatever it's been loaded with explode into the concrete a yard in front of Huxley's feet and send up a shower of debris that pecks at his face.

He feels something in his eye, something burning hot.

He can't close his eyes, or wince. He has to aim.

Nadine fires the revolver next to him and the man to the left stumbles.

Huxley pulls his own hammer back and fires three shots, taking the center man again, and then two into the right man.

The shadows are crumpled, moaning on the ground.

Huxley gives into the pain in his face and eyes, he bends a bit, eyes clamping shut and his fingers going to his face. He can feel the blood trickling down his face. He hisses curses to himself. He blinks and tries to open his eyes. His left eye is fine, but there is nothing but murky darkness in his right.

Nadine is sobbing. "Are you okay? Are you okay?"

He turns and puts his arm around her again, squinting his right eye against the pain of whatever is stuck in there, and trying to see with his left. "I'm fine. We need to keep …" he gulps for air as he drags her forward with him. "We need to keep moving. I'm sorry you had to do that."

"It's fine," she says flatly, but Huxley knows it is not.

There was no other way.

They make their way slowly through a mile of screams and bloodshed and fire.

He finds a man with a horse. He wears a sigil that Huxley doesn't know, and he is armed with a rifle. Huxley knows that he needs the horse—he is reaching his physical limit. But if Huxley tries to threaten the man for his horse, the risk is too great that he will open fire on them.

He has no choice. He is barreling forward.

Again, he tells Nadine to look away, and again she doesn't listen to him.

He shoots the man out of the saddle.

Yes, this is what I've become, my sweet girl. But it was so I could save you. It was so I could get you out of here. You don't have to love me. You don't even have to forgive me. You just have to live.

She cries out in agony as he strains to help her into the saddle. His one working arm is so overused now that it burns inside and out. The skin from fire, the muscles from acid of his body's own making. But he grunts and groans and manages to get her wounded leg over the animal's back. He thinks about just spurring it on, letting her get out of here, but she only has the revolver from his waistband, just a ball and cap with only two chambers left to fire, and she cannot ride the horse well with a broken leg.

He pulls himself into the saddle behind her. There is hardly room for both of them, but they have to make it work.

Mounted now, he rides at a steady, purposeful clip through the streets, always making sure that the burning husk of Old Town Jackson is at his back—that is the only way he can tell if he's going the right direction.

He is fading fast, he can feel it now. He keeps drooping in the saddle, his head nodding back, only the pain in his neck bringing him back to full consciousness. As the burning and looting becomes rarer, and the houses more spread apart, Huxley can see the night opening up around him, opening up into all of those farmer's fields, and he knows that they are out.

You're done. You made it out.

"We're out," he says, the words a jumble of consonants in his mouth. "We're okay. We're gonna be okay."

But they aren't. *He* isn't, anyway. A broken leg can be set. But he can't put blood back into him.

His life is forfeit anyway.

His thoughts are beginning to get nonsensical. One moment he has the presence of mind to stop the horse and ask Nadine to help him tourniquet his arm before he loses any more blood, and the next moment everything goes white and warm, like sand on a sunny beach. But he hears the crackling of thunder. Feels the drumbeat of rain on his skin.

His wife is there. Her hair is hanging in wet tangles.

He is on a beach. It is sunny and it is raining, all at once.

The beach is somehow also the field of barley, and he can see his wife there, and Charity is smiling at him and she kisses him. He looks out at the drooping heads, heavy with grain, and he knows the harvest will be good. Nadine is there too, and suddenly it is night, not a terrifying darkness, but a night filled with the blazes of stars so numerous they can't be counted. And she points up at them and smiles and calls him "Daddy."

He weeps.

She called me Daddy, he thinks. *Just like she used to, when I would come back from the fields and she would be excited to see me. Just like she did when she loved me, and I loved her, and I loved her mother, and her mother loved me, and everything was right in the world.*

She called me Daddy.

He weeps, and he laughs, and he smiles, and he is happy. Happy like he used to be.

And his wife, in the rain, in the sunny sand, in the field of barley, she looks at him fondly and she touches his weeping, laughing, foolish face, her eyes tracing the familiar patterns of him. Her hands are warm and soft.

"There you are," she says.

He swims through midnight waters, murky in their logic, and time is lost, inconsequential. He remembers things that he had forgotten, and forgets things that have only just happened. He sees Nadine as a toddler, full of laughs and nonsensical talk. He sees her face very clearly as a newborn in his arms. He sees his wife, still pregnant, in their tiny apartment, before all of this, before the world burned down to the ground.

His life parading in front of him, but it is stuck in reverse. He keeps going back and back, down to the roots, down to the elemental formation of things.

He is in college, feeling all the self-perceived genius of youth.

He is making love for the first time, an awkward frenzy of lust.

He is a child in church, fidgeting in his uncomfortable Sunday clothes.

"For now we see in a mirror, dimly, but then face-to-face," the preacher speaks. "Now I know in part, but then I shall know just as I also am known. And now abide faith, hope, love, these three; but the greatest of these is love."

The child version of Huxley stares up in silence at a stained-glass window.

The preacher: "Thus sayeth the word of God. And all God's people said …"

Ancient words on Huxley's tongue: "Amen."

Then he is sitting not in church, but in a classroom, but this is not his childhood classroom that smells of bright paint over old mustiness. Here he is not the pupil but the teacher, and he looks out across the gathered mirrors of his youth and he sees the opportunity there, the chances, the possibilities. He looks at one boy in his class and he recognizes his face.

He believes in these children. Out of love. Out of faith, and hope.

And then the walls of the school crumble down into ashes and the boy remains, no longer dressed in his fine clothes, or sitting on his desk. Now he is a naked desperate thing covered in dirt and ash and blood. All this boy's classmates are vanished and both Huxley and the boy knows where they went.

Into the ground.

They are dead.

All their hopeful promise extinguished. And the sky above them ripples with fire, a light show of blinding electricity.

He reaches out to the child, and he tries to call his name, but he has no voice.

Lowell …

Then he is falling.

Huxley comes to on his back, staring up at the sky. His body tingles and aches in the way that tells him he has just now struck the ground. The breath groans out of him painfully. Above him hovers night sky speckled to eternity and back with white pinpricks of light, and he can see the dark shadow of a horse and a girl, looking down at him. She is scared. She is trying to get out of the saddle, trying to help him.

She has a broken leg. She can't get out of the saddle.

He holds up a shaky hand. "It's okay, honey. I'm okay."

"You're not okay!" she sobs. "You just passed out!"

He looks at his arm. The last he remembers was her putting the tourniquet on him. It is tied tight and secure, his arm a dull, limp ache. How long ago was that?

"No, no," he says. His words are slightly slurred. "I just … fell asleep, that's all."

Nadine looks about, still frightened. "You have to get up!"

Huxley forces himself into a sitting position. That is a victory. Then onto his feet. Another victory. He grasps the pommel of the saddle and holds it there for a time, fighting off the lightheadedness. He blinks rapidly, trying to clear his right eye, and then remembers that something was shot into it and that he cannot see out of it.

Am I blind? Will my sight come back?

Doesn't matter now.

"How long?" he asks.

"What?"

"How long have we been out of the city?"

"I don't know. Maybe an hour."

Huxley is flabbergasted. He doesn't remember that hour. Was he passed out the whole time and only now toppled from the saddle?

It takes him three tries to get back into the saddle, but he makes it, exhausted, aching all over. He is sitting behind Nadine, and he can feel her small, bony body shivering against him. She is out in this cold night with just the flimsy dress she had on. No shoes on her feet. Her broken leg bouncing with every movement of the horse.

He struggles with the wool coat. How could he be wearing this when his daughter is shivering, broken in the saddle? He gets the coat off. The air is cold, but he doesn't even equate that to how he will feel after a few minutes exposed. He can only think about how it must feel for her. He puts the coat over her shoulders and wraps her tight in it.

She starts to object, but then remains silent.

Huxley spurs the horse on.

The cold is bracing enough to keep him conscious for a bit, though his eyes keep wanting to roll away from what he's trying to focus on—the road in front of them. And his thoughts are jumbled and disorganized. They flit from here to there with no real rhyme or reason. His brain firing awkwardly and randomly as he skirts the twilight edges of consciousness.

Nadine must have felt him swaying again in the saddle.

She gently touches his burned arm. It hurts, but he doesn't react to it. "Dad," she says. Trying to bring him back. Trying to keep his mind present.

Behind her, swaying almost drunkenly in the saddle, Huxley gives a faint, disastrous smile. "Yes …"

"Do you remember Mom?" she asks quietly.

He fights to keep his eyes open. "Yeah. 'Course I remember your mom."

"So … she's dead?"

The smile falters into a pale wisp, and then drops away. Nadine didn't know. When she'd been dragged away, her mother was still alive, lying on the ground. She must've suspected … but for a year and a half she didn't know. She didn't know whether her mother lived. Or her father. There must've been nights that she felt so stricken and abandoned …

But I'm here. I'm here now.

"Yes," he whispers. "She died."

Nadine takes a breath to speak, but hesitates for a few beats. "I … I think I'm forgetting her face."

Huxley doesn't speak, or react. Inside, he breaks. He is ground to dust. No stone left standing.

"I've tried to draw her," Nadine says, her voice strained with pain both physical and emotional. "I tried. But I could never … I could never remember what her *face* looked like. Is that wrong? Am I a bad daughter?"

"No, honey. You're not a bad daughter." He wants to offer more encouragement but he has to choke on his words for a short time until he can put some strength back into his voice. When he is steady enough, he says, "I can tell you about her."

I can only tell you, because I've forgotten the image too.

They are only words. But they're all I have left.

"Okay," Nadine says.

Huxley breathes slow, lets his eyes close. Sways with the movement of the horse. "She had hair the color of the barley fields when the sun was behind them—just like you. She had blue eyes that were bluer in the middle, and they sparkled when she smiled. A big smile. Beautiful mouth. She'd been a joyful person. A wonderful person. The best person I know."

They ride in silence for a time, Nadine seeming to digest his words, to construct them in her mind. Huxley wonders if it is familiar to her or not. Does the image he just spoke bear any resemblance to her dim memories?

"Maybe you can help me draw her someday."

"I'd like that," Huxley says.

But he knows he will not be given the time. He has a full tally to pay, debts accrued on debts.

He could just go. He could just run. With Nadine. They could go north, away from the Wastelands, away from the Riverlands, away from the EDS and their war for the Mississippi. They could go north and never look back, out of reach of Davies and the slavers and anyone else that might want to hurt them …

Lowell.

But he couldn't leave Lowell. He couldn't abandon him again.

Not even for your own daughter?

He looks at her in the saddle. Broken leg dangling to the left. But her shoulders are squared up to the wind, her face set with a sort of determination you don't see in people her age. It has only been eighteen months since they were separated, and yet there is the difference of a decade in this girl.

She is strong. She is very strong.

If Lowell dies, I will be lost.

That is still true. If he lets Lowell die, he will not be able to remember anything good about himself. He will be a soulless shell of a man, and he will live his life running scared and ashamed, always looking over his shoulder for Black Heart Davies, always haunted by his own weaknesses.

Nadine deserves a better father than that.

By dawn, they stumble upon a growing horde of refugees, and beyond, the span of the Mississippi river, that waterway so valuable that men will fight and die for its muddy banks. And it is here that his exhausted, injured daughter looks back at him.

"Where are we going?" she says.

He looks at her again, this girl with so many pieces of her mother in her. But pieces of him, too. And yet, she is not bad. She can't be bad. She's so young. And no matter how much of himself she has, she's still a good person.

I'm sorry, sweet girl. This is the way it has to be.

She might not understand now, but eventually … hopefully …

He starts down the hill toward the river. "There's someone I have to meet."

CHAPTER 11

At the riverbank, amongst the rest of the refugees, Nadine grows quiet. The refugees are quiet as well, for a group of what must have been a thousand. There are some that weep loudly and cry for the loss of loved ones, or the loss of their things. But mostly they stare at the waters, blankly. Some of them know what it is like now to have nothing. Will they become desperate too? Will they become dangerous?

The Riverlands is a country of summer-dried grasses, and lightning has just struck, and before this is all over, everything will burn.

The ferries come and go. The bridge is looking more of a shell now, the substructure the only thing that still spans. Explosions continue as holes are bored into concrete and sticks of some crude explosive are lit in them. Men crawl over the structure like swarms of ants, intent on its destruction. Now the destruction of the bridge makes sense. They are cutting the EDS off.

They have to wait for the large ferry, because the horse will not fit on the small boats, and Huxley doesn't believe he has the strength to carry Nadine. And so they wait. The morning sun warms him. Huxley fades in and out again.

The pain of his shattered arm stabs him occasionally.

Nadine also suffers, but she does it quietly.

An old woman, a healer, comes by. Huxley and Nadine are pathetic figures, but most of the refugees are injured or bloodied in some way or another, some of them carried in stretchers by their friends and family, barely clinging to life. Some of them lie by the wayside, dead in the journey. A young girl tags along beside the healer. He could imagine that this was Brie, half a dozen years ago.

Before her life had been destroyed. Before she grew hateful. Before she started killing more than she healed.

The girl carries a pitcher of water. She lets Huxley and Nadine drink from a ladle that she draws from her pitcher. The healer is there only to help. Not to make gold from these fleeing, penniless people. Huxley almost refuses her services—what injuries he has are his own fault. But he does not refuse the healer for Nadine.

Huxley helps Nadine down from the saddle. The healer puts a leather thong in Nadine's mouth for her to bite down on. It is wet from the mouths of others that have bit it along the way. Nadine doesn't seem to notice, or care. She clamps down on it, baring her teeth, squeezing her eyes shut. The healer sets the bone quickly while Nadine strains to stay still and not scream. Then the healer splints her broken leg with a few sticks fetched by the younger girl and smooths Nadine's hair.

"You'll be just fine," the healer says, kindly. She looks to Huxley, who leans against the horse, barely conscious. "If you won't let me tend to your wounds, at least let me put that arm into a sling. It'll only take a moment and a piece of cloth."

Huxley lets her sling his arm. The cloth comes from his own pant leg, a long strip of it from the bottom all the way to above the knee. The old healer works gently with Huxley's arm, always with a slight smile on her lips, as though nothing pleases her more than doing these kindnesses for others.

He watches her, almost with suspicion, and he hates that he is the foul one, because he can see that she is genuine. He is the schemer, the evil one. She is goodness and kindness. What right does he have to question her? He cannot even remember how to be kind to a stranger. He thinks maybe once he'd been capable of it, when he still had faith in people.

"Why are you doing this?" he asks the healer, unable to keep the suspicion from his voice. "You gain nothing from it."

She smiles at him, as though she expected his question. She is not taken aback. She is not offended. "What does it benefit me to gain the world, but lose my soul? I do this because you are a human being, and you are in pain. It is in my power to help relieve that pain. Why would I not?"

"Because you don't know what kind of person I am."

She finishes knotting the sling at his shoulder. "It doesn't matter what kind of person you are. What matters is the kind of person *I* am. I have no control over you, or the rest of the world. All I have control over is how I react to it. The world is full of people that choose to react by inflicting pain. I choose to react by taking it away." She seems good-humored about it. "We balance each other out."

Huxley's spirit is hardpan dirt that has been pierced. Underneath that, the things he'd kept down below for so long keep coming up. He has no control over them, but they burst out of him, unrelenting. He wants to be strong, but he can't keep it down anymore. Everything that has happened, all the deaths, and the murders and the bad things, and the good things, and his daughter and the memories that she brings and the goodness inside of her—they all just keep boring that hole bigger and bigger and it makes it all harder to control.

He takes the old woman's hand and kisses it. His own tears come down his nose and wet her wrinkled hand. He feels weak for his foolish tears, but they come against his will now. This is the nature of all the things that you sink down deep inside of you. They will eventually come out. In one way or another. They will come out in anger, or anguish. They will come out in blood, or in tears.

"This world doesn't deserve people like you," he whispers to the old lady.

She smiles and clasps his hands in hers. "Thank you for your kind words."

And then the healer moves on, her young apprentice in tow.

Still seated on the ground, Nadine is wiping tears from her eyes. She seems to be very deliberately not looking at Huxley. He doesn't know what to do, or what to say. Has he forgotten how to be a father? Or is he right to leave her alone in that moment?

On the river, the large ferry is trundling its gradual way back across the river.

Nadine, with trembling hands, reaches into the inner pocket of the heavy woolen coat that Huxley put over her shoulders, and she draws out the folded piece of parchment and the stick of charcoal, which has broken into three pieces now, each no longer than an inch.

"I found this," she says, still not looking up at him.

Huxley stares at it. Remembers the boys that died.

He has so much blood on his hands, so many souls on his shoulders … how could he ever be the father that Nadine needs? He is poison to those around him. But he has managed to succeed in one very important thing. He has taken Nadine out of bondage. He has freed her. He has seen her face, he has held her, even though it was briefly, and she has recognized him.

That is good enough.

What did he expect? That they would ride away into the north together? Or make it through the lines of war and sneak into the Eastern Democratic States? That he would build her a new life and till fields and be a father?

It seems beautiful, but how many beautiful things has he destroyed?

That is what I became. I became a destroyer.

Perhaps Davies is right. How long can you live with so steep a bill hanging over your head? The tally must be paid.

"You can have it," Huxley says. "Please. It's yours."

She opens the folded piece of paper. At the corner, Huxley can still see the muted stain of red.

"Is that blood?" she asks.

Huxley pulls his eyes away from it. "Yes."

Nadine considers it for a time, and then begins to draw.

Out of pure exhaustion, she falls asleep with just a few lines drawn, framing a face, though what face Huxley can't tell. He was never very good at understanding what she was drawing until he could see the finished picture. There were things that she did at the end, tiny details that seemed so insignificant sometimes, but which brought the picture to life. That was her talent. That's what made her so special to everyone.

The line of refugees continues to dwindle as the large ferry runs people and animals back and forth. It is a lifetime of laying down, taking a short nap, and then getting up and moving forward twenty yards, then collapsing again and sleeping.

When she is awake, Nadine draws, she adds small bits and pieces to the picture.

Huxley doesn't look over her shoulder. She never could stand that. She wanted to reveal it only when it was done. She knew that it was the finishing touches that made the picture real. She did not want anyone to see the groundwork sketches that came before.

It is midafternoon by the time they are able to board the ferry. It takes every last piece of gold in Huxley's satchel to pay for the passage of himself, his daughter, and the horse, and even then he has to empty his satchel and prove to the shipman taking the payments that he has no more coin.

Huxley is feeling less likely to pass out. But exhaustion is there, creeping over him like a heavy blanket. It seems to weigh everything down. Every limb a thousand pounds. When they find a quiet corner of the ferry, Huxley lays down. He has to lie on his back—both his arms scream when he tries to turn on his side. His eyes stay open for a brief moment.

His girl, seated atop the horse, her hair caught in the wind as the ferry shoves off for the western bank of the Mississippi, and the sun caught in the strands. *Like the barley fields*, he thinks again with a smile. She is drawing again, her red-rimmed eyes focused intensely on the paper, and he can almost imagine that the two of them are not where they are, but at a cottage that he built with his own hands, at the northeastern corner of a barley field, so many long miles away …

CHAPTER 12

She knows, Huxley thinks as he pulls the horse to a stop in the middle of a small dirt road that leads out of Vicksburg Landing. One that he has traveled before. And at the end of it …

She knows.

Nadine's eyes are bloodshot, her nose raw from wiping the snot from it with the rough sleeve of the woolen jacket. Sometime while he slept on the ferry, she had finished her picture and she had tucked it away in the pocket of the coat. She is crying again. She stays silent, but he can feel her shoulders shaking. He knows that it isn't from the pain of her leg anymore. He might have changed, but he still knows his daughter. He knows how to tell the difference between her physical pain and her grief.

The afternoon is turning to evening. Everything is golden, turning to ochre. The sun is in their eyes on this westerly road. It's not cold, except for when the wind gusts. There is a barren beauty to all of this finality. The way the sun dazzles between the trees like one last gift for him. Not a bad sunset to finish a lifetime's worth.

He dismounts. It is painfully difficult. Then he stoops down and struggles with the hobble. It is a two-handed job, and he only has one. But he manages to get the hobble looped around one hoof, and then starts on the other. Above his head, he can hear Nadine's breath—sharp and hitching. He has bent to this task as much to hide his eyes from her as because it is necessary.

I don't want her following me, he thinks, but he keeps his head pointed to the ground so that his tears can fall silently and without her seeing them. *She knows what I'm about to do.*

It's a vain effort. Even after wiping his eyes, he knows she can see that they are red, just like hers. He looks up at her, still sitting in the saddle of this poor, tired horse. He doesn't know what else to do. He wants more time. But more time was never part of the deal. And there are promises to keep.

It's only the second night. You have until tomorrow morning.

But Huxley knows that anything could happen between now and then. In the span of a night, he might die from his wounds, or at the least, become so sick and weak that he can't show up. And he will not have Nadine take him there. He will not expose her to Black Heart Davies. He must go while he still has the strength to go under his own power.

"Are you going to leave me here?" she asks, voice cracking.

"I can't take you with me," his own words are a struggle.

"Why?" she cries out, suddenly loud. "Why are you doing this?"

He lays a hand on her knee. She shoves it away.

It stings him, inside and out.

"Nadine, please," he begs, hanging his head at first, then raising it, not trying to hide himself anymore.

Her shoulders slump. Her eyes are locked on his. She sniffs loudly. "I don't understand. Why would you get me out of there if you're just going to leave me again?"

Your children always seem to know the words to cut you low.

Huxley puts his hand on her knee again. This time she lets it lie. He feels like he has to touch her, to make that connection, as though better understanding will be imparted through that contact. "Listen to me. I wanted you to be free. I wanted you to be safe. I wanted you to know that I didn't forget about you. You don't ... you won't ever know the things that I did to make it here. Honey ... I did things I'm ashamed of. And I have things that I need to answer for, okay? You can't just do whatever you want—you remember that. Every action has consequences." He struggles with the words. He struggles to make them make sense for her. "There's a boy in those woods, not much older than you, and he's waiting for me, just like you waited for me. And I made a promise to him, and to the man that's keeping him there. And now I have to go keep that promise, okay? I don't want to do it, sweet girl, please understand that I don't want to leave you. I want to stay with you. But sometimes you just have to do the right thing, and hope that it pays for all the bad things." He wipes his eyes, his nose. "If I stayed with you, those bad things would follow me, and they'd eventually find me, and then you might get hurt. And I can't let that happen. I won't let that happen. Do you understand? I want you to live. I want you to be safe. And the only way that can happen is if I go."

Nadine stares, shell-shocked. "So you're not gonna come back? You're never coming back?"

Huxley doesn't want to answer the question. "Nadine. The boy I told you about? His name is Lowell, okay? He's a good kid. He's smart. Listen to him. I want you guys to go north. I want you to get the hell out of this place. Go north and find a quiet place, find a community that'll take you in. Be safe. Live a good life. Do you promise me that you'll do that?"

"Don't go. Just don't go," she says, as though it is so simple.

"I have to, sweet girl. Promise me that you'll do what I'm asking."

The words are weak. "I promise."

He reaches up with a shaking hand and he touches her face, just one finger. He is scared to grab her and hold her like he wants to. He is terrified of her rejection of him. He does not want that to be his last memory, and time is growing short.

"I know that you understand," he tells her. "I know you don't like it either, but please don't hate me. Remember the good times, okay? If you can, remember your mother. Remember when we were all together. Can you do that for me? Can you remember me like that?"

She nods, unable to speak.

Huxley forces himself to smile for her. "Sweet girl. I have so much more to say. But I don't want you on the road after dark, okay? Lowell is going to come meet you. Wait right here for him. And then go back to Vicksburg Landing before it gets dark. And then north in the morning."

She squeezes her eyes shut.

"Hey." He gets her to look at him again. The next words are difficult to say. They want to stick in his tightening throat. "I love you … more than all the stars in the sky."

The words are like blows to her. He hadn't intended it that way. She rocks back, pulling away from him. He draws his hand back and he turns. *Best to go. Don't drag it out. Don't make it hurt any more than it has to. You've made things so horrible already. Just go. Go, and know that she'll live.*

He walks away from her.

"Daddy! Wait!"

He turns back to her, barely able to see her. He doesn't want to walk back, but he's pulled back to her side by some taut cord of instinct. It is not so easy to leave your daughter. It is not so easy to ignore her crying out for you.

When he is beside her again, she leans down and she throws her arms around his neck and she squeezes him like she used to when she was young, when she was trying to impress him with how strong she was. She's grown stronger, but it still feels so light around his neck. He puts his good arm around her shoulders and holds her like he's wanted to since she was ripped away from him.

She called me Daddy, but this time it wasn't a dream.

Or maybe it is.

She's the angel in this nightmare.

He pours a year and a half of pain and longing into that embrace.

He pulls away, hand on her shoulder. "I have to go," he says.

This time she doesn't try to stop him. She doesn't beg for him to stay. She must understand, just like Huxley knew. She understood from the moment that she saw him standing bloodied and murderous in that penthouse lounge. She understood that there would—there must be—a reckoning. She understood that he was only hers for a short time.

But it's not just a short time. I'm yours forever. Just remember me before. Remember me at the barley fields. Remember me under the stars at night. Remember me for the good.

She reaches into the coat that he gave her, and she pulls out the piece of paper, folded back on itself again. She handles it delicately.

"I want you to have it," she tells him.

Huxley takes it in his worn fingers. He begins to open it, but she stops him.

"Not here," she says, shaking her head. "Open it ... when you need help ... remembering."

He takes it gently. He doesn't mean to do it, but unconsciously he holds it against his chest. Jealously. Like an item of great value. He clings to it with the quiet pride of a poor man's sole possession.

"Okay," he promises. "I will."

CHAPTER 13

Huxley steps into the clearing.

"Mr. Huxley," Black Heart Davies calls out. There is a note of surprise in his voice.

He stands behind Lowell, the boy kneeling, still bound, but not hooded. The Black Hat must have heard Huxley coming through the woods. He has his pistol in his hand, the muzzle hovering behind Lowell's head. The boy looks up at Huxley and their eyes touch for a brief moment.

I'm here. I came back. I keep my promises.

Lowell is scared, of course, but relieved. And stricken. He wants to live, but he knows that Huxley's life is the only currency that can buy his own. There is a weight to that which the boy should not have to bear. Not with everything else that he carries.

"It's okay, Lowell," Huxley says to him, having to raise his voice just a bit to carry clearly across the intervening fifteen yards. His voice is steady now. He feels, in a way, bled dry of his emotions. His eyes still feel raw and red and crusted, but there are no tears left in him. Now it is time.

There is a sick feeling in his gut. But it is the feeling of letting go. That first initial plunge as you begin to fall.

It is okay. This is for the best.

Across from him, Davies eyes Huxley up and down, taking in how battered he is. His eyes linger on the revolver still stuck in Huxley's waistband. "Why'd you come armed, Huxley?"

Huxley raises his good hand to show he has no intention of making a move for the pistol. The paper is still held in his hands, between his fingers. He has not yet opened it. First Lowell goes free, and then Huxley can settle his soul. "I've come, Davies. That's what matters, right? I'm here."

Davies' tongue swipes over his top teeth. He gives Huxley a hard stare. "Did you think I would try to kill you both?"

Huxley stays motionless. "Don't take it personally." He makes a fractional nod toward Lowell. "Cut the boy loose. Let him go. You can have my gun. I didn't come for a fight."

"Hm." Davies' lips flatten out. "Alright. But you'll do exactly as I say. Or I'll put holes in you both faster than you can make a move for whatever ancient piece of shit is hanging out of your waistband. Am I understood?"

Huxley is tired. He has no energy left. He just nods, wearily.

Davies produces a knife in his left hand, keeping the pistol trained on the back of Lowell's head, and he cuts the boy's bindings with it. "Go," he tells the boy.

Lowell rises and walks unsteadily, holding his red wrists and rubbing them. He takes a few steps toward Huxley and tears spring up in his eyes, very briefly. His mouth works shakily, and then clamps shut, and the tears are gone. He is a hard person. He's had to be. That's good. It will keep him alive. It will keep Nadine alive.

Lowell stops just a few feet in front of Huxley. He whispers. "You don't have to do this. We could fight."

Huxley just shakes his head once. "Listen to me. Okay? Are you listening?"

"Yes."

"My daughter is on a horse a half mile toward Vicksburg Landing," he says. "Her name is Nadine. She's got a broken leg. Get her to safety, Lowell. Get her someplace safe in Vicksburg Landing, and then take her north, okay? Take her north, and keep her safe. That's what you need to do."

"Okay." Lowell is fighting his emotions again.

"Are you still listening to me?" Huxley asks.

Lowell takes a second. He swallows everything down. He nods. "I'm listening."

"Stop being afraid. Stay safe, but don't live your life in fear. You can't hold on to this life forever, and when you try, you do things you shouldn't. Remember that there are worse things than dying, okay? Live a good life. Be a good man. And take care of my daughter. I know you can do it. I have faith in you. You're better than what I made you become."

Lowell seems frozen in place.

Is he capable? He's just a boy.

"You know this isn't your fault, right?" Huxley asks.

Lowell says nothing.

Huxley shakes his head. "You saved me. The moment I almost forgot who I'd been, the moment I almost lost that one last, good piece of myself, you forced me to remember who I'd been. All of this? I earned it, Lowell. It's my tally." He looks at the ground. "Go, now. And remember what I said."

Lowell turns his body away from Huxley, away from Davies.

He walks away. His footsteps fading through the woods, and then they are gone.

It is just Davies and Huxley in the clearing.

Davies stands, pistol held straight out in his right hand, good aim, right at Huxley's upper chest. And he can fire as fast as he can pull the trigger. And Huxley has not even pulled his comparatively obsolete weapon out of his waistband. It is not cocked. He will die if he goes for it. They both know this.

"Very slowly," Davies begins. "With your thumb and forefinger only, take the revolver from your waistband and drop it on the ground."

Very slowly, with his thumb and his forefinger only, Huxley complies.

A gust of wind plays with the picture in his fingers. He wants to look at it now. He drops the revolver at his feet and focuses on keeping that invaluable paper from flying out of his grasp.

"Kick the gun away from you," Davies' voice carries over to him.

It is just background noise now. He complies, not for any reason but because he wants another moment to remember. Nadine knew he would want to remember. That is all they have. Everyone in this world. They just have memories. Memories of people they have loved and lost. Memories of better times.

He kicks the gun. It skitters through the dirt, just a lump of steel without a killer's hands on it.

Davies takes a few steps toward him. "Kneel down."

Huxley kneels, staring at the folded paper, and thinking about beautiful things. They are far away. They are hard to grasp sometimes. They don't belong in this world. They're from a different one. Why do the memories fade? Why can't they stay true for your whole life? The good ones always fade like the colors in a photograph, but the bad ones always seem to get worse. The blood gets redder …

No need for that now.

You're done with blood.

Go back. You were trying to remember …

But faces. Faces are hard to remember for some reason. At least, they've always been for him. He's watched them weather down like sculptures over eons, each day, each horrific thing, a year of rain and winds that scours away the detail from the carvings of his memories, making them plain and homogenous. But the real faces were anything but plain. They were alive. They were bright. They made his life beautiful.

She had hair the color of the barley fields when the sun was behind them. She had blue eyes that were bluer in the middle, and they sparkled when she smiled. A big smile. Beautiful mouth. She'd been a joyful person. A wonderful person. The best person I know.

He feels and hears Davies stepping around him, circling around to stand behind Huxley's kneeling form.

It's almost time.

He opens the folded piece of paper.

New tears, his last ones, hot and burning in his eyes.

There you are.

It is the picture he thought it would be. The one he *hoped* it would be. And it brings back every image of his wife, of that person that he lost to this world. Her face there on the page before him, remembered and brought to life with details that only Nadine could make. His wife, the love of his youth, the mother of his child, imperfect and ideal. The sight of her is like walking through the door of that cottage. It is faith. It is hope. It is love.

In the picture, she laughs, her eyes bright, her smile wide. How perfectly Nadine rendered her. He hopes that this is how Nadine remembers her. The best side of her.

He closes his eyes, that picture scratched out of charcoal like a key unlocking her, letting her back into his mind. He can see her now. Behind his eyes, he can remember everything that he'd forgotten. He can live there, in this imaginary land, for just a few seconds longer …

Davies' voice breaks in, but quietly, like a burglar in Huxley's dreamland.

"Who drew that?"

Davies is behind him now.

Huxley opens his eyes again. The light of the real world, even in the coming dusk, seems overly harsh. It washes away the patina of his imagined world. He looks at the picture in his hand. Then he turns his head. Out of the corner of his peripheral vision, he can just barely see the shape of Davies standing there, the pistol leveled at Huxley's head, as it had been leveled at Lowell's.

"My daughter drew it."

All is silent.

Huxley doesn't know why the question was asked. Can't really figure why he answered, other than because he has nothing left to fight this man with. He has come to pay his tally. Now he kneels and accepts his fate. The executioner stands behind him. His finger is on the trigger. Justice must be done.

He looks back at the picture. He is very quiet in his soul now. He has a stillness inside of him that he has not experienced in a very long time. So long that he wonders if he ever experienced it at all. It surpasses all his understanding, but he welcomes it nonetheless.

A shift of weight from behind him.

A rustle of fabric.

The light scrape of a boot in the dirt.

"Get up," Davies' voice says.

Fear snaps through Huxley, sudden and intense. *This isn't supposed to happen ...*

He turns himself again, but this time all the way, looking behind him.

Davies stands a little further away now. His pistol is still in his hand, but it is pointed at the ground. The grip that Davies holds it with seems lazy. The man, the rocky features ... something is passing through them. It is odd. Like hearing an underground river through a sheet of immovable stone. Nothing in his face actually changes, but Huxley can *sense* the cataclysm inside of the man.

He is staring at the picture.

"Why?" Huxley says.

Davies' face twitches at the sound of Huxley's voice. He seems to break from a trance. Then he looks Huxley in the eye. The pistol moves in his hand and Huxley thinks perhaps he only wanted to shoot Huxley in the face, for whatever reason, to look him in the eyes while he did it.

Then Davies holsters his pistol. "Get up," he repeats. "Go."

Huxley makes a sound, brings one foot up, then hesitates again.

Davies blinks rapidly. Something on the verge of collapse. He doesn't want it to be witnessed. The fact that Huxley is still kneeling there irritates him. He points into the forest behind Huxley. "Go, I said!" he snaps. "You're fucking free. Get the hell out of here before I change my mind."

Huxley is buzzing. This has all the surrealism of a dream.

He barely feels his feet on the ground as he rises. He can't feel the pain in his broken arm, or his burned arm. But he can feel his heart beat. Hard. And speeding up. He wants to ask Davies why, but it would be foolish. He can see the man's face straining under whatever is inside of him and Huxley doesn't want to be around when it breaks. It will be violent, Huxley thinks.

His brain keeps telling him, *You should be dead. You should be dead. This is not real.*

But he turns himself around. He starts walking with small, shuffling steps. He expects a bullet in the back. *This doesn't matter. None of this matters. He's still going to kill you. This is just a trick. Don't get your hopes up. Keep your head down. You're supposed to be dead.*

But his heart is soaring.

Terrified, but soaring.

"Huxley," Davies calls after him.

He's only made it a few yards. He is close to the woods. Is this it? Is this the bullet in the back? He stops where he is, but doesn't turn around. He braces himself for the impact of the bullet. Davies is a strange creature. As strange as Huxley himself.

"Your daughter," Davies says, his voice uncharacteristically shaky. "The picture girl. Tell her thank you. From the saddest man she's ever seen. Tell her thank you … for helping me remember."

Huxley looks back over his shoulder, words stricken out of his mouth, but hoping to look at Davies one more time, hoping that something in the other man's face will make sense of this. But when he looks, Davies has already turned, and he is walking quickly away into the darkening, deepening woods.

CHAPTER 14

Black Heart Davies stood as far out of the way as he possibly could. These parties, these soirées, he couldn't stand them. He went because he was required to go. To be there for his councilman. And because his councilman liked to brag.

"This is the infamous Black Heart," he liked to say, happily to those who hadn't met him yet. "Fastest gun in the Riverlands. Never seen him miss." Then the councilman would say, with a wink and a nudge, "He's the reason people do as I say."

More than the waste, more than the politics, Davies hated the parties because he hated being trotted out like this. He was a hero to some. A murderer to others. Cold blooded. Efficient. Everyone had a different characteristic of him that they'd built up in their mind. None of them truly knew him. It only served as a reminder that no one left in this world actually knew him, and it was a crushing, brutal reminder.

It drove him to drink.

Here, at House Murphy, watching his councilman and Councilman Murphy pretend as though they didn't hate each other, Davies put his back to the wall in miserable silence, and drank whatever watered swill they distributed to the *lower* guests. Black Hats were not supposed to drink when they were on duty, but Davies did not care, and it seemed that no one had the balls to challenge him on it, so he kept swiping drink after drink.

Nothing brought out the bad things in him more than these crowds. These fake friends and true enemies. Nothing could make him feel more lost and alone than being surrounded by all these strangers in this strange land, and sometimes it would feel so foreign to him that he felt certain he was dreaming.

Everyone thought him empty of feelings. And perhaps, in a way, they were right. There was a hole in him. But he could *feel* that hole. He just didn't let it show. He didn't talk to others. What would they think of him? In his business, weakness could get him a bullet in the brain.

Even if he could talk about it, he told himself there was no point. He told himself that his loss was not unusual. It was not special. There wasn't anyone over the age of twelve who hadn't lost someone or something that they'd loved.

Everyone's loss was only special to *them*.

He wondered sometimes how deep the undercurrent of pain ran in this burgeoning society. It seemed like it was a part of everything. But no one would admit it. Everyone refused to acknowledge that it existed. These parties seemed like a slap in the face to all of that, and he couldn't decide whether he thought it tragic or callous. Sometimes he thought this must've been what the ballroom of the *Titanic* would have looked like if everyone knew they were going to die and figured to keep the party going. Pop the corks and laugh, while death surrounds us.

Hours passed. The party wore on, interminable.

It was full dark outside. Everyone was drunk, or near drunk.

Davies was not an exception. The world was watery and dim to him. His thoughts were dark and cloudy.

He looked around the room, the guffawing buffoons of the so-called Great Council. His eyes traced a well-worn circuit, always coming back to rest on Mrs. Murphy and her newest prize, a young girl who sat on a stool beside a table with a thick ream of the best paper that could be pounded and pressed. The girl was maybe just entering adolescence. Twelve or thirteen at best. A skinny thing. She had no smile for any of them, but Mrs. Murphy and her guests seemed delighted by her.

Davies watched as councilmen and their wives posed for sketched portraits. They asked for the girl to draw silly things on them. Then they giggled quietly to each other. Everyone waited in expectation while the girl drew, her charcoal-blackened fingers moving about the paper, her eyes focused and intense, not letting anyone see until she was done. He noticed that she didn't look at them while she drew. It seemed that looking at them a few times at the beginning locked their images in her brain.

When she was finished, she revealed.

The guests laughed until they cried. They'd been drawn with monocles and top hats and furs made out of snarling foxes, the lady with a hat made out of eagle feathers, like an old Indian chief.

Gradually, the crowd died away and Mrs. Murphy grew bored of her newest amusement, as she was infamously prone to do. The girl remained on the stool with her ream of papers and her sticks of charcoal. When she was not drawing someone, she sat there and looked out at the party, and it seemed she bore the same distaste for them as Davies did.

His eyes moved on to the party, but over and over as the night went on, they kept tracking back to her. Eventually, she caught him looking.

She didn't blush or look down, or look away. She didn't seem scared of him. *She does not know who I am.*

Davies looked away and drank more of his sour drink.

The third time they made eye contact, Davies pushed himself off of the wall and walked over to her, a very slight sway in his step. Mrs. Murphy and her entourage were gone. The girl was alone.

"You're not drawing," he said, flatly.

"Do you want me to draw something?" her hand went to a paper.

"No."

"Okay."

"Why are you still here?"

"Mrs. Murphy told me to stay. In case she wants more entertainment."

"Entertainment," Davies sneered. He was drunk. He didn't mean to be aggressive, but he was blunt. "Why were you looking at me?"

"You were looking at me."

"That's my job."

"Oh."

"Do you know who I am?"

"No. Who are you?"

He regarded her evenly, taking another long draft of what he thought was some sort of mead. He didn't want to tell her who he was. What would be the purpose? To scare a little girl? To impress her? It was a silly question to begin with. A twelve-year-old slave didn't care about who he was, nor should she.

He rolled his shoulders, trying to force some of the misery off of himself. "What do I look like to you?"

It was an odd question, he knew.

The girl tilted her head at him, squinting as though he just spoke a different language. "What do you mean?"

"Put down your pencils," he said, and she complied. "If you had no pencils, if you had no paper, how would you describe me? I want you to draw me with words."

Why? He wonders. *To have some child confirm what everyone believes about me? Because you think children tell the truth and you want her to decide for you whether you're some gunslinging hero cop, or a slobbering monster with the blood of infants dripping down your fangs?*

You're ridiculous.

He drained his cup. "You don't have to answer that. Sorry."

She sized him up with an artist's eye anyway. "Do you want me to say? Or not?"

He smirked down at her, wishing for more booze. *The truth hurts, huh? Shouldn't have asked the question if you didn't want the answer. Are you scared of a little girl? Let her say what she wants.*

"Go ahead," he sighed. "Tell me."

The girl rubbed her fingers together, then wiped them off on her dress, leaving black smudges. "I think you're the saddest man that I've ever seen."

Davies snorted. "What do you know about sadness, little girl? You don't remember the Old World."

She shook her head. "I don't. But I used to draw for people. Sad people that had lost things in the Old World. I don't know how I could do it, but I could. I could have them tell me about the person that they missed, describe them to me, and I would draw them. I never knew the people I drew. But their loved ones ..." she shrugged, looking sad herself. "... I guess I drew them good. People would cry when they saw them. But in a good way. They wanted to keep the drawings. So I would give them away. Maybe it helped. I like to think that it helped."

Davies stared at her. The drink became cloying on his tongue.

"My Mom told me it was a good thing I was doing," the girl said. "She told me that it's been so long since everything happened, that some people had a hard time remembering the people that they loved. I hope that's not true. I'm afraid of forgetting what my mom looked like. Or my dad."

Davies swallowed hard. "Maybe you should draw them."

"Mrs. Murphy doesn't want me using the paper for *doodling*." The girl looked up. "She calls the stuff I want to draw *doodling*. She only wants me to draw what *she* wants me to draw. She says that if she catches me doodling she'll cut my fingers off and sell me as a bedslave."

Jesus Christ, Davies thought, but held his tongue.

The girl then reached across and grabbed a sheet of the paper. She adjusted her stance in the seat. Selected a piece of charcoal. "I don't like her drawings. I like to help people. Maybe I can help you." She looked at him. "Who was it? Can you remember their face?"

Davies' mouth worked. Half of him wanted to speak. The other half wanted to walk away.

I do not talk about this …

"My sons," Davies suddenly blurted out. Then he looked around, cautiously, as though afraid someone might have heard him. He looked back down at the girl, poised with her paper and her pencil, and he spoke, quieter then, like a secret being shared. "I had two sons. They were just boys. One was four. One was six."

And then, as though fighting against himself and losing, he began to describe them.

And the girl began to draw.

CHAPTER 15

Huxley steps out of the dark woods and onto the worn-out trail that once was a road. This is the spot. He knows, because he retraced his steps in the dim light, going by broken branches and disturbed leaves. His mind is giddy and scared, confused and elated.

This is the spot that he left his daughter on the hobbled horse less than a half hour ago, and now the road is empty. For a second comes the old fear, that feeling of separation. She is gone again. He does not know where she is, and he will never get her back ...

But he does know where she is. She is with Lowell. And they have left this place ahead of the dying rays of the sun, to make it back to Vicksburg Landing before dark.

Huxley stands in the middle of the road for a time. The wind whips his clothing. It is cold with the coming dark. The woods are silent. The road is abandoned. Here where he stands, where he left Nadine on the horse, the concrete is exposed, and it does not show any marks of travelers coming or going. It is possible to feel that none of it was real. That the woods were just a membrane between the real and dream world, and he has just walked through to the other side.

What do I feel?

The old familiar question, but is it necessary? Where before, Huxley had felt nothing, now he is almost struck dumb by everything coursing through him. He shakes as they all collide and spin around in him. He wants to laugh and cry, to run and to fall to the ground. He is in agony, and yet he feels pleasure in the wind, where before it had been cold and biting. He feels pleasure in the road beneath his feet, where before it had only been miles to cross.

Because before, he believed he had nothing to live for.

But now, he has everything.

What do I feel?

Alive. That is what I feel.

His heart is beating in his chest, and his limbs are moving as best they can—what other evidence does he need that he is alive?

He realizes that he is walking the road to Vicksburg Landing, one foot in front of the other, and he believes that he will make it. He has a *reason* to make it.

And from there, north, into some unknown. Into the vast and quiet hope of promises yet to be kept.

SPECIAL THANKS

I think I always knew what this story was about, but it took a long conversation with my incredible wife to drag it out of me. In the last few weeks of writing the rough draft, I found myself floundering for the right ending, but I must thank Tara for her uncanny insight into a story that she'd never read, which allowed me to find my way through a twisted and difficult story.

I have to also thank those who read *Wolves* and offered input and encouragement: my agent, David Fugate, a man of tireless work ethic; my partner, Joshua Gibbons, whose opinion I respect in almost all things; and of course, my pops, who's read everything I've ever written.

My sincere thanks to all of you.